FOR MY MOTHER

I

It was a period when the future seemed more present than the present itself. Place no less than time had been altered by the war. Our school was called St George's, and our exercise books still carried the Sussex address. When the telephone rang in the Lorna Doone Hotel, Morte Bay, I sometimes heard Mrs Stanhope, the headmaster's wife, pick it up and say, 'St George's, Crawley Down.' We had been evacuated since that fine May when artillery, or anti-aircraft fire, could be heard, and felt, as we sowed Carter's Tested Seeds in our individual gardens. In the months when British fortunes never ceased to falter, and when Britain's allies seemed so feeble that it was a condescension to play their anthems on the wireless, St George's resumed its life in North Devon, where Major Stanhope had been provident enough to secure the lease of the Lorna Doone Hotel. Other headmasters, with less foresight or greater faith in Mr Chamberlain, looked too late for similarly safe premises. Those who did not find them had to close their Kent or Sussex or Surrey schools, which lay under the path of the German bombers. One of them, Galen Quarles, had joined St George's as an assistant master; he was taking us for Latin on the day when Joe Hirsch arrived.

The Lorna Doone had a half-timbered façade calculated to appeal to the genteel holidaymakers who had patronized it before the war. There was a discordant, but impressive, stone porte-cochère outside the front door (which the boys were not allowed to use) and there had been two tennis courts, where Mrs Stanhope now kept Rhode Island Reds, across from it. We were lucky sometimes to have regular eggs, not dried. The valley on to which the hotel faced was narrow, with steep hills on both sides.

It opened on to a wider bay at the north end, with a cemented sea wall above the beach. The sands glistened from the retreating tide, though at high water you could see nothing but rocks, fringed with pungent seaweed. When the Blitz was hitting London, I did not go home for the holidays. My father paid supplementary fees for me to stay, with quite a few other boys, at the Lorna Doone. We spent those double-summertime days largely on the beach. Hugo Carmody and I built villages out of sand on the rocks. Our townships and colonies covered the limpet-bossed slate with fugitive civilization. Carmody modelled with brisk competence, a flop of fair hair over his thoughtful brow. Even in the different atmosphere of the holiday months, when we had no official lessons and when discipline was less severe (no one was ever swished), Carmody was always Carmody; I was always Jordan. He may have seen, from my letters, that I was called Michael, just as I knew him to be 'Dearest Hugo', from one of his mater's letters I had cribbed, but we would have embarrassed each other with first-name familiarities. Middle names were totally secret.

Carmody and I were in the same 'dorm', room 5, on the first floor of the Lorna Doone Hotel. There were three other iron beds. Each had a spare red blanket folded at the bottom during the day, so that we could cover ourselves during after-lunch rest. We had Sneyd with us in number 5, together with a couple of squits, one of whom was called Brasier-Creagh. (Double-barrels were both laughable and intimidating.) Carmody and I were in the second form; he came first in maths and I came first in Latin and Greek, which counted more. Hence I was top of the form, though I was not convinced of my superiority. There was something natural about Carmody's facility with figures: when he worked things out, he was right. He never strained or scratched his head. If I was clever, it was partly because I was also afraid.

I think it must have been a June morning in 1943 when Joe Hirsch came to St George's. The war had been going on for a good quarter of my life. I had never imagined that we could lose,

8

especially now that putteed Americans marched in the Devon lanes, but it was too soon to guess how and when we might win. Those whose fathers were in uniform walked and talked with a certain swagger. Carmody's father was a Brigadier; mine was a Major in the Judge-Advocate's department. Carmody's father wore red tabs and had gold braid on the peak of his cap. When I made sport of this, Carmody said, 'He can't help it, Jordan.' I expected him to recognize that my needling was not a reproach but an overture. When his blue eyes clouded with tears and his freckled face grew pale, almost transparent, I was as embarrassed by my sarcasm as I was excited by the power I seemed to have over my friend.

Perhaps I learned some of my sarcastic manner from Galen Quarles. He wore a gown which seemed ampler and more glossy than the other masters', velvet bows just below each shoulder and two swags of black material in addition to the slashed arms. These swags reminded me of the shorter legs of the crabs Carmody and I used to flush out from the recesses of the rocks. We once tried to make a sort of farm where a family of crabs would be housed. We were not sure whether they would be the masters, or the beasts whom we would exploit and finally slaughter. The pair we attempted to enclose in our easy walls soon lurched to freedom. Mr Quarles regarded our engineering with disdainful admiration. 'I am looking at the future,' he once said, 'and I cannot but wonder whether it will work.'

The architecture over which we took so much trouble was washed away by the steep tides, no matter how we reinforced the walls. We toted slate from the edge of the bay. The cliffs had shed stacks of it. The stones lay about, as big as elephants' ears, gummy earth impacted between them. There were caves under the lee of the cliffs, but we were forbidden to venture out of sight. Once I dropped a slate and chipped skin from my toe. Mr Quarles smiled as I fought my tears.

I liked to impress Mr Quarles. When we heard that he was to take us for Latin (if Mr Datchet had one of his spells), everyone else groaned, though never after he had come into the Residents'

Lounge, where St George's benches had displaced the hotel's brown sofas from the centre of the check-tiled room. The road from Ilfracombe came down behind the hotel, before going along the sea front, by the plum-coloured sea wall, and up again towards the golf course where we collected mushrooms after rain and sun had encouraged their sudden explosion. The Residents' Lounge was at ground level for those coming in from the Private Side, but was semi-basement at the back. The lane was above us as we sat doing our Latin sentences. There were high windows, opened by the manipulation of cords looped through an apparatus of winches well out of our reach. Anyone 'tampering' with the cords had been liable to severe punishment ever since Jenks managed to unlace them, when the stricken Mr Datchet was not looking. Mad Eric, the buttery hop, was told to climb the kitchen steps and re-thread the cords. A farce at which we were forbidden to laugh had followed: Eric leaned too far; the steps collapsed; one of the windows fell open with shattering abruptness. For a winter week, we had to have Latin in the sunless Sun Lounge. Carmody told Mr Oliffe, the maths master, who rode a motorbike in peacetime, that the principle of the pulley was elementary and that he could put it right, if anyone liked, in a couple of secs. Mr Oliffe reminded him of the old sweats' law: 'Never volunteer, Carmody, never volunteer.'

Mr Oliffe was very fat, but he had neat feet. He moved with agility. He could also do *The Times* crossword in under twenty-eight minutes. It was said that he had a private income, which allowed him to order a personal copy of the paper. When he had finished the crossword, he rubbed out the answers, with a special, almost transparent Art Gum Eraser, and blew away the traces before handing it to Mr Datchet, who solved it again, rather more slowly, while he had his tea.

There were three cottages in the westernmost corner of the bay. Mr Datchet and Mr Oliffe shared one of them; Mr Quarles had the second. The third, which was slightly apart, in the angle of the corner, was not occupied after another master, Mr Swindlehurst, had been taken to Ilfracombe in an ambulance with a bell ringing. The first two cottages were of brick, with slate roofs. The third was made of creosoted boards.

We could see only the lower part of cars and bicycles and vans as they came past the Residents' Lounge. You could hear them coming and then you would see the blur of spokes or the glitter of hubcaps, as they went by. In those few seconds, Carmody could identify a Morris or a Talbot or a Riley. (He could also identify friendly and enemy aircraft.) We always knew when Major Stanhope was coming back from Ilfracombe in his car because of the silence. 'The Major's,' Mr Quarles observed, 'is the car that doesn't bark in the day.' The reason for the Wolseley's silence was that the Major always switched off the engine at the top of the valley and coasted down. It was patriotic to save petrol. We would listen for the cough of the engine as the Major had to restart it for the reverse loop of his approach, which brought him back up between the clipped laurels, past the Rhode Island Reds to the porte-cochère which gave privileged access to the Private Side.

Mr Quarles had a way of drawing down his upper lip and creasing his chin. The look in his jaundiced grey eyes solicited laughter we would have been foolish to express. Mr Quarles was like one of those exiled dignitaries whose pictures we saw in the thin newspapers. The defeated were enjoying our hospitality. If it was terrible that France and Holland and once-gallant little Belgium (not so gallant the second time around, unfortunately) and Czecho-Slovakia and Poland had been unable to resist the Nazis, it was also to our credit and their shame. When, during the holidays, I saw their officers' funny caps (the kepis of the Free French, the off-centre square affairs of the Poles and the Czechs), it was not surprising that they had not been able to put up much resistance. By contrast, one Christmas our dentist, Gerald Lewin, came to see us wearing the cap of a Surgeon Commander R.N. After dinner, on my way to bed, I saw it lying on the chair in the hall of our flat. I took it and balanced it on my red ears. Only German officers had equally enviable caps. How did they manage to get the front of them to stand up so stiff and high? I sometimes drew pictures of German colonel-generals. In the desert, they had goggles as well as peaked caps.

'Sentence two,' Mr Quarles said. 'Jordan?'

'*Caesar copias suas Germanos oppugnare jussit*.'

Mr Quarles turned from staring at another boy, a habit of his when he posed a question, and looked at me with the sneer he reserved for those who answered correctly. If he approved in principle of those who got things right, they also deprived him of a certain pleasure. Virtue cheated him. His mouth turned down at the corners and his chin was oddly rumpled. 'That could be put in another, not to say a more elegant way, could it not? Fairfax?' He put the question to the boy directly behind him. Mr Quarles's descendants would, if Darwin was right, eventually have eyes in the back of their heads.

'You could use *imperare*, couldn't you, sir?' Fairfax was tall and wiry. He had merciless blue eyes. If his father had had red tabs, I should not have bothered to remark it. (In fact, he was a Lieutenant Commander R.N., and he had been on a Murmansk convoy, though we were not supposed to tell anybody if they asked us.) Fairfax's Latin was not reliable; he was not the kind of person who would ever need to bother when it came to academic matters. If his elongated wrists now protruded below his herringboned sleeve (where a cuff of lighter material showed how adroitly his mother, or some sewing woman, had retrieved another inch from the double tweed), his gestures promised that he would one day resume the handmade smartness which rationing rendered temporarily unavailable. Meanwhile his dandyism was shaped by his sense of himself, and of what he meant to be. He did not simply have a face, like Sneyd or Brasier-Creagh, Leach or Edge-Partington: he *wore* his face, as if it were a tailored article. He did not imitate the wilful creases to be seen on Mr Quarles's countenance (a word I associated with divinity, thanks to Hymns Ancient and Modern) but contrived an alarming impassivity. Fairfax never competed; he won.

'Perhaps,' Mr Quarles said, 'you would be good enough, Fairfax, to employ the machinery you suggest.'

The class raised their heads to the rubbery hum which promised that the Major had been to Ilfracombe. A few moments later, the Wolseley's monogrammed hubcaps rolled past the repaired window (it alone, owing to shortages, was not pebbled) and on down towards the sea wall. Mr Quarles smiled at the memory of his Holmesian quip, and so did we. 'Yes, Fairfax? You weren't saying?'

'*Caesar copias suas* . . .' Fairfax glanced at the black-and-white clock, as it quivered towards the hour, sighed and had to go on. '*Ut Germanos oppugnent imperavit*, sir.'

'Has that order been quite properly given, do you think?'

When the silence grew so long that it seemed fair to break it, I said, 'Shouldn't it be *copiis suis*, sir? *Imperare* takes the dative, doesn't it, sir?'

I turned in my seat, for praise, and found Mr Quarles's face rumpled with rage. 'And you, Jordan, sometimes take the confounded biscuit.'

'*Doesn't* it, sir?'

'A gentleman, Jordan, should you ever be asked, tends to look at the person to whom he is speaking. Since I am not, unless you or a qualified oculist advises me otherwise, completely cross-eyed, it should have been clear, even to the *meanest* intelligence, that my question was not intended for your *professional* ears, however irresistible the prospect of a bonus mark may have been.'

The longer the rest of the class favoured Mr Quarles with proof of their amusement, the less time remained for further use of the subjunctive with *ut*. 'Jordan may not recognize a gentleman when he is seen by one,' Mr Quarles said, brushing chalk from those vestigial sleeves, 'but he is quite right, if malapert, in remarking that our old friend *imperare*, whence *imperator*, as he would doubtless tell you, even if – perhaps particularly if – not invited, does indeed take the dative. Pray make a note of the fact, Fairfax.'

'I have, sir,' Fairfax said.

The clock uttered a whirring sound. Some noisy part of its

innards had been removed to avoid too ostentatious a striking of the hours, and quarters. Its husky murmur would doubtless be cured after the war.

'That is, it seems, as much of Rome as we shall have time to build today.' Mr Quarles took his books from the evacuated desk at the end of the lounge and gave me one last baleful glance, as if I had betrayed him, or myself, in some way I should be wise to avoid in future. He went out through the door with the wine-gummy coloured glass in its top half, which took him to the Private Side. I was glad that he had gone, but nervous at his departure; it left me to face Fairfax.

Gannet and Macintosh, who held office in his gang, were already regarding me with searing coldness. Fairfax said: 'Must you always?'

Carmody remained in his place, his arm bent around a drawing of a Messerschmitt ME 110E, on which he had begun work again as soon as the hour whirred. He might be my friend; he would never be my ally. 'Typical,' I said.

'Meaning?' Macintosh said. He already had hair down there. I had seen him in the bath. In the winter, we had to share our five inches sometimes. I shut the door and never sat in his. I splashed about, with my feet, and then dried myself, even though I was not wet. 'Meaning?'

'Typical Quarles,' I said.

'And what, pray, is typical of me?' He had opened the Residents Only door, behind me, and there he was again, without his gown.

'Coming in suddenly and giving me quite a shock, sir,' I said.

He appeared amused by my nerve. If he did not smile, he nodded. Then he said, 'You're wanted in the H.M.'s study, Jordan. Cut along there right away.'

The door shut again. 'Golly, I wonder what for.'

Fairfax said, 'Probably to get a half-holiday for knowing that *imperare* takes the dative.'

On my way past him to the door, I said, 'Sorry about that,

Fairfax,' as if my summons to the Magger had cancelled my misdemeanour.

The headmaster's study had Office on the heavy door. It was large enough for him to teach the first form and contained a row of high-backed hotel dining room chairs, on which they had to sit to face the Magger's questions. He had taken us for Latin once or twice, when Mr Datchet had one of his spells and Mr Quarles was already committed elsewhere. If you answered correctly after your neighbour had failed, the Magger told you to 'go up', and if several people had failed, a single brilliant answer could catapult you above them all. You numbered off at the end of the class and got as many marks as your final position warranted.

The high-backed chairs had been taken from the hotel dining room, which was now furnished with refectory tables and benches from Sussex. When I went in, I saw that there was a black handbag and an umbrella on one of the chairs. A dark-eyed woman, in a headscarf and a brown coat, with black shoes, was sitting on another. The Magger was standing, erect but not tall, in his leather-elbowed Harris tweed, by the mullioned windows. The study windows alone were made of the same ochre stone as the porte-cochère which shaded them. The Major's military moustache was yellowed from the pipe he smoked when off duty. He had puffy fingers, with a signet ring deep in the flesh of his left hand. Despite his engorged complexion, he was rarely angry. However, his mildness could make even Fairfax blink.

The study was full of things. There were filing cabinets and piles of text books and the serious desk with a gadget on it that pressed the school's address (the real one) into the writing paper. In a leather tub, there were cricket bats and tennis rackets (in screw-down presses) and walking sticks and, on the top of a filing cabinet, sleeved in a brown paper bag, three canes.

'Jordan,' Major Stanhope said, 'this is Hirsch.'

Joe was smaller than me, and narrower. He had the same dark eyes as his mother and black hair like mine. His shorts were longer than St George's outfitters supplied and they were made of foreign corduroy. They had a built-in belt of the same material. Georgians wore elastic belts in the school colours with a snake buckle. His sweater was brown with a beige band around the waist. It had a V neck, but with a covered button at the top. None of us ever had sweaters with buttons.

'Hirsch is going to be with you in the second form,' the Major said. 'I want you to be his friend until he finds his feet.'

The new boy sighed, as if the more onerous duty had been laid on him. His mother put her two shining feet in their black pumps together in front of her and aligned them, head down. Then she looked up, as if a decision had been made.

'He'll be in room 5 with you. He can have Carmody's bed.'

'Where's Carmody going to sleep, sir?'

'Miss Kellett will look after that side of things. You go with Jordan now, Hirsch, and he'll acquaint you with the general geography and take you into lunch.'

I went to open the door. Mr Oliffe was passing, with his famous suitcase. It contained penknives and sharpeners and pencil leads for revolving pencils and gummed reinforcements and national saving stamps (6d each) which he sold to us after rest, on Wednesdays and Saturdays. No one was allowed to have more than two shillings pocket money at any one time. Mr Oliffe kept the accounts and deducted the cost of our purchases from whatever had been handed in at the beginning of term.

'I would prefer to stay wiz my mother,' Joe said.

'She'll be just across the way,' the Major said. 'You'll doubtless see her from time to time.'

One of Joe's mother's lisle stockings had a darn in it, near the knee.

'I prefer to stay wiz my mother.'

'She wants you to go to school here,' the Major said. 'That's why she has brought you here. You mustn't be ungrateful.'

Joe's hostility seemed to be reserved for me. I might have been not only the witness but also the cause of his humiliation. 'If she needs me, she can call me, yes?'

'If she does, of course.'

Mrs Hirsch picked up her unsmart handbag and her heavy umbrella. We might have been in a courtroom, or a police station, where the formalities had ended, or been adjourned. The Major reached for his pipe. 'Cut along now, Jordan, will you, and show Hirsch the ropes?'

There were three alien suitcases in the checkered hallway, next to the door labelled Billiards, where the beaks had their common room. Two of the cases had metal corners and difficult locks. The third, which Joe picked up, was of chapped leather and had side pockets. None of us would ever have had attaché cases with side pockets. I feared for Hirsch if Jenks or anyone like that saw that he had an attaché case with side pockets, especially when it belonged to someone who said 'wiz' and had a belt made of the same material as his trousers.

Room 5 was at the far end of the coconut-matted first floor of the hotel. Its bay window overlooked the fuchsias around the back entrance, where Mad Eric parked his outsize bicycle. Once we saw him peeing into the fuchsias. He looked round and then he peed into the fuchsias. Mad Eric slept in a little room off the kitchen. 'That's Carmody's bed,' I said, 'which you're supposed to have.' Mrs Stanhope was coming along the drive with Mrs Hirsch. Mrs Stanhope was a big woman, in flat shoes, with grey hair and a piercing voice. It seemed to imply an element of rage at her sex, which prevented her taking command. Her deference to the Major was also a kind of threat.

'Why did he ask you to do zis?'

'Sorry?'

'The headmaster. Why you?'

'Search me.'

Joe Hirsch had put his case on the bed, unsnapped the locks and began to stow his things in the chest beside Carmody's bed. The Hag had already budged Carmody's clothes.

'I know why.'

'Where've you been until now? Where've you come from, I mean?'

'Manchester.'

'But where are you from really?'

'Where are you?' Joe Hirsch said.

'London.'

'Originally.'

'London I said. You're refugees, aren't you?'

'I know exactly why,' Joe Hirsch said.

He was supposed to be afraid of me. I was afraid of him. The hotel gong rumbled from downstairs. 'Lunch,' I said. 'We've got precisely ninety seconds.'

Carmody was talking about aero engines to Sneyd. The lunch was cold ham and salad. We had to finish the fat. If you didn't, you were told to think of the starving millions in Europe. As I chewed mine, I hated the starving millions. The lettuce came from Mrs Stanhope's garden where people had to dig if they had done something wrong. The only hot dish was boiled potatoes. They had been peeled by Mad Eric. He had gouged the black bits but failed to get them all out. Suddenly, I saw Mrs Hirsch through the butler's hatch. She was wearing a white overall and carried a tower of white pudding plates. Some of the crockery still bore the stamp of the Lorna Doone Hotel, but Mad Eric had smashed one whole huge stack early on and he was now forbidden to carry more than six plates at a time. Joe Hirsch ate his ham and then he reached for the salt and sprinkled his dark green lettuce and his knobbly potato.

'Any pepper?' he said.

'Staff only,' I said.

'Why?'

'It's a rule.'

'Aren't you going to introduce us to your friend, Jordan? What's his name? Is it pronounceable?'

'Hirsch,' I said. 'I don't know how it's spelt. Hirsch, this is Fairfax.'

Joe Hirsch spat out some fat and put it at the side of his plate.

'Aren't you going to tell him what's special about me?'

18

'Oh yes,' I said, 'of course: Fairfax takes the dative.'

'You mustn't think that everyone can talk to people like Jordan talks to people,' Fairfax said. 'Not even Jordan always can.'

'Takes the dative?' Joe Hirsch said. 'Are you mad?'

'Fairfax is the Saint,' I said.

Joe Hirsch rolled his eyes. He seemed too old for St George's, Crawley Down. He reached for some more potatoes and sprinkled salt on them. I expected Fairfax to disapprove, but he was looking with a certain favour on Joe Hirsch.

'He doesn't seem to know who the Saint is, Fairfax,' I said. 'He's a character in a book. The Saint. Simon Templar.'

'So you're a character in a book, are you?' Other people had finished eating. Joe Hirsch went on chewing. He spat out a piece of black potato and looked round. 'What's the point of that?'

'And Jenks is Bulldog Drummond,' I said. 'They're mortal foes. They've each got their gangs, you see, and they have this perpetual war going on. You can't ask to join them; you have to be asked. Like the commandos.'

'Who wants to join them?'

'It's the thing to do,' I said.

'And which gang are you in?'

'I haven't been asked,' I said. 'Yet.'

'Hard luck.' Joe Hirsch winced unpatriotically at the portion of roly-poly which had been passed down to him. A measure of watered golden syrup had been poured over it by Mr Oliffe. 'Christ, what's this?'

'I shouldn't say Christ if I were you.'

'Well, what is it?'

'If Mrs Stanhope hears you, she makes you wash your mouth out with soap.'

'I'd refuse.'

'You've got a lot to learn about St George's,' I said.

'And it's got a lot to learn about me,' Joe Hirsch said. 'So what do you think about that?'

To be perfectly honest, I wished that Joe and his mother, whose name was Hilde, had never come to Morte Bay. Although

Carmody and I still built our villages on half-holidays, his removal from my dorm fractured our friendship. Even when we were building another sea wall, higher than the earlier ones, in the defeated hope that it might resist the next tide, Joe Hirsch's gooseberry presence robbed the occasion of its previous intimacy. He seemed to share Mr Quarles's view: sand castles were puerile. Nothing that we did to pass the time really interested him.

On wet afternoons, when clouds hid the crests of the hills and the angry tides clapped the sea wall, we would be confined to the Residents' Lounge and the Sun Lounge. The sliding doors between them could be pushed wide open to create a stage where we improvised plays. A boy called Masterman once resurrected me, when I had died a dramatic death, by pulling my penis. Carmody had a collection of Dinky toys which he kept in a wooden box. It had a fastener, like a cedilla on its side, which latched into a metal eye. His collection included medium and heavy tanks with detachable chain-link tracks and turrets that really traversed, with wireless aerials on them. He had three-ton trucks with holes in their seats, into which little helmeted figures with pronged behinds could be fitted. The Bren gun carriers were complete with crew, and field-gun attachments. The ammunition trailers had couplings front and back. Carmody used to conduct armoured engagements against Denton, who didn't mind being the Germans. Personally, I made models of ships. My mother and I went up to town to get the kits in the holidays. The parts were roughly cut out, but had to be sanded and fitted together very carefully. The six-inch guns were made of special nails with small heads. Once everything was in place, I painted them battleship grey. It took ages to get all the finicky things, like the oerlikon guns, into place. I wished sometimes that the dexterous Carmody would help me, but he preferred to have battles with Denton. They elaborated their deployments by making huge maps out of cartridge paper, with rivers and hills. Their manoeuvres were very technical; they used terms like 'brigaded'.

One wet afternoon, I was working on H.M.S. *Exeter*, which had been so gallantly involved in the Battle of the River Plate, where it had helped to corner the *Graf Spee*, when I saw Fairfax go up to Carmody, at the far end of the long table where we had our things out, and pick up a three-ton lorry, with a camouflaged hood and helmeted driver, and turn it over for inspection. 'Exactly like the one I lost a week ago, on the beach,' Fairfax said.

'It's mine,' Carmody said.

'If it's yours, what colour is it?' Fairfax had the lorry behind his back now.

'Sort of green.'

'And underneath what colour is it?'

'Is it brown?'

'If it's really yours, you ought to know.'

Why was I excited at Carmody's ordeal? I was sure that he was being robbed. Yet I admired the way that the thief had made himself the judge in the case. Carmody knew exactly what his matériel consisted of and he was too honest, and too timid, to appropriate anything belonging to the Saint, of all people. I sanded my 'B' turret.

'It's brown.'

'Sorry, squit,' Fairfax said, 'but it's obviously not your lorry, because – look for yourself, if you don't believe me – it's decidedly red.'

Jenks, who had been whittling a stick with his tongue out, drifted over and was observing the confrontation between his mortal enemy and the neutral Carmody. 'Let's have a squint,' he said.

'The question is,' Fairfax said, 'is this lorry mine or the weed's? He says his is brown underneath, but this one's red, isn't it?'

'It's my lorry, Jenks. My mater bought it for me and sent it to me in a parcel. I soaked off the eightpenny stamps. They're in my album; I can show them to you. I call that a sort of brown, don't you, Jenks?'

The injustice made me breathless. I rubbed myself against the bench and the material of my shorts tightened sweetly. It was a trick I had discovered when racing to finish some maths for Mr Oliffe. Fear and pleasure came together as I sweated at my sums.

'You saw me, didn't you, Jordan, playing with it when I got it?'

'I'm trying to *do* something,' I said. Then I saw that Joe Hirsch was watching me. He smiled without moving his lips and came and sat on the table. 'Only I did see him playing with it actually.'

Joe was looking at the plans of H.M.S. *Exeter*. He might have asked me.

'There you are, Jenks.'

'Where am I?' Jenks said.

'"Where am I? Where am I?" You sound like a swooning maiden, Jenks.' Mr Datchet, with his walrus moustache and snorting manner, had come in from the Sun Lounge, where weeds did stamps, and approached the court.

'Purely coincidental, sir!' Fairfax said. He and Jenks smiled together, the best of enemies. 'Do you think it's going to clear up, sir?'

'We might manage a sortie from our beleaguered redoubt in due course,' Datchet said. When he used fine words, he cleared his throat afterwards, as if they had been no fault of his. The story was that he had been wounded in the First War, at Dixmude, and had a glass stomach.

'Pity we can't play cricket, isn't it, sir?'

'The greatest pity in the world, Fairfax. But there's a war on, I'm sorry to say. I advised them against it, but they would proceed.'

Fairfax and Jenks laughed, while a moist Carmody put the rest of his belongings in their wooden box. 'Sir,' Fairfax said, 'would you settle something? Would you say this is red or brown?'

As Mr Datchet cocked his head, he became aware of the anguish in Carmody's face. He looked without illusions at Jenks and at Fairfax. He even glanced, as if in the hope that I might be clever enough to flash him the answer, along the table to where Joe Hirsch was looking at my model. Mr Datchet looked at the three-tonner and said, 'More red than brown, I'd say.'

'There you are, Carmody! British justice. Totally impartial, you can't deny it.'

Fairfax put the lorry in his pocket and went into the Sun Lounge where Macintosh was using his tripod-mounted magnifying glass on some heavily franked penny blacks.

Joe Hirsch said, 'You're going to split that turret if you do it like that.'

'Well, it's my turret to split, isn't it?'

'You'll never get it to svivel like that.'

'Svivel?' I said. 'Von't I?'

He sat with his knees together in his unforgivable shorts. 'I had an uncle who made models.'

'Where?'

'Do it your way. I'm only trying to help.'

'Was your mother always a skivvy?' I said.

The next time the weather was fine enough for us to go again to the beach, I suggested to Carmody, as we were leaving our shoes and preparing for the sharp experience of going barefoot across the gravel, that we attempt something really ambitious in the way of a postwar city. My enthusiasm was compounded of shame (Fairfax still had that lorry) and of fear that Joe Hirsch had made trouble between me and my friend. I brought even bigger slabs of slate from the far corner of the beach. We constructed a concert hall with a stage you could actually see, if you bent right down. We were in bathing trunks only. Mr Quarles, in his sports jacket and flannels, and his brown shoes with a pattern of holes above the toecap, paced about looking hot and scornful. 'The little girls have an endless appetite for sand castles,' he allowed us to overhear him say as Mr Llewellyn came to join him.

Mr Llewellyn was not entitled to a gown. He would not have been a master at all under peacetime circumstances. He had grey, springy hair, cut very short, and fierce suspicions. He suspected everyone was imitating him, but he was incapable of detecting their mimicry: Welsh intonations did not strike him as unusual.

23

His resentment could boil up for no obvious reason. He would kick out with his black, military boots. He wore a blue shirt with a cream-coloured tie. 'It keeps them out of mischief, Quarles, doesn't it?' he said.

'This isn't what they'd be doing in Germany, by a long chalk. They don't baby them there like we do here. We shall never learn until it's too late.'

Carmody was doing something delicate – the control tower of our village aerodrome, I think – when he said, 'I've decided to tell my pater about Fairfax.'

'I shouldn't do that,' I said.

'People shouldn't be allowed to steal things and get away with it.'

'I shouldn't tell your pater if I were you. He'll probably give it back eventually.'

'Will you ask him?'

At the edge of the beach, on the limit of forbidden ground, Fairfax and Macintosh were collecting winkles and limpets from the jagged rocks. Jenks and Gladstone, one of the Bulldog's sly lieutenants, were dodging from cover to cover and creeping up on the Saint. If it was a comfort not to be facing Jenks's stinging accuracy, I wished that I could prove to Fairfax how brave I could be. If I could save his life, or something like that, I could then ask him to return Carmody's lorry.

'I think it's pathetic, don't you,' Carmody said, 'pretending to be the Saint and people and having wars?'

'Some people haven't got better things to do,' I said.

'Si pacem requiris,' Mr Quarles said, 'bellum para.' He made a sour face at our latest paradise. 'Utopia has never been my idea of a desirable destination.' He looked with greater approval over to where Fairfax had evaded Jenks and his men and was sprinting, with Macintosh behind him, to where Blessed and Taylor, two more of his gang, were in ambush. As Jenks and Gladstone gave chase, they were lured into a hail of winkles. 'Leadership,' Mr Quarles said. 'It can't be taught. Fairfax has it. Others not. What on earth is going on?'

Joe Hirsch was by the slipway and had called to his mother, who was walking, with a string bag of groceries, from the hotel entrance towards the black cottage where she had her quarters. Hilde stopped and came a few steps down the green slipperiness towards her son.

'You know what we could do when we've finished, Carmody, don't you?' I said, in a voice intended to distract Mr Quarles.

'What?'

'Bomb it.'

'Jordan,' Mr Quarles said.

'Sir?'

'Were you not deputed to be Hirsch's spiritual guardian and mundane mentor?'

'Well, sir . . .'

'I suggest that you honour that office. He's talking to strangers.'

'That's his mater, sir.'

'Who, during school hours, qualifies as a stranger. If he's going to stay with us, had he not better learn, as others have, how we behave in this country? Who better to instruct him than your excellent self?'

I sighed and started to go up the beach, making dents in the drying sand with my heavy heels. Joe was holding a jar of green shrimps up to his mother. 'For you, mutti.'

Hilde said, 'Share them with your friends.'

'I have no friends.'

'Of course you have.'

'I say, Hirsch . . .'

'You see?' Hilde said.

'Sorry, but Mr Quarles says you're out of bounds. You're to come down to where everyone else is.'

Hilde was wearing flat shoes and a black skirt with a white blouse. The sun gleamed in her dark eyes. She had one sinuous plait at the back of her head. 'How are you today, Michael?'

'I'm all right. I'm very sorry, but . . .'

'It's very nice of you to come and tell us,' Hilde said. 'Would you like to come and have tea with us in the cottage one day?'

'I'd have to get per.'

'Sunday,' she said. 'Get it for Sunday. Do you eat shrimps?'

'Sometimes,' I said.

'Share them with Michael, Osip,' she said.

'Jordan . . .' Mr Quarles was calling.

'We've got to go, Hirsch.'

Hilde turned and missed her step on the green stones; I caught her bare arm as she retrieved her balance. It had hairs on it. 'That was a near one!' There was modest ostentation in her slang, as if she were posing as a skivvy and wanted to prove that she was capable of being a different sort of woman entirely.

'It must be hells hard for you,' I said, as we went back down the sand towards Mr Quarles. 'Having your mater on the premises.'

'Don't you like your mother?'

'I wouldn't like her on the premises.' I dreaded getting near Mr Quarles. I stopped and looked into Joe's jar. 'Especially if she was skivvying.'

Joe jerked the jar. A gob of water got me in the eye. In an instant we were rolling on the ground. Joe was stronger, and angrier, than I expected. I tried to laugh, but we were really fighting. He got on top of me and knelt on my biceps. I bucked and tipped him off and rolled over. He got his hand behind my head and forced my face into the beach. 'Eat it,' he said. 'Eat it.'

I reached back and forced his hand away from my neck and suddenly seemed stronger. I toppled him and was about to mash sand in his face when I saw the Major standing above us on the slipway. 'Stop that at once.'

The jar of shrimps, still half-filled with water, was tilted but intact. Joe picked it up and said, 'Why can I not speak to my mother when I see her?'

'We were only playing, sir,' I said.

'Of course you may speak to her,' the Major said. 'Certainly you may salute her.'

'Salute her?'

'Whatever's appropriate. Now you'd better run down to the sea, both of you, and get rid of that sand.'

'I hate this place,' Joe Hirsch said, as we turned to go down to the advancing sea. 'I'd do anything to get away. Why are you so frightened of them?'

'I didn't mean it about your mother,' I said.

After tea, the whole school was told to stay in the dining room. The Major brought two strangers into the room. The piano was wheeled from the corner by Reynolds and Weigall, the head of the school. The woman sat down and put music on the rack. Monsieur Bergeret and Madame Donzeac were the representatives of our gallant allies, the French. They were making the rounds of schools like ours so that we would understand, as General de Gaulle had said, that France had lost a battle, but it had not lost the war. He and Madame Donzeac began by singing 'There'll always be an England' and then they gave us '*La Marseillaise*'. When invited to join in the chorus, the Major and his wife affected enthusiasm, but Mr Quarles pressed his purple lips together and was not to be seduced. Hilde Hirsch was with the rest of the domestic staff, except for Mad Eric, whose uncertain behaviour exempted him. I could hear her nice voice in the Marseillaise. She seemed more confident than Mr Datchet, who taught us French.

Monsieur Bergeret opened a small unEnglish attaché case and took out a box of paper French flags (the Croix de Lorraine in the white of the tricolor) and a collecting tin. Madame Donzeac, whose lipstick looked peculiar after her strenuous singing, dangled the tin while Monsieur Bergeret offered us flags. People fumbled and came out with some coins. Joe was looking at me. He had no money. I made a little questioning gesture, as if I might have failed to get some point. Was Madame Donzeac, whose hectic blonde curls fell over her shoulders, the reason for his nervousness? I looked over to where Hilde, aware of her son's distress, wanted to do something to help him and could not. It was a moment of power and pleasure; kindness and cruelty were one. Monsieur Bergeret was pinning a flag on Fairfax's lapel and touched his head. '*Merci*,' he was saying, '*vive l'Angleterre!*'

I took money from my pocket. I knew the joy of riches. I found another sixpence, which I was afraid I had lost, in the fluff at the bottom of my back pocket. I touched Joe's hand and slipped the spare tizzy into it. 'For the shrimps,' I whispered as Madame Donzeac's sticky mouth and demanding tin came towards us.

The war was elsewhere. It came to us in echoes. London was still being bombed; campaigns were being fought all over the world, except in Switzerland (home of the Red Cross) and Sweden (which sold wolfram to the Germans), but we lived in a cocoon of peace. Imagination flirted with the danger we were spared. Singer drew lifelike pictures of Stalingrad; 'street fighting' had a brutal allure. (North Africa was a piece of cake by comparison.) The crucial moment, we all knew, would be when Mr Churchill considered the time to be ripe for a Second Front. In the holidays, when I was allowed to go home to Court Royal, I saw SECOND FRONT NOW on the walls of railway bridges. The whitewash reminded me of the WE WANT WATNEYS hoardings.

One night I was dreaming of being on a destroyer, Gerald Lewin's cap on my ears and foreign shorts embarrassing my knees, when I was shaken awake. Joe Hirsch was jogging my shoulder. Flashes showed at the thinly curtained windows. At first I thought it was a thunderstorm. Then I realized that the Germans were bombing Cardiff, on the far side of the Bristol Channel. Sombre redness stained the sky. The docks were on fire. I had never seen an air raid before, but the whole scene seemed so familiar that I yawned and fretted my feet together. 'It's miles away.'

Then came the sound of engines; their stammer promised that they were German. The throb of Dornier engines was notoriously irregular. The informed view was that this lack of steadiness was evidence that Hitler would lose the war; allied engines were unfaltering. Joe opened the window and leaned out. I was afraid he might wake the Rhode Island Reds, as the invading Gauls had disturbed the Capitoline geese, and bring Mrs Stanhope out, possibly in her Wellingtons. The engines belonged to a single bomber which now came across the lurid sky, a tag of flame attached to one wing. The plane came lower and lower, fast. 'Junkers JU 88,' I said. 'He's going to crash.'

'No, he's not,' Joe said.

'He's going to crash right into us. We better tell someone.'

The tag of flame seemed to disappear. Then it was there again. The stiff bird thickened and filled the sky and then it swooped up and past us. There was no sign of flame as it surged along the valley and throbbed into the distance. 'He did it,' Joe said.

'He'll crash before he gets home,' I said. 'Bet you! Did what?'

'Put it out. That's why he dived. If you go fast enough, it goes out. Don't you know that?'

'Not always. They'll probably shoot it down anyway.'

'I'd like to run away from this place,' Joe said.

'I wonder what it's like to be German,' I said.

'You've got a sister, haven't you?' Joe Hirsch said.

'I might have.'

'Have you ever seen her?'

'What do you mean? Of course.'

'You know what she looks like then, do you, in the bath?'

'Zen?' I said. 'Zen?'

My mother sent me a model kit of the latest fighter-bomber. It had a complicated engine cowling, so I asked Carmody to help me with it. We were trusted with razor blades by Mr Oliffe, just for the afternoon, so that we could do the tricky bits. It must have been raining; we would have been outdoors otherwise. Brasier-Creagh came over and said that the Magger wanted to see Carmody in his study, soon as poss.

'What've you done now, Carmody?' I said.

Fairfax was sitting on the long table, scraping wax from the

29

cracks with a special bit of his Swiss army penknife and pressing it into a ball. 'Probably whipped some squit's most precious possession,' he said.

'Back in a tick,' Carmody said.

'I do like the niff of those paints, don't you, Jordan?' Brasier-Creagh said.

'We can't open them until the whole thing's finished,' I said.

How did we know that Carmody's father was dead? He went out of the room and he came back and we knew. He came back to where he had been working on the Mosquito and he picked up his half of the razor blade which Mr Oliffe had broken to give us and resumed work on the engine nacelles.

Mr Oliffe put one of his small feet on the bench by Carmody and simply watched him. I was filled with love for the maths master. It was a love such as I had never felt for my father. Mr Oliffe's tenderness made no demand on its object. Its goodness was entirely modest. It made me envy Carmody, who seemed unaware of it.

Fairfax had come back to the end of the table. He looked at me and he looked at Mr Oliffe. He took something from his pocket and held it down on the table as if it were alive. Then, with a convulsive gesture, he scooted the three-ton lorry along the polished surface. It stopped against the Mosquito instructions, in front of Carmody. Carmody blew a stubble of shaved balsa from the engine cowling and then he picked up the lorry and put it in his pocket. He was going to go on with the model, but then he started to cry. Mr Oliffe put his hand on Carmody's shoulder and stayed there with him. I started to bite my thumbnail, where it was juiciest.

Hilde Hirsch had made a bright little home of the black cottage. The cushions on the dull couch had been covered with her own material. She had books on the shelf and wild flowers in a cracked vase. The room where we had tea was so small that our knees touched. She had a small bedroom with a window at the side. The sitting room looked on to a wooden balcony, right over the rocks. She had made chocolate chip biscuits and served cocoa in bulldog mugs.

'Tell me something, Michael: did you go to church this morning?'

'It's compulsory,' I said. 'Unless . . . your parents come down or something like that.'

'Your mother and father don't mind?'

'They're not here, are they?' I said. 'These are very good biscuits. You didn't make them, did you, Mrs Hirsch?'

'Didn't I, Michael?'

'Why do you go to church?' Joe said.

'It's all very well for you,' I said. 'You've got your mother on Sundays.'

'You don't believe in it, do you?'

'This is England,' I said. 'This is England. You have to get used to it. My family's been here since the eighteenth century, if you know when that was. We've all got the same God, haven't we?'

'I wish we'd gone to America,' Joe said.

'I know someone who did,' I said, 'and they were torpedoed on the way over. His name was Richardson. He sang to people in the lifeboat and he had his picture in the *Daily Crusader*. I wish I could sing. You know French, don't you?'

'*Un peu*,' Hilde Hirsch said.

'My mother worked on a newspaper,' Joe Hirsch said. 'Before.'

'Isn't it awful about Carmody's father? He was on some special mission and his plane crashed. He may get a medal possibly. Carmody's being very brave.'

'People have to be,' Hilde Hirsch said. 'Where is your father at the moment?'

'Oh he won't tell us that, will you, Jordan? He thinks we're spies, mutti. He thinks we've got a secret wireless in the roof.'

'He doesn't think anything of the kind, Osip. Don't say things like that.'

'He wishes we were. He'd like to see us taken away, wouldn't you, Jordan? Under escort. By people with bayonets. Deny it.'

'What did your father do, before the war, Michael?'

'He was a barrister,' I said. 'I don't suppose you had them where you came from. Only barristers can become judges and wear wigs. He isn't a K.C. yet, but he probably will be after the war.'

'And your mother?'

'She's at home,' I said. 'She does voluntary work at the hospital and places. My sister's going to be in the WRENS when she's eighteen.'

'And what's her name?'

'Rachel. Which I don't like.'

'You don't like your sister?' Hilde said.

'Her name.'

'I can guess why,' Joe said.

'Can you? Why?'

'I can guess,' Joe said.

'I don't suppose you've got a sister or anything, have you?'

'I've probably got some cousins, haven't I, mutti?'

How could anyone *probably* have cousins? Hilde's nod suggested something that I did not quite understand, nor quite fail to understand. 'When's she going to be eighteen exactly?' Joe said.

'Probably next year,' I said.

'Probably!' Joe said.

'I think I should be getting back really, Mrs Hirsch.'

'So soon?' She went to a corner cupboard, on a bracket at the back of the room, and turned around with things in her hand. 'You've been so nice to Joseph,' she said.

There were American candy bars and chewing gum. 'Honestly,' I said.

'Don't be silly, Michael. I can always get some more.'

'He thinks they're black market.'

'They were a present. And I'd like to share them with you.'

'We're really not supposed to.'

'You know Leo and Brad, don't you, Osip?'

'I'll have them if he doesn't want them,' Joe said.

'We should share things. If you have any trouble, you can tell them where you got them from.'

'Thanks awfully, Mrs Hirsch, but I've honestly had enough.'

When I went into the second-form room for maths the following morning, there was a folded piece of paper on my desk. On it was written, 'Will you join us and take the oath?' Underneath was a drawing of a bulldog. Fairfax came in and gave me his unblinking stare. Did he know that I was being canvassed by his enemies? Or that I should much prefer to be solicited by him? He sat down in his place, without altering his expression, as Mr Oliffe and the others came in. Carmody sat next to me. If I took the oath, he would become a civilian; I should be practically forbidden to have anything to do with him. Jenks was not in our form, so I had until the end of the morning, at least, before I was obliged to respond. During cold milk, I saw Joe Hirsch was with Fairfax, so I had no opportunity to talk to the Saint. He was chewing gum.

We had history with Mr Quarles after cold milk, in the Sun Lounge. 'Until the British arrived in India,' he told us, 'there was nothing but chaos, misery and oppression. There was, in particular, no such thing as justice whatsoever. The French, of course, were trying to get everything out and put nothing in; likewise the Portuguese. And then came Clive . . . Are you thinking of joining us at all, Jordan, or do you, as usual, have better things to think about?'

Hilde was running, breathless, up between the laurels towards the putting green, breasts jolting. She turned and looked out at the bay and then she held her side for a moment, gasping, and seemed to be looking for help. She ran on towards us. 'It's Mrs Hirsch, sir,' I said.

'She may for all we know be bringing the good news from Aix to Ghent, but she does not, whatever her qualities, play any known part in eighteenth-century history. Hence . . .'

Hilde was tapping on the glass doors. Mr Quarles drew down his upper lip. The corners of his mouth became vertical. He made a heavy business of unlatching the sliding doors. 'I *hope* something is wrong,' he said.

'There's something in ze bay.' Hilde's fear made her foreign. 'Floating. I sink it's a mine.'

Mr Quarles smiled at Hilde and then at us. 'Carmody, you're the reliable one: go and tell the headmaster there may be a mine in the bay. I'm going to see. The rest of you . . .' He pressed the centre of his chin with one finger. 'Go out of these doors and straight along to the kitchen entrance and wait there, quietly. Fairfax, you're the temporary officer in charge.'

Joe said, 'Mutti . . .'

Mr Quarles pushed Hilde's shoulder, so that she turned towards the bay again, and then took her by the elbow and marched her down the drive. 'Assuming that there really *is* something in the bay.'

We went along the gravel, past Major Stanhope's study, where Carmody was knocking on the door. Mad Eric was attacking a tub of potatoes with a wicked knife by the kitchen entrance. He had a soft moustache, quite black, which never thickened and was never shaved. The rest of his moony face was blanched except for the busy eyes. He smirked as if we had come to enrol him in some escapade. I said, 'Don't you think we should change out of our house shoes, if there's going to be a full-scale evacuation?'

Fairfax said, 'Debatable.'

I said, 'I say, Fairfax, the Drummonds have asked me to, you know, join them.'

'Congratulations.' He took a strip of Spearmint from his top pocket, unsleeved its sugared pinkness and slipped it between his lips.

'I haven't decided yet,' I said.

The Major was bringing the rest of the school out of the front door. They were all still wearing their house shoes. The lowest form was laughing and chattering. 'It's as if the House of Israel had been delivered from bondage,' Mr Quarles said. 'As perhaps indeed it has in certain instances.'

'Where is my mother?' Joe Hirsch said.

'She has duties to perform,' Mr Quarles said.

'I want to stay with her.'

'You'll do what discipline tells you to do. You'll stay here until otherwise instructed.'

Joe walked along the drive to where Major Stanhope was lining up the rest of the school and checking that no one was missing. 'I want to stay with my mother.'

The Major put his hand on Joe's shoulder. 'She's with Mrs Stanhope. They're making some sandwiches. They're quite safe and I shall be bringing them along to join the rest of you in just a few minutes.' The Major fastened the unusual button at the top of Joe's sweater. 'You'll see her presently.'

'Self, self, self,' Mr Quarles said. 'All that's going to have to change.' He pushed the sleeve away from his watch with his other wrist. 'Confusion, disorder, lack of respect. These three, and the worst of them is lack of respect.'

I said, 'Sir, how many men did Clive have at Plassey?'

'It wasn't numbers that mattered, Jordan, then or now. It was battle-hardened discipline. Which we are, I'm sorry to say, sorely lacking in this establishment.'

'I'm a bit worried about my stamps, sir,' Carmody said. 'Do you think they'll be all right in the Sun Lounge?'

'Those who depend on others for their safety, Carmody, have always and will always be at the mercy of the fortunes of war.'

We walked past the fuchsias and up the long lane away from the sea, Mr Quarles at the head of the column, Mr Oliffe with the youngest Georgians at the back. Mr Quarles might have been leading us to the assault of some steep citadel where we might at last recover our pride, perhaps at the cost of our lives. It was not a retreat for him, but a crusade, a redemption, and a punishment. We should, he said, prepare ourselves to walk all day, if necessary. We might well have to sleep in the open. The July fields, with their tall and lolling hedges, did not make that prospect as disagreeable as Mr Quarles might have liked. The possibility of the mine exploding in Morte Bay and destroying the Lorna Doone Hotel was both thrilling and alarming. A new life might be forced upon us, or we might have to return home for the holidays before the due date, twenty-six days ahead. We passed a farmer leading two shaggy horses with thick shanks. One of the horses had a long black penis.

We walked and walked. Far beyond the range of our usual walks, we came to a crossroads and there was the Major with the Wolseley and Mrs Stanhope and Mad Eric and Hilde and the Hag. The boot of the car was open and I saw stacks of sandwiches and a big enamel drum, with a tap on it. Our emergency turned into a picnic. We went through a five-barred gate; its elongated diagonal had a curl at the top. We sat down on the grass, among crisp cowpats. They looked like the mines soldiers found in the desert. The sandwiches were not bad: egg, tomato, Shippam's paste and green rhubarb jam. The enamel drum had cocoa in it. It was not as good as Hilde's had been. After I had finished, I found some long grass and pulled out the inner tubes, where they went pale, and nibbled the sweetness. I also put some dandelion juice on a wart just below the knuckles of my left hand. If you did it every day, the wart went flaky and you could pick it off. Major Stanhope was sitting on a piece of newspaper, smoking his pipe, when Mr Quarles approached him. Mr Quarles had something on his shoe which he was removing with a twig. 'Major,' he said, 'I've been hoping possibly for a quiet word.'

The Magger looked up.

'Because may I say something?' Mr Quarles shot one leg out and lowered himself to the ground. He could turn ordinary actions into a form of reproach, even menace. 'Frankly, I'm not unduly impressed by this morning. It rather confirms something.'

The Major took his pipe from his mouth and looked into the bowl. He did something with the long nail of his little finger and then he replaced the pipe under his yellowed moustache.

'We have a relatively minor crisis and what happens?'

The Major dabbed a flake of tobacco from the tip of his tongue and rubbed it to dust before cleaning his fingers on the grass.

'Did anyone know where to go or what to do? Personally, I look at things under two principal headings: motivation, performance. And in the light of what I feel, headmaster, I should like to make one specific recommendation.'

Major Stanhope tilted his head downwards and looked up at Mr Quarles.

'Reds and blues,' Mr Quarles said.

The Major pulled his shoe to him and tightened the laces.

'We had them at Petworth. Officially organized, reds and blues divert a lot of otherwise indiscriminate energy into worthwhile channels. Are you aware of certain undercurrents? I'm sure you are. I rather admire some of them. Not everyone wants to play sand castles all day and all night. Reds and blues, efficiently organized, officially sponsored, create a competitive, yet disciplined, system throughout the day.'

'And what about the night?' Major Stanhope said. 'Do you also propose that there be competition at night?'

'Is this a bad moment, headmaster? They are supposed to be *boys*. Now if they were schooled to responsibility, through their colour-captains and thus to each other, we should have a more competent and – dare I say? – a more patriotic tone. How long is the war going to continue? And when, I wonder, will the country itself become aware that fifty per cent is less than a hundred per cent? These boys are going to go into the forces one of these days. They're going to be officers, sir, some of them, I trust. Some of them, I rather trust *not*.'

'I say, Jordan . . .' Gladstone was calling to me from a cowpat whose soft centre he was probing with a whittled stick. I shook my head and was busy with a thread in my jacket. Spying on grown-ups was too delicious to be abandoned.

'After the war, whatever the outcome, we're going to need the two great Os: order, organization. We shall certainly be able to dispense with sissification in all its forms. I hardly think that we need specifically to favour those who can build sand castles and arrange British Colonials, do we quite?' Mr Quarles barely managed to tolerate the courteous hearing the Major was giving him. 'It's nobody's fault that we can't have cricket, or proper football. Clearly no one can be blamed for moles in present conditions. I have in mind a comprehensive points system: games, work, turn-out, cooperative spirit, something that doesn't purely favour individualism and mark-grubbing, and then a weekly – possibly fortnightly – trooping.'

The Major urgently wanted his matches.

'At which points tallies would be entered on the chart of honour and the best cadet would kiss the banner.'

'Kiss?' the Major said.

'Or possibly salute. This country is in the state it is on account of the clever-clevers. They very nearly cost us everything. It mustn't happen again. If we're not ready for them after the war, we shall find them more than ready for us. They can always salute, or simply stand to attention, alone, in front of the ranks. I hope you don't resent my speaking as freely as I have?'

'On the contrary.' The Major got easily to his feet and brushed the sleeve on which he had been leaning. 'Freedom of speech is something to which I attach great importance. Before, during or after the war.'

Mr Quarles took longer to stand up. 'Excuse me, headmaster,' he said, as if he were now approaching the Magger for the first time, 'but where does one find a corner?'

'A corner? In the corner perhaps?'

'All right to go there?'

'Oh. You could always pop through the hedge while I talk to the boys.'

The Major called for us to gather round. I stood near Fairfax, but he made no recruiting move. Jenks came up beside me. 'What do you say?'

'If you really want me,' I said.

'I'm sorry to tell you,' the Major said, 'but the Bomb Disposal Squad tell me that the mine is still in the bay and they can't be sure when they will be able to defuse or explode it. Hence it is very unlikely that any of you will have the pleasure of doing algebra or irregular verbs this afternoon.' How was it that half of us knew to groan and the other half to cheer at this announcement? 'We've made arrangements to spend the night at Drake Hall, well away from the danger of blast if the mine does have to be detonated. I'm sure that you'll all be particularly careful not to give either Sir Greville or his wife any reason to regret their patriotic generosity. Now I want you to return your mugs to the car and form up ready to move off. It's quite a walk, but you can rest when we arrive. Miss Kellett has plasters if anyone's got a blister.'

Mr Llewellyn, in his stiff boots, watched Brasier-Creagh and Watson go to the Hag for first aid. Mr Quarles came through a gap in the sloe hedge with a new expression on his face. We did not have to stay in forms for the afternoon march, so I joined the group around Mr Oliffe, who claimed that one day man would be able to recapture the past, through mastering light waves. Everything that had ever happened in the world was out there somewhere, racing away from us at the speed of light, which meant that theoretically everything could be received, if you could get ahead of it, so to speak, and retransmitted. Whether it could also be heard again was another matter, since sound travelled at a different speed to light. At all events, history could be seen again as an endless silent film. It was possible that sound could be caught separately and then matched up, so that everything would reassemble as it had been before. We would then know precisely who had killed the little princes in the Tower. I wondered whether everyone would also be able to see how I rubbed myself against the bench when I had a hard piece of work to do.

We walked past a blacksmith's, where a horse had its hoof cocked between a boy's legs. A man in an apron hammered nails into it. It made me think of the Germans and the Japanese. We came to a main road, with a white line down the middle. We were just turning off, back towards the sea, when a line of Americans, in rimless helmets, carrying rifles and off-white packs, came round the corner. Mr Quarles put his hands behind his back and held each elbow in the palm of the other hand. The Americans did not keep step and they were talking. Several carried machine guns across their shoulders. One was holding his like a baby, in front of him. 'You have a problem, Weinstein?'

'My fucking back, sergeant.'

I said to Mr Oliffe, 'Their N.C.O.'s have got their stripes upside down, sir, haven't they?'

In the morning we had walked quickly, to get away from the danger; in the afternoon, we were allowed to straggle. They did not want us to arrive at Drake Hall too early and have nothing to do until bedtime. The house was no bigger than the Lorna Doone Hotel, but it was taller. The slate roof was steep and black. There was a sort of cage at the top, with a weather vane on it. The entrance hall had banners hanging from bossed poles. The material was tattered and might have been in a battle. A staircase with an elaborate balustrade went upstairs. The carpet was worn. We were instructed to stay on the ground floor unless expressly told otherwise.

In the Great Hall we found our red blankets, and pillows. We were going to sleep on the floor. I bagged a place by a suit of armour, near the door. The fireplace had unsplit logs in it. Coats of arms embossed the ceiling beams where they met the side wall. There were sullen portraits, on chains, and real swords above the mantelpiece. Two crossed halberds hung underneath them. Halberds went into people easily, but they did not come out easily.

The beaks went to have tea with Sir Greville and his wife. The Hag was busy with cuts and bruises. Hilde brought Mr Datchet a cup of tea and a biscuit; he sat gratefully in a big wooden chair to drink it. There was no one to stop us exploring upstairs. Joe said there were pictures of women. The women were large and fleshy and seemed to be floating in thin brown soup. I asked Joe whether Fairfax had invited him to join the Saints.

'Wouldn't you like to know?'

'He obviously hasn't.'

'Do you live in a house?'

'We live in a flat,' I said. 'It's much more convenient.'

'I'm going to have a house,' Joe Hirsch said.

We were down again on the half-landing, looking at a Cavalier. Mr Datchet came out of the Great Hall with his cup and saucer. He frowned at us, but the cup disarmed him. Joe said that we were interested in the painting and wondered what date it was. Mr Datchet asked him to find Mrs Hirsch and return the cup, with his thanks. Joe said, 'Of course, sir.' Normally he never called anyone 'sir'.

Supper was in the Refectory. It had long tables like the dining room in the hotel. At the far end, high-backed chairs were pushed up to a shinier, darker table on a stepped dais. Tapestries on the wall depicted threadbare naval battles. Galleons fired broadsides; a fire ship was bearing down on a moored fleet. I still wanted to go to Dartmouth Naval College. Jenks and Gladstone came and sat next to me. 'We've concluded this place harbours German spies,' Gladstone said.

'Debatable,' I said.

'Herr Kurt Vogel possibly,' Gladstone said. 'He's a master of disguise.'

'We're going to do a midnight scout,' Jenks said. 'It looks as if he's got an aerial rigged up on the roof.'

'We'll never get up there,' I said. 'And how –?'

'I've got a luminous watch,' Gladstone said. 'I'll know when it's midnight.'

'By the way,' Jenks said, 'you were talking to Hirsch before. You'd better drop him. I think he's been nobbled.'

'That's not what he told me.'

'All the more reason,' Jenks said. 'You know what they're like.'

We got up together, Jenks and his men, and paraded past Fairfax and Macintosh and Leach. Fairfax said, 'Does anyone happen to know that Jordan means a po?'

I huddled under my red blanket and went to sleep as fast as I could. With any luck, Gladstone wouldn't wake up; but he did.

He shook my shoulder and I saw his fat face in the moonlight. An owl was hooting. Gladstone wasn't wearing his spectacles and his lips were puffy. 'Got your torch?' he said. 'Because let's go.'

The cold floor of the entrance hall made me want to go to the lavatory. We climbed the stairs, under the Cavalier in his black armour (I couldn't resist giving him a burst with my torch, which had a special button for Morse), and then up to the gallery where the naked women floated, with gauze between their legs. We stalked past suits of armour, standing like metal shadows, and turned into totally unknown territory. There were oak chests under mansard windows. Jenks thought Herr Kurt Vogel might keep his wireless equipment in one of them. We opened a couple. They contained papers that made me want to sneeze. We came to a narrow staircase that went up into the roof. 'Aha!' Jenks said.

I said, 'No one's been up this in years.'

'How do you know?' Gladstone said.

I showed them the dust on the steps, and my fingers.

Jenks nodded. I felt clever, and relieved, when he started back towards the main staircase. We came to a door we had passed before. Jenks stopped and put his hand on the knob. Gladstone's glasses were repaired with sticky plaster on one side. Jenks had the door open. His torch frisked the darkness. He came back and signalled us in. I looked along the gallery, where the moonlight fell in icy panels, and then I had to go into the bedroom. Jenks's torch was going yellow. He shone it on an empty four-poster and on the walls. They were decorated with pistols and old guns. 'Aha!' Gladstone said.

Beneath one show of pistols was a tall chest of double drawers. Jenks opened a drawer on one side and then one on the other and made a zig-zag ladder to enable him to reach the pistols.

I said, 'I don't think we should, do you?'

Gladstone said, 'There's a war on in case you didn't know.'

A door banged downstairs. Jenks switched off his torch. We

stood in the darkness. The moon made a faint burn under the door. The windows of the bedroom were heavily curtained. Suddenly, there was a repeated thumping, not far away. 'What's that?' Gladstone said.

'Air lock,' Jenks said. 'We get it at home.'

'Obviously,' I said.

Gladstone said, 'That wasn't; that was a door.'

'Someone's been to the bog. Give me your torch, Blackie. Mine's giving up the ghost.'

I said, 'I can't do much without a torch, Bulldog.'

'There may be a secret compartment,' Jenks said. 'You'd probably best go and keep *cave*.'

I said, 'O.K., if you want. How exactly?'

'Go back and check everything's quiet. Here.' He handed me his waning torch and I went back to the door, opened it, and crept into the gallery. Jenks had *told* me to 'go back', so why shouldn't I descend slowly to ground level again? The head of the balustrade reminded me of the queen in a chess set my father had. I imagined the floor with knights and bishops on it. I stood there for a while and then I started to shiver. I started to cross the floor, making moves like a knight, to see if I could get back to the door of the Great Hall sort of by mistake on purpose. I was still keeping *cave*, of course. A door opened somewhere. I tried to make a quick bishop's move. A door opened behind me. I saw my shadow huge across the hall. I reached for the doorknob and felt a hand on my shoulder.

'Who is that?' Hilde Hirsch was wearing a long white night-gown with a dark brown cape over her shoulders. Her feet were bare and she was small.

I said, 'I was looking for the W.C. I need to go.'

'Michael!' she said. 'It's the middle of the night.'

'I still need to go.'

'How ever long have you been wandering about out here?'

'Not long.'

She put her arms around me and held me against her warmth. The cape was like underfelt. She folded her arms over me and

43

pressed me against her body. 'Come on,' she said. 'I'll show you where.'

She was opening the door from which she had emerged when there was a loud double crash from upstairs. Hilde looked at me with bright eyes and then she pulled me to safety behind the door. We were in a passage leading to the kitchens. A row of bells, covered with cobwebs, hung high on the cracked wall. Hilde opened another door and I saw a lavatory, without a seat, brooms and rusty tins piled next to it. 'Help yourself,' she said.

Nothing would come. I could hear doors opening and shutting and footsteps on the stairs and the beginning of voices. Mr Llewellyn was saying, 'What the . . . ?'

Finally, I really did need to go. Afterwards, we stood together, Hilde behind me with her hands over my shoulders and over my front, near the door which led to trouble. She bent and kissed the top of my head and left her lips against it. 'Don't worry.'

She opened the door and pushed me forward on to the cold floor. A torch beam struck the side of my face. Mr Quarles was on the stairs, in trench coat and slippers. 'And now what's happening?'

'Got them!' Mr Llewellyn had Jenks and Gladstone each by a long ear. He was wearing a macintosh and his big boots without socks.

'And where exactly have you sprung from, Jordan, at this hour?'

'I've just been to the lav, sir.'

'That's 'is story,' Mr Llewellyn said, coming down the stairs with the prisoners.

'He was not sure where to go,' Hilde said. 'I showed him.'

'May I ask what you're doing up and about at this time of night, Mrs Hirsch?'

'No,' Hilde said.

'Get back to bed, Jordan,' Mr Quarles said, 'immediately.'

'Yes, sir.'

Jenks and Gladstone had reached the same step on which Mr

Quarles was standing. 'Well, well,' he said, 'at least we know what's going to happen to these two gentlemen as soon as we get back to normal, don't we?'

Jenks patted the place next to him when I went into breakfast. I said, 'Nothing I could do.'

'One of the drawers had a crack in it. I went straight through.'

'You don't think it might have been a trap, do you?' I said. 'Herr Kurt Vogel can be pretty crafty when he wants to be.'

'Herr Kurt Vogel!' Jenks said.

Gladstone said, 'You were lucky.'

'Can't help it,' I said, 'can I?'

'You might have owned up.'

'What for? Don't you agree, Jenks?'

'No point,' the Bulldog said, 'that I can see.'

'We know what's going to happen to some people,' Macintosh said, 'don't we? Swish, swish, swish!'

'Shut up, hairy,' I said, slicing the top off my boiled egg. The smell was unmistakable. I put my hand up. 'I've got a bad one, sir.'

'Must've been intended for the curate, Jordan,' Mr Quarles said.

'What shall I do, sir?'

'Unless you can find one on the black market, or some similar source, you'll just have to make do with b. and b., won't you?'

'Not particularly fair, sir.'

'There's a war on, Jordan. All's fair in love and war, so they say.'

I sat with my niffy egg and looked at the smoking ships. Suddenly there was a distant explosion. It snowed dust for a moment. The Major got up from the head of the table and went out of the room. Mr Quarles said, 'That sounds like the signal for a spot of algebra later in the day, unless I'm a Dutchman.'

When the Major returned, he clapped his hands. 'Pay attention for a moment. As you may have heard . . .' He paused and laughter grew in the Refectory. We could guess, from the mock gravity of his expression, that the mine had exploded but that no one had been hurt. There was now nothing to prevent us from returning to the Lorna Doone Hotel. Gladstone was pressing his bread into a grey pat. 'One more thing,' the Major said. 'Sir Greville and Lady Drake must not even know, when they return to their home, that St George's has so much as been here. The best thanks we can give for their hospitality is to make sure that they have not the smallest reason to regret it.' Gladstone's bread was now a fluted pyramid. The ends of his fingers went white when he pressed on it. 'Go and fold your blankets and bring them, together with your pillows, to Miss Kellett in the entrance hall, where she'll tick you off.'

The mine had been 'destroyed by rifle fire' after being towed out to sea. Not a single pane of glass at the Lorna Doone Hotel had been cracked by the blast. Joe Hirsch said, 'Just my luck.' Carmody's stamps were where he had left them. I imagined the empty hotel, when we were marching inland, and I wished I could at least have seen it when it was deserted.

The next afternoon, we were back on the beach. It had happened to Jenks and Gladstone the previous night. No one else seemed to know exactly when. Jenks wore his blue bathing trunks so that you could see how accurate the Major's dozen had been. Gladstone wore khaki shorts, because he was a bit fat. The Bulldog led us to the far corner of the beach, where a tumble of slates hid us from Mr Datchet. Gladstone refused, but Jenks showed us all his marks. He was a cavalier and he had hairs coming. 'Right,' he said, 'now I've got a really diabolical plan.'

He led us round to where the cliff arched over our heads. A buttress of rock projected into the sea. There was a wig of turf on top of it.

'I'm sick of certain people thinking they can laugh at us,' Jenks said.

Spence, one of Jenks's smallest lieutenants, called out, '*Cave* Fairfax.'

We ducked into the recess of the rocks. Fairfax and Joe were trawling for shrimps and had come closer. 'Fancy him having a refujew in his gang,' Gladstone said. 'Just for what he can get out of him.'

Jenks said, 'Take a look at this.'

'Cripes,' I said, 'where did that come from?'

'What matters is what we're going to do with it.'

Gladstone said, 'Total war.'

What did the oval miniature have to do with warfare? It showed a man, in half-face, wearing a curly black wig. I thought of Macintosh in the bath.

'The Saint thinks he's so clever,' Jenks said, 'but we'll show him. Spence, come in here, because we've all got to swear an oath of utter and total and complete secrecy. This is serious.'

'Fucking serious,' Gladstone said.

We went back to tea talking together in a conspiratorial way, so that the Saint and company would twig that we had a secret. Afterwards, Spence and I sat together doing the paintwork on my Mosquito. Spence was good at camouflage. We whispered together until Macintosh came sauntering by. Spence said, 'Just as well we hid it in the cave,' and I looked at Mac and said, 'Sssh.' It was all rehearsed, like a play. Macintosh whistled, without producing a tune, and then went to report to Fairfax. I stuck R.A.F. roundels on the Mosquito with special glue and put the pin back in it, to stop it drying out. I winked at Spence, who had freckles. We liked each other because our little show had been successful.

The next time we were on the beach, Jenks gathered the Bulldogs together and made a loud speech about how we were going to collect ammunition over by the rotten boat, on the opposite side of the bay to the cave where we had our head-quarters. He raised his voice more than was realistic and sounded a bit false, but that was only my opinion. He led us all off, swishing a piece of bendy seaweed like an officer. Leach ran to tell Fairfax that we had all left the cave unguarded.

Before tea, a member of the first form always read out a bit from the Bible and then the Major said a prayer, which ended 'through Jesus Christ Our Lord'. Joe Hirsch always looked at me then. Usually, we then sat straight down to tea, but the Major sometimes made announcements, as he did now. He had been contacted by Lady Drake. A valuable piece of jewellery had disappeared from Drake Hall. 'Her ladyship is not accusing anyone from St George's of having taken it, but she does attach considerable sentimental importance to this particular minia-ture, which has a portrait of one of Sir Greville's ancestors on it. It's just possible that someone picked it up without realizing what it was and is afraid to give it back. Now, I very much hope that no one at St George's has seen it at all, and that it will turn up at Drake Hall, but if anyone has seen it, or has it in his possession, or knows who has, now is the time to say so. I shall take a lenient view if this miniature – it's about this size – is returned to me at once. I shall be less indulgent in due course.'

Jenks looked around so realistically that I almost expected someone to step forward. One thing was certain: even if the Saint was now stuck with the missing goods, Fairfax would never, never tell the Major how he had come by it. I trusted our enemies completely.

When no one reported himself, the Major announced that he had no choice but to make a thorough search of all our effects. It took place directly after tea, which was cucumber and Marmite, with margarine. We had to stay in our places while the staff went through our things. We waited and waited and then the Major came in and stood and looked at us. One master after another returned. Mr Llewellyn, Mr Datchet, Mr Quarles and even Mr Oliffe looked at us as if we were beyond redemption.

'Nothing?'

I wished we were doing Latin.

The Major said, 'There doesn't seem to be anywhere else we can look, does there?' His voice was old.

'Does there seriously not, headmaster?' Mr Quarles's mouth was drawn down as severely as I had ever seen it. 'Does there seriously not?'

The headmaster touched one of his eyes with the silk handkerchief from his top pocket. 'You'd all better go to bed,' he said, 'at once.' He cleared his throat when he had finished speaking. We filed out, murmuring 'Good night, sir' in our usual way, but we received no answer. Usually, the Major called each of us by our names when he said good night.

Mr Quarles was not in early school for Latin in the morning. We sat there waiting. Then we saw him and Mr Llewellyn coming up through the laurels, past the putting green and the glass doors of the Sun Lounge. Mr Llewellyn was talking, but Mr Quarles's mouth was particularly severe on one side. He walked towards the porte-cochere, never saying a word.

When Mr Quarles eventually came into the Sun Lounge, shrugging into his gown with the velvet bows, he told us to open our books. He put Joe on to translate. After the bell had gone, he said, 'Hirsch, you're wanted in the headmaster's study.'

On the way to Mr Oliffe for maths, in the Card Room, I went up to Fairfax. 'I say, can I talk to you possibly?'

'Have you got your tongue with you?'

'Because what's going to happen about Hirsch?'

'Your guess is as good as mine,' Fairfax said. 'Unless it's better.'

'Aren't you going to say anything?'

'About what?'

When the Major accused Joe of taking the miniature from Drake Hall, he denied it. But when he was asked how it came to be in his possession, he said nothing. Hilde was summoned. She begged him to tell the truth. But Joe had been long enough at St George's for her appeal to embarrass rather than move him. When she called him 'Osip', he glared. The Major may have guessed, or hoped, that there was an explanation which would acquit them both, but he was humiliated by their reticence. He must almost have wished that the miniature had not been found; Mr Quarles had had a triumph and would doubtless make great use of it. The Major offered Joe, and his mother, time to consider the implications of the discovery, but Hilde had no excuse to offer. Joe remained sullenly, almost happily, silent. Why should he say anything? By being expelled he would win the respect of those whom he was eager to leave.

While we were drinking our cold milk, Hilde walked along the gravel road towards the black cottage. Joe came into the Residents' Lounge to get his things from his locker. He never looked at me. I found Jenks in the bogs.

I said, 'What're we going to do now?'

'History, aren't we?'

'About Hirsch getting the blame.'

'The plan worked,' Jenks said.

'Yes, but honestly.'

'Him or us,' Gladstone said.

'It doesn't seem very fair.'

'All's fair in love and war, Blackie.'

'We swore an oath,' Gladstone said. 'And an oath's an oath.'

'Yes, and don't you forget it,' Jenks said.

After lunch we were told to go straight to the beach. Mr Quarles's sternest mouth deterred questions about the lack of a 'rest'. By the time we had shed our house shoes and were hopping across the sharp gravel, the Major had the Wolseley out in front of the porte-cochère. In his pierced shoes, Mr Quarles watched our wincing, barefoot progress with disdain. Hilde Hirsch came up towards us, carrying her two suitcases. My father had told me always to help women who were carrying heavy things. I said to Mr Quarles, 'Shall I lend a hand, sir?'

'Get on down to the beach if I were you, Jordan.'

Hilde put the cases down and watched us go past. Her forgiveness was a final rebuke. Carmody raced to catch me up as soon as we were on the earthy part of the path. 'I've had an idea,' he said.

'Save it,' I said.

I stood to one side, staring into the shrubbery as if I were after a purple emperor on a leaf. Everyone went past. Mr Llewellyn was with Mr Quarles, on the way to his cottage. 'It looks as if our allies will have to look elsewhere for their entertainment,' Mr Quarles was saying.

I said, 'Just going back to the lav, sir.'

Major Stanhope was putting Hilde's suitcases into the boot of the Wolseley. Joe came out of the Private Side carrying the case with flaps. He had all his foreign clothes on. I said, 'Can I speak to you, please, sir?'

The Major said, 'This isn't an ideal moment, Jordan.'

'It's rather important, sir,' I said.

We went inside. Hilde and Joe stood by the car. Mrs Stanhope was carrying a bucket of scraps to the Rhode Island Reds. ('They have the same lunch as we do,' was the standard joke.) The Major rearranged the pipes on the rack in front of him, and used thumb and forefinger to straighten his moustache. He waited patiently until I had said what I had to say. 'And why should I believe all this, Jordan?'

'Because it's true, sir.'

'So according to you Hirsch didn't take something he admits he had?'

'He maybe had it, sir, but he never took it.'

'And you know who did?'

'Roughly, sir.'

'You'd better get back down to the beach. I shall consider what you've told me and . . .'

'I never wanted to say anything, sir.'

'I can imagine that. Nor shall I advertise your . . . *démarche*.' The Major was a teacher. 'And now off you go.'

Carmody was building a headquarters for the British forces which would one day be garrisoned in Germany. It would serve as an example for the Germans, with its theatre and its church and its sports facilities. The prison and the barracks were concealed behind the public buildings and the airport. I helped Carmody for a while and asked him what he was doing in the hols. He was going to the Lake District with his mother. My mother and sister were coming down for a week in August, but otherwise I should almost certainly be staying at Morte Bay. Carmody, of course, now had his mother to himself.

I prospected for shrimps in the deep rock pools. Jenks and Gladstone strolled over to me eventually. 'What exactly do you think you're doing?' Gladstone said.

'Shrimping.'

'Who've you been talking to?'

'Carmody mostly. Why?'

'Have you heard the news?'

'No.'

'The Magger's giving him one more chance.'

'Giving who?'

'You know.'

'Do I?'

'The Saint's got a new hideout,' Jenks said.

'Where's that?'

'It's a bit difficult to recce,' Gladstone said. 'We think it's behind the flat rock.'

I said, 'I'll go and recce it, if you like.'

'It's a bit risky,' Gladstone said.

'I don't mind,' I said.

'I'm not sorry,' Jenks said.

'What about?'

'Hirsch. Even if he is what he is.'

'It was a hells clever plan,' Gladstone said, 'of ours.'

'Of *mine*,' Jenks said.

They took Spence and found some winkles and started bombarding Leach, who called up Fairfax and Macintosh as reinforcements, while I headed for the flat rock. I might have gone right round, at the back of the bay, and crept along under cover of the fallen slates without Fairfax and the others having a chance to guess what I was doing, but I had no wish for concealment. It was as if I were no longer a schoolboy. Joe Hirsch came down the slipway and I only pretended to duck behind some rocks. He looked over at me and then sauntered towards Fairfax. I scampered on towards the flat rock and crabbed my way across it.

There was little of interest in the hideout, apart from some shells and a stack of driftwood and a heap of old oranges, tough as leather, which had floated in ages ago from a wrecked cargo ship. I stayed in the hideout until I thought no one was going to find me, then I backed out and started down towards the flat rock. Fairfax and Macintosh caught me as I jumped down on to it and soon had my arms up behind my back. Joe Hirsch was in the middle of the beach, talking to Carmody. Macintosh sat on me while Leach went to find some whippy seaweed.

'We know what happens to thieves, don't we?' Fairfax said.

'And sneaks,' Leach said.

'Stand up,' Fairfax said.

'Get his things down.'

'Why are you a roundhead?' Gladstone said. 'As if we didn't know.'

They were careful where they lashed me because they didn't want any of the beaks to see the marks. They went on until Mr Quarles called us to tea.

Hilde Hirsch was pegging washing on the balcony outside her cottage. I did not look directly at her as I limped towards the slipway. I hoped that what Fairfax and Co. had done would wipe the slate clean, but I suspected that neither the Saint nor the Bulldog would ever want me again. Oh well, next term I should be in the first form, doing proper Greek and having Latin with the Major. I should have the chance to go right up to the top, if I timed my answers correctly, and there would be scholarship papers to do, in preparation for things that really mattered. Joe Hirsch was not hurrying, but I knew that he intended to catch me up. I did not really want him to thank me for what I had done, because it would make it even more obvious to everyone. At the same time, I felt that he and I now were two of a kind. We would no longer need to pretend to be divided by our silly allegiance to the Saint or the Bulldog. I stopped on the road, by the purple sea wall, and made out that I had got something in my eye. He came up to me, as I was pulling my eyelid down. He stood there and I thought we were really friends at last. He smiled, in a rather wise way and then, as he went on up to the Lorna Doone Hotel, he left a single word behind him, like a tip under a saucer: 'Traitor.'

II

My father never spoke of having fought in the war. He had been in the army and he had carried a revolver, but he had no illusions of having been a proper soldier. His career at the criminal bar made him an obvious choice for the Judge-Advocate's department, where a K.C. in his own chambers, Simon Edge-Partington, was a senior officer. My father's reputation was based on thorough preparation of even the dullest case. He could defend the indefensible with a professional zeal which never countenanced dishonesty: anyone who hoped that he might massage a witness was soon disabused. He never attacked the police, though he could be mordantly silent in the face of over-rehearsed officers. His capacity to stand in his place, swaying slightly, embarrassed for a man whose job could oblige him to say implausible things, made magistrates smile and caused experienced policemen to redden in the witness box.

Convention pleased, even amused him. He wore his black coat and striped trousers and bowler hat every day, yet each day he seemed to choose to wear them. He selected what turned out to be invariable. He always carried his furled umbrella, even in the hottest August. Simon Edge-Partington said that Jordan was more reliable than the weather. During the war, this regularity was disrupted, but my father tried to give disruption a certain form. He returned home to Court Royal whenever he could, often without warning, straight from a lift in a military aircraft. He rang the bell of our flat with his usual double-buzz, as though he had come direct from the Bailey. My mother's war work was done in the morning, when she ran the Wandsworth Borough car pool; her afternoons and evenings were nearly always spent at number 10, Trafalgar House, Court Royal. My father would not have liked her to be out when he arrived. Once, towards the end of the war, when I was more regularly at home for the holidays, the double-buzz sounded and I had my first sight of Colonel Jordan, in red tabs. My mother had invited a surgeon and his wife for drinks with two of his ex-patients. One of them was an American top sergeant called Nathanson, who had been wounded in Normandy. The warmth of my father's greeting, his refusal to be called anything but Samuel in his own home, and his apology for 'dropping in unannounced like this' served prompt, polite notice that the company should drink up and go. Why else did he suggest that they have another drink? Buddy Nathanson knew from my mother that Samuel was on the Control Commission and began to ask questions about the concentration camps. Was enough being done to punish those responsible for these terrible things? What did Samuel *feel* about it all? The presence of my mother and of Mrs Gilmour seemed to my father to make the conversation untimely. As he was going, Nathanson said something in a language I could not understand. My father's mouth went very straight and he said, 'Goodbye, sergeant.'

The next morning, he asked me whether I should be free on Saturday to do something with him. He spoke curtly, as if I had refused a proposal he had not yet made. 'You've got a suit presumably?' I had indeed: several pages of clothing coupons had been required for the regulation jacket and trousers with which I had recently been despatched to my public school. 'And a hat?'

'*Hat*?'

'Perhaps I've got one you can wear.'

'I don't want to wear a hat,' I said.

'And if I want you to wear a hat?'

'Whatever for?'

We were going to a service in the City. The roofless building in which the ceremony was held had been almost completely wrecked in the Blitz. Wild flowers grew amid the tumble of bricks on which hundreds of hatted, and capped, men took their stand. Incomprehensible prayers were chanted by bearded men in tasselled silk scarves. We mourned a catastrophe of which almost nothing had yet been said. It was a mass funeral without bodies. The truth poured on us, invisibly, from the clear sky and marked us for the survivors of a calamity we could neither remember nor forget. I stood there in a huge homburg; it had none of the glamour of Gerald Lewin's naval cap. I was proud and envious of my father after the congregation dispersed. His rank earned him the deference of the civilians and salutes from those in uniform. Some salutes were tinged with a certain familiarity.

We walked to the underground station at Aldgate East. I felt punished without being sure of my offence. My father pressed his lips together and regarded me with protective hostility. I had questions, but I did not ask them. I contented myself, once we were in the train and he was obliged to be sociable, with inquiring how badly damaged Germany was and what it was like to have to talk to Germans.

'Not very different,' he said, 'from talking to other suspected criminals, except that I understand them less well and they have an exaggerated respect for the uniform I happen to be wearing.'

'What exactly do you do?'

'Exactitude is not yet a part of my activities. Sir Robert says that our business is to turn chaos into mere disorder.'

'I suppose it's nearly all destroyed, is it?

'Some parts are. Others are surprisingly attractive. It depends where you are and what you're doing. My business is largely confined to reading large quantities of bumph. I'm not sure whether that's my good fortune or my bad. It keeps me out of mischief.'

Lieutenant-General Sir Robert Godolphin found my father a useful man. When the war ended, he was disinclined to release him. Not only was he a reliable officer, he was also a social asset. Sir Robert liked a decent game of bridge and he could not imagine why Colonel Jordan should not be happy to stay at Schloss Lowenstein for as long as maybe, drinking excellent stuff from the liberated cellar and making difficult contracts into which the General's forward bidding had landed him. 'Of course,' Godolphin remarked one evening, 'this is never soldiering in any legitimate sense, but I see no large objection to living off what's left of the fat of this benighted land while stocks last, do you, Routh?'

Major Routh was a short, black-haired, already florid young man, with serious spectacles through which he was known to read modern literature and books in yellow jackets. 'As an interim step, sir, it seems acceptable . . .'

'Quite right,' the General said. 'We're basically policemen without the appropriate boots. The sooner the Hun can look after himself again, *more Germanorum* unfortunately, the better for all concerned. Am I in my own hand?'

'Table, sir.'

'Thank you, Samuel. You don't agree, Hugo?'

'I don't disagree, sir,' Hugo Dickinson said. 'They need white officers for at least two generations, that's the problem. My lead?'

'As you won the last trick, we can afford you that liberty. Hang the Hun, remember Capua, don't you agree, Jordan?'

'Hannibal's men had no E.N.S.A. to keep them happy, did they, sir?'

'You're the educated man at the table. Clegg, we need more liquid ammunition here. Meanwhile, I shall plant a trump on Captain Dickinson's ace of diamonds.' Sir Robert gathered the trick he had just ruffed in his own hand and drew the rest of the trumps.

'Standing for parliament, Routh?'

'Yes, sir.'

'Then doubtless you'll be telling us presently what we have to do, and by when. Meanwhile, you're not privy, by any chance, to the inscrutable purposes of our possibly temporary masters across the water, are you, Jordan?'

'My access to high policy is of an extremely circumscribed order, sir. My office is to fry small fish.'

'Not too much oil. Circumscribed, did you say, or circumcised?'

'I happen to be both, sir,' Samuel said, 'but I confessed only to the former.'

'If more of our chaps were,' Godolphin said, 'they might conceivably be less prone to the clap and similar spoils of war. What's your view, Captain Dickinson?'

'I really wouldn't know, sir.'

'That rarely inhibits you from expressing an opinion. The rest of the tricks look to be mine.' He showed them the remaining cards in his hand. Three of them were diamonds, the suit he had ruffed earlier. 'Those are now good, are they not?'

'I doubt if they could be better, sir,' Samuel said, 'now.'

'Fascinating game, bridge. I thought I was going to go down when I first saw the dummy. Do you know Romania?'

'Is it a card game at all, sir?' Dickinson said.

'It's a country; in the Balkans, Hugo. And it's also where we should be at this moment, casting a baleful, prophylactic eye at Ivan's flank. They have remarkable churches, painted on the outside. Blue mostly. Impervious to weather, your Romanian exteriors, but not to H.E., one fears. We must hope for the best. They've lost the formula, I seem to remember. Their women, you might care to know, Routh, are grasping both in the figurative and – more importantly for the hedonistic calculus – in the anatomical sense. Very much your sort of thing, should parliamentary duties allow. If we'd turned right at Trieste, Hugo, we might have been in Bucharest even as I speak. Thank you for your expertise, partner. Goodnight, gentlemen.'

'Goodnight, sir.' Samuel neatened the cards as the General collected a dusty bottle from the elaborate side table and went under a gilded battle scene towards his quarters. 'Does he often revoke?'

'Did he revoke?' Dickinson said.

'He ruffed a diamond and later claimed the rest of the tricks by virtue of the good diamonds in his hand. A pedant might call that a revoke.'

'One either remarks it at the time,' Dickinson said, 'sir, or forever holds one's peace. At least in our mess.'

'I shan't forget your advice, Dickinson. However, it wasn't for me to claim a revoke against my own partner at that stage.'

'I meant no offence, sir.'

'I'm sorry to hear that,' Samuel said. 'It renders your remark unforgivable.'

Routh said, 'Did you know that Fritzi Kaufmann was a published author in Germany before the war?'

'There were rumours,' Samuel said.

'Awful little man,' Dickinson said. 'Squalid, awful little man.'

'He does his job,' Samuel said.

'Does he still write?'

'He still picks his nose,' Dickinson said. 'His big nose. In public. Thank God we don't have to have him in here.'

'Goodnight,' Samuel said.

'Does Bob-a-job do it deliberately, do you think?'

'Do you?' Desmond Routh said.

'I don't know how anyone can be a socialist,' Dickinson said.

'In the present state of the world,' Routh said, 'I don't see how anyone can be anything else.'

Fredy (Fritz) Kaufmann had been seconded to the Control Commission by the Ministry of Economic Warfare, where he had spent most of the war doing 'dirty propaganda'. As a civilian, and a talkative one, he had no access to the mess, though he was often in the Commission restaurant. His fluent German made him indispensable to Samuel during the first weeks of the allied military government, though his tendency to ask long and rhetorical questions could give those whom he and Samuel were interrogating more information than it elicited. Samuel's German was awkward, but unsparing. If he asked elementary questions, he stayed for the answers. He made formality into a pitiless weapon. His rectitude was without mercy. The businessmen and bureaucrats with whom he had to deal smiled at first, but seldom at the end of their sessions with him.

The war had been over for more than a year and a half before Samuel was able to return to civilian life. He had seen things which he proposed never to discuss with his wife. He resumed his striped trousers and his black coat, the bowler, the umbrella. He did not forget what he had seen and heard, but he set his face against allowing it to discompose him. The routine of the bar did not change, even if the courts were unheated. He wore two pairs of socks and a sweater under his shirt, but it was inconceivable to make any further concession to austerity. Deliberately not changing was his only acknowledgement that things had changed. When Mark Sweeting, the judge in the first trial in a new courtroom at the Old Bailey, began by saying, 'Now where were we before we were so rudely interrupted, Mr Jordan?', Samuel was the perfect man to pick up the cue.

The case concerned Francis Harold Rice. He was accused of murdering his wife. Samuel visited him in Pentonville to prepare the defence, but Rice was unresponsive. 'It doesn't matter to me, sir, what happens, one way or the other,' he said.

'Pleading guilty, Mr Rice, is very decidedly one way, if you'll allow me to say so. It leaves the judge no option. And I don't have to tell you what that means.'

'The black cap,' Rice said.

Samuel took the tea which a warder had brought in and breathed its steam. 'Plead not guilty, and we have a reasonable prospect of a manslaughter verdict.'

'How long will that mean?'

'It depends.'

'I was locked up in Germany for three and a half years, sir. After Tobruk. That'll do me.'

'It's not the least of the reasons why a jury might take a more lenient view.'

'I killed her,' Rice said. 'That's what I wanted to do.'

'Your wife –'

'Vicky, yes?'

'– she'd not only been unfaithful, which might be . . . she'd been blatantly so, had she not? We have your neighbours' – the Finches' – evidence –'

'You would have, I suppose, sir,' Rice said. 'Neighbours!'

'Someone who behaves like that when a man's fighting for his country –'

'I was making soup, sir, when I was captured. Some of the cooks could use a firearm, but the Major used to say that my soup was my best contribution. Vicky started her ways well before the war. They'll all tell you that.'

'Not if I don't ask them,' Samuel said.

'I suppose you must have had quite a lot of experience of people wanting to kill people, Mr Jordan, haven't you? Seeing what your business is. I don't hold with war myself. Silly, going out to kill people you never even met. They used to tell us they was bombing London, you know, in the camp, and I – I wouldn't necessarily tell anyone else this, but I used to hope and pray they wouldn't hit our house.'

'Very understandable,' Samuel said.

'I wanted her for myself. I didn't want her killed by accident, did I? It kept me going, that did: the thought of what I was going to do to her. I didn't want some bomb depriving me of the satisfaction.'

'Mr Rice, forgive me, but . . . you strike me as a very decent man –'

'You're not seeing me under normal conditions, Mr Jordan,' Rice said.

Samuel said, 'I don't want you waking up one night, after the trial, and realizing what's . . . going to happen, when it's too late to do anything about it. Spilt milk is beyond my competence to . . .'

'How can I say it wasn't premeditated, sir, when I never thought about nothing else for three and a half years and more?'

'The war –'

'Made no particular difference, if I'm honest about it. Not that I didn't see some sights. You must have yourself, I imagine.

Heads, for instance. I never saw a human head before the war. I never appreciated how small they were. I helped a butcher at one time, as a boy, but animals . . . you don't make the connection when you're young. I never saw a head as such until 1941. I thought about killing her on the first night. I didn't know what I'd married till then. Nor did Vicky I don't suppose. You can't learn to like cheese, can you sir?'

'Not if you're chalk, I don't suppose.'

'They say you know a lot of jokes, sir.'

'Do they? Who?'

'People who know you. You're a bit famous for it. There's not many people in life get to do exactly what they meant to do, are there? It wasn't that she laughed at me so much, sir, nor the men she had. It was the way she talked about my mother. She didn't know her and that was the way she talked about her. Not appreciated. Have you got a joke I could have to tell them at all, sir?'

'I only know the jokes I hear. My barber tells me them occasionally. I'm not sure they're very suitable.'

'I like an unsuitable joke, sir, in moderation. Where do you have it cut?'

'I go to a place in Great Windmill Street. There's the one about the smallest aerodrome in the world, do you know that one?'

'I don't believe I do, sir.'

'Under a Scotsman's kilt. There's just room for two hangers and a night-fighter. I'm not very proud of it, but there you are: short notice!'

'They'll probably like it, sir.'

Samuel put his cup on the green table. 'If you could avoid attributing it to me, my reputation might profit.'

'I'll plead not guilty for you, Mr Jordan, if you want me to,' Rice said.

Samuel held out his hand. 'For both our sakes, Mr Rice, why not?'

*

It was part of my father's regularity that he visited his mother whenever he could between the end of his work and dinner. Clarissa Jordan lived in Gloucester Mansions, Dorset Square, a considerable distance from Court Royal, which was on West Hill, Southfields. When Samuel was very busy, he was certain at least to telephone his mother. Kendall, the maid, always answered. Mrs Jordan had to be handed the instrument; reaching for it herself made her breathless and obliged her to speak to whoever had called. There were several callers to whom she was always too ill to talk. Her sisters, of whom there were four, were often among the proscribed, although never all of them at the same time nor always the same ones. Clarissa had taken to her bed in 1929, when she was fifty years old. In the early years, she had sometimes got up, wearing a zippered housecoat, and played Sunday afternoon bridge. I could remember pre-war afternoons when I sat and watched. While the next hand was dealt, she ate violet chocolates from Maison Lyons. Kendall supplied a damp flannel for her to wipe her fingers when she had finished. She hated sticky cards. The chocolates had petals of crystallized violet on the top and gave off a coloured smell. My grandfather appeared a mild man, with white hair and a polished forehead, but he was said to have had a fierce temper when he was younger. My father never spoke of it to me, but my mother told me that he had sworn that he would never raise his voice to her as a result of the storms he had witnessed. My grandfather died the summer the war ended. He had never had a day's illness in his life.

Samuel's visits to Gloucester Mansions had their precise form, like the rest of his activities. He gave his briefcase and umbrella to Kendall and put his head round the bedroom door. Where he put his head was a matter for daily decision. Sometimes he did it at the usual height, but then retracted it and waited for Clarissa to giggle. On other occasions, he dropped to his knees and his face appeared at the level at which a schoolboy might have been expected. If he was especially skittish, he would lie flat on the carpet. His mother would flap her powder puff in delighted reproach and a toothless smile promised him that he was forgiven, just. While Kendall boiled the kettle (the trolley would already be set), Samuel kissed his mother, chased her hand under the bedclothes until he had caught and pressed it, and sat down in the floral armchair by the bed. If Clarissa had not had an attack that day, she would put in her teeth for tea.

Samuel asked her what she thought of the world. 'I don't like Americans and I certainly don't like the Russians. I suppose you like the present government. How on earth did they manage to get where they are?'

'It's known as universal suffrage and majority rule, mother.'

'I never voted for either of them,' Clarissa said.

Kendall wheeled in the tea. She wore a black dress in the afternoon, with a white apron and bib. A silver cross on a thin chain hung on her humped bosom. She gave Samuel his tea and passed him a plate for his bread and butter and Madeira cake.

'Has the doctor been recently, Kendall?'

'Dr Cary-Saunders was here yesterday, Mr Samuel.' Her voice became a whisper perfectly audible to the old lady. 'She was very bad on Tuesday. *Two* attacks.'

'The pain from angina is the most severe known to medical science,' Clarissa said from the concave centre of her many soft pillows.

'Wind round the heart can run it an extremely close second,' Samuel said. 'But she's better today?'

'When I took her temperature this morning, Mr Samuel, the mercury *shot* up to normal.'

'But went no further than that?'

'It shot up to the very limit.'

Samuel ate his cake and refused a second slice. He looked at the travelling clock which his mother used always to take to Baden Baden in the days when she went there to take the waters and to dance. 'She's very well indeed, thank you,' he said.

'That's not what Dr Cary-Saunders thought. He said we were right to call him, didn't he, Kendall?'

'Touch and go, Mr Samuel.'

'First he touches and then he goes,' Samuel said. 'I thought you were asking after my wife.'

Clarissa sneezed into a lace handkerchief and had to catch her breath. Kendall found the smelling salts, took out the glass stopper and covered the bottle with a clean handkerchief for Clarissa to take a sniff. 'Is she . . . still . . . thinking of . . . returning to the stage?'

'She's not been on a stage for twenty years, mother.'

'As long as you're happy, dear.'

'I am,' Samuel said.

'She's waiting for you, I suppose.'

'That is often a woman's lot.'

'Are you going dancing?'

'Not tonight, mother.'

He bought the *Evening Standard*, for its bridge column, at Baker Street station and took the inner circle to Gloucester Road. There he changed to the Wimbledon line and walked up the hill from East Putney to Court Royal. The flats were built on the site of a great house. Some of the trees were said to date from the eighteenth century. The gardens had a generosity which the redbrick flats, with their narrow leaded windows and pseudo-manorial doorways, hardly matched. Trafalgar House had a rubberized hallway and a small lift with clashing gates. Number 10 was on the second floor. Samuel never discussed why he and Philippa had elected to live so far out. The good air and the nice grounds, with their terraced roses and banks of daffodils, their lilac and their prunus, were handsome enough to need no apology. The flat had three bedrooms: one for my parents, one for me and one for Rachel, when she was at home. We never had a servant, though my mother's Mrs D. came three mornings a week. The furniture had never changed for as long as I could remember. It was 'reproduction' and came from the store of a great-uncle-in-law, from whom my great-aunt Georgina had been scandalously, but not unprofitably, divorced in the days when she was a violet-eyed beauty. My father's rose bowls, trophies from his dancing days, stood on the sideboard, but there was no gramophone, until Rachel bought hers, and my parents never went to concerts. They did go dancing, but my mother was resigned to being less agile than my father's original partner, Gladys Padgett, of whom he would speak with flattering tactlessness. It seemed not to occur to him that my mother might resent being unfavourably compared with Gladys; my father assumed she would realize that no other woman now meant anything to him.

When I had been at my public school for two years, I was sent to a basement in Hammersmith where Gladys and her professional partner, Oliver Ricardo, taught ballroom dancing. The room was so cold that we often rumbaed and foxtrotted in overcoats. My lessons proved that dancing was not an inherited skill, but I only once failed to arrive, when the freeze was so severe that the trains could not run. One day, a blonde girl called Sally Raglan came to have the lesson after me. I was sixteen. I took one look at her, in her black coat with the fawn fur collar, a scarf over all that fair hair, and I thought that one day I would marry her. I had never held a girl's hand.

Just before the trial of Francis Harold Rice, my father received a call from Sir Robert Godolphin. He went to have lunch with 'Bob-a-job' later the same week. The Senior Officers' Club was in the process of re-hanging its pictures. The workmen were working in gloves in the lobby. Sir Robert was in mufti in the morning room, reading the *Burlington Magazine*. He was wearing mittens. He gave a little wave, when he saw Samuel reflected in a poxed mirror; the twiddly gesture was more intimate than any sign he had ever made before. 'When is this bloodsome weather going to end, Jordan?'

'My meteorology's no good at all, I'm afraid, Sir Robert.'

'Nobody's much is, to judge from this brass monkey business we're getting. Shall we have the same again?'

'I'm sure that would be very nice,' Samuel said.

'Same again, twice,' Godolphin said to the steward. 'Hermann Pfaff.'

'Where?' Samuel said.

'Mean anything to you?'

'He ought to be a heavyweight. And, in a manner of speaking, is. The banker?'

'Have they told you about this?'

'I was relying on you to do that, Sir Robert.'

'It seems there's something of a fiddly bit going on. They never gave you anything, did they? Gallantry award, anything in that department?'

'I was on secondment from the J.A.G.'s office, Sir Robert. Nothing very gallant involved in knees under a moveable desk.'

'Look here, Bob or Bobbie, if you feel so inclined. The Americans have suddenly elected to break cover trailing clouds of bumph. Forget rank: I've got my bowler hat hanging in the lobby. You've heard about Greece?'

'Greece,' Samuel said.

'That's where you and I should have been, Jordan. The only gentleman's war in the whole unfortunate episode. They even had an artist with them. Do you reckon Guy Falcon as a painter at all?'

'I'm not really up on him, I'm afraid, sir.'

'Look at this for a statement of claim. That's a little island I happen to know. Routh got into parliament then; talks a good deal. Booming chap, but not unamusing. Always ready to stand up and be counted, preferably twice. Unusually fine draughtsman at the very least. Falcon. The Yanks want him gone over again. Part of the price we pay. He was cleared once, as you probably know, by Brat Fothergill and what-was-his-name? Parsons. Now they want a second coat. Pfaff. Pfaff.'

'He was never formally arraigned, as I recall. There was no –'

'You recall correctly. Now they want to go again on him. They've asked me to put up a name, Jordan. What do you say?'

'It's very flattering.'

'In the yes or no department? They do eat rather out in Germany these days. It shouldn't add up to more than a couple of weeks *in situ*. Perhaps they should run our trains and we could run their consciences. Possibly three. They're good at trains, which we seem not entirely to be. Month at the outside.'

'I'm in the middle of a murder.'

'People might be grateful, in due course. You could do it in slices possibly. Not that gratitude pays the tailor. He needs prompt attention is the thing. He must either be in or out, not stuck in the breech. I never thought I'd be a railway guard. Hence the advertisement for a firm hand.'

'I'm not sure how good a ramrod I might turn out to be, Sir Robert.'

'The Yanks've bailed us out of Greece and you know what's going on in the unHoly land. You'll have able help. None of your Fredy whatsits, who's doing rather well for himself, incidentally. Do you know this chap Millom? He's said to be very able. Cambridge? Oxford? The Yanks trust you, Jordan, which is . . .'

'What Yanks are those, Sir Robert?'

'Don't underestimate yourself, Samuel. Leave that to the experts. They appreciate what you did on the Dieter von Hartmann affair.'

'I took him to be a common murderer.'

'With an uncommonly handsome wife. Hugo Dickinson was up to his doings in her subsequently, fortunate fellow. Rich too. It would be a service, if you could see your way to it, once you've got your chap off.'

'It's not very convenient just at the present, Sir Robert.'

'Very nice of you to look at it like that. Why don't you take silk? I'm sure you should. People would like it. Now, shall we see if we can make our way to the optimistically entitled dining room without getting ice on our wings or other parts?'

Samuel said, 'Sir Robert –'

'Nothing to thank me for.'

When Samuel looked up at the window of number 10, Trafalgar House that evening, he saw his wife Philippa, through the narrow glass, talking animatedly. The visitor was Buddy

Nathanson. He was having a drink with her and my sister, Rachel, who was reading history at Bedford College, London. She had a bedsitter in Holloway, but she came to Court Royal during the holidays. I wanted to talk to her and to have secrets with her, but we had been apart in the war and peace did not bring us much closer. We were less like a brother and sister than like two only children who happened to have the same parents.

Philippa said, 'You remember Buddy, Sam.'

'If you can spare the time, Nathanson, I can spare the dime,' Samuel said. 'How are you, sergeant?'

'Pretty good, sir. I've had a promotion since those days. I'm strictly private today!'

'Here on business? Who but a masochist comes to this country on pleasure?'

'Bud got in last night,' Philippa said, 'and we were the first people he called.'

'I've missed Europe. I'm hoping to do a little fund-raising here –'

'Are there any funds to raise? I thought the opposite the case. On whose behalf exactly?'

'I'm working for the Joint Palestine Appeal,' Buddy said.

Samuel said, 'Not a Joint to which I am greatly disposed to offer a slice.'

'What did I tell you?' Rachel was wearing a pink angora sweater and a slim black skirt. Her voice was quiet and distinct. 'Didn't I, mummy?'

'Have I been the subject of predictions? In my own home? Am I flattered? You're working against the British.'

'I'm not against anyone,' Buddy Nathanson said, 'unless anyone's against us. How do you see the situation developing?'

Samuel said, 'I'm surprised they let you into the country.'

'Well, you know who won the war.'

'Development, so far as I understand the process, takes place in darkened, even sealed rooms. One sees little and if one sees more, nothing develops at all.'

'That's a very British attitude, if I may say so.'

'Daddy *is* very British,' Rachel said.

'And where do you come from, young lady?'

'Oh Rachel's with me, sir,' Buddy said. 'I'm talking about the mid-East.'

'Impossible,' Samuel said.

'We've been in worse,' Buddy said. 'This time at least we have a chance. And we can see what happens when we rely on anyone but ourselves.'

'I was thinking of Britain,' Samuel said.

'Come on, Sam. Who's here but us? Who really comes first with you when the chips are down?'

'If it weren't for Britain,' Samuel said, 'some of us – perhaps all of us – would not be here at this moment –'

'Bullshit, Samuel.'

'We won't have that sort of talk. Palestine, if that's your topic, appears beyond rational solution. How much credit does that reflect on the parties concerned?'

'Nuts to credit. No rational solution; there has to be an irrational one. So let's tilt the table if we have to. And I think we do. Cry foul and tilt the table. We tried to play straight before and you saw what happened. You saw and I don't think you should forget it. Cricket is never going to be our national game, Sam.'

Rachel said, 'Buddy's asked me to go to Paris with him for a few days.'

'The thing being, I could do with some intelligent assistance over there. Rachel has French and if I have Rachel . . .'

'Temporary secretary! It fits in nicely just before the summer term.'

Samuel said, 'Is this a joke?'

'Beats the one about the owl and the parrot,' Buddy said. 'No joke.'

'Daddy, do you happen to know how old I am?'

'Don't tell me I've forgotten your birthday! I also know when your examinations are.'

'They're in June, when I shall take them. And not a moment

before. This is April and I also have some things I want to check in Paris.'

'It'll make a nice break for her, sir.'

'And what will it make for you?'

Philippa said, 'I'm going to go and do something about food.'

'Sir, may I say something? Because your daughter –'

'– is my responsibility.'

Rachel said, 'You see? And he talks about tolerance!'

'As rarely as possible. It's the best means of procuring it.'

'Sam, I'm a married man, thirty-four years old. I have a son and a daughter of my own. And a bald patch, right? Truly, you demean your daughter by suggesting –'

'All the suggestions have come from a quite different quarter. Am I to pretend that I welcome them?'

'It might be a courtesy,' Rachel said. 'I'm twenty-two and I've never been out of England. Unless you count Wales. I lived in a hole in Wales for seven months, decoding laundry lists mostly! That never bothered you.'

'You must do what you think right,' Samuel said.

'At what age do you seriously think a girl can safely see the Eiffel Tower without being fatally corrupted?'

'I'll go and see if Pippa needs any help in the kitchen,' Buddy said.

'And what will happen during the nights?'

'What happened when I was in the W.R.N.S.? Nothing; but in more interesting surroundings. Daddy, please don't do this.'

'He's acting openly against the interests of this country.'

'By taking me to Paris?'

'Who do you suppose is paying for this . . . jaunt? Since when do people call your mother Pippa?'

'Jaunt! Are you worried about the money?'

'That's rude,' Samuel said.

'But is it true?'

'A question can be neither true nor false.'

Rachel said, 'I expected better of you than this.'

'Generations exist to disappoint each other,' Samuel said.

'You mustn't take the British government for complete fools, you know.'

'Oh daddy, this really hasn't got anything to do with pulling the wool over Mr Attlee's eyes. *Swear!* A few days in Paris. Paris!'

'Who knows what you may want to do in a year's time? Paris with a married man.'

'I wish I could laugh at this conversation. I think I probably can, as a matter of fact, if I take a deep enough breath and don't scream first.'

Philippa was saying, 'If it weren't for cod and potatoes, where would we be?'

'You could always try the United States.'

'And ketchup. I don't think Sam would be very happy in the States.'

'Everybody else is. Here let me take that! You know, don't you, that when I asked your daughter —?'

'You were really wishing you could've asked me? Lucky you're not Pinocchio!'

'Your husband has really and truly . . . It came up and suddenly I thought, if she wants to come, why not? Jesus Christ, Pippa! Where's the big deal? Do I look like the Big Bad Wolf?'

'I'd call you grandma any day of the week.'

Rachel came in, looking bright. 'That's all fixed then,' she said. 'Anything I can do?'

When I came out of my room for supper, my father was alone in the sitting room, looking out at the dark gardens. After Buddy had gone, Samuel put on a silk dressing gown and his stiff slippers before telling Philippa that Bob-a-job Godolphin wanted him to go to Germany to make a report on Hermann Pfaff. It was, of course, the last thing that Samuel wanted to do.

'In that case, how are we going to prevent you?' Philippa said.

'The truth is,' Samuel said, 'if you don't mind my telling you it —'

'He made it awkward for you to refuse.'

'I could tell you that. It is true. But the truer truth is that Pfaff is a case I shouldn't much like anyone else to have. I'm not saying no one else is competent to look at it, but this is something I've known something about ever since we first got into Germany. It needs . . .'

'The Jordan touch!'

'I don't flatter myself, Pips, in the least, but if they want him investigated, it's got to be done properly, whatever anyone's motives. Whether people like it or not, to be frank.'

'Whether people like it or not is very much your department, I can see that. You think he's guilty, do you?'

'It's an inquiry, not a prosecution. It's up to me to report whether there's a case to answer, under a deNazification procedure. The Americans have turned up what they say is new evidence. We shall see.'

'Off you go then,' Philippa said. 'I'm sorry the war's over in some ways, do you know that?'

'There's still voluntary work to be done.'

'I could always work for the Joint,' Philippa said. 'You humiliated me with Buddy this evening. You won't do it again, will you?'

'It had nothing to do with you.'

'That was what was humiliating. Isn't Godolphin the man you told me cheated at bridge?'

'Inadvertently,' Samuel said.

'That's rather a neat thing to be able to do, isn't it?'

My father's eloquence could not prevent Francis Harold Rice from being found guilty of murder. There was a strong recommendation to mercy, but the confession of having planned his wife's death for several years made any other verdict impossible. Samuel offered him what condolence he could, though none was solicited, when he visited Mr Rice in the cells. There was always the appeal, of course. In the robing room, Samuel shook hands with prosecuting counsel and then went to take tea at Gloucester

Mansions. He had done his best, and would have preferred to win, but the verdict pained him no more than a defeat on the golf course. Rice's acquiescence purged it of anguish, while the same discreet exhilaration always accompanied the end of a trial, whatever the result. It was a comfort to think that Rice would probably be reprieved (the appeal was unlikely to be fruitful), but in any case there came the moment of release, when counsel went on his way, freer for the separation of his fortunes from those of the client. To hail a taxi and sling one's bag on the seat and know that it was on to the next one was a sweet divorce which had something in common with less excusable promiscuities.

Rachel and Buddy travelled to Paris by train and boat, via Folkestone and Dieppe. Buddy was more reticent when they were alone together than he had been when they were in the flat. Rachel was determined to be a sightseer. Her enthusiasm even for Dieppe, despite its brownish ruins, warned Buddy that she meant to keep him to his word: it was a trip, not a tryst. If she became younger, he agreed to be older.

His French was as bad as he had promised. It made her wince and it made her warm to him. He had people to whom it was important that he speak but with whom he could scarcely communicate without Rachel. Being an interpreter both promoted and reduced her. Essential at one moment, she was ignored the next. An English speaker rendered her superfluous and even suspect. She found time to go to the Louvre, where the rumpled, knowing Rembrandt gazed at her until her youth seemed to tick, under her long green coat with the little fur collar, like a bomb that must soon explode. She walked the alleys of the Tuilleries, charged with a desire that had no clear location in mind or body, a pulsing readiness for whatever it was that she was ready for. She burned with the spring which had hardly begun to pierce the iron city. Parisian women, their air of urgent purpose, their showy secrecy, and their shortness, seemed wonderfully solemn and comic. When men spoke to her, she answered them guilelessly. She laughed when they proposed a drink and walked on, shaking her dark head, enjoying the shift of the hair against her ears. One of them even clapped and called 'Bravo!'

She and Buddy walked down the rue St André des Arts one evening and were taken for lovers, even by themselves. 'Rachel,' he said, 'I have to talk to you. Because I didn't tell you the whole truth.'

'Nothing but the truth,' she said. 'Save it for court.'

'There's something I want to ask you're absolutely free to refuse to do.'

'I'm free to refuse to do absolutely anything you ask me,' Rachel said.

'I had another motive asking you here. You've done a fine job. I couldn't have handled these people without you, but I all the time had something else in mind as a possibility. You met Aaron and Léah. They liked you very much. And they agree with me, this is something you could handle better than anyone else we know. You heard – of course you did – about those passports from Holland. We have to get them – and some cash – to Rome by the weekend. This isn't anything you have to do if you don't want to.'

Rachel said, 'There's no connection between wanting and doing necessarily, is there?'

Buddy said, 'If I thought it was dangerous, I wouldn't ask. It's probably at best a slightly nervous bore, O.K.? Hours and hours in the train, someone meets you at the Termini Station, you give him the bag, you come back exhausted. You're someone the British don't know. Us they know. We can do it without you, of course, but will you do it?'

'I don't even know myself,' Rachel said.

'This may help. We're talking about kids who've been in camps. Kids were six and seven years old, younger, some of them, when their parents were gassed. You know what they did to some of those people? You don't. They hosed them with boiling water in some instances, Rachel, they boiled the flesh off their living bones. And now they won't let us have our own slice of territory. Good. We'll help ourselves. Will you help us?'

'Please don't,' Rachel said. 'Don't make me feel that you made me do this. I'll do it. Don't make me think I had to because of anything you said.'

Buddy Nathanson looked across the road and hit the side of his nose with a loose fist before he could look at her again. He said, 'I love you, Rachel Jordan. Sweet Jesus, do I.'

She said, 'I don't love you for this, Mr Nathanson.'

'You're the most beautiful thing I ever saw in my whole life. Everyone in the world should be the way you are.'

'This really does matter, doesn't it?'

'Very much. If you want the same things I want.'

'I don't know if I do or not. But I'll go. Rome? I'll go.'

He kissed her on the mouth, like a man, and he was not smiling. 'I love you. And it was never my intention to say that, or do this.'

'You had other intentions?'

'I promised your mother I'd take care of you, and here's what's happening!'

'You're turning me into a postman.'

'You never did it yet, did you?'

'Am I a fool?'

'Nobody who says you are ought to get anywhere near you, Rachel Jordan. Don't ever let them, will you? Do you want to come to bed with me?'

'Yes,' she said. 'But I'm going to Rome, aren't I?'

'One day –'

'I never listen to speeches that begin "one day".'

'This one you will. Because one day you'll go to a country that you helped to make, a country where you belong and where I belong. And then you'll know without any doubt who you are and why you are and where you are.'

'That's not the reason I'm going to Rome.'

'I don't give a rat's fart *why* you're going. I just love you for doing it.'

'Then what are you angry about?' Rachel said.

They went back to the hotel in the rue des Sts Pères. Buddy showed her the uninteresting luggage she would take to Rome. It was as if the stiff grey suitcase, into which she packed more clothes than she had brought with her (Léah Lacache came with a bundle of plausible padding), became the instrument by which she was to lose her innocence. The suitcase, whatever it contained, recruited her to an awareness of what she had never experienced. The long, dull journey turned out to be an adventure without excitement, a monotonous rumble through a landscape where, not long before, she might have been a species of vermin. She tasted the fear of memories she did not have, when the ticket collector slid open the door of her compartment and she bluffed him with the truth: her passport was valid; he took her smile for candour, not deceit. On the way to Rome she discovered the uses of herself. The small danger, the mystery of what precisely was under all that alien clothing, made her at once a cunning victim and a timid heroine. Her conscious thoughts were of Caesar and Napoleon, of Leonardo and Michelangelo, of an end to insularity. Only in abrupt dreams was she forced to put on the dirty clothes in her bag and to pretend that they fitted her, and that the grinning policemen, in their boots, were mistaken in their accusations that she was a fraud and a liar. Her dreams were a luxury; she lolled into them with weary relish and woke to trundling banality.

The case was delivered, to an ungrateful man, on the corner of the baths of Caracalla. Free of it, she looked back at the starchy marble regularity of Mussolini's Termini Station and checked her watch. Her train had arrived two hours late, but she still had a day in which to play the tourist that she was.

Samuel flew from Northolt to Frankfurt, where he was met in an official Humber by Owen Millom. Millom was tall and slim, with properly cut hair. Samuel was relieved both by his assistant's competence and by his Etonian manners. He was deferential to a distinguished K.C. (Samuel had taken silk at last) and he was unintimidated. Millom's deference depended on vanity; if he had been less sure of himself, he could not have been so self-effacing. His Oxford fellowship was waiting for him; he had already published papers on British foreign policy before the First World War to which other scholars made footnoted reference. At twenty-five he seemed to have personal experience of the last century. If he spoke German hesitantly, he read it well enough to have prepared Samuel's task with diligent skill. Owen had been working for the British Control Commission for longer than he had been promised would be required. He and Samuel were of the same mind: nothing but a complete examination of the dossier would satisfy their pride, but neither man wanted to stay in Germany longer than necessary.

Millom spelt out the brief on their first day in the office. 'We're to honour the American request to consider the documents and we're to – that's to say, you're to – I'm sorry about that – you're to report, without delay, on whether they warrant re-opening deNazification proceedings against our friend. It's been suggested that you might care to speak to Pfaff personally, though not under courtroom circumstances.' The banker had agreed to clarify any points which Samuel wished to press. Samuel was not happy that the interview should seem to depend on Pfaff's willingness to accord it, but Owen Millom, with a smile that acknowledged the 'Special Commissioner's' point, said that it was felt that an informal meeting might be more fruitful. 'The general feeling is that we want to get him out of our hair,' Millom said.

'While we still have some of it,' Samuel said. 'Oh I wasn't thinking of you, Mr Millom, I was thinking exclusively of myself, and H.M.G. You've got plenty of hirsute years ahead of you, I've no doubt.'

'You don't know my father, sir.'

One breezy blue morning in May, they drove to Pfaff's country house. It was large without being vulgar, tasteful without being precious. It seemed untouched by the war, just as its owner, still in his forties, was unfattened by it. Two brindled Borzois bounded up to the visitors and favoured them with husky attention. Dick and Inge were called off with accusing apologies and trotted away across the terrace, more condescending than chastened. The visitors were shown into the library, where French windows opened on to lilac and the bleaching remnants of flowering cherry.

Hermann Pfaff had reddish hair, fine but not crinkly, and a grizzled moustache; he looked as if he might have served in a good regiment. He carried himself well, but without stiffness. He was wearing brown tweeds, well enough cut to suggest a Savile Row tailor, but not so ostentatious as to advertise his name. He knew, and admired, England and he knew enough not to shout his admiration. His library was a big room, with leather chairs and buttoned chesterfields. The pictures were of varnished hunting scenes and family portraits. On side tables there were several chess sets, one red and white of Chinese origin, at which Samuel frowned, as if the ranged pieces already presented a problem.

Pfaff's lawyer was older than his client. Bruno Block's strict clothes promised that he had come from the city. A double sac of flesh depended from his jaw, as if (Samuel remarked later) he had pelican blood. The lawyer's ungainly apprehension made it seem as though he were being protected by his client. When Block began with a stumbling rehearsal of the findings of the tribunal before which Pfaff had appeared in 1945, the banker broke in. 'Whatever my motives, Mr Jordan, and I don't suppose that they are of interest, except for psychological purposes, I held myself at the disposal of the British authorities from the very beginning. Not everyone in Germany regards that as admirable, but there it is, it's on the record. Why deny it now? Nor is it a secret that some of us worked very hard to prevent the war in the first place. Not necessarily for any noble reason. Do you trust noble reasons? We guessed that catastrophic consequences would result, though none of us – I'm talking about innocent characters in the banking world! – guessed, or perhaps *could* have guessed, just how catastrophic they would be. It wasn't easy for us to even begin to articulate, let alone carry out or develop, a coherent policy. Coherence and treason often involved the same penalties. What are the facts? From 1943 onwards, I was actively seeking, through various channels which were still open to me, just about, to promote negotiations to prevent the collapse of the West. That's a shorthand – perhaps a little glib – for a process which has, alas, now reached critical proportions. I mention these channels because they were indeed almost wholly European. Is it a scandal that certain contacts were maintained right through the war? I hesitate, in the present circumstances, to give you details –'

'We may ask for them,' Samuel said.

'That will require a different kind of artillery, and perhaps some reflection on your part, before . . .' Pfaff went to the French windows, through which the sound of a mower was becoming obstreperous. He looked out, for a long moment, before it stopped and he returned to his seat by the unlit fire. 'This much I can fairly say, without being indiscreet: the Americans did their best to close those channels, while keeping others open. I can, if absolutely necessary, give you a list of American companies, suitably disguised as neutral corporations of course, which made it their business, often a very profitable one, to supply us – Germany – with a great variety of strategic material which various agencies, not least the R.A.F., made it otherwise difficult for us to obtain. Oh yes, right through the war. Some of the ruses employed might amuse you one day. The Americans' sudden desire to discredit me may have something – *something* – to do with my links before and even perhaps during the war with certain colleagues in the City of London. I'm not suggesting, by the way, that anyone in England was involved in treasonable activities, so please don't accuse me of doing so. Far from it. However, one can – in certain eyes – have the wrong friends as well as the wrong enemies. And often loyalty to the former is a greater crime than loyalty to the latter. Do they say that I was Nazi? Is that the essence of the matter? Because we can clear that up, again, right away. I was never a member of the Party although, and I say this without facetiousness, I sometimes wished that I were. Not because of the pressure they put on me, which was not inconsiderable, but because of the pressure I might then have put on *them*. *Now*, of course, it's rather lucky, but . . . What does perhaps need to be said, once, is that Nazism was – for most even of those who supported it – an expedient not a faith. Faiths are for the *petits gens*. Perhaps if some brighter people had joined in time to get a low number on their party cards, another rationale might have prevailed. Who knows? Back to our muttons! The Americans. The last thing they want is a united and independent Europe. The greatest fallacy in the world is the idea that because the wrong people have said something it is automatically false. To talk of Europe is to talk straight in terms which were not long ago put to crooked use. Granted. But how else can we face the future and its problems without dishonesty?'

'Philosophy may have to wait,' Samuel said. 'We've come to see you because certain allegations have been made on the basis of new documents suggesting that your wartime activities included the use of slave labour under conditions you, and your board, knew to be inhuman. What would assist us, and possibly yourself – if your time was indeed spent as you maintained it was when you were interrogated by the 1945 commission – is access to any undisclosed files, diaries or appointment books, or whatever else you may have, from the end of 1941 until the surrender in 1945.'

'I'm willing to go further than that, Mr Jordan. Whatever the technical limits of your brief, ask me anything you want to know and I'll try to tell you the truth. There are, by the by, some personal letters other than those in the British zone here. In Switzerland, for instance –'

'I don't believe zat Mr Chordan has any right to see ziss material,' Block said. 'It vill only confuse the issue.'

'Confusion *is* the issue,' Pfaff said. 'I don't offer that correspondence because I believe that you'll find it very edifying. It may well go some way to confirm your worst suspicions. Playing both sides against the middle is an old tradition in banking. How about some tea or some coffee? Forgive me!'

'Not for me, thank you.'

'Mr Millom. Tea? Coffee?'

'Thank you,' Owen said. 'Not.'

'I confess that I do rather envy certain people today. Not a very worthy confession, but there it is. Frankness is all! You know Fritzi Kaufmann, I think, Mr Jordan? He calls himself Fredy now, and why not? You know where he is these days?'

'I do not.'

'It won't surprise you to hear that he's operating in the American zone. I shouldn't be surprised if he weren't behind their present *démarche*. What puzzles me is that the Americans, for whatever reasons, are suddenly accusing me of something I never ever denied. Your own records will show you that I went out of my way, from the outset, to say that no German – *no* German – could claim to be innocent, least of all one like myself with the sort of responsibilities I was given. If I'm incriminating myself again, well then I am –'

'Herr Direktor –'

'Never mind, Bruno, for the moment. Please. It's undeniable that we – the board, myself, the German people – lent ourselves, knowingly, *en toute connaissance de cause*, to an iniquitous enterprise. For which we deserve punishment? Probably. Defeat *is* a punishment, believe me. What we didn't guess – and this is the folly of our conceit – was that our rulers were sincere. We thought they were cunning, dishonest, devious, calculating; we never supposed they were in earnest. We never supposed that they meant every ridiculous word they said. We Catholics always forget Luther! We forget with what glee a certain German tradition is willing to destroy traditional Germany. To our damnation, temporal and possibly eternal. We shall perhaps see. The business of the banker, Mr Jordan, is to make sure that he has his cake and manages to eat it too. If he can't work that elementary trick, he won't last long in the business of usury. It is a sorry defence to say that one was a coward by nature and upbringing, but there it is. I was never a Nazi; not out of virtue but out of . . . inhibition. Bankers keep their word, but everything else is negotiable!'

'May I suggest zumzing, Herr Direktor? Show Mr Chordan ze vatch you're wearing.'

'Oh. The watch. No, really . . . That's something a little bit personal.'

Bruno Block passed the gold watch to Samuel, springing the back as he did so. It was inscribed with the initials I.J./H.P. Underneath was, '*Semper*'. 'Do you know whose initials zose are, Mr Chordan? Do you know who I.J. voss, and is, zanks to . . .'

'I'm not sure that the Americans would think it relevant, and they might be right,' Hermann Pfaff said. 'I'm sorry Herr Block elected to show you that inscription because it reminds me of how little I did that I could have done.'

'Isidore Jacobson,' Block said.

'Possibly more of a genius even than Rathenau, who was a friend of my father's for many years. Jacobson taught me a great deal. Not enough, but a great deal. I sometimes think that if Isidore . . . What was it that Napoleon said about the execution of the Duc d'Enghien . . . ?'

'I think it may have been Talleyrand,' Owen Millom said.

'Worse than a crime, a folly?'

'Talleyrand.'

'Isidore gave me that before he went to Geneva in 1934. Isidore was a man of incredible selflessness, even though he was a Jew, I hope you'll understand my meaning, Mr Jordan, and perhaps even *because* he was, he could be dispassionate to the point of callousness. The most remarkable conversation I ever had with any man I had with Isidore Jacobson in this very room. 1934. About this time of year. I want to be very frank with you, even if it means that you lose all respect for me. Because at that time Isidore foresaw many possibilities, including what actually happened. He did not forecast what *would* happen – he was not a

84

man who traded in inevitabilities – but he foresaw that the world would lose patience with Germany at the very moment when patience was most needed. What made him so astonishing was that he saw that, at the time, Germany needed what we're now ashamed to call a 'strong man'. It was not a question of admiration, let alone endorsement, but of means to an end. And that end was Europe, civilization, if you like. I sometimes wonder what might have been the result if Churchill had come to Munich, as Prime Minister in 1938, if a man like that had confronted Hitler without fear and with his famous capacity for rhetoric and nerve. How many millions of men would still be alive? Churchill might have controlled his own supporters and been able to use his energy where, if we are honest, his instincts always inclined him, against Bolshevism. Imponderables!'

'When Isidore Jacobson's industrial interests and patents were Aryanized, Herr Pfaff, it was your bank, and its affiliated companies, which acquired them.'

'Thank God, yes. I was able to arrange that.'

'I wasn't aware of the divinity's part in the transaction.'

'Luckily, I was in a position to make sure that Isidore received a reasonable price.'

'Your valuation was seven per cent of the quoted value immediately before the 1933 elections.'

'Stock markets, as someone once said, go up and down, Mr Jordan, but not necessarily in that order. It may have been Izzy! All I know is that my old friend was – as you can see – touchingly, if unnecessarily, grateful. Highway robbery? Even that can be difficult to arrange without risk to the passengers! I managed to get all of Isidore's . . . compensation out to him in Zurich. That was not easy at all. Luckily, I had a good friend in London, who was Charlie Weeks. I hope he gets back into parliament next time because he's a hell of a man, I think. He was here not long ago. Do you know him? Perhaps one day I shall welcome Isidore Jacobson here again too. I hope so.'

'He may have a case for damages over the use of some of his patents.'

'Are you an expert in this field too, Mr Jordan? If Isidore has a case, please advise him to bring it and I wish him luck. Does this idea have something to do with why you have been sent here by the Americans?'

'This is the British zone, as you well know, and I'm here on the suggestion of the British authorities.'

'I like America, I admire it. Do you know "Chip" van Heusde? What a man! But what does America want? They're afraid of us, Mr Jordan; all their wealth, all their power can't quite buy off their fear. *That*'s why you're here. They must prevent Europe from recovering its confidence, its self-assurance, its belief in itself. Izzy saw it all coming in this room in May – or was it April? – 1934. He saw the future, many futures, which is what we too, without his genius, have to try to do. Let me be – was it Austen Chamberlain who used the expression? – "appallingly frank" –'

'Stanley Baldwin,' Owen Millom said.

'Mr Millom here is better than a library!'

'But not as good as a kitchen,' Samuel said.

'May I order something for you to eat? Forgive me!'

'Thank you,' Samuel said, 'not.'

'I've heard it said I consider myself indispensable to Europe, to Germany. I might *like* to think so, but in all honesty, no. The death of Anton Webern was a much greater loss than mine would have been if some drunken Yanks had happened to turn up at this house. The Gestapo might already have done the job for them in certain circumstances, but that's another story. We had them here a few times. No glorified accountant is irreplaceable. Only art is irreplaceable. My crime, Mr Jordan, morally if not juridically, is that I was in a position of power without responsibility. Or should I say the other way about? I thought there could be omelettes without broken heads! I cannot recover my innocence, if a clever person is ever innocent. As soon as we see that things could be otherwise, and we might still survive, we are compromised. Take Einstein. He was like a child in many ways, but what a child! He wrote to the president of the United States and told him an impossible truth: there was infinite destruction at the heart of the smallest finite unit. A European gave America the power to make Europe its slave. A Jew. That is the measure of our misfortune. That is why, if you like, you are here today. Britain is weak and impoverished and she must pay her debts in whatever coin, true or false, she can muster. Which reminds me of one of your own generals – you'd know him if I tell you his name – who supervised in this very room the loading and despatch to his own address of silver and porcelain and pictures that had been in my family over four hundred years. Well, Napoleon came back from Italy with his arms full, didn't he? You won't find many clean hands after a war. Imagine if you had come to Germany and found – let us suppose – a Resistance movement, men and women who had fought a brave and idealistic battle in the woods and the mountains against National Socialism and all its terrible ideas. Imagine that dedicated group, men and women with clean consciences, who had fought the good fight against all the odds and who, beyond a doubt, now had the moral right immediately to take over the government of this country. Imagine what would have happened to those men and women if the British or the Americans or the Russians had got to know of their existence. Good men and women are the last people in the world with whom any power would choose to deal. Shamefully then and luckily, I am neither as innocent as Dr Block could make me seem, nor as guilty as the Americans would like to paint me. I have no value; I may conceivably have a use. For better or for worse, I am a survivor, as you are, Mr Jordan. For better *and* for worse. Certainly I can be more use to the British government than any of those brave, immaculate members of the non-existent Resistance. The true horror of Hitler, if I may say so, Mr Jordan, is not that he was a heartless accountant but that he was a passionate moralist, an incurable romantic, a believer in the arts. Above all, sincere – only too sincere. Compared to such men, bankers are angels! In my vanity, I believed that no one could be more hard-headed or unsentimental than I. Therein lay my ignorance and my sentimentality.

'I shall send Mr Millom to Dr Block's office tomorrow for all the files and papers in your or his possession. I'm sure I needn't remind you that there are penalties for withholding anything relevant, whether or not specifically requisitioned. When we've analysed the material, we may, if we think it might be useful, seek a further meeting.'

'Of course. Whenever, wherever! You are certainly a man, if I may say so, who believes in giving the other fellow enough rope.'

'Is there anything else you want to say to us at this stage?'

'Only one thing really: I take it rather ill that you wouldn't drink a cup of tea in my house.'

'Self-denial,' Samuel said, 'also has its pleasures.'

'A very British sentiment, Mr Jordan, a very British senti-ment.'

Their driver was throwing a stick for the Borzois when Samuel and Owen came out of the house. Samuel sat in the back, his lower lip over the upper one, as they moved down the drive and through the ornamental gates. He looked at Owen Millom, finally, as if the young man had made some remark.

'You've spoken to Dr Block on other occasions, I take it, Owen?' Samuel said.

'Sir?'

'Dr Block – you've had previous conversations with him, have you not?'

'When I arranged our visit, sir, obviously –'

'The obvious sometimes deserves recognition.'

'Sir,' Millom said, 'if you imagine –'

'My imagination is not an article I was commissioned to bring. But why exactly are you here? To report to the Foreign Office, of course. But why should someone as bright as yourself agree to serve in the office of a dogsbody with quite such uncomplaining dedication? Remind me.'

'I do complain a bit, sir, at times. *And* look at my watch. But I was asked. Like yourself. It may sound naive –'

'If it did,' Samuel said, 'it wouldn't sound like you.'

Owen said, 'In a way, I must say I agree with Pfaff. Not that your suspicions about his involvements are necessarily –'

'Thank you for the necessarily,' Samuel said.

'Sir, if I've said something which leads you to think –'

'You've said nothing,' Samuel said. 'And that certainly leads me to think. Wherein lay your agreement, however reluctant, with Herr Pfaff?'

'When he said that justice wasn't a policy. Roughly. And rough justice least of all, he might have said!'

'It can't be discussed, but it can sometimes be put into effect. Can we doubt the justice of those who beat their sadistic guards to death with shovels? It's indefensible, but otherwise beyond criticism.'

'Justice is something static, sir, is what I mean, immobile, eternal. Life isn't; policy can't be. I'm not arguing against the punishment of criminals. Murder, for instance, clearly has to be – dealt with. But transferred across frontiers . . . the old equations seem not to work.'

'You make excellent fudge, Owen. I'm sure all your ambitions will be realized. Have I seen everything I should have seen?'

'Is that an accusation, sir?'

'Is it?'

Owen said, 'I don't mean to suggest that we should overlook what Pfaff did, or didn't do. But the Americans, as I understand it, sir, are actually employing former Gestapo personnel, and taking very good care of them. In fact, it may not be fanciful to think that this so-called new information against Pfaff has been leaked by people who are more interested in punishing him for his honesty than exposing him for his – what? – crimes, if you like. English ideas of justice simply don't travel – do they? – is all I'm saying.'

'You've been wasting my time, have you, Owen?'

'Not intentionally, sir.'

'With all this reading you've been giving me, and what's coming from your friend's office in the morning?'

'We're part of a process, sir, is all I'm –'

'It's a question of the required effect, is that the point?'

'I don't know that I should put it quite that way,' Owen said.

'I know you would,' Samuel said.

Mr Rice's appeal was due to be heard just before the courts rose for the summer. Samuel worked to finish his report on Hermann Pfaff in time to lead for the defence. What might have disposed another man to cut corners held him doggedly to his course. He read everything that was put in front of him. He sent Millom to ask again for whatever seemed too conveniently to be missing. His thoroughness found its target in his assistant. If he proceeded relentlessly against the banker, it amused him, though never to the point of smiling, to know that he was being more troublesome to Millom than tact or policy demanded. Impartiality too could be a kind of wilfulness. No acquittal could have been more damning than his final report. 'Circumscribed as I have been,' he concluded, 'both by the terms of reference and by the availability of evidence, I am conscious, as any reasonable man might be, of the uneven distribution of doubt in this matter. For if it is right that no one should be convicted if a reasonable doubt exists, it is difficult to conceal the fact that the doubts in this instance weigh against Herr Pfaff, even if they must lead to the view that no new charges, on the available evidence, can properly be brought against him. The documents offered by the American authorities add nothing substantial to what was investigated in 1945. The conclusion, albeit reluctant, must be that a case has not been made out for what would amount to Herr Pfaff's extradition.'

Samuel was in London in time for the Rice appeal. He travelled home, in an R.A.F. Dakota, with Owen and a weeping corporal, whose eleven-year-old daughter had been raped and killed near Bognor Regis. Rachel was at Court Royal for dinner on the evening of his return.

'Rachel went to Rome as well,' Philippa said.

'That's all right then,' Samuel said.

The telephone rang during dinner. It was Fredy Kaufmann. 'Is this a bad moment? Because I've got something for you. You haven't finished the report, have you?'

'Signed, sealed and to be delivered in the morning,' Samuel said.

'I've been in America. What did you decide?'

'Ask the minister in due course. I'm sure he'll furnish you with the details.'

'You've let him off. I can tell. You're mad. You've got to hold your report until I've seen you.'

'Impossible.'

'Nonsense. And you know it. I'm coming round to see you now. Right away.'

'I've only just arrived. I haven't seen my wife for five weeks.'

'She'll have to wait a minute. You too. I'll be there in ten minutes.'

'Fredy . . . Damn the man.'

Kaufmann arrived in a hire car. Samuel took him into the dining room and shut the door. Philippa had cleared the table. She and Rachel went into the bedroom.

'Let me get over to Wiesbaden, I can get you all the proof in the world. The man was in the S.S. There are photographs of him in uniform. Why would I lie to you?'

'Why weren't they supplied along with the other evidence?'

'Can't you tell the difference at your age, Samuel, between a dossier and a cookbook? They sent you a cookbook and you prepared them the dish they wanted.'

'I hardly think so.'

'Because you hardly think.'

'Fredy, behave yourself, please, or I shall ask you to leave.'

'I shan't behave myself and I shan't leave. Don't you know who I am? I know who you are, Samuel. You've fallen into every trap there is. I know what's in your report. Just what everyone wants to hear. You're severe on him, but you let him off. *D'extrême justesse!* The Jordan finger wags, but it is rude to point. You've done what you think H.M.G. would like, though not in the style they would like it. What you don't know is that you've done exactly what the Americans would like too. That's the point you're sitting on without feeling a thing. You've got a cork ass, Samuel. They got the evidence to you before they had to have it all, because that was the only time they would rely on you to turn them down.'

'What possible purpose could that serve?'

'Must I tell you? I'll tell you. They want Hermann to stay where he is, they need him to stay where he is, but they want him weakened. They want him to know which side his bread was buttered, and jammed. They wanted you to give him a message. And you were the messenger. They don't *care* what happens to Hermann Pfaff any more than the British do. So what have you done, Samuel? You've carried the whitewash for both sides. You know the saddest thing about you? You think you see through these people and all the time they pull the wool over your eyes and you think it's a judge's wig!'

'What right do you have to speak to me like this, Fredy?'

'None, hence every! Because you haven't used your head. I can prove that Pfaff not only knew about slave labour but actually interfered in the management of the camps. Actually visited two of them and made administrative changes, not wholly to the improvement of the inmates' condition of employment. Why don't you believe me?'

'Belief is not a commodity in which I'm commissioned to trade.'

'They chose the right man all right, didn't they?'

'If he was what you say he was, you can expose him at your leisure. If you can show me up as a dupe, by all means do so. I gather that your fortunes are prospering.'

'Do you wish they weren't, Samuel? Of course you do. Exposing him isn't the point. Exposing *them* is the point. You know what that man was; you've seen him and you know. What you don't accept is that your friends want him where he is, safe, and that's why they expose him to phantom dangers that enable people like you to give him a clean bill.'

'This is my house, Fredy. Be rude, but don't be loud, would you mind?'

'Manners makyth mannikin, Sam, and in your heart you know it. Your contempt for them comes out in neat phrases they think they taught you – "a commodity in which I'm commissioned to trade"! – and mine comes out as nose-thumbing, and picking, in public. You they like, me they don't. What've they offered you? They've offered you something, I'll bet my bottom dollar on it. What?'

'Now you'd better go.'

'You've rendered them a service. They'll make you pay for it, by giving you something, see if they don't.'

'There's no other way to run one's life except in a society.'

'Hang Plato; he'd hang us. You don't want to listen to me? I know who will.'

'In that case,' Samuel said, 'I mustn't take up any more of your time.'

'I'll give Hermann your regards, shall I?'

Samuel found two or three points which he tried to convince himself might form the basis of a successful appeal on Mr Rice's behalf. The third, suggesting a distinction between a wish and an intention, was a little fanciful, but it might go to show that a man could contemplate killing, as Rice admitted he had, without premeditation in the murderous sense. In court, Samuel spoke as if no other matter had been on his mind since the end of the trial. He was making his points in his usual measured way when quite suddenly he began to stammer. He stopped and swayed and checked his papers, while the appeal judges did polite things to give him time. He began again. And again he stammered. His jaw locked. His face was congested. He held the edge of the desk in front of him and then he blew his nose, as if he had merely sneezed. Dick Pearson-Davies leant across with a glass of water. He smiled shyly at his opponent and took a grateful sip. Their lordships bent forward, as if peering from the rail of a great liner in front of which a small boat had got into difficulties. 'Are you all right, Mr Jordan?'

93

'I must apologize to your lordships.'

'There have been graver offences,' the senior judge said.

Samuel took out his glasses and looked again at a document before him, from which, his frown suggested, some malign influence might have emanated to occasion such an uncharacteristic hiatus. He sipped more water and used a worn formula – 'if your lordships please' – to give his tongue a simple exercise. He soon recovered his fluency. When their lordships dismissed the appeal, with due attention to learned counsel's objections, they made reference to the customary eloquence with which he had expressed them. It was, of course, for the Home Secretary to make any recommendation to mercy.

Mr Rice was unchanged in his manner, and his manners, when Samuel went to see him after it had been decided that justice must take its course. He wondered whether there were any new jokes at all. The warders, it seemed, sometimes got depressed. Mr Rice was depressed only when he saw that they had deliberately allowed him to win at chess. He shook Samuel's hand as they parted and said that he quite understood the position. 'They can't make exceptions, can they, sir, or where should we be?'

Francis Harold Rice was hanged at Pentonville Gaol at the beginning of my summer holidays. My father took me down to the golf club on the first Friday of the hols and tried to improve my swing. I was not a good pupil: my only interest was hitting the ball as far as I possibly could. 'Technique first, distance thereafter,' Samuel said, but I made rage a substitute for steadiness. 'Moisten the lips and start afresh' was not a slogan to which I could warm. Afterwards, we drank shandy in the coconut-matted temporary bar (the bomb damage had yet to be repaired and no building licence was likely in the immediate future). My father said, 'I don't think you've had a very happy term at school, have you?'

'Not very,' I said.

'To be not *very* happy,' Samuel said, 'can sometimes, and to some people, seem the very apex of plausible hope.'

'That's a comfort,' I said.

'Facts are seldom a comfort,' Samuel said, 'but there they are. I don't suppose that it's of any great interest, but I don't think that I shall ever defend another murderer, if murderer he was. I don't think I have the right. The law isn't something that interests you, is it?'

'Not a lot.'

'I'm not sure that it interests me all that much,' Samuel said, 'on reflection.'

III

Whenever I saw Sally Raglan, during my vacations, she treated me with surprised kindness. 'Michael!' she would say, on the telephone, as if I were both the first and the last person she expected to hear from. My congratulations, when she won the Gold Medal at her drama school, meant more to her, she said, than anyone else's, yet if I invited her to come up to Cambridge for the weekend she would sigh and say only that she wished she could. If I suggested that she take part in some college production I was going to direct, she wished she could but she did not think that her tutor would approve. She was sure there were tons of available girls. As we grew up, we became sentimental about an adolescent closeness which had no actual history. Yet I always remembered her as she had appeared that cold morning in the doorway of Gladys Padgett's Dance Studio, bright-eyed above the fur collar of her coat.

Throughout my undergraduate years I was at once sociable and solitary. Solitude reminded me of my desires and of my lack of decisive purpose. If I wanted to say terrible things and to force people to the recognition of appalling truths, it amused me to ape the style and accents of those whose malice I intended to expose. My conformity, even when it affronted convention (my father deplored my haircuts, or the lack of them), was indistinguishable from that of the least heterodox of my contemporaries. The beauty of the city, the privilege of my situation, made resentment implausible. It might have been heroic to kick against the pricks; it was merely fretful to kick against the cushions. Our good fortune was an enviable kind of bad luck for someone who wanted to experience the cold bath of social realities.

When there was a competition for Young Playwrights, I entered a drama called *The Treasure*, based on the life of my mother's charlady and her family. The judges praised its dialogue, but the prize went to a knowing piece about a still-independent Venice, whose twentieth-century doge sought by sly diplomacy and sexual manipulation to maintain the serenity of his republic. A protégé of Guy Falcon, who had recently designed a 'controversial' *Don Juan*, created an astonishing *piazzetta*, with an undulating Bucentaur, in which the winning epigrams rattled like precocious hail. I auditioned for the part of the American ambassador, but my mimicry of Buddy Nathanson did not prevail. On the first night, I played snooker at the Union with a man in red braces who wanted to go into the hotel business.

I thought of Sally, but I was too far from her to imagine that she had the claim on my fidelity which I should have been happy to honour, had there been any hope of securing hers. Everything seemed to be a substitute for something else. Would I ever come face to face with the true thinginess of things? One afternoon, I shared a punt with a Trinity man whom I had met through the University Bridge Club. Louis Mendel's appearance was an embarrassment: he wore deplorable trousers and his asymmetric shirt was missing a button. He would plunge his hand below his belt, inside his trousers, and leave it there for several seconds before raising his fingers, like a bouquet, to his nose. He was said to be a brilliant mathematician (researching into 'fibre bundles'); he could execute double squeezes at the bridge table, while talking of other things. He approached girls without hesitation. I winced at his crudeness, but I was not sorry to profit from it when, after a single false cast, he fished two girls from the towpath into our punt.

Liz and Mo (Maureen) had come to Cambridge for the day, and the night, from Southampton, where they were student-teachers. Maureen sat next to me while Louis poled us towards Grantchester. She was rather short (and I was rather tall) and she had close-cropped brown hair and wide-spaced green eyes in a squarish, firm-jawed face. She wore purple lipstick, which glistened. She settled against me, as if I were precisely what she had come for, and crossed her bare legs. She wore boyish sandals, but her flesh was nicely rounded. After we had tea at Grantchester, Leo suggested that we all go to a dance that evening. He was prompt with improbable knowledge of some Scottish occasion taking place near the Catholic Church. The girls said it sounded like fun. They went to have supper at the hostel where they were staying and Louis gave me a wink; it was hard to believe that he was going to be a Prize Fellow of his college. 'Pushovers!'

I said, 'I don't think of women like that.'

Louis said, 'They think the same of us, don't they? Yours has done it already, if you ask me.'

Maureen's evening breasts were more easily visible in a white blouse with a V neck. She had put on silver eye-shadow and more gleaming lipstick. Her heels raised her against me and she moved with enough agility to make it seem that Gladys Padgett had taught me something after all. When Scottishness asserted itself to the point of crossed swords on the floor and pointed toes leaping over them, I proposed a walk across Christ's Pieces. Maureen gathered her things. 'Shall we go then?'

It was not a particularly warm summer's evening. She came into my arms by the bus stop. I liked the salty taste of her lips and the ardour of her unblinking gaze. I remarked, with easy treachery, on the bizarre dress and charmless manner of Louis Mendel and wondered whether Liz would be all right with him.

'Liz can take care of herself,' Maureen said.

'And so can you, I imagine.'

'If I have to,' she said.

Her kisses were keen, and she canted her hips against me, ignoring the tact with which I sought not to make my desire too obvious, but she did not part her lips. I put my hands on her breasts, outside the busy blouse. She seemed to nod slightly, still kissing.

'Oh Maureen,' I said.

'I know,' she said.

'I wish there was somewhere we could go.'

'True.'

'You can't come back to my rooms now, I'm afraid.'

'That's all right,' she said.

'Why don't you come for breakfast in the morning?'

'It's included at the hostel.'

'Well, come after. It wasn't really breakfast I was thinking about.'

'You'll have to be good,' she said.

'I shall be outstanding,' I said.

'I might,' she said, 'if you want me to.'

'To three places of decimals,' I said.

She caught my hand and put up that nice, square face to be kissed again. Her mouth opened this time, but when my tongue sought hers, it was as if she had none. Her mouth was hot, and empty. She slipped free of me and said, 'About nine then.'

I called on a classical scholar with military experience and borrowed a packet of contraceptives before climbing to my room. I was drunk with the luck which seemed to have made a female available to me without the preamble of promises or the hobble of love. Yet even as I told myself that I wanted Maureen without having the smallest interest in her feelings, I was touched by her cautious willingness. The salt of her lips remained on mine. I tasted the purple of her lipstick and was reminded of the violet chocolates my grandmother relished on bridge afternoons at Gloucester Mansions. Something in me seemed always to insist on a link between one experience and another. Why was I incapable of leaving a thing to be simply what it was? I tried to force my imagination to strip Maureen naked, but impersonal as my desire was, I also wanted her to like me. I should be disappointed if the weekend meant nothing more to her than I meant it to mean to me.

I woke dreading that she would not come, yet alarmed at the prospect of her arrival. The daylight was strikingly bright. We would see each other without polite shadows. When her sandals slapped the stairs and she gave a little hullo-knock on my open oak, it was as if she had come to haunt me. Was this the same girl? Had she had those freckles in the punt? Her legs were shorter! I greeted her with a ruthless smile; its remorseless warmth was a promise that I could handle this thing to my advantage. Over cornflakes and toast, I asked questions about her training course. Her awkward replies enabled me to patronize her; pity made me both fond and dismissive. When she had wiped the crumbs from her purple lips, I put my arms around her and kissed her. I wished now that she were Sally Raglan, or that Sally was there to observe my conquest. I thrust my hand inside her big-buttoned top and rummaged for a nipple.

She said, 'You weren't like this before.'

'Do these undo? Or are they bogus? You don't know what you've done to me.'

'I'd better be going!' The provincial sound of her voice advised me of the new distance she intended to put between us. 'I've got a train to catch.'

'What the hell did you come up here for?'

'You're not a very good loser, are you?' she said.

'I haven't lost anything yet,' I said. 'Worse luck.'

'You seemed so nice yesterday. I really liked you.'

When she leaned forward to refasten her boyish sandal, her breasts fell together in the deep vee of her blouse. I wanted to kiss and kiss her. She looked at me with unkindled eyes and stood up. While she made sure she had everything she came with, I stared at her, as if to net her forever in my memory and also to brand her with indelible regret. I wanted neither to keep nor to lose her.

As my time at Cambridge drew to an end, my father wondered what I intended to do with myself. I said that I wanted to take a look around. The committee had arranged to take our May Week Revue on a brief tour and then to the West End. There was talk of doing the show on the radio. Even after the Tripos, there were ways of postponing decision. I also wanted to work on a new, bolder version of *The Treasure*. Through writing revue material, I had discovered a small capacity to make audiences laugh; during our London season, I discovered the pleasure of being a smart clown. My heart might be dark with unsmiling rage, but how could I not masquerade as a very fortunate young man?

Barnaby Monk had been the editor of an undergraduate magazine where I vented my frustrations at not being allowed to direct plays by reviewing the productions of others. Barnaby encouraged me to savagery; he did not care how many enemies I made as long as my articles excited comment. In prevailing society, he maintained, to be scandalous was always to be just. He was slim and dark and wore white polo-necked sweaters and a black corduroy suit. If he was regularly described as 'elfin', he was an elf with a sharp tongue as well as those pointed ears. He spoke in the Union with a mixture of fulsomeness and impertinence; the one easily became the other. 'I hate you, sir, I *hate* you,' he once shouted at a cabinet minister, so loudly that his words had, as it were, been heard in London: one of the minister's colleagues invited him to dinner and suggested a political career. Barnaby had every opportunity to be whatever he wanted: he was a colourful chameleon, capable of standing out against any background. It was no surprise when he managed even to win Claudia Terracini from the arms of Jolyon Urquart. Our leading Cambridge poetess, with her tawny hair and her black stockings, her silver-buckled shoes and her slivers of allusive verse, had Mediterranean eyes and a red wound of a mouth unfamiliar with kind words. Barnaby never noticed the odds against her capture, not least, perhaps, because he was able to believe that she had captured him. Jolyon went off to lecture in California, warning Claudia that Barnaby was a fine spirit contaminated by journalism. She could be relied upon to relish the reference to Mr Eliot's verdict on Macaulay. Claudia combined reticence with daring: her few bold words dazzled as if on a black velvet tray. When someone asked if she were not Barnaby Monk's 'fiancée', she replied, 'I am his mistress.'

Barnaby wanted to be a journalist. It was not for lack of other prospects that he joined the *Sunday Crusader*; he believed in the importance of popular newspapers. They might be dishonest or badly written or superficial, but Fleet Street was the sole available means of challenging the unrationed complacency around us. He wanted to electrify, and shock, those who had revived the smugness and vanity which the war had promised to obliterate. Barnaby was expert in the social machinery of London; he revelled in the accuracy of unbelievable tales. All his knowledge was put to seditious purpose when he was taken on to the strength of 'Nelson's Column', the *Crusader*'s gossip page. It was an open secret that he would soon displace its editor, poor old Malcolm Spears. Benedict Bligh, who had joined the paper as drama critic, suggested that he give the column a punchy new title: 'Why not "Hamilton's Snatch?"'

Barnaby was scarcely established in Crusader House before he called me, at home, and suggested that I also work for the paper. I had not expected to hear from him again and I was flattered by his suggestion, though I could hardly fail to respond with sarcasm: 'Are my feet big enough for your footsteps?'

'No need to tread in them if they make you feel small,' Barnaby said. 'They asked me if I knew anybody who would make a good hack; I couldn't, so I mentioned you. Try it for a few weeks. If you don't like it, you can always write a swingeing drama exposing all the things about Fleet Street that everyone knows perfectly well already.'

I declined to work under Barnaby, but I was taken on as a second-string film critic and trainee feature writer. I told my father the news as if it were something I had arranged for his sake.

'Is that what you really want to do?'

'I don't suppose I shall ever do what I really want to do,' I said.

'And might one ask what that is, and why not?'

'I want to show people what the world is really like,' I said.

'And is that necessarily what one wants it to be like?'

'What attracts me more than anything else,' I said, 'is the grubbiness of Grub Street; the underbelly of reality, I haven't had much access to that.'

'I've never found underbellies particularly attractive aspects of anatomy myself, but each to his own.'

Barnaby and Claudia married and found a basement in Tite Street, below the blue badge of Oscar Wilde's house. They gave garrulous bottle parties where Benedict Bligh stammered fluently about the need for a theatrical revolution, and then a social one. I wished that I could move to a Chelsea address, and find a Chelsea woman, but I stayed in my parents' flat at Court Royal, as if graduation still lay in the future.

Sally Raglan too was living at home, off West Hill, not far from Court Royal. She was getting parts in suburban productions. It was comforting to imagine that we were twin souls, enduring a cloistered novitiate before launching ourselves into glamorous orbit. Even now, when proximity should have allowed me to see more of her, she was often busy. One Sunday, she said that if I really wanted to help her, I could come round to Cambalt Road, while she learnt her lines, and hold her hand. I said that it seemed like a reasonable place to start. 'What? Oh Michael! You'll have to promise to be good.'

'Goodness,' I said, 'is a threat, not a promise.'

The Raglans' narrow house was red brick, with a copper roof capped by a Victorian wrought-iron weather vane. The window frames were green and there was pre-Raphaelite glass in the front door. Major Raglan sold a little insurance and bought many drinks. Sally's mother, Anthea, kept the house neat and bright and wrote women's stories, under the pseudonym of Justine de la Corbières. Thanks to her industry, the swagged curtains had boxed pelmets and velvet ties. There were stacks of feminine cushions on the settee. Tasselled rigging held up the arms which could be let down hospitably for an overnight visitor. A collection of dolls of all nations lounged on the furniture and was ranged on a shelf. The Major and his wife played bridge on Sunday afternoons, so Sally and I had 33,

Cambalt Road to ourselves. She had put on serious glasses to study her acting edition.

'Pick it up from the top, darling,' she said. 'There.'

'You know very well how I feel about you,' I said.

'That doesn't mean I don't want to hear you say it. I stand up there. In words of one syllable preferably. I go over to the sofa. Do you know any?'

'I love you,' I said. 'If that isn't too complicated for you.'

'You make it sound like very bad news. I turn my back. Like the Fall of Constantinople.'

' "I love you" doesn't sound remotely like the Fall of Constantinople. More like the Siege of Lucknow.'

'History,' Sally said, 'was never my favourite subject.'

'Biology can be very enjoyable,' I said.

'If you really loved me,' she said, 'you wouldn't care –'

'If you *truly* loved me,' I pointed out, 'is what the great Gerald Pringle actually wrote at what I fear may well have been the height of his powers.'

'Buttons!' Sally said. 'O.K. If you *truly* loved me, you wouldn't care –'

'Gerald prefers "mind".'

'Fudge!' Sally said. 'You must be putting me off. We're dropping the book tomorrow.'

'From a considerable height, I trust.'

'Write something better yourself, if you think it's so easy.'

'I'm working on it,' I said. 'How long can you wait?'

'I hope you have as much success one day as *All's Fair* had in its time. You won't have anything to grumble about, if you do.'

'I'll find something,' I said. 'Why do you do these bloody awful plays with these bloody awful producers?'

'David isn't that bad. He just has this way of showing you how to do everything. I mean *everything*.'

'I can understand the temptation,' I said. 'Assuming that everything is something you're willing to do.'

'Which it's not. What would my mother say? The play does at least *work*.'

'The play does at *most* work. Plays should say something, preferably something very disagreeable.'

'I'm sure yours'll do that. Meanwhile, we really ought to think about doing it again.'

'Personally I was still thinking about doing it for the first time. Could that possibly be made to square with your plans?'

'Oh Michael!' she said.

'Right so far,' I said.

'Dear, dear Michael . . . I'm very, very fond of you . . . But we really do have to rehearse.'

'Constantinople never is going to bloody well fall, is it? Look at the time. It's way past 1453. They'll be discovering America in a minute.'

'You promised you'd be good.'

'This way, you'll never know if I am or not. I was told you were planning to be an actress, not a nun.'

'I did consider being a nun once,' she said.

'Should you perhaps give it further thought? I always thought an actress –'

'I'm not "an actress", Michael Jordan, thank you very much; I'm a real person.'

'I hope that isn't going to interfere with your career.'

'You're no different from all the others, are you?'

'Others? What others?'

'Now it all comes back to me,' she said, 'why I hate you sometimes.'

'As long as that's an advance on "very fond". Is it? Christ!'

Sally's expressive nose began to twitch. She blinked and tripped tears on to her powdered cheeks. Her tongue nipped left and right to catch the salt. Her lips quivered apprehensively, as if tasting a foreign dish. She thrust her hands under all the cushions for a handkerchief.

'Oh come on, Sall,' I said. 'No time for lamentation now . . .'

'You think you can say anything you like to me, don't you?' she said.

'Violet Elizabeth,' I said, 'come back here this instant!'

She shook her head seriously and scuttled out of the pink-and-beige sitting room. I picked up a magazine and opened it to Margaret Bradbury's advice column. Innumerable doors seemed to open and shut, as if Sally were in several parts of the house at the same time. Then the telephone rang. 'You might . . . answer it . . .' she called down to me with choked urgency.

The telephone might be ringing, but I could not see it. I followed a plait of white cord under the skirt of a Regency lady, complete with towering white wig and beauty spot, and discovered the receiver.

'Sally there?'

'Who shall I say is calling?'

Sally dashed in, blowing her dry nose, and took the telephone from me and sat feet-up in a floral easy chair. 'Kitson! How's Kitson and what does he want for a change? I've just been going through it with this friend of mine. An amateur. Because Kitson never suggested it. What? No. No one's said a word. Nary a syllabule. Rubbish! Everyone thought you were wonderful. Then she's lying through her uneven teeth. Tommy never! Then what Kitson should do is go to bed and have some lovely Freudian dreams. Of course: Fortnum's do them. I'll see Kitson in the a.m., looking lean and rested, and I won't drop the book until he winks me the tip! And I love Kitson!'

'Dear Margaret Bradbury,' I said, 'I'm racked with jealousy. Was that your leading man, do I shrewdly infer?'

'Someone beginning with Victoria Lock has been sowing seeds of doubt and suspicion. Actors are so *vulnerable*. You have to stake them like sweet peas half the time. Of course, I love Kitson dearly –'

'That sounds as if he's in trouble,' I said.

'– but I can't pretend that he's the ideal Victor Dangerfield.'

'You underestimate yourself.'

I thought that she was coming across the room to kiss me, but she ran to the window and pushed aside the lace curtain. Jack and Anthea Raglan were coming through the sprung gate and up the path between the inside-out tulips. Jack had his British Warm slung over his shoulders and wore a dark brown pork pie hat. Anthea took many steps behind him.

'Look who's, look who's!' Sally put her arms round her father's neck and kissed his flushed cheek, while Anthea unpinned her veiled blue straw hat to reveal *Chez Marcel* curls.

'Hullo, Michael. How are you?'

I said, 'Very well, Mrs Raglan.'

'Good evening, Major,' Sally said.

'That's very true, my dear,' Jack Raglan said.

'Did Daddy play very, very well?'

'I trumped everybody's aces, including your mother's.'

'Serves them jolly well right, say I!'

'And how is your writing going, Michael?' Anthea was watching Jack hold a bottle to the light.

'Still from the top of the page on down, Mrs Raglan. How about yours?'

'There are worse disciplines than the women's market! I may not be significant, but I like to think I'm getting better and better as time goes by.'

'And so you are, mummy. The last story was wonderful. You really should read "Gingerbread August", Michael.'

'The last one was "Jennifer's September",' Anthea Raglan said. 'It was set in Sardinia.'

'Oh, do you know Sardinia?'

'I based it on the Isle of Wight. With Italians. They've asked me to take on another *nom de plume*, did I tell you, Sall?'

'You should,' Sally said. She had her back to her mother and a hand on Jack Raglan's sleeve. 'Can I have sippers, Major?'

Jack Raglan tilted the cut-glass goblet to his daughter's lips. 'No gulpers now!'

'I'm thinking possibly Baroness Calvi. I suppose you don't believe in romance, Michael.'

'Implicitly,' I said. 'Can you give me the name of a reliable supplier?'

'Jack faced death and destruction more than once in the Royal Marines, and when things were at their very worst, what helped him to come through unscathed? Ask him!'

Sally stood on tiptoe to kiss her father on the forehead as he took a manly dose of gin. When I said that I ought to be getting home, she touched her father's lips and gave him a look which the acting edition would have qualified as 'roguish', before crossing to give me a real pal's kiss. 'You will come again, won't you, and see us, soon?'

On Saturdays, eager for mundane experience, I worked as a reporter. The *Sunday Crusader* expanded its work force and took over the newsroom occupied by the *Daily Crusader* on other days of the week. I looked forward to the clatter of Royal Sovereign typewriters and the professional panic which hung over the low-ceilinged room, with its scabby olive walls and dust-furred ventilators. The news editor, Bernie Platt, and the chief sub, Vic Fidgin, presided at a long table in the centre of the room, their subordinates beside them. Copy went on to spikes or was passed to the subs for improvement. Wet proofs came up from the presses and were graded according to their likelihood of making the paper. At first I had been apprenticed to the Labour Correspondent (who was also the Naval Correspondent and, not infrequently, 'Our Political Staff'). Brocky wrote all his copy in longhand, with a soft pencil, a paragraph on each flimsy page. His vocabulary was limited and his spelling uncertain, but his stories were seldom spiked. He had joined a local newspaper as a boy; the street had been his school. His intelligence was in his nose: he knew where to sniff out a story and he detected a fraud instantly. He managed to be both ruthless and kind: his criticism was a line through my copy, but he raised his glass to me when my first piece made the Scottish edition and rejected my gratitude with a shake of the grizzled head that did not interrupt the flow of mild and bitter. On the day that Brocky said, 'You're ready to fly solo, son, so bugger off and leave me alone, will you?' I felt that I had at last achieved an honest graduation. For a while, in tribute to him, I even smoked Woodbines.

Bernie Platt came over to me one Saturday morning and leaned his garter-sleeved arm on my metal table. 'You're a well-travelled young man, aren't you, Michael?'

'I've been to Knokke-le-Zoute,' I said.

'Fancy a trip to Knokke-le-East Finchley at all? You speak the lingo, don't you?'

'Well,' I said, 'I can do the hand signals.'

'This Mrs Neville's been through on the blower – husband and little girl've disappeared into thin air. *Verb. sap.!* So why don't you get down there as fast as public transport can carry you and take a sniff of the prevailing?' He looked at what I was typing, a report on the sly use, by certain German manufacturers, of British mailing lists; it was technically known as 'slipstreaming'. 'That's not a semi-colon in there again, is it, Michael? Did Brocky never tell you that on the news pages all semi-colons are full stops? Think on, lad! You know what happens when semi-colons creep in? I get a call from the country. And that doesn't always mean congratulations. Here's the address. Show respect and understanding and come back with the dirt.' Bernie looked at his service watch. 'Oh all right then, take a bloody taxi.'

Bothwell Court was a grey block of thirties flats with metal windows. There was a sheaf of gilded leaves in a copper vase on a console by the lift, but the fourth floor, where number 27 was, had linoleum in the corridor and fly-mottled light fittings. When I pressed the bell, there was a whirring noise.

'Anthony?' A woman's voice was calling through the door.

'Michael Jordan,' I said, '*Sunday Crusader*.'

An adjacent door had opened. The neighbour wore a quilted housecoat and her thick brown hair was in curlers. She made a gesture for me to come over.

'Just a minute,' the voice said from behind the closed door.

'Excuse me,' I said to the neighbour, 'but do you know these people at all?'

'I could see you later,' she said. 'Elevenses?'

She shut her door as that of number 27 opened. A grey-suited, silver-haired woman in tartan slippers and a good deal of make-up looked out. 'No photographer?'

'Absolutely not,' I said.

'Why not?'

'Oh, I thought – my editor thought – it might be better – more – I can always get one later, if –'

'I hope we did the right thing to call you. Because this is a terrible, terrible thing that's happened.'

'Suppose you tell me all about it, Mrs –'

'Davies,' she said. 'Tina Davies. I'm her mother, the person who called you, rightly or wrongly.'

Jackie Neville was sitting at the kitchen table. Her cigarette was reddened by lipstick for almost half its length.

'Does she usually smoke?' Mrs Davies said. 'She's smoking. Well, he's come. You wanted him to come; here he is.'

I said, 'Mrs Neville –'

'Can you see what kind of a state she's in? She's out of her mind. That's the only reason she said to call you.'

'Mother, could I speak with this – alone, do you think, please?'

'Her father's had to go to business. That's Mr Gerald Davies. Otherwise, believe me, he'd be here.'

'*Mother!* Can I please have *two minutes* –'

'Is she usually like this?'

Jackie lowered her chin to the red-and-white oilcloth covering the table and bumped her chin up and down between the cereal packets. She was black-haired and wore a blue cotton overall, with scalloped buttons down the front.

Mrs Davies stood close to me. 'Will I ever allow that man back into this house? I'm not going to answer that question. That is one question I'm not prepared to answer.'

Jackie said, '*Mother!*'

She worked as an usherette in a local Regal. She was out alternate evenings. Her husband, Morris, was a clerical worker in the Ministry of Transport. They had lived with Jackie's parents, in Bothwell Court, ever since the birth of little Tessa, who slept with them in the back room. She could show me how much space they had in there, if I liked.

'And how old are you?'

'I'm twenty-two,' she said. 'Four years in the one room. Three of us. He didn't like it; of course he didn't like it. *I* didn't like it.'

'We should call the police right away, if you ask me,' Mrs Davies said, from the hallway.

Jackie got up and shut the kitchen door. 'Do you want anything?'

'Not for me,' I said. 'And has he threatened to do something like this before at all?'

'What has he done? Do you know what he's done? He's taken my Tessa, that's all I know, and I want her back. The police can't do anything. He's her father. What can they do? How old are you?'

'Twenty-four,' I said. 'Has he maltreated you in the past?'

'How should I know?'

'Been cruel to you?'

'I wouldn't say so. He's never well, not really. It's his lungs, from when he was in the mines. South Derbyshire when I first met him. He comes from round the corner, but that's where he was. His chest.'

'Bevin boy?'

'They wanted me to marry someone else. Older and richer. Norman Wallace. But there was something about Morris; at the time. I couldn't help it. I work. But where can we go? I expect they were right, in a way. I've got these, haven't I, but how long are they going to last? Especially after a kiddie. Only what's he done with her? That's the reason I called you. Are you experienced?'

'Is he a violent man at all, Mrs Neville?'

She said, 'Jackie. I think of Mrs Neville, I don't think of me: I think of his mother. Cat. I nearly died with Tessa and now this has to happen. I come back dog-tired and has he even left a note? I've seen *Up In Arms* sixteen times this week. And now this. Can you imagine? When did he ever change a nappy? Do you know how thick the walls are in this flat? That doesn't exactly help, does it? So now what are you going to do?'

'I presume Neville is N,e,v,i,l,l,e, is that right?'

I telephoned a quick draft of 'YOUNG MOTHER'S HEART-RENDING APPEAL' to the *Crusader* office from the booth on the corner and then I came back and buzzed the neighbour's bell. She had taken the curlers from her hair and put on a pair of high heels, without stockings. She was still zipped up the front. 'He used to come in here,' she said, 'did Morris. To visit. My husband was killed in an accident while he was in the R.E.M.E., so we had something in common. We had nice talks. We discussed me going with him. He read a lot, you know. He thought about things. How could I, with my two at school? You have a very nice voice. I expect you know that.'

'Going where, Mrs –?'

'Oh no! Oh no! I'm not having my name mentioned, even by a dark brown voice like yours. I trust a voice before a face. I work on a switchboard, as you may or may not have guessed. You can call me Denise, if you want to, between these four walls. He'd been planning it for ages. Of course he had. There was the passport to get, wasn't there? I've never been to Paris, have you?'

'What makes you think he's gone to Paris?'

'That's where his friend lives. He trusted me, Morris.'

'Friend?'

'He met during the war. This Frenchman. He kept up with him. Engineer. He was with him down the mines; I don't know if you know about that.'

'You wouldn't know whereabouts exactly, I suppose?'

'They pay for information, don't they? I've got this address he gave me.'

'Have you really? How extraordinary!'

'Don't misunderstand me,' she said. 'He was lonely; so was I. I wouldn't take money; that's not why I'm talking to you. It's 147, rue de Crimée. The name is Jouves, Félix. Think they might send you over?'

'They might,' I said. 'If I hurry.'

'I'll come as your secretary,' she said. 'Do you have a secretary?'

'Of course not.'

'Now I suppose you've got what you wanted, haven't you?'

'Let's say I've made a start; thanks to you, Denise.'

'If you were married, I wouldn't have any trouble with you at all, would I? Dark brown disappointment, that's how you're going down in little Denise's diary as things stand at the moment.'

Bernie Platt looked at his commando watch and mouthed calculations. 'If you catch the two-fifteen plane, I don't see why you shouldn't file in time. You can get most of it written while you're in the air, can't you?'

'Look, there's no absolute certainty he's going to be in Paris.'

'Well, if he isn't, you can have a good time and when you get back, you can look for another job, can't you?'

'What about a photographer?' I said.

'I'll get the number for you. This American: Dave de Soto – Dave de photo! Watch the mademoiselles, won't you? They all swear they haven't got it. They all bloody well have.'

The rue de Crimée was sombre with heavy apartment buildings. An advertisement for Suze, blue on yellow, filled the steep narrow side of an irregular structure overlooking a vacant lot. An articulated lorry was close against the wall of 147. I had to squeeze along to the archway where metal post boxes might tell me where Jouves, Félix, lived. I went through to the central courtyard. A cinder path took me to entrance F. The path was edged with wine bottles driven neck-downwards into the ground. Two wire 'trees' were freighted with empties. Gritty washing hung on tiered frames.

Morris Neville was wearing a skimpy blue suit and a collarless shirt. He had waxy skin and he had not shaved. It was as if minute black wires had been forced into his chin. His eyes were pale blue; the pupils appeared to be surrounded by a black line. He took me down a creaking corridor to glassed sliding doors. The furniture in the little sitting room was close together; it might have come from somewhere else. There were crocheted antimacassars on wide, upholstered chairs facing each other across a table loaded with silver-framed photographs. Morris sat opposite me and stared at me across the frames. I had to make the first move in some game whose rules he assumed me to know.

I said, 'Your wife is very upset.'

'The man who owns this flat,' Morris said, 'if you make any trouble for him –'

'I'm not in the business of making trouble for anyone, Mr Neville.'

'I thought you said you were a journalist.' He fingered one of the photographs, of a soldier with a 1914–18 chest, as if to hold himself to a frown which his own humour seemed to threaten. 'He's the first real man I ever met in my life. He opened my eyes.'

I said, 'Jackie told me you were down the mines.'

'I never thought about politics before I met him. He told me to come here any time I wanted to. People say things sometimes; he meant it. How's she taking it?'

'She's very upset.'

'People don't want to know the truth, do they?' he said. 'They want to deceive themselves, they want to deceive other people. Start with yourself, the rest soon follows. You're educated, aren't you? Well educated?'

'Money passed,' I said, 'if that's what you mean.'

'Félix works for the C.G.T. The Communist Trade Union.'

'I know.'

'How do you know?'

'What the C.G.T. is. Your wife wants her daughter back. What're you going to do about it?'

'You've settled for England, have you, as it is?'

'Can I see her, Mr Neville?'

114

'Suits you, does it?'

'I wouldn't say that it was made-to-measure exactly, but . . . I manage to wear it, roughly. Are you a Communist?'

'I haven't brought any secrets with me, if that's what you mean. I wish I knew some. You want the world to be different, is that it, but you don't want to do anything to change it? I'm not having her grow up to be an usherette.'

'How're you and Tessa going to be any better off here than you were in Bothwell Court?'

'I could kick you out of this flat,' Morris Neville said, 'into the street, and there's nothing you could do about it. I don't know why I don't.'

'Don't you, Mr Neville? I think I do.'

'Yes? Why's that then?'

'I think you want to go home.'

Morris considered the photographs and then he had me by the throat and he was pushing me back against a creaking armoire which rocked with the impact. He held me there and I tried to swallow. There was coloured glass displayed on a hanging shelf by my head. It was no good breaking things. I said, 'Why else did you give Denise this address? Your neighbour.'

Morris said, 'The bitch!'

'The necessary bitch. How else would I have got here? Or does somebody else know as well?'

The glass doors slid apart. A man in a beret stepped into the room and turned chalky eyes in our direction. '*Félix n'est pas là?*'

Morris let go of me. 'He's gone out.'

'*Comment?*'

'*Le monsieur dit qu'il est sorti, monsieur.*'

'You're lucky,' Morris Neville said. 'You can go anywhere you like, can't you?'

'I really would like to see Tessa, Mr Neville. Where is she?'

'You want her to be dead, don't you? That'd just suit you nicely. Well, they've taken her to the zoo.' He laughed and then he sniffed. 'Denise!'

I looked at my watch. 'Could I possibly use the telephone, do you think? I'll give them the money.'

Dave de Soto drove a blue jeep and wore a denim suit. His crew-cut hair had golden streaks. He told me that he detested animals and little girls, but he took some good shots of Tessa with a baby elephant. I sat at an uneven metal table in a café by the Gare d'Austerlitz and revised my story about the cross-channel tug-of-love which was tearing a family apart. I smiled as I scribbled; the composition of something I had read, and despised, a hundred times elsewhere might have been an entry in a competition for clichés. As I anchored the scribbled sheets under the St Raphael ashtray, I had a sense of being a heroic nonentity: a reporter. I could imagine how my life would be devoted to meeting lower and lower standards. How much ingenuity I should have to display in order to give no hint of being able to do better!

Dave de Soto took me to the *Crusader* office, Avenue Foch, from where my copy could be passed to London. He talked of all the people he knew (his 'fun-group' he called them) and I wondered whether he might not suggest that we spend the evening with them. When I asked him to suggest somewhere I could stay, he mentioned a hotel in the rue Jacob, shook hands and jumped into his jeep. 'Gotta run, Michael.' I collected my suitcase from Les Invalides and went to the hotel he had mentioned. Alone in Paris, I could scarcely admit my innocence of the city even to myself. I walked down the rue Bonaparte to the *quais*. The bookstalls were already locked. I craved print if I could not have company. I bought a copy of *L'Express* and sat in a café drinking a *fine* I did not want.

I crossed the river by the Pont Neuf and walked and walked. If I could have transported myself to Court Royal, in time for one of my mother's dishes of 'Spanish rice', I should hardly have resisted. Paris was grey and alien. The June evening seemed chilly; I sweated and shivered. I walked along the rue du Faubourg-St Honoré and found myself, as if it were a destination I knew to be there, in the narrow streets around Les Halles.

Prostitutes paraded outside pretty hotels. Some leaned over the sills of downstairs rooms, smoking and showing their breasts in silvery, off-the-shoulder tops. Others braced one leg against the wall, to show their shape. You could hardly pass without grazing a shiny knee. *'Tu viens?'*

I had to keep a hand in my pocket to hide my excitement. The standard price was a thousand francs. The hardened heels and brittle hair, the lurid mouths and sticky mascara, filled me with disgusted desire. The occasional beauty, head tilted to catch the light, body jiggling a little, as if some tiny motor were idling within, caused me to stop and stare, dizzy with opportunity. Less than a quid! I observed the brazenness of men with humbug amazement. One became involved in a negotiation, which finally required pencil and paper. Despite what Bernie Platt had said, I was more afraid of making a fool of myself than of a disease. What exactly did you do when you went upstairs? How did you persuade them that you were interested in them personally?

Families were having dinner in the restaurants of the *quartier*. I was dizzy with the simultaneity of things. My desire went beyond lust: I wanted to possess the whole multiplicity of the scene, to possess it from every angle at the same time. Fear and conceit were indistinguishable. I wanted to do terrible things to these women and I wanted to understand them, to possess their stories as well as their bodies. The garishness of the streets, the indifference of it all to my own existence, caused a kind of vertigo. I stood for several minutes watching one of the most majestic tarts, in front of a hotel whose white paint and neat lettering suggested that it might be less infested than the others. I swore I would go and talk to her, if she looked across at me with any sort of encouragement. A French officer, in kepi and burnished boots, came round the corner and went up to my tart. She was all in white. Her breasts were superb. Her bare legs had dimpled knees under a flared skirt. Her thonged sandals were unscuffed. As the officer spoke to her, he tapped his swagger stick against his breeches. She nodded and pointed. He gestured to her with his stick, to go ahead of him and followed her into the clean hotel. I sighed at her infidelity and walked away.

I had a ham sandwich and a glass of beer in one café and a cup of coffee in another. I made my way, in a ragged circle, back to the Left Bank and sat down to read *L'Express* in the Royal St Germain. Might some existentialist take me for an intellectual? All the philosophers in the café respected my solitude. What made me as I was and not as I wanted to be? Only the thinnest membrane seemed to separate me from a world to which I could find no access.

'*Pardon, monsieur, mais vous n'êtes pas par hasard le Lone Ranger?*'

'*Excusez-moi, monsieur, mais vous vous trompez de numéro.*' I was ready for facetiousness at a moment's notice, though I had no notion of who had spoken to me or of precisely what he had said. Only after I had replied, with a brusqueness suggesting that I had no wish to be interrupted in my study of the Mendèsiste position on the European Iron and Steel Federation, did I suspect that the leather-jacketed young man in front of me might be someone who actually knew me.

'*Je vous explique pourquoi. Parce que, à l'époque, moi, j'étais en quelque sorte Tonto.* Tell me the truth, are you or are you not a certain Michael Jordan? Because if so, I just may be your oldest friend in the world. Or at least in this *arrondissement*.'

'Jesus Christ,' I said. 'Joe Hirsch!'

'Right second time,' he said. 'You haven't changed a bit. How's school? Alternatively, what're you doing in Paris?'

'I've got a rendezvous with destiny,' I said, 'but I'm not sure it's going to show up.'

'It is. It has. Come and join us. Or are you still hoping she's going to arrive?' Joe took me by the arm and led me to one of those groups from which, a few minutes earlier, I had thought myself excluded. How did he come to know Stafford Canning (an ex-president of the Union, I recalled, and now first secretary at the British embassy) or Justo Linares, who had just returned from a secret mission to Madrid on behalf of the banned Spanish

Socialist Party? Justo shook hands while blood seeped from his head and was staunched by Pierrette Lévi, a slim, fair girl in a loose black windcheater and narrow black trousers.

Stafford said, 'Jordan, Jordan! Didn't I see you performing in some sort of revue in London at some point?'

'One of the many things I should never have done.'

'You should do more of them. I practically pissed myself at that thing you did about Bertie Russell.'

'I'm not sure that that was me,' I said.

'*J'ai failli me pisser*,' Stafford said to Pierrette, '*à ce type qui faisait une impression vachement drôle de Bertrand Russell. Le grand savant anglais.*'

Pierrette said, 'I know very well who Bertrand Russell is, Stafford.'

I said, 'May I be the millionth visitor to say how well you speak English?'

'Typical!' Joe said. 'The English always think it's a sign of intellectual distinction for any foreigner to be able to order a cup of tea without getting coffee.'

I said, 'How's your mother these days, Joe?'

'Pierrette teaches the damn language. She's very well. She's in Harrogate.'

'I do remember a sketch you did now. It was rather a hoot.'

'I did several actually.'

'And this one was rather a hoot.' Stafford crossed his ankles and leaned back in his chair, fingertips together, and closed his eyes.

I said, 'What happened?'

Pierrette said, 'He was at a demonstration.'

'It looks nasty.'

Pierrette said, '*Justo, mon amour, tu dois aller au lit.*'

'*On a toujours Ramon à rencontrer.*'

Stafford Canning rolled his head and opened sudden blue eyes. 'Were you ever a practising bugger at all?'

'For some reason,' I said, 'I've always preferred women. Perhaps because I never went to school with any of them.'

'I've never wholly understood females. The anatomy looks simple in the diagram, but they turn out to be unbelievably complicated below the waterline, one finds.'

'Canning, you're pissed,' Joe said.

'The trouble with trying to drown my sorrows is that all the little sods have got gills. I drown and they get bigger and bigger. Don't worry about Justo, comrade Jordan. He likes having his head bashed in. He goes round looking for hefty people to do him the honour. It's known in his addled patois as keeping up the struggle against Fascism. He gets Frog coppers to run a Moch on his nut and persuades himself that Francisco Franco sleeps less easy o' nights on account of it. *No es verdad, compañero?*'

'You're a Foreign Office shit, Canning,' Joe Hirsch said.

'Present, and correct.'

'Shit is right,' Justo said. 'Because let me tell you something: I was in Madrid in 1945 – August 15th, 1945 –'

Stafford pulled my ear towards his lips. 'Never trust accuracy.'

'– and I'll tell you something, my friend – the whole place was red, white and blue. All the women were wearing blue skirts, white blouses, red scarves . . . Why?'

'Never answer optional questions.'

'They were waiting for the British.'

'Let 'em wait,' Stafford said.

'Not the Russians, not the Americans. You people. There were no guardias on the streets – Franco was packing his bags in the Redondo. Everyone knew it was all over for the little bastard. The British had only to raise their little fingers –'

'More exercise than any of us felt like taking.'

'Canning, you're a bastard.'

'Something for which more than a little finger has to be raised.'

'The Provisional Government was in St Jean de Luz. One word needed to be said. No one said it. Why? Why? Tell me why.'

'Easy. We didn't want Stalin taking his holidays in Gibraltar.'

'Stafford, *tu es vraiment méchant, toi!*'

'*Tu viens coucher avec moi, ma petite Pierrette?*'

'*Pour quoi faire finalement?*'

'*Tu me traites en tante de ma plume? Je vous quitte définitivement. Non, non. Je me sauve.*' Stafford stood up and then bent to kiss Pierrette, who touched his nose with her delicate finger. 'If you want a winning slogan to take back to England with you, Jordan, try "Yanks Go Home". High time they did. High time I did. Joe, are you giving me a lift or do I take the Citroën into my own hands?'

'How do you come to have a car?'

'Expect me to live out of a suitcase all my life?' Joe said. 'Are you here tomorrow?'

'Tomorrow's almost here,' I said.

'Lunch? Only . . .' He tapped his watch. 'We've got Ramon . . .'

Pierrette said, '*Ramon, c'est une ordure . . .*'

'*Allons, Pierrot. C'est une ordure qui nous attend.*'

'*Pas moi,*' she said. '*Une fois, ça suffit. C'est une saleté.*'

Joe said, 'Suit yourself. Michael'll buy you another drink, won't you, Jordan old scout?'

'With pleasure.'

'*Merci, mais j'ai un assez long trajet à faire. Et le Métro . . .*'

I said, 'I'm on expenses. Lord Muck, my legendary proprietor, can send you home in a taxi. Please.'

'*C'est gentil, mais . . .*' She was putting her cigarettes and lighter into a straw shopping bag she had under the table.

'Please,' I said. 'I really do need to improve my English.'

She looked at her watch, made a tight mouth and sat down. Joe was signalling to me through the glass as he and the others went into the night. I frowned at him. Pierrette lit a new cigarette and we began to talk. We talked and talked; I told her about Morris Neville and his hopeless hope of a new life. The more I talked of him, the more I seemed to be talking of myself. The futility he found in England, the domestic round, the sumptuous banality, these were things which threatened us all with disreputable comforts. I displayed my rhetoric to flatter and challenge the pale girl who took one cigarette after another from her packet of *Gauloises Jaunes* and lit them with a frown which made each a little experiment to be greeted, when smoke came, with contented relief. Her throat emerged slim and yellowy-white from the black sweat shirt. It was like a strong stem of a flower plunged in a dark vase. I did not try to imagine her body. She was those grey eyes, that throat, those restless hands. Her voice was at once brisk and hesitant. Her words were furred by smoking. She cleared them with a discreet agitation of her throat, hardly a cough, a gesture of impatience at her own gentleness. Her pity for Morris Neville reproached my con-descension. 'What do you suppose he imagined he might find here?' While I gazed in admiration of her subjunctive, she breathed smoke from flared nostrils. A charge of blood pulsed, hidden humour, in her upper lip. 'Seriously?'

'Oh,' I said, 'what have you got? A mixture of ooh-là-là and the workers' paradise. Somewhere where it's possible to *be* serious. A place where you don't have to be what other people have decided you're going to be. A chance to be yourself, a self that isn't their you, but your own. A world without parents perhaps. *Familles, je vous déteste!* One thinks one knows why people do things. At least, I think I know! But there's always an element in the equation which you assume to be a zero and isn't necessarily at all. I never met his mother, for instance. Jackie – that's the wife – she said one word about her: "Cat!" Perhaps she was the butler who really did it.'

Was Pierrette's frown because she was considering my psychological algebra or because my remark was too obscure? She said, '*Le pauvre. L'imagination trop précise, c'est la marque des petits esprits*. How would you translate that?'

'If you know exactly what you're looking for, you're a bit of a fool. Or something like that.' We talked for a long time without the smallest threat of silence. Then, suddenly, the road of words had run out. She went about the business of another cigarette. Finally, I said, 'You were here in the war, of course.'

'Of course,' she said. 'But not here.'

'Not in Paris. Just as well, I imagine. I imagine. *Sans précision!* I imagine without knowing. The birth of sentiment. You were in school presumably?'

'Yes, I was. Near Annecy. In the Savoie, if you know it. Near Switzerland.'

'With your family?'

'You're good at interviews.'

I said, 'Forgive me.'

'I was with my grandfather. Most of the time.'

'You see . . . no reason why you should . . . but what happened here, in Europe . . . the things that happened . . . it's almost impossible for us to believe that it was really the way it was . . . that it really *was* at all. We want to understand it, we want to think we know about it, that we *can* know about it, and yet . . . It's a little like Stafford and women!'

'*Il connaît bien les femmes, Stafford.*' Pierrette took a trace of tobacco from her mouth. Her tongue was red. She looked at the scrap of tobacco and rubbed it away on her leg. '*Croyez-moi.*'

I said, 'Then it's not like anything I can think of. I was very lucky being where I was and nothing makes you more arrogant than luck, does it? It even allows you the luxury of feeling sorry for yourself because nothing much ever happened to you.'

'Do I understand everything you say to me always?'

'If you do, you won't like it very much. It's the English fog; calculated to confuse you and passing itself off as a romantic haze! You're a teacher. I was never taught by a woman in my whole life.'

'Then perhaps it's time,' she said.

'Perhaps? It *is* time. Do you want something else to . . . ? I could never meet anyone like you in England. There isn't anyone like you in England. I'm very, very glad poor old Morris had a friend in the C.G.T. Did he bring you up then, your grandfather?'

'Yes.' She made a long word of it, containing memories and reservations.

I said, 'Was he – is he – what sort of person, I mean?' One of my tenses gave her pain. I went on with brazen caution, not knowing exactly where it hurt. 'Is he a teacher too? I don't mean to . . .'

'He was a doctor,' she said. 'And a teacher. He taught medicine.'

'He's dead?'

'Yes.' Again the word was heavy with what she knew and I did not.

'But . . . ?' My prompt was ignorant and falsely tender. I wanted whatever she was keeping to herself. 'Or . . . ?'

'A man came to the house one day during the war and shot him.'

Love and greed were the same. I loved the pain which made her vulnerable; I wanted, at the same time, with the same appetite, to heal her wounds. It was not only that I wanted her to the point of comedy (how would Priapus ever get out of the café without looking ridiculous?), it was also that I loved her tragedy, whatever it was. The death of her grandfather, however it had happened, seemed to have happened for me. I put one finger on one of her narrow fingers. Her nail was blanched by my pressure. I said, as if it were a phrase from a book I never expected to be able to quote, 'Will you come back with me to my hotel?'

She tasted her lower lip and took the basket from below the table and put her cigarettes and her *briquette* into it. She pushed the straight, fair hair behind her ears. They were naked and delicate, without earrings. She was unadorned. There was no trace of make-up on her face. With the look she gave me at last an English girl would have been saying no.

The woman behind the counter at the Hotel des Deux Continents gave me my key. I led the way up the stairs. The room was at the back. The window opened on to a well. There was the big bed and a basin and a bidet behind a screen. Pierrette put her basket by the screen and looked at me without a smile. I was noticing that she was taller than I expected, even in her flat pumps.

She said, '*Tu m'embrasses?*'

Her tongue thickened against mine. I felt her ribs against my chest and her hands in my hair as she pulled my mouth against hers.

She shucked her shoes and folded her arms across her chest and drew the windcheater over her head. Hair floated and settled around her ears. She ducked forward to unhook her bra. I kissed her throat and then her pale, blue-veined breasts. She said, '*Attends*,' and turned away to take off her black trousers. There seemed to be too much of her for me ever to be able to kiss and touch enough. She pulled the bed open while I took off my clumsy clothes. How should I ever last long enough to please her? She was sitting on the bed, knees to her chin. I looked at her and she made a little movement of her head. She lay down next to me and I felt the grain of her against me and it was as I feared.

I said, '*Quelle honte, quelle stupidité!*'

'*Ni stupide ni honteux. Ça se produit.*'

She fetched a towel from by the basin. My desire was so great that the fiasco hardly interrupted me. She touched me with those pale fingers and I was repaired. She kissed me nicely and then, with a change of mood, took us away from niceness. Her mouth bit at mine, her hips butted against me. We were not friends any longer. She pulled me on to her before I could worry again and drew me into her and her head was hanging back, eyes closed, and pleasure thickened her throat.

I turned out the bright light and opened the curtains. Her body was silvered by the sweat which burst out of us. We rested and then I was ready again, and again. I could not tire of her pleasure. My desire was for hers. Nothing and everything was a surprise. I might have done everything before that I did now for the first time. Nothing that she did had ever been done by her with anyone but me. We made love and we slept and we made love again. I wanted to stay in her forever.

I woke again at dawn. The bed was empty next to me. I sat up and saw Pierrette standing by the window, one foot on a chair, a cigarette in her fingers. She had put on her wind-cheater.

'I dreamed you were leaving. We were in the café and you put your things in your bag and you walked out.'

'Not yet,' she said.

'Never,' I said. 'God, look at this bed!'

'*On a travaillé un peu!*' she said. 'Don't worry. We're not the first people . . .'

'Yes, we are.'

'You're very romantic.'

'Come back to bed. I'll show you how romantic.'

'*Tu es une merveille*,' she said.

I said, 'I'm not like any of those people: Stafford and the others.'

'I never thought so,' she said.

'I was jealous of them the minute I sat down at your table. I didn't want you to know them. I wished I could have you all to myself. Right from the very first moment. There are so many things . . . so many questions I want to ask you.'

'No, I don't,' she said. 'Not very often. No, no one has. Ever. I promise. As soon as I saw you. There are your answers.'

I said, 'I'm never going to let you go.'

'*Sois gentil maintenant. Il faut que je parte.* It's very late.'

'Too late. So late it's early. *Donc tu restes.*'

'*Miko, sois sage!* Please, it's time to go now.'

I said, 'You're not married, are you?'

'Of course not.'

I kissed her ringless fingers. 'I'm not going back to London.'

'*On va travailler chez la C.G.T.?*'

'Unless you come with me.'

'And what will she say?'

'Who?'

'Your mistress. Your girl friend.'

'I don't have anybody but you. I don't ever want to have

anybody but you. *J'ai besoin de toi, tu sais? A jamais. Tu seras ma vie toute entière.*'

'You speak nice French.'

'What's wrong with it?'

'Please don't.'

'Is there someone else?'

'Do you think I came to life last night, so that you could meet me and bring me here?'

'Of course. Do you love him?'

'It's a long story.'

'Tell it. The longer the better. *On a tout son temps*. I want to know everything there is to know about you. Start with the war. Tell me what happened.'

'For a long time I was very lucky,' she said, 'very, very. And then, later, I was not so lucky.'

'Tell me about your grandfather.'

She began to tell me things. She grew up in her grandfather's house. Her mother loved and was sometimes cold with her. She knew, without knowing the model, that the coldness came when her mother saw the absent father in the child. She carried her father's image, though she had no memory of him. His name was not hers. She was a schoolgirl who lived with her grandfather. Le Professeur Lévi remained steady and grave and practical. Surgery, he said, was a kind of plumbing. '*Il ne faut pas drama-tiser les choses*' was his slogan. Most things were very ordinary and very simple. He included death among them.

When the Jews were ordered to register at the Mairie of St Louis-le-Grand, Professor Lévi made no objection. He went and his daughter and his granddaughter went with him. The law was the law. He continued to work at the hospital, although he was now forbidden to teach. He was denied petrol. His car was confiscated. He walked. Humiliation did not affect his pride. Pierrette went to the lycée. She learned to show nothing, like her grandfather. Sometimes she pretended that she too had a little white beard. No one knew when they would be arrested. She hid her dread behind phantom whiskers.

Her mother wanted to take her to Oran, in Algeria, where they had cousins. Pierrette cried: she wanted to stay with her Pépé. Her mother went to Marseille to get a ship. She was arrested in the big *rafle* ('*Les Fridolins étaient partout*') and sent to Drancy. In St Louis-le-Grand, commune d'Annecy, nothing seemed to change. Except that 'hair grew on me, that was all. I didn't like it, but . . . it grew. My grandfather called me Mademoiselle then! Everyone knew that the Americans were going to win the war. He was sure we would be safe now. Also, he had a colleague, who'd been one of his favourite pupils, and this man owed my grandfather a great deal, and said so. He was political; he knew the right people; he would protect us. We were safe; fear became a secret with me. I almost liked it. It didn't really frighten me until the Germans and their friends too began to know that they would lose. My grandfather would never discuss this. He went on in the same way, being good. I wasn't so good. Perhaps it was my father alive in me. It made me guess things, know things, want things. I asked Jacquot finally to arrange something. Switzerland was not far away. He could get me there.'

'Jacquot?'

'My Pépé's colleague. Jean-Claude his name was; they called him Jacquot. He said sure he'd do something for me. I told Pépé, because I was pleased the way Jacquot had said he'd do it for me. My grandfather wasn't angry, but he was . . . irritated; I had acted without him; that was what I liked, of course. I wanted to get away from St Louis-le-Grand because it was something I was arranging for myself, by myself. I had changed. Men looked at my breasts in the street. I was glad. Let them. I went back to see Jacquot again. I had a secret, like the hair. Don't now, please. Then one day someone in the Milice, if you know what that is —'

'Was,' I said. 'The Vichy Gestapo.'

'This man was killed. Le Gros Riri, they called him. He had a bar. And a car. Henry Lemayieu. With an *ygrec*. Some F.F.I. men came and killed him one day, O.K.?'

'It is with me.'

'We were at home one day soon after this. I was doing my homework. Pépé was ranging his stamps; he loved to range his stamps. Simone, the maid, was making soup. *Potiron*. Pumpkin? Yes. A man came to the door. I heard the ring. Voices. More. Very loud. And then I heard a man say, "*Le Juif Lévi*." The man came upstairs. He was in the next room. He said that one of their men had been killed and that Pépé must know about it. He would give my grandfather three minutes to say his prayers, if he wished to say them, and then he would empty his revolver into his body. I was sitting at the desk with my book. My grandfather said, in a quiet voice, that he had nothing to do with the death of the *milicien*. He deplored all deaths. The man said that he was "*désolé*", but the decision was made. The Jews had wanted war; they wanted the death of France. There was a silence and then I heard my grandfather say, "*Mon pauvre ami!*" And then he said, "*Il y a un enfant à la maison*." The man said, "She won't be hurt. My word of honour. Three minutes by my watch." I sat in the little bureau with my Corneille and all I could think of was Jacquot. How could I get to his house in less than three minutes? Two and a half. Two. One and a half. The telephone was in my grandfather's room. One minute. In one minute he was going to die. I looked out of the window at the lake and the summer flowers. A boy in a check cap was putting a stick to a wooden 'oop. The future was already out there, clean and bright. I saw it as it was and as it would be, as I would see it and Pépé would not. There it was. *Impeccable!* I heard the first shot and I looked down at my text. "*Mes yeux ont vu son sang*." We all had to learn it. They still do. There were several shots. Simone was screaming. The man met her in the doorway as he was leaving. He told her to shut up. "*Une Française*," he said, "*tu n'as pas honte de travailler dans une telle maison?*" He called her "tu" in such a way! He went down the stairs and out into the street. I ran into the next room and stood with my grandfather. He was small now he was dead. Someone came in. A patient worried about his 'ealth. Then I looked up and saw that the man with the gun had come back into the room. Was he going to break his word and kill me too? I saw the lake and the flowers and the boy with the 'oop and I thought after all I would not live to see the future. The man pushed me aside like a curtain, with the back of his hand, and he raised his gun at my grandfather again. I tried to stop him, although I knew Pépé was dead; it made no difference. The man – his name was Le Commandant Brault – he frowned at me and he said, "*Excuse-moi, mademoiselle, mais il me reste toujours une balle. Je lui en ai promis toutes, et je tiens toujours mes promesses.*" Then he fired the last bullet into my dead grandfather. These are the things you really want to know? That last bullet, it went into me, do you understand this? I felt what he could no longer feel. It went into me. I was dead and I was alive. I would never be one thing again. I thought, "Jacquot!" The only man. The people in the room – they were all confused, frightened, ugly. I loved Jacquot. No one else. I loved him and I'd always loved him. I ran out of the house, ran, flew, along the lake, past the boy in the check cap, all the way to Jacquot's house, rue Pasteur. He was in his office. Thank God, thank God! He was writing notes for his *fichier*. Doing his homework like a good doctor. He had clean hands; he smelt nice. His nurse was wheeling her bicycle out of the hall. She said, "*Bonsoir, mademoiselle,*" and I smiled. Nothing had happened here. Jacquot patted my hair. He held my hand. He wanted me. I knew it; he knew and he wanted me. He was afraid I blamed him.'

'Why?'

'Ouf! He would have all my grandfather's patients now, for one thing. What did I know? What did I imagine? Everything in the world! It's not nice, but that's the truth. Jacquot was the friend of that bastard Brault. I imagined that they had laughed together . . . planned it all between them . . . the worse the better now, if you can understand that. I was not afraid and nothing else mattered: he loved me, he wanted me. All the things he'd done, all of it was for me. I was the thing he wanted, and I wanted that. We were in his little – office. A narrow bed like a shelf along the wall. A sheet, a pillow like a parcel. An eye chart.

The letters getting smaller. You read the little ones and it's like a reprieve. That is where it first happened for me. I was fifteen years old. You like to hear this?'

'My God,' I said, 'he certainly . . .'

'Was it him or was it me? I wanted it to happen. Quickly. Before something changed. I said, "Oh", and I pleaded, but I needed him. I needed him to hurt me. I was glad, when he did. In the middle, the telephone was ringing and I hoped it was that fat bastard because now Jacquot was in me, it was too late. I would survive now. Jacquot's face was thick with the blood in it and the hunger. His eyes . . . I thought of the boy in the cap, with the 'oop; 'oop? Why do you smile?'

'Hoop.'

'I saw his fat, spoiled face and the pouty mouth, you know, as if he still took his mother's milk, and I wondered if one day I might marry that hairless boy and spoil him myself. He was so awful! Hoop. The telephone was ringing and Jacquot was not finished and I was wet and he was talking on the telephone and it almost made me laugh. He was naked and his voice was dressed. "*Elle est avec moi, mon commandant. Je m'en occuperai.*" I looked at the wall and it was not yet six o'clock. The time I had set myself to learn my Corneille. An hour and a half. He came back and finished on me and I knew I was safe. Are you hungry?'

We dressed and went out into the brightening morning. Bells were ringing, Place St Germain des Près. The first waiters were hosing the pavement in front of the Café des Deux Magots. We went up the rue du Dragon to a *boulangerie* and bought croissants, two each, and sat on the kerb outside Raffi to eat them. Crumbs stuck to our lips like brown petals of confetti.

In the days that followed she was in Jacquot's power, but he was also in hers. The death of Professor Lévi was not reported, but it was known. For the moment, it was an execution, but everyone knew that it would become a crime. The people of St Louis-le-Grand were a jury to whom it would fall, in time, to give their verdict. Jacquot knew that Pierrette was his hope of profiting both from the war and from the peace. He might do what he wanted with her, but he could not afford to lose her. She was the witness of both his guilt and his innocence. After a few days, he sent her to a chalet in the mountains. The house of Pierrette's grandfather was sold and Jacquot bought it. He said he was keeping it for her. For the first time he acknowledged that the allies had won the war.

There was a guardian called Albert at the chalet. He brought things to the chalet and gave them to Pierrette, things to eat and things to read, things for when Jacquot next came to see her, clothes and perfume. Jacquot said that they were stolen from the Germans' special stock. Imagine if they knew who was wearing their stockings and touching their perfume to her throat and little breasts!

I said, 'Let's go and get some coffee.'

Albert was in the Resistance. He took people over the mountains. They came at night. Sometimes they hid in the cellar for several days. Pierrette thought of them in the darkness and felt superior to them. She had Jacquot; they depended on Albert and on luck. He took their money and their jewels and then he led them over the mountains. Sometimes when he was gone, Pierrette heard shots. And then one day the Germans disappeared. There was more shooting than there had ever been before. One night the Resistance killed over eighty *miliciens* on the edge of Albert's village. Frenchmen had cars again, crowded with young men with guns. Flags flew from them. They hooted as if victory were a wedding. Albert had a uniform.

'Jacquot was arrested presumably?'

'He was questioned,' Pierrette said. 'But he had helped a lot of people. He had helped me. They asked me; I told them. Some people were shot, others . . . But Jacquot . . . he was someone people liked to like. He looked so nice. He *was* so nice. He is so nice.'

I said, 'Pierrette, will you marry me?'

She said, 'Do you understand what I'm telling you?'

'Will you? *Je t'aime. Je t'aime vraiment, du fond du coeur. Je t'aime d'amour.*'

'*Je t'aime aussi.*' It sounded like a contradiction.

We were in the Royal St Germain. I took her hands and breathed on them as if they needed warming. There was a threat of winter in her pale eyes. 'I want to live with you. Last night . . . it was wonderful, but it was only the beginning – before the beginning even. I want to start all over again, and again, and again.'

Pierrette said, 'Miko, I'm going home now, to give breakfast to my daughter. She will be worried about me, do you understand?'

'You said you weren't married.'

'*Mais que tu es anglais finalement!*'

'I'm sorry. How old is –?'

'Quite big now.'

I said, 'How old is she, Pierrette?'

'Ah, you begin to judge me now. Is that nice?'

'What's her name and how old is she?'

'How quickly men can join the police, isn't that right? Her name is France. She's nearly five years old now.'

'The war's been over for nine.'

'You're good at dates.'

'Do you still see him?'

'I see him.'

'Is he married?'

'He doesn't come to Paris very often. A doctor; of course. People don't like a doctor who isn't married with a nice family. Goodbye now, Michael.'

'Please don't go. *Je t'en supplie*. Three minutes.'

Pierrette took her watch from her wrist. She folded the strap under the face and put it in front of her on the table and rested her chin on her hands. I said, 'It's true: I don't know much about the world. I want it all to have started today. Clean of everything and everyone before you. I want to be with you forever and marrying you is all I can suggest to . . . What else is there in the

133

world that I can say or do? The things you tell me, they're meant to warn me, to threaten me, but at the same time – and you know this – they're the very things that make me want you more than ever. I want you not because I'm young and innocent and English and never did the things . . . or else, possibly, yes, because of that, because I'm tired of having to be like people I'm not really like at all, even though I'm like them. The truth is, I love the things that happened to you. I envy you them. I love you because of *everything*, your courage, your shame, your cunning, everything you are, everything that happened to you. I don't want to change anything about you. You think you've already given me what I wanted. You have, and I still want it. You haven't, because you're still there. I want you to be there as long as I'm alive. Marry me, Pierrette. Yes?'

'Go home now, Miko.'

'You don't even know what that means.'

'You're not a Yank, but go home. To England.'

'What can I do in England? Be English! Play their game. Oh I can; quite well. You know the only thing I learned at school, university? How to cheat by giving the right answers. How to please examiners. England! What's wrong with it? You can be anything you want in England, as long as it's not yourself. You can say anything you like, as long as it's not what you'd like to say. I want to stay here, with you, where no one takes me for anything except what I am. Stay with me, Pierrette. Tell me this hasn't been . . . one of those things. It's not one of those things; it's the only thing that's ever meant anything to me at all.'

'*Je voudrais bien rester avec toi, tu le sais bien . . .*'

'You can. You must.'

'I can't and I mustn't. And if you love me –'

'Then I don't. Is that what you want me to say? I want to marry you; I want to give you a different sort of life. You and . . . France. If . . .'

She said, 'I've told you things, things I never even told myself before. Last night, today, now, we were married, if you like. And now, I have to go. And so do you.'

'You don't need him. I'm quite clever, you know. I can do things to make money, if I want to. If that's what you want me to do, I'll do it. I can put sugar on things if I have to. You don't need him.'

She leaned bloodless fingers against my lips and the breath sighed in her nostrils. The little second hand on her watch went up past three-quarters and peaked and began a new minute. She took the watch and put it in her black pocket and then she stood up and walked past the swabbing waiter at the door of the Royal St Germain and out into the boulevard carrying her basket and brushing one side of her hair behind her empty ear.

I heard the ghost of her grandfather whisper, '*Il ne faut pas dramatiser les choses.*' Especially, I said to myself, if you want to be a dramatist. The treason of art held me to where I sat. My pain was already diluted and forking into possibilities. What had no meaning might still be used. My present was already doubling for the past: present pain was prospective pleasure. Tenderness curdled into knowledge: the unique was a precedent now. Who next would take my penis between her lips and look at me at the same time, promising to like whatever I wanted? Pierrette was gone and yet I saw her. I spied and reported to myself. She was on the steps of the Métro. Might she still be caught? Life was too single for my character. The little sentinel at the entrance to the Métro platform was clipping Pierrette's ticket. I heard her say, '*Merci, madame.*' She put the punctured ticket in her purse, for another time. Was she even thinking of me as she waited, Direction Porte de Clignancourt? Perhaps she had made up the whole story of Jacquot and St Louis-le-Grand. Perhaps she would be in the same café in a night or two and some other story would be told to some other innocent. Perhaps she would tell them what a fool I had been. No, I did not believe that. I believed her. I kindled again at the memory of her body and the thought of her 'ah, ah, *ah*'. How close pride and contempt were! How I longed to be Jacquot, powerful, corrupt and inescapable! I wondered how long it would be before the kiosk in front of the

Café des Deux Magots had copies of the English Sunday papers and whether little Tessa, on the baby elephant, could possibly be on the front page.

IV

'You can't use words like Kierkegaard in a family newspaper, old man,' Bernie Platt said. The news editor used to come into my cubicle to drink his mug of tea on weekday mornings. I had ceased being a reporter and had become a 'special feature writer', a position which left me three mornings a week to write plays. 'You'll frighten the voters.'

'Bugger off, Bernard,' I said. 'I'm not expecting anyone to know who he is.'

'Far be it from me to give advice to one who has passed far beyond my uneducated orbit, but you're writing for the spike, my clever lad. You've heard the latest, presumably?'

'The one about the Englishman, the Egyptian and the Suez Canal? No. Have they gone and nationalized it?'

'Official.'

'The unsurprising tribute the wily wog pays his erstwhile imperial master. Anything Britannia could do, he can do better. You can't blame him.'

'Bugger blame him,' Bernie said. 'Bomb him.'

'Is that what the call from the country recommends to this independent newspaper over which his lordship exercises no control whatsoever?'

'You're very cheeky these days. Rich aunt left you a fortune, has she? What else do you recommend?'

'I believe in reason.'

'And how do we drop that on people in a form that makes any sort of a lasting impression?'

'There has to be some other response apart from violence, doesn't there, Bernard?'

'And so there is, sonny boy, and always was, assuming you can get used to sitting with the thin end of the wedge stuck up your backside.'

'Tell you what, Bernard,' I said. 'Why don't we bomb the bastards?'

The licorice-black telephone on my green metal desk began to ring. Bernard collected his tea and patted me on the shoulder. 'One thing about war that's rarely true of reason: it's a great knicker-dropper. Kierkegaard!'

'Hullo, Kitson,' I said, 'what's the latest? Yes, I know about that: I work for a newspaper. I meant about the play. November? Do people in Colchester go to the theatre in November? Well, you're the resident expert. If you're putting my play on, I'll certainly be there, whatever the temperature or the state of the Middle East. Then I'll certainly be there. Listen, on casting: any chance of one Sally Raglan playing Tessa? I thought perhaps . . . Fair enough, if no fairer than that. I'll tell her it's all your fault. And it is. Of course, I am; more pleased than I can say. Tomorrow Colchester, Wednesday week who knows where?'

Barnaby Monk said, 'You're very skittish.'

'Sorry,' I said. 'I didn't hear you knock.'

'Knocking is something I leave to you. After the way you laced into them last week, I presume Pinewood Studios have been plying you with offers of lucrative employment.'

'My telephone has stopped ringing,' I said. 'What can I do for a man in your position?'

'Solve this one for me. What the editor is. Four letters, beginning with C.'

'King doesn't begin with a C, does it? And country-lover is too long. I give up.'

'How can you work for a paper that thinks Nasser and Hitler come out of the same basket?'

'I just imitate important people like Barnaby Monk and bite on the bullet.'

'First tragedy, then farce. Don't you agree?'

'Farce is a very difficult form,' I said. 'I'm not sure that Eden's up to it.'

'There comes a time when a man has to stand up and be counted.'

'I don't object to being a bean in your row, Barnaby, as long as it doesn't involve being tattooed on the wrist while the rest of the company looks the other way and sings along with Vera Lynn.'

'How do you seriously expect to keep your friends, if that's the way you talk to them?'

'Oh Barnaby! Should you really be telling me how much you love me in his lordship's time and air-space? I'm supposed to be knocking out eight hundred words on the New Drama, to coincide with the first, and perhaps the last, night of a break-through play about a boilermaker who responds to the iniquities of the English class system by turning into Big Ben. I need my wits about me, so unless you're willing to be one of them . . .'

'I'm on my way.'

'Of course you are, dear boy. Unless we're all very much mistaken about you.'

'Is your sister an actress, by any chance?'

'Hullo, still here? Certainly not. She's the next best thing to a don, if you really want to blow the gaff on her. And to which don is she the next best thing? A certain Owen Millom. Fellow of Merton. She's his research assistant, index-compiler and I don't know how much further it goes, or there is to go. What makes you ask?'

'Claudia saw her looking very glam in some mag.'

'Rachel has looks and she also has brains. Rather like that Claudia woman who went and wasted herself on some Barnaby Monk or other. Whatever happened to him?'

'So someone's putting one of your plays on, are they? I might do a bit about it in the column, nearer the time. Assuming we're all still here.'

'What are hell and high water,' I said, 'compared to ambition?'

'Do you imagine that people like you for talking to them like that? Or don't you really believe that they're there at all?'

*

Rachel had been working with Owen Millom for nearly two years. When Millom asked her to assist his researches into 'the consequences of the consequences of the peace,' an assessment of the impact of the Treaty of Versailles beyond continental Europe, there was no perceptible distinction between thinking about it and accepting. She liked Oxford and she liked Owen. He admired her intelligence and he respected her opinions. When the work was ready for the printers, he was courteous enough to say that she deserved to be his co-author rather than an acknowledged 'invaluable help'. Rachel set about correcting the proofs with regretful competence. As soon as they were returned, she would have to think about what to do next. Owen ordered a celebratory lunch, which came to his rooms under the usual college lids 'to keep it tepid', and told her that he had been invited to do a stint at the Foreign Office.

'The question of course being, is the F.O. a case of power without responsibility, which is rather an attractive option, or of responsibility without power, which is less so?'

'Very tempting,' Rachel said, 'for a historian to observe the political process right in the lion's mouth.'

'But what chance does an adviser have of having his advice taken? And if it is, will he want it to be? Wisdom after the event is often folly before it. What're you thinking of doing next?'

'Once the index is checked, I shall take a breath, deep, and a bath, deeper, and then I thought I might go to America, North.'

'Whatever for?'

'New York, Chicago, San Francisco.'

'You'll only find they're all full of Americans.'

'They'll make a change from alphabetical order, won't they?'

'I'll tell you one thing I thought you might do, if you felt like it.'

'I'm always open to suggestions, during office hours.'

'Marry me,' Owen said. 'Does the thought appal?'

'Appal? No. Appeal? Rather. Stun? Somewhat. More than somewhat!'

'I'm not too sure of the drill in these matters. What do you say? More roly-poly?'

'To the roly-poly, no.'

'Should I speak to your father, I mean?'

'It might be advisable from time to time,' Rachel said. 'He admires you very much.'

'And I him. You have a lot in common. That capacity for passionate accuracy. I've been dreading the end of our little project. Our *parvum opus*! I thought it was because I didn't want to say goodbye to Oxford. And then I realized it was because it meant saying goodbye to you. I'm not, as you must long have realized, a great expert in the diplomacy of the heart.'

Rachel reached across the heavy table and touched his white hand. 'May I ask you something, Owen?'

'Absolutely anything you like.'

She looked at his smooth face, which she had never seen unshaven, and at the monogrammed cuff-links that showed below his blazered sleeves. 'No,' she said, 'I don't think I can.'

He had a nice smile. He leaned back while Trench, his scout, removed pudding dishes with intrusive tact. Rachel had time to be touched by the confusion of sophistication and helplessness in those clever, uneasy blue eyes. Owen switched his knees from under the table and seemed to guess at the nature of Rachel's unspoken question.

'Life,' he said, 'really can be the most serious imaginable kind of absurdity at times, don't you agree?'

'Is our subject foreign or domestic policy at this point?'

'You'll be doing me the greatest honour in the world.'

'Let me think about it a little, Owen, will you?'

'I ask nothing better. Have some vile coffee from a very nice jug.'

Barnaby Monk's favourite lunch-place, so he promised, was 'Sid's Cafe' in Farringdon Street. There were unpainted wooden partitions between the hard booths along one wall and a stool-lined counter where Sid and Dot did a steamy business in combinations of eggs, chips, mushrooms, bacon, sausages and beans. When prevented from going to Sid's, Barnaby sighed in places like Simpson's or Scott's or the Mayfair Club. When he asked me to join him at Sid's, I knew that there were important topics to consider.

'It comes down to a simple question, M. Jordan: are you with us or are you not?'

'Look, I'm flattered to be invited by the *Sunday Crusader*'s redoubtable columnist, but where's the party exactly and who's on the Central Committee?'

'I've talked to Leo Quaritch and Peter Cartwright. All we're trying to do is make sure that the paper isn't hijacked by the jingos.'

'In that case, hadn't you better start putting water and hard tack in the long boat? Because what the hell kind of a ship do you think you're on? This is mutiny, Mr Christian!'

'Never mind the undergraduate imitations. I thought you were a socialist.'

'Just because I voted for you as President of the Union doesn't mean I have to risk my by-line does it?'

'You know your trouble, Michael? You think that just because you say something, you can't possibly mean it. You turn being a trimmer into a form of intellectual distinction. It won't wash.'

'Then it must use more perfume. If you think forming a pressure group of guilt-ridden Oxbridge know-alls is going to change the editorial line one iota – even if there are iotas in it, which Bernie Platt will be doing his best to avoid –'

'And if you think that bombing Nasser is going to help Israel –'

'I'll tell you something, Barnaby – no, I'll tell you two things. No, I'll just tell you the second one: in the end, there'll be some shaming little compromise and Downing Street will announce it as evidence of British firmness, resolve and willingness to pay blackmail as long as the bill isn't presented in public. Well, they just may not say the last bit. As for our great newspaper, it will, as a call from the country will confirm, have been crucial in holding the government steady as she goes, for which we shall take our fair share of the credit and our lily-livered rivals' circulation. As for you and me, we can like it or lump it, or dislike it and lump it. A choice as agonizing as it is vacuous.'

'There's a kind of conceit in underestimating yourself the way you do, Michael.'

'I shall never accuse you of it, Barnaby. O.K., I'll pull an oar with you in the long boat, Mr Christian, if I have to. With my usual bad grace. But don't suppose that the skipper is going to step quietly over the side when you ask him to.'

'Are you willing to sign a round robin is what it boils down to.'

'Get Robin round here and I'll have my ball-point sharpened. What course are you actually recommending as the socialist solution? A Fabian bookshop within hawking distance of Port Said? Or really tough measures like pelting them with copies of *Tribune* until they cry "Halt, enough!"?'

'If Nasser has to back down, the Tories are in Downing Street for another five years, minimum.'

'Long live Gamel Abdul,' I said, 'if that's the size of it.'

When Stafford Canning telephoned me at the *Sunday Crusader*, his tone suggested that we knew each other very well, although my only encounter with him had been at the Royal St Germain on the night that I met Pierrette Lévi. I had given her my address, but I had no expectations of hearing from her again. The memory of our time together was at once reassuring and inhibiting: how could I ever find anyone as beautiful or as tragic or as significant again? I went out, as the expression was, with various girls, but I clung to the importance of Pierrette and judged other women by her impossible standard. Stagnation took on a romantic allure. I judged romances, and marriage, in the light of a single, sublime night, in which I had made love half a dozen times with a beautiful woman whom I scarcely knew. When Stafford announced who he was, I was as excited, for a moment, as if it had been Pierrette herself. Could I spare a few minutes? We met at the National Gallery, in front of the Rokeby Venus.

'Back views are often best, aren't they?' he said. 'I've got something I want to tell you and it'd be prudent if we didn't advertise our meeting.'

'What's up?'

'I've got some information I think someone capable ought to have. Rather disreputable, it might amuse you.' He was in a grey, pin-striped suit and his O.W. tie. I was slightly surprised by the rust-coloured suede shoes. He lifted his long, thin nose, as if he had sniffed a dish he did not fancy, and led the way out to the portico, where the traffic in Trafalgar Square seemed to make our conversation less noticeable. 'There's a secret meeting in prospect. The Israelis, the British, the French. To finalize and coordinate the particular game of charades they're planning to play. At a place called Senlis.'

'Good spot for a rendezvous,' I said, 'if you know your French theatre, as I'm sure you do. How come you know about this?'

'I've seen and I've heard.'

'And what are you suggesting I do? And, if you'll take supplementary, why?'

'What about a speculative article toying with the impossibility that secret talks are in train with a view to creating circumstances under which shining armour could be donned by ourselves and the frogs while leaving Ben-Gurion with the spoils of a nicely limited little war, to which Britannia and Marianne, the self-righteous sisters, could put an officious end for their own shabby purposes. Why? Because I don't like fraud. Duplicity is one thing, set to the right kind of music, but this is worse than humbug; it's going to lead to the definitive collapse of hitherto relatively stout parties. It's also going to let the Yanks into the Middle East in a big way. Have I said enough?'

'One small point. When I get picked up by the Special Branch, where do I say I got my information?'

'What's wrong with your ripe and ready imagination? Can such things conceivably be *true*? The British fomenting a war they then step in officiously to forbid? You've got to be joking, haven't you? To deny is to confirm.'

'Why me? You must know stacks of people in the press who'd be better placed to blow the gaff, if that's–'

'Not all that many. And those I do I'm not inclined to trust.'

'What makes you think you can trust me?'

'You wouldn't want it to get about,' Stafford said, 'but I strongly suspect that you're a person of great indignations. Correct me if I'm right.'

'You want me to take a risk you're not prepared to take yourself.'

'Hole in one.'

'How can they hope to get away with it?'

'Conspiracy makes for loyalty. Pols may be divided about the right thing to do, but once they've done something wrong, they stick together like a nun's knees. Anthony can't trust the cabinet to hold steady unless they've all got something to be ashamed of. The ignoble lie is a powerful adhesive.'

'And what's your motive, Stafford?'

'I don't like hypocrites.'

'A diplomat?'

'The government should learn to leave lying to properly qualified people. No, deception is one thing, self-deception is another. Once a society gets an appetite for lies, it loses the capacity to swallow anything else. I can give you enough details for Whitehall to know that the cat is well and truly debagged. Things like whose unofficial car had a head-on discussion with a tractor outside what small village and who offered Normandy oysters as a special treat to the advance party from Tel Aviv.'

'What if they could bring it off – give the Israelis a free hand and then slap their wrists gently for taking it and leave themselves in command of the field? Isn't it conceivable that the trick might work?'

'Have you any conception how big a hat would be needed if all this were to be kept safely under it? The best service we can render this country is to pull the plug long and hard as soon as may be. Before the Yanks and the Russkies tell us to make an arse in front of the whole bloody world. Which they surely will, in due course, which isn't all that far off, believe you me, Michael.'

Stafford's sudden anger, which seemed to have me no less than the conspirators for its target, startled me by its passion. His manner had been almost facetious; his disgust was pitiless. I rode back to Court Royal on a 14 bus, excited and dismayed by his information. He had paid me a perilous compliment which made me conscious that I had arrived at the age of twenty-five without knowing a single contemporary whose advice I trusted. Stafford's confidences flattered and alarmed me; I could imagine that I might do as he wanted simply because I feared his scorn and desired his good opinion. That evening, fearful that I was proving myself too immature for the challenge, I told my father the whole story as we sat in the living room at Court Royal, the blue curtains half-drawn, a storm muttering on the horizon.

'It's a facer,' my father said. 'Why did he tell you about it, do you suppose?'

'Perhaps because he knows that the reasons why I would hesitate to use what he told me are the same ones that might drive me to do so. Shame is sometimes more reliable than courage, don't you think? He's daring me to keep quiet. Knowing that if I do I won't be the man I'd like him to think I am, even if I'm not.'

'Close friend?'

'Distant acquaintance. I quite like him. I like liking him. I like him liking me. I don't know why really.'

'Don't you?'

'Why should one want to be wanted by someone one doesn't want oneself? I must be one of the rare public schoolboys who never got involved in anything like that. You went to a day school, you wouldn't necessarily . . . I never had the smallest inclination; prudishness probably, dread of . . . something. Other people. Stafford plays the old English trick to perfection: he condescends by treating you as an equal. I could swear that he's in earnest, but what about exactly?'

146

'He's teasing you, you think?'

'If I write the story, and it gets printed, he's got me one way. More than I've got him, because I've done it for him, and he hasn't done anything for me. And if I don't, he's got me the other: I've let him down. Beyond all that, of course, if I want to be a journalist, it's a chance I absolutely ought to take.'

'If.'

'You certainly can string out a two-letter word, dad, can't you? He half expects me to do nothing. You know why, don't you?'

Samuel said, 'Presumably he wants to know something secret about you, just as you do about him. It makes you conspirators without a plot. Not that I know the chap, of course . . .'

'Do you know me?'

'I've never been convinced that paternity was a particularly close relationship,' Samuel said. 'It's very good news about the play.'

'You'll come to the first night, I hope, if the world lasts that long?'

'If invited, we shall be there.'

'By the way, something I've been meaning to raise: would you like me to pay you some rent? For living here?'

'Why?' Samuel said. 'Are you thinking of leaving?'

We sat in the darkening room, with the lightning flaring behind the building opposite. It reminded me of the blackout, when electric sparks from underground trains were enough to light up the city. Suddenly, my father was talking again, his face in shadow, his voice almost dreamy, yet not without its usual hint of unsmiling amusement.

'When I was sixteen years old, I spent an afternoon with a wounded captain in the Buffs in his suite at the Grand Hotel, Eastbourne. He said he wanted to show me his stamps. After tea, something happened. He apologized and asked me to be sure never to tell anyone what we'd been doing. Since I knew no words to describe what he'd been up to, I concluded that stamp collecting must have some disreputable aspect. A couple of years later, I was called up. The philatelist was now a major in the camp where I did my O.C.T.U. The breakfasts were singularly unpalatable: slabs of greasy bacon. I decided to declare my religious aversion to it. My request for a different diet had to be made through this particular major. Can you, as a theatrical expert, make a face compounded of equal portions of dread and contempt? In which recognition and ignorance make the same promise to see you in hell as soon as enemy machine guns can be summoned to do the job? That was what I saluted.'

'Did he make you go on eating greasy bacon?'

'That would have been to exceed his powers. I was given a fresh egg every morning. There was very nearly a mass conversion to the law of Moses, but closer reading proved it to involve a sacrifice few of my fellow cadets were disposed to make.'

'I'm not sure that I would ever have had the nerve.'

'Ah,' Samuel said, 'but then you never collected stamps. Why did I tell you that story?'

When I had written a draft of my 'Too True To Be Good' article, I showed it to Barnaby. I was pleased enough with it to think that it might appeal to Leo Quaritch and perhaps serve as a lever to dislodge the jingo faction from their control of the paper. Barnaby put on his serious glasses and cocked his head, in his usual way, before going at it, pencil in hand. Half-way through, he got off my desk and went and shut the door.

'Hot stuff,' he said, 'but irony is a caviare that shouldn't ever be served to the masses. Frankly, there's no way Leo's going to let this into the paper. It's neither fact nor fiction, is it?'

'You've never tasted better red herring though, have you, Barn?'

'It won't do for the leader page and it isn't exactly sport, is it?'

'What occurred to me was that someone who had a regular niche might be able to smuggle it in casually. You're not the same Barnaby who writes that *Crusader* column by any chance, are you, Mr Monk?'

'I never use things in my column I haven't written for myself.'

'If you're going to be a man of integrity,' I said, 'there's nothing further to be said.'

'I'll show it to Leo, if that's what you want. I suspect he'll think it's too soon.'

'It's premature, he ejaculated! And in a couple of days, it'll be too late. Sorry I bothered you, Mr Christian! Off you go and have cocoa and ship's biscuits with Mr Bligh.'

'Can they possibly bring it off, do you think?'

'Would that make it right?'

'It'd make it interesting. Why don't you write a straight story and dare them to deny it?'

'Are you going to come and see me in chokey? It'd be D-noticed before the Special Branch popped in for a friendly word.'

'I could make it a gossip item in the Diary,' Barnaby said. ' "At a Chelsea party last night, a certain young playwright, soon to be famous in Colchester, did a brilliant impression of a secret meeting in Northern France at which –" What the hell does that look mean? I'm trying to find a way –'

'I know you are: a way of making the world-renowned Barnaby Monk omelette – no broken eggs.'

'I hope you never seriously need me, Michael Jordan.'

'Under what circumstances could reality take that kind of improbable turn?'

'I just might be editor of this bloody sheet one of these days.'

'Oh sir, forgive me! If you're going to be above criticism, allow me to be one of the first not to criticize you. For a giddy moment, I had visions of us resigning together on a matter of principle, but I'll be better in a tick.'

'I'll tell you who would publish it: the *Weekender*.'

'Alternatively, more people would get a chance to see it if I sealed it in a lead-lined casket and dropped it in the North Sea.'

'Can Anthony really be up to anything so totally misconceived?'

'The man who said, "What would I do with a million Jews?" Impossible.'

'So that's why you've got it in for him, is it?'

A few weeks later, I was commuting to Colchester for rehearsals of *With This Ring*. My *News Chronicle* told me that the Israelis were approaching the Suez Canal and that the British Prime Minister had warned both sides to behave themselves. Nothing of what Stafford Canning had revealed had been printed in the *Sunday Crusader*, though my article had been praised and pirated by the gossips. I wrote to Stafford detailing the whole comic process, but I never decided where it would be safe to send the letter and finally put it in a drawer.

Frank Kitson indicated that I should take my usual place not too near the front of the stalls. In his denim suit and Viking beard, Frank himself stood with his legs crossed, an assessing finger to his lips, while Ronnie Tanfield and Viola Peasland (in one of her first parts) did my suburban stuff on stage.

'I was going to cross uncharted seas, Tessa. I was going to hack my way through virgin forests –'

'There's no need to talk like that, Dennis, even if we are married now.'

'Do you care what happens to me, Tessa, or to my plans?'

'I love you, Dennis. Doesn't that mean anything . . . to yoooo . . . ?' Viola's voice wilted as if it were coming from a wind-up gramophone as Frank clapped his hands and sprang on to the stage.

'Why have I stopped you, poppety? And don't say to spare myself further punishment.'

Viola said, 'Oh golly, was I supposed to sit down on that bit?'

'No, golly, you're supposed to sit down on this bit.' He goosed her nicely. 'You're playing it as if it were comedy, darlings.'

'Isn't it?' Viola said. 'I thought –'

'Yes, it is. But the author doesn't want people to know that, remember?'

I had sat quietly for three sessions. I walked down the aisle and waited for a cue to speak. Frank ignored me. I said, 'Frank, it might help –'

'Later, Michael . . . You'll get your invitation when the time comes. Meanwhile, read the chapter on helpful authors in my new book. It's very, very short.' He put his arm round Viola and took her for a private walk. 'I think you really do love him, poppety, at this point, don't you?'

'Frank,' I said, trying to be agile as I lumbered on to the stage, 'surely –'

'Michael, with all the will in the world, what I was trying to convey could be more forcefully expressed as *shut up*.'

Annie Rose, the Assistant Stage Manager, had been sitting in the prompt corner; her competent modesty was such that I had hardly noticed her until she clapped her script shut and dropped it on the floor.

Frank said, 'Out! Out.'

I said, 'Frank, don't lose your head.'

'Out! Do I look like Louis the Sixteenth?'

I considered the beard. 'No, but you are beginning to take on a certain resemblance to Charles the First.'

Annie Rose was wearing cotton trousers and a maroon tank top. Her thick brown hair bobbed about her burning ears as she collected her script and her white tote bag.

I said, 'I don't mind you telling me to shut up, Frank, much, but when it comes to shouting at someone who's done absolutely nothing –'

'Look, shall we just scrub round the whole flaming production?'

'Production?'

'I'm not all that convinced about this play. If you think you can rehearse the actors, why don't you bloody well rehearse them?' Kitson turned and walked, without haste, into the wings.

Viola Peasland called after him, 'Fra . . . aaank,' but Ronnie Tanfield put a hand on her arm. She repeated the gramophone effect and Kitson could be heard swearing about amateurs. Viola puffed her cheeks. 'What was your point?'

'Mightn't it be funnier, and truer, if you said "I love you", as if you were in a rage? As if you were saying you hated him?'

Viola said, 'I *love* you.'

Annie Rose smiled and nodded at me from the prompt corner.

I said, 'I'd better go and . . .'

Ronnie Tanfield crossed his legs and put a finger to his lips. 'Michael, will you please rehearse the bloody actors? You've probably got all of twenty minutes. Because two pints of black and tan and Kitson's going to be back on board like a pygmy refreshed. On your marks . . .'

The shrill tyres, falling glass and the louder sound of the silence that followed fetched us all to the Stage Door. Frank had slammed out of the theatre and walked straight in front of a printer's van. We sat with him by the kerb and Annie fetched cushions and a blanket. He sucked his beard into his mouth and did not like to look at his shattered knee. His skin was very white where the beard bent.

The Israelis were destroying two Arab tank brigades in the Sinai and the Russians were poised to cross back into Hungary. Everything that Stafford Canning had told me had been justified by events. As Armageddon threatened, I was in the theatre having the most enjoyable afternoon of my life. Not for a second during the rehearsal did it occur to me that there was anything more worth doing. Not a fraction of my energy or attention was distracted from the sweet task to which, by chance, I found myself committed.

When we broke, I telephoned Leo Quaritch to explain the situation and crave a few days' leave from the paper. There was no room in Ronnie and Viola's digs, but Annie Rose offered to put me up. She rented a couple of rooms above an antique shop in the Dutch quarter.

'Sofa, Michael; Michael, sofa. The rest you can work out between you. I'm afraid I don't run to pyjamas, and I don't think my nighties would particularly suit you.'

'I shall be absolutely fine in my skin, thanks.'

'You were very good in there today.'

'Just as well, considering –'

'– what I let you in for? Is that what you were going to say?'

'Of course. If you were responsible, you must be my fairy godsister. Thank heavens Frank isn't too bad or I'd be feeling even more guilty than I do. Christ, we open on Tuesday, come what may, as long as it isn't Khrushchev's rockets. Can I really keep our frail little ship on course in the meanwhile? If yes, say yes. If no, say yes.'

'Easily.'

'Nice room. Do you like living on your own?'

'Well, I'm not always mad about other people's hair in the plug hole.'

'Is that the voice of rueful experience?'

'You haven't come up here for chapter three of my autobiography, have you?'

'I'll find a pub or somewhere tomorrow.'

'Just concentrate on your actors, would you, please?'

'If you insist. What do you actually think the right thing for us to do is?'

'Us?'

'You and me and the other members of Her Majesty's government.'

'Get an early night,' Annie said. 'And meet again in the morning.'

'I do appreciate this,' I said. 'Your sofa's being an absolute brick to let me sleep on it like this.'

'The last man who did it didn't care for it one bit.'

'He must have had bigger ambitions than I do. You're probably very well shot of him. Bet he was an actor.'

'You lose. He was a musician.'

'Which he thought gave him the right to your bed.'

'And breakfast.'

'Your breakfast is in no danger from me. And the acme of my musical knowledge is recognizing Ravel's Bolero. Did he mean a lot to you?'

'Yes,' she said.

'Maybe he'll be back. Not tonight, I trust, but –'

'He won't. He's dead.'

'Do you ever get the feeling that you might have said the wrong thing? I'm sorry. How come?'

'He drank; he drove; you shouldn't.'

'Did you like him very much?'

'Not all that much. I just happened to love him rather a lot. It's all right, this isn't going to turn into a memorial service. It was quite a while ago now. His name was Edmund Askew. I pronounced it "a-skew". It turned out I was right.'

'Do you feel guilty?'

She shook her head. 'Stupid. For thinking it really mattered all that much where he slept. Better luck next time. Someone in insurance perhaps. Or a sensible clergyman who doesn't ride his motorbike under lorries.'

'I hope Frank's going to be all right,' I said, 'eventually. *Clergyman*? Didn't you ever want to be an actress?'

'When I can be on the book instead? I'm rotten at being anyone but myself unfortunately. And I'm not always brilliant at that.'

'I think you're pretty good at it,' I said.

'May I say something, Michael?'

'And cue Annie!'

'Don't feel you have to entertain the actors all the time. Make sure they entertain you. I hope you don't mind my saying.'

'How dare you give me really useful advice?'

The dress rehearsal went quite well, except for a door which opened the wrong way and had to be re-hung and then stuck when Viola was making a tearful exit. I began to believe that we might do more than get away with it. Some of the London press had promised to come down. I hoped and feared that Benedict Bligh would make an effort to abuse me in the *Sunday Crusader*. I loitered in the manager's office as people began to arrive. Frank Kitson came gallantly up the steps from the High Street on his crutches. His name was, of course, still in the programme as producer.

My parents arrived on the same train as Benedict. I greeted

them and had my eyes on him. My father was in a dark suit, of the kind he might have chosen to wear at a nondenominational service, and my mother was in a black silk dress covered with white polka dots. I saw how she might have been quite an actress and I suspected, from her radiant modesty, that she regretted that she could not be recognized as anything but the author's mother. If she was prepared to rejoice in my local and temporary fame, she would have liked to have been noticed for herself. She and Samuel waited in the foyer for Rachel and Owen, who were driving over from Oxford, while I went back to appear calm and confident, between bouts of nausea, for the benefit of the actors.

Benedict Bligh and his wife, Karen, who had been previously married to Warren Landau, the screenwriter and socialite, had brought Stanley Hendrick with them from London. Stanley had two plays running in town, one in the West End and one in the East End. Benedict had observed that 'once again we have been reminded that the English theatre is a place made brilliant by Irishmen'. I had asked Ted Wilson to keep an eye open for Benny and to make sure that drinks were offered. Stanley was a thirsty man.

Rachel and Owen did not reach the theatre until people were moving into the auditorium. Rachel could hear a loud voice and thought that the curtain had already gone up. Stanley Kendrick was performing in the bar. 'The country,' he was saying, 'is split from top to bottom and that's a prospect to be relished, my masters, by all lovers of liberty, a gash to be explored with libidinous enthusy-musy, a gorgeous gusset in which boundless pleasure may be invested . . .'

Owen said, 'How very nice to see you again, sir.'

'The name is still Samuel. Did you ever meet my wife, Philippa?'

'Once, I believe. This is a very nice occasion, isn't it?'

'I hope so,' Philippa said.

I checked the dangerous door as the national anthem made everyone stand up again. Benedict was still in the bar, acknowledging the Queen by standing on his head and smoking a

Balkan Sobranie through a foot-long cigarette holder. The cast had seemed pleased with the presents from the antique shop below Annie's flat. I had found Victorian scent bottles, with silver tops, for Viola and Marie and an R.S.M.'s parade cane for Ronnie. Annie had wrapped them for me. I went and looked through the spy-hole in the tabs and saw a dark young man in a black leather jacket and black corduroys coming down the aisle in an urgent way which suggested that he had come from a much more important occasion. It was Joe Hirsch.

As the curtain rose, and the play passed beyond my control, I became a spectator of my own fate. The flaws and naivetés in the characters and the dialogue were borne in upon me as if I had known nothing of them before. I waited for the first laugh with numb anguish. How could I have been so unsubtle as to call the Briggs's family pet, a caged budgerigar, 'Britannia'? When the audience laughed at the first exchanges between Marie and Ronnie, I was relieved and a little ashamed by their generosity. Could it possibly last? The scene continued:

IRIS: What're you doing, Dennis?
DENNIS: I'm feeding Britannia.
IRIS: With your feet, Dennis.
DENNIS: I'm standing on them. Isn't that what they're for?
IRIS: Look at my carpet, Dennis. Look at those marks. You could at least take your shoes off.
DENNIS: They've still got feet underneath. I hope.
IRIS: Should you perhaps see a doctor, Dennis?

The laugh was followed by the sound of one person clapping, loudly. Stanley Hendrick was coming down the aisle. The method of his progress suggested that a very high sea was running. He stopped and leaned on the rail in front of the orchestra pit. 'Author, author!'

Benedict Bligh said, 'Stanley, behave!'

Stanley Hendrick said, 'This is how I behave.'

'Sit down and shut up.'

DENNIS: I should see an ornithologist.
IRIS: Oh my goodness me! When did this start?
DENNIS: I'm getting smaller and smaller. I'm
growing feathers. Yellow ones. On my extremities.
Move over, Britannia, I'm going to crawl in and
live with you. Hurry up. I think I'm going to
lay an egg.

Stanley's intervention had distracted the audience, but now they seemed to recover. Their laughter, to my ears, was a little forced: a reproach to the drunken celebrity rather than a response to the play. I loitered by the stage door and finally stepped outside and walked in the cool. Through the window of a bluish room in the Dutch quarter, I saw the Russians in the streets of Budapest. I stood there, an absurd peeper, and cribbed the vileness of the world, as incapable of affecting it as I was of altering the nature or the prospects of *With This Ring*.

I stepped back inside the stage door to hear the last words of the act. Steady applause greeted Viola's curtain line when, after the sound of a prolonged street accident, she came in (through that damned door) and looked at her horrified family for a long time before saying, 'Dennis, I'm afraid I've scratched the Consul.'

My parents were in the Stalls Bar. Philippa had a brandy and soda, while Samuel made do with orange squash. 'I hope the father isn't supposed to be me,' he said.

'He's not remotely like you,' Philippa said. 'Is the mother like me?'

Samuel said, 'No-o. One or two phrases perhaps.'

Rachel said, 'Daddy, really! She's nothing whatever like you, mummy. He ought to be ashamed of himself.'

'That's rather a harsh judgement. He's still very young, after all.'

'I'm talking about you, daddy, and you're not as young as all that.'

Samuel winked at Owen, who sipped his gin and tonic and

scanned the company in the tight bar. Stanley Hendrick had a glass in each hand. It did not augur well for his behaviour during the second act.

'What's he got against suburbia?' Samuel said. 'Some of my best friends are suburbanites. They don't invade people; they don't nationalize anyone's belongings and they very rarely arrive for work by tank or parachute. Wherein exactly lies their sin?'

'I do think they're doing it awfully well,' Philippa said.

Frank Kitson gave her a modest smile and swung his stiff, blanched leg towards the door. Stanley Hendrick drained a glass and put it down on the bar, which proved to be a foot higher than he had imagined. 'It's the black day of the working class, my masters! To think that once upon a time, without a vestige of irony, we sang songs to Comrade Stalin, all together, boys! For the sake of Comrade Stalin, we drove the White Guards back!'

Owen Millom took the opportunity to ask Rachel whether this was the right moment to say anything to her parents. His tact seemed to amuse her. 'No hurry,' she said.

A young man was looking at her. He was tall and fair-haired and his glance suggested that she ought to recognize him, although she had never, to her knowledge, seen him before. He looked at her and then at Owen and then he was coming towards them. 'You probably don't remember me, sir, but you taught me for a brief period. At Oxford.'

'David Lucas,' Owen said. 'May I introduce Rachel Jordan? My fiancée.'

'Congratulations.'

'What're you doing with yourself these days?'

'I'm hoping to get off to West Africa, as a matter of fact, if I can manage it before they call me up again.'

'I thought you had the makings of a scholar at one point.'

David Lucas said, 'He must be thinking of some other member of the Boat Club. I hope you'll be very happy.'

Rachel said, 'Thank you.'

I checked the demon door again, just in case, as the audience came back. Annie Rose was dowsing an umbrella, ready for Ronnie's entrance. He came into the wings rubbing his lips together. He looked as if he had overdone the number 5 rather, but it was too late to change anything now. The curtain rose as Annie anointed Ronnie's macintoshed shoulders with water from her basin and the play resumed.

> DENNIS: I don't want to rise slowly to the
> top, or halfway down, Tess, or not even as high
> as that. I don't want to end up committing
> suicide by throwing myself out of a basement
> window. I don't want to be safe, and sorry.
> I want to catch life on the wing. I want to
> fly before I croak. I want to be a man before
> I die. Better whole-cock than half-cock, or
> no bloody cock at all!
> IRIS: Oh my goodness, Tessa Binge, what have
> you married?
> DENNIS: You want to see what she married?
> (Begins to undress) By God, I'll show you.
> IRIS: (in a panic, calls) Harry, you'd better
> ring for the police.
> DENNIS: And the fire brigade, and the ambulance.
> The more the merrier. (Crows) Nine-nine-nine!
> Nine-nine-nine! Music, maestro, please!

As Ronnie signalled to the pit, Annie put on a record of 'I'll Build A Stairway to Paradise' and my liberated hero began a dance over his mother-in-law's furniture which the audience had just begun to applaud when Stanley Hendrick lurched to the front of the stalls and began to sing, 'For the sake of Comrade Nikita, they broke the workers' ranks/ for the sake of Comrade Khrushchev, they shot the toilers down/ For the sake of Comrade Eden, we couldn't do a fucking thing . . ./ For the sake of Christ and decency/ Let's drive the buggers back!'

IRIS: What's got into him? It's not that
new cereal, is it? My carpet! My put-u-up!
My combination radiogram and cocktail
cabinet with mirrored interior!

Stanley took the applause to be his due. 'For the sake of
Comrade Khrushchev, we'll bring the Russkies back/ For the
sake of fat Nikita, we'll cut off the workers' works!'

Joe Hirsch leaned over to say something to Benedict Bligh.
The critic shrugged. Stanley was a force of nature with which he
did not care to tangle. 'As a fully paid-up coward, I wish you the
best of luck.'

Joe said, 'Out he bloody well goes.'

He thrust past the knees between him and the aisle, grabbed
Stanley by the scruff of the neck and began to march him out of
the theatre. Hendrick was drunk and he was strong and he
resisted loudly, while Viola and Ronnie, on stage, performed
their mild revolutionary dance. David Lucas saw Stanley's fist
smash into Joe's face and jumped up to assist in the eviction.
There was no further chorus from Hendrick as they marched
him through the swing doors into the foyer and then urged him
into the street.

When the curtain fell, there was instant applause. I could not
help reading a measure of apology in it. People resented Stanley
at least as much as they admired my play. There were some calls
of 'author, author!', but I knew better than to step on to the
stage. The actors had been told on no account to signal to me.
Annie came and kissed me and Ted Wilson shook my hand and
said, 'The first of many, I hope.'

When Rachel came up to me and put her arms around me, I
realized how rarely we touched each other. She looked so lovely,
her eyes brilliant with sympathy, that I thought that the play had
perhaps gone better than I feared. It was as if my petty success
had gone to her head. 'They loved it,' she said. 'Everyone did.'

'Not everyone quite.'

'You're not going to let one drunken idiot spoil your evening.'

'Drunken genius, according to Benny Bligh. He may be right.'

Ted Wilson said, 'One nice straw in the wind, Michael: Frank's just been offered a play to direct at the Court. Oscar was in front.'

Joe Hirsch came bounding across the stage, where people were holding their glasses up to Annie, who had red in the right hand and white in the left. He imitated a cock and gave me the thumbs up.

Rachel said, 'Thanks for what you did.'

Joe said, 'Who are you?'

'Joe!' I said. 'Rachel, this is Joe Hirsch. We were at St George's together. This is my sister, Rachel.'

Joe said, 'You're exceptionally beautiful.'

'What're you doing here? I never realized you were even in England.'

'Are you an actress?'

'I'm a historian, sort of.'

'You're just the sort of historian I like. I should have been invited, if only to meet you. Why have you kept her from me?'

'Careful, Raitch,' I said, 'because this man's motorized mayhem.'

Joe said, 'We really mustn't keep you, Michael. Your sister and I have very important things to discuss.'

Owen came with a glass of white wine and put his arm through Rachel's. 'Most enjoyable evening! I do hope London nibbles.'

Joe Hirsch said, 'Who the hell is this?'

'I think you ought to meet my fiancé,' Rachel said. 'This is Joe . . . Hirsch. Owen Millom.'

'How do you do?' Owen said.

Joe looked at him and said, 'Why?'

'Why not?' Owen said.

'I know you,' Joe said. 'Where from? I've seen you on television. You were talking about Germany. I disagree with you totally.'

'I can see how you might be an acquired taste,' Owen said.

'Is that a soft answer?'

Owen turned away, with dismissive patience, and shook my hand. 'Congratulations. Pity about the singing Irishman, or was that in the script?'

'It was a pity, wasn't it?' Joe Hirsch said. 'And what did you do about it? Or anything else? You smirked. You and your shit friends.'

I said, 'Joe, please . . .'

'Surely you mean "Joe, thank you".'

'Owen Millom, get thee to a nunnery!' Benedict Bligh, a white-faced intellectual harlequin, was holding out a long, limp hand. 'The best Ophelia of his day, and quite late into the night, so we're given to understand! Did the sports master ever tell you that nunnery is another term for brothel or were you as lament-ably ill-informed as the rest of us?' He put the question to me, while watching for its effect on Rachel. 'You haven't seen Stanley anywhere, have you?' He looked at Joe. 'You don't happen to remember where you put him, I suppose?'

'You ruined Michael's play,' Joe said.

'I'm not claiming credit for a single line,' Benedict said.

'By bringing that drunken bum with you.'

'Administrative error,' Benedict said.

'That's English for a shit's trick, isn't it?'

I said, 'Joe . . .'

'I've also got to take him home with me.'

'He's in the street,' Joe said. 'Being sick into one of his shoes. I wish it was one of yours.'

Benedict said, 'One comes all the way to the sticks in order to be abused by shoeshine boys.'

I said, 'Look, why not have a drink and . . . ?'

'You don't need this kind of talking banana,' Joe Hirsch said.

Benny Bligh said, 'Michael, before I was put in my lowly place by your muscular friend, I was intending to offer you an apology, if not full-length grovel, for our liquid chum Stanley. I thought as a fellow author he might add lustre to the occasion.

He didn't. If there's any humble pie going, I'll grab me a slice. Failing same, sorry.'

'The least you can do,' Joe said, 'after fouling up the evening is to say in the paper just how good the play was.'

Benedict turned his colourless face to me and grinned toothily. 'Unless you're very, very careful, I may well do so.'

Owen Millom emitted a trill of laughter. Benedict put an arm on Owen's shoulder and whispered something in his ear, before winking at me and waving a languid finger or two.

Joe Hirsch said, 'You can't possibly marry that man.' Rachel smiled, as if she had been paid a compliment which she could safely ignore. 'Why do you say you're going to when you know you shouldn't? Why?'

'Because I am.'

Joe said, 'Is it because of them?' My parents were standing by the staircase which Ronnie and Viola had climbed to their naive paradise. 'You can't do it.'

'You don't know anything about me.'

'Yes, I do. And you know I do.' Joe was speaking with savage intensity. There was nothing ostentatious in his rage. It was hardly audible. 'You're not going to do it. You can't.'

'Are you drunk?'

'Are you sober?'

'Very.'

'You're afraid of yourself. Or what you'd be if you weren't.'

Rachel said, 'Please leave me alone.'

I was kissing Viola for a local newspaper when Joe came across to me. 'She can't possibly marry that idiot.'

'He's not an idiot, whatever . . .'

'He is and she can't.'

'He's a very bright fellow and they've known each other a long time. What's it got to do with me?'

'Can't you see that she's desperate for someone to tell her she mustn't on any account do it?'

'I see no signs of desperation.' Then I looked at Rachel and saw that she was almost as white as Benedict had been. Her upper lip glistened with sweat. Meanwhile, Owen was being polite with Samuel and Philippa. The reassuring glance he gave Rachel provoked a one-sided smile.

'Mr Jordan? My name is Bob Sander. I'm an example of low-life you may have to get used to, if you go on writing plays as good, or better than this one. They call me an agent on my passport; they call me other things elsewhere, but that's the burden I have to bear. You don't need me. I need you. What do you say?'

'It sounds like an ideal arrangement,' I said, 'or does it?'

'It does. Do I call you Michael, Mike or what?'

'Michael in preference to Mike,' I said, 'and Mike in preference to what.'

'I think you have a future. I'd like to be a part of it. When can we have a meeting?'

Owen was shaking hands with Samuel and then he kissed my mother on the cheek. Joe went suddenly across, took Rachel by the arm and dragged her into the wings. She did not reject or refuse Joe's furious passion. He did not amuse her, yet she was amused. He did not offend her, yet she was offended. Owen said, 'What is happening here exactly?'

Joe's mouth was raw with Rachel's lipstick. He wiped it on his handkerchief and showed the redness to Owen. 'You are a man who could smile at anything. Anything.'

'I think you'd better get out, don't you?'

'Come with me,' Joe said. 'Come with me now.'

Rachel stood there with Owen's arm through hers. Her mouth was smudged from Joe's kiss. She took a handkerchief from her bag and wiped the bruise. Joe's contempt was for more than Owen, or Rachel; what he had seen, what was happening, confirmed some long suspicion about the world. He thrust his lower lip upwards in the disdainful rehearsal of a kiss and then he strode to the stage door.

There was quite a pleasant review of *With This Ring*, by a second string, in the *Daily Mail* and brief, initialled encouragement in the *Telegraph*, but I was scarcely hailed as a new planet overnight. Relief and disappointment were part of the same emotion. The play was too simple, in scope and tone, to cause any kind of a sensation, but I still hoped that Benedict might like it enough, or be embarrassed enough by the behaviour of his guest, to make amends to a colleague. On Sunday morning, I was up early, waiting for the sound of the papers being wedged into the letter box at Court Royal. I carried them into the sitting room. In a sudden sweat of optimism, I saw that Benedict's column was headed 'The Young Play of the Decade'.

> Before Mr Khrushchev puts a tank in my office or Mr Eden drops paratroopers to separate critics from their natural prey, let me take a deep breath and offer a deep bow to a powerful, original and shameless new talent. Before the apocalypse reminds us all of the intellectual qualities of those who follow the paths of glory (more gory than glorious), I wish to declare that a return visit this week to see Stanley Hendrick's *Irish Eyes* has served to consolidate my view, stated with appalling frankness in this column a month ago, that the only English plays of genius are those written by Irishmen. In a week of Saharan barrenness elsewhere, Hendrick's anarchic baroque masterpiece sticks out like a naughty deed in a goody-goody world . . .

My father said, 'Why has your friend not reviewed your play?'

'Please hazard a guess,' I said. 'I lack the wit.'

'Presumably he didn't think it was fair.'

'Then why come all that way? You obviously didn't like it yourself.'

'Was it designed for me to like?'

My mother said, 'That awful Irishman did rather put custard on the goose, didn't he?'

'He's the one Benedict's whole bloody column is about.'

'Perhaps he's waiting to write about your play when it comes to London.'

'If it comes to London, it'll be in an old macintosh with a cap pulled well down over its eyes. I'm going to resign from the *Sunday Crusader*.'

'Why walk before the umpire raises his finger?'

'Bad losers never wait for impartial decisions. Their editorial line on Suez is an absolute disgrace.'

'Since when do you write editorials?'

'I don't collect stamps either,' I said. 'And if is indeed a very long word.'

Philippa said, 'I wish you two would speak a language I could understand occasionally.'

Rachel and Owen were supposed to be coming to London at the beginning of December. Their move from Oxford had been delayed, not to their disappointment, by the political confusions of the autumn. The humiliation of Eden, and of Britain and France, made the Foreign Office reluctant to hasten changes, for fear not only of having been wrong but also of appearing to acknowledge the fact. However, a flat had been found in Ennismore Gardens and Rachel started to crate the books which Owen might need in London. It was a nice exercise in empathy to choose without asking, though she verified her selection now and again, for the pleasure of having been right. When he came in, one cold morning, from an appointment in the Randolph bar with 'someone from London', she asked whether he would be wanting Moneypenny in town.

'Improbable.' Owen hung his umbrella over the open door to the bedroom and took off his slim blue overcoat. 'Rachel . . .'

'Present.'

Owen pulled off rather orange gloves. 'Before going any further, one thing goes without saying.'

'You sound as if you're about to say it. And to go further.'

'You are without exception the most understanding and worthwhile woman I've ever met.'

'Is that good for me or bad for women?'

'Rachel, I'm not going to beat about the bush.'

'What are you going to beat about?'

'They've been on to me from London. Did you ever know a man called Aaron Nathanson?'

'Why?'

'You evidently did.'

'I knew him as Buddy. Has something happened to him?'

'Did you do something for him at one point? A favour?'

'It wasn't a favour; it was something I did. Why? Because they've been on to you from London. My father was right.'

'He knew? How?'

'He knew Buddy, and he knew London.'

'The F.O. is very jumpy just now.'

'Perhaps you should encourage them to go and jump.'

'You never told me about this before.'

'I never imagined you'd be interested. I doubt if you would have been now, if all things were equal, but they're rarely that, are they? To tell you the truth –'

'It is perhaps time you did.'

Rachel pushed the library steps into the corner of the room and dusted her fingers.

Owen said, 'The thing is –'

'Ah, the thing! What is the thing?'

'A story started floating around London – emanating from the offices of the *Sunday Crusader* they discovered – about collusion between ourselves, the French and the . . . the Israelis, over – well, what subsequently – emerged.'

Rachel said, 'And what has this to do with how worthwhile and understanding I am?'

Owen said, 'Did you by any chance have anything to do with it?'

Rachel said, 'I don't remember seeing anything about collusion in the *Sunday Crusader*, or anywhere else.'

'There wasn't anything. They spiked it. The question remains, where did they get their information? Come on, Rachel. They suspect it came from your brother, don't they?'

'Come on where exactly? My brother's name isn't Nathanson. I don't know anything about it and I never told Michael anything. By what conceivable means would I know something that the papers don't know? I know virtually nothing after 1938.'

'It isn't that I don't believe you, but your friend Nathanson was involved in certain, well, discussions, secret . . . If he happened to speak to you and you happened to . . . inadvertently, when speaking to . . . your brother. Are you going somewhere?'

Rachel had taken her coat from the hook behind the door. 'Aren't I?'

'My dear Rachel, I'm only asking you to understand my problem.'

'My dear Owen, I can do better than that: I can solve it.'

'Please appreciate that I have no overriding need or wish to work in the Foreign Office, but if I'm to do so –'

'Poor Owen.'

'Poverty is not my first anxiety. Are you still in contact with him, or them? That's all I need to satisfy myself about.'

'If I tell you I'm not, will you believe me?' Rachel had woollen gloves which Philippa had knitted, blue with red. 'Because I'm not and never have been. Well?'

'My first loyalty is, of course, to you.'

'And that's not a very easy thing to forgive, is it?'

'I simply have to know where I stand.'

'Goodbye, Owen,' Rachel said.

V

Bob Sander said, 'Michael Jordan – Aubrey Jellinek.'

Aubrey said, 'But not necessarily in that order, of course.'

Bob said, 'Well, that more or less completes my part of the bargain, doesn't it? So can I have my money now, please?'

'By which he means our money,' Aubrey said. 'No one could call him altruistic exactly, could they?'

'I think he'd probably prefer a cheque,' I said.

Robert Sander and Associates had taken new offices in Old Compton Street, though scarcely on the strength of my enrolment as a client. My first play had been amiably received at Colchester, but it had lived no longer than the two weeks of its provincial run. While contemporaries like Barnaby Monk, married and with children, advanced effortlessly it seemed, into adult life, I remained in my parents' home, unable to find a good reason for moving out. I was working on a new play, slowly, but I was glad of the odd jobs which Bob Sander was able to find for me in television and, occasionally, in films. I cursed the interruption to my serious work even as I welcomed its postponement. I had substituted one kind of journalism for another, though I was at least relieved of the need to report to the *Crusader* offices where Barnaby Monk's position had been strengthened by the promotion of Leo Quaritch to managing editor.

'Mr Chalk, Mr Cheese,' Bob Sander said. 'I'm a man who keeps his promises, if there's nothing more profitable to be done with them, and I promised I'd introduce you two characters to each other, much as I may wonder whether you can ever really want to work together!'

'Which one of us do you think he suspects of having scruples, Michael?' Aubrey Jellinek was a year or two older than I, but he gave an impression of confidence and suaveness (the cavalry twill trousers, the yellow waistcoat with the bone buttons), to which my Harris tweed jacket, tubular green corduroys and polo-necked sweater, with snagged stitches, offered no convincingly Bohemian contrast. Aubrey was clean-shaven to the point of pinkness. His almost rimless glasses were a prop which elected him immediate chairman of our meeting. His button-down collar established his transatlantic affinities. He had spent the war in Kansas City (and Chicago) and he had the guiltless optimism of one for whom other people's misfortunes had, through no fault or cowardice of his, been a blissful opportunity. He had been transported from the suburbs of Birmingham to the picture-windowed ranch-house of an American cousin, through which he had observed the brilliant prospect of the American way of life. He returned to England at the age of sixteen already able to drive a car and date a girl. He had a suitcase full of records and sheet music and a determined idea of where he was going. Neither a couple of years at Dover College, nor his time in the army, when he served as 'Entertainments Officer, B.A.O.R.', though they anglicized his tone, had altered his ambition. His latest song 'Partners' was already being requested by housewives.

'I caught your last play,' he said.

'You must have been standing in very close at first slip.'

'Best dialogue I've heard in ages.'

'And?' I said. 'Or is it but?'

'Both,' Aubrey said, 'Both. *And* I want you to do a musical comedy with me. *But* I'm afraid you'll think you shouldn't.'

'Or couldn't.'

'Not an expression you should be familiar with. Has this unbelievably devious agent of ours – I hope that's what he is, because if not, we'd better shop someone else! – has he told you what a straight-down-the-middle show-bizzy kind of character I am? How can I possibly seduce someone as . . . as *significant* as your intellectual self into writing something as mundane as a West End musical? I mean, what possible interest could a

Michael Jordan have in confecting mountains of whipped cream and collecting enough royalties to make Croesus wonder where he went wrong? You do the chattipoos; I do the songs; Bob does the business . . .'

'Draw breath, Aubrey, draw breath! It's Wednesday. Wednesdays, he breathes. It's in the contract.' Bob was enjoying the drawstrings on his new ice-blue drapes. He widened and narrowed the view of the yard where his second-hand Austin Healey stood in a pinched slot next to the emergency exit from an Italian restaurant.

Aubrey said, 'So, next item on the agenda: how do I persuade you to sell me your soul?'

'I'm not sure that I believe in souls. What do you actually have in mind?'

'Oh, you believe in minds, do you? Laugh at me, if you will, and you probably will, but I happen to think that – deep breath and out with it! – *Zenda* is the best idea I ever stole, or at least appropriated. What do you think?'

'As in the prisoner thereof?'

'You're getting warmer,' Aubrey said. 'Hey, you didn't tell him about it, did you, Bobert?'

'Of course,' Bob said. 'That's why he never bothered to show up. He hated the whole idea.'

I said, 'You won't believe this. Unless someone's already told you, of course, but *Zenda* was the first thing I ever adapted for the stage.'

'It was you I stole it from!'

'At prep school. We rehearsed the whole thing and then the costumes arrived from London. And the swords. The headmaster suddenly had visions of his best scholarship prospects being run through by Black Michael and associates and he cancelled the whole production.'

'You've just had a change of headmaster,' Aubrey said. 'Are you conceivably on, dare I hope?'

'Put it this way: when I'm off, I'm usually gone by now.'

Aubrey held his hand out. 'You owe me a quid, Bobert.'

'How could I know about him and his headmaster?'

'Pay up and I'll buy us a celebratory lunch, all expense spared.'

'I haven't said yes, you know, only —'

'You haven't said no, though, have you? And that's what Boberto said you'd say. It's not only the ayes that have it, it's also the maybes. It won't take more than a few minutes of your valuable time.'

' "Let's be partners! How do you do?/Can this lead to tickets for two?" ' Bob Sander remembered what the housewives were asking for and played it gently back to us.

Aubrey said, 'In reply to your question, Michael, I believe in a strictly fifty-fifty relationship, right down the line, round the corner and back up the other side. Fifty for you, fifty for me and a big kiss for the man who made it all possible, the one and only Bob Sander.'

We went to Schmidt's, in Charlotte Street, and had Wiener schnitzel and cream caramel and coffee and there was change from Aubrey Jellinek's winnings. I said that I would read *The Prisoner of Zenda* again, as if this allowed me the dignity of a choice I felt, with dread and exhilaration, that I had already made. Why not hitch my wagon to Aubrey Jellinek's ascendant star? It would be no great drag to do again in my twenties what had amused me in the days when Major Stanhope commanded my destiny. If it would be no stylish credit for me to get to the West End in such pedestrian circumstances, who knew what more valuable opportunities might follow? I was as flattered by Aubrey Jellinek's overtures as I was disdainful of his mundane ambitions. It was, in a way, convenient to find a partner who was both entertaining and of no consequence. If all went well, I should have the reward of success, of a kind; if, for any reason, the whole thing collapsed, I should have the sour pleasure of having proved to myself that I should never have become involved with such triviality. I promised Aubrey that I would let him know within twenty-four hours and spent the afternoon watching a Polish film of unremitting realism. It was preceded by a short in which Guy Falcon, in crumpled khaki, loped around ancient Ephesus, revealing the 'palimpsest of history' to be found in its impacted archaeology. Falcon's bearded intelligence, the frown with which he confronted the hot questions of antiquity, made me long for access to the high culture he found so suggestive. When the doomed Poles moved through the sewers of Warsaw, on their stinking and dignified way to a death which the prologue made inevitable, I wondered where, in recent English history, one could find a story so tragic or so immune to the humorous touches with which, so they imagined, British film-makers paid tribute to the Shakespearian tradition of light relief. Acceding to Aubrey Jellinek somehow became for me a gesture of contempt not for myself but for the local climate which made working with him seem so natural.

The end of Rachel's engagement to Owen Millom had not disposed her to return to Court Royal. She had found a job, in the editorial department of the London University Press, and she took a room in Gordon Square, a few minutes' walk from her office. She was doing work she liked and she had her modest independence. I slightly envied her routine acquaintance with the academic *gratin* whose manuscripts she edited with a diligence which, on the occasions when I watched her, after I had called in for a sherry before the theatre, or to collect a discounted book she had obtained for me, seemed tinged with restrained passion, a sort of decorous sensuality that made her smile at the proof sheets in front of her, as if they had paid her some sly compliment.

One afternoon, when she was checking some references in Greville's diaries, her telephone rang. She rather assumed it would be one of her professors (Owen Millom had been particularly generous in recommending her to his colleagues) and she said 'Rachel Jordan' in what she thought of as her 'head-girl' voice.

'Miss Jordan, I do hope you're going to forgive me.'

'Perhaps if you'll tell me who you are and what you've done exactly . . .'

'That sounds more like you. For calling you out of the blue like this. My name is David Lucas. I don't imagine for a moment that you remember –'

'You were at my brother's first night,' she said. 'Colchester.'

'I want to ask you an immense favour.'

'If you bring the manuscript round, I'll read it as quickly as I can.'

'I beg your pardon? Oh. No, no. Nothing like that. Something much more important. Are you conceivably free for dinner tonight?'

Rachel said, 'Tonight?'

'I've only just got back to the U.K. Otherwise I'd've been more . . . trepidatious? Does that exist?'

'I can check for you,' she said, 'but I hope not.'

'I do very much want to see you again.'

'Tonight?' Rachel said. 'All right.'

'What did you say?'

'I said "all right". Was that not –?'

'Can you seriously be free?'

'Where shall I see you,' Rachel said, 'and when?'

She reached Maurer's before the rain started and sat at the table David had reserved. People came in with dripping umbrellas and lank hair. They had shiny smiles on their tilted faces. She watched, without knowing who he was, as a tall man in naval officer's uniform made anxious excuses to Madame Maurer and looked from table to table. When he removed his rain-blackened hat, she saw that it was David. She looked away, as if trapped in an indiscretion. 'Terribly sorry,' he said. 'Chapter of accidents. I thought the esteemed parents were in town. They thought . . . Never mind. Boring story, you've probably heard it many times before: no keys, no clothes and I'm late. Things can only get better.'

Rachel said, 'I had no idea you were a sailor.'

'I'm not: I'm an engineer in fancy dress. You were never meant

174

to see me like this. It's simply that I did my national service in the navy, after Oxford. I always liked boats. At least I did until they made me do the washing up after Suez.'

'I was in the Wrens at the end of the war,' Rachel said.

'You weren't old enough.'

'They still took me,' she said.

'And I'm not in the least surprised. I'm not permanently committed to a life on the ocean wave or anything like that. This is just something they've kitted me out in to make sure I got the respect I wasn't necessarily entitled to while I was out in Egypt.'

'I didn't realize that was still going on.'

'You weren't supposed to. And it isn't. However, there was a certain amount of junk to be cleared out. The morning after the night before ended up by lasting quite a few weeks, I can tell you. It was the Frogs who did most of the scowling. As far as they were concerned, it was 1940 all over again. But t'other way round. This time we shopped them instead of them shopping us.'

'I should have thought that might have given them a certain amount of perverse pleasure.'

'You should've seen them when the ceasefire came through. I'd just arrived. They dragged me off the plane to Accra pretty well, because Bill Fell wanted me to help him clear the canal. Very nice of him, blast his eyes. Anyway, tears and lamentation was what I arrived to. Tears of rage mostly, against us. The Frogs said we couldn't understand what they were going through, because we'd already lost India. Our empire was up the spout already, but they still had some of theirs to lose. Algeria mainly. And now, thanks to us, they would. They were all very emotional about it. One of our chaps – a four-ringer R.N. – told them that it wasn't losing India that knocked the stuffing out of the British, it was losing Gracie Fields. This Frog looked totally discombobulated. "Gricee Fields? Gricee Fields? Vere are zese Gricee Fields precisely?" Old Marwood said, "Even with your perfect English, *mon capitaine*, I doubt if I could explain." Much laughter among our chaps, ditto sullen resentment *du côté français*. Never the twain shall meet, I'm afraid. Are you as hungry as I am?'

'I rather think I may be,' Rachel said.

'Then why am I talking so much when we could be ordering dinner instead?'

His hair had dried. It was thick and blond. He caught her looking at the two and a half gold rings on his sleeves and at the strong wrists that emerged from them. Madame Maurer came and took their order in her brusque, conspiratorial way. She could be abrupt and sentimental at the same time.

Rachel said, 'How did you find out where I was?'

'I'm afraid I called Owen Millom. I wanted to see if the coast was conceivably clear.'

'You're certainly very maritime in your . . .'

'I probably could have put that more elegantly. The truth is, I spent a lot of time out there wondering what the hell I was doing, and why. I had no personal reason for hauling wrecks out of the bloody canal and I wasn't even sure why I was doing it, or we were doing it. To hide the fact that we'd cocked up the whole operation and had to pretend that we were still in charge, dictating the course of events we'd actually failed utterly to control? To apologize to the Egyptians while appearing to give them a lesson in salvage technique? To open the waterway before people realized that having it closed made virtually no difference to anything and that all that talk about suffocation was a lot of nonsense? There was some abstract amusement value in getting the various hulks to pop up out of the murky depths, but it all went on much too long. Sunken ships are cussed things; they never quite come up the way you expect. But I didn't *care* if we ever cleared the bloody waterway or not. Which led me to think how wonderful it might be really to care about something, or someone. Isn't that the damnedest way to come to appreciate there's only one person in the world you're aching to see?'

Rachel said, 'What did Owen tell you about me?'

'He said you'd decided not to get married and then he gave me your telephone number.'

Rachel nodded, as if he had confirmed what she feared, and then she stood up and moved away from the table. David was cornered on a banquette behind the table, other diners on either side of him. When he saw Rachel collecting her coat, he made no ungainly effort to follow her. He understood. His voice carried across the room. 'I never discussed you with Owen. I had no wish to do so. I fell in love with you the first moment I saw you.' Rachel did not hurry to leave, but she was leaving. There was nothing angry or playful in her attitude. She had to go, that was all. 'You don't believe in these things? They happen. To be perfectly honest, I rather think it's the only thing of the remotest importance that's ever happened to me in my life.'

He spoke the last words to Rachel's absence. He appeared neither surprised nor embarrassed by her departure. What he said was the truth; he did not mind who heard it. He sensed her anguish without any notion of its cause. He was sure that he was not guilty of hurting her and he had no greed for the blame. He took money from his blue pocket and put it on the table, collected his cap and his coat and went out after her into the Soho rain. He saw her hesitating under the arch which cut through to Charing Cross Road. She turned her collar up over her ears and huddled forward into the downpour. He had time to catch and retrieve her by the arm. 'I may be a fool, but I don't understand. And I'm not letting you go until I do.'

Her face was slashed by the coloured rain. Neon signs made hundreds and thousands of the droplets. 'It was very nice of you to ask me.'

'Hang nice,' he said. 'What did I say, or do?'

'It's nothing to do with you,' Rachel said.

'If it's seriously Owen that's bothering you, he gave me your number and that was it. Finish. I swear.'

'I'm not what you think I am.'

'Yes you bloody well are,' he said. 'You're a very beautiful and extraordinary woman and I want to marry you.'

'Sailors imagine —'

'Hang sailors, and their imaginations. I'm not a sailor. I'm an engineer in borrowed clobber, as you very well know.'

She said, 'There's truly no sense in both of us —'

'Both of us is the only thing that matters to me. What's sense got to do with anything? Have you noticed the world at all recently?'

Rachel said, 'Anything after 1938 goes to another department.'

'I love you and I want to marry you.' He pulled her back under the narrow shelter of the archway and kissed her clean and chilly lips. She stiffened against him, but he was not deterred. And then she was returning his kiss with a ferocity compounded of threat, anger and desire. Her emotion swamped them both, but he was not intimidated or amazed. He held on to her and felt her shudder and wince and cling to him.

She said, 'Did he not tell you what happened when we went to bed together?'

'I don't want to know anything about that.'

'But did he tell you?'

'He told me nothing.'

'That's exactly what happened.'

'I'm not in the least surprised. What ever possessed you to think that anything else was likely to happen? Poor you! Is that why you split up?'

'He said it didn't matter. I had the feeling that he didn't regret it. It created a sort of bond between us.'

'Shame's a rotten bond. And you should never feel it. You more than anyone. I hardly know Owen. He thinks I read medieval French, when actually . . . Do you think we could possibly find somewhere slightly more suitable to continue this?'

She looked at him unappeased. Her kiss might never have been offered. She stood apart from him and shuddered again at the bending rain as it glanced from the rooftops and boiled on the cobbles.

David said, 'What exactly do you suspect me of? I'd appreciate knowing. I'd actually appreciate knowing pretty well anything you feel like telling me. Starting with the name of your teddy bear when you were seven years old.'

The whites of her eyes caught light. 'Alphonse. I chewed his ears.'

'Lucky Alphonse.'

'I don't want you taking me for the promised land,' she said.

'I want you to be my wife. Not my territory. I love you. Sorry, but I can't think of anything more original to say. I've never felt it before. I shall never feel it again.'

'No?'

'No.'

'How do I know that?'

'Because I say it. Because I mean it and you know I mean it. Because you're what you are and no one but a fool would think he could lie to you and not be found out. Why do you hesitate? There's you and there's me and no one else matters a damn.'

There were many books in Rachel's room. It was large and rather sombre, with tall narrow windows overlooking the square. She liked the brown propriety of the panelled walls. The demanding formality of the place, its assured modesty, reminded David that he might love Rachel but that he hardly knew her. He stood, with damp shoulders, looking at a line drawing framed above her walnut work-table. It was a nude portrait, from the back, of a woman who had to be Rachel herself. It was inscribed: 'G.F. for R.J. "For and against".'

'I see him when he comes up to London to scowl at dealers.'

David said, 'You don't have to explain anything to me.'

She said, 'He'll never leave his wife. At least not more than once a week. I don't think I ever wanted him to. I'm very happy living alone.'

'Are you?' he said.

'Not really.'

'I love your smile. That smile. I love your frown too.'

She said, 'I met Guy after Owen and I . . . He had a book he wanted the press to do. I was the one who had to tell him no, with the usual pious regrets. He made it his business to prove to me what fools they were, and I was. Now we're friends. Friends! I like him partly because he's so blissfully unhappy, so irretrievably beyond easy consolations. He thought he was going to be the great English master, the arbiter whose generosity would license and regulate at the same time. It never occurred to him that people could read his generosity for selfishness or ambition.'

David said, 'I wish I could do things like that.'

Rachel said, 'I could never marry an artist. He'd always have something more important to him than me.'

After meeting Aubrey Jellinek, I worked almost all night. My new play became luminously clear to me. It was called *Security*. Harry Sandheim, a refugee businessman, fearful of losing his postwar prosperity, hires a bodyguard to keep his belongings safe. Wolf Wolf, the security man, is diligent to the point of becoming the gaoler and, in the end, the ruthless exploiter of the man whose family he has been commissioned to protect. His henchmen take over the house and abuse Sandheim's lovely daughter. I had not intended to write anything as black as the play which emerged, but I began to take an almost brutal pleasure in the humiliation of my family; I laughed out loud at their fears and degradation. I seemed to have no control over the inventive cruelties I wished on my characters. The bodyguard too turned out to be a Jew.

The next morning, I had a call from Wendy Savage, Sally's agent, asking me to go and see Miss Raglan in her dressing room at the Playhouse that evening. She was starring in *A Story So Far*, Oliver Chisholm's verse play about Napoleon and Josephine, who were being played by Ned Corman and, of course, his wife, Irene Jameson. Sally had the second lead part of Marie Walewska, the pure-hearted Polish girl who was persuaded to seduce the Emperor for patriotic purposes. Oliver Chisholm's lush language had been the subject of a catty and doggerel attack by Benedict Bligh ('Chiselled Chisholm, dictionary-dazzled/Flatters phoneys, facetiae-frazzled/With alliterative addenda/And kids the bourgeois it's on a stylish bender' etcetera), but the lure of Corman and Jameson, and the promise of circumlocutory improprieties, enabled the Playhouse box office to triumph over critical anathemas. If I was disposed to agree with Benedict's opinions (or at least to relish their tart expression), I could have wished to emulate the conceits I deplored.

'You rang, madame?'

'Michael! Darling! You got the message!'

'I think I must have, or the coincidence would verge on the miraculous. How are you, Sall?'

She kissed air close to my mouth. 'Sticky as anything! You haven't come in specially, have you? I just wanted you to know that Aubrey thought you were brilliant.'

'Are you suggesting that I'm not?'

'He's only afraid that you'll be much too clever for him.'

'Where did he get the idea that I won't? You'll never believe what it is he wants me to do with him.'

'Darling, please! You know how easily shocked I am! On the other hand, I think *Zenda*'s a honey of an idea.' She was taking serious trouble over her make-up. It was as if she were two people: both the impatient user of her own face and body and the patient creature undergoing assessment. She looked at herself, winced and went to work again, smoothing and highlighting. Her own prettiness did not quite meet her requirements. Marie Walewska's innocence was cunningly applied. 'I think you'll do it superbly, what's more.'

'Surely you mean "What's less". Come to sunny Ruritania/ Where life could not be zanier/ Come and do a wild mazurka/ Be a shashlik, not a shirker! I didn't realize you were involved.'

'Why else do you think Aubs got in touch with you?'

'You mustn't think about me so much. Benny B.'ll only catch you at it and start writing forgivable things about us in his column. Dear Christ, imagine what he'll say about a musical of *Zenda*.' I sprayed the dressing room with indiscriminate machine-gun fire. 'To put it mildly.'

'Big bugs to Benny B., say I. He hated this piece, but look at the queues. I'm longing to play the Queen of Ruritania and make everyone cry and cry. You'll do it so nicely. I told Aubs if he could get you, he could get me, but not otherwise. Satisfied?'

'I sometimes suspect we don't have the same definition of satisfaction.'

'Patience, Michael, patience!'

'We don't,' I said.

'You were never this way when we were reading Gerald Pringle together. You used to be so correct I was afraid there was something wrong with you.'

'That was last year's line, madam. Allow me to show you a more recent model. Are you free for dinner after the show? I promise to be very, very incorrect.'

'I'd love to,' she said. 'Oh buttons! Tonight I can't. I can't tonight. Can we do it some other time?'

The door of the dressing room opened and Ned Corman came in, wearing Napoleonic breeches and a typically false nose. '*Ah madame, ainsi tu me trahis!*'

'My oldest and dearest friend, Michael Jordan. We danced together when we were children.'

'I was a child,' I said, 'you were already Sally Raglan.'

'My name, the lady has omitted to mention, is Ned Corman.'

'I believe I know it,' I said.

'Sally told me about your play.' He spoke in a voice without apparent make-up. 'If you ever write something suitable for me, I hope you'll keep me in mind.'

I said, 'Believe me, I should be very . . . and as a matter of fact . . .' I stood up. 'Well, I'd better be on my way . . .'

Ned Corman said, 'When I say goodbye, Mr Jordan, I say goodbye. Meanwhile, pray stay, unless you have someone better to do.'

'I thought perhaps you two –'

'*Eh bien, mon amour, mon ange!*' Ned fattened his voice to Napoleonic richness with comic speed. '*Il connaît tout, ton petit ami?*'

'*Tout, sire, sauf la verité!*' She too could resume the Raglan huskiness quite effortlessly.

I was less upstaged than disqualified by their performance. As he welcomed me, Ned Corman dismissed me; I was an audience they scarcely needed. Sally's kiss made me the salt for Ned's tail.

'I shall await your manuscript, sir.'

'And, sir, you shall receive the same.'

'*Zenda* comes first,' Sally said.

'*Zenda?*' Ned Corman said. '*Ah que la trahison est douce/ Entr'un auteur et une méchante puce!*'

'Aubers needs you,' Sally called out to me as I went into the concrete corridor. '*I* need you.'

'We all bloody well need you, Mr Jordan. Do we not!'

The call-boy was knocking on doors, but he stood aside to allow Irene Jameson to pass. Ned's wife was still a great beauty, although there was a tightness about her mouth which hinted at bitterness at what she feared might be the conspiracy of time. The brilliant scorn she visited on casual eyes, like mine, or the call-boy's, was quite impersonal. It was the same look she would have given us had we been mirrors. She saw herself in our eyes and was as anxious as she was flattered by the sight. Her voice was the terse evidence of unnecessary doubts. 'Who are you?'

'I'm just leaving,' I said.

'Shall I call you Mr Leaving? Or plain Just? Have you seen my husband at all?'

'I think he's in with Miss Raglan, Miss Jameson,' I said.

'I have very much the same impression, Mr Leaving.'

'Actually, my name is Michael Jordan. I'm one of your greatest admirers.'

'I very much doubt if you come in the first five hundred.' The sound of Beethoven's *Eroica* filled the theatre with recorded richness and came tinnily over the Tannoy. 'I suppose you think you're never going to die.'

'I leave immortality to my betters,' I said. 'I've seen every film you were ever in.'

'On no account tell me your favourite. Are you a critic?'

'Absolutely not,' I said.

'Then be comforted. There are lower forms of life than you, Mr Leaving.'

Ned Corman came out of Sally's dressing room and offered an imperial bow to Irene. 'I thought I heard your voice, sweet wife.'

I was again the mirror of Irene's quest for confirmation both of her charm and of its conceivable disappearance. She wanted and distrusted me.

'They're ready for you, Miss Jameson,' the call-boy said, 'Mr Corman.'

'And we,' Ned Corman said, 'are more than ready for them, are we not, my love?'

Joe Hirsch had told me to come and see him whenever I wanted. There was something demanding in his promise of hospitality and I had not yet visited him in Primrose Hill. I did not want to go there now: I had no confidence that I should find him sympathetic or that he would have reliable advice to offer. I telephoned Barnaby and Claudia's number, in the hope that domesticated cynicism could arm me against the lure of Aubrey Jellinek or their mocking connivance encourage me to yield to it. They had gone to the theatre.

Joe Hirsch said, 'You didn't really come round here for advice. You came for permission. Why from me?'

I said, 'I wanted to talk to someone. And when I couldn't find anyone, I naturally turned to you.'

'I know exactly why. You were afraid Pierrette wouldn't approve of you doing a musical comedy.'

'I can't believe Pierrette would care one way or the other. I don't suppose she even knows what musical comedies are. Do you hear from her at all?'

'Do you? Over and done with? Have you ever written anything about her? You should.'

'I doubt it. It's a kind of flippancy, being serious about things you've never experienced, imagining you can have any idea of what people like that went through. A kind of greed possibly, wanting to have their lives for your own purposes. There's something untouchable there. Sacred and obscene, not for others.'

'Pierrette had it easy compared to some people. You should talk to my father sometime.'

'Is he around?'

'Not often.'

'The terrible thing is —'

'You can be jealous of pretty well anything, can't you? Including people who've been in concentration camps. Almost anything turns into a privilege, something to resent. You think you're the only person in the world who has disreputable thoughts! Far more than art, they're what unite us, Michael, make us one. In the end, the camps'll be yet another thing they'll be saying give us an unfair advantage. Auschwitz will be one more Jewish racket. An old school tie we won't let anyone else wear. The next stage is being persecuted for having been persecuted, and living to tell the tale, or some of it. You didn't just love her, did you? You wanted to have what she'd had. The flavour of the true cross.'

'I haven't come up here to talk about Pierrette.'

'You came to get a sniff of her, though. I'm the nearest thing this side of the Channel. What do you think of the place?'

'It's fine, if you don't mind six flights.'

'I'll put in a lift one day. Who the hell can that be?' The street bell had rung. 'Are you expecting someone?'

'You're the one who lives here, Joe. Don't . . . .'

'Then she's probably for me.' He opened the window and leaned out. 'Key coming!' When he was in again, he said, 'Do you know Jessica Flam?'

'Presumably no relation of Chester Flam, a man of property?'

'His daughter,' Joe said. 'Or so she tells me.'

'And you never knew until you had her dress off and saw the tell-tale mark. By which time it was already true love.'

'I never talk about love. I leave that to playwrights. I never tell people I love them. Jessica and I are partners, that's all. I wanted you to be the last to know.'

He had the door open to allow light to shine down the top flight of attic steps.

I said, 'Isn't she married? What kind of partners exactly?'

'Business.' Joe took Jessica in his arms and kissed her on the mouth. 'And that's the kind of business we do.'

Jessica was wearing a flared black coat with a white fur collar. She had black curls and a heart-shaped face with a straight, or straightened, nose and gleaming eyes. She wore more make-up than her prettiness required; there was defiance in such a shameless show.

Joe said, 'Jessica, this is Michael Jordan. Kiss her if you want to.'

Jessica threw the coat aside and revealed a dark red silk dress with a shirred neck. She had unexpected freckles. 'Behave yourself, Joseph.'

'And lose what's left of my reputation?'

I said, 'How do you do?'

'Spoken like a gentleman,' Joe said, 'if not by one.'

'Why do I stand for this?'

'Because it's the national anthem, isn't it?' Joe found new words for God Save The Queen: 'I am an English Jew, I am an English Jew . . .'

'Have your joke,' I said, 'but don't expect me to stand to attention for it. I came round here –'

'– to get forty lashes and an O.K. from the Beth Din for wanting to write a musical with Aubrey Jellinek. I only gave him ten, so he's sulking. Jessica and I are starting a new magazine. Have you ever been to Israel? You should go for us.'

'I don't want to be a journalist.'

'You're a bit choosy for a hack, aren't you?'

I said, 'He was a lot nicer before you arrived, Jessica. He must like you a lot.'

'Why don't you?' she said. 'Write for us?'

I said, 'What're you calling this mag of yours?'

'We're thinking of *Here and Now*.'

'Think of something better,' Joe said.

'How about *Black and White*?'

'See it in *Black and White*! Not bad, Joseph.'

'The oracle, she speaks! You could always be our film critic if you won't go to Israel. They won't make your movies? Tear theirs to pieces instead. You can't join 'em, lick 'em! Michael's written a brilliant script about the scandal of capitalism and he can't find a financier who'll put money into it. Mad! Perhaps you can get your father to contribute to his own tumbril.'

'White-wall tyres?' she said. 'Why not?'

'Talking of transport, I have this last bus to catch. It may be a long way to Tipperary, but try Southfields.'

'You're not still living with your parents?'

'Begin that with *nonne* when you translate it into Latin, because you know you expect the answer yes. No one else has offered me the same standard of accommodation.'

'You should buy a place of your own.'

'Everyone should,' I said, 'it'd solve the housing problem in no time.'

'What do you reckon I'm paying for this place? Guess.'

'No idea. After a lightning survey and bearing in mind the height above sea level, I'd say a fiver a week.'

'It's paying me,' Joe said. 'I own the house, don't I? I've got tenants downstairs. You could do the same thing if you put your mind to it.'

'When I put my mind to that kind of fence, it trips and breaks its neck. No head for heights or business.'

'You think there's something sordid about having to do with money, property or the control of your own destiny. You're an innocent little Jewish lamb whose highest ambition is to be hung for a British sheep.'

I said, 'Goodnight. Nice to have met you. Some of you.'

'He's afraid we're going to start screwing before he's down the stairs. That's why he's got that sprinting expression on his face: hear nothing, see nothing, know nothing, do nothing. Otherwise, please yourself. One more windowless wanderer pretending to be at home in this demi-paradise. That isn't a rosy future you see ahead of you, boychik, it's the furnace they'll wind up throwing you into, whether or not you drop your aitches. Do you seriously still think the English are different? Or that you are? You're not; they're not.'

'In that case, why bother going down all those bloody stairs? I'll jump straight out of the window. You don't believe it and I don't believe it. You and Aubrey Jellinek have a lot in common – you both want to get people to do what you want them to do by pretending you've got a couple of complimentary tickets to a gilt-edged future. Admit one and friend. Sorry to be playing extra time, Jessica, but every now and again –'

'Go ahead,' she said. 'Kick and scratch. He needs it.'

'You know what I am to him, don't you? The Jew he doesn't think he has to be and no one is ever supposed to suspect him of being. As long as he isn't seen around with me too much. Hence the nocturnal visit to the ghetto gate.'

'Crap,' I said.

'What do you believe in?'

'I don't particularly believe in anything, least of all belief.'

'You particularly believe in *everything*. The empire, the public schools, British justice, the United Nations, the Central Committee of the C.P.S.U., the House of Lords, the Jockey Club, the A.A.! There isn't anything you don't believe in. You still think all the people who run them are properly qualified and that only you – and I – and Jessica – have to apologize for your existence and wait for guidance from above before we so much as give each other a kiss. You think the Nazis were qualified to do what they did. You think they were serious, grown-up people with a Big Idea that has to be puzzled over and understood and respected. The truth about people like you is that you're so busy seeing the other man's point of view you forget to have one of your own.'

'And the truth about truth is, it's true whatever you say or I believe. Whoever you are and whatever you've been through, or not. The truth is true for Jews and Gentiles and for anyone else who happens to be listening, or not, and it's quite important that we shouldn't let them forget it, though not necessarily at this late hour when they're understandably anxious to get to bed.'

'He really is a bit English, isn't he? The limp bit that never rises to an occasion if it can be adjourned to a later date. Have a nice time working with Aubrey Jellinek. A lot of jelly and not all that much neck.'

I said, 'At least you've got a title for your crappy magazine.'

Jessica said, 'You mustn't pay any attention to Joseph.'

'Michael . . .'

'Well, what?'

Joe said, 'I am your best friend, aren't I?'

I finished the first draft of *Security* and sent it to Bob Sander before making a decision about working with Aubrey. In the final scene, Harry Sandheim is reduced to playing bridge, with marked cards, in the company of three scoundrels, one of whom is, of course, Wolf Wolf, his protective persecutor. I had the idea that all three of them would, in the end, put on Hitler masks as they proceeded to fleece Harry with fair play. In his determination to pretend that the past did not exist, Sandheim would be obliged to relive it as farce.

Bob said, 'I read it at a sitting. The best so far. And the most uncompromising.'

'Is that another word for disappointing?'

'I shall be disappointed if it is, Michael, but there are a few things . . . They're never going to allow the daughter to be stark naked on stage, are they?'

'She can sit in a chair. Screened by other bits of furniture. No one's going to have to see anything the Lord Chamberlain's never seen before.'

'There's also the language.'

'Is English a serious problem with a London audience?'

'Michael, I'm not the enemy. I wish I was. I'd surrender without a shot being fired. Save your ammunition.'

'You don't think anyone's going to want to put it on.'

'Tell me where to send it and I'll gladly supply the stamps. It seems to me, Michael, that the logical next step –'

'I don't want to write crappy musicals. Ned Corman said he wanted to see my next play. This is it. He'd make a marvellous Sandheim. Think what a change it would be after Oliver Chisholm!'

'No reason at all why Ned shouldn't see what's good for him, once he's got *Zenda* out of the way. He's longing to play Rudolf Rassendyll. Which is not the least reason why it makes sense for you to –'

'I don't believe it.'

'Aubers played him a couple of the projected songs at a party of mine the other night – a few people after the theatre – quite impromptu –'

'That's all right, Bob, no call to blush scarlet.'

'With Ned and Sally committed – two of your greatest fans – it seems a shame to let them down. Particularly Ned . . .'

'Now I remember what "uncompromising" means; it means "not wanted on voyage", doesn't it?'

'They're waiting on your decision. Which you did promise Aubrey . . . What do you want me to tell them? If you want them to find someone else, I think you owe it to them to say so before the end of the week. Personally . . .'

I went round to collect Rachel, who was coming to Court Royal for a dinner she was dreading. Happiness made her both beautiful and prickly. At lunchtime she had broken the news to Guy Falcon of her intention to marry David. He wished Rachel well and dared to suggest that she could rely on his availability whenever such reliance appealed to her. He took his relationship with her so seriously that he could respond to its rupture only with amusement. She made no effort to convince him that her feeling for David transcended her desire for an artist whose boldness was the function of a certain despair. The prodigy is always old before his time. In Guy Falcon's case, it now seemed that his time might never come. He had committed himself to a view of art, and of England, which depended on assumptions to which flashier talents were indifferent or hostile. He had become the enemy of those who did not even take the trouble to dislike him. His work was derided by a younger generation (in years scarcely junior to him) who took Guy's fame for granted: why else would they declare it undeserved? Rachel's presence on his arm at the Fitzroy or the French pub or the Eight Bells had served to exasperate those who saw in his early eminence an unfair promotion and in his beautiful companion an unmerited dividend. Rachel knew that her break with Guy appeared to confirm the departure of the god who had once cherished him. He had been in Greece and in Alex during the war and had once declared himself, on an official form, to be a 'gnostic'. He was told by the adjutant that the English for that was 'C. of E.' He smiled and made no objection; when he objected, he always smiled.

My mother followed the kidney soup with roast chicken, roast potatoes, peas and bread sauce. My father very much liked bread sauce, which his mother's housekeeper, Kendall, made to a special recipe. It had required a brave effort on my mother's part to request it from her. Kendall had omitted some minor, but crucial, ingredient (the cloves, I think), with the result that Samuel was pleased by the appearance of the sauce but muted in his appreciation of it. The news of Rachel's intention to marry was answered simply by the word, 'Congratulations'. Carving then became a demanding activity. Plates were passed in silence. Samuel, having precipitated the tension, seemed puzzled by our uneasiness. When he spoke, he felt obliged to use the tone we sometimes referred to as 'summing up', though we never advised him of the fact.

'A distinguished judge,' he said, 'once observed that people attach entirely too much significance to the person they marry.'

'Distinguished judges,' Philippa said, 'often say a lot of very undistinguished things.'

'I should not necessarily deny that. Nevertheless –'

'That is a denial, daddy.'

'Allow me my say, Rachel, at least for another day or two. Nevertheless, if red-haired people were obliged by law to marry only the red-headed, righteously indignant persons would almost certainly chain themselves to railings in pursuit of their inalienable right to marry blondes, or brunettes, or whomever the iniquitous law forbade.'

Rachel said, 'I think you'll like David when you meet him. Chained or unchained.'

'I'm making a philosophical point. The odd thing, if I may finish, being that once the red-haired had finally, and after who knows what courageous campaign, gained access to the blonde or the brunette, and been given the freedom to let the heart rule where once antiquated custom prevailed, no one would, if my guess is correct, turn out to be very much happier than before. The more freedoms we appropriate, the more absurdly we enmesh ourselves in new misfortunes.'

Rachel said, 'I don't remember your having any objection to Owen.'

Samuel said, 'When did I ever object to anyone? If that is your decision, what right has anyone to question it? My only intention was to amuse the company. Poor Yorick, I now know how he felt.'

'Your jokes,' Philippa said, 'have always had a way of making tears run down people's cheeks without first making them laugh.'

'I confess myself confused.'

'You're confused, dad. Others are contused.'

My remark seemed to sting my mother. She stood up and reached for empty plates and clashed them together. 'Does everyone have to be clever all the time?'

'Delicious dinner,' Samuel said. 'Exactly what I had for lunch.'

Philippa stumbled on the way to the kitchen and banged the door when she had reached it.

Samuel said, 'I'm afraid you've upset your mother.'

'I was taking her part,' I said.

'Ah, that's the one she often likes to play for herself.'

Rachel said, 'I shall marry David whether anyone likes it or not.'

'As long as you like it, and he likes it, why worry about anyone else? Unless you do, it hardly seems worth the —'

'Worth the what?' Rachel said.

Samuel said, 'Aren't we getting smoked salmon and champagne? I'm not coming!' He stood up as Philippa came back, oven-gloved hands holding a cabinet pudding. 'It's your decision. After all, you're over twenty-one, aren't you?' As Rachel leaned to kiss him, Samuel gave me a wink. 'Well over.'

Suddenly the three of us were giggling together, as if something had been agreed, or at least talked about, while Philippa was out of the room. When we tried to straighten our faces, we laughed all the more. Philippa put the hot dish on a mat depicting Buckingham Palace and started to weep.

Aubrey Jellinek's 'studio' was in Abbotsbury Court, a block of mansion flats near Holland Park. There was one big room and an alcove with a built-in bed behind a tidy velvet curtain. A white upright piano, a Heal's pine sofa (bright green cushion) and matching chair and a coffee table with tiled top gave the room a businesslike modernity. There was something unguarded about Aubrey's idea of himself. His metal shelves contained song books and professional gazetteers and volumes of jokes and anecdotes and bound editions of *Reader's Digest* publications. Framed photographs of self and girls, self and celebrities, self at first nights, stood on his top shelf and on the radiogram. The clean bathroom had copies of *Esquire* and the *New Yorker* and *Variety* in the neat corner. There was not a moment to be wasted in the pursuit or rehearsal of success. Aubrey was a good host. Coffee (in 'Big A' mugs) was waiting when I arrived for our sessions; the cookies were always crisp. Aubs would have nothing to do with anything that was stale. The room was always aired and the bed was already made and curtained off. Girls were talked about; none was ever present. The telephone rang, often, but I never felt excluded or *de trop*. When we went out to lunch, Aubrey always wanted to pay. 'I'm the one with the dibs *pro tem*; when things change, the smokers'll be on you.' Paying my share, when I insisted that I should, seemed like a form of self-assertion.

It went against the grain to admit it, but working with Aubrey was fun. When I set off from Court Royal in the morning, with the sheets of dialogue I had confected since our last conference, I felt sick with shame, but Aubrey was winningly cheerful and amusing. He was an excellent mimic and a well-informed, unmalicious gossip. Although the lyrics were his business, like the music, he welcomed my suggestions. The show was always referred to as 'ours' and he agreed that I had every right to a number or two in it, if I could come up with a suitable contribution. His capacity for speedy composition was enviable. We would plot a number one evening and the next day he would sit down and offer me 'a brand new slice of ham'. I winced and applauded at the same time. How could I resist, or admire, a number like 'Never Ever Again', designed both for Flavia and Rudolf and for the ignoble market for which its unspecific words were perfectly tailored?

The copy was propped on the white piano and Aubrey did his busking stuff: '"Never ever again/ No parting, starting/ Over again/ Love like this/ Perfect bliss/ Never, ever again/ It's once in a life time/ Husband and wife time/ Now and forever/ Never ever again!"' Or something along those laughably predictable but conceivably commercial lines. What do you think?'

'A characteristic stroke of genius ends Act One with a whimper that is also a bang. Knockout. How do you do it?'

'Let's not change the subject, shall we? Then we reprise it at the end, when old Sapt is about to escort Rudolf to the frontier and we know that he and Flavia will never see each other again. Not a dry hankiepoo in the house or I'm a Dutchman, *mein freund*.'

'Wasn't that where Sapt was going to do "Goodbye, Englishman!"? My modest little contribution to the rhyming repertoire.'

'Yes, sir, that's your baby and you're right to defend it. O.K., got it: we can bung "Goodbye, Englishman!" in before the last reprise. Flavia turns up, against Sapt's orders, for a final farewell . . . You can tickle the book to that effect, can't you, without typing your ribbon to cinders?'

'I don't want my only number so far to be swallowed up or even –'

'Michael, it's our show. Ours. "Yours" and "mine" don't come into it. We're the three musketeers, only we're a man short. And what about that for a musical when we have a spare morning? I'm really pleased we're working together, but you have to trust me. You have to trust yourself.'

I said, 'I thought you said you couldn't write music.'

'I can't. Oh. I've got this friend – you haven't met him – Larry, who's an arranger in his spare time, when he's not composing violin concertos and immortal things like that. He dots it out for me.'

'Not Larry d'Artagnan by any chance?'

'Larry Page. Larry d'Artagnan!'

'Incidentally, Aubrey, who's going to direct this show of ours?'

'Musicals aren't really your *tasse de thé*, are they, directorially? I think there's a good case for you having a hand in staging the book, if that's what you want to do with your time, because I know you've got a new play to tidge up, but we can talk about it when the time comes. Let's settle the words and the music and then we can fight about who does what. I can't wait for Sally to see the new scenes. By the way, one thing, in case it's worrying you: I never cut in on my partners. Women are all very well, bless their beautiful hides, but they rarely write first-class dialogue.'

'Shall I tell her you said so?'

He sat straight down at the piano. ' "Shall I tell her you said so?/ Ned so!/ She has talent and skill/ And may I add she has looks/And cooks?/She's not quite over the hill/ She's a queen, she's an angel/ Change'll/Always be for the worse/ Her life deserves a sonnet/ On it/ But why go from bed to verse?"'

'You're not making this up, George, are you?'

'"Oh I love and adore her/ For her/ I'd give up the Nobel Prize!/ Oh those beautiful lips/ That can and those thighs!/ They're a delectable sight/ And remind me of hips/ That go — *bump* in the night!"'

When the words and the music were complete, Aubrey asked if he could take them down to Tyler's Barn, the Cormans' country house, for the weekend. He happened to have been invited and wasn't it a perfect chance to clinch Ned's allegiance to the project? It was hardly Aubrey's fault that an invitation had come for him and not for me, but I agreed only gracelessly to his plan. My resentment was appeased, not entirely dispersed, by the report of Ned's enthusiasm. Irene was going to make a film in the new year, produced by Charlie Lehmann, who was coming to London specially, so no diplomacy was going to be necessary to persuade her not to play Flavia. Our first choice, Sally, could pass for second best. When the contracts were signed, and I had received my half of the advance (for the 'book'), I asked Sally to come out to '96' for a celebration.

'To celebrate what exactly?'

'I wasn't going to show you till later.'

'Can I wait that long? What?'

'I've taken the plunge — *a* plunge — and found myself somewhere to live. Now seemed a better time than never, so that's what I've done. I'll take you there as soon as they play two sambas in a row.'

She was wearing a white dress with puff sleeves and a blue sash. A slight tan gave her the appearance of having returned recently from an expensive holiday, though not with me. Even when Sally gave me her whole attention, as she seemed to be doing, something made me feel jealous. She danced close to me; she smiled like a very dear friend; she held my hand when the music stopped and her eager breath suggested that we and the evening were young, yet the keenness of her glances around the room, her very enjoyment of the place I had taken her, seemed to serve notice on our intimacy.

'You've turned into quite a dancer,' she said, after I had managed not to step on her on the crowded little floor, where chassis-reverses were luckily out of the question, no matter how many lessons one might have had with Gladys Padgett, teacher of repute. 'No one would think you were the same person I danced with in the old days, would they?'

'Not if they wanted to retain my good will. Sall, are you happy about Aubrey directing and me just, well, supervising the dialogue?'

'If you want to be around, it suits me down to the grind! Frankly, I care more about the next thing you write than anything else.'

'It's already written,' I said.

'I know, and I want to be in it. Up to my neck.'

'Wait till you read it,' I said.

Sally sipped her Matéus Rosé (my notion of economic luxury). 'What makes you think I haven't?'

I said, 'Oh just a little thing like the fact that I gave strict instructions that it wasn't to be shown to a soul.'

'I hate strict instructions, don't you, darling? And I'm not really a soul. Bob did make me promise not to let on, but I find it so hard to deceive you.'

'What did you think?'

'Turning it into a film is a brilliant idea.'

'So brilliant it's the first I've heard of it.'

'With you directing? Don't say no before you say yes, because it's much more what you ought to be doing than . . . oh look! Benny Bligh! Put him in a dinner jacket and he turns into a penguin with malaria.'

'Perhaps it's time to go, what do you say?'

Sally said, 'I love Benny. He's so wicked.'

Benedict saw Sally waving and steered his wife towards us. Karen was in a strapless maroon dress which showed more of thickening shoulders than appetite desired. There was something brave in such ostentatious indifference to age and fashion. She had heavy antique rings on her fingers and gold hoops in her ears. Her hair had been brown, but it was greying at the roots. She had recently published her first novel, *Seconds Out*, and had abandoned make-up, except for a little mascara and a welt of lipstick, to mark the independence it had brought her. She looked at once more contented and more truculent as a result of bestsellerdom.

'So this is where the workers of the world unite!' Benedict said.

'Well, who've you been very, very disappointed to see in such a rotten play tonight, big Benny?'

'Sally Raglan thinks nothing of being the brightest ingénue wasting her time on Oliver Chisholm *and* putting words in my mouth. I can think of all sorts of things I'd sooner she put there. Both of you shall appear in a thoroughly scandalous, but not actionable, light in my Thursday column, see if you don't.'

'Promises, promises,' I said.

'You remember Karen.'

'Congratulations on the book,' I said.

'Charlie Lehmann is nibbling,' Benedict said.

'I hate to drag you away from the quality, Benedict,' Karen said, 'but the royal carriage is without and her brainless little ladyship will shortly be within.'

'I must go and bow and scrape. Such is democracy! Why don't you both join us later? Or have you better things to lick than princesses of the blood? Probably, probably!' As the Blighs moved on, Benedict mouthed inquiries at Sally. There was something at once flattering and demeaning in being the subject of so complex and so vacuous a curiosity. Benedict blessed the ordinary with scandalous allure. His malign glance turned my pre-production celebration with Sally into an amorous rendez-vous. She gleamed with wicked eyes.

'I do adore Benny,' she said.

'Love *and* adore? What's left for the major prize winners?'

'Do you think he was serious? About us joining them later?'

'I think he went a little beyond his station,' I said. 'Surely little ladyship decides who joins them and who merely gawks? Personally, I shall be quite happy to get out and breathe something more oxygenated than cigar smoke, what about you?'

'We didn't come out for an early night, did we?'

'I wasn't thinking of going home for one,' I said. 'I'm longing to show you my place.'

'Imagine if we got her to come to our first night! Isn't it worth hanging around to see what develops?'

The princess was greeted by what was said to be her favourite Lionel Hampton number. She was small and seemed to move in an airmail envelope of silver light. Her tall and saturnine companion appeared to have renounced personality as the price of promotion. He might have been doing something rather shameful. He passed the other patrons of '96' just as a man in custody, but not yet convicted, might sidle through the spectators at the door of a courtroom. Sally was checking her appearance in the mirrored back of a clean spoon.

At St George's, Crawley Down, we studied a green booklet in which, among other elements of English usage, there was a section on correct forms of address. We learned how to apostrophize a bishop, a duke, an earl, a judge, the Pope, a magistrate, a countess and a baron, as well as a king or a queen or a princess. I hoped and dreaded that Sally and I would be summoned to the princess. If I could have wished to avoid formality, I was hardly less apprehensive of casual conversation in which the little green book had afforded me no instruction. I almost wanted Sally to be commanded to the presence without me. To be thus humiliated might be a kind of election. When the waiter came with a note and we had to go across, I wondered only if I should have to dance with the princess. Oh that I might be spared the samba!

Her Royal Highness had not only seen Sally in *A Story So Far*, she had even seen me in the undergraduate revue to which Benedict made prompt allusion. He was the advocate of a generation of iconoclastic playwrights, whose outrageousness he underwrote and whose language he made a point of speaking, especially where it might excite offence. Royalty, I discovered, is never offended: if it is amused, it stays; if it is displeased, it leaves. The princess stayed. Benedict was a fluent courtier: he had no stage fright at all. He stammered only at reality. In the tradition of the fool, he breached all the rules except the one requiring him to entertain. He mocked the princess's escort so deferentially that she was moved to protect him, so leaving him more defenceless than before. Benedict trod the line between insinuation and impertinence with an infallible sense of balance. Like the clown on the high wire, he lurched and faltered only to establish his sure-footedness. His revolutionary ambition was realized in impudent snobbery; he took a gambler's risks, rendered nerveless by the knowledge that he was playing in a doomed currency. The princess might withdraw her favour, but she would then be condemned to the company of her polite companion. If she chose to be teased, if she wanted at once to enjoy and escape from her dignity, she had to endure Benedict's obsequious insolence. In the extraction from H.R.H. of confessions about the stupidity of her family or the charm of guardsmen (about whose alternative sources of income she was persuaded to admit that she knew), and in the mixture of innuendo with assumptions of aristocratic forthrightness, Benedict proved a master. There was no society in which he would not dare to apply for the jester's role. Living dangerously, he could live anywhere. His scorn for society and his desire to shine in it had a common origin. Nothing contemptible was wholly unattractive in his eyes. Rising and falling were a single operation with him. The plot of *Zenda* provided an excuse for speculating on the value, and likelihood, of virginity in royal brides. He wondered whether Flavia, that pure romantic figure, did not know from the beginning that Rudolf Rassendyll was not the king to whom she was betrothed. Her passion was triggered by the prospect of being deceived into marriage with an impostor: only thus could she experience 'the real thing'.

What did H.R.H. think? The danger of self-revelation made the princess sharp, rather than witty, but she was piqued into volubility. Double-talk was her only means of coming clean. Certainly, she did not get up and go when Benedict provoked her. Before she did leave, soon after one in the morning, she had promised to come to the first night of *Zenda*.

In our taxi, Sally said, 'He's such a *schemer* is Benedict! He knows just what he wants.'

'If he did,' I said, 'he'd never be able to get it.'

'Oh Michael,' she said, 'what an evening, really!'

Her lips tasted of strawberries. She sipped my tongue and leaned her golden head against me. Her arm went round my neck and her eyes closed and opened and closed again as she settled with a hyphenated sigh into new and longer kisses. My hand found her breast and she shivered, to allow my fingers to pass more easily under her dress. Her nipple stirred and stiffened. I loved her little gasp of apprehensive encouragement. What did it matter whether it was involuntary or not? If she was acting, she was acting as I wished. Like a disinterested stranger, I congratulated myself on the skill of my campaign. Hope made me cold.

The taxi stopped on Chelsea Embankment. For a moment I could not understand why. Was the driver about to complain at our embrace? He said, 'Is this where you meant, guv?' I looked out at the droop and swoop of the Albert Bridge and the rumpled waters as they moved against the piers, and then I realized that I now lived here and that I had only to get Sally's heat from the taxi to my barge for all my adolescent dreams to come true.

'This is fine,' I said. 'Come on, Sallifer. Our stop.'

She looked out and it might have been raining. She said, 'Oh darling, would you mind frightfully if I took him on?'

'As you ask: yes.'

'Don't think I wouldn't love to see where you live, but I've really got to go home.'

'This is home,' I said.

'Oh Michael, it isn't that I don't want to. It's just that there's something I need.'

'I suspect I may have the very thing.'

'I doubt it. The last thing in the world I want to have happen seems to have happened. It's probably all your fault, getting me excited like this.'

'Are you *sure*?'

'You can't argue with the moon, darling. I wish you could, but you can't. Bad luck, isn't it? But there it is: *and* I shall probably be rotten at the read-through in the morning.'

'Sod the read-through.'

'You wouldn't call me first thing, would you? In case I oversleep. I may have to take something.'

'Sleep here,' I said. 'There's plenty of room your side of the bed and then there'll be no risk of my having to read Flavia to cover your unprofessional behaviour.'

'Darling, I've got to go, honestly, or I'll disgrace myself. I'll take care of the cab.'

She waved to me like a princess as she was driven away. I took my ache across the wooden gangplanks to the black barge which I had rented. It smelt of low tide.

The read-through of *Zenda* took place in a rehearsal room near Finsbury Park. It was convenient for Aubrey, but not for me. When I called Sally's number, before I set off across town, there was no reply. Aubrey was already in the hall, where trestle tables had been arranged in a square with a missing side. Annie Rose, the stage manager, was setting out scripts and yellow pencils, while Aubers strummed his hit number, 'Never Ever Again', on a black upright. By way of evidence that the show was really in production, a proof of the poster was spread on the end of one of the tables.

Aubrey said, 'How was your memorable evening, Michaelovich?'

'It had its moments,' I said, 'you thoroughgoing shit.'

Aubrey said, 'Oh, I want to talk to you about that.'

'I don't want to talk to you about it,' I said. 'I'll talk to Bob Sander about it. I'll talk to my solicitor about it. I'll talk to the Archbishop of bloody Canterbury about it.'

At the bottom of the poster, in immodest letters, was an additional credit, which had never been mentioned to me: 'Devised and Produced by Aubrey Jellinek.'

'I already have, mate. He's not interested. Michael, it's a simple misunderstanding. This is only a proof —'

'And I know what it proves.'

'I don't think that line ought to be in your final draft, mate, quite honestly.'

'What do you know about honesty, apart from what you read in the papers?'

'Would I put this here if I wanted to deceive you? It's a printer's error.'

'Putting it in the proof? I'll say.'

'Why turn hiccups into scarlet fever? I'm going to give them a right rollocking as soon as we've finished the triumphant read-through. You can come with. Trust me, Michael. I trust you.' Aubrey looked quite pleading. Ned Corman, in a brown hat and a tweed cape had put his head round the door. Aubrey said, 'Yes, can I help you?'

Ned put on a husky, alcoholic's croak. 'Dear boy, you're not expecting me to sing this morning, are you?'

'Just dance, Ned, just dance.'

Ned did a few tottery steps. 'That's all right then.' He stopped and took exhausted breaths, with a wink for Annie, leaning both hands on the table. 'What time is it by your ticker?' His tongue lolled comically from his lopsided mouth as he scanned the poster. He swivelled his eyes towards me and I was not sure whether his silence was deploring the artwork or registering my relegation. Annie Rose looked at Aubrey and then at me and shook her head, just once.

I said, 'Nice to see *you* here.'

She said, 'We can't spend our whole lives in Colchester, can we?'

'Unfortunately.'

Aubrey said, 'And how is her majesty this a.m.?'

Sally said, 'Eversowell, ta very much.' She bent to remove the bicycle clips from her painter's overalls.

Annie said, 'It's going to be a lovely show.'

'Every line understandable at the back of the stalls,' I said. 'No sly ambiguities here!'

'I wouldn't say that to look at you,' Annie said.

Jack Fairbairn, who was playing Colonel Sapt, came in with Gerry Lake, who was going to be Fritz Von Tarlenheim. Jack had grown a military moustache and carried a silver-knobbed cane. There was an invisible helmet and crest on his head.

I kissed Sally's cheek. She looked tolerant and surprised, as if I had taken advantage of the occasion. 'This is your alarm call,' I said. 'Are you awake?'

'Oh darling,' she said, 'I went to the park first thing. Did you phone? You are sweet! The bulbs were unbelievable. The colours!'

'Well,' Aubrey said, 'we all seem to be here, some of us, so why don't we make an encouraging start?'

'Before we do,' Ned said, 'Irene was hoping to get along this morning to wish us all luck, but she had to stay overnight in Hastings, poor lamb, on her movie. More munn, less fun! She sends everyone love and longs to catch up with us in Plymouth or Southsea or somewhere maritime like that.'

Jack Fairbairn said, 'A tiny point: there's a line of mine that was in an earlier script, the one I agreed to play, and it doesn't seem to be here any more.'

'Tell you what, Jack,' Aubrey said, 'let's rehearse the lines we're actually going to use, and then, if there's time, we'll rehearse the cuts, what do you say?'

The general laughter did not appease Jack Fairbairn. He gave me a malevolent glance to which I responded, out of cowardice or a desire for almost an ally, with a wince of sympathy, even though I guessed that Aubrey would make me responsible for the curtailment of Jack's part. The 'book', after all, was my minor province.

The cast laughed nicely at my (and Anthony Hope's) jokes, while Aubrey sang and mocked his own songs with a verve that dispelled resentment by fostering the prospect of a success. I was both pleased and displeased. If things went well for me, they would have to go better for Aubrey. Were *Zenda* to be a hit, how could I escape *The Three Musketeers*? Yet how could I wish for failure? Aubrey's performance, as he mimicked the company and coaxed them to believe in him and in themselves, was that of a man who had no doubts. As we moved from the rehearsal room to the theatre in which, if all went well in the provinces, we would open in the autumn, Aubrey cocooned everyone in Ruritanian *Gemütlichkeit*. What he satirized he also believed in. Even as I sighed at his demands for new scenes more insipid even than those they replaced, I conceded that he had a flawless ear: only when he endorsed my revisions did I wonder how it was that I had become the eager supplier of merchandise more cloying than *marrons glacés*. Somehow, the more irksome the work was, as I typed on some hotel table while the others were rehearsing, the more inescapable my bondage seemed to become. I dreaded the hours when I had nothing intolerable to do, when I walked the streets of Plymouth and Nottingham and Southsea, looking in vain for degrading temptation. Aubrey both lacked originality and displayed extraordinary ingenuity. Where did he get the idea of introducing a court jeweller to Strelsau, in order to create a balletic tribute to a local Fabergé, an egg which would hatch a 'clockwork' chorus for Queen Flavia's birthday? He went up to London overnight and came back with the 'top line' of the new number and the sleepy choreographer, 'Big Miguel Cartuja', with whom he had had a working breakfast on the train.

It was a tribute to Aubrey's dedication, and his assumption of my availability, that I postponed mentioning Rachel's wedding until it was not much more than a week away. Would he regard me as a deserter if I spent the weekend in London?

'We don't want to lose you,' he said, 'but you've obviously got to go. I wish I could be there myself, but somebody's shoulder has got to be to the grindstone, hasn't it? It goeth well, don't you agree, mate? Two more weeks on the uphill part and then we roll into London town! You have a good time with smokers and shampoo and we shall try and plod on without you. Any luck with that tiny tidgeypoo on the farewell scene?'

I watched Rachel's wedding as if it too were a rehearsal, a scene for which an unseen director might, at any moment, have an improvement to suggest. Under the ratepayers' chandelier in the Chelsea Register Office we went through the motions of solemnity for some purpose which no one quite knew, without the sanction of a God who, for tactful reasons, could not be represented. David's parents seemed to have been cast in parts they were not entirely sure how to play. My father was at pains to put them at their ease, which left them only very slightly uncomfortable. He assumed that they would enjoy the self-deprecation of his speech, which contained no overt reference to Jewishness while somehow ascribing to the Lucases an expectation of heavily accented foreigners and peculiar food. My father combined blandness of expression with an ironical tone. Modesty in him was always tinged with condescension; deference was salted with disdain.

As I watched Rachel and the man she loved, I set myself against ever making municipal promises. How demeaning it seemed for them to have to play the children's parts, for the sake of a family show from which society had withdrawn its favour! The hired clothes were the symbol of an embarrassment we had procured for ourselves; for want of a larger public, we had to act for each other. Yet David and Rachel were married and set apart; they had seceded from the accidental world I lived in and had emigrated to another, where certainty replaced the scepticism on which, in a society without absolutes, it depended for reinforcement. If society had insisted that the ceremony was a required certificate for their love, David and Rachel would have challenged its importance, but since it was regarded as an almost superfluous rite, it could become evidence of their seriousness. I was torn between amusement (as if I could share their ambivalence) and envy. If I rejoiced, glumly, at my now unquestionable apartness from Rachel, since David had decisively come between us, rendering unnecessary those affectations of closeness which had, in fact, disconcerted us both, I could not deny the luxurious pain of that detachment. My smile, as Rachel said goodbye, alluded already to a lost paradise of confidences which, in fact, we had never shared. Only eviction carried intimations of bliss. The feeling that she shared this unfounded memory made me aware of the desire she lived (it was not a matter of mere appetite, her love for David) and of the jealousy it aroused. I did not desire my sister so much as I desired her desire. It made me think of a film in which a crew on an old ship are captured by cannibals whose discovered existence seduces the sailors into speculation as to which of them will be put in the pot and how he will taste.

When David and Rachel had driven away, I was faced with a lonely night in my barge, and then with a Sunday morning in London, with lunch at Court Royal at the end of it. I decided that I might as well return to Southsea. I had been away since Friday morning and we were due to open on Tuesday. I wanted to give Aubrey no reason to accuse me of unprofessional absence. With any luck, there might be some kind of a party going on at the hotel. I could do with some meaningless experience with Patty Carson or little Renée, if Sally was too busy for me.

None of the cast was in the hotel. Everyone was said still to be at the theatre. It was past ten o'clock when I pushed open the stage door and saw Annie Ross in the little office, trying to be patient on the telephone. 'I'm sorry to bother you at home, Mr Kimmins,' she was saying, 'but it's only because I can't bother you at the office. You may have sent them, but they're not here. We've been here all day; we shall probably be here all night. I know it's difficult, but I want you to put them – or another lot – in a car and get them down here. Your best, on past form, Mr Kimmins, isn't likely to be good enough. I'm not doing anything of the kind. When I scream . . . Thank you.' She put down the telephone, made a weary face and then screamed, twice. 'No plumes for the British ambassador, no medals for His Majesty, no sleep for the wicked, or even for the innocent. No one expected to see you tonight, Michael.'

'Anything right?'

'They've done the new number – without the Order of the Bath – seven times and Aubrey's still tinkering.'

'What new number?'

'When the British ambassador gives the king Queen Victoria's love and instructs him in how to be an English gentleman. How long have you been away? Oh and how was the wedding?'

'Bibulous. How did the run-through go?'

'It didn't. It's still with us. Ten hours in labour and we still don't know if it's a boy or a girl. Sheer bliss.'

'I had no idea it was going to be another invasion of Russia. Aubs said everything was under control when I left. He even said not to hurry back. He talked about Monday, but I thought . . .'

'Perhaps you'd better get scrubbed up,' Annie said, 'and into the delivery room.'

'How's Sally?'

'Knockout,' Annie said.

'You don't think she's a little young for Ned?'

'That's just the age he likes them, isn't it?' She was checking one of her lists. She took the pencil from behind her ear and rubbed her scalp with the blunt end. She looked tired and brave and just a little uncomfortable. 'Michael –'

'Annie, is something going on?'

'Plenty,' she said.

I wanted to stay in the little office with her, but then I heard Jack Fairbairn's I-have-done-the-Classics voice as he said, 'I will not give in to blackmail, Mr Producer!'

Aubrey said, 'You speak for all of us, Jack.'

'Not intentionally,' Jack said. 'I have just one substantial number in the show. And about thirty lines. Thirty-eight at the outset. Of which you now propose to cut about eighteen.'

'Twelve,' Aubrey said.

'You should have been an accountant,' Jack said.

'And you,' Aubrey said, 'should have been an actor.'

'That's it,' Jack said. 'That's it, that is definitively it.' He turned to Ned Corman, whose frogged jacket was unbuttoned and whose attention was devoted to Sally. She was being professional about a bit of business which had not been going right. She tried it again and it clicked and she leaned her head against Ned's Balkan breast and closed her eyes. Jack seemed to have left belongings in all the corners of the stage. Collecting them required considerable marches. When he was looking for his pen, very close to Renée Peterson (Black Michael's mistress), she said, 'Jack sweetheart!'

Jack Fairbairn said, 'I will not be a sprat to catch a mackerel.'

Aubrey said, 'Jack you may be, sprat you will never be. No one's cut anything yet. We're simply trying to evaluate the options. What we all want more than anything else, Jack, is a successful show, isn't it? Why else do you think you're here?'

Jack said, 'Don't try and smooth me down like a – like a –'

Ned Corman said, 'Don't look at us, Jack. This isn't the prompt corner, old cock.'

There was a moment, the French's edition would have said, of pure horror. A corporate intake of breath might well have been indicated. But Ned Corman's outrageousness defused the situation it also brought to a head: the breaths taken in with horror emerged as laughter. Jack Fairbairn said, 'You are pure evil, Ned Corman,' and then he was laughing too. 'Blast you!'

Only Aubrey, in blue shirt sleeves and Fair Isle waistcoat, seemed unrelieved. As I stepped out of the wings, in my best suit, he gave me a razor-edged smile. 'About time too! Where the hell have you been?'

'My sister got married,' I said. 'Remember?'

'Married! I should think she's had twins by now. With another set in the pipeline. Now where are you going?'

'Back to the hotel to find your apology waiting for me. If it isn't, I shall draw the necessary conclusions.'

Aubrey took long steps after me into the wings where the

dungeon of Zenda was stacked against the wall. 'Michael, come on, we're partners. If we can't say unforgivable things to each other, who can? This is no time for argy-bargy.'

'Give me a time and a place where I can call your sister a whore in front of the assembled company with impunity and I'll be there.'

'I'm trying to make your show into a hit. And I could do with some help. You can take a joke, can't you?'

'Where the hell did you get that idea?'

Ned Corman said, 'Are you two having a good holiday? How's the weather been?'

Aubrey said, 'Action stations, Michael! We'll be right there, Ned. D-day, Michael. We're hitting the beach. Don't let me down now. Please. If I said something stupid, I apologize. This is my hand, O.K.? All for one and one for all. It's the only way.' He put his arm around my shoulder and we walked back towards the stage. 'By the way, you were right: we may – *may* – have to cut "Goodbye, Englishman!"'

I said, 'Jack'll go through the roof. And so will I, dammit.'

Aubrey said, 'You can use the same hole.'

'It's not only his only number in the show; it's also, as you may recall, my only number in the show.'

'Yours and mine don't mean anything now. Trust me, Michael. Trust yourself, because you were the one who saw that "Goodbye, Englishman!" – good as it is, and it is – was getting in the emotional way of "Never Ever", which is our banker. Trust me, Michael, and consider the options carefully before you say anything.'

'Including "fuck you"?'

'Abuse is a luxury. Wait till we've had a hit and then you can afford it, to the sound of trumpets.' Aubrey clapped his hands. 'Right away then, everybody, if it has to take that long. Have we got playback for "Suddenly"? Ted?'

'All set, Aubrey,' Ted said, from the flies, and then there was a flash and the whole theatre went dark. The EXIT signs brightened in the black.

'Off we go then,' Aubrey said.

'Shan't be a tick.' A working light went on and we were all glaring whitely at each other. 'Chat among yourselves for a moment or two, boys and girls.'

Sally said, 'Was it a lovely wedding and did Rachel get my wire?'

'It was; she did. Thank you very much.'

'Don't worry, darling,' Sally was on tiptoe to kiss my forehead. 'It's all going to be wonderful. Ned's been magic today.'

'I hear the girl hasn't been too bad either.'

'Aubs is on the gravity tank though, squadron leader. Don't lean on him too hard, will you?'

Jack Fairbairn was saying, 'I've always been a team man, always. Ned, you'll bear me out?'

'I've never known you to give yourself a second thought,' Ned said. 'A trouper, Jack. Through and through. Always were.'

Sally said, 'Jack's such an old fraud. *And* he can't sing. Your number doesn't sound half as good as it should. It's the sauce, isn't it?'

'If "Goodbye, Englishman!" goes, I go.'

'It's something I thought we ought at least to discuss – how goes it, chief? – because it's the only honest way,' Aubrey said. 'We're all in this together. Alternatively, I can go through the show tonight and tell everyone what I've decided in the morning. This seemed like the mature way, but . . .'

The lights came on. The cheers and applause made Aubrey smile. How had he had time to shave during the course of his day? His cheeks were as smooth as his tongue.

'Look, chaps, we've got a hit on your hands. You should've seen the cleaning women during the farewell scene! Let's not ruin our chances by over-egging the omelette. It won't damage anyone's plans if we run for eighteen months, will it? Hands up!'

Jack said, 'I haven't agreed to start a new life as an extra.'

Ned Corman said, 'Jack old man, why don't you sleep on it?'

Aubrey said, 'I'll resist the obvious.'

'Rather late in the day for that, isn't it?' Jack said.

'I'm sorry?'

'Likewise your apology, Mr Producer.' Jack stood up and walked off the stage. We watched him go.

Sally had her arm through mine and held me to her. 'Oh, I do so wish you'd been here all day.'

'I'll be here all night,' I said, 'if that's any use to you.'

Ned Corman stood up and straightened his trousers and put his hands through his hair. We were waiting for the playback when Ned dropped the character of Rudolf and became himself. Irene Jameson was coming down the aisle in several thousand pounds' worth of ranch mink. She might have been cued for a scene calling for the entrance of an undoubted star at the peak of her beauty. If she was no longer a girl, she was a magnificent woman. 'Work, work, work,' she said. 'Do you people never stop?'

'Darling!' Ned jumped over the orchestra pit and stood as still as an acrobat in the space in front of the first row of seats. 'Don't tell me you've wrapped.'

'All good overage comes to an end,' Irene said, and then she was in his arms and they were lovers, oblivious to the presence of those for whom they were performing. Antony greeted Cleopatra, Benedick Beatrice, Romeo Juliet, without smudging her lipstick or disturbing her hair. 'Whatever's wrong with Jack Fairbairn?'

'Darling, do we have time?'

'I met him on the way out.'

'He's been on it for years.' Elyot made Amanda smile. 'Presumably he gave you all the good news?'

'Yes.' Irene was my father's equal in the protraction of simple monosyllables.

'Change of plan frankly acknowledged,' Aubrey said. 'I suspect we've all had more than enough for one night . . .'

'What way is that to talk to a lady?' Irene said.

Aubrey blushed. Bold speech from women turned him into a small-town boy. 'I suggest a resumption at ten in the morning. If Jack isn't here, Quentin, perhaps you'd make a point of being? A promotion to Colonel seems more than likely to be gazetted.'

Sally said, 'Darling, is it too late for something to eat, do you suppose?'

I took her to a fish restaurant across the green from Queen's Hotel. We moistened our old hake with a bottle of Château Court-les-Muts. David and Rachel had gone to the Dordogne in his M.G. How long would it be before I could afford what Aubrey called 'a wagon'? The wish to be done with the humiliations of *Zenda* warred with craving for the independence which royalties (and film rights) might bring.

Sally and I walked towards the hotel arm in arm. I stopped in the middle of the green and kissed her. She said, 'Oh darling, I'm totally exhausted. We've been on parade for hours and hours. My knees are giving.'

'That sounds promising,' I said.

'Just think,' she said, 'Rachel's married. Lucky, lucky thing!'

Ned and Irene had been served with *foie gras* and champagne, compliments of the Italian manager. We could see them through the modernized doors of the dining room. Sally put her arms round my neck as Ned and Irene threw down their napkins and came in our direction.

Ned was saying, 'I've missed you so much.'

'Have you?'

'Ask anyone.'

'I already have. I asked Jack.'

'Didn't he tell you?'

'He did indeed.'

With unobtrusively neat timing, we were all standing together at the lift. 'I hear you're quite wonderful, Miss Raglan,' Irene said.

'Ah, but I *know* you are, Miss Jameson!'

They were determined to appreciate each other's poise. Sally, as the younger, deferred to Irene when the lift doors opened; Irene, as the queen, took precedence without hesitation. Ned put his hand on my shoulder and gave me one of his lop-sided smirks. Buttons were pressed.

I said, 'I suppose I'd better go and report to Aubrey for the night shift.'

Sally said, 'Oh darling, don't do that. Not now. Please. Take me to my door at least.'

Ned rolled his eyes for Irene, whose lips twitched and then were straight again. He took her hand and did his notorious nonchalance as we all got out at the fourth floor. 'Goodnight, children, goodnight!'

'Goodnight, goodnight. Sleep well.' Sally might have been their daughter.

As Sally and I walked down the corridor, Irene turned to Ned and I heard her say, 'Is she . . . ? Are they . . . ?'

'Grew up together, my love. Why? Do you fancy him?'

'I'm going to kill Jack Fairbairn.' Irene was still looking at us when we reached Sally's door. I kissed her on the cheek as she opened it. She put her arms round me and tugged me against her and into the room.

She was very slim when she came out of the bathroom. She jumped into bed and put her arms and legs around me and laughed. Then she kissed me thoroughly and lay on her back, awaiting inspection. Her breasts were smaller than I expected and were lightly chalked with powder. She had powdered her tuft of golden hair too. I could hardly believe that she would not still find some way of denying me, but she lifted her knee when my lips grazed her thigh. Her leg rolled to one side so that I could taste the powder. She said, 'Oh darling, oh Michael, oh lover!'

I made her pay in pleasure for the years I had waited since I saw her in the doorway of the basement ballroom. She would be sorry for what she had denied me, and herself. My desire was sustained by revenge. What I did for her and what I did to her were the same: love and its counterfeit were one. As she cried out, loud enough to challenge the discreet architecture, I was pounding with an emotion too strong for identity: I felt without knowing what I felt. I stayed in her and began again. I told myself that I did not need the encouragement of the educated fingers that found their way under her thigh. I withdrew and turned her over and began again. Her breasts were hanging into my palms and her back arched. I wanted to be her master. I thought of other things and of nothing else. She put her head down on her pillow and I pumped her slim hips. She said, 'Oh my goodness! Why ever didn't we do this sooner?'

'I did propose it,' I said, 'but I could never find a seconder.'

Sally flopped down at last and grinned over the turreted pillow. 'She must have been wonderful.'

'Who's that then?'

'Your *petite Française*.'

'*Christ!*' I said.

'What's the matter?'

'What's the matter? What do you think?'

'Oh darling, *that*'s all right,' Sally said.

'How can you be sure?'

'I read the instructions very carefully. Better safe than mother.' She turned and propped herself on one arm. Her tight breast glistened and bobbed. 'Darling, I know it's not for me to say . . .'

I kissed her softening nipple. 'Say it, say it. What?'

Sally said, 'Jack Fairbairn.'

'Emendation to the foregoing,' I said. 'You may say anything but Jack Fairbairn.'

'He's a trouble-making old sod. I wish —'

'I wish the same thing, but we open on Tuesday. How can we possibly dump him?'

'You do agree he makes Banquo look like an ideal guest?'

'I thought we didn't make references to the Scottish play when we hadn't got our clothes on. Jack *is* a bit of a pill, I grant you.'

'I was only thinking that if we cut "Goodbye, Englishman!", which is truly a lovely, lovely number but it does seem to hold things up a bit, and sort of deflect the story at the last moment —'

I said, 'You haven't by any chance been in bed with uncle Aubers among an already large cast, have you?'

She twisted away from me and was sitting on the edge of the bed, fighting with her dressing gown sleeves. 'Doesn't what – what happened – doesn't it mean anything to you at all?'

'It means everything,' I said.

'Then everything doesn't mean very much.' She kicked her feet into her slippers and walked towards the door. 'When I think of how much it meant to me.'

'Where are you going? This is your room. Is there any sense in reporting to Aubers at this hour?'

'And I thought you really loved me. Do you think I'd ever have let you do the things you did if I imagined for a second that you were going to be like this? I was trying to *help*.'

'You can't seriously blame me for being suspicious about Aubrey. He's always up to something.'

'Never with me, honey. You have my solemn word. I don't think he's got a hair on his body, do you? I certainly don't want to find out. Anyway, doesn't he have somebody?'

'Don't know, don't care. Yes, probably. I don't think he needs her more than once a year.'

'It'd be like being in bed with the Wall's Ice Cream man, wouldn't it?'

'You know what he wants, don't you?'

'He won't be getting it from little Sall.'

'My name off this show.'

'Over my dead body,' Sally said. 'Ned feels the same way.'

'It's been discussed then, has it?'

'Not in so many words.'

'In a few terse Tacitean phrases?'

'You're over my head, sweetie. I'm a simple suburban miss, remember?' She lifted her slender, cool arms and put them round my neck and had to kiss me again. She settled against me and one of her hands dropped into my lap. It was as if her fingers smiled at what they found. 'Oh love!'

I said, 'God, I wish we were making that movie, just the two of us.'

'We will, Michael. I promise you. In good time. Just so long as

216

you don't blame me for getting you into this?'

'This?' I said. 'Any time!'

'I meant the show,' she said.

'To hell with the show. God, you're beautiful. You're so beautiful.'

'Oh that is nice. You were right.'

'I often am,' I said.

'It's just lovely. I'll have to upset you more often.'

'What the hell does some bloody musical comedy matter to me anyway? I never wanted to do it and it was never mine in the first place, was it?'

'I was sure that was how you felt. Will this really work? Oh, that's nice, that's lovely! You're absolutely right: it'd be really silly to be upset about the new scenes.'

I said, 'New scenes?'

'What do you think we were rehearsing all day? He did show them to you, didn't he?'

'New scenes. You mean the new number. The British ambassador.'

'That's all part of it. He's simplified the dialogue in a few places and he's rewritten the first meeting between me and Ned, so that we get to "You're A Different Man" more quickly. I assumed you knew. Oh, don't go away!'

'Well, well, your excellency! There's *another* new number for you.'

'Do I understand?'

'That's what they call ambassadors, isn't it? Your excellency? How long have you been rehearsing this particular little bit of business? You'll get the Order of the Bath for this, my pretty darling.'

'Michael, where are you going? What's the matter with you? It's not very nice of you to treat a girl like this.'

'You were on your way before. Don't let me keep you now. Tell him I've taken it very badly indeed. As he might expect. I'm going to see Bob Sander as soon as I get back to London and if I have any rights at all –'

'Michael, what's this got to do with *me*? Why are you being so vile? Do I really deserve this after . . . ?'

'Isn't it a little late in the second act for the virgin sacrifice number?'

'No one's saying you're not hugely talented, but you weren't here, and when a scene doesn't work, you have to do something about it, don't you?'

'Well, this one doesn't. So what are you going to do about it?'

'And you say you love me! You don't love anything except . . . You've just taken advantage of me, that's all. You make me feel disgusting, ashamed, and . . . defiled. To think that I seriously thought that you and I . . . it's horrible of you. Horrible!'

'He's a crook and a shit and you let him use you. Tell him I said so.'

Jack Fairbairn and I were the only people on the platform for the early train to London. We ignored each other at first and then we drifted closer together and finally we climbed into the same compartment with our bags and our wads of newspaper. As the train did its double lurch before rolling out of the station, I said, 'This is the one for Siberia, isn't it?'

Jack Fairbairn said, 'Waterloo.'

The princess was at the first night in Shaftesbury Avenue. The lights advertised NED CORMAN and SALLY RAGLAN in AUBREY JELLINEK'S ZENDA. The show was, of course, devised and produced by the author. Benedict Bligh wrote:

THE FLAVIA OF THE MONTH

Emigration is not only to another place, it can also be to another time. On the Rings-a-Belle-Epoque face of it, *Zenda* ignores everything that happened after 1910. It cuts modern history dead. Dedicated to profit and floss, it heaps sugar on candy and is no more acid than Château Yquem. The songs make Sigmund Romberg sound like an innovator and the wedding waltz was probably found in the Strauss family's abandoned picnic basket in the Vienna woods. Here is an olde worlde where a villain can be recognized by the curl of his lip and the thickening of his eyebrows. In the only Balkan state whose classier inhabitants speak perfect English (the lower orders stick to Mummerset in the country and have difficulty viz their consonants in town), Ned Corman's Rudolf Rassendyll has, as one would expect of our most versatile and ageless *primo don*, little difficulty in taking the king's part at very short notice. *Zenda* might be a rather stale slice of *Forêt Noire*, a gyp off the old Bach, did it not offer, with brazen coyness, so dated a contrast with the kind of theatre to which, in sermonizing mood, I have lent my socially conscious approval, that it becomes the flavour of the month, perhaps of the year. Its charm may be the result, in large part, of a calculated assault on our tear ducts (the better to gain access to our wallets), but not the most cynical script-conference could procure a performance of the heart-rending, nicest-possible-kind-of-lust-stimulating quality such as that given by Sally Raglan. Miss Raglan has always threatened to be very good indeed. Her threat is now proved to be, like her bodice, anything but empty. A star is not born; it has come of age. You would swear, if you were as naive as I, that you were witnessing a real romance between the Englishman and the princess who is his for today but never tomorrow. The plot is old enough to belong to the department of MittelEuropan antiquities; the dialogue creaks like Black Michael's dungeon door; the songs are of the kind which, as it was once witty to say, you go into the theatre whistling. What matter? *Zenda* has nothing whatever to recommend it except a great actor on holiday from all the things he ought to be doing and an actress of such beauty that all further resistance, as Rupert of Hentzau remarks, is pointless. Only being British can prevent Sally Raglan from entering the lists of world stardom. Aubrey Jellinek's direction is most admirable when it stands aside like a flunkey and lets Rudolf and Flavia transform improbable pap into the food of the gods – and the dress circle, and the stalls. This one, *mein damen und herren*, vill valtz and valtz.

VI

My life on Chelsea Embankment was that of a gregarious hermit. I told myself that I had chosen and enjoyed my solitude, but I took no great pleasure in it. When I turned on the wireless, songs from *Zenda* poisoned my fugitive complacency. The stink of the Thames, at low tide, reminded me of the realities of what others took to be a romantic life. I had turned my back on triviality only to be conscious of the thinness of my own purposes. I worked on a new play, telling myself that I was grateful for the silence entailed by the inability to afford a telephone. Why then did I find reasons to call Bob Sander and why was I depressed all morning by an absence of post? I swore to Barnaby and Claudia, when they had me to their new house in Norland Square, that I rejoiced in being an absentee resident in London, no longer obliged to mundane regularities. Yet if I resisted journalism, I accepted scripting jobs in television. When I broke off my serious work to meet a deadline, I rejoiced in prompt applause from producers and directors for whose intelligence, had they not had power over me, I should have had no time at all.

The day was at once endless and too short. If I had no company in the evening, I would go up to the King's Road and see a film on my own. Pubs repelled me. I hated the smell of beer even as I envied the conviviality of those who seemed so easily to make friends. I was not a humbug, because I knew my own absurdity, but I could not quite remain the unswerving artist whose vanity could carry him, without a wistful glance, through the wilderness days. At night, mortified by how little I had done, I would type in the silence, rattling the keys with a fury which passed for passion. My loneliness was an act of principled resentment; it made sense to me only if others were aware of it. It was a performance.

I listened with apprehensive hope when I heard footsteps on the gangway which linked the barges to the shore. I sighed when there was a knock on the door and told myself not to hurry to open it. I threw the candlewick coverlet over my bunk and checked that the books on my packing case table were of suitable quality. Who knew what emissary of high culture might not be at my narrow door? I was a peninsular Philoctetes, semi-marooned in my rueful serenity, determined not to yield to the world's demands, but not wholly incurious as to the form they might take. Alone, I lived in the light of a phantom companion whose good opinions I sought to deserve and of whose mockery I did not fail to be aware.

The footsteps which came to my door one Thursday morning had heels. The knock was of nervous knuckles. I typed on for a couple of speeches, until my Underwood keys interlaced. Then I cursed in the Bohemian style and took a long step to the door as the knock was repeated. 'Michael?'

'He's not here.'

'Michael,' Sally said, 'you're not going to be horrible are you?'

'Are you in a position to expect me to change the habits of a lifetime?'

'Please. Because it took quite a lot of courage for me to come here like this.'

'I'll tell you something funny,' I said, 'well, fairly funny. Totally unamusing really. I never got your lovely, lovely letter sympathizing for the way Aubrey Jellinek – you remember Aubs – double-crossed me in spades, diamonds and clubs. Hearts he left to you, didn't he? Oh, it's all right, it's all right – I know why: you never bloody well wrote it, did you, darling?'

'I say, number one, the flak's hells thick over Chelsea Reach this merry a.m., eh what? Perhaps we should scrap the mission and return to Biggin Hill, before we get seriously pranged!' She ducked under the low lintel (wearing a red and white ski cap with a big bobble) and took off her short duffel coat. 'Oh honestly, Michael, you're so old-fashioned sometimes!'

'You spotted the crinoline,' I said. 'Like it?'

'You were the one who walked out. Nothing to do with me. Oh, I didn't *blame* you, but I did feel a bit let down.'

'Little Red Riding Hood, what big eyes you've got! Do you want anything? Presumably, because why would you be here otherwise?'

'It's no use waiting to be invited, is it? I didn't know men went into Purdah until I met you. Talking of invitations, are you conceivably free the weekend after next? Ned and Irene are having some people down to Tyler's Barn and they wondered if I'd ask you.'

'No, thank you. No, thank them.' I sat down again at the typewriter and dirtied my fingers on the snagged keys. 'Who?'

'Who what?'

'Are they having down?'

Sally said, 'The bear who lived on a barge! Sore head and all! Charlie Lehmann mostly. Irene's producer on *Royal Highness*. He's got a movie he wants to talk to you about, but I'm sure you're right to stick to *Water Police*. That episode you did about the theft that never happened was brilliant.'

'If you did my play,' I said, 'I wouldn't have to get seasick, would I?'

'I couldn't help *Zenda* running as long as it did, could I? I hope you got something out of it eventually. I thought we could drive down to Tyler's Barn together. It'd give us a chance to really –'

'I haven't got a car. And we'd never both fit in one of my Dinky toys.'

'We can take mine. You know how much Ned admires you. It's a real opportunity to mend some bridges.'

'Not as much as he admires you, from what I hear.'

'You've been reading Benny Bligh's column.'

'Hasn't everybody? Including Irene, presumably.'

'Ned's very worried about her, Michael. She's so . . . unpre-

dictable. That's why he wants this weekend to be, well, *civilized*.'
She took cigarettes and a folder of matches from her tote bag and
looked anxiously at me, as if she had more business to do than
the dialogue would quite cover. The gleam of wordless panic in
her eyes reminded me of how much I had missed her. 'It's for her
sake that . . . oh *buttons*!' As she struck one of the weak matches,
it flared and ignited the others. She flipped the folder from her
on to the black floor. It turned into a flat firework, spurting
flame. I put my shoe on it and that was that. 'Oh darling, I'm so
sorry.'

I kissed her cheek and felt her breasts against my shirt. 'No
need to take your clothes off just for that,' I said.

She said, 'I have missed you, in spite of all the horrid, horrid
things you always say to me. We did have a wonderful night
together, didn't we? Whatever you say.'

'Yes,' I said.

She grinned and looked at her neat watch.

'Is that the time already?' I said. 'You must fly!'

'Be glad you're not an actress. I've got to go and see a beastly
man with eight hands who wants me to be in his new musical. I
wish I didn't. Saturday week. Ten o'clockish? I'll come and call
for you, if you like.'

'Give Aubrey my love,' I said.

When Sally had gone, I could wonder why I had given in so
easily, but I could also persuade myself that I had given in more
coldly than she might imagine, which left a little secret change
from the transaction. Even without a witness, how truthful was
it possible for me to be about how I felt? Sally's betrayal was,
after all, an aspect of her charm. Would she have been so
delicious and so accessible, in Queen's Hotel, Southsea, if her
desires had been the expression only of her feelings? How sweet
and how bitter it was to know that she had been so ingenious in
the promotion of her career, in the seduction of the great world
whose good opinions she craved! Her body had responded to
ambition as if it were a wholly natural and irresistible thing.
It had moistened and stiffened her, I did not doubt, more

thoroughly than my well-read caresses. (Oh the hours at Charing Cross Road counters, in my second-hand years, reading about the perfection of marriage – always marriage – by the variety of positions and the anatomical accuracy of one's strokes!) She had come back, not for more love but because – I feared and hoped – there was still some profit to be gained by her ability to produce me, no matter how much of a rabbit I might be, from her fetching little hat. It was both demeaning and delicious to be the subject of such calculations. My independence was defined by those who sought to compromise it.

When Joe Hirsch sent word, through Bob Sander, that he would like to see me, I took pleasure in reversing the charges from the call box on Beaufort Street, but I did not fail to get in touch. *Black and White* was edging towards sales of seventy-five thousand. Its mixture of satire and obsequiousness, of gossip and chic, of muck-raking and trend-setting meant that no one could say that he had liked it or that he had not seen it. Scorn was a form of endorsement to which Joe made no objection, as long as those who despised the magazine also subscribed to it. His office in Bothwell Court had a W.1 postmark and a W.C.2 ambience. It was stacked with books and records, the evidence more of how keenly he was solicited than of artistic preoccupation. There were a couple of black leather chairs and a draughtsman's board in the window. They deserved a larger space than they occupied, and a smarter address; they were the mute promise that *Black and White* would soon be moving. The stairs were narrow and uncarpeted and the rest of the staff worked in partitioned hutches on the ground floor.

Joe said, 'Cigar?'

'You didn't really say that, did you?'

'Chester wants to talk to you.'

'Since when did you smoke cigars?'

'Since Havanas got hard to get. Why shouldn't I? Jessica's father. He wants somebody to do something for him on film. I thought of you. He's a good man to have in your corner.'

'If you want to see it turned into an office block he is.'

'Imagine if we could interest him in feature films.'

'We? As in me and you?'

'There are things that need to be dealt with. Capital punishment. How do you feel about capital punishment?'

'I'll let you have a list of candidates if you promise it won't be quick or painless. Where do I see him, if I see him?'

'He's not like you imagine, Michael, you know.'

'And how do I imagine him?'

'The cantilevered shoulders, the stainless steel tie, the Fort Knox cuff-links, the monogrammed condoms . . .'

'He really isn't like that? I don't want to see him.'

A few days later, I set off, in clean corduroys and an open-necked grey shirt, to see Chester Flam in his Belgravia office. The building wore his company's grey-on-grey logo, in steatite relief, but it was disappointingly unpretentious. The lobby had a black and white checkered floor and the hot lift had Axminster walls, but the penthouse advertised the modesty of its owner. He could hardly be reproached for the charm of the view or for the generosity of the cold cuts. He ate only a single slice of turkey. The model of his latest development was the smoothest of toys, but there were no expensive pictures or intimidating furniture. His secretary was called Beryl. She must have been fifty and, judging by her looks, very competent.

'Do you know Harrow Green at all? It's not near Harrow and it's not green.' When we inspected the model, I could almost see over Chester Flam's head. He was in his mid-fifties and wore a brown suit with a reddish stripe, like a thin trace of pencil on brown paper. He seemed to have elected to be neither flashy nor a counterfeit gentleman. His voice was of the same pattern: he spoke quietly, without low-life affectations or transplanted plumminess. His brown hair was, I suspected, wirier than it had been but it was not yet grey. He had a fighter's nose, with a horizontal nick in it, as if a big hat had once been forced down over it. 'You know what I do, don't you, Mr Jordan?'

'I'm told you buy up property that nobody wants until you've bought it. And then they want it so badly you can get a bad name by selling it to them.'

'Have some more to eat. The cheesecake's not bad. Personally I'd sooner live another couple of years, but it's all according. Harrow Green is somewhere I want to do something a little bit special. They had a land mine in the war, one of Mr Hitler's, killed an auntie of mine. I'd like to do something'll knock their eyes out. I'm a man runs into a lot of opposition, you may have heard. I'm not surprised; I'm not angry. Are you one of these young men's supposed to be angry about everything?'

'Of course.'

'You like to say things to people, don't you? For me, anger is a luxury. I must still be saving up. You, you can afford it, enjoy yourself. I've got Ronald Bird and Associates working on it, if that means anything to you. The best. Six-acre site. They win a lot of prizes: never cut a corner unless they put a nice kerb on it. Taste. I like the best. You get the top people and then you see what they can say about what you're doing. They'll find something. That's my little pleasure, if you must know. Not money, doing things properly, to see what the rest of them make of it. Harrow Green. Here's what's in my mind: a little educational exercise. Documentary record of the whole development. From the first stages, which are now, to the topping out which is . . . whenever, or – if past experience is anything to go by, when it comes to contractors – a little later than that. You don't wear a tie. Is that for health reasons?'

'Yes.'

'What's wrong with you then?'

'It's to prevent anything being wrong with me.'

'Car's downstairs. If you want anything else to eat, you'd better put it in your pocket. Joseph Hirsch an old friend of yours?'

'I'm too young to have old friends,' I said. 'We were at school together. Were you born in England, Mr Flam?'

'Antwerp,' Chester Flam said. 'But I came to England before I

227

had to apologize for being here. I don't. I don't apologize for anything.'

There was a green chauffeur-driven Jaguar XJ6 at the door. Chester Flam sat in the corner of the car and asked me if I minded a pipe. His small, manicured hand held the tassel by the window. He looked out at London as if it were his favourite reading. Now and again he would glance through the back window and smile; one could not be sure whether it was because he had won or lost a bet, or with whom.

'St George's, Harrow Green.' We had stopped in a barren tract of land, somewhere north of Wembley. In the middle of the beaten earth was a large Victorian church, a dusty layer cake of red and white brick. The red had staled into brownness and the white into carious grey. The windows had been punctiliously vandalized: each diamond pane smashed individually. Wide steps at the front, with a central banister, went up to a boarded double doorway. Below the steps, the obscenities on a wooden hoarding were signed Isaiah. 'Would you call that a thing of beauty at all?'

'Presumably it would have to depend on the deal.'

'Believe it or not – that's a building some crackpots want to put a preservation order on. Blackmail? Not necessarily. Blackmail I can pay. I think they believe what they say. Beautiful! I can't see it. Who's Harrison Digby, mean anything to you?'

'The defender of Madeira cake, Marble Arch and the heroic couplet? Is he threatening to rhyme you with spam?'

'Young Hirsch says you're clever.'

'He doesn't mean any harm,' I said.

'This Harrison's threatening to come to the public inquiry. He's never given me trouble previous. Now he's coming to the inquiry, bringing the press, making a stink. He's going to have people there, we can have people here. You, Mr Jordan.'

I said, 'Are you hoping that the presence of a film crew will shame him into withdrawing his objections, is that what I'm doing here?'

Chester Flam said, 'I want to make a point. You always talk this way to people? You'll have a free hand.'

'The one that's tied behind my back presumably.'

Chester Flam took new flame to his pipe. 'If I've wasted your afternoon, I can have you driven home right away. Or are you so clever you want to walk? Better for you.'

Bob Sander told me that for some reason Chester had liked me. He wanted to see what kind of a film I might make. What real purpose could he possibly have in persisting? Was it simply a matter of vanity, the refusal of rejection? His character did not suggest it. The deal he proposed was hard to resist: no interference from him or his people, all expenses paid and a couple of thousand for myself. He was even prepared to hire union labour, so that the finished product could be shown in public. He might find some way of interesting one of the television companies. It would all take more of my time than I ought to spend on such peripheral matters, but I was being paid to experiment and, most attractively of all, I was being offered my first small command. Resolved not to give Chester quite what he expected, I could see no reason not to accept.

Harrison Digby wore a sagging yellow cardigan, a chapped sports jacket with scuffed leather elbows, flannel bags with a school tie for a belt, and a pork pie hat from under which well-known wisps of grey hair blew in the breeze. He was so unreluctant to perform for our camera that I almost suspected collusion between him and Chester Flam. His pink face and puce lips flowered with good will as he prepared to perform a little elegy he had written. 'Immense fun,' he said, 'all this, don't you find? Indecent fun!'

In a quiet tone, I said, 'Action', as if I had said it before.

Digby walked up the steps of St George's, with his shooting stick under his arm, turned and declaimed:

'We took the Met or the lurching trolley,
Peered at the Pink 'Un damp from the brolly.

Then the sirens wailed at the Heinkels' whine
And fire bombs fell on North West Nine.

The dawn came up and still St George's stood.
Proudly we said, 'It's there for good!'
To hell with Hitlers and with Neros!
V for victory and a land for heroes.

The world's made safe, and Britannia's free,
Long live the king and now what's for tea?
After the war, no time for England's flags.
Down with St George's, up dragon money-bags!'

'That was excellent, Digby,' I said.

'Do you want to do it again?'

'We're just checking the gate, but I think we can go straight into the church now, if that suits you. You're very expert.'

'Mr Bumble does his best,' Digby said. 'This is a building I've always adored. A marvel of confidence on the part of old Blair Keating, don't you feel that? The soul-factory! Suburban magnificence! I love it! These bricks were made in Edgware, the white ones, Dawson Road, and the red ones came from the old London Brick Company – Ebenezer Stout's outfit – in Nine Elms. Look at all that space left for God! As if He were some kind of dirigible, due to dock at any time. No, Blair Keating wouldn't have accepted that. He would have preferred to look things up in a kind of metaphysical Bradshaw; he believed in divine punctuality. What concrete and rust civic centre can take the place of that sublimely dotty St Pancras of the spirit?'

Digby was so untroubled by his own grotesquerie that it became a theatrical prop, a cunning adjunct to his performance. As he seduced the unit, I began to think that the whole film might as well see the St George's issue through his eyes. Artless and artful, he sweetened his prejudices with delectable detail. He stood for an England without doubts or certainties, a middle ground of lazy, hard-working, credulous, sceptical, parochial, imperial, penny-wise, pound-foolish people whose dignity was absurd and whose absurdity was not without majesty. Helplessness and self-sufficiency were indistinguishable in Digby and in the England he sentimentalized so ruthlessly. It was a pleasure for both of us, I guessed, to consort so amicably in the hope that we were making fools of each other. Digby amused and depressed me: he was the amiable representation of a society from which I should forever be excluded. When I went from our last session of filming to Gloucester Mansions, to see my grandmother, I felt as if he had beaten me in some game whose rules I could not follow. His jolly friendly handshake made me a better loser than I had any wish to be.

I put a sheaf of narcissi on to the cuff of Clarissa's linen sheet. She lay in a cleft of pillows, in a clean, lacy nightgown. Her profile, softened by age, might have been taken from some smooth, obsolete coin. 'I hoped I should find you in,' I said.

Kendall said, 'A cup of tea, Mr Michael?'

'Of course he wants a cup of tea. *And* bread and butter. Or a tea cake? He's a growing boy.'

Kendall giggled and went into the little kitchen. After the death of my grandfather, Clarissa had taken a smaller flat in the same block. The furniture had had to be moved in on her; a walnut armoire, with its oval mirror, stood close to the head of the bed, like a monocled visitor. There were Dresden figurines on the commode. The bedside table held bottles of medicine, a tortoise-shell talcum powder container and perfumes for which there might be a call. Medicines and cosmetics went together.

'Your sister got married,' Clarissa said.

'She seems very happy. They're living in West Africa.'

'Is he English?'

'He could hardly be more so.'

'Your father . . .'

'He's English too,' I said. 'Have you seen him recently?'

'He's very regular. He always comes, and if he doesn't come, he calls.'

'He's very fond of you.' I spoke as if I were measuring words in a spoon and dropping them into the old woman's ear. Intimations of immortality were strengthened by her tenacious frailty. If she could live as many years as she had, what could prevent me from lasting forever?

'I'm his only mother,' she said. 'Did we do the right thing?'

'When did we do anything else?' I had no notion what she meant, but the suggestion of complicity was easy. I had only to be my father and the trick was easily turned. 'About what, granny?' Incitation and warning came in the same package. 'That was nice and quick!'

Kendall, in a frilled apron now, was lifting the trolley over the edge of the Persian carpet.

'Has he got his bread and butter?'

'And his Fuller's cake. I know what Mr Michael likes. Two slices!' She made sure that everything was in place and then she went back into the kitchen, only a pace or two from the bedroom. 'If there's anything else, you've only to . . .'

'You can never trust them. Her sister comes. Ada. They whisper together.'

'They don't want to disturb you, granny.'

'What've they got to whisper about? They get their wages. I'm an old woman . . .'

'You're only saying that.'

'You're like him,' she said. 'Your father. I never tried to influence him, never mind what they say. It was his father. Do you remember your grandfather?'

'Of course,' I said. ' "Can't stop," that's what he always used to say, wasn't it, in the mornings? When he was off to the office. "Can't stop." Like the White Rabbit.'

Her face came round the snowy corner of her pillow. 'Do you know what little fingers are for? For turning men round is what little fingers are for! And that's just what she did.'

'Who is this we're talking about, grandma?'

'She doesn't like me.' Clarissa had gone back between prongs of softness. Her pillow projected on both sides of her head like a plump wimple. 'Your mother.'

'She may not have seen your best side,' I said.

'Jeremy Lascelles said that I had the shortest, straightest nose he'd ever seen. You don't remember him. I had four dances with him that night. Gossamer, that's what he said I was. They played the Blue Danube, the last waltz. He would've married me, but for his family. You know the only thing I ever used? A little powder, a little lavender water. I married your father instead.'

'Grandfather,' I said.

'I could've floated away, he said, if he hadn't held me tight. Do you want a tea cake now?'

'I'd sooner have another dance.'

'I should've been someone else entirely.' She came forward again and put a finger to her lips. 'They listen to every word. You're never safe and you're never free. He was killed in the war. He didn't carry a gun, but he was killed all the same. Just a cane. They said I was beautiful and a beautiful girl could be anything she wanted to be. I only wanted to be beautiful. He came to see me in Eastbourne in his uniform. After he'd been wounded. I had the smallest, straightest nose he'd ever seen. And then he went away and he was killed, they said. Do you know why people marry people? So that they don't have to marry anyone else. When did you get married?'

'I didn't, grandma.'

'You've got children.'

'You're thinking of Samuel,' I said. 'Your son. I'm Michael.' I looked round the pillows to make sure that she was all right. Her hazel eyes were waiting for me. The lace had slipped from her white shoulder. 'Your grandson.'

'How's your brother?'

'I have no brother, granny. I've got one sister, and that's all, Rachel. The one who's got married.'

'The smallest, straightest nose he'd ever seen.'

'You still have,' I said. 'Why do the English attach so much importance to noses?'

In an abruptly younger voice, Clarissa said, 'You're not an American, are you?'

'No,' I said. 'Are you?'

'The English are quite right,' she said, 'about everything. What's your mother's name?'

'Still Philippa Jordan,' I said.

'No young girl is a natural liar,' Clarissa said. 'It comes with marriage, lying. I always believed in the truth, until I found out what it was.'

'Grandma, you can be very Delphic.'

'I could tell you all sorts of things, but . . .' She made warning eyes in the direction of the kitchen, where Kendall was making quietly busy noises. 'I daren't.'

'Oh I think you could be pretty daring if you wanted to be,' I said.

'One thing I'd like you to know.' She made a beckoning motion with her right hand. I leant across the bed. 'One thing I've learned over the years.' I put my ear close to her lips. She blew into it and began to giggle. She laughed and laughed. Her breath grew desperate with amusement. She needed her smelling salts, but she could not bring herself to abort the pleasure which racked her. The tears stood in her crinkled eyes and she gasped in the bed. 'There!' she said.

Kendall was in the doorway, light glinting on her golden cross. As I thanked her, I undid the bow of her apron and she giggled as she always had when I was a small boy. My grandmother glared at Kendall and went low enough in the bed to be invisible in the mirror which faced her.

As I pressed the button for the lift, it flared ENGAGED. When it arrived at the fourth floor, my father stepped out. He was wearing his work clothes: black coat, striped trousers. 'Hullo, dad,' I said, 'are you expected?'

'Quite a few are born that are not expected,' he said. 'How is she?'

'Much the same.'

'Poor mum.'

'Have you been working?'

'Well, I've been,' he said. 'Whether or not I was working is for his Lordship to say. They've made Maurice Lanzmann a judge.'

'Ought they to be ashamed of themselves?'

'Many are called and he was chosen. How's your filming?'

'I'm not sure if I'm for the defence or the prosecution. I did a sequence intended to make Harrison Digby look like King Canute, but I'm afraid he might just turn the tide after all.'

'May you not be rather embarrassed, in view of who is paying the piper?'

'I said I'd do it only if the choice of tune was left strictly to me.'

My father made a march of the few steps from the lift to his mother's door. 'I suppose they'll give him a knighthood in due course.'

'He is at least a man who does things. Chester makes me sarcastic, but he wants to do things, now, in the future. He's a megalomaniac without pretensions. I'd sooner spend time with Digby, I think, but I don't want him to win.'

'I was thinking of Maurice,' my father said.

'They might offer you one one day, mightn't they? Would you accept?'

'One neither solicits honours nor refuses them.'

'I thought that was women,' I said.

'The right kind of woman is an honour,' Samuel said.

'You certainly play well out of bunkers still, don't you, dad?'

'Never ground your club and keep the head down. Why don't you write a comedy? We went to a terrible one on Tuesday. I'd sooner go to one of yours.'

'As soon as I've finished with St George's and its environs, your order will have my personal attention. Not that we necessarily laugh at the same things. Have you heard from Rachel recently?'

'Your mother has, I believe.' He pressed the bell. 'Has she heard from you at all?'

Sally was only an hour late when she came to collect me in her white TR II. There was a rust-edged crater in the nearside door. 'Pity about that,' I said.

'Not really,' she said. 'He's going to pay for the whole car to be re-sprayed, the man who did it, even though I don't think it was his fault. He said it was worth it to get my name and address.'

'How did the meeting go? With the man with eight hands?'

'Oh, darling, haven't you got a memory! It was all right. But do I want to get locked into another long run? I shall be old before I've made a film with my favourite writer and then he'd look even sulkier than usual.' She drove as if it were a part-time occupation. In the hope of keeping her attention on the road, I told her, at length, of my ambivalent attitude towards Chester Flam and his opponents.

'I want to give someone a nasty surprise,' I said. 'But who? Whom. Lenin said it all, most of it. It's a marvellous plan, the development, which turns out to be the work, in large part, of someone I was at prep school with, called Hugo Carmody. Our school was called St George's too, which adds Ossa to Pelion in the coincidence department.'

'You couldn't talk Portuguese, could you, for a bit? I'd have a better chance of understanding what this is all about.'

'Sorry. For a brief moment I had the idea you might be interested in what I'm doing.'

'You'd think we were married or something, the way you expect me to keep up with all the intimate details!'

'If I have to choose between marriage and something, I'll take something. Who else is going to be down this weekend?'

'Only the people I said, as far as I know. It's just a chance to relax in the country and sop up some fresh air. Have you got Ned's map? Because is it left or right here?'

'Left. *Right*. I always want to go both ways, don't you? When peace broke out in ancient Rome, they closed the doors of the temple of Janus. Mr Facing-Both-Ways. An end to duplicity. In modern England, that's the only temple they ought to leave open, wouldn't you say so? War or peace? No: War *and* Peace. Mr Tolstoy had it right.'

'It's no use, I've never read it.'

'You've read the *title*, haven't you?'

'Why ever did I say I'd drive you down here?'

'That will, I am sure, as the synopses always say, emerge in due course.'

We turned in at stone gateposts, between sandstone gryphons grasping blank menus, and passed a rural Gothic lodge before driving between low white fences towards the Queen Anne farmhouse and the thatched Suffolk barn from which the property took its name. Sally spat pebbles against a beige Rolls as she made a tight turn and stopped the TR. The sky was buoyant with tufted clouds; the hope of heat made Sally lean her golden head against the black leather and breathe in the country.

Hall, the Cormans' butler, in a silver-striped waistcoat and gartered shirt sleeves, came out for our bags. He did not need to be told that, despite fond appearances, we were not sharing a room. We were shown to the door of the drawing room and I heard Sally's voice singing 'Never Ever Again'. French windows opened from the plaster-ceilinged room on to a flagstoned terrace which went the length of the house. A rococo double staircase curved down to the roses.

'Here comes our leading lady now,' Ned Corman said.

Sally pivoted and looked behind her. 'Where? Where?'

'How are you, Michael? How nice to see you again!'

'How nice to be visible again!' I said.

Ned thrust his tongue into his cheek and rolled his eyes. He was wearing plus-fours the colour of Dijon mustard and an olive-green turtle-necked sweater with a flat cable-stitch motif. Charlie Lehmann, in a pale grey suit, with a black tie and gold pin, was swinging well-pressed legs on the terrace wall. He was tall and sallow and his black hair was cut short with a peak in the front. His beard already darkened his chin. He had on black and white Oxfords. He seemed both young and old, successful and modest. He cannot have been more than forty-five and he had produced his first film at twenty-one. When Ned took me out to meet him, he jumped down from the wall and held out a slim, waxy hand. Ned said, 'Michael Jordan, as promised.'

'Bob Sander sent me the script of *Maximum Security*. I admired it very, very much.'

'When do we start shooting?'

'I wish.'

'That doesn't sound like a date to put in my diary exactly.'

Charlie Lehmann smiled. 'Whenever you say something nice to an Englishman, he fixes bayonets. Why?'

'We're educated to take just about everything from a stranger except sweets.'

Irene Jameson and Mireille Lehmann came through a gap in the yew hedge. Each took a separate staircase to reach the terrace. Hall came out of the house with a tray of champagne in frosted blue Venetian glasses. Mireille had thick auburn hair and wore a velvet dress the colour of crushed raspberries. A ruby necklace, with matching earrings, clasped her neck and relied on the smoothness of her skin. She and Irene smiled as they came together again at the top of the stairway; they might have conspired to be each other's flattering reflections. Irene's famous face, with the green almond eyes and the rather thin, but mobile mouth, the remarkable cheekbones and the narrow nose seemed to trump Mireille's by its assumption of the world's attention. Irene wore a neat black suit, with a gush of red silk scarf at the throat. Tiny emerald earrings were her only jewels, apart from her wedding ring. She went into the drawing room and was so, so glad to see Sally.

Mireille said, 'Ned Corman, your house is a marvel. That barn! Those beams! I'd like to transplant it lock, stock and barrel to Bel Air.'

'Sorry, my darling, but I'm keeping the barrel.'

'For scraping,' Irene called.

'And you should see the picture gallery, Charlie. It puts Edie in the shade.'

'Why don't we let's call and tell her?' Charlie said.

'Pay-phone in the hall.' Ned did his tongue-in-cheek, eye-rolling stuff for my benefit.

'Did you tell Mr Jordan how much we liked his script? I think he should make it.'

'Mrs Lehmann, I thought you looked like a very intelligent woman with a great deal of power and influence. Please use them with this gentleman.'

'How can I make a picture called *Maximum Security*? My contract stipulates that all my movies have to have either Love, Spring or Princess in the title.'

'We could always call it *Maximum Security Princess*,' I said. 'I thought those days were over.'

'Those days,' Charlie Lehmann said, 'have very, very long sunsets. Your fiancée is very beautiful. And very, very talented. My God!'

I said, 'I have yet to meet my fiancée. Would you be good enough to introduce us?'

'I'm sorry. I was given to understand . . . I must've misread the stage directions. I thought you two . . .'

'Oh we do. I love her and she loves me. But rarely on the same day.'

'She ought to be a big, big star.'

'She has time,' I said.

'Nobody has time,' Charlie Lehmann said. 'Time has us. Somewhere in the world, it's already tomorrow.'

'Not in England,' I said. 'In England it's already yesterday.'

'I love England,' Charlie Lehmann said. 'Don't you?'

There was movement inside the drawing room. A pale figure in white trousers and a bull-fighter's shirt, with string-tie, had arrived and was drinking from Irene's champagne glass. 'It's so nice to see a noble house like this in the hands of honest *arrivistes*. It's much too good for the aristocracy.'

Ned Corman shook the newcomer's hand. 'Goodbye, Benedict.' He kissed Benedict's wife on the cheek as she came in. 'Hullo, Karen.'

Benedict said, 'It's going to be that kind of a show, is it, folks? I see!'

Sally said, 'Mireille, do tell me, is your family French originally?'

'Only its windows. My mother read a lot of novels when she was pregnant. They gave her the idea that French women were proud and resilient and knew how to handle themselves.'

'And has that made you very self-satisfied? You're among friends.'

'Not while you're around, Benedict.'

'Women are very coy about masturbation, aren't they? Why is that, do you think?'

'You must ask the vicar, Benedict,' Ned said. 'He's coming for tea.'

Hall said, 'Luncheon is served, madame.'

As we went towards the dining room, past the Edwardian cabinet in which Irene's Oscar and Ned's Stage Golfing Society trophy were displayed, Benedict said, 'Hall won't be happy until he can say "Luncheon is served, my lady".'

Karen, now quite grey, said, 'Nor will my lady, will she?' I could understand both why Benedict had married her and why he would divorce her.

Irene saw me quizzing the cabinet and her lips toyed with things she might have said. She put her hand on my tweed sleeve and gave me a long close-up of those green eyes. 'Are you very, very keen on golf, Mr Leaving?'

The meal was served on a long oak table. The hand-cut surface was puddled with the glare of the sifted sun. The narrowness of the Jacobean style brought us almost knee to knee. Eight of us occupied scarcely half of the length of the table; it was as if the dull people had been left out, or had not yet arrived. The Portuguese maid was called Maria by Irene and Teresa by Ned. Her severe grace put the company on its best behaviour. The heavy silver, the Limoges plates, the cut-glass goblets in which the Château Grillet (my first taste of it) was served, and the Georgian bonbon dishes suggested that the Cormans had collected whatever possessions had not been inherited from tasteful ancestors through diligent connoisseurship. Yet Ned, at the head of the table in a Louis XIII armchair, gave the mocking impression that everything he touched and saw had been recently imported by the property master. Even as he vaunted himself on his establishment, he played the upstart understudy, pitched into a richer part than experience or ambition warranted. When he raised an issue of professional concern, he acted as if we must know more about it than he: 'Can someone please tell me where, when and if it is all going to end? Are these so-called developers not going to rest until they've pulled down every last theatre in London and put up their perfectly appalling office blocks in their unnecessary place?'

'That's capitalism for you, Ned. You remember what Bert Brecht said.'

'Only with the greatest difficulty, Benedict. Not many laughs there!' Ned seemed again to be performing for my benefit. He was like a recruiting poster which appeared to beckon personally to everyone in the room. 'What we really ought to do is to send Mistress Raglan, here present, as a deputation to Mr Flam. You could throw yourself at the rich man's feet, my sweet, for the greater glory of Thespis. Well, you could start with his feet.'

Sally rippled with wilful laughter. 'You have to get up so early in the morning, don't you, to be insulted by famous people who live this far out of town?'

'If you fancy an early night, madame, you have only to persist in your scruples.'

Mireille said, 'Where has that nice host of ours got to? I don't seem to have seen him for some time.'

'All ladders and no snakes is what some people think the game is.' Ned threw his remark on to the table like a gambler, to see what it might produce.

Benedict said, 'I find the ladders much more alarming than the snakes myself. You always climb a snake, given the right gym teacher, but sliding down ladders can be hazardous for the anatomy. What we really need is an enlightened government policy for the arts: lavish funding and brutally unfair discrimination against the young and the beautiful. The old guard would then mount definitive productions of the weariest classics and there'd be every reason for the frustrated *jeunesse* to produce work of true revolutionary quality. If uncharacteristic sincerity embarrasses you, pray chat among yourselves.'

Coffee was served on the terrace. There were red-eyed *petits fours* and powdered truffles and that crunchy coffee sugar it was tempting to spoon from the bottom of the cup. Again I had the feeling that we were in a borrowed place and that the owners, or the audience, might at any moment reveal themselves. Somewhere, if only in the kitchen, real people were working to service a game of charades in which, I suspected, everyone else was more aware of what the word might be than I was.

Benedict was wearing yellow Moroccan sandals. When he sat down on one of the white chairs by the skirted coffee table, he seemed to have more limbs than anyone else in the company. He folded down like some contraption whose assembly instructions had not been properly followed. 'If they're looking for a commander-in-chief for the Old Guard, a man who can shed fresh dust on any proceedings, why not you, Ned? You seem to have taken belated refuge in the kind of above-the-titled modesty that any large sum of American money can buy. How could you possibly have lent yourself, even at extortionate rates of interest, to that cream of vegetable muck I saw you drowning in in Leicester Square, one ill-advised morning last week? *Hannibal the Great*? I never hope to hear the word *cunctator* used so often in public again. And you complain about Mr Flam! "Short live the theatre" seems to be your common motto. May I assist you, distinguished host, with the beam in your own eye? Handkerchief anyone?'

Ned invented another woeful expression. His tongue came out so far that I could believe that it might curl upwards and engulf his nose. 'Benny sweetheart, if you're going to bring me presents all the way from London, I should prefer something I can *wear* rather than shove up my . . .' He made the arrival of Maria, or Teresa, the reason for tactful bathos. '*Nose?*'

Mireille said, 'Quite suddenly, I feel like a brisk stroll to the horizon and back. Well, not necessarily back.'

She took my arm and we went down towards the roses and along the strict yew-walk which led towards a paddock where a U-backed grey hunter was cropping clover, nervous chestnut trees behind him.

Ned said, 'Presumably you're getting all you need, Mistress R., from the reportedly brilliant young man who's making off with Charlie's wife?'

Sally said, 'I hope you think you're being funny, Nedward. In which case you're merely failing. On the other hand, if you seriously mean any of part of this, you're simply being disgusting. *And* juvenile.'

'Juvenile?' Ned said. 'Now you're talking!'

Irene's lips curled into the most tolerant of expressions. Charlie Lehmann was eating truffles as if they had been prescribed, bravely. Mireille winked at me as we walked along the weedless path towards the paddock. One of her eyes was more than enough.

Irene said, 'Darling, I don't know what's the matter with you.'

Ned said, 'It starts with a tickle in the throat, and then it spreads to other selected venues. Why shouldn't the young lady do for the sake of the theatre what Walewska did for Poland?'

Sally said, 'Irene darling, I'm sorry, but really . . .'

Ned called out, 'Don't forget to take young Sir Gollyhead with you if you're making a dash for home, *ma petite*. London's a hell of a long way for him on a retired nag.'

Irene caught the tearful Sally at the drawing room door. Sally said, 'It was such a lovely, lovely lunch, Irene dear. But . . .'

'And it's going to be an even better dinner. Some people are coming who so want to meet you. Please . . .'

Sally had to accept the arms outstretched to her. How sad that Irene's muscles no longer had quite the firmness they had shown when poor Mary Queen of Scots bade farewell to her lover in the 1938 hit! 'If you really want me to . . .'

Benedict unlaced his legs and reached for more coffee. 'I can't bear it when people kiss and make up,' he said. 'It seems so uncalled for.'

Mireille and I had taken a path which led into the walled vegetable garden. Green raspberries fattened in neat rows. Scarlet runners climbed taut rigging. Unseen gardeners announced their impeccable attention. I said, 'Do you understand all this?'

'I don't try.' She made it sound like a form of intelligence. 'I'm an outsider.'

'We both are,' I said.

'Why are you here, if you don't belong?'

'Why are you?'

'I belong to Charlie.'

'People don't belong to people.'

'Of course they do. Are you in love with her?'

'I swore I wasn't when I said I'd come. Now I'm not so sure.'

'Then you're not.'

'You don't belong to him.'

'Do I not?' The air buzzed with hot insects. The lichened walls, orange and purple, reflected the heat and the sound. 'Have you any idea how comforting it is to be a possession?' Mireille had seemed older than I at lunch, of another generation, to be respected and mocked. Now her beauty beat back along the stream of time, shedding years. 'Anything is better than being a Canadian.'

I said, 'Don't you love him?'

She leaned against my arm. I weighed her like some rare commodity, to which the rubies were cheap dressing. 'You want to know what love means in my life? Love is what leads to abortions in Cleveland in the middle of an Ohio winter when you're eighteen years old, your folks think you're in St Jean-de-Vite and you didn't know the sonofabitch was married. Or a sonofabitch.'

244

'I always assume beautiful women have some sixth sense . . .'

'Beauty isn't a moral quality; it's a perishable blessing, where it isn't an unreliable curse. Haven't you noticed how some people have to keep checking in the mirror to make sure they can still recognize themselves?'

I said, 'Irene looks wonderful today.'

'Yes. Do you have any idea whose plan this party is going according to?'

I said, 'I feel as if I'm taking part in a game of charades and everyone knows the word except me.'

She looked at me and I blushed, at her keenness. Did she suspect that I had resurrected a remark I had already made, if only to myself, and paraded it as spontaneous? 'You're afraid they're cleverer than you,' she said. 'That's the only stupid thing about you.'

'You're quite an education, Mrs Lehmann.'

'I'm not the kind of teacher who's ever going to be satisfied with apples, believe me. Pack your bag and get out of here.'

'Before your husband offers me a job?'

'He likes to have his own way, and his own people. He admires resistance, especially when he can overcome it.'

'Don't all rich people, and most men?'

'Go and do terrible things, Michael. Things you can be ashamed of later. There's nothing worse in the world than to realize you have nothing in your life you wish you'd never done. You wait for other people to be bad for you. You want to be there while they do it, but you don't do it yourself.'

'You could've been a movie star. You were right not to be and you wish you had been, right?'

'I thought I was choosing reality, but reality's something you only imagine you can have. Reality is what people make up to excuse not using their imagination.'

'Come with me,' I said, 'and I just might go.'

'Get a couple of tickets for the day before yesterday,' Mireille said, 'I just might be your girl. But you can't. And I'm not. I belong to Charlie Lehmann.'

A Standard Vanguard was coming between the white fences. It had a substantial package on its roof-rack. A bearded man was being driven by a hennaed woman. He frowned at the landscape as if trying to remember where he had seen it before. Sally's voice was calling from the terrace: 'Michael? Mireille? Come and see! Michael? Mireille?'

'We seem to be wanted,' I said.

'They must be afraid we're enjoying ourselves.'

I was struck by the courage of beautiful women. How frequently they had to find comely defences against their admirers and against those who envied them! And how often they were the same people! It seemed wrong that Mireille should have only mortal suitors from whom to make her selection. Perhaps she thought money permanent enough to be stained with immortality.

The bearded man was introduced to us as Guy Falcon. I had seen his work in the Tate and in Albemarle Street. Claudia Monk's first novel – *An Easy Life* – had had a jacket which he had designed; it depicted the Sibyl at Cumae suspended in her display jar. Guy's wife, who wore a loose brown dress and wedge-heeled straw shoes, was called Wendy. She had the self-effacing aloofness of a clever woman who was seldom invited anywhere except on her husband's account. She untied the string on the large, flat package with capable briskness. The tar paper lolled open to reveal a portrait of Irene Jameson. Benedict squatted on the floor, knees up to his ears, blanched and bony as a punctured harlequin. Guy Falcon, in a denim suit and collarless Greek shirt, frowned at his own canvas like a critic.

Irene was portrayed in a Renaissance pose which both disdained contemporary fashion and parodied the tradition to which it paid tribute. She was shown in one of her most famous parts, Lola in Gerald Pringle's *All's Fair*. There was the long latticed shutter of the Juan-les-Pins hotel where she was first discovered with Osbert Monkhouse (Ned Corman) and the edge of the balcony which Peewee Pargiter (Clarkson Walters) climbs to steal her jewels and lose his heart. The bedroom visible through the half-open shutter reproduced Cedric Griffin's 1937 Broadway set, with the cockleshell bed, the soaped mirrors, and the notorious practical shower. 'I haven't kept my word,' Guy said, 'because I said it wouldn't be flattering. I can only say that to be unflattering it would also have to be untruthful. That would be more than any fee could procure and less than Irene deserves.'

'He is obviously lying about something, isn't he?' Benedict said.

On the back of an anomalous chair, at the limit of the interior, where the lattice took slices from them, the star's street clothes had been draped. She might just have removed them. And as we looked at the picture, with its exaggerated height, it was as though a spotlight began to shine more brightly on the anomaly. The clothes were of today. The Balenciaga coat and dress, the Hermès scarf and – cast aside so hurriedly that they had spilled on to the toppled shoes – the silken underclothes must have been what Irene wore when she went for the sittings. Guy Falcon frowned at his work. Could somebody have done something to it without his permission? His eyebrows were a bushy circumflex above his bold nose. He flicked at Irene's painted knee with a long little-fingernail, as if that solved his problem.

Ned Corman said, 'I never thought anyone could do you justice, my love, but I was wrong. For the first time. Because Guy has. Justice indeed.'

Sally clapped and everyone except Benedict joined in. His admiration was too sharp for politeness. A master of malice himself, he had perhaps been shocked by the disconcerting innuendo in Guy's effusiveness. The setting of the figure, too low in the frame, made it seem that Irene was slipping down towards oblivion. The regality of her smile was both accurate and pretentious. The picture was both bland and astringent, inoffensive and lethal, like a property dagger which could draw real blood.

When Irene looked at Guy with an air of gratitude, Ned smiled, as if she had done something which had never gone quite so well at rehearsal. Mischievous and ageless, she walked up to Guy and raised a hand, apparently to caress his face. In the same affectionate gesture, she yanked his beard. Guy clapped his hand to his chin like someone mortified to have forgotten an important appointment. Irene turned away, cheeks ribbed with rage, and Ned had her in his arms. Sally produced the rich chuckle which had, on its own, received critical acclaim.

Ned said, 'No permanent damage, I trust?'

'Your wife is quite a strong woman.'

'Has to be, cocky, to hold on to me. Get the cheque all right?'

Wendy Falcon had made a ball of the now knotless string and was smoothing the tar paper into portable form. 'Yes, thank you.'

'We're all going to have tea shortly.' Irene could have been to her caravan, had a little rest and come back for a fresh take. 'I think the drawing room, Maria.'

'We've left the dogs,' Wendy Falcon said.

'Surely they can amuse themselves,' Ned said. 'You've got the television, haven't you?'

Guy said, 'I could use a cup.'

Irene said, 'I'm not sure that they're meant to be used.'

Sally whispered to me, 'Can that really be the line, do you suppose?'

The tea was as traditional as the house seemed to deserve: there were even crumpets in a chafing dish. Kendall would have been proud of the thin bread and butter, the home-made conserves (Cook's secret!), the egg and cress sandwiches. Harrison Digby would have said 'Scrumptious' to the Madeira cake, 'Golly!' to the Dundee.

I was on a chintz Chesterfield next to Guy, whose beard I half expected to ooze blood. I said, 'Do you think painters can really see things in their subjects' faces that ordinary people can't see?'

'Certainly. Green for instance. Most people don't see the green.'

'I was thinking of things like whether they're suffering from a mortal disease –'

'We all are. It's called life. Next question.'

'– or have a streak of cowardice or nobility or –'

'Looking at you, I'd say you . . .' Guy narrowed his eyes and touched the mole by the side of that nose. 'You have an older sister!'

'She doesn't look older,' I said, 'but yes, I do. Impressive! Are you guessing?'

Guy looked away, towards a russet drawing of a naked woman, hips canted at a provocative angle, thighs deeply shadowed. 'Poor André. Got very fat. Guess.'

'You can't have told from looking at me. I guess you're guessing.'

'I'm not licensed to play the fortune-teller without a brush in my hand. My fingers see better than my eyes. I only guess when I already know. Michael Jordan. You've got her eyes, or some of them.'

I said, 'Now I . . . Did you ever actually *see* Irene in *All's Fair*?'

'It's awfully good of you to ask me all these questions. I hope they're for your benefit. What do you think, if you think?'

'1937? I doubt it.'

'Wrong. I was in New York when I was eighteen. Designing a ballet for Igor Nekrassov.'

'At *eighteen*?'

'I was a slow starter,' Guy said.

'I always envy the way some people manage to be at the centre of things, while the rest of us are still wondering whether we just might get our house hockey colours at last. How the hell did you get to be in New York just at the right moment?'

'I was fucking Anita Goldman. And I was extremely talented. The ticket came from Cook's.'

'And what was the ballet?'

'Oh I'm afraid that was *Orpheus and Eurydice*.'

'But you never looked back.'

'That was probably my big mistake.' He made his beard bristle for Wendy, who already had her tea. Guy could wink without batting an eyelid. 'Why do people marry? It's somewhere to bung one's stuff.'

I said, 'My sister has one of your pictures hanging in her room, or did have.' The portrait of Irene Jameson, leaning against one side of the cherry-coloured mantelpiece, was a varnished mirror of our hostess, who seemed again and again to check her appearance in it. 'The camera lies. You tell the truth.'

'Consult our prices,' Guy said. 'I don't tell the truth; it tells me.'

Benedict flopped on the plump arm of our couch like a wingless stork. 'You're very pretentious this afternoon, Guy.'

'That's because it's my afternoon off. Unpretentiousness is such hard work one must relax somehow. Am I ever going to get that cup of tea?'

Irene's lips nearly said something which amused her and then she poured milk in a saucer and handed it to Guy. '*Monsieur est servi*.'

'You've been mistaken for a pussy, Guy!'

'Not mistaken at all.' Guy took the saucer in clawless paws and sipped it with feline delicacy. 'Recognized.'

As Guy cleaned his whiskers, with the back of his hands, I became aware of the cat's cradle of relationships suspended in the often photographed room. I had no notion of what my own place might be, but the others announced themselves as the players, or witnesses, of an imminent drama. It presented itself to me, not as a theatrical scene, with a single text articulating the complexities, but as a sequence of images, their simultaneity separated into discrete strands as light is winnowed by a prism. I saw again, as if it were running through a movieola, the quivering politeness of Irene Jameson as she handed the saucer to her feline assassin. I saw Ned Corman, blank of hope and humour, as his wife took a step towards something beyond the means of his agile clowning to repair. His fingers fretted Sally's shoulder, not in the seigneurial manner which, in the theatre, so often allowed desire to rehearse as courtesy, but as a blind man might grope for guidance. His hand fluttered and then leaned hard enough for

Sally to tilt and almost laugh. In that miraculous moment, when my eyes were blessed with a fly's ability to scan in all directions, it was Mireille whose motionless animation rang like a shrill, inaudible alarm. Irene's portrait glowed before us with a naked-ness in which not even Benedict could take scandalous pleasure. It was a magic lantern show with a single, telling side. Wendy was looking, chin up, at Guy Falcon. I read her flare of hennaed hair as a reminder of what she had been when he first saw her. It reminded him how recklessly he had poached her from the husband who had been his friend. Her docile possessiveness combined the allure of Eurydice with the competence of a bank manager. Only I myself, in the still business of missing nothing, became reduced to nullity, a fleshless point of view. The footage of the afternoon ran through me as if I were a machine. Mireille's glaucous eyes swallowed the scene like scorching drops from which she was too proud to flinch. As for Charlie Lehmann, he saw Ned Corman's fingers drop from Sally's shoulder and find nowhere to go other than his pocket – an actor who had forgotten his business. Sincerity is what art, and fraud, can never have; it does what art can never do – embarrass.

Tyler's Barn preserved the appearance of antiquity, at the price of renovation. The old barn now provided separate bathrooms for each of the six guest bedrooms. I had a blue room, with wood-pinned beams and a swagged view towards the paddock where the old grey hunter was saddled with the last of the sunlight. By the time I had had a bath (wondering, like a schoolboy, whether I was really dirty enough to require it), lights had come on in the main house and in the ship's lantern outside the front door. More people were evidently expected.

Sally was in the next room. Her bathroom was adjacent to mine and shared ventilation with it. I thought of her naked, not more than a couple of yards from me, and I wondered what chances there were of a rap at my door, then or later. How would she look in the accessible nightgown, or pyjamas, in which she wanted to ask me a serious question that couldn't wait? What a liberation to have not the smallest inclination to trust her! I ought to have been incapable of loving a girl who always did exactly what suited her, but Southsea excited irresistible memories and cruel prospects. Even as I told myself how worthless her promises were, I looked forward to their renewal and to the teasing pleasure she might give me, and I her.

How could I have been surprised, or hurt, or shocked, at the voices which bubbled from the next bathroom and incited me to thread them into sentences whose content I seemed to know already? The need to supply the connections turned me into an accomplice. Was Sally in a fluffy yellow robe, cinched at the waist but generous at the neck, so that her pouty breasts, powdered and put away, were only a very marginal element in the conversation? I thought of bare feet on furry carpet, the slight upward tilt of clean, slim big toes.

'. . . come in here now . . .'

'. . . in the bath . . . Nothing to make her . . .'

'. . . come down here at all . . .'

Ned said, 'Benny . . .'

'Trust him, trust him . . . I don't know . . . never happen . . . can't happen . . .'

'. . . little darling . . .'

Shame and curiosity, wanting and not wanting to know, made a spy of me. Power and powerlessness charged me from the same source. I ached to be told why I had been brought into the plot and what role I was expected to play. The only shame in an audition is not even to be offered a part, or a lie.

'. . . miserable . . .'

'. . . my sweet darling . . .'

'. . . talk to Irene.'

'. . . spoil everything for all of us . . . patient . . .'

'. . . feel patient . . . so unhappy . . .'

'. . . time . . .'

'. . . love me . . .'

'. . . anything in the world.'

'. . . dishonest, Ned, so terribly dishonest . . . vile . . .'

'. . . marry you . . .'

'. . . think about it any more . . .'

'. . . I swear . . . when we can . . .'

'. . . do with me . . . you . . .'

'. . . she's like . . . for yourself . . . for ever, my pretty, pretty one!'

'. . . just when I think . . . you . . .'

'. . . do without you . . . see you crying . . .'

'. . . hate . . . love . . .'

'. . . understand . . . the only one . . .'

'. . . don't . . . don't . . .'

'. . . have to . . .'

'. . . her house . . .'

'. . . anything in the world . . .'

'. . . not now . . . please, please . . .'

'. . . prove to you . . .'

'. . . unfair . . . unfair . . . oh . . . oh . . . so, so unfair . . .'

I looked at myself in the magnifying mirror. I advertised the excitement of exclusion. Surprised by what did not surprise me, I was lanced by what left no new scar. I bandaged myself in my Adamson's suit and stood at my window, watching the grassy slab of light from the next room in the hope that Sally's shadow might fall on the black lawn below our windows. Any evidence of her independent life filled me with murderous affection. Of which of his women had Byron once said, 'I cannot live with thee or without thee'?

I buffed my black shoes under the bedside carpet and went into the soft corridor. The barn had been joined to the main house by a panelled overpass which, being of recent construction, seemed more authentically antique than the rest of the place. The beams had been taken from a demolished mansion; the light fittings were Jacobean pewter sconces.

Benedict Bligh was examining a portrait of Edmund Kean in one of his electric performances. Having exchanged his Moroccan slippers for a pair of patent pumps with silver buckles, he was wearing a smocked Guatemalan peasant blouse with a vivid collar. Red, orange, blue and gold, it came to flashy points in front and hung behind in a brief apron between his shoulder blades.

'Well, well, Benedict,' I said, 'you've been given your colours at last!'

'What's he saying? If anything? Or is he simply counting the house? Are you really planning to marry Mistress Raglan?'

'Is that a well-known columnist's question?'

'Go abroad is my advice.'

'When do you take it?'

'I won't pretend to be your friend, Michael, because I'm not anybody's friend. Bastards can't be. I'm telling you because the words come out of me in that order. You've got the idea that you're still very young. The abiding sin of the precocious. It makes them old before their time. Look at Guy Falcon. When's your film about Chester Flam going to be finished?'

'When he stops giving me enough money to make any more of it, I expect, don't you?'

'Why do you choose to be used?'

'It makes one feel cunning, I suppose. Being a cog in someone else's machine gives one the illusion of commissioned irresponsibility.'

'Chester Flam is a ruthless operator with affectations of good taste. There's only one conceivable excuse for having anything to do with that kind of character. Let him down, Michael, as you value your soul. Show him up for what he is. Give him more than he asked for and I can guarantee you his ingratitude. A masterpiece is never what anyone had in mind. Jews can never be safe; playing safe is their only stupidity. Every clever answer is a kind of conformity. You think you can vanish in a puff of good marks. I won't let you. Wear your gabardine as if it were ermine. Make them wish you were dead and they'll never be able to forget you. Or are you the kind of Pinocchio who thinks that your nose'll get smaller every time you tell a lie?'

'Children, children!' Karen had opened a heavy door and stepped into the gallery. She was in a dark crimson dress freckled with black spots. Her heavy arms hung bare, three tortoiseshell bracelets, like mottled curtain rings, slanted against her thumb. 'Will you boys never leave your old schools?'

'Where else,' Benedict said, 'can we have unlimited access to swishy canes and newly laundered buttocks? What man has savoured the fullness of life's joys who has not once said, in a situation that brooks no denial, "bend over"?'

Ned's library had been designed and stocked by an antiquarian bookseller who wrote cynically sentimental thrillers. It was divided into four booths, each with a double lectern and a jointed green-shaded lamp. I wanted to check of whom Byron had made the remark which nagged me. I was trying to guess how it might be tagged in Nicolson's index when I heard Sally's voice again, the business-like register this time. How cleverly her make-up-free tone promised that no performance was taking place at present!

'It's very tempting,' she said, 'but I can't make up my mind without talking to Bob, you do know that, don't you?'

'As long as you say "Yes" right away,' Charlie Lehmann said, 'you can always make up your mind later.'

'Will the studio really accept me? I may have made a film or two, but I've never been in a movie.'

'With open arms,' Charlie said. 'And similar cheque books. My advice: run to the latter. I'd like to make a three-picture deal with you just on the strength of that laugh of yours, but I don't think Bob Sander would like it.'

Sally said, 'It depends so much on how the script turns out. What did you really think of the screenplay my . . . my friend Michael did?'

'He has the eye; he has the ear. Would you like to have him work on it?'

'I'd *love* him to,' Sally said. 'I can't think of anyone better. But comedy? Does he have the experience?'

'I did talk to Jake Lewin,' Charlie Lehmann said, 'at one point.'

'Jake Lewin!' Sally said. 'Who did *An Honest Woman*? The best!'

'It's always been good enough for me.'

I found the quotation just as I heard the door shut behind them. The person with whom and without whom Byron could not live was John Cam Hobhouse, his dull, reliable travelling companion.

Brian Routh, M.P., and his wife, Davina, whose fine fair hair was spun into a slightly dated beehive, had come over from their cottage, near Yoxford. Only when she got up to go in to dinner did it become clear that she was lame. Routh wore a plum-coloured, frogged smoking jacket and a floppy velvet bow tie. His longish hair was streaked with grey; he might have been playing an older man in an end-of-term production. His shirt was escaping from his cummerbunded waistband. Over the pear salad, with which dinner began, he offered reminiscences of life under the Allied Military Government in Germany. Inside knowledge, of secret agreements between enemies and secret hostilities between friends, was his stock-in-trade. He whispered at the top of his voice. Nothing amused him more bitterly than the delinquencies of those he was assumed to support, except the inadequacy of those whose failings should not, in view of his socialist allegiance, have disappointed or surprised him. His wife, who must have heard his stories before, was often their target. She sat, restored to beauty by immobility, in a gold-threaded Italian evening blouse which displayed her gleaming shoulders and deeply divided breasts, and refused to be distressed by her husband's provocations. He had turned the promotion of outrageous opinions into a substitute for holding office, which electoral chance and maverick vanity had put beyond his grasp. When he had finished his quails with *pommes Dauphine*, *purée* of artichoke and *choux au verjus* and his cabinet pudding, he put on Churchillian glasses to consider the cheese. 'Once one's missed the boat, as Anthony did, there's no sense in trying to remain water-borne. It simply leads to ungainly splashing. This country was finished, thalassocratically speaking, when we failed to smash Nasser. Europe became our only available destination and the entire Tory party had to be turned around to get us there. How? By making sure that any other policy either failed, through incompetence, or was ruled out, by expense. Nothing has succeeded so well, in the last five years, as failure. The government's strength lies in the country's weakness. A little toddle to the corner will soon be all the exercise we can be trusted to take. We resemble more and more an old people's home, liberally marked by samplers advising us to watch our step and get an early night. Britannia today is tied to America's apron-strings and lucky to be able to keep the bow straight. The Tories will be shown up for vacillating poltroons if we reveal any signs of cutting a fresh set of teeth, when they're all ready to buy false ones from Uncle Sam. As for the Labour party, it can't point out how far we've fallen without confessing a nostalgia for the days we're absolutely committed to regard as both bad and old. No one, therefore, is in a position to steer us anywhere except towards the rockiest of futures.'

Benedict cut himself a difficult segment of Chaours. 'May one ask a question of tonight's speaker?'

'One may ask one,' Routh said.

'On a matter of personal information then: how do you manage to sleep at night?'

Ned said, 'Hullo, Benedict's back!'

'I'll tell you. I avail myself of one of the apertures in the charming lady sitting on your left; I then read a bad book highly recommended by some hack colleague of yours who presumably needs the money and I then drop off without the smallest difficulty; and what the hell do you bloody well mean?'

'I mean that to a simple soul with only a mortal capacity for keeping down an excellent dinner, it's something of an effort to stomach your particular brand of sauce. It requires more than a propensity to contradict yourself whenever you open your loud mouth to deserve a reputation for paradox. It also demands more than an ability to let your own side down in order to qualify as Winston-come-again.'

'Ladies, shall we – perhaps – would you like –?'

'I'm not going to say anything to offend the ladies, Irene. I'm just going to say something to offend the gentleman. Because how can anyone with declared socialist principles consistently take the reactionary line, no matter how many apertures of delectable stringency may be available to him, and still manage to live with himself, even on his wife's money?'

'I heard you were a pansy, Bligh. I didn't know you were a buffoon.'

Irene said, 'I really do think that this conversation ought to be, if it ought to be at all, *entr'hommes*.' She stood at the head of the table, her uncertain fingers playing an invisible piano. 'Mireille . . .' She looked at Karen Bligh for a prompt which was not offered. 'Please . . .'

'Why don't you all bloody well sit down and smoke a cigar through one of your many apertures?'

'I knew Grand Barrail was a good wine,' Ned said. 'I didn't know it was quite this good.'

'It was excellent,' Charlie Lehmann said. 'It just doesn't seem to mix all that well with Mr Bligh.'

Routh was saying, 'You poor bloodless clown, do you really think Gamel Abdul Nasser was ever any sort of a socialist? You must be a bigger idiot than even your advertising leads one to believe.'

Mireille said, 'If you two go on being absolutely vile to each other like this, might it not eventually turn quite nasty?'

'What the world needs, before it's too late, is some really dedicated and far-seeing cowardice at the top. The idea that smashing Nasser would've increased Britain's stature by a fracture of a cubit is bigger rubbish than even an elected turncoat can be expected to get away with.'

Routh said, 'If Anthony had simply given orders, instead of taking advice from the Chiefs of Staff, we could have had friend Abdul back selling dirty postcards within the week. When the Chiefs play politics – as they always do – the politicians have to become generals, as Winston did, or no one's left to sound the charge. Anthony's nerve went in 1916, but no one spotted the fact until forty years later. *Ecco tutto*.'

I said, 'Wouldn't the Americans have sunk sterling?'

Routh said, 'Who the hell are you?'

I said, 'I'm the man who just asked whether the Americans wouldn't've sunk sterling if we'd actually –'

'So? Let them. We'd either have been obliged to abandon our absurd pretensions to world economic importance or – much more likely – the Yanks would've had to patch the ship they'd holed and help bale it out. Of course, one side of Anthony was so excited at the idea of being pronged by the Arabs that he couldn't decide which way was up. People like you, Bligh, want to take morality out of the bedroom and bring it into politics. Leave it under your pillow is my advice, where it does the least harm. You want to turn this country into a pansies' paradise, that's fine, up to a point, because a spot of tickle-your-tum never did much harm, but when it comes to practical politics, leave it to people who've spent ten minutes or more at the sharp end, I should.'

'You know your trouble, Routh? You've got bigger tits than your wife.'

Routh said, 'By Christ . . .' His chair fell backwards as he started to find his way round the table towards Benedict, who found time to wink at me as he reached for an unoffered cigar. 'By Christ . . .'

Irene said, 'Oh please – please – not in my house –'

'I'm going to punch this stick of poisonous celery on what's left of his syphilitic nose.'

Benedict swivelled to face the lurching Routh and drew on his Romeo y Julieta. 'Go ahead. Help yourself. Only I warn you, I shall have you in court, and the newspapers, like a shot. Never expect an ounce of chivalry out of me, you pathetic transvestite sonofaBlimp.'

Ned was tracing something in the spilled salt in front of Sally. She cancelled it with a slim finger and made a naughty face in my direction.

'No jury in this country would convict me if I took you outside and did what your mother should've done years ago, assuming you ever had one.'

'Brian, come on,' Guy Falcon said, 'enough of this mature behaviour.'

'He wants his physiognomy adjusted.'

'He's only trying to entertain the company,' Guy said. 'He doesn't want hitting, he wants reviewing.'

Irene said, 'There's coffee in the drawing room. And brandy. There's everything you want. Won't someone come with me?'

Mireille was first to Irene, but Sally ran to be with her too. Irene was as pale as the moon. On the way to the door, she gave a hectic smile and uttered a silvery laugh. Karen reached across the table for a cigar with half a yawn and a clack of bracelets. She looked very bored.

'Hey,' Benedict said, 'don't leave the sinking shit. Hit him before he hits me. What are women for?'

'It's no surprise that you haven't found out,' Routh said. 'Posing as a coward doesn't stop you being one.'

Benedict said, 'If you want a duel, fatso, you can bloody well have one.'

I said, 'Benedict, you've really more than earned your supper. Many congratulations and hadn't you better . . . ?'

'Oh, don't spoil things, Michael,' Ned Corman said, 'again. Do you mind?'

'Choose your weapons,' Routh said.

'Soup,' Benedict said. 'At ten paces. Michael, pop and see if cook's got any good throwing broth, there's a born second.'

Irene turned back from her escort. 'Oh do please stop, do please. There must be something else you can do . . .'

'Too late for charades, Irene. And not really enough talent for them.'

'Ned, do you want me to call the police?'

'They're having a little boyish fun, darling. Benedict, that'll probably do, won't it?'

'Do what?'

'Enough, Benedict.' Ned had played Wellington, as a separate-card cameo role, in Victor England's *Thin Red Line*. 'I mean it.'

'Like you meant that elaborately staged little spat with the tasty Miss Raglan, who is no more involved, at the hip-joining level, with Master Jordan here than I am with the poxy Major Routh, who remains the best argument against sleeping with his wife that anyone's ever likely to come across.'

Irene said, 'I thought they were secretly engaged. They *are* secretly engaged. Bene*dict*!'

Karen said, 'Oh for God's sake, Irene, don't fall for this nonsense.'

'House lights!' Irene said. 'House lights!'

Mireille said, 'What the hell are you playing at, Ned?'

'It's called "A Few Friends for the Weekend". Any number can play.'

'Check again. I think it's called "Murder"!'

Routh said, 'You do know, don't you, not that I suppose you give a damn, that you've got the whole thing arse-up, don't you?'

'Well,' Benedict said, 'if it's all the same to you, it is my favourite position.'

Karen leant across me to draw flame from a candle. I said, 'Is he as much fun as he ought to be?'

She said, 'Is anyone?'

The heat, if not the embarrassment, had gone out of the evening. Some people were standing, others were sitting; some seemed committed to leaving the dining room, others to staying. It was as though we were waiting for the director to bounce up from the stalls with an organizing idea. Benedict passed Brian Routh his glass and raised his own. When Routh presented his, Benedict clashed them together. Sparks of glass bled and tinkled on the oak. Irene wept.

Guy said, 'Shouldn't we perhaps . . . ?' He took Irene's moist hand. 'The dogs of peace can be no less demanding than the dogs of war.' His politeness implied resignation. He always knew how to remind people that he had better things to do, and did them better than they. 'Goodnight. My salutes to your sister.'

'I hope we shall meet again,' I said.

'But not on this blasted heath.'

261

'You started this, Falcon,' Ned Corman said.

'As commissioned,' Guy said.

I collected shards of Waterford glass from the table. There were, of course, servants to clear up and I probably more irritated than assisted them by my action but it appealed to me to be the last to quit the dining room. When they came in and found me with a palm full of tiny daggers and diamonds, Teresa and the butler may well have thought that I was seeking to conceal some clumsiness of my own. By the time I reached the drawing room, Benedict and Routh were discussing Claudia Monk's novel, which they decided that Charlie Lehmann should make into a movie with Sally and Ned. Charlie said, 'Now can I decide what you should both do?' The portrait of Irene Jameson was no longer leaning against the mantelpiece.

When I heard repeated banging, I tried to fit the hammering sound into the pattern of the evening. Was Hall repairing something in the dining room? Then I realized that someone was rapping again and again on the front door like a demented auctioneer. I strode out and opened it. Guy Falcon stood there, mouth half open, too close for a visitor.

'Hullo. Forget something?'

'Fire,' Guy said. 'Upstairs.'

He ran past me, stretched his arm high on to the banister and was gone, with simian agility, towards the upper bedrooms. As if it might be a naiveté I should later regret, I yelled, 'Fire. Fire.' Then I scrambled after Guy.

We ran along the corridor under the eaves. Everything appeared normal: shining doors, correct curtains, a sword-chest with a Delft bowl of mauve roses. A drift of grey smoke, no more than a shaky line at the base of a door, stopped us at the end of the corridor. Guy looked at me and then he knocked. 'Irene?'

I tried the door and, for some reason, was not sorry to discover that it was locked. 'She's done it on purpose.'

'That's a comfort.'

I said, 'We'd better do the wrong thing, hadn't we?' I shouted, 'Fire!' yet again and then I took a step back and charged the door.

It hurt my shoulder but it did not budge. Guy rumpled his beard and bent to look at the brass lock. He gentled me out of the way, braced himself against the slope of the eaves and raised his knee high in the air before crashing his heel against the door, right by the lock. Wood ripped and he hopped. A black shoulder of smoke barged us out of the way.

I threw myself on the floor and crawled on my forearms into the room.

Guy said, 'Don't be an ass.'

I could hear people running along the corridor as I inched into the bedroom. I had the feeling less of heroism than of escaping from the others. On the floor, against the wainscoting, was Guy's portrait of Irene, blistered and scorched where she had poured paraffin or lighter fuel on it. Across the room, Irene was on the four-poster bed. Flames had scaled the drapes. She lay very flat among many little fires like nasty birthday candles. I cannot say why, but the first thing I did was to kick her portrait towards the door. Confused voices promised that I had an audience. I was choking but I was not afraid; the presence of the others seemed to guarantee that I should survive. If anything, I was happy. I crawled towards the bed and reached for the unringed fingers that spilled over the edge. I was almost there, when strong hands on my ankles dragged me backwards, grating against the carpet, and out into the corridor.

Ned was saying, 'Irene! My darling, my life!' He stood on my hand as he fought to get past me into the bedroom. 'Let me get to her, you swine.'

Guy said, 'Get out of it.'

I stumbled to my feet, coughing and coughing, among the people in the corridor. They did not seem greatly to like me for my efforts. Guy hauled Ned Corman out of the burning room and banged the door shut. Wendy had hot fingers from the portrait.

'Open the door, you bastard.' Ned gathered himself to get back into the room. 'This is my bloody house.'

'You'll only burn it down,' Guy said. 'It's too late.'

Sally said, 'Ned darling, he's right.'

'Let go of me, you damned bitch. I'm going in.'

I said, 'Don't be a bloody fool, Ned. It's not possible, believe me . . .'

'What're you doing here? How did it happen? How? How?'

Brian Routh said, 'You did well.'

I said, 'I didn't get anywhere.'

'Just as well.'

The sound of the fire engines' bells gave an excuse to go back downstairs. Smoke came with us. Wendy Falcon was carrying Irene's portrait.

Guy said, 'Women.'

Flames were snapping out of the roof before the fire brigade had their equipment in place, but the main structure of Tyler's Barn was saved, although the water brought down the famous plaster ceiling in the dining room and swamped the library. Ned Corman went to London with Benedict and Karen the next day. He never returned to the house. It was sold to an advertising agency as a conference centre and hospitality facility.

Sally was in tears most of the way to London. The death of Irene was, of course, a shock, but so too was Ned's wordless departure. As we drove into town, I was aware that I had an opportunity to prove myself to be the one person on whom Sally could, after all, rely. I could imagine everything she was fearing and hoping. How could I fail to take advantage of my chance? I was neither too scrupulous nor too weak; I was indifferent. It was not only that I felt disgust at Ned's belated loyalty to Irene or that I wanted nothing more to do with him or his intrigues; Guy Falcon had, in a way, behaved worse than anyone else, except when it came to practical resourcefulness, but I still hoped that I should see him again, even if his portrait had poisoned the house it was intended to adorn. Although no one could be sure why Irene had taken it as she did, whether it spoke too loudly of the end of her beauty or simply boasted of Guy's cursory seduction of her, the admiring malice of the artist had brought the curtain down in flames. The rest of the company had turned into a collection of characters assembled in order to create enough suspects for the tragedy to have a first act. I had, perhaps, been the biggest dupe of them all, but my memory of J.T.C. drills – how to enter a burning house was a standard item – had acquitted me of utter superfluousness. Sally kept saying, 'You were the only one, Michael, the only one!' I was pleased, but I had no illusions: I had flinched from dragging Irene off the bed, when I first went into the bedroom, because I was afraid she would come to pieces. I avoided even touching that roasting flesh which had looked so irresistible at the Globe Cinema, Upper Richmond Road. Beyond everything else, however, I realized, as Sally drove tearfully towards the Embankment, that my desire for her no longer existed. Sob as she might, I did not feel the urge to comfort or possess her. Was she waiting for me to invite her in when I took my bag from the trough behind my seat? I kissed her on the cheek, as if too stricken by the tragedy to be anything but honourable, and stepped on to the gangway. We smiled wanly at each other as she drove away.

Joe Hirsch was sitting on the roof of my barge reading a manuscript. 'Heard the news?'

'All the news I want to hear.'

'They've gone and burned down St George's, Harrow Green.'

'Have they just? Who?'

'Person or persons. You thought I was talking about the Jameson woman.'

'Have some respect, Joe, could you possibly for people?'

'If people want to set fire to themselves, what's to respect exactly? You see what it means of course.'

'It means Sally Raglan and Ned Corman will be free to marry when the smoke has cleared. Yes, I do.'

'The fire.'

'It means person or persons have rendered Chester Flam some service. For which, it can safely be assumed, they will have their reward; half on commission, half on delivery?'

'Slander,' Joe said. 'Aren't you going to ask me in?'

'I'm tired, Joe. I'm shagged out. What do you want exactly?'

'I've brought you the new issue of *Black and White*. An interview with Claudia Monk complete with intelligent nipples visible through new Italian knitwear. You like?'

'Tell you what I'd like better: some back-lit interviews in the charred ruins with the masked incendiaries of North West whatever. It'd give the little film some much-needed uplift, wouldn't it?'

'That's partly what I want to see you about.'

'I wondered why it was my birthday. Want some tea?'

'Got any wine?'

'I offered you tea. Deliver your message, O wing-heeled emissary, and then we'll see whether we've got a corkscrew.'

'Chester feels the film might be misinterpreted, especially now. He doesn't want to waste your time. You have been paid. For not very much as yet. You should be grateful.'

'Why throw good money after better by showing the world how a throwback like Harrison Digby once stood between us and an architectural masterpiece which can now be built after all?'

'It was a bit of luck.'

'Not to mention a bit of good management.'

'Why would Chester sponsor anyone to make a film, as he did, with all the expenses involved, if he knew all the time that it was going to be completely unnecessary?'

'How many peanuts to the pound today, Joseph, in early trading, any idea? And ever heard of the term "alibi"? Mr Quarles'll remind you what it means, but I bet you know! Elsewhere, where I suggest you go.'

Joe said, 'You always want to think the worst of people.'

'It's often better than they deserve.'

Joe raised a one-more-thing finger to me at the door, but I shook my head. He did the same and I was alone again. There was now no reason for the public inquiry at Harrow Green to be anything but a formality. Planning permission was granted for the development along the lines of Hugo Carmody's blueprint, but Chester Flam was distressed by persistent suggestions of sharp practice. Harrison Digby was a good-humoured and pitiless enemy. His humour had rattled Chester more than the clever schemes of those who sought to take over his company or suborn his partners. Chester could cope with sharks, but he was defenceless against eccentric sports. When, after some months of saying that he would do no such thing, he sold the Harrow Green site to an insurance company, he donated a hundred thousand pounds of the profit to a fund for a new St George's, to be built on a neighbouring estate. Five tower blocks and a shopping precinct were put up on the six-acre site, leaving room for a prize-winning outer belt of terrace houses which were soon demolished in a road-widening scheme.

VII

We sat at a soft-cornered, hexagonal table of knotless pine. Brandy balloons and coffee cups suggested the end of a convivial occasion. Barnaby Monk, now Associate Editor of the *Sunday Crusader*, was at the head of the table, in a narrow-lapelled blazer, pink shirt and crocheted black tie, very thin. He frowned and moved things in front of him and tilted his head to one side and said, 'Suppose we were preparing an agenda for the next decade of the world's existence . . .'

'Optimist!' Benny Bligh said. 'What makes you give it that long?'

'Trust you to be quickly in, Benedict.'

'And quickly out again, fair Claudia. The whole operation need not take more than a few moments of your increasingly valuable time.'

'We have certain areas of generally agreed policy, don't we? Decolonization, fairer distribution of natural resources, religious toleration, an end to racial prejudice, equal opportunities for all the talents, um —'

'Pass the platitude barrel,' Benedict said. 'Barnaby wants to give it another scrape. After which he will probably turn it over and bang it several times on the bottom.'

'Do you not think,' Gordon Knight said, 'that religion and tolerance are contradictory? Tolerance is the first means by which the *philosophes* set about damaging religion. As soon as theology admits the possibility of an intellectual republic, it has as good as abdicated its crown.'

Benedict said, 'What this country seriously needs is a large measure of pectoral liberation. I spell that t,i,t,s. I am, as it happens, a founder member — and I use that word advisedly — of the pectoral liberation front, and I use *that* word advisedly also –'

'It truly is a credit to your prep school, Benedict, that you show so little inclination to leave it.'

'Claudia publishes one novel, lavishly praised by those to whom she threatens to play Rapunzel, and suddenly she's everyone's headmistress!'

'Benedict should have been born in the South Seas,' Harriet Beaumont said.

'One of my main reforms – and I do recommend it to your executive, Harriet – will be the right of anyone confronted by authority in any of its pretentious garbs, to demand that everyone present strip off, *instanter*. Imagine High Court judges without the drag. If we could but see them in their sorry flesh, all purple wattles and wrinkled dugs –'

'Oh Benedict, *please!*'

'No need to say please, Claudia; in your case, *when* will be quite sufficient. Half the things that scandalize the judiciary are less pernicious than they are, and a lot more amusing. Hands up for mutual masturbation.'

'Benedict ought to be available on the National Health,' Quentin Beaumont said. 'He'd have the nation up and about in no time.'

'One thing I should certainly crack down on: immigration. There are far too many people in this country already. Apart from Jews and Blacks, I should ban all new arrivals.'

Harry Pearce came in, both hands raised in commanding surrender. 'People, people! It's fine, it's lovely, it's going very well. But as this is only a pilot programme, let's have an interim post mortem, before we're dead, shall we? Because some of you aren't getting too much of a shout. Eight people may be too many, of course –'

Quentin Beaumont said, 'I'm very happy to go for a walk and possibly to be gone for a considerable time.'

'Me too, because aren't you going to get into trouble if you have too many people from the Left?'

'It's all right, Harriet,' Benedict said, 'I'm a socialist. That ought to help balance things out.'

Harry Pearce glanced at his clipboard. 'Michael, I wonder if you'd do something for me.'

'Do I hear the running of an early bath?'

'Take over the chair. I'd like to bring Barnaby into the general conversation a bit more.'

I was flattered and criticized at the same time. I had sat listening to my contemporaries with the feeling that I was incurably younger than they. Harriet was one of the new Labour members of parliament and Quentin was already a university lecturer. Claudia Monk's first novel, *Family Circles*, had turned her not only into a literary celebrity but also into a beauty. She was wearing a long-sleeved, scoop-necked dress of gold and green silk. There was a black velvet choker about her supple throat. Her tawny hair looked more luxuriant since the press had saluted her talent; her frown had the radiance of a smile she had no longer any need to display. I had known her as Claudia Terracini, a very English-seeming girl blessed with a name more glamorous than its owner could quite sustain, for all her terse and timeless Mediterranean poems. When she married Barnaby, and took his monosyllabic name, she appeared to have advanced into being someone altogether more plausible: she *was* Claudia Monk, where she had only affected to be Miss Terracini. Now that she was being photographed and interviewed, under her old name, it was as if she had split her new skin and proved herself entitled to be the improbably named girl I had first known. Barnaby was both proud and sulky: he possessed a wife to whom he was obliged to establish himself all over again. She had married him because he was destined to succeed: beautiful and deferential, her future was depended on his. Now he feared that he had been right to fear that she might be cleverer than he. She showed no symptom of discontent as we came down the stairs from the studio, her arm latched over Barnaby's, unsmiling at Benedict's latest effrontery. Her shoes matched her dress, a showy conformity.

There was a wrinkled menace in her dutiful smartness.

'You did well,' Barnaby said.

'You did better,' I said.

'And Benedict – alas! – did best.'

'He will yet turn the lavatory wall into the artistic locus of his generation, won't you, Bligh?'

'Michael, you shouldn't be here, should you? Why aren't you in Algeria?'

'Despite my sallow cast of countenance,' I said, 'I'm not an Arab. Nor do I wish to get my feet black, only then to be obliged to remove them from somebody's magic carpet.'

'Writing plays about people who drop their aitches and – rather too late into the second act – their mass-produced knickers is no recipe for redemption. The drama needs a serious subject. Algeria has to be seen.'

'When do you leave?'

'I'm a registered coward,' Benedict said. 'But the gypsy he say, doctoring film scripts for Charlie Lehmann, no matter how toothsome his wife, is no ticket to eternity. Ten shillings, please. I can get you into F.L.N. headquarters. I've got contacts in Tunis through Jean-Pierre Jumeau.'

'Very smart,' I said. 'I know the Algerians are right and that history's on their side, but am I on history's?'

Gordon Knight had put on his bicycle clips and was wheeling his Raleigh by its taped racing handlebars from the porter's office towards the numbered glass doors of Alhambra House. He wore the orange polo-necked sweater in which he had been photographed after writing *Joy and Anguish* while living in a disused deckchair store in Regent's Park. I regarded him with envious pity. How could he have read all those books, without the advantages of scholarships and with the advice only of public librarians? The enthusiasm which greeted *Joy and Anguish* was at once immoderate and patronizing. When the critics discovered a new Saul among the prophets, their congratulations were as much for themselves, on discovering so rough a diamond, as for the jewel they saluted. As he threaded his handlebars through the rotating doors of Alhambra House, I called out, 'Good luck with the new one, Gordon.'

Benedict said, 'You know that Quentin's already done the definitive hatchet job on *Left, Right and Religion*, don't you?'

'Who's been peeking at other people's proofs before they're even in the pudding?' Quentin Beaumont was tall and severe. His profile might have encouraged him to be an actor, and a seducer, had he not been apprenticed to rigour by his intellectual precociousness. He and Harriet advertised the breadth of their minds by their marital proximity. He was a sceptic for whom her Catholicism was neither an embarrassment nor an absurdity. His willingness to embrace a woman dedicated to antique superstition was a warrant both of his love for Harriet and of his capacity for logical and emotional finesse. The two of them advertised that the unlikely was, in the England they hoped and intended to sponsor, a viable way of life. The one had no doubts at all, the other made doubt a method; together they announced synthesis to be the love of equals and opposites. Benedict Bligh described their closeness as 'a comedy without errors or laughs'.

Claudia said, 'Michael, do you want to come back and have a very little to eat for supper?'

'Sounds delicious,' I said.

The Monks already had their three-floored place in Norland Square although the square itself was still rather too far west for smartness. I was impressed by the size and solidity of their establishment. The Victorian furniture suited the psoriatic stucco of the house. Its weighty sombreness suggested a marriage rooted in generations of settled propriety. I recognized proleptic cunning in Claudia's domesticity; she had prepared this dutiful homeliness before literary success revealed her to be more than a mere housewife: modesty served vanity. The Welsh dresser with its blue freight of Delft, the floral Chesterfields whose sagging centres testified to ancestors of substantial *poids*, the double-parked books and the knickknacked corner cupboards, the unmodish portraits in bargain frames (aged by their dust), the hinge-fronted Victorian doll's house on the laundry table by the window over the long, seedy garden, these things insisted on stability, even as *Family Circles* announced Claudia's scorn for its pretences.

Barnaby opened a bottle of Marqués de Cáceres and poured it into thick, dignifying glasses. It was not difficult to pretend to be grown up with the sound of a crying baby coming down the stairs. I could imagine Claudia working a shoulder of that figured silk down her golden arm, a breast compressed and then coolly liberated. The supping silence of little Caroline gave the image a stirring reality. On second thoughts, Claudia would probably unzip the dress and let it slip forwards down her arms. 'You're damned lucky, Barnaby, I must say, aren't you?'

'Think so?' Barnaby took good fortune to be an unfair accusation. 'What do you really think of Claudia's book?'

'How much of it is true, as a matter of interest?'

'You'll have to ask her,' Barnaby said. 'Is there a film in it?'

'I'm sure Claudia has megaphonic agents to push her wares with far more volume than I can contrive.'

When Claudia came down the stairs in a thank-God-that's-over cotton dress with big buttons down the front, she had shucked her golden shoes and was wearing schoolgirlish sandals. 'She's such a pig! In one end and out the other. Nature is disgustingly unsubtle, isn't she? Has anyone done anything about food at all?'

'We've done something about drink,' Barnaby said.

'Time I got round to this impressive second novel – such a difficult hurdle! – about a woman who's expected to give suck to all age groups and never gets a drop in return.'

'Here, suck this,' Barnaby said. 'Michael's been telling me what's wrong with your novel.'

'Does he lie to you about everything?' I said.

'If a man can't conceal things from his wife,' she said, 'who can he conceal them from? Why aren't you married, Michael?'

'I've read too many highly promising first novels. And all the best women are already spoken for.'

'This one can speak for herself, can't she, Claw?'

Claudia took Barnaby's proffered hand and clamped it over her mouth for a gag before nodding agreement. Then she bit the drumstick of his thumb. 'Did you hate this afternoon as much as I did, Michael?'

'It rather depends on whether it comes to anything.'

'How can what you feel about something depend on its consequences?'

'Easily,' I said. 'The sensation of being recruited into an army in which one would never have chosen to march always has a certain piquancy. The trouble is, being invited to be outspoken always disposes me to reticence.'

'If they want to make you resident chairman,' Barnaby said, 'which they may well, don't hesitate. You'll get your plays put on if you're the king of that particular castle even more easily than if Ned Corman wants you worse than a knighthood.'

'You'll almost certainly be the nap selection,' I said, 'not least because you have favours of your own – or other people's – to dispense. Space in the paper? Up you go!'

'Does anyone fancy omelettes?' Claudia reached for the bottle and replenished her hazed glass. 'There are plenty of eggs.'

'Nice idea,' Barnaby said.

'They're in the fridge.'

Claudia took the bottle to the Chesterfield in front of the cold fireplace and put her feet up. I sat in the honest tub chair by the dangling tongs and smiled at a copy of *Family Circles* on the cut-down table between us. 'The character that interests me most is Ludovico. Was he your father – or shouldn't one ask?'

'One shouldn't and he was. An opportunist wop Fascist who walked out on my mousy Mancunian mother when I was three years old. I never saw him again until well after the war, by which time I was sixteen. His name isn't Ludovico, it's Reynaldo, but otherwise . . .'

'The strangest thing about being at university with people is that you never know anything about their families.'

'I had a father and a mother,' Claudia said. 'Never a family.'

'Well, you've got one now.' The back of one of her ankles was quite callused. There was a tab of thickened skin there. 'When you say he's a Fascist . . .'

'Was,' she said. 'There's no point in being a Fascist without Fascism. It's a system of graft, not a collection of ideas. He's a Christian Democrat now. He was in South America for most of the war. B.A. Clever him. Plenty of time to make sure the coast was clear before he sailed home.'

'And did you really go to see him, all by yourself, when you were sixteen?'

'That's not very young anywhere except in England. Mind you, not *everything* that happened in the book happened in literal fact. Not that father-daughter incest is all that unusual. Or all that unpleasant necessarily, I imagine. Were you shocked?'

'Why did she do it? Because he'd been a Fascist or because he'd let her and her mother down?'

'Perhaps she wanted to avenge her mother; perhaps she wanted to make sure that nothing that had happened to the mother was going to happen to her. Perhaps she was avenging herself *on* her mother. How does one explain the inexplicable?'

'Is she still alive, your mother?'

'She lives in Letchworth. And if you want to know, she assumes I did it for the money. The book. She's been teaching the violin for twenty-five years, living in two rooms in the school grounds. Money's rarely a bad reason to do things.'

'I've had my omelette,' Barnaby called from the back of the house. 'Do you want me to have yours?'

I said, 'He's got another family now presumably?'

'Of course. It was much more awkward for him to introduce me to them as his daughter than to have them assume I was his latest mistress. One aged him; the other made him younger than ever. You want me to have slept with him, don't you? I wanted to. It was about the first time I ever wanted to do anything. I even knew exactly how. Me on top. *Così!* So much for virginal innocence!'

'Small wonder no one wants to be a bloody cook these days.'

Claudia put her hands on the cut-down table and leaned

across to me, all that new golden hair tumbled about her face, and kissed me on the lips. Then she stood up, as if I had given offence. I followed her to the kitchen where a plastic-aproned Barnaby was tilting a bulging omelette on to an unaffected stoneware dish.

Claudia said, 'Have you ever met Barnaby's father, Buck? He's the top copy and Barn's the carbon, aren't you, *marito mio*, serviceable but faintly smudged?'

'People like Barnaby and I tend to keep our fathers well away from each other.'

'Claudia likes to think my father would have shot hers, given a tenth of a chance. Reynaldo represents everything Buck spent half his life fighting against.'

'Buck is bliss,' Claudia said. 'A gentleman Communist. Where but in England, or Italy, do you find one of those?'

'What did he think about Hungary?' I said.

'Oh he left the Party long before that,' Barnaby said. 'Or rather he always said that the Party left him.'

'Did he ever actually shoot anybody?'

'Notice the subtlety with which Michael seeks information. He also extracts wisdom teeth without anaesthetics. When he finally chucked the Party, they told him, as a leaving present, that a man he'd helped to trail in Madrid in 1937, as a Franco spy, was actually a Trot. The evidence my father unearthed and presented to the tribunal was planted specially so that he could find it. He was the sort of witness no one could disbelieve. The man he fingered was a German refugee who'd come back from New York to fight for the Republic. They shot him in the back of the head. I found myself one day trying to persuade Buck that they'd been lying and the man really was a spy. He said it really didn't matter which was true. I was rather horrified, probably because he was right. Finding your parents are honest is rather a shock to the system, don't you find?'

'Do you think we could ever possibly be like that? Can you seriously imagine killing someone, or delivering someone to be killed? Not me.'

'I shot at someone in Somaliland,' Barnaby said. 'I never knew if I hit him or not. Either he's still alive or I'm a killer.'

'And what did you think as you were firing at him?'

'What a bloody idle section I had with me in the truck. They should've been quicker on the trigger than I was. My animus was directed entirely at them. Normal, I should suppose. Did you never get a shot off at anyone?'

'No great opportunity at Camberley,' I said. 'Or even in Versailles, where I was briefly.'

The ghost of a tune, played and then replayed on a muted piano, seemed to drift in from the garden. If it was haunting, it was because it promised a popularity it had yet to achieve. The player stopped and began again and seemed, as he resumed, to have added a new, appealing element. It was as if one were hearing for the first time something already famous.

'Larry's at it already!' Claudia said. 'Did you know him? Larry Page? The demon lodger. He was a choral scholar in Barnaby's college. I can't wait to get him out of the basement and a nice, untalented *ragazza* from Foggia into it.'

'You see where the ruthless streak is in our family, don't you?' Barnaby saluted his wife with a straight arm. '*Duce! Duce!* Benedict was right about Algeria, Michael. We can send you there, if you want us to.'

'And stash your nanny in my barge? Sorry, but I've got other commitments, and I'm not really sorry at all. I'm doing a documentary about Guy Falcon for the B.B.C. Don't tell me I'm wasting my time. It gets me behind a camera, which is what I want. And in front of a rather interesting man, whatever your shit of a critic may have said about his last show.'

'The nice thing about you, Michael is . . . What *is* the nice thing about him, Claw?'

'He always helps with the washing up.'

The sound of Larry Page's composition was louder in the street. He had a separate entrance, down the service stairs, to the white room in which I could just see him as I left the Monks. Some haughty modesty prevented me from approaching him, though I thought he would write excellent music for my documentary.

At one moment it seemed that I was a fortunate young man, with interesting contemporaries and happy prospects, and at the next, wondering whether I should take a bus or walk back to Chelsea, I was plunged into incurable solitude. Walking through Holland Park, I tasted the soreness of my soul like some painful and delicious ulcer. What a comfort it was to have busy days in my diary! And yet what a pointless life I was leading and how I longed for some shaping purpose! I was so desperate, in the midst of all my small hopes, that I almost rang Benedict to ask him to smuggle me into Algeria. Absurdly, it was less the danger which inhibited me than the fear of rejection. Was my French inadequate for conversations with *gauchisants* intellectuals like Jumeau, whose existential company I craved in the days when I was in Paris and met Pierrette? I could imagine too easily how comic it would seem to the F.L.N. to have a Jew seeking to prove himself in their midst. If I were Algerian, or French, I might have had the passion or the ironic sophistication to handle the paradox; as an Englishman, I should be either a fool or a dupe. I lacked the assertive neutrality of a doctor, who could be both partisan and Samaritan. Imagination lamed enthusiasm; its fanciful ingenuity demobbed my militance. I had enjoyed the army because, in the lucky lacuna of the twentieth century in which I was called upon to slope arms, and later to be saluted, there was nothing but playfulness in my soldiering, unless it was tedium. When I strode around, after being commissioned, I was torn between a feeling of pride and one of imposture. Was I now really of the same stuff as those who led their men over the top, armed only with a steady accent and a swagger stick? I feared that I had a greater affinity with plausible rascals who defrauded old ladies and hotel receptionists: I could act the officer but I flinched from officiousness. Deception was nicer than responsibility; it was more sincere.

*

I made no strict plans for the filming I was to do with Guy Falcon. When we had had a preparatory drink at the Savile I assumed an intimacy which I should never have dared without the corporation's warrant. Even as I made it plain that I had nothing but contempt for the regular structure, I was emboldened by its warrant. Guy and I were both happy to be pirates with assisted passages. Arithmetic promised that he was only eleven years older than I, but his long reputation and his aging beard, his rumpled ruefulness and astute resentment, the roster both of his dated achievements and of his important friends, put a generation between us. When I mentioned Irene Jameson, with mournful tact, his blue-grey eyes, under the mobile brows, were prompted to complicity, as if we had to pretend to regret.

The occasion for making the film was that Guy had been commissioned to design the stained glass for the new church of St George, Harrow Green. As we sat in the Sandpit at the Savile, I was flattered by the speed with which our rapport developed. As if on some involuntary movieola, on which a subconscious editor had bracketed a trial reel, spools of the past were spliced together in my mental viewing theatre. I saw the little drawing, and its inscription, in Rachel's old room, and I saw Guy's face, and his wife's, at Tyler's Barn; I realized that he was capable of his present geniality not least because it allowed him again to savour what he could no longer enjoy. Pleasure graced him with a charm which I could not resist, even as I recognized its duplicity. Treachery was more sensitive than candour, and more entertaining. Guy's intelligence was at once ruthless and scrupulous, egotistical and magnanimous. Teasing and wooing were indistinguishable: he enabled me to understand, with a shiver and a smile, how one might know that a man was a traitor and yet be loyal to him. He had been dropped into Greece during the war and told me of a liaison officer whom they had suspected of commerce with the enemy. As if amused by my inquisitive apprehension, Guy gave a dry account of the tenderness with which the final trap had been prepared for a principled traitor, whose political sophistication rendered him too clever for obedience and too arrogant for caution. Guy saw in this man, who had been shot by a companion on a patrol, a complete adult, unconfused by furtive frivolity. 'The opposite of an artist. A phoenix that never flinched from the ashes. You never get bread sauce with that kind of fowl. How is she these days? The queen. Your sister.'

'She's out in Africa. West African Federation, as it's soon to be.'

'She did the right thing, blast her lovely eyes. When are you coming down to The Old Mill? If I know anything about your lords and masters, you'll have to grind exceeding fast to finish within your schedule.'

The plan for the film took shape only after I had finished shooting. Loops of processed stock hung, like dark and gleaming *pasta*, from the hooks in my basement office. I felt as I had when in command of a platoon, commissioned to give orders without understanding how anything actually worked. What a liberating bluff to find oneself so authoritative and so lacking in mechanical competence! My editor, Simon Young, acted out a courteous pretence of not knowing what should be done until I suggested it. Yet I proposed resection without being able, if Simon had not been ready with his scissors and paste, even to stick two ends together. But if my practical skill was negligible, my hunches were not vacuous. Was my instinct for film made keener by the absence of practical qualifications? Art, like poker, was a game in which the bluffer was not necessarily a fraud.

My fine cut began with panels of pure colour. Scissors cut into them; their unoiled progress was grimly surgical. Then there was a face: bespectacled Jesus, in attendant agony, as the Roman soldiers became savage carpenters. Guy had prepared many charcoal sketches on which I dawdled. He gloried in doing more than was required, aggressive generosity. Out of economy, I had myself played the interviewer, though I was determined never to appear in shot. My voice was heard to ask, as Guy jaundiced Jesus with a panel of yellow perspex, 'Do you believe in God?'

'I believe in Gods,' he said.

'How do you feel about being commissioned, in 1961, to do a crucifixion?'

'Unenriched.'

'*Méchant*,' I had said, but I removed the foreign flirtatiousness from the screened version. 'Are you a Christian?'

'I am and I'm not. I'm for and I'm against. That fraudulent genius Pablo P. once called God "The other craftsman". If only he'd had the wit to say "the other charlatan"! Now you see Him, now you don't. He may not exist, but He undoubtedly creates. The truth of the sea, the lie of the land! Where does man end and God begin?'

I put another Jesus on the screen and held on that stubbled, civilian deity as he watched a legionary frown for the right nail.

'Nothing in this world can be trusted to be only what it is. A thing is what it is *and* another thing. Nature specializes in vile economies. The father's living procured the son's dying: hammer and nails, the carpenter's and the executioner's kit. Nice and nasty.'

He had incorporated scenes from a football match among the crowd at the foot of the cross. The fans were fat and hungry for the others' agony, bilious with impersonal animosity. Hatred banded brothers more easily than love.

'Are you being fair to the crowd at Calvary, do you think?' My voice galled me with its sensible tone.

'All pity gloats,' Guy said. 'The soldiers didn't hate him, nor did the women, but think of Peter. The rock of the church was split all right. Those three denials were affirmations of a kind, but what kind? The soldiers cursed Him, not because they gave a damn about theology but because He was another job of bloody work before the weekend. Like art. I curse Him myself: why won't He agree to be easy to do? Fair to the crowd! The crowd always wants whatever it's going to be a little bit ashamed to have had, a bit of the other. Every witness is an accomplice. If Christianity hadn't institutionalized guilt, would the church have survived? We measure the sun by the shadow it casts. Marriage may be a perishable business, but adultery is made in heaven. Life lights the fuse for death; artless truth makes lying into a craftsman's trade. What kind of intentions is the road to the City of God paved with? Never ask!'

I said, 'Is the bishop going to understand this set of windows, do you think, when it's finally installed in St George's, Harrow Green?'

'I don't ask to be understood. If I'm understood, how can I have done anything? Misunderstand me, chum, or I'm bloody well kaput.' Guy let his belly sag, in sudden, exhaling audition for some spent Silenus. 'Portrait of a man famous when he was twenty and who is now working his way towards oblivion. How else am I to be remembered?' He cocked his beard forward with a rumple of the chin. 'Can she really be happy with that man?'

'How do we ever know what makes anyone happy?'

'Money helps,' Guy said.

I said, 'You don't mean that.'

'You don't know much about art if you think it gets done A.M.D.G. Have you seen Beethoven's rates for concertos, symphonies and sonatas? Very competitive. No reasonable offer refused. Nothing about the moral worth of the commissioner or the spiritual preparedness of the composer. What did the soldiers do when Jesus was *in extremis* above them? Argued about the rate for the job. And what does art do with the crucifixion? Anything better? I'm not telling you what you want to hear, and that suits you fine, doesn't it? Look shocked and I know I've made you happy. No one can honestly ever have what he wants. Art always delivers what hasn't been ordered. Otherwise it would be like logic, a recipe for those who are never disappointed and never anything else. Aythankkew.'

I ended with Guy's larky bow and then superimposed the indifferent crowd, some modern and some 'biblical' faces, a spectrum of survivors down the ages. I left a note for Simon, thanking him for his patience and trying it with a few further trims and tricks, and then I walked out of the windowless office into a bent corridor where I was abruptly deflated by the pettiness of what had seemed, all afternoon, a significant challenge. Why had I dedicated days and days to a little film about a painter? Who needed yet another instalment of the convenient cant about the importance of art in society? I told myself that I should now be better able to progress to making real films, though I had to admit, as dusty sunshine made me sneeze, that I had agreed to be diverted from what I found demanding and unendurable. I was evading the comedy of a world which had trumped tragedy and rendered it naive, in order to provide consolation for those who liked to believe that there had been no incurable caesura between what had been plausible before 1939 and what could decently be maintained since. The confusion of my thoughts was matched by my inability to find my way out of the building. I found myself going over a 'spur' and coming into another set of corridors. A girl backed out of a room and turned, handbag hanging next to a gleaming nyloned leg, towards the lifts. I caught her up and stood by her shoulder for a moment. Then I said, 'Excuse me, but didn't we once spend the night together?'

She looked into the blush of the afternoon sun. 'Thank heavens it's you,' Annie Rose said. 'And aren't you lucky I didn't slosh you with my handbag?'

'The line was irresistible,' I said. 'What's a disreputable girl like you doing in a nice place like this?'

'As it turns out, nothing whatsoever. I came, I was seen and I failed to conquer. They were supposed to be hiring someone, but they're not. At least not me. I thought I might become a script editor.'

'You don't want to do that,' I said.

'And just as well.'

I said, 'Do you know how long it is since we were doing that little play of mine at Colchester?'

'It was just last week, wasn't it?'

'God help us, over four years.'

The lift came and we stood side by side, waiting for the doors to shut.

'I loved that little play,' Annie said. 'It was so nice.'

'And so were you, by God.'

She flowered without the sun. Her lips bulged into a new smile and she looked at her feet and then, with a chuck of her head, directly at me. The lift stopped. The doors opened. I noticed the pucker of her pierced ear. I could imagine her, at her early morning mirror, deciding that a B.B.C. board might not approve of her favourite earrings. The lift doors shut on us again and we were going up. At the sixth floor, the doors opened and no one was waiting. I said, 'Now we know who lives up here: immortal, invisible God only wise. The Supreme Executive who could give us everything we want, if it weren't better for us to struggle along with a reduced budget. You're not still living in that little attic of yours in Colchester, are you?'

'Am I not? All I need now is to find that I've been evicted in my absence.'

We were again at the ground floor. The doors opened. She went out so briskly that I feared that I had offended her. I watched her being independent for a moment and then I called out, 'Annie . . .' She stopped by the doors and looked round, as if she might have dropped something. I said, 'I happen to have here, by pure chance, two tickets for something that really shouldn't be missed.' I took two pound notes from my pocket and rubbed them in front of her eyes. 'To my chagrin and relief my oldest friend seems unlikely to show up after all, so what do you say, as long as it's yes?'

The Amadeus Quartet was playing at Kenwood, in the open air. I dreaded the humiliation of being unable even to achieve entry to so modest an occasion, but it proved an easy paradise. The musicians at least had resolved the contradictions which baffled me. Their language was uncompromised by the wanton perversions of speech. The continuities of expertise transcended the slaughterers' century. Because I knew so little of music (my father, the dancer, could scarcely carry a tune, though he never missed a beat), I was delivered from informed attention; I could only accept a beauty I could not dwell upon. Incapable of knowledgeable modesty, my mind pestered me with dramatic ideas. I felt in my pocket for a pen or pencil and had neither. Not looking, Annie opened her bag and came out with a Venus. I scribbled in the margin of my programme and then I watched her profile, the straight nose cuffed with wax-pink flesh, the unblinking, rust-lashed eye caressed again and then again by the fall of the lid. She turned to me with a girlish wince, as if she feared that I had disliked what so enthralled her. As she clasped her bag again, over the recovered pencil, and was ready for the next movement, I was dizzied with overwhelming affection. I felt, in one swoop of amazed appetite, as if she had been in my life for years and years and I had been too cheap to realize it. I wanted to repair all at once the shortfall of attention. The practical evidence of desire caused the face-down programme to rise and then slip from my lap. I hid my embarrassment by reaching into the shadowed grass for the elusive paper. When I came up with it, people were already clapping.

During the interval, I could think of nothing to say. I suspect I seemed taciturn, bored perhaps. Annie looked at me with bewilderment, but she did not lose her composed humour. We took our places and the Mozart, at once familiar and abstruse, required the silence which I craved. It restored Annie to me as she had been when I realized how much I, yes, liked her. Affection outranked love in that sweet mood. I revelled in a calmness which had never before preceded the wish to touch a girl. Perhaps I thought she was lucky. Who was she, after all, but a little provincial stage manager? As I sat there, aware of every breath she drew, of the past proximity of her flesh, she leaned her head against my shoulder and closed her eyes. She was sleeping with me before we had so much as held hands!

The piece ended. The audience clapped. Annie opened her eyes and looked up at me with flattering alarm; I might have been a wicked stranger. I put my arm around her and kissed her on those pink, pouting lips. Her eyelids fluttered and then closed and she leaned her face into mine. We were lovers. The kiss was broken by the shuffle of the audience as it abandoned hope of an encore and began to consider buses and trains. We stood amid the emptying, slatted rows and I took her hand to my lips. She put her hand to my face and touched my mouth. I said, 'Annie Rose.'

We walked to Archway station and I ran into the street and flagged down an unexpected taxi. As we rode across town to Chelsea Embankment, we kissed and kissed. I refrained from putting my hand on her breast or trying her legs. I wanted to impress her with my discretion and to give her no excuse for refusing me. When, perhaps by mistake, her hand fell into my lap, and stayed there, I was a little shocked.

I led her across lurching gangways to the barge. It was getting dark, but there was no mistaking who was sitting on the roof of 'Ariel', feet dangling over the curved lintel of the red front door. 'Oh Michael, darling, darling! Thank heavens!'

'Sally, I can't see you now.'

'I'm sorry if it's inconvenient.'

'It's not inconvenient.' Annie's hand was cold in mine, and then it was not there at all. 'It's impossible.'

'You're the only person in the whole world I can talk to.'

'Count again.'

'Something too too terrible has happened.' Sally was wearing a brown check donkey jacket and had a Turkish peasant scarf knotted under her trembling chin. Desperation had frayed the skin on her bottom lip. Tears glinted like promises in her hugely frantic eyes. She made an irresistible effort to be polite to Annie: 'Hullo, how are you?'

Annie said, 'Hullo.'

'I'm Sally Raglan.'

'I know. And I'm Annie Rose.'

'Of course! How *are* you? I wouldn't normally do this, ever, but I simply must talk to Michael. It's life or death.'

I said, 'They're not going to let you play Flavia in the film of Aubrey Jellinek's immortal musical!'

'Oh my God,' Sally said, 'aren't they? It's one thing after another. Where did you hear this? Oh Michael, you are an absolute bustard: you shouldn't joke about things like this. Can we possibly go inside?'

Annie said, 'I'd better perhaps –'

'No, we can't,' I said. 'And you'd better not, Annie. Sally's just going. You don't seem to understand: I don't give a damn about the world coming to an end. Annie and I are going to get married.'

Sally took it well for a second and a half and then, to my embarrassed delight, she howled. Her mouth was a hoop of dark and baleful noise. She seemed to have no teeth, simultaneously a baby and an old woman.

Annie said, 'You shouldn't make jokes like that.'

I said, 'No joke at all. I mean it.'

Annie turned away and started across the swaying planks for the shore.

'Have you by any chance seen the evening paper?'

'No,' I said, 'and I don't want to. If you've come to sell me a copy, please go away. When I want one, I'll contact the circulation manager.' Even as I raged, I was conscious that it was easier, and more enjoyable, to be angry with Sally than to chase after, and recapture, Annie. 'Please go away.'

'Ned's going to marry Sylvia Sherwood,' Sally said. 'How can he? How *can* he?'

'It couldn't be because it's exactly what you deserve, could it?'

'I hate him so much. For what he did to us. If you knew how I fought and fought to stop them slinging you off *Zenda*. Oh Michael, you know how much I love you and how much you love me . . .'

Annie was waving at taxis on the embankment. I shrugged Sally's arm from my shoulder, weak as a dreamer. 'I'm sorry if you're unhappy –'

'I'm not unhappy. I'm desperate. Desperate, I tell you.'

'Dialogue by Gerald Pringle,' I said. '*Annie.*'

Annie was opening a taxi door when I reached her. I fumbled for money to appease the driver (the flag was already down) and could not decide what part of her to grab. She said, 'I'm going to miss my train.'

I said, 'Excellent news. I love you. I want to marry you. Do you want to marry me by any chance?'

She said, 'I don't know.'

Sally was walking along the gangway towards the black pit of the river. Only someone convinced that she was not alone could have conveyed abandonment simply by that droop of the shoulder, the hand on the railing which seemed, like a sulky child, reluctant to keep up with the rest of her body.

'I think she's going to chuck herself in,' Annie said.

'I'll go and give her a hand,' I said.

The cabbie said, 'What's going on?'

I said, 'Hold on, I'll go and get your next fare and be back in half a minute, a new world and Olympic record.'

'Stupid games,' the cabbie said.

I ran across the road and called out, 'Sally, Sally . . .'

She faltered and looked back and the lights of the Albert Bridge bloomed in her eyes. I grabbed her urgently by the arm and hauled her to the ticking taxi. I pushed her into the back of the cab and shut the door and held it shut until she gave the driver some sad destination; then I scanned the shadows for Annie. She was striding towards Beaufort Street. When I caught her, she looked both unaccusing and implacable. 'I hated that.'

'How about some Italian food? Think that'd go down any better? I've opened an exclusive little restaurant for two. Please don't let Miss Raglan poison the pasta.'

She sniffed, through one nostril, it seemed, and tilted her head and I thought: so this is my wife. We went back to the barge and I bolted the door while she hung her interview coat on the brass hook next to a passe-partouted playbill from Colchester. When we kissed this time, I slid my hand over her breast and found the nipple already sprung. Male absurdity made me faintly scandalized by her body's annunciation. When my fingers found her moist, some rakish department of my brain sneered at my unnecessary declarations: I had published the banns when I might have enjoyed her without their benefit. I thrust my hand deeper between her unstockinged thighs. She pushed me from her and sat straight. 'Do you always serve black smoke with your spaghetti?'

I ran to the stove. 'It's O.K. The burns are only second-degree. This sauce will live. Official.'

Annie said, 'I suppose we should try doing one thing at a time.'

I said, 'I've never found that to be anything like enough.'

She said, 'Then what do you want to get married for?'

'Only to stop you going back to Colchester.'

She did not smile and she did not frown. She considered me. She thought about me and she doubted something. Her expression cleared and then her chin was suddenly a gathering of tiny crevices that quivered together. She laughed and she cried. The contradiction of her feelings made me busy with the supper: looking at her was a kind of spying. All of her decisions were made as I unstrung the *pasta* from the saucepan into a glass dish. I knew that she would come to bed with me and I knew (with a taint of disappointment) that neither persuasion nor cunning would now be needed. We ate our smoky food and talked about other people, for instance Frank Kitson, in ruthless alliance. The years during which we had been acquaintances were read, in retrospect, as a long ritual of courtship which culminated in the moment when, without modesty or brazenness, Annie took off her clothes and arranged them on a narrow ladder-backed chair I had bought, green and black, in Fulham. Somehow I expected her to be wearing more layers than she was. Her nakedness was offered before I was ready for it.

She said, 'Look, have you got anything at all?'

I said, 'Don't worry.'

She said, 'I'd sooner not. Hence my question.'

I said, 'Yes, I do. I'm sorry.'

'Don't be. I'm not.'

Naked, we resumed our strangeness. Her earlier lovers crowded my imagination. Desire faltered and then it was more urgent than the books advised. Our eyes lost their complicity. My widish bunk seemed too narrow for our awkward eagerness. I considered some adroit transfer to the floor, but dared not propose it. I probed and seemed to be refused. I feared that I should not be able to last much longer. And then I realized, in a futile gush, that she was not testing me at all, and there was blood on me, and her, and the sheet.

'You should have told me,' I said.

'Meaning I should have warned you.'

I said, 'It'll get better. Much.'

'It better, hadn't it?'

I kissed her rumpled forehead and put my arm round her damp waist. 'You were waiting for me all this time.'

'Was I? I wish I'd known.'

'You know now. Dear Annie . . .'

'Oh please,' she said, 'don't write me a letter yet. Give us another chance!'

When I said, 'I love you and nothing else matters,' I felt a little magnanimous. Her virginity was not a gift I valued. I was touched and I was slightly vexed. The tincture of resentment, at finding that Annie was everything I might have hoped she was, armed me with an almost cruel resolution to make her happy. When, in the small hours, she cried out at the discovery of what I was determined that she should find, I smiled into the darkness, as if I had a secret accomplice.

She said, 'Oh honey!'

I said, 'Many happy returns.'

She said, 'I'll never smell fish without thinking of this moment.'

I said, 'I can't guarantee that that's fish, but by all means think it is. This particular river is a strange umber god.'

She said, 'Do I have to like Eliot?'

I was going to marry a cleverer girl than I had supposed, and just as well. 'You don't have to like anything you don't want to,' I said, 'and I very much doubt if you would anyway. I, on the other hand, must tell you that I find it very hard to distinguish

Mozart from Haydn from Schubert, unless I've got the crib available.'

She said, 'I've never forgotten the way you looked at my sofa.'

'Love at first light,' I said. 'Perhaps I'm really marrying you for your *meubles*.'

Annie said, 'The trouble with marriage is, it involves so many people, doesn't it?'

The telephone rang while we were having bendable cornflakes with not enough milk. I said, 'Hullo, possibly.'

'Mr Michael? This is Kendall. From Gloucester Mansions. I'm sorry to call you so early, but we've lost your grandmother.'

I said, '*Lost* her?'

'She's dead, Mr Michael. And as Mr Samuel and . . . your mother are in the South of France, I didn't know who else to call.'

The old lady lay among her pillows with a napkin knotted under her jaw. In death she had become the Jewess she was so determined not to be in life. I could not help thinking that she had, as she liked, had the last laugh. My father would have to be recalled from La Napoule. Like a cunning baby, who need not even cry to command attention, she lay there causing a commotion. It was as if even with her eyes shut she could see how awkward she was making things. Kendall stood in the doorway, pious with mischief, hands joined under the usual cross. 'Will everyone be coming to the funeral, do you suppose, Mr Michael?'

'Who exactly do you have in mind?' Death had slimmed my grandmother into a parcel of grey flesh; a false modesty seemed to enfold her. All the cosmetic pots and medicine bottles with which she had played turned into antiques and remnants. Her stillness teased us, who were obliged to act as if she both could and could not censor our conversation. 'Well?'

'My lips are sealed,' Kendall said. 'Your grandmother told me everything, but as a Christian, I have to honour my word to her.'

I still had no car of my own. There was nowhere convenient to keep it on Chelsea Embankment. When I had money, I took taxis. I drove my father's Alvis to the airport, a courtesy which was also, ridiculously, a kind of escapade. I never borrowed his car and I had the keys only in case an emergency required its evacuation. I was not sure how he would take his mother's death, but he proved more amused than distressed. 'At least she waited till we'd had two weeks,' he said.

My mother made tea when we got back to Court Royal, while my father and I sat together in the drawing room, anxious to say appropriate things, though neither of us, it seemed, was deeply moved. 'Poor mum,' he said, once in quiet rehearsal, then in definitive performance, with a glance at me that appeared to hope that he had said enough.

I said, 'Dad, what did Kendall mean by saying *everyone* in that loaded way? Any idea?'

My mother said, 'She's the world's worst troublemaker. Sam, I'm going to have to pop down to the High Street. Mrs Fidget hasn't exactly distinguished herself: no milk, no eggs.'

'And I thought I was going to greet you on your return with some good news! I've met someone I want to marry.'

'And what,' Samuel said, 'is the good news?'

'Sam, really! Someone we know?'

'I thought he didn't approve of bourgeois institutions.'

'Her name's Annie Rose,' I said, 'if you'll excuse the interruption. She was A.S.M. on *With This Ring*.'

'Well, at least she's not an actress,' my mother said. 'I'll leave you to pour the tea.'

'Can we manage that?' my father said. 'Is she Jewish?'

'Does it matter?'

'Does it not? What does her father do?'

'He's a chemist,' I said. 'Dad, when Kendall –'

'Do you mean that he lectures on chemistry or –?'

'I mean he fills in prescriptions. In Worthing. What exactly –?'

'I was almost thirty when I married.' My father might have been telling me something for which he found it only just possible to forgive me. 'And I once made a bit of a fool of myself over a woman. She said she couldn't have children.'

'You proved her wrong.'

'Someone certainly did.'

'And is that the skeleton that's prevented us from using the cupboard all these years? Does mummy know? Ah. But you never wanted me to. Why?'

'What happened happened to a young man who wasn't your father. Who didn't even know your mother. I owe you no account of my life, least of all at that stage.'

'Some people might maintain that it was a matter more of honour than of accountancy. The fact is, you preached one set of morals and lived another.'

'Remind me when I mounted the pulpit. The occasion escapes me.'

'You have one built in,' I said. 'Why else do you always make certain things seem beyond question, beyond appeal? You wanted me to be good, and proper, when you'd failed to be any such thing yourself.'

'Not an unreasonable desire. I never offered myself as an example.'

'You sounded like one,' I said. 'You acted like one. You still do. What was her name? May I know that?'

'Is this really quite the time? Olive Peachy. She worked on the Baltic Exchange. I was a young barrister. She liked to dance.'

'And do other things.'

'Very much. I've never consciously sought to regulate your life in that regard.'

'I thought you were a moralist; you were really afraid that I'd turn out like you. What happened finally?'

'My mother gave her money to go away. I didn't think she would, but she did. I was rather offended, truth to tell. Her word turned out to be her bond. Rather unflattering that. She had the baby in Malta, I believe.'

'Is she still alive?'

'It's conceivable.'

'And the child? Likewise?'

'She kept her word,' Samuel said. 'I kept mine.'

'Keeping one's word can sometimes be remarkably like bad faith, don't you think so?'

'You're in love,' my father said. 'It makes you cruel.'

'Truthful,' I said. 'What are you going to do about Kendall?'

'I shall endeavour as always to keep my fingers from her throat.'

'She's worked for the family for over forty years.'

'Are you recommending generosity?'

'You've never much liked me, have you?' I said. 'I'm not the sort of son you ever intended to have. I'm not sure I'm the sort I ever wanted to be. Neither of us has quite got what we were looking for out of me, have we?'

'You're thinking of getting married. I congratulate you. I also warn you: things will never again seem as simple as they do now. Is she pregnant?'

'No,' I said. 'I shan't be needing you to supply her with a passage to oblivion.'

'You assume that if something is neatly phrased, people will forgive you for it. That's because your mother never knew how to refuse you anything. The world, however, is not your mother. It seldom forgives what it fails to forget. You can go too far.'

'It's a destination I dream of.'

'I must go to Gloucester Mansions,' Samuel said. 'Shall I need an umbrella?'

He checked his appearance in the hall mirror, as if he were going to see a mistress, or a critic. His mother had saved him from marrying an unsuitable woman, only to have him marry a suitable one. Infuriated by what she could never openly challenge, Clarissa took to her bed not long after her son's marriage and he never risked breaking her heart, although it proved a durable organ, by facing her down. A coward with courage, my father could sustain the loneliness of a champion, and of failure, but other people were to be finessed, rather than honoured. He had never craved money, but he had learned its abrupt uses, when Olive Peachy was bought off. Women excited and alarmed him. His mother's ruthlessness left him forever in her debt and he paid lifelong interest on it.

Clarissa's death gave me a warrant for inquisitiveness. Perhaps my love for Annie also liberated me, as my father's for his wife had never quite liberated him, but liberty and indifference, even hostility, were too blurred for facile definition. I had the feeling, as I helped my mother to put away the groceries, that I was doing certain things for the last time. Court Royal would never again be the fulcrum of my emotions. I remembered Bothwell Court and the condescension with which I had quizzed its inhabitants. My mother became the object of solicitous coldness which enabled me to interview her in a new voice.

'Why didn't you ever go on with acting?' I was being helpful at the fridge door. My question was a polite charge for handing her eggs and butter and ice cream and bacon. 'It seems such a waste.'

'Perhaps I did,' she said.

'You've acted happy, is that it?'

'One can act what one is, don't you think? He wanted me to be his wife. Won't you want yours to be? He never loved that woman, you know. You're free to imagine what you like, but he never did. It was a sex thing. And what's so marvellous about being an actress? Who are you to tell us how we ought to live? That bitch Kendall!'

'I hope he's going to look after her,' I said.

'Men always want you to be full of variety and absolutely the same. It takes quite a bit of doing.' My mother hung the mauve shopping net behind the kitchen door. 'You don't have to worry. I shall be very nice to her.'

Annie came to Clarissa's funeral. I hardly realized how generous it was to agree to be introduced to the family under such circumstances. I wanted everyone to see our happiness and to prove to Rachel, who had flown back from Fort St George with David, that I would soon have a life of my own. Annie came, perhaps partly out of tactful curiosity. She watched politely as the two almost identical, uniformed, rankless attendants pushed the coffin on a two-wheeled trolley, along the Willesden paths which Clarissa would never have deigned to tread in person. There was sadness, and its counterfeit, in our procession. The masks of tragedy and comedy properly overlap. Neither David nor Annie had known Clarissa in life; my mother hated her; I had played with her like an antique baby. If my father felt distress, it must have been diluted with relief. He would no longer be torn between conflicting duties, but nor would he again know the sweet pinch of duplicity. His mother's death buried a youth which had been prolonged into late middle age. We walked back from the graveside with an older man.

My father believed in the necessity of humour. He was uneasy with sustained solemnity, although it was often he who sponsored it. His certainty that he was always logical debarred him from any effort to inhabit another's point of view. The routines of the law, where levity spiced tedium, were parodied in his home: both judge and advocate, fair and partial, stern and bending, he liked to preside over his domestic court.

We had cold food at the flat after the funeral. David and Rachel moved like dancers who heard music inaudible to others. There was grace in their movements, an awareness of each other in even the most trivial activity. The passing of a plate, the offer of a napkin, the joint attention to another's remark, the common response even to the fall of sunlight on one or the other, declared their unity. They appeared so happy that they had not the smallest urge to boast of it. Ordinariness disguised them like unjudging gods, immune to mortal muddle yet tactfully mundane.

My father said, 'I did consider chucking a box of Maison Lyons violet chocolates in there with her. I don't know how much she's going to like heaven without them. Poor dad! Do you think he'll be obliged to spend eternity with her? How he must have hoped she'd live forever! I know what he'll say when he sees her.'

'Can't stop,' my mother said.

Can my father still have supposed that the dead milled about in another world staffed by bottomless angels? Did he see his parents inhabiting a milky and transparent spiritual concourse where there was neither marriage nor giving in marriage? Did we not all know that Clarissa had been tipped into the oubliette to which, in her harmlessly savage way, she would have been happy to consign most of mankind, and that all of us, like Phlebas the Phoenician, had a brief day and a long night ahead of us? What Jew could now give credit or honour to God?

My mother said, 'I was surprised not to see Kendall.'

My father said, 'Were you?'

I felt a surge of affection for him, a sort of relief such as one experiences as a schoolboy when a conundrum suddenly resolves itself and one thinks, 'I *love* Latin!' He must have paid off Kendall, on condition that he never again had to clap eyes on her. I poured David another glass of Château Cissac. 'Do you see any Africans at all?'

'See them? Of course. I work with quite a few. Do you mean socially? We don't have many to dinner. We don't have many people to dinner at all these days. Billio keeps Rachel pretty busy.'

Philippa said, 'I'm longing to see him again. I do hope he'll be all right without you.'

'There has to be a first time,' Rachel said. 'And the Sextons do have two of their own. These friends of ours. *And* a very good girl.'

'Do you actually *like* it out there?' I said.

'I do,' David said. 'Lots of bridges to build. The twilight of empire is the dawn of opportunity, as my boss rarely fails to remark once the sun is over the yardarm.'

'What're the rest of the company people like mostly?'

'He's hoping you're going to say dreadful,' Rachel said.

'The expats generally.'

'Hyde's a pretty decent outfit. They have their limitations – unlike the rest of us – but we don't depend on them, do we, Raitch, inordinately?'

'The company even funded us to come home,' Rachel said, 'which was rather decent of them, on condition David carried a letter to the chairman and saw one or two bores before we go back.'

'Well,' Samuel said, 'here we are! He can see us.'

'Perhaps they could find me a job,' I said.

'I thought your fiancée was going to do all the work in your family,' my father said.

'No,' Annie said, 'I'm only going to make the money.'

'According to Moses, Michael,' my father said, 'if you were a scholar there could be no objection to such an arrangement.'

'Somehow,' I said, 'the word fiancée always sounds like a genteel term for a pregnant bride, don't you think so?'

'Daddy,' Rachel said, 'when ever are they going to make you a judge?'

'I'm getting a little long in the tooth, and short in the claw, for such positions. The bench is a lonely perch; perhaps I shall be better off where I am.' Samuel gave Annie a particularly nice smile. 'After all, if I want to feel isolated, I can always rely on my family.'

The ghosts of my grandmother, and of my unknown half-sister or half-brother, moved among us and, because they were invisible, we pretended not to see them. After we had eaten, I took Annie back to the barge. I wanted her to stay the night, but she was determined to return to Colchester for a production meeting early the next morning. She meant to resign from the theatre, but not to let its new director down. When we made love, I forced her pleasure out of her as if to avenge a petty defeat. The touch of coldness which her nice obstinacy provoked had an unexpected consequence. When I first saw her again, I had liked her so much that I loved her; now, resenting her show of independence, I fell in love. I feared that it was the man, not the appointment with him, which commanded her return to Colchester. When she was dressed, I wanted to have her again. I said, 'You don't even have to take your clothes off if you don't want to.'

She said, 'I'll see you at the weekend. And we'll have lots of time.'

'Tell you what: I'll cancel the screening for Frank and come up tomorrow.'

'You've still got some editing to do, you said.'

'Why can't you get the first train in the morning?'

'Save it for Saturday.'

'It won't keep. Annie, I love you.'

'And I love you.'

I said, 'Perhaps I should call Sally Raglan.'

Annie said, 'Please don't say things like that to me.'

'Saturday. No excuses.'

She said, 'I don't need excuses.'

The memory of the new boldness which she had showed in bed (did women too read furtive books on technique?), turned her into an elusive stranger whom I could believe, with horrible eagerness, to be deliberately teasing. I dreamed of her body, without closing my eyes, as if I had never possessed it. I had thought myself her benefactor and now became a zealous suitor. My offer of marriage had been a gesture of levity and exhilaration. I could not have made it unless I had assumed that marriage was no longer to be taken seriously. Now, as the result of a fancied grievance, I was afraid that she might not be serious about marrying me. Something close to panic hobbled my conceit. I wondered how I could possibly support her and yet I was determined to do so, like a good husband. I did not want her to have alien appointments; I wanted her with me, always, like a good wife.

I was reaching the end of my twenties without the smallest warrant for adult life. I had patronized David, asking him about his relationships with the Africans, as if I would have chosen to be in intimate rapport with them. In fact, however, I had no society of my own. What, practically, could I do? I wrote dialogue. In order to make a living, I had to prove myself capable of what I disdained in others. Every time I pleased a television producer, I endorsed my own degradation. My smile at his praise was a whore's professionalism. How could my classical education, with all its lordly subtleties, have issued in such servility? It armed me with a fatuous vanity. Unable to distinguish a gasket from a piston, I despised mechanics; incapable of making an untrembling speech, I sneered at politicians; fearful of penury, I deplored commerce.

Even my admiration for Guy Falcon was tainted. As I sat in the darkness of the basement viewing theatre and reviewed his grizzled frown, I wondered how well I should speak of him if he were an applauded candidate for immortality. His failure made him succeed with me. I ended the film with a sequence about Judas Iscariot. In extreme close up, Guy said, 'The traitor is always the facer, isn't he? Why did he do it? Money? Principle? Perversity? The hope of the fame Erostratus was after when he put a match to the Artemisium? If you can't be the man who makes the masterpiece, be the one who wrecks it.'

There then came a shot of the mock-up of the stained glass window, with light forced through it from behind. The face of Judas, saintly with dedication, bore a defiant resemblance to Guy himself. Art was the allegiance which made him the considerate executioner. Guy Judas looked at Jesus without guilt or hostility. There was no more ardent impersonation, his reverence implied, than that of the disappointed follower. Judas judged God, on Guy's reckoning, and his judgement proposed a power that could trump omnipotence. What more absolute arrogance, or independence, than the artist's could be conceived?

I cut from Judas to Guy looking through the perspex and then I overlaid Iscariot again. When pale Guy walked out from behind the brazenly discolouring veil, he contrived a new betrayal, comic and insinuating: his walk slumped to a trudge; his noble expression became satanically gormless. '*Ars longa, vita brevis,*' he said. 'In other words, you need a big arse if you want to survive very long in this life.' He then turned to me, behind the camera. 'You won't use that, will you? No, you won't use anything that gives the impression there's anything in English art that won't please the vicar and his ladies. Play safe, old son, and you just may play for England. You'll always disappoint them, of course, but that's precisely why they'll go on putting you in the team. Nought not out, the popular British score!' I had bought his bluff and left every word of his sour speech in my final cut. The film ended with his spent face fading to leave the crowning crucifixion in shot. Jesus was nailed through one hand; the other reached toward the viewer, a parody of imploring salutation.

The lights went up. Frank Kitson sat at the control desk at the back of the theatre, next to me, as if waiting for me to say something. I remained resolutely silent. Finally, he said, 'Can I be very frank with you, Michael?'

I said, 'If I can then be very Michael with you, Frank.'

'Is that worthy?' Frank took the top of his beard under his teeth and let it out, bristling. 'If I'd been Head of Arts at the time, I would never have commissioned this. Why? Because the man you put up on that screen is someone I detest. *Detest.*'

'Then you should on no account go to bed with him.'

'Let me be specific over one thing: blasphemy.'

'Go,' I said.

'He seems to be pursuing some infantile feud with God, not creating anything that belongs in a church. And you, if I may say so, seem to glory in that. I can only beg you to do one thing: think again, with a pair of scissors in your hand.'

'I'm not recutting it,' I said.

'We can always find someone else. I'd sooner not.'

'Would you, Frank? I think you're quite excited in your trousers about the idea. Your predecessor, whose name shall be nameless, gave Guy a written assurance – on headed paper even – that if he made himself available, he could choose his own director – how else do I come to be at the receipt of custom, and abuse? – *and* that the resultant work would definitely be screened, assuming certain givens, which not even you could easily deny. Now how are you going to hit me on the head?'

'He had no right to do any such thing,' Frank said. 'Those stained glass windows – they're repulsive. Don't you find them so?'

'The way he's linked the image of Jesus with the victims of the Nazis? The crowd at the foot of the cross looking like the good people at a Monday morning suburban station? The slight hint of Tory politician in Pontius P.? The picnic air on Calvary, with the sandwiches very slightly salted by the sounds of terminal agony? Disgusting! If the Gospel can't be good news, let's crucify the messenger and call it standards. Time-servers always do.'

'One day, Michael, you'll meet a real enemy. And then you'll realize just how tolerant people have been.'

'And what exactly have you been tolerating, Frank?'

He pushed himself to his feet, hands on the directorial console. 'I'd appreciate seeing that letter you say was sent to Falcon.'

I said, 'You shall see a copy, as soon as I get one made. Did you hear that Annie Rose was getting married?'

'Little Annie!' he said. 'Is she really? Anyone I know?'

'No,' I said. 'Not really. Me.'

'What on earth do you want to go and do a thing like that for?'

'You know something, Frank? I shouldn't like to have to be you twenty-four hours a day.'

When I told Annie something of this conversation, she smiled one-sidedly. She was only half-amused. What had passed between Frank and me smacked of complicity: we had made her a topic. She feared now that I might one day blame her for the vigour of my resignation from Frank's department. I imagined that I had been her champion, but she could see, I guessed, that I had less defended than made use of her. My indignation somehow conceded the validity of Frank Kitson's surprise. I had done her a favour and she suspected that she had done me a disservice for which, one day, I should blame her.

I said, 'On the contrary. I've got better things to do, haven't I,

302

than direct run-of-the-mule documentaries. One should always burn one's boats before setting sail, don't you agree?'

It was curious, and a little disturbing, to be pitched into formality with Annie at the very moment when I was rejoicing in having no secrets from her. We were sitting in her little flat above the antique shop in the Dutch quarter of Colchester. The sofa which had doubled for a bed was newly covered by a fringed blanket, with dancing figures on it, which she had bought in Hammamet. The other small additions – the water colour of La Rochelle, the gourds in a cork crock from Ramatuelle, the pine corner cupboard with its petty crew of theatrical dolls – reminded me that Annie was capable of living without me, that her existence did not depend on my attention. I was touched by her independence and I was eager to put an end to it. Later, as I lay for the first time in her bed, I wondered how often her nakedness had glanced off the long, narrow, Regency mirror above her green-lacquered dressing table. How had she felt when she came from London after our first night together? Had she sat on the end of the bed and tried to see what difference it had made to her to have had a man?

We made love decorously that night, as if our parents might be in the house. When we kissed afterwards, we were merely affectionate. The prospect of marriage trailed its limiting sanities. We were colouring passion with prudence. Somehow my row with Frank Kitson had tainted the blitheness of our intimacy. My father's warning came back to me: I was at the end of my youth. I had not greatly enjoyed it, but to lose it was a curse.

In the morning, Annie brought breakfast on a Florentine tray. She had been an earnest traveller, taking modest holidays where there was something cardinal to see. Her early morning face was pale and girlish. I loved her pink feet, braced on the boards as she put the tray over me and on to the sheet. Her hair was rusted by the East Anglian sun and bobbed in copper springs at the nape of her neck. I touched the droop of her breast under the white cotton. Everything was so nice.

I said, 'Annie, I don't know why, but I have to get out of this country.'

She said, 'Can I come?'

I said, 'You're the best thing that ever happened to me. I can't believe my luck.'

She said, 'Thank you.'

I said, 'I want to go somewhere I can work and work without any of them being able to get in touch with me. Guy Falcon recommends Greece.'

'I've always wanted to go there. I've never been able to afford it.'

'He knows an island where you can live for practically nothing.'

'Have we got practically nothing?'

'I'm going to sell the barge,' I said. 'Plus contents, if that's a plus. That'll provide a few bob, apart from what's in the bank.'

'Are you sure you want to?'

'Burn your boats and sell your barges! Imagine what'd happen to it while we were away. Will you terribly mind giving this up?'

'Not very much.'

'Will they store your stuff for you somewhere? I love this little flat, but . . .'

'Do you?' she said. 'So do I.'

Harry Pearce called me a week before the wedding. He had decided that Benedict Bligh should become the chairman of *While We're On The Subject*. I said that I should not have been available in any case, but I should have preferred to have been able to refuse the job. Harry said, 'Maybe we'll be able to find something else to do together one day.' I was seized by dread I was eager to deny: would anyone remember me by the time we returned? Annie's willingness to do what I wanted made it impossible to confess my apprehension; she wanted it more than I did. Loyalty spawned dissimulation: we were going to get married and then we were going to Iskios. My trust in her was greater than my trust in myself.

I loved her and I dreaded the wedding. I could not bring myself to make any preparations for it. David and Rachel had returned to Fort St George and I turned their absence into a reason for not inviting anyone else. Barnaby and Claudia would probably have come, so would other of my university friends; Aubrey and Sally and even Ned Corman and his new wife and Bob Sander and Charlie and Mireille might have been free, but I flinched from their recruitment. Did I feel ashamed of Annie? Not in the least; she was not only pretty, she was also wonderfully true. Did I fear that if I asked my friends she would have to ask hers, and all her relatives too? I was not marrying her family, nor was I obliged to love them. Her parents proved friendly and shy. Her father had grey eyes with keen black centres and a flushed smile, at once anxious and oddly brazen; I read it as a professional dressing to cover an uneasy private personality. He reassured others without being sure of himself. He could never know, I imagined, whether the customer who walked into the chemist's was carrying a prescription against death or would ask for contraceptives. His presence at the Chelsea Register Office, wearing a grey suit and silvery tie, was somehow official, despite the absence of the white coat. He spoke softly to my mother on the damp steps and exchanged correct handshakes with my father, as if at the beginning of a sporting competition for which they had not yet changed. My father's courtesy to Mrs Rose, whose blue two-piece was slightly rumpled from the train (and whose hat had travelled in a box, to protect the veil and the fruit), was as impeccable as any he might have shown to someone he was genuinely pleased to see.

The only other witness to the ceremony was Annie's cousin, Sean, a bearded builder from the Isle of Wight who had won the M.C. in Sicily. (Annie's sister, Ursula, was married and lived in Melbourne.) I did not even have a best man. Sean produced the ring from Cameo corner. I had no feeling of being truly present at the ceremony. When I woke that morning, I was appalled by what I had brought upon myself. I was incapable of saying whether it was merely the mechanics of the occasion which dismayed me or the idea of marriage itself. Did the day or the years appal me? I wanted already to be further down the track: as it was, I could not see any difference between the trap and the escape. Faced with the reality of the morning, I decided to despise the whole ceremony rather than admit how humiliated I was by having no one to parade as my best friend. Should I have invited Joe Hirsch? My dread of his scornful presence seemed only to confess my own scorn for the whole prim business. How could I declare to the world, even if it showed no interest in the declaration, that Joe was the man whom I trusted and felt closest to among my whole acquaintance? How was it that I lacked an easy relationship with any Englishman of my own sex? I could almost believe that the skimpiness of my friendships had pushed me into marriage. If I had had male friends in whose rude or subtle company I could abandon my suspicions and lose my uncomfortable self, I might have been able to prolong my bachelordom, reporting conquests and sharing triumphs with beery mates. It was too late to take refuge in male solidarity. I dressed and shaved in the barge for the last time (the lease was already under offer) and I began to sentimentalize my hated solitude as soon as I closed the low red door and straightened up, no obvious Bohemian in my pin-stripes, and looked out at the hazed charm of Turner's Reach for the last time as an unmarried man.

As I stood in front of the registrar, alone, it was as if I had been delivered, for some ritual reason, to an arranged marriage. I was the rigged victim of some antique machination against which there was no appeal. It was part of the procedure that I had to act as if I were happy, but when I heard the rustle of my approaching bride, I glanced at her with the wary politeness of a guest being offered an unfamiliar delicacy. It would not have amazed me to be faced with a girl whom I had never seen before. Should I have had the nerve to refuse her? Annie herself seemed, for a blurred second, to be just such a female, chosen at hazard by external forces I was too weak to challenge. We smiled together with brave feebleness, the tulled, perfumed Annie and I, in my

Sunday suit, my tie, my black shoes and socks (my big toe came through the hidden hole in the right one). She touched my hand with the back of hers. 'Hullo, little one.'

VIII

' "We took the stinking steamer from Piraeus and reached Iskios at 3.30 in the morning: very convenient. Pitch dark; the Styx itself. Then a cigarette glowed in the windy underworld beneath the old British-built tub. A small boat was rowing out to our anchorage and we were urged down the swaying ladder to where Charon was leaning on his oars. Shades of Jugurtha plunged into his cold bath! Hands reached out of the night for us and our bags. Mind that typewriter, you're dripping on my dreams! The little boat bobbed like a maritime yo-yo." '

'Rather an overdone image,' Barnaby said. 'The lad must've heard you were the new queen of literary London.'

Claudia said, 'I doubt if he could have heard that particular pin drop, even if he were in the theatre at Epidafros.'

'What a lot you two have in common!' Barnaby said. 'It's a wonder you can stand the sight of each other! Listen to this: "*Off the Ration*, with its echoes of austerity and monkey-nuts business, is an authentic breath of stale air. In *Have a Big Cigar*, it offers a show-stopper of a number in a show that cries out, like a British heavyweight's title fight, to be stopped before anyone gets seriously hurt." Knock, knock, who's there? Benny B.! Go on with Michael's encyclical. The clichés were stinking slowly in the West.'

Claudia said, ' "Our cottage is above a scimitar of untrodden sand littered with grey spuds of pumice. You walk up to the village shop, forty-five minutes in Regulo number seven heat. Peasants never pass without leaving us a little Greek gift: a few flowers for Annie or a stale biscuit for me . . ." '

Barnaby said, 'Who the hell was Jugurtha?'

'Wasn't he one of the many barbarians butchered to make a Roman triumph?'

'All your questions are knowledgeable answers, aren't they? Why did he marry this girl? Probably to spite you. He's certainly taken a lot of trouble over your letter.'

'It's addressed to both of us. He loves her and she loves him. That always used to be a good reason for marrying people, didn't it?'

Barnaby gathered his hooped and annotated morning papers and removed his serious spectacles (narrow rectangular lenses, black frames). He frowned at Claudia with boyish blindness. 'I must away to inspire my team of idealists in their ceaseless search for a better world.' As he bent to kiss her, Claudia spotted a tonsure of baldness on the crown of his neat, squarish head. 'I'll see you this evening, when the battle's lost and won.'

'Monk by name,' she said, 'and Monk by nature.'

He made a provisional skullcap of his palm. 'But not by vocation, *cara.*'

The fine day made Barnaby wince as he stood on the step of his clean house. No good news was wholly appetizing to him, unless it concealed surly possibilities. The brown lightweight macintosh on his grey worsted arm suggested access to a darker diagnosis of the day ahead than might be available to the common Londoner. Across the street, a new Sunbeam Alpine, pillar-box red, made stopping into a form of acceleration, demanding a surge of power. Its owner hurdled his unopened door, stiff briefcase in a high hand, and strolled towards Barnaby's basement gateway. The gymnast was wearing a badged blazer, with nautical buttons, cavalry twill trousers and a graph-paper shirt, with a silk, school-colours neck-square. The sunglasses offered Barnaby a double view of himself.

'Congratulations,' Barnaby said.

'On what?'

'I have a choice? The car. Not a scratch.'

'Proves I haven't yet exposed it to the best cats. Did you see what Benny Bligh said about the show?'

'Not yet,' Barnaby said. 'Good?'

'Rave,' Aubrey said.

'I was wondering: would you be willing to give a frank, no-paunches-pulled interview to one of our features people, about how you fix your tax?'

'Do I get the fee in used oncers?'

'What fee?' Barnaby said.

'What interview?'

'Seriously, what do you do with all your loot?'

'Donate eighty-six per cent of it to my favourite charity, don't I? England, Home and Beauty. Any less charitable ideas would be very welcome. A hit show doesn't necessarily make you rich, Barnaby, only handsome.'

They parted with cordially unfriendly waves, as if they had rehearsed a number to which they might return. Each gave the impression of having got the better of the other. Aubrey's idea of fame relied purely on being recognized. It did not matter to him what people thought of him, provided he was what they were thinking about. He never resented sarcasm because it never wounded him. He gave such an impression of flattered amiability that Barnaby, while consciously plotting some sapping article on the iniquity of ill-earned wealth, found himself pacing the underground platform with the words of 'Never Ever Again', from Aubrey's *Zenda*, booming in his head.

Aubrey went down the area steps a little more clatteringly than his desert-booted tread required. His clumsiness was loud with tact: he did not like to surprise Larry Page undressed or unprepared. The bleakness of the whitewashed brick and scuffed floorboards in the basement room, where Larry worked undistracted by pictures or books, his blinds down against the world, seemed to keep the composer in a state of permanent adolescence. Even his stubble appeared an unconvincing disguise. His tarnished curls had lost their golden lustre, but it was as if he had deliberately saddened them with ash, which he could easily wash away. His shirt was buttoned, where it was, into inappropriate holes and it had not come back recently from the laundry. Yet its flannel, like the yellowing trousers, the whitish shoes, recalled days of propriety when Larry's economical bowling kept him in the school team. Aubrey saw him as an inverted dandy, whose dishevelment did not wholly disqualify him from being conscientiously smart. Even with an open neck, he wore a superior, if invisible, tie.

Larry sat down at the big piano and propped words and music in front of him. His casual performance was both an audition and a condescension. He treated Aubrey's lyrics with such respect that his disdain for them was unmistakable. His fidelity to their spirit was as ironic as it was appropriate.

'The girl of my dreams
Never read Sigmund Freud –
The girl of my dreams
Would be quite annoyed
By Vienn-easy,
Free'n'easy themes.
She never, it seems,
Has a hair out of place
And that dream of a face
Is gold unalloyed!
Will you be mine, Dream Girl?
Name the place, name the time,
I'm the prose – you're the rhyme,
My peaches'n'cream girl!'

'Love it,' Aubrey said, quietly springing the locks on his briefcase.

'Dream Girl,
I walk in a daze,
Whole hours, whole days,
Without knowing your name,
Or the name of your game.
But all the same,
You're my dream, girl!

I love you so much you
Might not believe me –
There's nothing to touch you –
So don't deceive me.
It's the truth, not lies –
You've opened my eyes.
Dream Girl, Dream Girl, Dream Girl.'

'Not bad, mate,' Aubrey said. 'Not baddy-poo.'
Larry consulted the plaster rose blooming whitely in the centre of his ceiling and affected to pluck new inspiration:

'So please open your thighs –
Cos I'm bursting my flies,
I've got such a high rise,
Dream Girl, Dream Girl, Dream Girlll!'

'There you go again, proving why I can't take you anywhere.' Aubrey took a ballasted envelope from his briefcase. 'As promised. We're really going to have to find you somewhere more convenient to live.'

'I like it here.'

'So do I,' Aubrey said, 'but do I like getting here? Forty minutes in the traffic this particular a.m. The time-and-motion boys are never going to okay it, maestro. I've brought a couple more lyrics, when you can spare the time from the concerto. How goes it?'

Larry threw heavy hair from his brow and flared his nostrils and played some painful bars. When he looked again at Aubrey, his pupils were black nail-heads in the centre of his green-golden eyes. 'What do you think?'

'Very impressive, mate.'

'Good old Rachmaninoff,' Larry said. 'How's Melanie?'

'She'll be even better, and very grateful, if you can get these numbers scored. Everyone's after her to get this cabaret act together. She sends you her love, hasn't forgotten you yet, although I'm still living in hopes. She stops the show every night. Even Benedict said so this morning.'

'Does she know where her catchy little tune comes from at all?'

'Am I the man to conceal vital evidence from the jury? It's your decision, mate, to do things the way you've decided to do them. It suits me if it suits you, but if you ever want to break radio silence, tip me the wink and we'll change the rules of the game.'

Aubrey went back to his new flat in E, Albany. He had bought the lease and contents from the executors of a professional bridge player and amateur antiquarian. The walls were chocolate-covered ('My favourite flavour') and the woodwork was milk-of-magnesia white. There were Corinthian columns on each side of the complicated walnut chimney-piece, with imperial busts on them. The floor-to-ceiling shelves were impressive with books. Aubrey felt perfectly at home in a décor which he would never have chosen for himself. His gramophone was concealed in a Provençal *armoire*; his L.P.s were narrow volumes directly beneath North's Plutarch and Greville's *Diaries*. The leather sofas and wing-chair might have come from the kind of club he was not interested in joining. The four-poster bed had blue drapes on brass rings and a Regency commode at its foot. The bathroom had brass taps and a claw-and-ball bath, with a high rail for those sumptuous sheets in which Aubrey liked to wrap himself before taking the call which had drawn him from the tub. He lived like Aladdin, forever discovering new treasures in the cleverly lit cave. Success and 'Sesame' had something in common. Money gave him a past as well as a future.

When he had changed his shirt and put on a lightweight check suit, with slip-on shoes, he went to meet Melanie Tucker for lunch at a club in Berkeley Square where there was, famously, no menu. The proprietor recited the day's dishes in an apostrophizing litany which seemed to be offering each alternative for the particular delight of sir and madame. A patter of applause, which Aubrey redirected, with a denying flourish, to Melanie alone, greeted their arrival. They talked together, after they had sat down, as if they had come to this public place only in order to find some privacy. Aubrey signed the bill with an American pen as big as a carrot and announced that there was something he wanted Melanie to see. She walked ahead of him, on those long, dancer's legs, past admiring eyes. When she looked back, her face was filled by the scarlet of her smile and the salted almond-shaped (Benedict Bligh) dark-brown eyes above it, with a tilt of nose between them. She had worked hard for her first-night glory in *Off the Ration* and there was still something almost tearful in the happy surprise with which she acknowledged her triumph. Aubrey was proud of her, not least because his own ruthlessness had, as she told her interviewers, contributed crucially to her success. She had never expected such applause. The leading lady, Yolande Pettit, who had had to be satisfied with an ovation, kissed Melanie again and again as the audience called for another big cigar. (Aubrey, who did not smoke, pocketed the Romeo y Julieta which Victor Lamont sent across the restaurant to him.)

They walked down Bond Street, past a large (48″ × 36″) water colour of gasoline trucks which Aubrey bought, but did not stop to pay for, in a brassy gallery.

In South Molton Street, he indicated a summer suit, pleated skirt and nautical blouse, behind the invisible glass of a couturier's shop. The top had stripes graded through pale to dark pink, a white collar, with a squared bib behind, and a graded pink tie in the front.

'It's lovely, Aubrey, but you're not buying it for me.'

'In which case, you ain't having it, Miss Melly.'

Melanie said, 'Oh come on.'

Aubrey traced his eyebrow with a rake's finger. 'That's a different matter entirely, my dear.'

She said, 'I could always try it on.'

'That too is a different matter entirely.' He leaned on the door and it yielded behind him and he became a footman, briefly, bowing her in. He stood with the saleslady while those lithe, silken legs moved intriguingly behind the latticed door of the fitting room. When she stepped out and did a tiny horn-pipe, he played the bosun's whistle, before making the saleslady his umpire: 'Perfection?'

'I'll take it,' Melanie said. 'On one condition.'

'Not granted. It's not for sale to you. Ask the lady.'

'Then why is it in the shop?'

'I'm afraid it's already been sold, Miss Tucker.'

'Then it shouldn't be on show.'

'Bought and paid for, I'm afraid.'

Melanie said, 'Aubrey, you're a stinker.'

'Let's hope this will put me in a better odour. How can I take you to one of Bob Sander's Sunday shindigs if you're not properly dressed? Do you like it? Will you hold it against me?'

'Any time you say.'

'Wrap up madame's previous costume, please. I'm sure it would suit somebody.'

'I loved that dress,' Melanie said.

'Off with the old and on with the new.'

'Now what? she said.

'Now *when*,' Aubrey said.

After finding the right shoes, they had tea at Fortnum's. He told her of his many plans. Aubrey liked to spread his ambitions in front of him as though they were certain to be realized, apart from a few tidgey-poos. He composed his history in the future tense. Over buck rarebits and coffee milkshakes, he announced his latest idea, a musical about Good Queen Bess. Would Melanie consider dying her gleaming dark hair? 'I don't like putting you in a wig, even though I know she wore one. It turns out your lights, a wig.'

'I'll do anything you want me to do,' she said.

There was less submission than determination in her voice. Her father had been a regular soldier, in the Indian army. Her mother had been the captain's lady (Maynard Tucker had no prospects of a colonelcy). When the time came for the little girl to go to school, she was shipped back to England. Patriotism insisted that she take the translation without complaint. In fact, she had small urge to cry. She learnt on the quayside how easy it was to be congratulated for what was much less difficult than others supposed. When, some years later, a Surrey headmistress told her that her father had been killed, while supervising the transfer of files from Calcutta to Rangoon, she prolonged the spasms of grief long enough to cause Miss Lefroy to begin sobbing herself. It was wonderful to be contagious without herself suffering from the affliction. The dancer and the dance became so indistinguishable in her that she seemed as effortless as flame, and left as little residue. She was all motion and all stillness. When the audience laughed, as it did in *Off the Ration*, it was because whatever was left of her personality simply elongated her legs to the point of parody and tilted her grace into controlled absurdity. She had a stage presence so utterly without remainder that when the curtain fell she seemed to be lessened by the reprise of reality. Falseness was her truth, not because she was a liar but because it was so totally consuming. She could respond to any choreographer and take any direction he suggested.

That evening they drank old brandy in Joel Wexler's hand-blown balloons and then they danced to Aubrey's American L.P.s. She said, when they stopped to kiss, still flexing to the samba, that she really ought to be going. He smiled at the generous cue which encouraged him to say that she really ought to be staying.

He found her a quilted hanger for the sailor suit and soon she was sitting on his Tuscan bedspread and bringing her knees towards her pointed little chin in order to peel off her stockings. She had the practised modesty not to look at him as she undressed, so that he had the pleasure of being a licensed spy. When she was in her slip, the fleeced blackness a dark triangle at the base of the silk, he wanted to dance with her again, to the smoky music from the other room. His nimble shoes threatened but never touched her toes. He went at last into the bathroom and returned in a blue, monogrammed dressing gown.

She was already in the linen bed. He took her in his arms and said, 'There's nothing to you, little dancer.'

'That's what I was afraid you'd say.'

'It's nice to lie like this.'

'I've had such a heavenly day,' she said. 'You've given me everything I ever dreamed about.'

'Have you ever had this effect on a man before, my darling?'

She said, 'This is the first time . . .'

He comforted her with a new set of plans. 'I'm going to make you into a great, great star, little Melly, but you'll have to trust me completely. Me and no one else. Trust me and I'll trust you and we can really go places.'

She said, 'You're not angry with me, are you?'

'Does this feel like anger? Do I want to marry someone I'm angry with? We're going to spend half our time in Europe and half in the States. We shall be the happiest, most enviable couple in the whole wide world.'

She said, 'It is my fault, isn't it?'

I liked to walk to the village by myself for provisions. When I had written a sufficient stack of pages, I left Annie in the cottage to read them. My presence made demands: if she laughed, I wanted to know what was funny and if she did not, I wondered why. The steep path at the end of the beach was like a rock ladder. Who could have inserted those stony rungs in the craggy face? I recalled the Athenian night attack on Epipoli, which might have turned the course of ancient history. Failure and success were a stumble apart.

I had tried to interest Annie in the Classics, but she flattered me with more knowledge than I possessed; she feared that I should despise her ignorance, when I wanted only to persuade myself that I had not wasted all those years on dust. Alone, I tried to remember whether Cleisthenes had preceded Pisistratus or vice versa. My capacity to string a few Greek words together impressed and intimidated Annie, but I winced at the poverty of my vocabulary. In the village, I sat over a cup of glutinous coffee *sketo*, with a copy of *Ta Nea*, and tried to apply Thucydides to modern Greek politics. There was one grocer and one green-grocer and one butcher on Iskios. I bought whatever was available in the greengrocer's sacks and some lamb chops and minced beef from the butcher and honey and *vitam* and tinned food from the grocer. The baker was on the way back to the beach. A loaf of his *milevko* lasted us for two days.

I had come up in heat, but a storm could gather with sudden vehemence in the spring evenings. The horizon was hedged with clouds like cauliflowers. Below them the sea turned as black as Poseidon when he was making trouble for the homegoing Odysseus. I bought my bread and was past the bolster of stone wall below the cemetery before the first rain starred the path. The stone ladder glistened by the time I reached it. Potatoes and beans and the tins of peaches I had bought from Michaelis weighted my arms to my sides. My local sandals, with their tyre-soles, skidded on the quartz. I gasped and muttered as I lurched through the storm. I made a joke of my incompetence: in comedies, no one gets killed.

The cottage stood on a terrace above the beach. I went past some thatched huts, partly pillaged for firewood, which had been put up, so Michaelis told me, by an Athenian who had once intended to establish a nudist colony. The local priest objected and his sermons made life impossible for the entrepreneur. Most of the work had been done by an Iskian builder, but once it was completed, neither he nor his workers supported the Athenian. Now the bay was returning to its previous state. Our cottage had been built to shelter mules. It was behind a silvery screen of olive trees and had two rooms, one twice the length of the other, divided by a wall without a door. We had to go out of the living room and along the terrace to get to the bedroom. Our bed was an iron frame, with rickety brass ends. Unplaned planks supported a mattress filled with straw. The roof of the cottage consisted of thick clay on top of wooden beams cross-hatched with bamboo. Yellow daisies had seeded themselves on the roof, among thistles and grass. A fig tree, its early leaves all thumbs, drooped by the well, below our narrow terrace. Beyond the well, discreet with a sacking doorway, was the earth closet.

The rain was running from my neck into my sandals. I was both naked and dressed as I clambered up the spill of slates at the corner of the field between the beach and home. The radio was talking as I stopped by the numbered, unpainted door, savouring the last moments of sour solitude. The news came, in special English, from the American Forces Network in Akrotiri, Cyprus. Three masked men, it was announced at dictation speed, had walked into a hospital in Algiers and machine-gunned wounded patients as they lay in bed. 'A nurse and a doctor were also shot. A spokesman for the Secret Army Organization said later . . .' The sound was cut off. Had Annie been indifferent to what froze me where I stood? Behind the door was someone who, in all sorts of ways, I did not know, whose actions lay beyond my understanding.

She was sitting by the uneven table, with her glasses on, a pencil in her fingers, my pages in front of her.

'What's so funny?' I said.

'If you could see yourself!' She took the netted groceries from my clawed fingers. 'Can I make you a hot drink?'

'I don't think you'd find it very difficult. You have only to pour me into a saucepan and heat me up. What do you think? About the play?'

'Horrible,' she said. And at that moment, the radio was talking again: General de Gaulle had reiterated that the only way forward was what he called 'a peace of the brave'. The storm had caused a break in transmission. 'You never really went and told your housemaster about those two boys being in bed together, did you?'

'If I did, do you want a divorce?' I took a threadbare towel and sopped up the water from my involuntary shower. 'You've no idea how easy it is to become a credulous prig if your father's willing to pay high enough fees. Does Solomon come out looking like a total creep?'

'So far so odious,' Annie said.

'No sense in creating a worm if it isn't a surprise when it turns.'

She was wearing jeans and a white turtle-necked sweater. I took off her glasses and kissed her. 'You'd better put something on,' she said.

'It's not really necessary for what I had in mind.'

'What happens next is what I want to know.'

'Surely you remember.'

'In the play,' Annie said. 'Michael, behave yourself.'

'On a remote Greek island? With the sex-mad wife of my choice? In a thunderstorm?'

'We're not sending any child of ours within a hundred miles of one of those schools.'

'Child of ours? You're not getting subtle, are you? Or careless?'

'Hopeful,' Annie said.

'I never want to go back to England, do you?'

'Never's a very long time.'

'That's what I like about it,' I said. 'I want to stay here at least until the sun comes out. *Greece*. It has to sometime. Without anyone to tell me how uncommercial, unattractive or unequivocal I'm being.'

'What exactly is my office then?'

'I'm afraid there wasn't anything green except the usual beans. You don't need an office to shell *koukia* in, do you?'

'You don't have to entertain me all the time, you know.'

I said, 'Have I done something wrong? I'm not necessarily Paul Solomon, you know, if that's what's disgusting you.'

'No one's disgusted.'

I said, 'Oh I brought you the paper. All the two days' old wet news you want to read.'

'Michael, I'm never going to learn Greek, you do know that, don't you? And do you think there's ever going to be anything to eat apart from broad beans?'

'Pythagoras wouldn't touch them, so you're in good company. He thought they might be old friends transmogrified. Come to bed.'

'Then what'll we do tonight? Anyway, it's pelting.'

'We can use the floor in here. It's probably softer. Are you suggesting we're limited to once every twenty-four hours? You don't have to learn Greek if you don't want to.'

'Of course I want to,' she said. 'It's just that I can't, *pethi mou*. Do you think anyone's going to want to put it on?'

'We'll see when I've finished it. If I ever do. Perhaps I shouldn't bother.'

'Blackmailer. I just thought it might make a book.'

I said, 'I don't know who I am when I try to be just one person. I'm like Whitman: I entertain multitudes. Well, I may not entertain them but I keep them off the streets, some of them. Dialogue is the natural form of those who don't want to be anyone in particular. Will you be here for next week's lecture? I shall hope to see you then.'

'I can't wait to find out where you're going. With the play.'

'Do you want me to spoil it for you? It'll be the work of a second. You really did get the job after all, didn't you? Script editor! The only outstanding problem is salary basically, but then the great thing is satisfaction, isn't it?'

Annie said, 'The first scene between Eely and Barnes is too long. Otherwise . . . it's coming along nicely.'

'Nicely? You prize bitch, aren't you?'

'Nicely *and* nastily.'

'You wait,' I said. 'You ain't read nothing yet.'

'*J'attendrai le jour et la nuit . . . j'attendrai toujoooooorrrs . . .*' Annie's gramophone ran out of drive, as Viola's had on the stage at Colchester when Frank Kitson was throwing his weight about. The allusion reminded me, with sly generosity, of what we had escaped; Annie made exile into a privilege.

'Oh,' I said, 'you do speak a little Greek, do you?'

'*Kookia, kalemera, kookoo,*' she said.

'*And* French!'

We smiled, friends. The storm nattered on the roof and then, in an abrupt, brown mess, on the table, on the floor, on the typewriter. I grabbed the Olivetti and scrambled under the table.

Annie said, 'Room for one more inside?'

She joined me in the narrow dry. 'You see? There is a life after television. It's cramped, damp and unpaid; it's also not to be missed. Do you know what reality is for, Mrs Jordan? It's for running away from and then writing about. What do you suppose could ever conceivably impel us to go back to it?'

Bob Sander's Sunday evenings had begun at the time of his divorce from Carol, when he gave a housewarming for his new place overlooking Hyde Park. There was a delivered buffet under the Oxford-blue silk curtained windows, in front of lattice-boxed radiators. The guests were a mixture of his own clients and those who might be interesting to or interested in them. Bob's hair was longer and more bulky than it had been when, as an articled clerk, he had first noticed how much money people in show business could earn. He was already married to a nice girl and had two nice children by the time the success of Robert Sander Associates proved to him how right he had been to change course and how unwise to suppose that Carol Rigby was the best he could do for himself. He had assumed himself an ordinary bloke, but ten per cent of Ken Haller and Aubrey Jellinek, and others, persuaded him that he had miscalculated. Carol's voice grated where once it had seemed smooth; her idea of fun was monotony. He tried to make her realize how unhappy she was, but her inability to guess that he was sleeping with his secretary or that the children irked him meant that it took a long time to be shot of her. The flat in Hyde Park Gardens was the advertisement of his freedom.

'I'm a big, big fan of yours, Miss Tucker,' Bob said, having opened the door on Melanie and Aubrey.

'Master agent, master manipulator and red-hot fan of M. Tucker! Can't be bad, can't be baddy-paddy! I said I'd bring her and here she is!' Aubrey looked at the polychromatic marble table in the hallway, the eagled mirror above the walnut console

(Louis XV) and the gleaming checkerboard floor. 'You've had men at work, Roberto, since I last saw these unpromising premises!'

'I don't know if they were men,' Bob said, 'but they certainly worked. And charged. Like the Light Brigade!'

'Into the Valley of Debt? He can afford it, my love.' They went through into the murmurous drawing room, with its two four-seater sofas, its glass display tables (one with Napoleonic mementos, the other with famous theatrical props, including the first Lady Windermere's fan), its thought-about spaciousness, its yards of Spanish carpet, grey, white and blue-to-match-the-curtains. Bob was too busy to attend to these things himself. Besides, he wanted nothing in his flat that he was capable of thinking of for himself.

'Who's that scowling at me from among the caviare? One of the workmen?'

'Don't get excited, Aubs: Dave scowls at everyone. Dave Hitchcock? *One Man, One Vote?* You don't read novels, you don't go to the cinema, you haven't been to the theatre? Why should you have heard of him?'

'I thought he was bigger than that,' Melanie said.

'He will be,' Bob said. 'He's only just come to me.'

'The footballer!' Aubrey said. 'Is there going to be a kickabout at all?'

'Not on my carpet, if I can help it.'

'And the girl?'

'Lovey Rudge? I'm surprised you noticed her,' Bob said.

'She certainly starts with two huge advantages, whoever she is.'

'Let me introduce you to several fascinating people, Melanie, before they get disappointed.'

Dave Hitchcock said, 'Wrong on all counts. I'm not interested in tax planning because I don't want to take home a penny more than any ordinary worker.'

'Are you married then?' Lovey Rudge said. 'And is your wife here?'

'Socialism is just as much about private behaviour as it is about public ownership.'

'Does that mean she is or she isn't?'

Jack Palgrave said, 'Is that an argument for paying more tax than you have to? Tax planning's not illegal, after all.'

'That doesn't mean it isn't immoral,' Hitchcock said. 'People didn't fight in the war to make things safe for plutocrats.'

'I spent four years in submarines,' Palgrave said, 'just like you, presumably. The last thing I want to do is encourage anyone present to do anything immoral. Except for Miss Rudge here, of course.'

Lovey was checking that the gold cross was still there between her breasts. 'I really don't know what you're talking about.'

'Champagne's not all that much of a drink,' Dave Hitchcock said, 'so far as I can see.'

'Perhaps you should get some new glasses.'

'I'd sooner have honest beer and honest people.'

Aubrey said, 'You're Lovey Rudge, aren't you?'

Lovey said, 'No need to tell me who you are.'

'In that case I'll remain anonymous. I just came over to tell Mr Hitchcock how much I admired *One Man, One Vote*.'

Jack Palgrave said, 'He's writing the sequel. *One Man, One Veto*.'

'If you weren't a pensioner,' Hitchcock said, 'I'd bloody well flatten you.'

Felicity Hale, in a caramel-coloured linen suit (made for her in Málaga) and a ruched silk shirt, offered a plate of canapés to Charlie Lehmann, who was in a narrow, dark suit, his face rather sallow above the ivory shirt and square-ended Italian tie, its frieze of red figures like the parade of some discreet triumph. 'May I ask you something, as an admirer?' she said. 'Why do you never produce films about things that matter?'

'What sort of questions do you ask as a detractor, Lady Felicity?'

'You have so much taste and so much power.'

'You should meet the people I have to go on my knees to for money. They taste horrible.'

'What makes people like you come and live in England?'

'And who are people like me?' Charlie Lehmann said. 'I live here, because you never come across the nasty, aggressive type of woman you find in California. And because Jack Palgrave says it's a good idea. There's also the wonderful food you get everywhere except at Bob Sander's on a Sunday evening.' Charlie's expression contrived to be a frown for Felicity and a smile for Melanie Tucker at the same time. 'We came to London because my wife liked the idea of somewhere it took three hundred years for anything to be really old.'

'I was christened Brenda,' Lovey Rudge was telling Aubrey 'but all my friends call me Lovey.'

'You have extremely lucky friends. Have you also got an overseas partnership? And what's the point exactly?'

'I haven't even got a partnership in England.'

'That's not easy to believe.'

'The point,' Jack Palgrave told Aubrey, 'is that you can vest all your overseas earnings in it, provided you don't have more than a forty-nine per cent interest, and the whole lot falls out of tax. And then, if you have someone to go partners with who bears any kind of a resemblance to my old shipmate Archie Sharples, who lives in Guernsey and doubles for the Good Samaritan, although he does have a few day to day running expenses, you get to keep a good deal more than the statutory forty-nine per cent. If he takes a shine to you – as Arch did to Peter Perkins, alias the Great Perk – he creams off a mere Bob Sander's worth, alias ten per cent, and the rest is yours to do what you like with, when you like to do it, once the partnership winds itself up in x years' time.'

'Sounds like a man worth meeting,' Aubrey said, 'and shining for.'

'Are you likely to be around in July? He's threatening to blow into town.'

'Are we?' Aubrey said.

'I will, if you will,' Lovey Rudge said.

'Why doesn't she ever say things like that to me?' Jack Palgrave said.

'Because you're very ugly,' Dave Hitchcock said, 'and a lot too old.'

'I thought that was probably it,' Jack said. 'If you feel inclined, we can all have lunch, some of us.'

'Didn't you think it was wonderfully paced, for a first screen-play? And scrupulously intelligent? It had an extraordinary plangency, didn't you feel that Charlie?'

'I don't know that I register plangency, Bob. I don't think I have the instrumentation. I know one thing, though: I wish we could persuade Michael Jordan to stop being happy for long enough to make the script a little bit unscrupulous.'

'He just sent me his new play.'

'Plangent? Are the movie rights available?'

'All the rights are available,' Bob said. 'Who am I going to find to put on a brilliant satire on the public schools with an all-male cast except for the matron, who has a moustache?'

'Can we call him?'

'Only if you have a very loud voice. There's no telephone. Claudia has the right to do a polish. She's a very remarkable girl.'

Lovey Rudge said, 'Your fiancée is looking a little left out.'

Aubrey said, 'I don't know who you're talking about.'

'Bob told me you and she were engaged.'

'I just broke it off,' Aubrey said.

'I wish I could be in something of yours,' Lovey said.

Aubrey said, 'Likewise.'

Melanie Tucker took off the buttonless waistcoat first (cut like a tropical mess jacket) and then, leaning two fingers on the buffet, she shivered out of the pleated skirt. The pink-to-rose stripes came over her head in an easy thrust of her arms. She went on her steep, rosy heels, in her short pink slip, to where Aubrey was standing with Lovey. She had her clothes over her arm, as if she had just stepped out of the latticed door of the booth where she tried them on. 'These are yours,' she said.

'See what happens,' Aubrey said, 'when some sailors have too much juice?'

Melanie looked as well-dressed in slip and shoes, her slim legs and tight behind beautifully displayed, as she had in her costume. Humiliated and unabashed, she opened the fire-safe door of the drawing room (it was pulled to again by a brass chain on a spring) and went towards the evening.

'Wait a tick,' Dave Hitchcock said, 'I'll come with you.'

Charlie Lehmann said, 'I'm going, Mr Hitchcock. I have a car with a driver.'

In the early spring, the river bed was filled with water from the mountains which rose, pitted and slabbed with strokes of jostling rock, behind the cottage. After the snow had melted and the rains abated, the boulders greened and then dried. By early April, we could walk up the river until it contracted to a path which demanded a leader. Tamarisks burst from the base of walls defining the property of owners who rarely visited their birthright. As the valley narrowed, it grew greener. Fig and almond trees brimmed the courtyards. We came to dilapidated houses, with outside stairways to wide terraces and unglassed French windows. Oleanders put out spear-headed leaves.

One of the farmhouses stood between the dry torrent and a tributary which came down from the monastery, once the hideout, so we had been told, of three British commandos, who surveyed enemy shipping from its tiny white eminence. There was something about this farmhouse, its walled yard and stone-bonneted well, its rotting round seat under the parrot-tree, which lured us into thinking of it as somehow ours. The cottage where we were living belonged to Nikos Plakeotis, who collected three hundred drachs a month in rent. The ruin had no owner. Chickens from a neighbouring run were its only inhabitants. We went inside and found crockery, unlabelled medicine bottles, even a book or two. I dreamed of owning the place. When I shared the dream with Annie, she smiled. I was not sure whether she was indulging me or concealing misgivings. My desire was partly a function of what I imagined to be her dread. Now and again, when I left her in the cottage, I would hurry along the river bed, to where it narrowed and divided, as if to visit a lover.

Aubrey's white piano had been repainted for the Albany flat. He had had it stripped and French polished. It had a concert stool. Before he played 'Dream Girl' for Lovey Rudge, he had her lean on the corner of the piano, where she could inspire him. When he had finished improvising words and music, suspicion and admiration widened the big brown eyes. 'That's never the first time you sang that song to someone.'

'I swear to you,' he said. 'This is also the first time I've ever proposed to anyone. So will you?'

Lovey said, 'What?'

'There are alternatives? Marry me!'

She said, 'This morning I'd never even met you.'

'And tonight it's spring!' He stood up and took her in his arms. The crucifix was lifted almost horizontal by the embrace. 'When *Off the Ration*'s a Broadway hit, and the one after it as well, we'll have a split-level ranch house in Beverly Hills, with a maroon Rolls parked outside, and an all-white Alfa-Romeo Spider twenty-eight hundred for my one and only. We'll have an indoor and an outdoor pool and a little place on Lake Arrowhead for summer getaways. You won't have to do any more wet-shirt movies because I shall personally vet all your scripts. Nothing's too good for the woman I love.'

'Love means a lot to me,' Lovey Rudge said.

'And you shall have a lot for it,' he said.

She said, 'Please don't do that.'

'What's the matter?'

'Everyone does that. You're special. I don't want you to.' She unzipped the black skirt she was wearing and stepped out of it. Then she hoisted the crimson top. The black velvet straps loosened and she blanked her face before emerging again, hair tousled into thick brown froth. The slip came off next and she was in a D-cup red bra and black panties. The suspenders were budded with red rosettes. He played another chorus while she stood there, one knee crooked against the other. When he stopped, she sat on a leather chair to untrip her garters and then peel the black stockings. Her legs were brown. She turned her back to have him unlatch her bra. Then she skipped a step away, shorter than he now, and turned to show him her treasures. The only thing she was still wearing was the gold cross.

Lovey said, 'There you are: everything there is to see. You're not disappointed, are you?'

Aubrey made to speak, but played dry, to make her smile. He cleared his throat and swallowed and said, 'Have you seen the bedroom?'

She said, 'Now I want you to do something for me.'

'I can't imagine that there could be any difficulty there.'

'Make sure she's all right,' Lovey said.

'She'll be fine,' Aubrey said.

'Or I shan't be happy.'

Larry answered the telephone. Aubrey had gone into the little den, which was twice as high as it was long, in order to give Lovey the chance to surprise him in the four-poster.

'What's the matter?' Larry said. 'I can hardly hear you.'

'Truth to tell, me old mate, I'm a bit shattered and battered. Mel's given me the long walk, short pier routine. Could you possibly buzz round to her place and give her an impromptu in E flat minor on the front door bell? Just in case she could do with a brilliant new talent in her life? Only don't tell her about me calling like this, I shouldn't. *Bonne chance, mon brave.* One man's poison, eh? How's the new tune coming?'

'I'll play it to her,' Larry said.

'Behind my back! There's an old friend for you!'

Lovey was in her skirt and high heels. She was shrugging her way into the crimson top. 'Did you get her?'

'Everything's fine. *Was* fine. What's going on? I thought it was bedtime.'

'I wanted you to see what you were getting,' Lovey said. 'You saw.'

'And when do I get it?'

'When we're married. When I'm really yours in the eyes of God and man.'

Aubrey said, 'Do I have to hobble around like this until we've been in front of the preacher?'

She said, 'You are funny.'

'Maybe. But do I?'

She said, 'Why don't you sit down there and nursie'll have a look at the problem.'

He said, 'What're you doing?'

She said, 'You don't want lipstick on it, do you?'

Sometimes, after we had made love, Annie fell asleep before me. It became a sweet treachery to outlast her. As soon as she was happy, she was sure that I was. One night, when she had cried out as if scalded by pleasure, and then quickly fallen asleep, I slipped out from under the sheet and stood naked in the lozenge of moonlight from the little window. Still gorged, my penis hung in a thick bracket, making a shadow like a ridiculous nose. I picked up my sandals and a pair of shorts and went out of the cottage.

The moonlight smelt of thyme. The moon was a brittle coin milled by the jagged headland. I went past the fig tree and along a boundary wall which sloped down to the river bed. The old farmhouse was wearing a cap of shadow. The yard was salted with moonlight. The steps to the terrace looked so snowy with brilliance that I feared I would leave footprints on them. My heart was as busy as if there were people sleeping in the empty rooms. I seemed to be picking the rusty lock of their past.

The house was the summer place of a family isolated by forces which swarmed at them from a history they had assumed to be dead. They had now to be what they had never before acknowledged themselves. What might have united them prised them apart. The father began to hate, because he feared, the dark woman who had given him children he was powerless to protect. She was the proof of his weakness, just as his son and daughter were the witnesses of his fear. Alone, he might have been strong enough to save himself, but they hobbled him. Only by having a secret from them could he endure what he could not prevent. On the last occasion when they visited the island (where he had been born), he brought diamonds from the capital and cached them in the courtyard. None of the family knew what he had done. Now that he had a secret, and a distinction, he could curb his resentment. He knew that when the Germans came and took them away, the villagers would swarm like locusts. They would steal anything they could find. On the way to the boat, under guard, he looked at the Iskiots with savage contempt. Their greedy steps would take them over a dowry more valuable than anything they might pillage.

The man died in a gas chamber, with his son, whom he could love as long as the boy did not know what his father knew. The mother had died in the cold train. The daughter survived. She never knew of the riches which her father had buried. Without a dowry, she could not make the marriage she might have. Money would have given her the contempt she needed to give herself to a good husband. As if I had contrived her in order to justify it, I stiffened at the ghost of that dark, unsmiling girl. Suddenly I was seeing Pierrette. I tried to blink her away and put an alien face on my shadow, but imagination was obstinately specific. I had plotted against myself and Pierrette watched me mockingly, as I sat on the stone bench and looked out at a sea all candled with broken moonlight. Defiant and furtive, I listened to the scuffle of nocturnal life.

I pissed in the river bed as if it were a pleasure and then, sour with relief that I had not stumbled on some dangerous truth, or stubbed my toe, I climbed again to the cottage. Annie was on the terrace, in her nightie (a petty disappointment, her reluctance to be chilly and naked).

'Where've you been?'

'Hyde Park Corner and back. I went to have a pee.'

'You've been up to Tara, haven't you?'

'I wanted to be sure there were ghosts.'

'And are there?'

'Don't worry,' I said, 'they don't speak English.'

Claudia said, 'What brought you to London?'

'Alitalia. I wanted to see you.'

'A woman presumably.'

'Of course. My daughter.'

'For years you never even acknowledged my existence.'

'For your sake, and your mother's. Then I read your book.'

'You're not short of money by any chance?'

'Do you need some? Isn't he good to you, your husband? Is he faithful?'

'You wouldn't think much of him if he were, would you? What do you really want?'

'To see my lovely and talented daughter. They're going to make a film of it now, is that right?'

'Spaghetti, spaghetti!'

'What did your mother think when you wrote a book like that?'

'I'll give you her telephone number. You can ask her yourself. Do you want me to give you her name as well?'

'This book, to be honest, when it's published in Italy, people are going to come up to me and say . . . well, what are they going to say? What are they going to think? I have a family, you know, to consider. Children. Your brothers and sisters. And *their* children. Quite frankly, have you no sense of responsibility, saying things like you do? I didn't want to tell you this, but I may not have very long to live. I'm waiting for some results, I'm not unduly optimistic.'

'You're wonderful,' Claudia said. 'Wonderful! A work of art: no one could have imagined you. Spaghetti, spaghetti!'

'I remember your visit to Lucca. You were fat and you were very – what? – timid. You just looked at everything. And then in this book . . . terrible! I come to London and what do I find? A beauty, I must say!'

'You really don't know what you've come for, do you? But you'd like it to be something. In your shabby little heart, you haven't quite ruled out anything, have you? There's no dividend that you wouldn't be glad to take.'

'Please don't do that, my God! Put your skirt down. Sometimes I don't think you're my daughter at all.'

'In that case, why not have a look a little higher up? Not bad are they, for a wife and mother? Try not to look like a Fascist. You can't, can you?'

'Let me tell you something: you have the luxury of accusation. I had the poverty of experience.'

'Very articulate, I must say, for a Wop.'

'You're the same. You want to be, if you're honest.'

'Honest? With my pedigree? You turned me into an English-woman, didn't you, to punish me for existing at all?'

'A girl belongs with her mother.'

'And a son with his father in the *casini*, right? I was the evidence you wanted destroyed.'

'*Claudia, sia gentile. Sono tu padre, sai? Sia discreta, ti prego.*'

'You don't feel too discreet to me. Isn't it nice not to know people? To owe them nothing? And then pay them back? Oh I am glad to see you!'

Barnaby said: 'What's he doing here? Out!'

'I'd like you to meet my father.'

'Out, I said.'

'I am the grandfather of your daughter.'

'What is this? A linguaphone lesson? I won't have this man in my house.'

'Now I understand: *he* made you write this terrible book.'

'How did you get into this country? You ought to be in prison.'

'What a fool, I must say! What a badly educated personality!'

'Do you want a boot up the backside?'

'A man who doesn't trust you, Claudia, that is a man you

should never never trust. I'm going, I'm going. What people though, I must say!'

Claudia was waiting when Barnaby came back from slamming the door. He had taken off his tie. It swung from his hand. 'Did you know he was coming?'

'No questions unless you have a warrant, inspector.'

'Did you invite him?'

'I'm going to tell you just one thing. One: someone who hasn't got the elementary guts to be happy with someone else hasn't got any rights over them whatsoever.'

'My rights are between my legs,' Barnaby said. 'And I won't have a Fascist in my house.'

'Fascist! What do you care? Because who do you work for? What kind of a socialist works for his lordship? Your kind! You always wanted to be told what to do by someone you could despise. Is that your idea of socialism, *husband*?'

Barnaby said: 'If I ever find he's been here again . . .'

'Do you think I don't know about you and the Weeks creature?'

'I'm warning you, Claw.'

'It may amuse you to know that you kicked out the wrong father. Remember that next time you come in here and find Buck with his clothes on.'

'Very funny. Why don't you put that in a book?'

'If it's funny, why aren't you laughing?'

'She's not a creature,' Barnaby said.

'You're not necessarily going to like all this,' Felicity said.

'I hope that's what I'm going to like about it.'

'My uncle Joss opened quite a few doors, some of them into remarkably evil-smelling corners. Chester Flam is quite a resourceful fellow. With fingers in more pies than you could easily count.'

'What else are fingers for?' Joe said. 'Or pies? You said you wanted to do something controversial.'

'I'm still wondering why you said you wanted me to.'

'Tell me what flavour pie you're serving, and where the fingers go in.'

'For instance, there's a Lichtenstein holding company in which Chester and a certain Hermann Pfaff seem to be equal partners. Aren't you encouraging me to saw the branch you're bloody well sitting on?'

'Why shouldn't two clever men go into business together?'

'And why should they want to keep it quiet? You're up to something. What?'

'You ought to put on a bit of weight. That's the only thing wrong with you. What do you really want to do?'

'Piss standing up,' she said. 'Jewboy.'

Joe said: 'When my father died, or was . . . accidentally . . . he didn't leave much. A bunch of papers, some photographs. One or two of which might make hot illustrations for your piece. Hermann Pfaff in S.S. uniform. Even Chester might be a little embarrassed.'

Felicity said, 'What're you up to, Mr Hirsch?'

'Most things you care to suggest. Unless you'd rather I suggested them?'

'Doesn't Mr Flam have a daughter you're rumoured to know rather well? Oh, and isn't she also a partner of yours in this very mag?'

'You do your job; I'll do everybody else's. I commissioned two and a half thousand words, Lady F. When do I get them?'

'What's she going to say when you tar her dad with Hermann's brush?'

'Put it to Chester, see how he reacts to what uncle Joss had to say.'

Felicity said, 'Hoping he'll buy you off?'

Joe said, 'Have you got anything on under those trousers?'

'You'll go too far one of these days.'

'One of these nights, I'll go a hell of a sight further than that, if you like. And you will. Got your diary with you?'

'I've got a good mind to go somewhere else with what I've found out.'

'You've got a very good mind,' Joe Hirsch said, 'and that's why you won't. What does your stuff add up to without mine? A row of beans, but who'll want to plant them? You and I, Lady F., have very good reasons for sticking together. Much more fun than sticking separately, anyway, don't you think so? But if you really want to go, that's your business.'

At Easter, natives of the island came back from Athens to honour their origins and display their wealth. The icons were paraded from the palm-fringed *plateia* at the peak of the village. The bearded priest exchanged his everyday purple robe for a less stained and more sumptuous surplice. The streets were insipid with incense. Steps were whitened. On Easter Sunday Annie and I were invited to the Plakeotis house for roast lamb. There were two portraits hanging high above the strict family photographs: Edward the Seventh and Queen Alexandra. Touched by the antique piety which promised long respect for Britannia, I dared a mawkish toast. Michaelis was puzzled. I pointed to the royal images. He shrugged. He had no idea who the couple were.

After dinner, finding it easier to speak Greek than to listen to it, I mentioned Guy Falcon and his wartime adventures in Crete. Had they had good relations with the Englishmen who had been dropped on Iskios? Michaelis was a small, wary man, with very short sight: he had to frown even to see how beautiful his wife was. He said that the only people they had disliked during the war were the Italians. The one German on the island had been a good man (*kalo pethi*), but the four Italians were louts. I should ask Anna. His wife smiled and looked at Annie, as if they shared memories as well as names. When the English landed, three of them, there was a miniature war on Iskios. Eventually the Italians killed the German and brought his body to the English. A couple of nights later, one of the Englishmen got very drunk and called the Italians cowards and traitors. One of the Italians drew a knife. The Englishman shot him and then the others. He wounded one of the other Englishmen who tried to intervene. In the morning, they threw the Italians into the sea. Michaelis told the story as if it were a joke. Anna was looking at Annie, who understood only what I translated. As I did so, Anna would almost laugh, one hand encouraging Annie's elbow, as if she were helping her through something, a little birth.

I was writing in my spiral notebook about the good German and the Italians and the Englishmen, trying to make a tiny Iliad out of the story, while Annie was peeling potatoes in the cottage, when I heard the peck of donkey hooves in the river bed and then saw the bobbing head of Giorgios Galatsios, tutting as he came up through the flat-footed cactus. The sun was a hot plate in the blue morning sky. The shadows in the rock were complicated keyholes. Giorgios had a passenger astride the mule in front of him (he himself dangled both legs on one side of Phryne's rump).

'Michael Jordan?'

'Never heard of him.'

'That's what they're all saying in London,' Bob Sander said. 'You certainly live a long way from the station.'

'*Yasoo, Giorge! Poo echete vree afto to pethi?*'

'*Echi phthai me to Canari.*'

'You haven't been sitting on the dock since three o'clock this morning?'

'This character found me a bed in the village. I slept.'

'You don't look it. Annie, look who's here.'

Annie came out in shorts and a football shirt of mine, red and black.

'Hullo, Bob. Just passing?'

'Sorry about the short notice. I had to go to Athens and they said your island was just round the corner.'

'Is there any beer left in the fridge, Annie?'

'I thought you said you had no electricity.'

'Look and see,' Annie said. 'It's your department.'

I went to the well and reeled in the rope which plumbed it. There was a promising clink as I raised the net from the bottom. 'You're in luck, if you're willing to drink something as mundane as *Fix*. What's the good news you couldn't wait to tell us?'

337

Annie said, 'I hope you like beans.'

'Anything,' Bob said. 'Charlie Lehmann wants to make a movie out of *For the Good of the School*.'

'It's a play,' Annie said.

'And it'll make a marvellous movie. This is paradise, isn't it?'

'Then you must be the snake,' I said. 'The other parts are already cast.'

'I can see why you wouldn't be in too much of a hurry to leave. I'm talking Charlie into letting you write and direct. And since that's his idea anyway, it's not proving too difficult. Should I not have come?'

Annie said, 'Michael's on a new play.'

'And I've just thought of something else I want to do. You remember what Michaelis was telling us last night? Imagine if it didn't happen quite like that, but there was a period when they all agreed to have a truce, the German, the Italians, the English . . . A time out of war. 'An Outbreak Of Peace'! How's that for a title? And then something happens and the war starts again, between the seven or eight of them. There'd have to be a girl.'

'Am I in the way at all?' Bob said.

'He really wants to let me write and direct? What kind of a snake are you, Sander? Can I write it here?'

'You know Charlie,' Bob said. 'He's got a few things he wants to talk to you about.'

'I'm not going to talk to him unless you've made a deal first.'

'And I'm not going to let you, am I?'

'You ought to finish the play,' Annie said. 'And then decide.'

'I don't think Annie's all that pleased to see me,' Bob said.

'How much . . . ?'

'The magic words; I wondered when I'd hear them.'

I said, 'There's a house here I'd love to buy. I can't imagine it'd cost very much. Where I'd be happy to live for the rest of my life.'

Jessica said, 'You must be mad.'

'Would you sooner I resigned as editor and took the whole story round to Barnaby Monk? He'll print it like a shot.'

'I thought it was pronounced shit. Have you considered what the libel damages could be?'

'JEWISH FATHER SUES PET DAUGHTER SENSATION. Think what the stink could do for circulation. I reckon we could be over a hundred thou easy. Onward and upward, Jess, isn't that the motto?'

'You don't have to tell me it's yours. You don't seriously think that little *shikse*'s going to marry you, do you, by any chance?'

'She says the baby's mine,' Joe said, 'and I have some reason to believe her.'

Jessica said, 'I want world rights in this article and I'll pay you top whack for your shares in the company and I want you out of this office in one hour flat. What do you say to that?'

'When can I have the money?'

'We won't go,' I said.

'You should do what you want to do.'

'You're right. And we won't. Can you imagine hiring anyone less suitable to work on Claudia's script than Dave Hitchcock? Charlie must be crazy.'

'Imagine coming all this way to tell you a thing like that,' Annie said.

'Well, it wasn't exactly his prime purpose. Bob was very . . . diplomatic, I thought, didn't you? After all, messengers have brought worse messages, haven't they?'

Annie said, 'You want me to be the one who makes us stay here, don't you? When you're the one who likes it.'

I said, 'Meaning you don't?'

'We'll go back tomorrow,' she said, 'if that's what you really want.'

'Why do we always have to be ashamed of the things we really want? I want to buy the farmhouse. I want to be able to come here whenever we feel like it. I would've been happy to stay here *forever*, you know that. And you also know you wouldn't. So where does that leave us? The money won't last forever: I have to rely on Bob for a slice or two of the bacon, don't I, even if *The*

War Effort comes out?' Annie, be on my side, please: you're the only one who ever was.'

'You're afraid of upsetting people who ought to be afraid of upsetting you. You're bowing to pygmies. That's what I hate.'

'I'm afraid of you,' I said, 'that's the truth. Because I can't deceive you. You know what worries me most? Not being good enough, not being quite good enough. Do you remember Philoctetes?'

'Not really,' Annie said.

'The greatest archer in the Greek army. He got a septic foot and it stank so badly that the Greeks dumped him on the island of Lemnos and tried to win the Trojan War without him. But then they realized that they needed him, however ghastly his socks were, so they sent Odysseus to persuade him to come and finish the script. He said he didn't want to, he'd finished with the people who'd ditched him, to hell with them.'

'And finally he went.'

'Ten per cent of the gross,' I said.

'Finish the play first,' Annie said. 'He said to think about it.'

'To hell with Odysseus. Where's the typewriter?'

Annie went back into the cottage without smiling. I looked down at my feet.

'Write *and* direct,' I said. 'It beats sacking Troy.'

'I was sure you wouldn't come,' Charlie Lehmann said.

'It's always a dirty trick to give people everything they ask for,' I said.

'What do I do for an encore? This is it, Wakefield.'

The Rolls stopped on the corner by an Italian restaurant with a yellow awning over the Bayswater pavement. A northern sun shone on the white building next to the Trattoria where Charlie had found somewhere for us to stay. Wakefield carried the bags from the Rolls (I took my typewriter and the case with my manuscript in it) and we went up narrow stairs to the second floor.

Charlie said, 'I guess I really have you to thank for Michael being here.'

Annie said, 'I wouldn't say that.'

'Nobody but Greeks should have babies in Greece, from what I hear,' Charlie said.

I said, 'There's a bit of truth in that, isn't there, darling?'

Annie said, 'I'm not having it for six months.'

Charlie unlocked the new door and we went into the next flat. There was a sitting room overlooking the yellow awning and a bedroom, with a big, low bed and a wall of louvred cupboards, and a bathroom with bright fittings. No one had stayed in the apartment before us.

Charlie said, 'It's kinda small.'

'So are we,' I said, 'for six months or so.'

'It's near me,' Charlie said. 'That's the only disadvantage. I had Wakefield fill the ice box, in case you get tired of spaghetti.'

Annie said, 'The thought of a bath!'

Charlie said, 'Michael, can we talk for a minute?'

The sitting room had two short, fawn Chesterfields in front of the brassy fireplace. There was an unused wastepaper basket under the blank desk by the window. The walls were striped white and platinum on a matt ground. There were no pictures. A quartet of mint magazines had been fanned on the marble table between the sofas. *Black and White*'s cover was of Sally Raglan in Elizabethan costume.

I said, 'Charlie, before we start, I hope you know how thrilled I am. I never thought of *For the Good of the School* as your sort of movie exactly.'

'We may have to call it *For The Good of the School Princess*,' Charlie said. 'It's going to be wonderful and Albie can't wait to do it with you. Did you hear about your friend Mr Hirsch?'

'I didn't hear about anybody,' I said.

'His group got the franchise for the South-East. Tower T.V. Hasn't he been in touch? He will be. He's deputy chairman and he's also getting married. To a human torpedo. Alias Lady Felicity. Is that wise?'

'I must call him,' I said. 'No, I mustn't.'

'Michael, since we talked on that snap-crackle-pop of a line from your island, a few things have happened.'

I said, 'There's a problem? There's a problem.'

'Albie. Dick and David had an option he was sure they weren't going to take up.'

'How long does it mean waiting?'

'Only six months. Please don't be sore.'

'Why did we have to come back? When did you hear this?'

'You were already on the boat. Believe me . . .'

'Charlie, Charlie, Charlie . . . I always wanted to say that.'

'Well there you are, now you said it. Do you want to hear plan B?'

'Annie said you really wanted to get me to come back to London so that I could work on the script Claudia wrote for *Family Circles*. That's not true is it?'

'Oh, it's not? Michael, listen to me.'

'You're never going to get that script right, never.'

'That's why I want to throw a big bunch of money at you so you can.'

'That's not the kind of work I want to do, Charlie. You know that. I told Bob . . .'

'And he told me. Why else am I going to give you five thousand bucks a week for ten weeks?'

'Why not let's do *For the Good of the School* on stage first? That's where plays ought to be done. We don't need Albie for that.'

'I don't produce plays. I produce movies. And I have a deal for *Family Circles*. Horrible people are relying on me, Michael. I have your friend Ken Haller to direct.'

'He's not my friend.'

'Well, I still have him. Pay or play. I prefer to play. Have you seen *Harry England*?'

'He finally made it!'

'No, but it's out. I hated it. It's tearing up trees. Michael, you have to help me. You're talking to a drowning man.'

342

'The water sure rises fast where you live. You were on top of the world a week ago.'

'That was when you said you were coming home.'

'I thought better of you, Charlie.'

'You and my mother both. We have to shoot before October one. That's tomorrow. Aren't you a little bit provoked by the evident challenge this represents? Do be. Please.'

I said, 'Why me? Why not Jake Lewin?'

'All the other untalented bastards were busy,' Charlie said, 'or untalented.'

'I'm seriously not very happy about this,' I said.

'Michael, I can't make you happy. Only rich and successful. Settle?'

'Annie's going to . . . Charlie, you're not drowning. Sharks can't.'

'Does that mean we have a deal?'

I said, 'How's Mireille?'

Charlie said, 'She went to the States. She hasn't called, so I guess everything must be fine.'

I said, 'How long is she going to be away?'

Charlie said, 'I wish you'd ask her if you speak to her. I haven't necessarily closed with Bobby yet. Maybe the studio would go a little higher.'

I said, 'Annie's going to despise me.'

Charlie said, 'I'll talk to Bobby. You do believe me, don't you, that I didn't know this was going to happen?'

'I'm working on it,' I said.

When Charlie had gone, I sat turning the pages of *Black and White*. Sally was thrilled to be working with Aubrey Jellinek, who had created *Zenda*, her first real success for her, single-handed. *Young Bess* was proving a terrific challenge, but the songs were superb and it was wonderful to think of doing a thoroughly British show.

What was I going to say to Annie? When I heard her in the kitchen, I took a deep breath and went to tell her that I was more or less committed to working on *Family Circles*. She had had a bath and washed her hair. It was fired by the sunlight and her face was still brown from Greece. She was wearing white trousers and a black tank top, with the sleeves pushed up to her elbows. She said, 'Michael . . .'

I said, 'Annie . . .'

'You won't be angry if I say something, will you?'

'Ditto.'

'I love it here.'

I said, 'You did marry me for my money! Correction: for Charlie's money.'

'You don't despise me, do you?'

'Of course, and you can despise me. What a great basis for a relationship!' I took her in my arms and slid my hands under the black top. 'My beautiful big-breasted wife! What a cunning bitch nature is!'

'Hurry, hurry, while stocks last!'

'I always did have a thing for milkshakes.'

'Those aren't meant for you. Oh well, until the other customer shows up.'

'We're going to be able to buy that farmhouse. If Giorgos really means it about *trianta chiliades*.'

'Whatever that means.'

'You know perfectly well. Thirty thousand drachs. I'll make that much in a week. Less. Jesus, some people are lucky!'

'How long can we stay here?' Annie said.

'As long as we like. You like. We all like. We won't lose what we had in Greece, will we?'

'That's up to you,' Annie said, 'isn't it? When do you start work on that bloody bitch's script?'

'Darling, I hope you're going to believe me . . .'

'Oh so do I,' she said. 'So do I.'

I was with Charlie in the office which he had had made with tartan walls in the basement under his apartment, talking about what I was going to do to *Family Circles*, when his new telephone rang. 'Mrs Lehmann is calling you from the United States.'

Charlie said, '*Darling*?'

I heard a woman say, 'Chuckie?'

Charlie's smile died. He said, 'Mother!'

IX

Annie said, 'These cups are new, aren't they?'

'After thirty years,' my mother said, 'I decided to throw caution to the winds.'

'And what have you been doing since then?' my father said.

'You stay where you are, Annie. I'll put them in the sink for my Mrs Fidget.'

I said, 'You never liked her and you never get rid of her.'

Philippa said, 'If I liked her, I should worry about losing her, wouldn't I?'

'This chap Hirsch,' my father said, 'you know him, don't you?'

'He's grown a bit since we used to play on the beach together.'

'Become quite a power in the land. One of his producers called me up. Harry Peace? Pearce?'

'Careful, dad. Or on your dressing room they'll pin a star. Do they want you to go fifteen rounds with Benny Bligh?'

'It's come at a very awkward time,' Samuel said. 'They want to reopen something that's been dead and buried for a good many years. Hermann Pfaff.'

I said, 'I didn't know that people who'd been dead and buried for a good many years drove to work every morning in chauffeur-driven Mercedes, or had worldwide commercial interests.'

'I might have guessed you'd not be sympathetic.'

Annie said, 'What's all this about exactly?'

'Another time,' Samuel said. 'This isn't something strangers . . .'

I said, 'Dad, this is my wife, Annie. The mother of your next grandchild, unless Rachel has some news she hasn't shared from distant Fort St G.'

Samuel said, 'There are other topics apart from Herr Pfaff.'

Annie said, 'Who is this man and why does he have to spoil our evening?'

I said, 'A long time ago, dad headed an inquiry to see if this Nazi banker —'

'The inquiry was to determine if he'd been directly concerned with war crimes as defined by the inter-allied Commission. On the evidence available, I couldn't conclude that he had. It's always possible that I was wrong.'

'Why do they want to deal with this particular issue again now?'

'Perhaps you'd like to ask your friend. Some woman's involved, I believe, the interviewer. Felicity something?'

'Hale. You can always refuse.'

'Rather attractive. I can refuse, but if they go ahead with the programme anyway . . .'

Philippa said, 'There's a rumour that they're going to appoint two new County Court judges next term. A scandal is the last thing your father needs.'

'Why should there be a scandal?'

'Why else should there be a programme? Scandals excite and amuse. We've seen evidence enough of that with handy Mandy and her friends.'

'If they've discovered something that you weren't told, how can that reflect badly on you?'

'I hardly think they're seeking my co-operation in order to enhance my reputation. A cleft stick is not a comfortable lodging. If I do the programme, I allow myself to be put in a bad light; if I refuse, I appear to have something to hide. Your friend doesn't have some personal reason for pursuing this matter, does he? Have you discussed it with him at all?'

'I rarely see him,' I said. 'And if you're suggesting that I put him up to it, I didn't.'

'My notorious lack of imagination inhibits me from any such conjecture.'

'Couldn't we talk about something else?'

'We could try teaching Annie bridge,' I said, 'if talking about things that really matter puts an intolerable strain on the social fabric. What was your off-the-record impression of Pfaff?'

'A very plausible shit. A shit in cellophane, but a shit none the less. However, I wasn't commissioned to adjudge his moral worth. Few of us, I suppose, would 'scape whipping in an ideal world, from which, luckily, we have so far been spared. Annie perhaps, but the rest of us ... If our system of law were dependent on sincerely held views, civilization would cease to exist. There are, after all, an enormous number of people in the world over whose death I should not lose a moment's sleep, but whom I should, as a matter of duty, do everything in my power to save. In the same way, there are – or, as Maurice Lanzmann would insist – there *is* an enormous number over whose lives I'm similarly indifferent. If Pfaff had been killed, in a rage or by accident, it would be no loss to humanity; his survival may be due to luck or cunning or even – though I hardly think so – destiny, but it's a matter of no significance whatever. I may have wished him dead, but I could not find evidence to validate my ambition. He may, like the man in Humphrey Clinker, enjoy the smell of his own excrement, but I take leave to doubt it. All the same, he has to live with it. Perhaps that's his just punishment.'

'A convenient view,' I said.

'You always think you can jump up and down on the ice with impunity. Some of us happen to know just how thin it is. Only those with very small experience of the world could possibly be confident that the heart should have priority over the head in these matters.'

I said, 'Are you afraid that Felicity will take the view that you're making a special category of murderers and thieves out of people who might prove useful to the City of London?'

Philippa said, 'It's very good news that Sally Raglan likes your script so much.'

Annie said, 'I think perhaps –'

I said, 'Look, dad, I'll have a word with Joe.'

Samuel said, 'It's up to you. I suppose I shall soon start being called grandpa by everybody. What do you call your father?'

Annie said, 'As a matter of fact, I call him Merlin. After the wizard. He always used to be boiling up potions, so . . .'

The front doorbell rang. I looked at my watch. It was twenty to eleven.

'Improbable,' Samuel said.

My mother went into the hall and opened the door. Samuel smiled at Annie, as if he and she had planned some surprise. He could conjure moments of wishful intimacy out of nothing. At such times, he saw the world as a joke which it was a small privilege to share with him. Annie blushed and her lips quivered and she looked down at the mustard-coloured carpet.

Philippa said, 'Guess who this is!'

The visitor was young, with black curly hair and freckles. He was wearing Levis and a tartan shirt and had a boulder-sized knapsack over his forearm and against his knee. He wore work boots with leather laces that went round metal studs.

'I can't begin to imagine,' Samuel said. 'Buddy's boy!'

'My name is Jess Nathanson, sir.'

'Buddy's boy!' my father said. 'I'd never have guessed.'

'I sure hope this isn't an intrusion.'

'At this hour? Unannounced?'

I said, 'I'm Michael. This is my wife, Annie.'

Philippa said, 'Do you want something to eat?'

'If it isn't too much trouble, Mrs Jordan. Dad said to say hullo to everyone.' Jess allowed the rucksack to drop to the floor and bulged his lips. 'I'm a man of unimpaired appetites, I have to admit that.'

'What brings you to London?' Samuel said.

'Heap big silver bird. I heard it was the place to come to if you wanted to observe a total breakdown of traditional manners and morals. Sounds a great subject to major in. I also wanted to see your National Gallery. I'm studying to be a very great painter. It's also entirely conceivable that I could wind up with my own T.V. show.'

I went into the kitchen, where my mother was waiting by the stove for our stewed chicken to get hot again. She kept her back to me for a moment and then she turned and her face was oddly bright, bold, as if daring me to say that she looked different. I said, 'He's got his nerve, I must say. Are you going to let him stay?'

When we went back into the living room, with his food, Jess was saying, 'I figure there's always a market for comedy, right? So I finance my painting with selling material. You know what a comedy script is worth today in New York? Plenty.'

'Perhaps I should become a comedy writer,' Samuel said.

'I can always use a partner, sir. Hey, this looks terrific. Sir, do you agree with me, that we'd be making a great mistake to put troops on the Asiatic land mass in any considerable numbers?'

'You and I, Jess – it is Jess, isn't it? – might be very ill-advised to start putting troops anywhere at this late stage.'

'Jess,' Philippa said, 'where exactly are you planning on staying the night?'

'May I use your telephone? I have a king-sized address book of kids I once gave candy to when they were visiting the States.'

I said, 'A lot of people in London go to bed at night. Some of them even fall asleep. Especially at this hour.'

Jess said, 'Great being on the show with you folks. Thanks for the hospitality and which is the way to the Y.?'

Annie said, 'If you need somewhere for the night . . .'

'Your wife is psychic, Michael. She has gifts.'

'We have a sort of a spare room. If you don't mind sharing with the broom.'

'Hey, that broom and I are going to get along fine. This is very nice of you.'

I had bought our first car, a grey Standard Ensign with red upholstery. We drove back to Bayswater, the three of us, all smiling, though not, I suspected, at the same joke. The so-called spare room scarcely had space for the boarding-school bed with which it had been furnished. A square frosted window overlooked the mews where Wakefield washed Charlie Lehmann's Silver Phantom.

Jess said, 'Does your broom usually stay out this late? I'm going to have to come to some kind of a *modus vivendi* with that stiff bastard.'

I said, 'If there's anything else you want, hesitate to ask, won't you?'

'Huh? Oh. Hey, that's good. I hadn't heard that one before.'

'Use it, use it.'

In the bedroom, Annie was still smiling, fingers on her dome. 'Do you want to feel the bean? *To kouki!* He's doing his exercises.'

I said, 'I say, you don't think you could be pregnant or something, do you? What on earth made you ask him to stay? You're not hoping for something in dad's will, are you?'

Annie said, 'They didn't want him. He's all right. And after all, this isn't costing us anything. He won't stay long, will he?'

'Just don't get too maternal *avant la lettre*, O.K.? He's learnt to walk. Let him.'

I played tennis with an old pro in a covered court in Hall Road, off Maida Vale, once a week. When he was not teaching, Frank would sit in the room behind the showers drinking Heinz Scotch Broth, cold, from the tin. I booked the court in one of Frank's free periods and invited Joe Hirsch to play. He arrived in a white Jaguar. At the end of the hour, I was leading 5-4 in the second set, having lost the first on a line call which made me shake my head quite a lot. We were both naked under the showers before I mentioned my father.

Joe said, 'Oh is that why you let me get away with that call?'

'No, the call is why I'm not going to let you get away with this.'

Joe said, 'I'm sorry, but you're still in the bunker.'

'You haven't taken up golf now? I suppose your pa-in-law's got his own bloody course. The one thing that matters to my father at the moment is being made a judge. He's coming up to sixty, the chances are minimal, but this kind of thing could kill them stone dead.'

'Pfaff was in the S.S. Your father –'

'My father did an honest job. He may not have had all the facts –'

'The British government rigged the whole thing. They had to find someone who they could say had every reason not to give Pfaff the benefit of the doubt. The necessary Jew. Your father; I'm not blaming him.'

'The British government –'

'Can't you see how ridiculous you make yourself, defending people who're stronger than you are?'

'And what do you make yourself attacking people who've done nothing but their duty, after all this time?'

Joe reached across and squeezed the bulb of my soft penis with his wet hand. I jumped away and he laughed. 'What are you going to do? Run and tell someone? I read your play. Shit hot. Michael, I'm your friend. I don't have any vendetta against your father. It's Pfaff I'm after. And all the other little Pfaffs who were taken care of by the gallant allies for their own sordid little reasons.'

I said, 'Every new civilization is cannibalized from the last. You couldn't nail every Pfaff in the world without bringing the whole bloody thing down around our ears. Think of the German scientists. Where would we be without those shits? The only people you're ever going to get are the ones you're allowed to get.'

'You think we're being set up like your dad was? Red faces in certain quarters don't suggest it. Anyway, this isn't really in my hands. Felicity and Larry run their own show.'

'Balls. How is Felicity these days? Did you ever get the wedding present we sent you? We never got the one you sent us.'

'I wasn't invited, was I?'

'How's your mother?'

'Fine. She's living in Belsize Park. I bought her a little place. She's got a Lebanese lover. She shares him, but she's got him.'

I said, 'Remember me to her.'

352

Joe said, 'Do you feel guilty about having other women apart from your wife?'

I said, 'Not in the least. I don't have them. Annie happens to be pregnant with our first child, for Christ's sake.'

'Hence my question. *Fra uomini*.'

'Joe, do me one first and final favour: lay off my dad, O.K.?'

'If Felicity thought I was trying to manipulate things, she'd be all the more . . . Tell you what you could do – *should* do – ring her up, take her out to lunch. Play tennis with her! Give her the point when the ball's on the line. She fancies you.'

When Joe said he was my oldest friend, I almost believed him. If I almost hoped that he would let me down, was it because I wanted to see my father put through Benny Bligh's hoops or because I should then be exempt from further obligation to Joe? What, after all, did I owe him? Surely the debt was to me, and yet I felt the need to pay interest on it. How could I begin to weigh what Pfaff had done against my schoolboy redemption of Joe from the expulsion he craved? What act could be measured against another? There might be a rhetoric of morals, but there could never be a mathematics.

As I opened the door of the flat, I heard laughter: Annie's. She was in the kitchen putting food in front of Jess Nathanson.

'Oh hi, Michael. You deserted your wife, so I figured why not move back in?'

'Where've you been, Jess? And when are you going back?'

'Six countries. Several of them Spain. Land of Contrasts.'

'And how was El Caudillo?'

'I really felt at home. My next car will definitely be an Auto-da-Fé. Can Nathanson conceivably be Sephardic? The Prado? Major major. Only one drawback: I could never find a Spanish girl who was open. This poses certain problems to a healthy kid like me, but why disgust you with them? Falling in love with Goya was a terrific experience, but a three-dimensional *maja* would have been a welcome plus. Forgive me, but I'm very young.'

'Is your painting as good as your patter?'

'Is it ever? I run neck and neck with myself. I sky out in the a.m., that's why your wife is looking so happy, in case you're wondering. This represents only a temporarily intolerable intrusion. O.K., short notice, but at least you haven't had to dread my coming, have you?'

'Jess, are you on something?'

He jumped up and looked at his chair. 'This isn't here? I fly without wings! Tomorrow I make an exception. America: think I'll still recognize it? I can't wait to tell my dad about your mother. He still carries that torch, in case you didn't know. And now I've fallen madly in love with your wife. You're lucky there's something between us. Two out of two. The luck of the Nathansons.'

'Jess,' Annie said, 'anyone ever tell you you talked too much?'

'This is London, isn't it?' Jess said. 'Where the swings are and the roundabouts are never going to get to catch up? Come on, guys! This is little Jess Nathanson, the kid who means no harm; don't kick me, I'll kick myself. I'm Jewish, aren't I?'

I said, 'I promised I'd go and see Claudia about the script. After all, it's her novel.'

'And your promise,' Annie said.

The Monks's house had fresh paint on the railings. Inside, there were new, William Morris curtains, operated by tight rigging. A stack of review copies was on the table next to the Guy Falcon bronze of two naked females, a woman and a girl, a breath apart. It was entitled 'Mirror, mirror'.

Claudia's hair was tight to behind her head, where it was clawed by two amber combs before bushing into golden freedom. She folded her legs under the Mexican skirt and nagged a thread on one of the new buttons on the sofa. It had been recovered to go with the curtains, and the wallpaper. 'I'm quite jealous,' she said. 'You've shown me how screenwriting's done.'

'Sows' purses out of silk ears is quite a speciality of mine. Have I ruined it for you?'

'I'm certainly not taking my name off it, if that's what you're

354

hoping. What does the awful Lehmann man think of it?'

I said, 'He likes it. I like Charlie.'

Claudia said, 'When I went to see him, he wanted me to work with him stripped to the waist.'

'Why hasn't he ever asked me to make myself at home like that?'

'Why do men like tits so much?'

'Probably because they were brought up on them. Have you got anything you want to raise with me? On the script. Or shall I let Ken Haller go ahead and mutilate it?'

'I'm told your wife is very nice.'

'You must come and see us, when we get a big enough place, you and Barn.'

'He's got another woman.'

'Oh.'

'It's been going on for quite a long time. Revenge for the book. She also has big tits. I expect you knew. Biggish. Felicity Hale. Barnaby's been saying for some time that he ought to get into television. He decided to tunnel. Joe Hirsch is a friend of yours, isn't he?'

I said, 'I always knew it was a small world, but I had no idea it all fitted into a single bed. He hasn't left you, has he?'

'We're being as civilized as we know how. We only quarrel in front of the children.'

I said, 'I never know quite how to take you, Claw.'

'That's because you secretly believe that everyone else is really as happy and ordinary and incorruptible as you are.'

'Unprovoked, Claudia, calling me names like that. How's the new book coming along?'

'Limps and bounds,' she said. 'I keep telling myself it isn't about me and then I start raining cats and dogs all over the keys. Don't be sorry for me, will you, just because Barnaby's taking a hack's revenge? I did rather start it, for one thing, if only by wanting him so much when I first met him, and for another, I really do believe in freedom, even for myself, and even if I don't want it. How can anyone believe in fidelity, after all?'

'There are things that can't be believed in but can still be lived, aren't there? A little humbug I still have at the bottom of my wartime tin. God help me, I got all my ideas about life at a time when there weren't any new ones available. From wartime newspapers. It may be rough if the Jesuits have you before you're seven, but nothing like as terrible as being in the grip of the Ministry of Information between seven and fourteen.'

'I stole something last week.' Claudia went to a drawer in the knee-hole desk in the corner of the clean room and came back with a red cylinder which she held in front of me. Suddenly she thrust a stick up from below it and a jack-in-the-cylinder jumped out, in cap and glasses. 'Don't you think it looks like Barn?'

'You *stole* it? Why?'

'I wanted to know what it would feel like.'

'And how did it?'

'Like drowning without water. I had to lean against the wall of the Midland Bank. It was very, very *something*, but what I couldn't say. I was catching my breath when I heard this man, calling. "Excuse me, excuse me." I felt completely naked, as if all my clothes were slipping off, melting snow from a roof. It was the man from the shop. I had this under my coat and there he was, the vessel of doom in a black coat and silly trousers. I looked at him and I was ready to kill him and to plead with him, to do whatever he wanted *and* spit in his face. Then I saw that he was holding out my handbag. I'd left it on the counter.'

'You thought you didn't want to pay for it, but you obviously did.'

'Exactly what Benny Bligh said.'

'Damn.'

'In another world, who knows what he would have done, if he'd known what I'd taken? Instead of which – thank you very much and home to tea. England! I despised him and I also wanted him, right there in the street.'

'You missed paying him with the only thing you think men really want.'

'In reality they'd always sooner be feared than wanted, wouldn't they?'

'Fear lasts longer, doesn't it? And what would women always sooner be?'

'Easy!' Claudia said. 'Admired from behind.'

'You've still got your lodger!' I said. 'And still inventing old favourites by the sound of it. Did that girl from Foggia never show up?'

'Poor Larry! I've grown accustomed to his tinkle. Benedetta lives upstairs; nearer the children.'

I said, 'I thought I was going to hate working on the script, but I didn't. It was astonishing, what you can tease out of somebody else's work if you approach it shamelessly.' I kissed her at the door without putting my hands on her. 'Thanks for the *imprimatur*.'

The Alfa-Romeo 2800 had grey paintwork and white leather upholstery. Aubrey was putting up the canvas roof, glancing at the untrustworthy sky. He wore a tweed Raglan and a deerstalker hat. 'Hullo, mate!'

'Wrong number,' I said.

'How's it going?'

'Towards the underground,' I said. 'Can't stop.'

'You haven't changed, have you?'

'I like the hat,' I said.

'You like? You take!' He swept the deerstalker from his head and backhanded it to me. 'Right over the stumps!'

'I wish I'd said I like the car.'

He made to throw the keys (on their golf ball ring). 'I was thinking about you only yesterday.'

'Something you ate?'

'Because do you know Bill Cater? We were talking about a musical about Moses.'

'There must be worse ideas,' I said. 'I just can't seem to think of one at the moment.'

'What about him and Pharaoh's wife?'

'Wasn't that Joseph?'

'You can see why we need you.' Aubrey said, 'Why do you like making enemies?'

'I only really like having enemies who like me.'

'That's true,' he said. 'That's *true*. So you went and married our little Annie Rose.'

'And you went and married your big Lovey Dovey!'

'Sally Rag wasn't too pleased.'

'You two will just have to work things out between you.'

'She'd like to take it to appeal. She . . . next time perhaps! What're you doing about tax?'

'Paying it.'

'Yes? Well, there's a man you have to meet, if you're going to start making a living wage: Archie Sharples, mucker of mine. Fabulous character, D.S.O., D.S.C., lives in the C.I. He takes seven and a half per cent of your overseas earnings and keeps the rest for you under his pillow.'

I said, 'I don't have any overseas earnings.'

'If you ever do, give me a bell. He isn't nice to everyone, unlike me, the Arch, but you never know.'

I said, 'What do you think about The Old School as an idea for a musical? The history of England seen as the pageant of a spoof public school?'

'I only wish I was here to lift it off you! Good to see you, mate. Love to Annie. She always was my favourite.'

I left Aubrey hurriedly and with reluctance. He gave optimism a chromium finish; he might be bright and flashy, but he lived in the world. The horrors passed him by; he was not callous, merely ignorant. The absence of shame transformed all doubt into energy. He was a machine so fired by ambition that he left no trace of exhaust. His face was angelic; neither a sign of age nor a hint of vice deformed it. He went down the stairs to Larry Page's basement with a periscopic wave of the hand, the captain of his easy fate. Even the Alfa looked as though it had been driven exclusively on parquet. As I waited for the Central Line train, I wondered if he had conceivably been serious about making a musical out of Exodus.

Annie went into labour towards midnight on January 20th. I drove her through dramatic streets (with a Vivaldi sound-track) to the Middlesex Hospital. She smiled at my urgency, lolling in the corner of the Ensign, bravely smug, knowing that the night would be hers, and its. I was not allowed to stay with her.

'Goodbye, you two,' I said, and headed back to Bayswater. I pretended to be disappointed by the severe Sister, but I left the hospital as if reprieved. The new life which Annie carried was also a small death. If I had ever been irresponsible, would I ever have another chance? Annie's eagerness for the pain ahead of her was touching and mortifying. I was relieved not to be its witness. I could even contrive to resent it; her lack of apprehension made my own disreputable.

The next day, I had lunch with my father at Crockford's. There was still no news from the hospital. After lunch, we went up to the five-shilling room. In a tight lift, Samuel made a joke of the appointment of two younger men as County Court judges. His last chance of the bench appeared to have gone. 'Imagine them choosing Willy and Nilly, the broker's men! They were probably right; I don't suppose I should've been a very competent judge.'

'At least you don't have to feel it matters what you say on the box now if you decide to do it. Nothing hinges on it any more.'

'Except my honour perhaps; an expendable commodity.'

'Table up,' Mrs Gold said, as we walked in.

My father said, 'I suppose only one of us had better play. The bridge table is the one place where my son and I don't care to oppose each other.'

'Oh come along,' Mr Morris said, 'we'll take you on, won't we Marie?'

If I could not be with Annie, what was wrong with playing a rubber or two? Yet my eye went constantly to the clock and the telephone in the corner of the stuffy room. We played a few hands without incident and then I became declarer in four spades. Marie Gold thought for a moment and then she led the jack of hearts.

Mr Morris sighed and turned to my father, who was putting the dummy on the table. 'What was your first bid?'

I said, 'Is that a proper question at this stage?'

'You're an expert on propriety?'

'Not particularly, but I can recognize an attempt to pervert the course of justice when it's wearing size ten boots and blowing a policeman's whistle.'

Mr Morris, who was a very small, very rich man, in a double-breasted brown suit and crested tie, failed to see my joke. 'I've been a member here thirty years, no one ever spoke to me like that before. Do you mind if we add up right away?'

The telephone rang. Mrs Tooth, the hostess, answered it.

'You have no business asking the bidding, Leo, once the dummy goes down.'

Annie's frail, triumphant voice said, 'We did it. You and me and him. He's got two of everything you ought to have two of and one of everything else.'

I went back to the table with a loud secret. 'A boy. Six pounds ten ounces.'

Mrs Gold said, 'Mazeltov.'

My father stood up and put his arm around me. Good news made him bite his lip. 'I suppose there's no possibility of champagne, Dorothy, is there?'

'Of course,' Mrs Tooth said. 'Indian or China?'

Leo Morris said, 'I didn't realize. Congratulations. He was under emotional strain. Do you want a cigar?'

We called him Daniel Lawrence. He had colic for the first ten weeks of his loud life. We had little sleep and little time to do anything except appease our red son. The only way to stop his crying was to put him in the car, in his carrycot, and drive round London. I would leave Annie to get some rest and go on my own. Aubrey Jellinek's tunes came over the radio like aural treacle. Daniel slept until I turned off the engine. I used to sit outside the flat, in neutral, reading.

Annie was patient and kind and single-minded: Daniel was her fond obsession. I was her husband, not her lover. I could find no fault in her, but I found some in myself. I inquired about a house big enough for a girl from Foggia. I wondered when Annie could be weaned from maternity; her devotion isolated me. Colic passed; teething arrived. Parenthood transformed Annie and me into co-operative strangers, clock-watchers who affected an intimacy strained by impatience and frayed by long hours. Her breast, which had once enraptured me under a cotton nightgown, was a drooling parcel too evidently designed to appease rather than excite.

After the usual postponements and difficulties over casting (and credit), filming started on *Family Circles* in early June. Ken Haller and I had worked in acrimonious harmony on the last draft of the script. I had the ideas; he had the authority. It was no surprise when he wanted to be credited as co-author. I asked Ken what was so attractive exactly about Naboth's vineyard. He did not seem to take the reference. Bob Sander applied massage in the right place and Charlie Lehmann found another percentage point to procure a measure of grace from Ken.

Maximum Security had been translated and was being put on in Paris. At least I would get sole credit there. When invited to go, I decided, sullenly, that I could not leave Annie. I preferred to bank my disappointment. The producer called me after the first night to report a respectful ovation. The press spoke of *'dialogues fort intelligents, des ironies à la fois cruelles et pertinentes, à faire grincer et à faire rire.'*

Annie said, 'I wonder if she'll go and see it.'

I said, 'Who's she exactly?'

She said, 'You know.'

I said, 'Oh. I doubt it. She probably doesn't even remember my name. Much it matters. Have you got time to look at a couple of houses sometime? The awful Margo's sent one in Chelsea, i.e.

Fulham, that looks as if there must be something wrong with it, considering the price.'

We had made an offer for 19, Seymour Walk, which even had a little garden at the back, when Charlie Lehmann called from the location. I hoped that he was going to tell me that Albie was free of the overage he had been doing on his movie in the South of France and we were clear to set a date for *The Good of the School*. I guessed that it was more likely that something had gone wrong with *Family Circles*. It had.

'Michael, it's not your fault. But we had to recast the English doctor. And the actor we have isn't short and fat, like the dialogue, he's tall and thin. We also have a problem with the little boy Ken would like to talk to you about.'

'I never discuss Ken's private life with him.'

'I'll send Wakefield to pick you up.'

'I've got a car,' I said. 'I just don't want to come to Shrewsbury.'

'Nobody does, but that's where they are. There's a nice little hotel.'

'I hate being away for the night.'

'You don't want to direct *The Good of the School* after all?'

'Directing is one thing, slavery's something else.'

'One night,' Charlie said. 'What kind of servitude is that? Everyone's longing to see you.'

'Tell them not to blink,' I said. 'One night.'

I drove off to Shrewsbury with a better conscience, since I did not want to, than I would have to Paris. *The Good of the School* had branded me beyond repair: I could be freed only on the promise of new chains. As I left Annie, I thought only of my return. The hitch-hikers with their short menus did not slow me down. The sooner I was done with Ken, the sooner I should be coming the other way again. Even Daniel called me back with his toothsome smile.

*

They were using a big Victorian country house near Shrewsbury as a composite source of settings. Claudia's novel was set, in part, in provincial, wartime England, which recalled my own exiled immunity in Devon. She and her mother had known the humiliations of decorum on a small budget. It was difficult to separate her heroine, Monica, from the girl I had first known at Cambridge. Claudia's scholarly distinction had combined accuracy with display. It amused Miss Terracini to be more English than the English; her seriousness was unsmiling mockery. Perhaps we had something in common: I liked to make them wince; she preferred to make them cringe. I was attracted by a characteristic of hers without finding her character attractive. When I attacked the screenplay, I had not questioned her too thoroughly about the quotient of truth in her book: I preferred to imagine how she might have seduced her father rather than to hear the details. The perverse was more interesting as metaphor than as meaty fact. It was a suggestive coincidence that Sally Raglan was to play Monica: I remembered how she had embraced the Major when her parents came home and reduced my chances of investigating their grateful daughter more thoroughly after we had finished reading Gerald Pringle.

I arrived at the location (hooped in red on the hand-delivered sketch map) as the unit was finishing lunch. Sally threw relieved arms around me in front of the sweatered sparks and mechanicals. '*Finalement!* How are you, darling? We've *missed* you!' Oh that little frog that lived in her throat! 'Everybody adores what you've done.'

'Then I may as well go home, mayn't I? Charlie says that Ken's been blaming everything on the script except the things that work.'

Sally kept her arm round my waist as she said 'And cue Kenneth Haller!'

Ken was not a tall man, even when he was angry. He expanded but he did not grow. He was angry now. His light blue sweater seemed to flare with the rage it contained, just. Ken's anger was not loud; his frown was. The careful placing of his feet, as he kept pace with Terry Shields, the first assistant, suggested that he was walking on coals, on which he might shortly invite Terry to join him, barefooted.

'The kid was upset,' Terry said.

'If he was upset, why didn't he bloody well cry?' Ken twisted one whitening eyebrow. 'His mother said he could cry whenever he wanted to. *She* certainly can; why doesn't he?'

'He was trying, Ken. It just didn't come.'

'We hired him on the understanding that the waterworks worked. Perhaps we'd better get someone else.'

'Continuity problem. He's already been in the scene at the airport.'

'At least make them unhappy, Terry. Treat them like you treat Brigid. Hullo, Michael, at last.'

'Don't you mean at least?'

'He's been here thirty seconds and he's rewriting the director.'

'Well,' I said, 'he can't recast him, can he?'

'Your picture's got a green light, I can see that,' Ken said. 'If he doesn't cry on the first take this afternoon, stick something into him. You may be against Fascism, Michael, but I'm beginning to see its points. Have you spoken to Charlie? Are you coming to Italy?'

'I'm not all that sure I'm coming here.'

Sally said, 'It's all going so well, I was telling Michael –'

'Aren't there a thousand and one things you have to go and do, Miss R.? The actress's life is one of selfless dedication. I have things to quarrel with Master Michael about. Can't you possibly at least stay a week?'

I said, 'My wife –'

Ken said, 'Michael, I'm delighted that you're the happiest couple in the world, but are you sure that happiness and this business belong together? What I need ideally is a brilliant writer who isn't pussy-whipped and preferably never wants to go home a moment before the director has him bundled off the set. Can you think of anyone? The script needs at least a full week of on-the-spot therapy.'

'Can this be the same set of flawless pages with which you said it would be an honour to be associated?'

'The present scene between Monica and her mama is a little bit nya-nya, to put it politely. When she first talks about going to Italy.'

'It shows us why the husband walked out.'

'It'll also show us why the audience will. It just ain't working, dear. Have you brought your needle and cotton?'

I said, 'Suppose – suppose Monica sees how excited her mother gets – assuming she does – when she talks about Giancarlo. The mother thinks she's showing how she despises him, but every word she says contradicts that impression. That might be quite a scene.'

'If only we had someone to write it. That way Monica realizes what was wrong with the marriage, which wasn't necessarily the father at all.'

'Nor was it that her mama was the dry stick she's always supposed. On the contrary, Giancarlo was horrified by how much she wanted, which was a bigger volume of *asti spermanti* than his cellars could well contain. Italian men, myth and reality, a symposium. English women, their unfair reputation for coldness. *Soit?*'

'You're the expert on the ladies, Michael, I simply press my nose to the glass.'

'Oh, is that what happened to it?'

Terry Shields returned with a courtly cough. 'Big Bill Benson's got something he'd like you to have a look at, sir.'

'I'm on my way. Meanwhile, I hope you've over-dosed Master David with tear gas. Take Mr Jordan to the office and show him the instruments of torture, will you, Terence, and then come straight back down to the set? Do you really want to be a director? Ninety-nine per cent of the time it's about as creative as clearing up dog mess with your bare hands.'

Terry took me to an uncurtained room on the first floor, overlooking a stone-faced lily pond with a mossed fountain in the centre. Trestle tables held collections of props for later in the shoot. One had been cleared to make room for a typewriter and a stack of paper. I settled, with docile rage, to serve my sentence. I hated working away from home, in over-large rooms to which other people had access and on unfamiliar machines. I should have been incapable of writing a coherent word, but I found myself humiliatingly competent: the weaknesses in the old scenes were as manifest as the solutions to them. I was already wondering if I could get away before nightfall when the door opened and a dark head looked round it.

'I know it's awfully silly, but I'm afraid we're lost.'

She was a slim woman, in her thirties, wearing white trousers and a fringed black and white top. Her high heels seemed to make her dizzy: as she steadied herself against the doorway, I saw the anxious face of a freckled boy behind her arm.

'I think they're shooting in the kitchen,' I said. 'I'm working in here.'

'I'm so sorry. I'm Jilly Brandt. This is David.'

'So I imagined,' I said. 'I'm Michael Jordan. Otherwise known as the writer. That's why you've never heard of me.'

'I've seen all your plays,' she said.

'They're almost directly below this room, I think, slightly in that direction. You'd better hurry. Good luck, David.'

She shut the door carefully and I went on working with brisk cheerfulness. Birds came and applied careful feet to the verge and dipped their bills in the ornamental pond as the characters chatted under my fingers. After nearly an hour, when more than half of the work was done, I could not resist going downstairs. Sally, in the part of Monica, was telling her little brother of her decision to leave home and go and find her father. At the end of her declaration David Brandt was supposed to cry. As I arrived, I heard the clapper-boy say, 'One-four-one, take twelve.'

Ken Haller said, 'And action', in a voice which sounded as if it were done shouting and was now resigned to modesty.

Sally said, 'And you'll most probably never see me again.'

As she quit the kitchen, in her 1948 coat and hat, the camera moved in on David. Ken watched; the cameraman watched; we all watched. The boy looked at Sally's disappearing back and then directly at the camera and his freckled face was engorged with effect. Mrs Brandt was chewing one of her little fingers as if she had not eaten for days.

Ken said: 'Yes, well, we can cancel the chara to fun-filled Firenze for a start, because we shall be in this god-awful house till Christmas, at least. When's Easter? Because we shall probably be here till then.'

Mrs Brandt said: 'You frighten him.'

Ken said, 'Well, he has very unrewarding ways of showing it.'

I said, 'Ken, if David can't cry –'

'Who let you out of solitary confinement?'

'– perhaps there's a good reason for it –'

'Supply it, dear, and men shall rise up and call thee blessed. Alternatively, stay in your own part of the boat.'

I said, 'Look, his sister says she's buggering off for good. The obvious response is that he cries –'

'It's your script, Michael –'

'Very good of you to say so. So, is it necessarily all that brilliant for him to do so? Never mind the stage directions. Perhaps it's better – and truer – if, against all the expectations, the kid isn't sorry at all. We close in for the tears and instead we get a sort of crooked smile.'

'Is he up to crooked smiles, Terence? Ask the lady, will you? Why the hell weren't you here earlier, Michael? Never let it be said that I'm harsh and inflexible. I'm harsh and flexible.' Ken took a breath and squatted down to where David was watching us with uneasy eyes. 'David, I don't think you should cry and I don't want you to cry now, all right? All you're going to do the next time is look up into the camera and stare at it. Just stare, all right?'

Mrs Brandt was looking at herself in her hand mirror. She had dark brown eyes and black kiss-curls over her ears. She said, 'You are a nice man, aren't you?'

I said, 'It's not in my contract, but it's better than working.'

'Very quiet, please, boys.'

The clapper-boy said: 'One-four-one, take thirteen.'

'And action, Sally.'

'And you'll most probably never see me again.'

As Sally walked out of the room, the dolly was rolled forward and the camera sank down towards David. There was panic in his eyes. His face grew pink and swollen. He quivered with uncertainty, then he burst into tears. He stopped, in mid-sob, and bit his lip and gave a sheepish, dreadful smile. The camera went on running. Mrs Brandt and I looked at Ken Haller. 'And cut,' he said. 'Brilliant. Not quick necessarily, but brilliant.'

'Check the gate.'

Sally's hand pressed my shoulder and her lips were by my ear. 'My best little bacon-saver!' she said. 'What an afternoon you've spared us!'

I said, 'Thanks, kid. Wanna have dinner after the show?'

There was a place with pink walls in the town where she said they did quite good scampi. We drank a bottle of Muscadet and played old friends. I wondered what she thought about when she had to cry on cue.

'I think about us,' she said, 'in the taxi . . . that night . . . and how different things might've been if the moon had been a little kinder to me.'

'I don't believe a word of it,' I said. 'I don't mean I don't appreciate it, but . . .'

'Well, what makes you cry?'

'Oh hundreds of things, starting with the bit in the Swiss Family Robinson where the snake swallows the donkey. The Marseillaise, the Greeks saying *ochi* to Mussolini, the Grand Fleet sailing out in 1914, the thought of you doing another musical with Aubers . . .'

'The first script was terrible, darling. I only wished you were working on it.'

I said, 'And I only wish you were working on me to get me to. You aren't, are you?'

'That's unworthy,' she said. 'Pity there aren't any sweet women's parts in your new one.'

'You don't feel like playing the matron? We're making it into a movie, didn't Charlie tell you?'

'Of course. You ought to find *something* for me to do. Just to prove you've forgiven me. I can't remember what for.'

'So tell me, what've you been doing for it, stuck up here in Shrewsbury?'

'You've got very bold in the tongue, Michael, since you got married. Benny comes up from time to time, when he can.'

'That must be a comfort to you both. Where is he tonight?'

'It's his box night, isn't it, silly? He's cutting two ears and the tail off some cringing celeb. He might be down later. I wish you were directing this. Ken's marvellous, but he doesn't understand women, does he?'

'Do you remember once telling Charlie Lehmann that you didn't think I was the right person to write a certain script?'

'I never did. What makes you say a thing like that?'

'That weekend at Tyler's Barn.'

'You know she had twin boys, don't you?'

'Did she? Who did?'

'Sylvia. *And* she's preggers again. Imagine Ned doing the wheelies in Regent's Park. They've bought one of those houses in Cumberland Gate, with a *lift* in it. If I said that to Charlie, which I don't remember doing, it was probably because he wanted you to do something which wasn't right. You're such an old grievance collector! I really don't know why I go on loving you in spite of it all.'

'Mazo de la Raglan,' I said. 'How's your mama? Any new pseudonyms?'

'She's still at it. They're reading *Freda on Finisterre* this week on *Woman's Hour*.'

'And the Major?'

Her eyes were huge with tears. 'Surely you know? You don't? He died last year.'

I said, 'I'm sorry. We were in Greece.'

She nodded and swallowed. She bit her lip and looked away while I paid the bill. As we went out into the purple, provincial evening, she put her arm through mine and held tightly to me, head against my shoulder, hair on my cheek. She stopped under the lee of one of the empty boarding houses and had to find a handkerchief.

I said, 'I would've written if I'd known.'

'It was very sudden. Not unexpected, but sudden. Heart. He was a wonderful man. I sometimes think he was the only man I ever really cared about. Except for you.'

'And Ned. And . . .'

'Please don't be unkind. Not now.'

I said, 'Later perhaps. He certainly loved you very much.'

Sally said, 'Can we just stay here and . . . ? I'll be all right in a minute.'

Locals were getting into their cars outside the hotel by the time we got back to the Salop Arms. Sally had stopped to repair her face in the window of an antique shop and gave the men unspoilt smiles. Their looks made me feel lucky. While we were waiting for the lift, with our heavy keys, I said 'God, how I hate single beds!'

She said, 'I've got a big one.'

'Lucky you.'

'I don't suppose Benny'll come tonight, if you want to come in and talk. If he does, we can all three talk.'

'I think I've done enough talking for tonight, darling, thank you.'

'Maybe tomorrow?'

'I'm going home tomorrow,' I said.

'That's not what Ken told me.'

'Well, that's what you tell Ken.'

The lift stopped at her floor and I opened the slack gates. She put her arms round my neck and looked irresistible. 'Nobody's ever going to know,' she said.

'Oh yes they are,' I said, 'because I'm going to tell them. We've both behaved like very good ships and passed very properly in the night. Night, Sallifer. Sorry about the Major, truly.'

She took the cue to be gallant and I shut the gates and went on up to the third floor. Rather as I had expected, my room was the furthest possible distance from the lift. I had to walk past the fire buckets, with their dead cigarettes, and along a threadbare corridor in order to be as near the town clock as possible. It was striking eleven, with a regularity that promised relentless punctuality all night. A door opened and I saw bare feet, red toenails, and a floral housecoat. Mrs Brandt whispered, 'See you in the morning,' and then opened an adjacent door, with light behind it. When she saw me, she hesitated and then she said, 'I do want to thank you. I was so afraid this afternoon, before you arrived –'

'Never be afraid of directors. They're all paper tiggers: they always act as if they want you for breakfast, but they rarely do.'

'You've no idea what it meant to me, and David. You see, we're a little bit like the woman in the story, and the little boy: my husband was killed in Korea. He was in the engineers, clearing mines, and one went off. When the war was already over.'

I said, 'I'm sure everything'll be O.K. now. See you in the morning probably.'

I wanted to call Annie but I feared she would be asleep. I got into the narrow bed, its clamminess reminding me of boarding school, and read Claudia's typescript. Nicola, the heroine, was married to a super-reporter who jetted all over the world on brave, 3000-word expeditions. Meanwhile, his wife, who had been much the cleverer at Cambridge, applied herself to nameless domesticity. Nappies and sick hamsters, dry rot and valetudinarian house plants filled her parish. Her returning husband was not warmed by the home fires which she tended with such meek distinction. Fidelity was greeted with a sigh. The scorn with which she revealed his friends' considerate attempts to seduce her evoked no laughter from Barnaby's double. When she discovers about the women he has had in New York, Capetown and Cairo, he would have her believe that they were, in a way, evidence of his generosity. The willingness with which Nicola agreed to be lectured on the selfishness of loyalty was conveyed with *pétillant* dryness. She was an author from whom one flinched in admiration.

The knock on my door had a surprising firmness. It was as if I had ordered something. When I opened it, there was Mrs Brandt again, with pom-pommed slippers on.

I said, 'Something wrong?'

She shook dark curls. Her hair was more done than it had been earlier. I looked at my watch: twenty minutes. I heard the clash of the lift gates and the threat of footsteps. 'You were so kind . . .'

I said, 'Come in.'

I had the door shut, but not locked, before the incoming guest came round the corner. The town bell sounded half-past. There was a whirr before the bong. Mrs Brandt said, 'I'm Jilly, in case I didn't tell you.'

I said, 'Look, Jilly . . .'

She unzipped the floral front of her housecoat from strict neck to below her navel. She said, 'Please.'

I went and pulled the curtains and came back to her. She had had time to step out of the pom-poms. Naked, she was very small. Her elaborate hair was the biggest part of her. Her flesh was white and her breasts larger than imagination had designed them. I said, 'Mrs Brandt . . .'

She said, 'Please.'

I put my arms around her as if to clothe her nakedness. I was appalled and, she could tell, thrilled. She held her face up to me seriously. It was as if I had lured her into this. Had I? Desire displaced doubt. It was better to be a man than a prig. When I kissed her hot mouth, the breath from her nostrils seemed to scorch my cheek. She put her hand down and pulled the cord of my pyjamas. I was shackled and smiling as we fell on to the bed.

I had never before been promoted and reduced to the office of a stud. If my kindness had primed her, Jilly soon had no interest in who I was. I was flattered at first and then, in my vanity and humiliation, I began to be sly. My enthusiasm ceased to be gleeful and became an imposture. Pretence released me from apprehension. How often, even with Annie, in the safety of marriage with a trusting woman, had I had to remind myself to think of mashed potatoes in order to prolong what should have been a mindless conjunction of blood with blood! Now I was worried neither by the fear of comparisons nor by the shortcomings of sincerity. I was a sexual worker, emancipated by my fierce servitude. I could do things to Jilly Brandt which I should never attempt with Annie. I was a boy out of school.

She was a solid dream destined to be gone by morning. I recalled her whispered desires as if they had been uttered, with rare directness, by a phantom whose heat both warmed and froze. I was pleased with myself and I hoped that I should not be cursed with her again. She had been so sincere when she finally said, 'I'm *com*pletely satisfied, *com*pletely,' that I was sure that she would honour her word and never reveal to anyone what had happened.

I saw her again, playing ball with David in the unsunny garden, as I walked to the Ensign, after delivering the last revised pages to Ken during a lunchtime huddle over roast beef and potatoes baked in their leather jackets. Pleased, he was sulky at having no good reason to detain me. I waved to Jilly as if we were both obliged, in the British tradition, to pretend to indifference for the sake of some higher morality. Had that really been the woman who knelt by the side of my bed and looked back at me over her shoulder and whose hand came between her legs, at just the right moment, to sound my horn? How pretty she was, and what a relief never to want to see her again!

I drove to town like two new men. Had I not at last become a member of the club to which Bob Sander and his clients had long been admitted, though I should never admit it? At the same time I was also a good husband; I wanted nothing more than to be safely home with Annie. I had left London piqued by a marriage in which I no longer played the grateful part; I was returning enriched by a secret account on which I swore I should never draw. I gave a lift to a pretty hitchhiker, from Watford on into town, and heard that she wanted to be an actress. I advised her to get a good agent and was sure that she would have had dinner with me, if I had not wanted to get home. I stopped for flowers at a puddled lay-by.

Annie was watching Benedict Bligh on the box. I frowned at the voice of his 'guest', as if at a conundrum: it was my father. I said, 'I thought it was next week.'

I put the flowers on the couch and we sat in the blue glimmer as Benny drew on his notoriously long cigarette and then did one of his sudden forward hunches, as if an intellectual scrum was about to be formed. 'What made you elect to ignore the evidence on Pfaff's direct involvement with factories using slave labour?'

'Who'da thunk it?' I said, 'Benny B., the conscience of the nation!'

'The same thing,' my father said, 'that makes the referee refuse what the crowd consider a good goal after the whistle has gone. It may be good, but it's not a goal. The rule of law depends on both law and rules. You, like the crowd, want emotion to override the rules. Perhaps I should prefer it myself. But whose emotion? Yours and mine and why not Mr Hitler's too? The rules are part of the law, Mr um Bligh: once their application is optional we don't have justice, we have totalitarianism. Is that your wish? It's not mine.'

Benny looked under his arm, as if a coach were on the touchline, and then he said, 'Didn't you rather allow yourself to be used by the British Government of the day?'

Samuel said, 'I've never regarded the British crown as a disreputable employer. Have you, Mr um Bligh?'

I said, 'Neat.'

'They didn't pick just any old legal hack to conduct their inquiry, did they?'

'Good of you to say so.'

'They picked a Jew, didn't they? Someone whose acquittal of Pfaff would seem kosher indeed.'

'I'll tell you something improbable, perhaps naive, perhaps conceited; it never occurred to me that that could be a factor.

Nor does it matter. Happily, motives count for nothing in our system. Our justice is what it is precisely because it has safeguards against partialities, certainly ways of trumping them in the long run. I wish I could have known – or taken into account – all the supposed facts you've brought up tonight. But it's precisely because I regret personally having stuck to the rules that I'm glad I did. It's what distinguishes us from the Nazis. They can't refrain from condemning the innocent; we, in certain circumstances, can't help exempting the guilty.'

Benedict made smoke and leaned forward, for a final inaudible word, as the closing captions began to roll, under the usual worthwhile listening music.

'He did rather well, didn't he?'

Annie went into the kitchen, without the flowers. There was a glass on the floor by the sofa. I picked it up and followed her. The glass still contained a slop of liquid. I sniffed it.

In the kitchen, I said, 'Are you all right?'

She threw her head back and the light flared on her face. 'Aren't I?'

'Did it upset you, the programme?'

'Programme?'

'You're upset about something.'

'How was Shrewsbury? Did they all love you?'

'This isn't like you.'

'Perhaps this isn't me,' she said. 'Is this you?'

'Annie, come on: what the hell's up?'

She said, 'You haven't done something.'

'It's not your birthday? Or have you gone and changed the date?'

She said, 'You haven't asked me something.'

'Since when do you drink whisky on your own? Is Danny all right? Are you all right?'

'Right as rain. Righter! And rainier!'

'O.K. What have I not asked you?'

'The thing you always ask. Were there any calls?'

'Oh. That can wait, can't it? Were there?'

'Yes.'

'Well? Bad news? Charlie?'

'Good news and bad news, I suppose. Good news for you –'

I said, 'Must you be so coy?'

'Am I being? *Sorry*. You fucked someone last night. That's not coy, is it? Do you want some pickle with that?'

I said, 'What exactly . . . ?'

'That was the message, timed at six forty-three. Is it true? Don't say it's not, because it is, isn't it?'

I said, 'Who the hell phoned you?'

'A friend. It's always a friend, isn't it? Someone who wanted to be helpful. And was. Can I have some more scotch, please?'

'You know you don't like it.'

'I don't like anything much.'

'Did they say who it was?'

'Yes. They said it was you and a woman. I suppose that's a comfort. But not much of one.'

'On the phone, was it a man or a woman?'

'It was a woman, it was a Wednesday, what does it matter? You must feel very good. I bet you've got a hell of an appetite. Is there anything else I can get you?'

I said, 'How could anyone do a thing like that?'

'The very question I've been putting to the panel. They couldn't come up with a really convincing solution. Can you?'

I said, 'I can't believe it was her.'

Annie said, 'I couldn't believe it was you. We seem to have a genuine crisis of faith.'

I said, 'Can I tell you about it?'

'No.'

'Please. Annie, I love you.'

'Don't fling all your high cards on the table right away, isn't that what you always tried to teach me before you discovered how hopeless I was?'

'This has nothing to do with you and me.'

'I don't think you should write films. It makes you come up with such rotten lines.'

376

'O.K., I won't.'

'How was the great Ken Haller? You see *Harry England* got an award?'

'Annie, please forgive me.'

'Aren't you even going to cry first? Shall I put on the Marseillaise?'

'Who told you that?'

'You did, didn't you? It wasn't in the paper, was it?'

'I'm going to tell you what happened whether you like it or not. She came into my room, this woman. I was nice to her during the afternoon –'

'You're nice to everybody. Mr Softy, aren't you? Hard on the outside, gooey in the middle.'

I said, 'She came to my room in the middle of the night. I couldn't think why at first.'

'But you cottoned on like a good 'un, I'll bet.'

'I was sorry for her.'

'You have a *pension* for unhappy ladies, don't you?'

I said, 'Penchant.'

'A soft spot. But it gets hard given half a chance, doesn't it? Don't you bloody well grin at me. The first opportunity you get –'

'That's not quite the case, as a matter of fact, your honour. In fact, the irony is that Sally . . .'

The telephone was ringing.

I said, 'I'm not here.'

'That makes two of us.'

'Who's taking care of Daniel then?'

'If it weren't for him, do you think I would've been here when you got home?'

'Then I'm very glad he's here.'

Annie picked up the telephone and held it out in my direction. 'Careful: it might be someone wanting to talk to me. You'd better get there first, hadn't you?'

I heard my father saying, 'Hullo? 3491?'

I said, 'Hullo, dad. Sorry . . .'

Annie went out of the room and seemed to walk further away than there was room to go in the little flat. Doors shut and re-shut. My father wanted to know whether he had seemed evasive or priggish. I was embarrassed that he should apply to himself terms which, in my anger, I had secretly used myself. I could jib at his certainty, but his doubts were painful to me.

I said, 'I don't think you came across as self-righteous at all. Who said you did? Ah well, that's what friends are for. Interviewers always pull that trick. Just like leading counsel. Dupe? Certainly not. Do what Aubrey Jell always does: tell everyone what a triumph you're said to have had. They'll probably give you a knighthood. Believe me, dad, you did fine. I was going to call you, but . . . I just got in. Before. Sleep well. And to mummy.'

The bathroom door was locked. Annie was very quiet. Had she gone to sleep in the tub? I rattled the door.

'Are you going to stay in the bath all night?'

She said, 'Probably.'

I said, 'Who could have been enough of a swine to do a thing like that?'

'Precisely the question I put to myself. But you managed it, didn't you?'

She came out of the bathroom finally in a long nightgown, with a light blue cotton dressing gown over it, hair brushed back and cinched at the back. She looked like a good schoolgirl. 'Aren't you going to have a bath?'

I said, 'I had one this morning. I had one this morning. I'm sure it can't have been her. If you'd seen her –'

'Oh I do hope you haven't got a photograph.'

'Oh for Christ's sake, it just can't be that terrible. It *can't*. When you think of the things that happened in the war –'

Annie said, 'You've been a shit. O.K. Don't bother to go for the double and be utterly despicable as well. Leave something for another time, why don't you?'

'All right,' I said, 'all right, I've played the fucking penitent, I've made myself look pathetic and ashamed, but if you really

378

want to know I had a bloody good time. I really enjoyed myself. I felt like a benefactor. Someone who could do it whenever he wanted, whenever *anyone* wanted, king of the castle, top of the world. Do I wish it had never happened? Oh yes, in a way, and in another way . . . It didn't mean a thing, and there's no reason why it ever should, but it wasn't high treason, Annie, it wasn't anything to do with you in the slightest. It's not the great tragedy of our time; it doesn't even register on the Richter scale. Compared with . . . compared with . . .'

'Comparisons aren't merely odious, they're also cheap and – and – I'm not going to cry. I'm not, I'm *not*.'

I loved her furious, wide-eyed face. I was as good as her: I knew that she dared not blink because the tears would spill. Understanding became desire; separation became identity. I said, 'Sweet Annie . . .'

She said, 'Just don't try putting me in your coffee.' There were no tears now; her eyes had swallowed them. 'I thought we were *friends*.'

I said, 'And so we are. Of course we are.'

Her smile was vinegared with pain. 'I'm a very old-fashioned girl, I'm afraid. I didn't think I was, but I am.'

I said, 'If I ever find out who did it, I'll . . .'

'Thou art the man, Michaelovich.'

I said, 'I'll make it up to you, I swear.'

Annie said, 'Just don't buy me anything, all right? Don't buy me the nicest thing you can think of, that I'd really, really like, because I wouldn't.'

I said, 'The cheap bastard who . . .'

She said, 'I know, don't worry. I'll get over it.' She undid her hair and shrugged it on her shoulders. 'Feel like a fuck?'

I put my arms round her and bent to kiss her. She dodged my mouth. 'Oh no,' she said, 'it's a little soon for kisses, don't you think so?'

Ten days later, Ken Haller had a heart attack during a night shoot. Charlie Lehmann flew back from California and asked me to take over the direction of the movie. I told Annie that I was going to refuse, but she said that she would walk out if I failed to take the opportunity. I did not believe her, but I took her at her word. We went to Italy and I finished *Family Circles* with Ignazio Naldi and Sally Raglan. Sally and Annie became very good friends.

In the late autumn, Maurice Lanzmann died, leaving an unexpected place free on the roster of county court judges. It seemed that certain people had much resented the suggestion, on Benny Bligh's programme, that they had chosen my father with the specific purpose of whitewashing Hermann Pfaff. It is possible, of course, that Samuel would have been promoted in any case, although his age was now against him, but the imputation made his appointment an unexpected certainty. His television appearance secured him the advancement which he might not otherwise have had. I did not have time to thank Joe Hirsch for arranging it.

X

As the band of the West African Rifles, in their red and white uniforms and pipe-clayed pith helmets, played God Save The Queen, the Union Jack twitched on its floodlit flagpole above the dusty lawns of what was, until midnight, Government House, and began to descend. The faces of the guests caught the gleam of the strung lights as they watched the proceedings, not quite sure whether they should be solemn or cheerful. The Princess who had arrived from London earlier that day resumed chatting bravely with Sir Stafford Canning and Wesley Idun. From where Rachel was sipping the white wine deemed suitable by the Commonwealth Office (represented by Horatio Peace, the Minister of State in Mr Wilson's government) H.R.H. had the animated appearance of a tiaraed salesgirl. Both Wesley and the Governor General (soon to be transitional High Commissioner) were listening to the Princess's remarks with tilted heads. She was small and they were large, and the band, having concluded the British anthem, was playing what both men took to be the preamble to that of the newly constituted Federation. This composition had demanded some tact of the European musicologist commissioned to provide an impartial blend of the traditional airs of the South, the Centre and the North. Stafford Canning tried both to stand to attention and to be inclined in a courtly fashion. His hook-fastened collar chafed his shaved throat; his chest hair came very high. Wesley, in his black cotton outfit, with the Maoist collar and breast pockets and the Nehru-style cap, displayed less stiff respect; it might look immodest to defer too ostentatiously to his own signature tune. The West African Federation was the result of his long, loud and eloquent campaign first to alarm and then to reassure the colonial power.

As the Green, White and Orange flag of the W.A.F. (a cluster of cocoa pods in the centre) began its tugged ascent, the festal lights dimmed and then went out. There was a murmur among the crowd. No one was sure whether the darkness had been stage-managed or was another of those temporary eclipses to which inhabitants of Fort St George, now (on the stroke of midnight) Libertyville, had to accustom themselves. The continuing steady beam of the searchlight (operated by one of Colonel Samson's élite units) suggested that all was going according to plan. The guests clapped as the band went into the finale with wilful unity.

'At this point,' Rachel's neighbour whispered to her, 'your prayers are solicited.' He pressed an electric detonator and there was a splutter and then a surge of rockets which fizzed into the sky and unzipped patriotic stars over the gardens. Green, white and orange, they hung for a few moments before being gulped into the darkness. Another volley followed. The coloured lights which played Tarzan between the palms flickered and then, to diplomatic cheers, came on again. The buffet and the bar were there once more.

'*Plus ça change,*' Rachel said.

'Optimistic view.' Trevor Flint, in a white dinner jacket, maroon cummerbund and bow tie, checked his appearance on the back of one of H.E.'s spoons and then came up to Rachel. 'Would you like the pleasure of that dance I promised you?' He led her to the braced floor which had been laid by Colonel Samson's engineers and glided into the anniversary waltz. 'I thought Poker Ramsden might be causing you some grief.'

Rachel said, 'Too busy pressing buttons.'

'He makes over fifteen thou a year arranging these shindigs apparently. Better pension than most sappers manage to get together.'

Bunty Flint was standing with David. She did not dance. 'Your wife always looks so happy,' she said. 'It's rare for a beauty to do that. What's the explanation? I'd've done anything to make Trevor happy.'

'He looks pretty happy to me,' David said.

'That's because he's dancing with your wife. He married me because someone told him I was clever; and I married him because someone told me he was handsome. Both of us were correctly informed, but . . . You're a lucky man, David. And she's a lucky woman. How long are you going to stick it out in the W.A.F.?'

'Rather depends on how long the W.A.F. does. Johnny Quashie doesn't look totally thrilled with this evening's proceedings, does he? Sunglasses at midnight look a little ominous, don't they?'

'You should get Trev to engineer you a plummy little niche in the U.K. Time you had a telephone that worked and a cupboard that didn't turn everything green. Time we did, come to that.'

'I wouldn't get the chance to build bridges in all directions in the U.K., Bunty. This is a first-class place for second-class men, isn't that the old . . . ?'

'No one whose wife looks like yours does can possibly be second-rate.'

Horatio Peace had been urged to say something appropriate to Wesley Idun. 'I enjoyed myself very much, sir. So, I know, did H.R.H. She could scarcely tear herself away. And I'm sure you're 'aving a good time too, sir.'

Wesley was nodding before Horatio had finished, as if he recognized the tune. 'You don't have to call me sir, sir. I've known you as Horatio long enough to be sure that I can always rely on you to call me Wesley, except in a tight corner, of course.'

Horatio's Commonwealth Office minder smiled at his chief's genial humiliation and caught Rachel's eye as she and Trevor stepped back down on to the lawn. 'Hullo, Rachel.'

Rachel said, 'Hullo, Owen. Do you two know each other?'

'I'm Trevor Flint. And you're Owen Millom. How do we do? More important, how will they? Three in one and one in three? Three provinces with little in common but an appetite for big cars and places round the Lancaster House table. Can't see it myself.'

Owen said, 'It worked for England, Scotland and Wales.'

'Catholic, Muslim and more or less C. of E.?' Trevor formed his lips into a sceptical, bloodless roundel. 'You'll be off back to London, of course, long before I've finished my duty dances.'

Rachel said, 'How are you, Owen?'

'All the better for seeing you. Not witty, but true. I've only got to take one look to thank my lucky stars you and I never got married.'

'Can that be the nicest compliment I was ever paid?'

'If ever I saw someone who should've married the man she did and not the one she didn't, thou art the woman.'

'How long are you in Fort St G?'

'As long as my masters in London want to leave the Right Honourable H. Peace out here in the hope that he catches blackwater fever or whatever the local malady is.'

'I think you'll find it's backwater fever,' Rachel said.

As he and the Minister of State watched the Coat of Arms of the West African Federation flare and then fizzle on the great trellis built for their explosive display, Colonel Samson said, 'I am indeed serious. In my father's time native riflemen had to bring in one rebel hand for every cartridge they'd fired. Not that anyone could ever tell for sure that it had ever been attached to a rebel arm, of course.'

Horatio Peace said, 'But *why*?'

'To stop the ignorant bloody savages from firing off a whole clip before they were so much as in range. There's only one thing those Northern province jokers ever began to understand, Mr Peace, and that's a whiff of grapeshot. But don't worry: we'll keep them in order, you'll see. Or else.'

Wesley Idun said, 'Now then Julius, you're not alarming our guest, I hope?'

'Those days are long past, I trust, Colonel.'

'Don't you worry, Mr Peace,' Julius Samson said, 'I was at Sandhurst, you know. They taught us only the nicest possible ways of killing people. Nothing to distress the ladies.'

Horatio said, 'I earnestly trust you'll 'ave no cause to kill anyone at all.'

'As long as you don't get up to any of your divide-and-rule tricks, Horatio, why should we?'

'We've put a lot of investment in the Federation, Mr President. We only want to see you succeed. Personally, I very much 'ope –'

'I was joking, Horatio. I'm always joking. You know that, don't you, Stafford? Even when Stafford was shoving me into pokey, I was still the life and soul of the party; you'll bear me out, won't you?'

'You were always very sporting about it, sir, I must say.'

'I played croquet for Balliol, Stafford! The most character-forming part of my invaluable British education. Did you ever study croquet at Sandhurst, Julius, or were you too busy with Alexander the Great? The Granicus was nothing compared to the triumph of posting the Master twenty minutes before Hall.' Wesley winked at Stafford and looked closely at the medals on the Colonel's spangled chest. 'Are you sure that one isn't for croquet? If not, what?'

Samson moved his head slightly as he answered. 'I think that one is just there to complete the set, sir.' The motion combined deference with a hint of disdain. 'I didn't like to say no.'

'Have you enjoyed yourself, Stafford?'

'A very happy occasion, Mr President.'

'The monkeys taking over the zoo?'

Horatio Peace pondered the bottom of his glass, while Stafford said, 'In Darwinian times, sir, you might say that one set of monkeys is replacing another. Not that I should put it that way myself necessarily.'

'You see how the High Commissioner designate can go through the tightest of hoops without so much as touching the sides? The steady hand, Julius, the unblinking eye, the merciless appraisal of possibilities, how shall we acquire the virtues of our erstwhile masters unless we learn to play the same game? The day you make a clear round and rap that sphere against the barberish pole – nice, eh? – I'll make you a bloody Field-Marshal, see if I don't. And you can have medals right down your striped trouser leg!'

Trevor Flint said, 'One man seems to be having a good time at all events.' He had an arm round Rachel's bare shoulder and supported his behind on the white-aproned buffet table now badged with signs that the evening was coming to an end: empty glasses, rouged cigarettes, unfinished sandwiches and canapés. 'I want you to pop up to Port Victoria or whatever we're now instructed to call the place, because the Northerners are going to want ·a new landing strip, and a V.I.P. lounge, if I know anything, to match what Wesley's giving old Mustafa at Lordship Cove. They're also going to want to ship their cocoa out of Porto Vic instead of driving it down here for the pleasure of putting it in Wesley's people's surf boats, but that's a little way down the road yet. See what you can do to make Johnny Q. your best friend, David. Take Rachel with you, if nanny'll let her go! I can't say fairer than that, can I, and you can't do fairer, can you?'

Rachel could hear Wesley Idun, who had Stafford Canning by the elbow. 'You still believe the secret of the West is your high moral values. Or you still believe that we still believe that. We don't: we know that the secret of the West is the maxim gun and the howitzer, of both of which Colonel Samson is a master. He can also slo-ope arms, slow march and drink his fellow officers under the table. His time in Camberley was not wasted. Nor were his nights in Virginia Water. You have the furtive hope that you've infected him with that contempt for lesser breeds which is the true purpose of an English education and the true majesty of the English law. No soap. Neither I nor the gallant colonel has any intention of affording you the pleasure of seeing Tweedledee and Tweedledum agreeing to have a battle. The heart of the darkness, Stafford, is right in there.' Wesley drilled a slim finger into the centre of the High Commissioner's forehead and pressed until the tip was mauve. Stafford smiled. 'Julius and I, on the contrary, are going to have a ball, aren't we, old friend? We are going to waltz into the future without stepping on each other's tootsies in the least. And if Johnny Quashie or H.M.G. thinks any different, they're going to get egg on their fizzes. The Federation is here to stay. Like you and me, Julius.' The lights flickered and then they went out. This time they stayed out. 'Our secret weapon, gentlemen of England: we can see you and you can't see us.' Wesley laughed and laughed.

Fort St George's first European section had been built on high enough ground to oversee the original battlements which protected the old slave ships. The expansion of the commercial district caused a white retreat to the landscaped suburb where Rachel and David lived. There was sparseness in the luxury; the gardens were young and yellow (water was a problem) and potholes had appeared in the widened roads before the last layer of tar could be applied. The Lucases' Triumph Herald groaned as David drove down Coronation Street towards the Freedom Roundabout, where the coastal highway and the road to Idun International Airport met to the north of the city. They combined in a dual carriageway which carried three lanes of traffic half a mile along the waterfront before it narrowed to join the old road into the town centre. Work was in progress to prolong it to Liberty Square.

'I think we're going to need a new shock absorber before the century's out,' David said. 'Hear that wheezy noise, Billio? Tell-tale signs that go oh-no in the day.'

William sat in the back, with Monty, the golden labrador, and the picnic basket. Sunday morning at the beach club was a routine with the Lucases. David turned right at the roundabout, which had been newly shaved for a plinth on which the Great Liberator's statue was due to be unveiled by H.R.H. The local joke was that it would have to be unveiled before it was installed, because it was still on a truck at the docks, but the ceremony was promised for Tuesday.

The beach club was half a dozen miles from Fort St George. They drove past market gardens which supplied Fort St George with tomatoes, eggs, peppers and okra, from which Unity, their maid, could devise a number of dishes, all of them cheerfully disliked by David. Then there came a section of scrub, with shanties on it. Tribesmen from the North hoping for casual work congregated there. They were not popular nearer Fort St George. The Herald passed a police jeep whose crew had stopped two Northerners, in yellow and black shirts, issued to them, no doubt, by Johnny Quashie's party. The two tall men stood motionless in front of their khaki inquisitors, waiting with impassive apprehension.

Rachel said, 'I hate it so much.'

The club house was a palm-fronded circular building. Hyde International had installed a bar, changing rooms and showers. At the weekend there was a buffet. The Herald lurched down a wide earth road to where high, handmade gates had been propped open by Gus, the ex-regular R.S.M. who took care of the place. He had nailed the gates together from driftwood and plaited them with barbed wire. A turreted ant hill grew beside the entrance, like some knobbly sentry box. There were palm-leaved 'umbrellas' and wooden lounging frames along the beach. Trevor Flint, in khaki shorts and plastic sandals, head in shadow, body exposed, was on his towel mattress, attacking the airmail *Daily Telegraph* crossword with a sharp pencil.

' "Did Henry James say oh for them?" 3,5,2,1,4. What the hell can that mean?'

Bunty said, 'The Wings of a Dove.'

'Of course,' Trevor said. 'Why? Morning, Billio, morning, Monty, morning the Lucas family in general and in particular. Are we getting a quorum at all for tip and run, David, have you heard?'

'I'm hoping to turn my arm over before lunch,' David said. 'Lovely day.'

'Bought and paid for on our behalf by the Great Liberator no doubt. Salaam, salaam.'

There was the crack and echo of a shot and birds panicked from the trees beyond the fence. They were circling to settle when another shot made them raucous again. Monty bristled with his nose up. 'Oh do stop pretending to know what it all means, Monts,' David said. 'You've never been hunting in your whole spoilt life.'

'I suppose we can't persuade you to play second slip, Rachel, can we?'

'You know you don't want women interrupting your flannelled fantasies, Trevor.'

'All my fantasies involve women intimately, didn't you know that?'

Rachel went to find some shade in which to read Claudia Monk's *Wife and Mother*. She was wearing an apple-green 'playsuit' which left her long legs to brown while she swallowed Nicola's cool story.

William said, 'Mummy.'

Rachel turned a page and said, 'Here I am.'

'Should that man be there?'

Rachel lowered her sunglasses and looked. William was pointing beyond the mild breakers to where a black man was swimming out to sea. The club had been sited well along the coast in order to provide safe bathing for the English community, but the breakers were still intimidating. No one was allowed to go beyond them.

Trevor Flint said, 'Stupid clown, what's he doing? Presumably he knows. Not one of ours to judge by his engine cowling. Let them do the needful, if needful there be. Here are the Sextons at last. Time to pick up sides.'

David said, 'A little rescue practice wouldn't hurt anyone. He doesn't look too buoyant to me.'

'How the hell did he get out there? Must be quite a swimmer.'

'Time we checked whether that motor's really up to the job.'

'I never liked the boy scouts,' Trevor pushed himself to his feet and dropped the tissue *Telegraph* by Bunty's canvas chair. 'Ready and unwilling, I suppose.'

William said, 'Can I come, dad?'

David said, 'Next time.'

They ran out the rubber dinghy. While Trevor was still making a performance of getting aboard, David already had the engine going. He steered towards the breakers which began to butt the soft floor. As he opened the throttle, Trevor looked back with a Jellicoe jut of the jaw towards the people on the beach.

The swimmer seemed indifferent to their mission. If he heard the approaching rescuers, he showed no eagerness to be saved. Although he was low enough to seem waterlogged, he swam on, his face buried in the sea. His arms flipped with thin elegance. He appeared to have neither fear nor purpose as he moved out to sea.

David said, 'When we get to him, Trevor, grab him under the arms and haul him inboard backwards, all right? Don't be in too much of a hurry or we shall have you both in the drink.'

'Aye aye, skipper.' Trevor made his first trawl for the swimmer, but silky flesh slipped through his hands. 'Bugger, frankly. What's the matter with you, man? What the hell do you think we're here for?'

David said, 'Take over here, sir, will you? Keep her steady, don't get too close to him. Come on, sonny. No obligation to make things as difficult as you possibly can.'

Trevor said, 'He looks bloody awful, whoever he is.'

'Sea water's a rotten tipple,' David said.

Margaret Sexton, in a pink bikini with a polka-dotted tutu, stepped over with hot toes to where Rachel was inspecting William's moated grange. 'One excitement after another!'

'Remind me of the last one,' Rachel said.

'You didn't like the fireworks? Don't let Poker Ramsden hear or he might come and give you a private rocket! What a hero David is, I must say! I know he was naval, but he does do the intrepid bit rather well. Tim can't always keep on an even keel when he's on *terra firma*.'

Trevor called out, 'Has anyone had the rudimentary intelligence to ring for an ambulance? Or don't free countries run to them on the weekend?'

David was helping the swimmer out of the dinghy and laid him on the damp sand. Their heads were close together.

Rachel said, 'We'd better get him to a doctor. Fast.'

David was smiling. 'Guess what. He *is* a doctor.'

The swimmer propped himself on his elbow, head dangling. 'Green as a lizard,' Trevor said.

David said, 'Got the car keys, darling?'

William said, 'We don't have to *go*, do we?'

David said, 'Give us a hand here, Tim.'

They took the swimmer under the arms and walked him towards the Herald. He was rubber-legged, but his eyes seemed untroubled by his feebleness. They appraised the club house and the English faces with accurate neutrality. Noticing was a kind of comment, to which a British determination not to behave differently was the only response. Trevor Flint said, 'If he turns out to be a fast bowler, bring him back. The attack's going to be dangerously short without you, David.'

Margaret Sexton said, 'Why doesn't Billio stay with us and play with Alexander? We'll drop him home later. And Monty.'

William said, 'Mummy, can I?'

His name was Jerome Leblanc. Rachel brought tea to them on the wide veranda overlooking the strip of garden at the back of the tin-roofed house. He said, 'You're waiting for me to thank you for saving my life.'

David said, 'Not a bit.'

'Oh a *bit*, surely.' The volume came back into Jerome's voice as if he had been incorrectly tuned.

David said, 'What the hell did you think you were doing out there?'

Jerome said, 'I was thinking of swimming to America.'

'Five thousand miles away?'

'I had all day.'

Rachel said, 'Do you know what's happened, again? Excuse me, but . . .'

391

David said, 'Unity's left the freezer open and it's leaked all over the kitchen floor?'

Rachel said, 'I hope you're both hungry. Because we have a lot of limp goodies to eat up. You will stay, won't you?'

'Drowning gives people a hell of an appetite,' David said. 'Of course he will. Nice ordering doctors around for a change. Are you working out here, or what?'

'I was.' Jerome looked at his feet in David's slippers and dipped a spoon in his milkless tea. 'Hyde has its own hospital, they tell me.'

'They're right and they're wrong. We have a sick bay, you might say. We employ a good many people and some of the things we do can get quite hairy, especially when people don't follow the instructions on the packet. You get bossy, they resent you; you get lax, they cut people's feet off.'

'The white man's burden.'

Owen Millom and Stafford Canning took a walk after tea at Government House. Workmen had left ladders and buckets, tool boxes and coils of wire all over the place. Wesley Idun was planning to move into the white, pillared building across from the New National Assembly as soon as the High Commissioner could be accommodated in the old West Africa Steamship Company's offices on Prince of Wales Drive (it would be renamed Marcus Garvey Avenue). The two white men walked through the now peeling wooden houses of the old 'Ridge' district and crossed into a section where windowless warehouses, ventilated only at clerestory level, had been built for the baled cocoa which the surf boats would run out to the roadsteads where large ships had to be loaded. Leggy boys were playing football against a door with a new padlock on a rusty chain.

Owen said, 'How can one feel jealous of people who have absolutely nothing?'

Stafford said, 'I used to like boys. I don't much any more. Why do you suppose that is?'

'Perhaps you're afraid they won't like you?'

'Like oysters,' Stafford said. 'It's rather demeaning, isn't it? You and I being able to take a stroll through a recently liberated colony without any danger of a hostile mob?'

'I had a word to London,' Owen said, 'about your little idea. They thought they just about might manage to spring to it, if the Treasury agree.'

'It's rather in the vaseline department, but there you are: one must do what one can for one's country, as long as it's nothing much.'

'Are you a patriot, Stafford?'

'I used to like the truth rather,' Stafford said, 'but ever since Suez that's involved rather a stretch. My country wrong is still my country, however, don't you find that?'

'You still enjoy your job?'

'Being a servant's remarkably exhilarating,' Stafford said. 'We know where everything's kept, we know precisely what our masters do, on their limited incomes, and we remain within nose-rubbing distance of their dirty laundry. Omniscience is a nice compensation for lack of omnipotence, wouldn't you say? We're a couple of housemaids, Owen.'

'I always did like bombazine.'

'Unsatisfied desires are the only really enjoyable ones, so the vicar tells me.' Stafford returned the flabby ball to two grinning boys. 'What's Poker's game finally, in your view?'

Owen said, 'He seems harmless to me.'

'And to me,' Stafford said, 'but that doesn't make him so. Don't your chaps have any kind of a rundown on him? He's in no apparent hurry to get to his next port of call. Perhaps you could get Harold to raise the British yoke from some other oppressed nation so that he can go and hawk them some sparklers. I wouldn't mind him out of Johnny Q.'s parish, which is where he does his hunting.'

'He's very thick with Geoffrey Hyde, isn't he?'

'And Geoffrey Hyde is far from very thick. How much longer are you going to be here, Owen?'

'Until Horatio tires of shaking hands and stepping on toes and Harold can bear to have him back.'

'Where did he get that centre parting from? And those extraordinary turn-ups? If he stays much longer, they'll probably start worshipping him as a god. No one's ever seen his like before.'

David said, 'I don't think we've done anything to be ashamed of. At least there's been no serious bloodshed. Compared to Algeria, it's been a pretty smooth operation. Isn't that to our credit?'

'It's to your advantage. Now shall we talk about the weather?'

David said, 'Well, at least Unity didn't freeze any okra. So we're let off that.'

'You will have it,' Jerome said. 'Bloodshed. Or they will. You'll regret it officially, but it'll come as no surprise and rather a comfort: see how badly they managed without us! Any true revolution has to be founded in blood, which is why, apart from cowardice, you've been so careful not to shed any. Seats round a table at Lancaster House are no alternative to battle practice.'

Rachel said, 'You don't even come from here.'

'I lack your advantages,' Jerome said. 'This is excellent.'

Rachel said, 'Have some more. Unity'll take most of it home with her. Whatever we don't get through. Whenever her family comes from up country, she leaves the freezer open.'

David said, 'What exactly did you do in Algeria, Dr Leblanc?'

'I was Dr Leblanc.'

'You changed sides, you said. Why?'

'At first I thought I had no side. Isn't that what made me become a doctor? The invisible, colourless, *useful* man. The man in the white coat with no insides at all. What did I do? I learned that neutrality made a fool of me. I don't like being a fool. I wanted to find a way of changing and not changing. To tell the truth, I shot a French officer.'

Rachel said, 'Someone you knew?'

'A patient. A torturer. It takes it out of them. He was lying in

394

bed. I was the only person who could get to him. So I did. Dr Leblanc. Is it time I left?'

'Unity's made up a bed in the spare room,' Rachel said. 'But we've got a lot of eating to do before then.'

David said, 'You never had a wife or children?'

'I have absolutely nothing,' Jerome said. 'Nothing and no one. Good companions.'

'Is that from choice?'

'Choice and necessity, the identical twins.'

'That's balls, you know.'

Jerome smiled at Rachel, to congratulate her on David. 'You must have a very healthy husband. He dares to correct a doctor.'

Jerome went up to bed soon after eating two portions of unfrozen ice cream and stewed apples. William had gone straight to his room as soon as the Sextons returned him from the beach, where he had made seven runs and nearly caught someone. Unity cleared the table and then went home with two heavy shopping baskets. Rachel and David smiled, as usual, and as usual made no comment. Rachel called out, 'William, I'm counting down from two hundred.' She picked up *Wife and Mother* while David sighed again over a plan for a rural bridge deep in Centre province which had fallen in once already, thanks to inadequate footings on a crumbling river bank.

'Nine, eight, seven, six, five . . .' Rachel marked her place and began a slow climb to William's bedroom. 'Four, three . . .'

She was on the landing when hands came out of the darkness and made her gasp. 'Billy, don't ever do that again.'

'Don't be frightened,' Jerome said.

'What the hell are you playing at?' It was a courtesy to keep her anger secret from David.

'I couldn't see you.'

'Turn on the light. It is working for a change.'

'It wouldn't help.'

'Mummy?' William had not wanted her until she did not come.

'You're not blind, are you?'

395

'Yes.'

'You weren't blind at dinner.'

'No. But I am now.'

'Do you often go blind?'

'Sometimes,' he said. 'Kindly take me to the door of my room.'

'This isn't some kind of a joke is it?'

'Of course.'

When she opened the door of the spare room, she jumped back. It was a blizzard of moths and other insects. The light was on. The window was open. She said, 'Look what you've done now.'

He said, 'I should like to.'

She said, 'You'll be bitten to death.'

He said, 'I shall be all right.'

In the morning, Rachel said, 'Now I think he's gone deaf.'

She knocked again and then opened the door. The spare room was empty. The bed was made. Jerome might never have been in the house. On the floor were some parched moths, like chaff on the waxed boards.

'De bird, he flown?' David said. 'I wonder if he's left a note propped on the mantelpiece.'

Rachel went to the central market to buy spices from her favourite stall later that morning. Owen Millom waved to her, discreetly, from the aromatic depths of the barn-like building. Horatio Peace, in rumpled tropical trousers, had stopped by a stall where carpets and fabrics were being unfolded for him by a market mama of rare size and energy. 'You give me ten pound W.A.F., master! Ten pound. You ask them, very fair price.'

The two Security Men, in new shiny suits, turned their backs and frowned into the crowd.

'We 'ave to bargain with 'er, presumably, Owen?'

'I imagine that's the usual form, minister.'

'It don't seem a 'ell of a lot for a blanket, ten pounds W.A.F.'

A mustachioed Syrian, with hairy arms, across the aisle from the mama, said, 'Offer her five.'

'You shut your damn mouth, Ali, you hear me? Eight pound W.A.F.'

'My advice is that five would be an appropriate price.' Horatio smiled, as if playing a brave part in some local game, while the mama and the Syrian jeweller shouted abuse at each other. Horatio affected to look at some of the Syrian's bracelets, waiting for the mama to reduce her original price. A young black slipped through the crowd and thrust a yellow and black flag into Horatio Peace's hand. 'Wave the flag for us, mister. Support our side. Give us a wave.'

Horatio smiled his electioneering smile and waved the yellow and black flag. Owen, who disliked bargaining, had turned away from the stall and was too late to prevent Horatio from being photographed by another young black who popped up from behind a fruit stall. The Security Men (known as the Tintin Macoutes to Owen and Stafford Canning) flung themselves at the photographer, but he tossed his camera to a confederate before skipping free and shimmying towards the door. The Security Men had their guns out and punched their way into the crowd.

'Stop that man. Stop or I fire.'

Rachel saw the photographer running at her, the guns levelled behind him and then she was pulled down on to a heap of green mats.

'Don't get trigger-'appy, lads. No 'arm done. Never get trigger-'appy.'

Owen said, 'I think we'd better get out of here, sir. And may I take that?'

'Local team, is it?' Horatio said. 'Feelings run 'igh evidently.'

Owen said, 'Those are the colours of the Northern Province, sir. Johnny Quashie's people. We have to hope that photo doesn't come out.'

'Mine never do,' Horatio Peace said.

The mama said, 'Five pound W.A.F.'

''old on a tick,' Horatio Peace said. 'Must take something for Mrs Peace. She would've loved to be here but she 'ates injections, can't stomach the things. Needles give 'er the willies. No one's got 'urt, 'ave they? No damage done?'

Rachel said, 'You're a quick thinker. As well as a very neat folder of a blanket. Thank you.'

Jerome said, 'Do you want some tea?'

'Why not?'

They went to a stall where a thin man with a straggly grey beard tended two big urns. He put unsteady brown cups on the blistered green counter.

Jerome said, 'You should get out of here. You disguise yourself as a wife and mother, but you know.'

Rachel said, 'And what do you disguise yourself as?'

'I've told you.'

'You disguise yourself as what you are, Dr Leblanc. So do I. And where are you going to go? Or do you belong here?'

'I may not belong. I have a use.'

'You must miss France.'

'Yes,' he said. 'It's curious: you can miss France without missing the French.'

'You could go there now, couldn't you?'

'I've already been. I was sent there two years ago, by my grateful friends the Arabs. After they'd won the war. They needed me when they were fighting, but I wasn't the sort of doctor that liberation was intended to liberate. They persuaded me to go and improve myself, professionally, by studying with a professor in Paris, René Poulain, who'd been a sympathizer. Each of us was rewarded with the other. That's never necessarily a good recipe for a romance, would you say?'

'Rachel!' Margaret Sexton said. 'Big world! Haven't seen you since yesterday!'

'Hullo, Mag. You know Dr Leblanc, don't you?'

'I recognize Dr Leblanc, but I couldn't say I knew him. How are you today? Better than yesterday, I can see that.' Margaret, in a white cotton dress with a gilt acropolis on the front and a gilt frieze around the hem, of warriors with shields and spears, pulled Rachel to her by the upper arm and lowered her head and voice. 'The last time I sent Maudie to market on her own, the price of everything doubled and the average pound weighed ten ounces, so now I go with her and we don't have shouting matches any more. The girl cooks like an angel and lies like a trooper. Tim says it's better than lying like an angel and cooking like a trooper.'

'Thanks for giving Billio such a nice time yesterday.'

'Oh Alexander's longing to get on a spaceship with him again soon. They've got several galaxies they hadn't explored yet. I hear you're going up to Porto Vic in the near future. That always used to be Tim's patch rather. You don't get the feeling that Sir Trevor's giving him a taste of outer darkness at all, do you, Rachel?'

'He just likes to shuffle his pack.'

'Does he pinch you at all? He pinches me. He should've been a pasha, should Trevor: he thinks women are only good for one thing. What were you trying to *do* yesterday, Dr Leblanc, if you don't mind my curiosity?'

Rachel said, 'He was trying to swim to America.'

'Much too far,' Maggie Sexton said, 'and not all that nice when you get there. Sorry to interrupt you. I'd better go and see how many eggs there are in Maudie's dozen.'

Rachel said, 'It must have been strange going back to Paris. Weren't you . . . uneasy? You can't have been sure quite which side wasn't going to forgive you first.'

Jerome said, 'I was promised I could go back to Constantine afterwards and head up a new psychiatric unit. If the French had hated me, as I expected to hate them, I might have been more . . . single-minded, if you like. But I found myself something of a hero, at least with some people. I had an excuse to like what I'd sworn to hate. Is that woman a friend of yours?'

'Her husband and mine both work for Hyde.'

'I met people who knew the man I'd killed. The officer in the hospital. They didn't know that I was the one who . . . They talked about how he had been in the Resistance. They made him real for me without knowing what they were doing. As a torturer, I had never thought about him again. As a man, he began to haunt me. I did not think I had been wrong to do what I did. I don't now. But every year – on the anniversary of what I did . . . I have . . . certain problems.' He looked steadily at her over his cool tea. 'You can get away from Africa, and you should. I have a more difficult trip to make: I have to get away from myself.'

Rachel said, '*Bon voyage.*'

Wesley Idun said, 'What's the explanation of this, Sir Stafford?'

Stafford took the *Port Victoria Clarion* from Wesley's hands and needed his spectacles before he could answer. 'May I say first of all, Mr President, off the record, that your old friend 'oratio was caught on the hop? Without his specs. He's probably colour-blind and he meant no conceivable harm.'

'He's done some. And by colour-blind you mean the old British disease: he can't tell one nignog from another. This is a very grave incident, Sir Stafford.'

'As I understand it, sir, your people have seized most of the copies of the *Clarion* and Johnny Quashie has himself said that it was a case of over-enthusiasm.'

'And how do I prevent this appearing in the foreign press? Evidence of British sympathy with Johnny Q.'s secessionist ambitions.'

'The British Government, as the Prime Minister has emphasized again and again, stands four-square behind the Federation. I thought the unveiling went exceptionally well, sir. Very fine turnout.'

'A lot of ill-mannered hooting. Some of your people didn't appreciate the traffic being held up. Dammit, Stafford, when a British Prime Minister emphasizes something again and again, you can be sure it means no one believes a word of it. The Prime Minister should have come here himself.'

'If, as I earnestly trust is not the case, Mr President, you mistrust our sentiments, you can surely appreciate our interests.

Our investment in the Federation renders us your keenest supporters, if only because we have the most to gain, and the most to lose. Take Hyde International . . .'

'That may well be what I shall do. Take Hyde International. I have to prove that I'm in charge in my own house, that I'm not a stooge of outside forces. I don't rule out nationalization. Oh, you're very diplomatic, Stafford. I admire you. But you know – and don't imagine I don't – that I've got you off quite a nasty hook. It looks as if Wesley Idun has humiliated the British and you've been wonderfully sporting about it, welcoming us into the Commonwealth, sending us a tiara, refusing to wince after being kicked in the pants. You all think how you can go on pulling the strings without having to run the theatre. And if the chance comes along to make a better deal with Johnny Q. or Julius Samson . . . I'm warning you, my dear old friend, and you can pass this particular parcel right round the next all-white party you go to: if you and Trevor Flint think you can run with the hares and hunt with the Quashies, it won't wash. Because if I get this kind of trouble again, I shan't hesitate to put the blame squarely on imperialist interests. I've read my Machiavelli.'

'The subtle Nicolo would long have despaired of the British, I fear. If we really had some sly plan for taking advantage of the present situation, would we have worked quite so hard, do you suppose, sir, to prevent it ever coming about?'

'Of course! How could you – or I – have persuaded my people that the Great Liberator had indeed lifted the imperialist yoke, unless you first cracked the whip and threatened scorpions? You were very obliging in your show of wrath, and in return what did I do? I yelled and shouted and asked the Russians to wait in the next room. They're still waiting.'

Stafford said, 'I do remember some of your chaps breaking windows in the British Council Library.'

'After closing hours, Stafford. Be fair. We didn't want anybody badly cut while reading the airmail edition of the *New Statesman and Nation*. And in return for your barbarian boxer's incompetence, I agreed to have a single deliberative assembly, with a nice free opposition and a speaker with a wig on his woolly head. Likewise judges and policemen with English motorbikes. Who made a fool of whom, Stafford? Honestly.'

'Honestly, sir, no one made a fool of anyone.'

'Stafford, sit down. The price of cocoa has been falling for the last three months. Johnny Q.'s people are talking about oil and even possibly uranium. I'm hoping the cartographers can prove that the mines belong to Central Province, but I can't be sure. What if Johnny offers Julius Samson the presidency in return for a looser form of association? I think Horatio Peace should either resign or be replaced.'

'Forgive me, sir, but that would be a great mistake. All the good publicity of the last weeks would be compromised. You know very well that poor old 'oratio meant no harm whatsoever . . .'

'The ideal scapegoat therefore!'

'No, sir. Wait till you've got a crisis before you despatch anyone into the wilderness with the sins of the world attached. This is the time to be magnanimous, build on your popularity, prove your confidence. Your own people are your judges now, just as you always wanted them to be.'

Wesley said, 'Oh Stafford, what fun it all was when you had all the cards in your hand! What fun to go straight from jail to the Constitutional conference! If the cocoa price continues to drop, we shall all be dependent on the oil boys in Porto Vic. Imagine. You made me promise my people all kinds of benefits once you'd lowered the Union Jack, knowing I could never deliver. Now the opposition can do the same. And I'm in your position, except that I don't have a pension and Eastbourne waiting for me.'

Stafford said, 'I'm not sure, sir, whether this is a tactful moment, but I do have something for you in the outer office.'

There was a green coffin-like box on two chairs. Wesley clapped his hands and laughed. 'Machiavelli was an Englishman!' He pushed open the gilt cedilla which fastened the lid and revealed the Army and Navy mallets, the championship-quality hoops, the coloured clips, the red, black, yellow and blue balls.

'Very fine, Stafford. Very fine indeed. But where is the lawn? They haven't sent the lawn. Half-measures, old friend, but better than no measures at all. Fun and games, the British idea of hard work! Poor old Horatio!'

'We have to be ready for all eventualities, David, and I never said that, did I? Pass me that stack of bibles! Hyde doesn't want to be identified with Master Wesley or anybody else. We're not in the business of nailing colours to mastheads. You may be Nelson; I'm the vicar of Bray. We want to do heap profitable business with whichever worthy happens to be shelling out the cowries. At the moment, putting my wet finger to the prevailing zephyr, it looks as if Johnny Q. and his boys just might be the better stayers. Worth an each-way bet at all events, like any other dark horse. Put it this way, though never say I said so: whoever comes out on top, we have to be sure we supplied the rackets and the balls. Whichever best man wins, it'll all be thanks to us. Tell you who you might see, incidentally, when you're up in Porto Vic and that's our friend Poker Ramsden.'

'He's not about to sell fireworks to Johnny Q., I trust, is he? I'm not sure that I like Colonel Ramsden.'

'Oh I'm sure you do, David.'

It took a week for Carlos, the Portuguese mechanic at Britannia Garages, to get the new shock absorbers fitted on the Herald. Rachel basked in guilty liberty when finally she and David rolled, without groaning lurches, past the strident statue of the Great Liberator and turned north along the coastal highway for Port Victoria.

David said, 'He'll be fine with Maggie. Kids don't miss their mamas as much as their mamas like to think. One tit is much like another.'

Rachel said, 'Is it? Thanks.'

He touched her white-shirted breast. 'Tell me something: what would you say if I said I was thinking of looking for something else to do?'

Rachel said, 'Hurrah. Followed by when. Followed by what.'

'And never mind why? Because something's going on that smells of fish. God help me, I thought I was out here to build bridges. The only question is, if not Africa, then where?'

They passed a tall black man in shorts, standing on the verge with a transistor radio to his ear. He raised a thumb for a lift without even looking to see whether David would stop.

Rachel said, 'What about South Kensington?'

Soon after the province border, on the Mampong River bridge (built by Hyde International in the fifties), the road looped east, to avoid a coastline dimpled with lagoons. It took them through the fringe of the rain forest which, in this part of the Northern Province, came down almost to the sea. A benched truck, which served as a supplementary bus, stopped near where David had pulled up to have their picnic. A couple of passengers jumped down and were handed their bundle. They walked down a narrow path, between the umbrella trees, the woman with the bundle on her head, directly into the jungle. David said, 'Deep in the heart of Texas!'

On the outskirts of Port Victoria, they had to slow up. A firing squad of black-and-yellow-shirted militiamen, under an officer in a camouflaged boiler suit, were laughing and pointing their rifles. Rachel was relieved to see that their target was only a lifesize portrait of Wesley Idun. When they fired, the hammered target fell backwards in the dust. It proved to be an old road sign with 'PORT VICTORIA – 3' on its pimpled white face.

The town had always had certain claims to be the rightful capital of the colony. It had a deep-water harbour. The local tribe, first converted to Catholicism by Portuguese missionaries who had been able, for a while, to protect them from the slave-traders, was hard-working and cohesive. It was precisely their intelligence which had inhibited the British, when they became the masters of the coast, from offering them too much prestige. It was prudent for the colonial power to flatter the less favoured majority tribe of the Centre. It was assumed that the

Northerners would have the wit to see that the white men would never have demoted them if they had not thought particularly well of them.

The Grand Hotel was run by an Indian called Harry Sinha. It was built in the colonial style, with shuttered bedrooms opening on to wrought-iron terraces overlooking Marina Drive. The ground floor had recently been re-modelled, with plate-glass doors and an American Bar. There were telephones in all rooms, but only one line to which they could be connected. Rachel went to take a shower while David tried to get through to announce his appointment to Johnny Quashie's office.

'How goes it, darling?'

'Luxury unlimited,' Rachel said. 'A veritable torrent of cold cocoa. Form queue this side.'

'Good country for wild-goose chasing, this. Johnny's not at home and I can't get Flinters in under two hours, which probably means tomorrow morning. We may as well enjoy ourselves.'

'I never expected to enjoy anything much else,' Rachel said.

David threw his clothes back into the bedroom and joined her under the trickle of brown water. They were laughing together when there was a scorching of tyres, the sound of metal rumpling into stone, falling glass, shouting and cries of pain. When he had opened the reluctant shutters, David could see that a lorry with a load of yellow-and-black Northerners had crushed a Federal jeep against a warehouse wall. The driver had gone through and over the windscreen; another soldier was holding his head and looking at the blow. A third had been caught by the Northerners, who were standing around him in a goading circle. Two others, one with a Sten gun, ran across the wide street and into the hotel. One of the Northerners ripped the belt out of their prisoner's loops and pulled his trousers to the ground.

David said, 'I'd better go down.'

Harry Sinha had locked the big doors behind the soldiers. One was a sergeant who was bleeding from a blow on the head and had a ballooning knee. The lance corporal with him was

405

ready to shoot. Harry Sinha was saying, 'The telephone is unfortunately not operational at this stage.'

David said, 'Get them out of sight, quick as you can. Get them into the bar. Isn't there a back way out? Go with this gentleman, sergeant, all right?'

The unwounded soldier helped to get the hopping sergeant out of the sight of the crowd, whose faces were massed against the thick glass. For the moment, they seemed less threatening than in search of entertainment. The hotel might have been a cinema showing a film of which they had heard unenthusiastic reports. But they might decide to come in at any second. David preferred not to hear the screams in the street.

'Thank God for you, sir,' Harry Sinha said.

'The best thing,' David said, 'would be to get them out the back fast. Can you find a taxi that'll come to the service door?'

'I can, sir.'

'And then get me through to Hyde International in Fort St G.'

'More problematical, I'm afraid, but I'll do what I can.'

David walked back into the main foyer. The big doors were holding but wariness had yielded to rage on the faces of those locked outside. David ambled up to the mouthing silence and waved apologetic hands. He indicated, with an administrative shrug, that the key had been misplaced. He supplemented his elaborate faces with an amusing mime of the manager searching for the spare key. The quicker-witted of the crowd were pleased to guess what David's gestures were intended to convey. His little show breached the mob's common ambition and turned them back into individuals. With a courteous final sweep of his hands, proposing that they move along, he turned and took the steps two at a time back up to room 19.

Rachel opened the door and saw blood on his shirt and hands. 'Not mine, so don't worry,' David said. 'Unless we're very careful or very lucky, Flinters is going to have to send a Panzer division up here to get us out of this.'

'I wetted a towel,' Rachel said. 'The pipes were making

406

ominous noises, so I thought we'd better have something to get the muck off. Here!'

'There's my graduate wife!' The telephone rang. 'Bless his heart, even if it is a wrong number.'

Johnny Quashie sent a car from his personal fleet and three of his men to escort them to the provincial Prime Minister's residence. The car was a big Austin, with a black and yellow flag on the wing. The streets seemed quiet, but they passed a crowd of cheering Northerners gathered round something that lay in the dust. David shielded Rachel from seeing the sergeant's stripes.

Johnny Quashie's office was in one of the oldest buildings in Port Victoria. It had been the bishop's palace during the Portuguese tenure of the coast. St Peter's church was across a courtyard symmetrical with tubbed palms and citrus trees. Johnny Quashie was sleeved in a great blue and yellow robe, the colours slanting across his body. The solid black shoes visible at the ends of his outstretched legs suggested that his robes concealed a complete European outfit. Rachel had not wanted to come, any more than she wanted to be left alone, but David said that the invitation specifically included her. It was a preliminary, social occasion; besides, he did not propose to leave her at the hotel.

'Wesley, let us face it, just now he's drunk with vanity,' Johnny Quashie said. 'I find him impossible to talk to. We have the British to thank for that, of course. They made him their great enemy so that he could then become their great friend. They don't like complications, but that's not what we're here to talk about, is it?'

They drank a locally bottled fruit juice in frosted glasses. The room had a slow fan in the high, vaulted ceiling. The stuccoed walls were hung with traditional weavings and masks. On Johnny Quashie's desk there was a heavy brass bird, balanced firmly on splayed claws, an ancient gesture of friendship from a chief in Dahomey. It looked solid enough to kill and delicate enough to fly.

'You had a spot of trouble this evening, sir,' David said.

'You know, I've been begging Wesley to pull the Federal people out of N.P. I don't think he necessarily means any harm, but it's very provocative.'

A male secretary, slim in a cotton suit, knocked on the open door and came and whispered to Johnny Quashie. The Prime Minister put a hand on the man's shoulder and then, having heard the message, stood up, smiling. 'You will have to excuse me for a moment.'

Rachel and David looked at the masks and then out of the window. 'What's going on, oh interpreter of omens?'

'He's very keen for us to see him as the father of his people, isn't he? But why us? It's too subtle for my size twelve shoes, I'm afraid.'

'What a nice surprise! Mrs Lucas! Not to mention Mr Lucas!' Poker Ramsden was standing in the doorway, taking a frosted glass from the secretary. 'We seem to be getting a bit of static.'

'What's the latest state of the parties exactly?' David said. 'And what's J.Q. up to?'

Ramsden joined them at the window. 'You remember the old line, Lucas: "I am their leader – I must follow them."'

'Ledru-Rollin,' Rachel said.

'I beg your pardon? Seen a friend?' Ramsden winked at David.

Rachel said, 'What're you doing here, Colonel Ramsden?'

'My friends call me "Poker". Improving my mind, catching up with the wild life, observing the improprieties. Johnny's under some pressure from not a few of his chums. They're all for closing the Mampong bridge and declaring a separate state before Wesley can so much as get his stamps into the local P.O., let alone Julius Samson's tanks. I can't say I blame them, do you?'

'Hang blame! I don't want to get caught the wrong side of the border.'

'No one does,' Ramsden said. 'Is this supposed to be gin?'

Rachel said, 'We've left our son in Fort St G.'

'This is all between them,' Ramsden said. 'Teething troubles. Bound to happen. J.Q.'s people've got the brains and quite a bit of brawn and Wesley's got the seat in the United Nations and his face on the national lav paper. For my money, Johnny and his chaps ought to have had the running of the whole show from the outset, but they were loyal to the Crown and made no trouble when Wesley was yelling his head off in Britannia Square and frightening London half to death. Free-DOM, free-DOM! The chairman told London what the score was, but they had other plans. I had a word with Trevor Flint earlier in the proceedings. All's quiet on the central front.'

'Did you so? I couldn't get through.'

'I pulled some local military plonkers and managed to raise him. He wants you to up stumps and get back to Fort St G., *quam celerrime*.'

David said, '*What?*'

'Bit of a pardon-my-French nuisance for you, but that's Africa, isn't it? Land of contrasts. Asked me to pass the word. Safest thing.'

'When exactly?'

'First possible moment. If Johnny decides to go for broke, much as one may sympathize, it's best for all concerned if we're not seen to be in his camp when he does it.'

David said, '*We?*'

'You and I and the lovely lady on my left.'

'I thought you were just observing the wild life.'

'Do you like Wordsworth at all, Mrs Lucas? Because do you know what I do for the most part? I wander lonely as a cloud. But I am a cloud with the odd silver lining. I do think you'd be well advised to let me be your father, *pro tem*. If this is the calm, I think it may well be the one that precedes the storm. The road to Fort St G. may not be all that plain sailing in a little while.' There was a distant but prolonged natter of small-arms fire, as if to second Ramsden's intelligence. He uncapped his stainless-steel watch. 'I think the best shot would be to doss down under Johnny Q.'s generous auspices, then take your bus to the airport in the small hours. I happen to have a Piper made for three waiting on the runway.'

'I've had the bloody suspension repaired on my Herald,' David said. 'Are you suggesting we ditch it?'

'The fortunes of peace,' Ramsden said.

Ramsden proposed that they set their alarms for 4 a.m. The streets then would be deserted and they could walk to the Grand, collect the car and be away soon after dawn. Until the pubs closed, so to say, the hotel was best avoided; according to some reports, there might be a little trouble in store for Harry Sinha. They had waited in his office another hour, but Johnny Quashie failed to return. No one appeared to know where he had gone, nor was anyone noticeably surprised by his absence. Rachel suspected that everything spontaneous had been arranged beforehand. Soldiers came and went across the courtyard. At one moment the bells of St Peter's began to ring. Ramsden proved able to raise some food (no okra, but plenty of fried plantain, which David liked) and seemed determined to establish his competence.

'Good man in a tight corner, it must be admitted.'

'Let's hope it gets no tighter,' Rachel said. 'I only wish we could swim for it personally.'

'Don't rely on Flinters to push the boat out to save us. Better stay on dry land.'

'I'm never going to be able to sleep on this bed,' Rachel said. 'I hate not feeling you next to me.'

'Shall I come and crawl in?'

'Has that door got a lock?'

David said, 'I'm damned sorry about this.'

Rachel said, 'We'll be all right, won't we?'

'Pipers are tolerably reliable,' David said, 'and Ramsden's been around. I reckon we're in good hands.'

'Unfortunately,' Rachel said, 'I don't like him. One bit.'

'Me neither. It might be easier on the floor.'

'Put both the beastly mattresses on the floor. Why didn't I think of that? This was going to be a *break*!'

'Could be worse,' David said. 'You're not keeping this thing on during negotiations are you?'

Rachel said, 'Roll on, South Ken.'

They slept together on the floor and were woken by Ramsden's knock. 'Tea's up.' He left it for them and came back when they were dressed, carrying a kitbag with his 'tackle' in it. Rachel hated the trust which she could not help putting in the man. He might be a joke, but he was a joke who knew his way around. It was an unnerving reassurance to see, from the shape of the bulge, that he had a revolver in his kit.

The airstrip was deserted. The Piper was outside the soaring hoop of corrugated iron which served as a hangar. When they drove up to it, they saw the bad news. Someone had taken a sledgehammer to the cockpit. 'Damn and likewise blast,' Ramsden said. 'They must have had some jokers out here. I wondered why there wasn't anyone on duty. Took it for a Federal kite presumably.'

'What happens now?' Rachel said.

'Plan B comes smoothly into operation,' Ramsden said. 'Once we've decided what plan B is. Lucas?'

David said, 'How long's the plane been in this condition, Ramsden?'

'Academic rather, that. Can't say until we hear from the pathologist. Thieves in the night, I presume. I'm very much afraid there may be some bodies in the bush, but that's not our part of ship, is it, commander?'

Rachel said, 'I want to get back to Fort St G.'

'*Quam celerrime*,' Ramsden said. 'Caesar mustered his forces, peppered the enemy and assaulted the fort. Luckily it's still early. No one'll be moving yet.'

'Who do you expect to be moving?'

'Look, I'm very sorry the clipper service isn't running, but at least we shall get your machine back to Fort St G. for you, shan't we? You don't think my presence'll put an undue strain on your new shock absorbers, do you?'

David drove. His and Rachel's straight faces were amused and irritated by the same thing. Ramsden sprawled in the back, the rim of his panama hat on his red nose, whistling to himself. He had found a couple of gerry cans of petrol in the hangar, one of those pieces of well-placed luck which seemed to be his stock-in-trade. There was at least no anxiety about fuel.

The umbrella trees by the side of the road thinned and the sun freckled the road. They crossed a plank bridge over a dry torrent and went through a quiet village. Women with ribbed pots on their heads paraded by the well, silhouettes inked on a silken day. Ramsden squirmed sideways and put his feet on the folded roof. He began to sing quietly: 'May I have a piece of cake, oh may I have a piece of cake? May I have a piece of cake, may I have a piece of cake?'

David and Rachel felt no urge to join in the chorus. Ramsden seemed delighted by his own company; he continued the refrain as the miles bounced by. They were nearly at the end of the forest region when they heard shots. Ramsden ceased to repeat the words, which was a blessing, but hummed instead.

They came to where wooden billets had been laid across a culvert. A jeep was parked across the narrowest part of the road, where it joined the bumpy bridge. Behind it, a truck, with Federal Government markings, had been stopped. Militiamen in yellow-and-black jerseys and khaki shorts had opened its door. The driver, in overalls and a peaked cap, was pissing into the culvert. It was as if the golden arch secured him from trouble: the longer it lasted, the better his chances.

David said, 'Keep smiling through, folks.'

The driver of the jeep looked at his officer (in full camouflage kit and black beret) and was encouraged to back slightly out of the way. The militiamen were tossing stacks of new, identical books on to the side of the road. The golden arch wilted and the driver, perhaps prompted by the presence of the Europeans, gave a hopeful smile. 'You see? No guns. Only books. Sir . . .' He called to David. 'I am delivering books for schools in Northern Province. Will you tell them this?'

David said, 'Morning.'

The officer said, 'Routine check, sir.'

'May I have a piece of cake, oh may I . . .'

The books on the roadway were entitled *A Shorter English History*.

David said, 'What's the problem?'

'No problem, sir. Open the boot, please.'

Ramsden held Rachel's eye steadily while David unlocked the boot. She looked back at him with deliberate lack of complicity. He tilted his head back, with a silent gasp, like a surfacing swimmer, and then switched his head to look at the camouflaged officer. He regarded him with the same unsmiling humour he had shown towards Rachel. Did they know each other? The officer closed the boot and made a suave movement with his hand.

David said, 'Any chance of giving that chap at least a glass of water at all?'

'He's not thirsty, sir. Safe journey to you.' The officer indicated for the jeep to make way.

David said, 'Poor sod.'

'Drive on, Lucas, is my version of events. We're not in charge here, are we? *Le jour de gloire est arrivé.*'

The militiamen had wound a rag around the driver's face and over the top of his peaked cap. They started to spin him around in the road as David drove on. He watched them in his wing mirror until there was a curve in the road. 'I hate that sort of thing.' Several shots frightened the birds: three, four, five.

'Boys will be boys.'

They were approaching the Mampong bridge when they saw a tall, thin soldier in Federal uniform sitting, legs apart, by the side of the road, head hanging down as if he were studying some intricate work.

'May I have a piece of cake, oh may I have a piece of cake?'

The soldier raised his head and snatched a gun from the verge.

Ramsden said, 'Foot down, corporal.'

David said, 'Look here, Ramsden . . .'

The soldier waved his Sten at them, like a friend. As David slowed, having seen blood on the man's shirt, he started firing, one-handed. The other hand hung bloody by his side. The Herald swerved and slithered in the dust as bullets pecked the driver's door.

Rachel said, 'No, no, no.' She turned and yelled in Ramsden's face. '*NO*.'

David said, 'Oh Jesus, Raitch. Oh Christ, darling.'

Steering with a hand that still seemed strong, he turned half-towards her. She felt wet weight against her arm. The soldier was in the roadway behind them, with the gun dangling by his side, like a disappointed passenger. Ramsden said, 'Get your foot down on that accelerator, woman.'

David said, 'Oh Raitch, I wish we were in South Ken. I truly do.'

Rachel said, 'No. No.'

David said, ' 'fraid so, my life.'

Ramsden said, 'Budge him over, budge over yourself. We're getting out of here.'

'Fuck you, Ramsden,' Rachel said.

'More than possibly, but we'd better get him to a quack.'

'You dirty, filthy bastard. Fuck you forever.'

Ramsden drove down a rutted track and through a village where flared chickens scuttled on tiptoe at the car's approach. David lay against Rachel's breast. She held him hard, under the arm. The 'hospital' was a shack with a tin roof. There was a motorbike without a front wheel padlocked to the gatepost. Ramsden walked into the surgery. '*Run*, you shit,' Rachel said. Jerome Leblanc came out, running, with a stretcher.

'One good turn deserves another,' Rachel whispered to the hair beneath her lips.

In the surgery, she waited with savage patience for Jerome to say what she already knew. He looked at her and his lips winced at the corner and he took up David's hand and laid it on his chest. Rachel agreed with what he had not said. Her chin gave brief assent and she turned and walked back into the palm-fenced heat and out to the car. Ramsden leaned over and opened the door. A buzzing red rag in the grass indicated that he had cleaned the seat. Rachel walked past the open door and on toward the puckering chickens. Ramsden started the engine and came slowly after her. 'Please get in the car, Mrs Lucas.'

Rachel did not stop. 'You pretended to want to help us. You wanted us to help you. You knew your plane had been smashed up.'

Ramsden said, 'Think of your boy, Mrs Lucas. Get in the car.'

She stopped and looked at him. 'Who told you you could drive?'

He said, 'I can't tell you how sorry I am.'

'My car. I'll drive.'

Ramsden got out of the car and held the door for Rachel, covering the bullet holes with seasoned tact. He waited to meet her glance, but she put the car straight into gear. He scrambled behind the boot to get in the other side. She changed up and accelerated away from him. He loped after her, indulgent and red-faced. 'Mrs Lucas, Mrs Lucas, please.'

She slowed down. He smiled in the wing mirror and walked towards her. She reached into the back and flung his kitbag on to the grassless chicken run. Then she thrust the car into gear and spat dust at Ramsden as he flapped his arms and grew shorter. A pregnant woman, walking wide-footed, a child on the crook of her arm, passed Ramsden and went into the fenced compound. He walked furiously into the surgery.

'She's driven off. She's taken the car and she's driven off.'

'There's nothing she can do here,' Jerome said. 'Will you please go out and shut the door.'

'I need transport. Where's the telephone?'

'What telephone?'

'I can't believe it.'

'The legacy of empire,' Jerome said. 'I have a patient.'

'There's half a motorbike in the yard. Where's the other half?'

Jerome lifted a string which went round his neck. There was a key under his shirt.

Ramsden said, 'Can I possibly have it?'
Jerome said, 'Wait outside.'

The woman in the white Herald drove steadily and without haste. She began to meet other cars and buses after she had crossed the Mampong girder bridge. She overtook and she was overtaken. Farmers were loading boxes of produce in the area near the Beach Club. She waited while a lorry that had shed its overloaded freight of bundled waste paper was hauled into the side by a tractor. A policeman, in blancoed belt and white helmet was particularly keen to tell her why there had been a delay and to help her round the obstacle so that she might continue towards Libertyville. The spilled consignment, fretted by the sea breeze, broke and paperchased across the flat fields. It was nearly evening when she reached Freedom Roundabout. Several military vehicles, with thick indented tyres and narrow, visored windscreens, were leaving the city. The Herald went up the hill to the house. She parked on the far side of the street and waited. Just before six o'clock, Unity came out of the house. Her shopping basket elongated one arm as she walked down the cooling road towards her bus stop.

Rachel drove the car in a deep semi-circle and parked in front of the house. There were letters on the hall table. She recognized her brother's writing. There was a strong smell of polish. Unity was quick to use it, but less eager to wipe it off. One of David's blueprints was still spread on the coffee table. A pipe rack, a tub of sharpened pencils, a small Ashanti mask and a set of old keys held down the corners. She lifted the keys and then the mask. The plan rolled up.

The telephone was ringing. She took a breath. Doing nothing was an activity she laid aside reluctantly; her voice was slightly stern when she picked up the receiver. 'Yes, it is,' she said. 'I'm afraid he's not here at the moment. What? Yes. Oh, hullo! How are you? Just a few minutes ago. He's still up country. I drove myself. I'll remember. No, no, I've got plenty to do here.'

She went upstairs and into the bathroom. It was still her face she saw in the mirror. David's shaving things were on the marble shelf. He had unscrewed the haft of his Gillette, ready to insert a new blade from the blue dispenser. She slid one from the plastic clasp and felt its oiliness in the palm of her hand. Her fingers were red and ribbed where she had grasped the steering wheel. She closed them on the blade until it bit. Blood made hyphens between her fingers. She relaxed her hand, as if another mild duty had been performed and opened her fingers. When she turned it over, the blade did not fall. She paddled her hand until the bloody thing tinkled in the basin.

Jerome plumbed the baby's nostrils and cleaned the glistening white mess from its new body and then laid it on the mother's breast. He went to wash his hands in an enamel basin. Ramsden was roasting with furious respect. 'You like to make people sweat, do you, doctor? Three and a half bloody hours. I need some bloody transport. It's life or death.'

Jerome looked to the side of the room. David's body was under a short sheet. 'I can do you a certain amount of good, if that interests you. Likewise bad under certain circumstances. I need that motorbike and I need you to drive the bloody thing, sadly. Three hundred quid W.A.F. Just to the provincial boundary, perhaps a little further. What do you say?'

Jerome dried between his fingers. 'Five hundred.'

'Let's get on with it then.'

'First you're going to do something,' Jerome said. 'Like a gentleman.'

It was dark by the time they had sawn wood and made the coffin. Ramsden worked with docile indignation. He was so angry as to be almost amused. He liked and he hated Jerome for the vindictive calm with which he imposed his will. They made the coffin and they put the body into it and they nailed on the top and they carried it out of the surgery into an outhouse and put it on trestles. Jerome padlocked the door and put the key on the string that went round his damp neck.

'And now can we go, please, doctor?'

'What makes you think I'm going to keep my word, Colonel, when I'd like nothing better than to see you in hell?'

'I think you know the answer to that one: to prove you're my equal. To make it plain how much you distrust and despise me. People rarely let their enemies down, don't you find? That's what friends are for. So what about it? Shall we dance?'

Jerome smiled without altering expression and took the other key and opened a green metal cabinet in the surgery. The second wheel for the Norton was in there. Ramsden opened his kitbag and spilled banknotes on to the table.

Stafford said, 'I hope I'm not too late, Trevor.'

'The bottle still has something in it, Stafford, and there's always another one where the first one came from. Can we give you something to eat?'

'I'd appreciate a private word, if I may. I've just come from Wesley.'

'I thought I could smell funk,' Trevor said.

'I want you to tell me the truth.'

'You're asking a businessman to break the habits of a lifetime, Stafford, but fire away.'

'Are you funding Johnny Q. to chance his arm?'

Trevor put his hand in his inside pocket and produced a crocodile wallet.

'There you are: count what's in it. I think you'll find my full week's wages. Don't be a buffoon, Stafford, it's not your usual style.'

'What made you send young Lucas rushing up to see Quashie?'

'David's one of my senior men. Old time is still a-flying. I have to keep my chaps on their toes and to do that I sometimes have to keep them on each other's. Tim Sexton's getting a little slow on the turn. I thought it was time I made him jump. Do I really have to read you selected passages from the executive training manual at this stage, Stafford? How does that suit you?'

'Less gin, more tonic, if you don't mind. H.M.G. –'

'I never thought of you as a man who needed to add a Dutch uncle to his family, Stafford, but really! H.M.G. are turning into the kind of rats who swim towards sinking ships and try to clamber aboard. After torpedoing them. And then have the nerve to talk about ruling the waves. Because you've checked out, Stafford, thrown in your hand – use whatever image you like. It's all over, Mr Governor General! And you think you're going to go on as before.'

'Trevor, certain guidelines have been set out –'

'Have they so? Well, I'm not a bloody guide, let alone of the girl variety, so keep your dainty fingers out of my elasticated drawers, would you be so kind? Your pinko masters in Whitehall or wherever they spend their evenings want all of the gravy and none of the attendant grease and muck. That's what socialism is, isn't it, letting other people bake the cake and then helping yourself to the biggest slice and all of the icing?'

'Wind, Trevor.'

'If you don't like the pong, old chum, get your nose out of the ventilator shaft. The wind of change was never going to niff of roses. If weasly Wes can't keep his bloody federation in one piece, if it ever was one, it's going to take a lot more than the king's men, in their present state of panic and disarray, to put Humpty together again.'

Stafford said, 'Bluster, Trevor.'

'And if you can't put Humpty together again, there's only one thing to do with him, and that's make the best omelette you can, which is what, although you'll never admit it, you rely on us to do. You're going through the motions Stafford, is what you're doing. I know it; you know it. And what am I up to? Something called contingency planning, which is what you people used to do before you took up full-time bishop-bashing. I have to keep my options open, whatever Brown Owl has to say. Isn't that precisely what your precious P.M. likes to do in between rummaging under Britannia's skirts trying to bring her off twice in quick succession?'

'Do you want to see the U.N. in here, Trevor?'

'We've still got a veto, haven't we? We haven't got much but we should still be able to run to a veto.'

'You know what the Americans say, don't you Trevor? Where did you get that "we" shit, that's what the Americans say.'

'You mustn't talk dirty to me, Stafford; I blush.'

'Trevor, I'm warning you –'

'I don't think so, Stafford. I think you're covering your tracks; different operation altogether. Because the truth – if that commodity has a market at all – is that you and your masters are in no position to warn us about anything. It may interest you to know that the chairman is actively considering up sticks and shifting our whole operation to Geneva, so don't fall into the temptation of threatening fiscal revenge. It'll only rebound on your tiny heads, all right? I suggest you drink up and then leave me to run my shabby little business in my own shabby little way.'

'I don't like . . .'

'With the best will in the world, Stafford, your likes and dislikes are no large concern of mine. And if you want to pull rank, forget it, because you don't have any in this house, or in this country. Pop along home and shove your cocked hat up the orifice nature intended for it. I imagine it's about as much fun as you can hope to have after office hours.'

'My information was,' Stafford said, 'that your chairman was more than interested in a peerage. I take it that was as lacking in substance as Wesley's fear that you've been pumping cash into Johnny Q.'s coffers through an account in that place you mentioned so casually just before. Geneva, that's the one. Good night to you. My best to Bunty.'

'Stafford . . .'

'No, no, I must go and put my cocked hat where it'll be happiest for the night.'

   . . . my best friends think I'm making a serious mistake doing something so parochial, but my enemies are afraid I may have done the right thing. After the success of *Family Circles* in Berlin, and elsewhere, they all expected me to vanish in a puff of dollars, instead of which, what am I doing? A black-and-white number about England, home and ugliness! Just the thing to make the New Cinema clique yelp that I'm queering their pitch and pitching their queer. (The homosexual element in *The Good of the School* has caused eyebrows to flutter no end.) Any chance of you and David being in London for the première? Annie, Daniel and the replaceable Carmen – improving under a steady hail of blows, hot and cold – are clamouring for a break before I do my final cut, which means that we shall almost certainly be on Iskios before the summer reaches red-alert temperatures. I wish you and D. and Billio would harness your horses to the wind of change and join us in the cottage. Why is it impossible?

The letter stuck to Rachel's hand when she tried to put it down. Blood had oozed through the gauze covering her wounds. It was as if a sensible third party was in the house with her. She could not decide whether the real Rachel was the one who wanted to die or the one who advised her of the duty she had to live. Pitched between prudence and savagery, she picked up the telephone after reading the jolly letter from London and said that she wanted to make a call to England. There was a three-hour delay. She cursed and smiled and replaced the receiver.

In the time she had been back in the house, she moved silently, as if playing some new game which required her to disturb nothing, do nothing which would advance her into the future. She held the present to her like some frail trophy which might be shattered even by too deep a breath. She did not turn the lights on as darkness felted the windows. She promised herself that she could make out the shapes of the furniture without needing to advance the hour by using a lamp. In the gloom, she was without substance, a bodiless spirit, naked of sensation, immune to time. She even telephoned Margaret Sexton and took pleasure in the normality of her voice as she made sure that William was not being too much trouble. Margaret assumed that she was calling from Porto Vic and was eager to assure her that Billio would be fine with them at the beach house at least until the day after tomorrow. Rachel moved the receiver back and forth from her lips as she spoke, to give the notorious 'P.V. effect', which made it seem that some aural tide was gushing into the room in which she was speaking. The pleasure of conspiracy seemed to be something she could share with David; it kept him with her. At least it postponed his absence.

The Norton's headlight snubbed the road and then speared the trees as Jerome's front wheel bucked on the uneven surface. Ramsden only yelled to him to go faster. Jerome's hopes that the Englishman would be alarmed by the pace were in vain. Ramsden knew that the doctor would like nothing better than to fling him into the ditch or have him ask for a safer speed. The contest made them an involuntary team. Each was laughing into the wind they had generated, heads tucked to the side, as if from a common danger.

They hit the main road fifteen miles short of the province border. Vehicle lights shone as they came towards the Mampong bridge. Ramsden tapped Jerome on the shoulder. 'Pull up here. We might even find a hot meal.'

As Jerome eased the throttle, more lights went on, plating the roadway with metallic brightness. 'Poker, is that you?' Julius Samson was sitting in a six-wheel reconnaissance car. 'Where in hell's name have you been?'

Jerome saw half-trucks and lorries parked in a clearing where buses and trucks could be checked before crossing into Centre Province.

'I've brought you a visitor,' Ramsden said.

'We're practically on the bloody start-line, old boy.'

'Who might be worth entertaining,' Ramsden said, unslinging his kitbag from his shoulder, 'before it's too late.'

Jerome twisted the throttle and the Norton jumped forward,

the headlamp needling between two jeeps and thrusting into the girdered blackness beyond.

'Stop that man, damn you,' Samson said.

The Norton whirred between the brackets of the bridge and then took off on to Centre Province macadam. The improved surface would last only long enough to give a rich impression to those entering Wesley Idun's domain, but it enabled Jerome to be well clear of any pursuers before they could be organized. Exhilaration made him clever. He guessed that Samson would send word to those in rear echelon to watch out for him, but his knowledge of the back roads and tracks enabled him to avoid interception. He knew that he could not go back to N.P. so he drove on to Libertyville. He was almost at Freedom Round-about when he saw a jeep parked without lights near a rusting, tyreless bus. Its engines started as its crew spotted the Norton. Jerome accelerated for a few hundred yards and then his engine died as he rolled down towards the statue of the Great Liberator. He threw the Norton aside and ran. The jeep came after him, but without using its siren, if it had one. Jerome vaulted a fence into a back garden and ran again.

When Rachel saw the jeep's lights, she crouched on the waxed, sticky floor of the hall, holding her side. The jeep's lights painted a transitory coat of brilliance on the walls and ceiling and went away up the street. When she heard a tap on the screen door of the terrace, she called out, 'David, you'd better bring the .45. Someone outside.'

'Mrs Lucas? Mrs Lucas.'

'My husband is just coming downstairs. You'd better go away.'

'Jerome Leblanc. Let me in, please.'

She walked to the door and snapped open the clip that held the sliding screens together. Jerome came in, blacker than black, a negative shape. When he bent and found a lamp and turned it on, she gave a terrible cry, 'NO. No, no, no.'

He said, 'Is someone here?'

'No one.'

'I didn't know where else to go. They were after me. I think they probably want to kill me.'

'What do you want?' Rachel said. 'Because help yourself.'

Jerome said, 'Do you have any tea?'

'You're a ghost, I'm a ghost,' Rachel said. 'I see through you and you see through me. No one else can see us at all.'

Jerome said, 'That's what we have to hope.'

Rachel said, 'If people can go blind when they want to, why can't they die when they want to? Doctor.'

She spooned Earl Grey in the pot and they sat in the kitchen with the light above the stove making thick shadows for them. He said, 'You're going to have to make contact with them sooner or later.'

'Later,' she said. 'Once I tell them, it's true.'

'Ramsden knows already. And so does Samson. They may try to make some use of it.'

'They can do what they like about it. I so wanted something to happen on the road back from that place you . . . I don't want to go back to England. I don't ever want to see anyone I know again, not even Billy. I thought I might take him to Israel.'

Jerome said, 'Israel . . .'

'From the day I got married I never thought about being Jewish. It meant nothing to me; it meant nothing to David that I . . . Or did it? I don't know what men think, except that I assume they do. I was his; he was mine. We were us. I thought. Now . . . I'm thinking of turning Billy into a regular little Jew, with a gun in his hand. You wouldn't like that, would you, you and your friends? Perhaps I'm the one who should have been shot today, do you think? If the world were a properly run place. What does the doctor say?'

Jerome said, 'This is hardly the time . . .'

'What time shall we have then? A quarter to five? Ten past eight? Eight past ten? Believe it or not, Dr Leblanc, but until tonight – or this morning or this afternoon, depending on where you think we are – London, Algiers, Moscow, Timbuktu – I never really felt I was Jewish. Now I feel it's the only thing I am. A Jewess, with a hot black box! I've probably gone blind, wouldn't you say?'

Johnny Quashie said, 'You have orders to move on Porto Vic? I can't believe that, you know.'

'Would writing constitute proof for you, Johnny? Because I have them in my briefcase: any military action on your part and I move to restore order, arresting anyone who tries to stop me. Signed Wesley Idun. Why else am I here in strength?'

'If I may make a point, gentlemen: as soon as the Great Liberator hears a white man's been killed – and he may have heard it already – Wesley's going to need a scapegoat. Because imagine the London press. And you're the easy man to accuse, sir. Your Yellows have been beating people up in Porto Vic and points south . . .'

'I can deny it categorically.'

'Rule one,' Ramsden said, 'denials confirm: confirmations deny.'

'But Julius has just admitted that it was one of his men who . . .'

'A good Sandhurst man,' Ramsden said. 'He wants to take responsibility, where honour obliges, but how can he do that and become Mr President as well? So now where do we go for honey?'

'What the hell's in your mind, Poker? Because we haven't got much time.'

'Let me see those signed orders, will you, Julius?' Ramsden flipped through the papers which Julius produced from his black, twin-locked briefcase. 'It's not here! How amazing!'

'Everything's here,' Samson said.

'Then where are the secret orders from Wesley instructing you to make sure a certain white man gets killed by some of your chaps dressed as Johnny's yellow boys in order to give the Federal forces under your loyal command every excuse to move in on Porto Vic?'

Julius Samson said, 'I don't like this, Poker.'

'It's not all that likeable,' Ramsden said, 'admitted. But what comes further down the road'll possibly be more to your ascetic taste. Salutes, promotions, limousines, seats at the Commonwealth conference table. Tea with Madge at the Palace earned by a reputation for devotion to duty. We shall need a typewriter and a heap of suitable bodies. Your chaps can doubtless manage that for us. And the necessary snaps thereafter.'

'One of these days, Poker, I'm probably going to have to deny that you ever exist.'

'One of these days I may not have to,' Ramsden said. 'Meanwhile, ay haves me uses, so why not use me?'

Jerome said, 'I liked him.'

'But you didn't like *us*!'

'Should happy couples expect single men to like them?'

'I didn't altogether like you. I thought you wanted a reason not to like David. I didn't think I came into it.'

'Only because you cursed me with the virtue of your prejudice. Black skin, white conscience. When people save your life, they tend to think they've given you back something you want to keep.'

Rachel said, 'I was nettled when I found you'd gone. *And* when I saw you again. Because I was glad to. Your tact was a little insulting, I realize. As if we didn't matter.'

'Other people's happiness always shows one the door.'

A cock crowed in the greying darkness. Rachel said, 'I don't want the day. That cock is fast.' The joke made her cry. He left his cup and came round the table. Blood had dried to rust on her shirt. She said, 'There isn't anything that remotely begins to be what I really want.'

Jerome said, '*Viens*.'

He was standing over her and she fought up at him, like a child, with futile fists. When she stood up against him, he smothered her rage with the insides of his arms, like a stalling boxer. She had to get away from him to strike him as she thought

426

she wanted. He did not prevent her hands meeting his face. And at the end, without triumphing or smiling, he again said '*Viens.*'

When Trevor Flint was woken by the telephone, at four o'clock, he had a whispered conversation with someone whom he called 'Reverend' and then he sat up, head against the wall behind the bed, the mosquito net crepitating as he rolled his hair against it.

Bunty said, 'What're you doing, T.F.?'

'I'm doing what I get every opportunity to do when in bed with you, Bunts: thinking. Because they've gone and shot young Lucas.'

'*David?* Who have? Why?'

'That's what I'm thinking about.'

'How absolutely horrible!'

'Isn't it? Nice chap.'

'Do you mean he's dead?'

'He's dead,' Trevor said, 'but not necessarily buried.'

'What're you doing to do?'

'I'm going to ask you to give me five minutes of uninterrupted silence while I consider the matter in all its aspects.'

'Who was that just now on the telephone?'

'If you'd be so kind.'

'What about Rachel?'

'Unharmed by all accounts. She got clean away. Luck of the Irish.'

Ramsden said, 'Is that sweet music, Julius, or is that sweet music?' A helicopter was nattering towards them out of the dawn sky. 'I said I'd have a taxi waiting for you and there she is.'

'I wish Wesley would agree to go quietly.'

'Quietly isn't within his range, old boy, least of all when it comes to going.'

'I still say we could offer him an ultimatum.'

'Forgive my spelling, Julius, but spell it out I shall: there isn't a bloody penny on standby in Switzerland for them as faints on parade.'

'The first thing I do,' Samson shouted, 'when I'm in a position to do it, is have you put on a plane, Poker, with a one-way ticket.'

'And I shall be more than happy to be in Scotland afore ye, Julius. Now let's stick to plan B and stick close. Trevor's putting some bromide in Wesley's tea, so it should be smooth sailing into G.H. *Aut Caesar aut nihil*, Julius, if you remember your French. Shit or bust if you don't.'

A jeep was coming along the road to where the helicopter was low enough to make everyone hold on to their hats. There was a plain wooden coffin in the back.

Wesley Idun looked green in the early light. His rumpled face was womanish and petulant. 'How do you know this at this hour? Why not last night? Why now precisely?'

'Little birdies fly up and down this lovely land of yours, Mr President. Telling us sometimes one thing, sometimes another. This one happened to be a nightingale, but I wasn't too sanguine about the song it was singing. Hence my alarm call.'

'We'd better get Stafford over here.'

'Stafford! My information is that Samson and co. are going to be coming this way before Stafford's even decided which bra to put on. You've got either to face down Samson or climb down yourself. Sir.'

'I can bloody well throw you in the chokey for this, Flint. I think you've known about this plot, if plot it is, for a hell of a sight longer than a couple of hours. On the other hand what reason do I have to doubt Julius Samson's loyalty, except your word?'

'I doubt if we've got time to press that one to a conclusion, sir. What you've got to do, if I may presume to point it out, is make a lot of promises rather sharply to all the majors and captains and lieutenants who happen to be within hailing distance and get them to park their wagons in a tightish circle around G.H.'

'I can't fathom you, Flint. You never wanted the Federation, or me. I know what you've been up to, my friend. So why this change of front now?'

'For God's sake, sir. I'm trying to run a company. Our interests and yours are coincidental at many points.'

'I think I get it, Flint. I think I get it. You're putting Poker Ramsden up shit creek, aren't you? Am I right or am I wrong?'

'When were you last wrong, Mr President?'

Wesley Idun smiled and looked at his watch. 'Faith unfaithful kept him falsely true. Remember? The *Dunciad* was it?'

'I didn't go to Oxford myself, sir,' Trevor said, 'but I can imagine.'

Two three-ton trucks, with troops strap-hanging inside, were moving down towards Freedom Roundabout by the time Trevor had left Government House and was driving up towards the Lucas house. The statue of the Great Liberator was wearing a school blazer and cap. Trevor parked the Jaguar by the kerb and approved of himself in the tilted mirror. He combed his hair and tightened his belt a notch and went up the three wooden steps to the front door and jangled the bell.

Rachel said, 'What do you want?'

'Rachel, my dear, may I step inside? I've just heard the news. I can't tell you how sorry I am. Are you all right?'

'No.'

Trevor said, 'My dear girl, you haven't been here all night on your own, have you?'

Jerome, in David's dressing gown, was leaning on the balustrade. Trevor said, 'I don't know what to say.'

'That's an improvement.'

'You – you brought her back here presumably, doctor?'

'If you tell anyone he's here, Trevor, I'll kill you.'

Trevor said, 'You can trust me, Rachel. In every respect. But the sooner you make yourself scarce, doctor, if I may say so, the better all round. Do you need transport?'

'I mean it, Trevor.'

'Rachel my dear, nothing whatever's going to happen to anyone.'

'David will be home soon, will he?'

'I want to get you and Billio on a plane to London as soon as ever we can. This is no place for you to be, and I expect it to get worse.'

'And if I won't go?'

'Alternatively someone could fly out from London, if that would . . .'

'I'd sooner go to bed with Dr Leblanc.'

'Rachel, please, David . . .'

'You go to bed with Maggie Sexton, don't you?'

'She needs treatment, don't you agree, doctor? Come with me, Rachel, now. You can see Bunty.'

'Why should I want to see Bunty? Do you ever want to see her?'

'I've always had the highest possible regard for you, Rachel.'

'I'm sorry about that. You prefer women for whom you can have the lowest possible regard, don't you?'

'How long have you been here, doctor?'

Rachel said, 'What if *he* came to London with me?'

'Rachel, for heaven's sake. We shall do all we can, but in the nature of things the press are bound to be there to meet you. Dr Leblanc wouldn't want to . . . would you, sir? All right, laugh. I agree: I'm sweating like a fat pig. I wish I was anywhere else in the world, but I'm not. For heaven's sake, let's try to think of other people. Think of Billio.'

'Billio, of course! A woman is above all a mother, isn't she? *Is* she? What are you above all, Flinters?'

'A hard-pressed businessman with far too many pots on the Aga to be able to watch them all. Think of David if you can't think of anyone else.'

'What did he say?' Rachel turned to Jerome. 'Did you catch?'

Trevor said, 'Dr Leblanc, could you conceivably have the vestigial grace to let me speak to Mrs Lucas alone for a few moments? It might be a good plan if you put some clothes on, preferably your own.'

'Don't worry, Mr Flint: I'm not going to London. No one

thinks I am.' He went into the bedroom and shut the door.

Rachel said, 'Fuck you, Trevor.'

'Rachel, David still has certain rights. Not least to be honoured by those he . . . leaves behind. Also to have his son properly looked after. The company will, of course, do its part, but we must send you . . .'

'If I want to stay here, I shall stay. I'm not your bloody parcel: you're not sending me anywhere.'

'Billy has the right to a mother who conducts herself with dignity, and decency. You really must put some clothes on. Do you want him to travel to London alone?'

'He can come with us,' Rachel said.

Jerome came down the stairs in crumpled trousers and sweat-stained shirt. 'Get out of this house now, will you, please, Mr Flint?'

Trevor said, 'I want you to get dressed, Rachel, and come out to the car. Don't tell me what to do.'

'Outside,' Jerome said.

'By Christ . . .'

'I'll bring her out to you in a minute.'

'Sound fellow.'

Rachel said, 'I want to stay here, with you.'

'You can't, and you know it.'

'You're the only person . . .'

'It isn't true and you know that too.'

'What about last night?'

'You wanted an enemy you could see and feel, and trust.'

'You despise me, is that it?'

'I pity you and I admire you and I think you very beautiful. As if it mattered. You can't stay with me and you know you can't.'

She said, 'Why did you come to this house last night?'

'To save my hide. I was frightened and I wanted you. Nothing to be proud of. I also loved you, but that may not have been the prime motive. *Je t'aime toujours. Peu importe. L'amour, c'est quelque chose de pourri dans le monde actuel.*'

431

'*Le monde actuel*,' Rachel said, 'is a fake from top to bottom. A fake and a fraud like that fat bastard on the stoep. Only the impossible is worth anything at all.'

'What you had with your husband –'

'That *is* the impossible, isn't it?' She touched his head. It was almost a blow, the way she flung her hand out at him. 'And what's going to happen to you?'

'It already has, Rachel.'

'Goodbye then, Dr Leblanc.'

Major Gambaga had fanned his squadron of light tanks in front of Government House. Poker Ramsden flew in from the sea and saw that three troop transporters were now stationed by the Freedom Roundabout, the men still inside. Samson's forces were advancing from the Beach Club area and would soon reach Libertyville city limits. Trevor Flint's white Jag was driving across town, along the ridge, towards the new development on Africa Point, where the Sextons lived.

Ramsden banked over Government House and crabbed towards the sea. No guns were pointed skywards. He traversed the column approaching the city and headed for the vehicle park where Johnny Quashie was waiting to be wheeled towards G.H., once Julius Samson was in the president's place to receive him. Ramsden's gloved hand clapped the Colonel's thigh. 'Almost there, Sambo.'

Rachel walked slowly down the path to where the boys were colonizing Mars. Monty ran towards her, bristling and wagging his tail in a confusion of attitudes. William, with a saucepan on his head, pretended not to see Rachel until she was too deep in his air space to be ignored. Then he said, 'Oh no, not you! Do I have to come?'

The leading vehicles of Samson's motorized brigade halted short of Major Gambaga's tanks and three officers went forward in an open reconnaissance car. The sound of the helicopter began once again to fret the air. Sir Stafford Canning's car was at the gate of Government House when Wesley Idun looked out.

Wesley was shouting, 'Arrest those officers, Major. This is your president commanding you. Those men are guilty of high treason.'

Major Gambaga could not hear. He was, in any case, outnumbered and without confidence in the willingness of his squadron to obey an order to fire on Samson's forces. The three officers pointed to the helicopter which was now hovering over the watered lawn on which Wesley Idun proposed to set out his croquet pitch.

By the time Stafford Canning had gained admission to Wesley's office, the president was standing by the window watching the future arrive more promptly than he could ever have imagined. 'What can one expect of such people?'

Stafford said, 'What exactly is going on?'

'Oh, exactitude! Is this the time?'

They watched like absentees as the helicopter clattered in over the tanks and leaned towards the green. The soldiers on the ground were frowning upwards. Samson, in his Sam Browne and his black cap, could be seen through the ribbed blister of perspex. Everyone was ready to salute him. The helicopter dropped like a bomb. At one second it was steady, the next it fell, as if on purpose. There was a froth of fire all around it and black smoke and then the loud swell of igniting fuel. Stafford and Wesley winced. Their elbows came up in front of their faces.

'Saved, Stafford, saved! By British engineering! I'm not Kerensky after all. I'm still the king of the bloody castle, you old coot.'

From Barnaby Monk, in Libertyville, West African Federation.

The mysterious figure of Colonel Ralph 'Poker' Ramsden seems to be at the centre of the attempted coup in the recently independent W.A.F. The pilot in the fatal helicopter crash which decapitated the coup by also killing

Sandhurst-educated Colonel Julius Samson, Ramsden was rumoured to be the paymaster acting for a group of Paris-based financial interests eager to carve up the mineral-rich ex-colony.

The whistle appears to have been blown on firework-salesman Ramsden's double game by Trevor Flint, the Libertyville boss of Hyde International. Flint's suspicions were aroused by information about a secret landing strip in the oil-bearing North Province. The local Prime Minister, Johnny Quashie, pretended to go along with Ramsden's coup plans but remained loyal to President Wesley Idun, with whom he had an emotional reunion at the presidential palace yesterday afternoon.

'The Federation,' a tense but beaming president told me in an exclusive interview this morning, 'has been tested and found true. Prime Minister Quashie has proved himself to all concerned to be both very brave and very calm. We go forward together.'

The accidental killing of Hyde International engineer, David Lucas, 36, by separatist irregulars, probably led to the President's intelligence service getting premature wind of the plot. 'We were always a step ahead of the hot-heads,' Wesley Idun told me, 'thanks to the efficiency and steadiness of my best officers.'

The High Commissioner, Sir Stafford Canning, confirmed that the President had always been on top of the situation. 'President Idun was concerned above all to avoid bloodshed. His main purpose was not to secure his own position, but to steer his young, potentially strong country through its first major crisis.'

'Democracy,' President Idun told me, 'is a tender plant, not necessarily indigenous to West Africa. We must take care of it and it will grow and prosper. If we are patient we shall all be able to take comfort from its shade and its fruit. I have been in touch with Her Majesty personally, and with my dear old friend Horatio Peace, and I know that we can count on the staunch support of our British friends.'

The plane which had brought Barnaby to Libertyville took William and Rachel to London. As the captain announced that they were landing, William was colouring the animal book which he had been given by the stewardess. Without looking up, he said, 'It's sad, isn't it, mummy, having to leave Monty?'

'Very sad,' Rachel said.

XI

I was working happily in the dubbing theatre with Albie, applying final touches to *The Good of the School*, as Rachel's 707 scored the runway at Heathrow. I had volunteered to meet her, but I was not reluctant to be dissuaded. A copy of the movie had to be ready for a delegation coming from Venice to choose entries for the autumn's film festival. Show business ran on a disconcerting calendar: we catered for an orderly future despite the chaos of the present; always planning ahead, we were perpetually behind. Aubrey Jellinek's postponed musical, *Bess!*, which should have opened two years earlier was only now in rehearsal. If the end of the world was left in the hands of producers, the final judgement would be held over owing to casting-budgeting problems. Who said that hope was a function of incompetence?

Aubrey had been supervising the movie of *Zenda* ('Another way of saying he's been re-writing it,' Benedict Bligh maintained). California was the only place which offered a choice of Ruritanias; Twentieth Century Fox had provided the Balkan capital most to Aubrey's taste. His overseas partnership grew richer to the tune of half a million dollars. In those modest times, it seemed like a good deal. He and Lovey sent me a thirty-fifth birthday card from the Bel Air Hotel, where they had rented a cottage while they negotiated to buy their house in Mulholland Drive. Aubrey flew back to London to attend casting sessions for *Bess!*, but Sally Raglan was already set to play the Virgin Queen. ('Woman,' Aubrey wrote on the two dozen roses he sent her, 'you is my Bess now!') By the time Melanie Tucker auditioned for the part of Lady Ralegh, Aubrey was already on the way back to Los Angeles. Melanie performed 'Swisser Swatter' with erotic elasticity, but she was not given the role. The associate director was obliged to tell her that the part was simply not important enough for her. She said that anything would be better than nothing, but he was sincerely sorry.

That was the summer when Sally Raglan's voice was always on the radio in my little green Mercedes 230SL when I drove back from the studio to Seymour Walk. I groaned every time I heard that intro, and Aubrey's words, but I never quite brought myself to punch up something more cultural. Had Sally ever wasted herself to better effect?

> I've wandered
> Lonely as a cloud,
> Only as a cloud's allowed –
> Squandered chances,
> Been led dances,
> Stayed bloody and unbowed!
> I swore I liked
> To play that way,
> Hitched and hiked
> To stay that way.
> Other girls could bill and coo,
> Get a thrill from Who's with Who –
> But me, I wouldn't fake,
> Me, I couldn't take . . .
> Romance!

Who but Aubers could have given Sally words and music so alien to the cant of the age and still sent her directly to number one, profiting from a breach between one Beatles' single and the next? The movie in which Sally sang the song, 'Irish Eyes', did not contain a single frame in which she appeared. The song had been added at the last, desperate minute, when Little Siobhan's misadventures in London left too many dry eyes in the preview house. 'Dosed with Jellinek syrup,' Benedict Bligh had written subsequently, 'the flat soufflé could be passed off as a Belgian waffle, which the public in its darlin' guilelessness decided was the flavour of the month. Do people perhaps watch the movie with their eyes shut? In that case, more paying customers will have not seen "Irish Eyes" than any other picture in the history of the seventh art.' Aubrey's words, Benedict observed, were packed as tightly as chorus boys' trousers and the tune fitted them 'like Supertrans'.

> But now today . . .
> I'm not the same,
> I find the game
> Has changed its name –
> 'cos – wow! today . . .
> One man, one wife,
> Now *that's* the life!
> I beg your pardon,
> But a garden
> And a house
> Are what I crave –
> I'd even rave
> At a kitchen ladle –
> As for a cradle,
> That, I'm afraid'll
> Make this cat Miss Mouse!

Waiting for three empty number 14 buses to clear the entrance to my street, I even joined in the last part, seduced by no shortage of swinging strings:

> One man, one wife,
> Isn't that what life
> Is all about?
> So fall about
> To see a fool
> Who's lost her cool,
> Burned her boat,
> Turned her coat,
> Filled her moat,
> Sown her oat,

Cleared her throat
To say . . .
One man, one wife,
For the rest of my life,
On the crest of my life,
Riding high,
You and I!
Call me a sap, I
Mean to be happy
For the rest of my life,
In the nest of my life,
The best of my life
Is set to be,
Is yet to be . . .
With just you and me!

'You and me!' I said, and managed, with two tyres pinched against the pavement, to squeeze into the narrow street where I hoped I would find Annie waiting.

'How are you, William?' Philippa said.

'It's very nice to be in England again. Where am I sleeping, grandma?'

'You look pretty wide awake to me, Billio.'

'Mummy, do you have to call me that all the time? I *am* eight.'

Rachel said, 'We're not going to stay with grandma and pops. This flat's too small for people of our age.'

Philippa said, 'You know what's still here, Billi – William? All of your uncle Michael's old Dinky toys, remember?'

Philippa took William into the spare room to drag the boxes from the wardrobe. Rachel went into the living room and almost smiled at the bogus African head on the double-leaved Victorian card table which had once been in Gloucester Mansions. Philippa came back, like a tactful magician, having made William disappear, happily, for a while.

'I nearly didn't come back to England. Who wants to be that poor Mrs Lucas?'

Philippa said, 'One always does the thing one doesn't want to do. You feel so bad if you don't.'

'You sound like daddy.'

'Just don't tell me I look like him. Do you want tea? What are you going to do with William?'

'I suppose he'll have to go to boarding school. The English answer to all big problems between the ages of eight and eighteen. Mummy and daddy Lucas say he'll need company of his own age. They're being very helpful and brave.'

'Damn tea. I'm going to have a drink,' Philippa said. 'Will you?'

'I shall have to take Bill – William – down to see them. Not for me. I'm afraid they'll be wonderfully kind and understanding.'

'And what about you?'

'I shall look for a suitable scrap heap.'

'You're still young, and very beautiful.'

'One owner! Lowish mileage! Offers?'

Philippa said, 'At least . . .'

Rachel said, 'He was shot to death sitting as close to me as you are, mummy. Closer. At least nothing. *Nothing.*'

William said, 'Sorry, but didn't there used to be some battle-ships? American ones. On sort of wheels.'

Rachel said, 'Go and play with what you've got, darling, now, will you?'

Philippa was on her feet. 'They ought to be somewhere, William. I know!'

'You see, grandma, I do want to have a battle if I can.'

When Philippa came back, she said, 'He looks so like David sometimes, doesn't he?'

'Yes,' Rachel said, 'damn him.'

Philippa took a long sip from her gin and tonic and then she said, 'You know, I sometimes think nothing ever really happened to me at all. I'm still waiting.'

'You fell in love with daddy. How is he?'

'Judging. He likes it. They laugh at his jokes. And probably, he says, at his judgments. He said I was the one thing he wanted and I took it for granted that he was what the one thing wanted. He told me on my honeymoon that if I ever had anything to do with another man, and he found out, he'd divorce me. I laughed. He didn't.'

'That was how you knew it was a joke presumably. And if he didn't find out, was that all right?'

'I don't even have a cheque book,' Philippa said. 'He gives me everything I need, of course, but absolutely nothing else.'

Rachel said, 'Don't envy me, will you?'

'Darling . . .'

'Oh yes! Nothing's so awful that people can't wish, just a little bit, that it had happened to them. Even the Gentiles think, somewhere along the line, that it's unfair that the Jews had so many frightful things happen to them. Being murdered does rather amount to an unfair advantage, doesn't it?'

Philippa said, 'I'm sorry to say so, but I've never really felt very Jewish.'

'You and granny Jordan!' Rachel said. 'Sisters under the skin!'

'I met your father when I was much too young.'

'Did you never have anyone else before you met him?'

'*Have*? Good heavens! There were a few fingers after dances. A knee or two. My mother told me that men didn't like slices from cut cakes. I believed her.'

'Mine said the same.'

'What did she know?' Philippa said. 'I was on your side about going to Paris with Buddy, wasn't I?'

'My memory is that you abstained.'

'You went, didn't you?'

'But I didn't go further than that, did I? I wanted you to be jealous, I think, to be honest. I always had a probably unfounded suspicion that you and Mr Nathanson had a bit of an *amitié amoureuse*. No?'

Philippa said, 'Secrets! Aren't they absurd? When Sam was away being a colonel, I used to go with Buddy sometimes for rides in his jeep. The roads were empty, pretty well, unless you hit a military convoy. Endless, they were. Always with their headlights on! He loved old castles and country houses. Anything historical – whatever had happened before America did. I learned more about England with him than I did at school, *much*. We acted as if we were very old and very respectable: married people, after all, both of us. *And* Jewish, I suppose. You were always very secretive, you know, even as a little girl. You locked yourself in the bathroom when you were two years old.'

'I remember.'

'You can't! You weren't frightened; I was. It was as if you'd got away and *I* was locked in.'

'So you saw a lot of historical places?'

'We got as far as Walsingham on one occasion. Your father must never know this.'

'Then you must never tell him,' Rachel said. 'What happened at Walsingham?'

'Walsingham? Nothing. We had a picnic, I think. Oh I see. One day – I've never told anyone this, why should I? – we were going to go to Cowdray Park. He wanted to see the ceiling in the great hall of Arundel House. He always came to collect me from the flat. He'd honk his horn and down I'd go. The neighbours could think what they liked: I didn't have anything to hide, did I? On this particular day, I looked out and he had someone else with him. I was surprised at how disappointed I was, almost angry. Buddy with a buddy, as your father would have said. His name was Frank Brown. Very unusual! He was a top sergeant – could never *quite* believe they didn't have their stripes on the wrong way up, but there we are. How do you do, ma'am? Hope I'm not in the way! Of course not. Not much. It was as if I had made up my mind that on that day I was going to . . . do something I'd never done before, though I'm sure I wasn't, and he was in the way. Frank was tall and dark, with a Ronald Colman moustache, and that was about all I noticed about him. We went round Arundel House and then we went to have coffee – they *called* it coffee – in one of those half-timbered hotels with thatched roofs that Americans think of as our equivalent of the great pyramids. There was a piano in the corner of the lounge and Frank went over and started to play. He'd been at the Juilliard, it turned out, whatever that was. I don't know if he played well or badly; he played well enough for me. When Buddy put his arm round my shoulders on the sticky sofa, I turned straight back into the colonel's lady: stood up and said it was time to go home. Frank went on playing. Liszt? Mozart? Heinrich von Kitsch? I stood there and, it's true, my knees began to . . . I reeled! Finally, he nodded at me and shut the piano, folded back the busy little brass candlesticks and put on his cap and his top-sergeant's face. Why am I telling you this now?'

'Because I'm dead,' Rachel said, 'and you can always talk to the dead.'

'Going through Liphook, the engine had a coughing fit. Finally we had to pull up, on the Devil's punch bowl. Buddy opened the whatsit and got some very hot fingers. He seemed to know what the trouble was and off he trotted to find whatever would take care of it.'

'Leaving you and the pianist in the finals.'

'He was quite embarrassed. I think, Frank. He started to whistle. I waited till he'd finished and then I kissed him. It was like crawling under a fence when you were a little girl. Forbidden territory! Forgive us our trespasses! Why? Because they're so much fun, I suppose. I kissed him and then we did other things. It was as if I'd always done them. It didn't hurt one bit. I wasn't anybody in particular at all. No one nowhere doing nothing! When Buddy came back with whatever it was – could it have been a fan belt? – we were sitting there like good children. I never saw Frank again by myself. After V.E. day he was sent out to the Far East. He was killed by a truck in Tokyo. Buddy wrote and told me. Other news.'

'Were you very unhappy?'

'I was rather relieved, to tell you the truth.'

'Grandma, can I take these with me, do you think?'

'I'm sure that'd be all right,' Philippa said. 'Check with Uncle

443

Michael when you see him, because that's where you're going to stay, isn't it, for a while?'

William said, 'What were you laughing at just now?'

Aubrey said, 'Straight from the coast. Don't say I don't ever do anything for you, mate. While the customs men were checking Lovey's cleavage, your old chum went clean through on the blind side. How's the new number coming?'

Larry Page took the cindery envelope and popped it behind the lid of the piano before he began to play.

'And vy did chew not let me hear ziss before? I've had a headick since Vensday. What a last-minute-Annie you are, big L.! I'f a good mind to titch you a lesson, but on second thoughts I'll go on taking zem from you. Good keed! This'll slot into the last act like a bishop slipping into a warm sailor. How can you seriously still be living in this room?'

Larry said, 'Melanie auditioned for Lady Ralegh. You turned her down.'

'Where did you get that from? Because it's balls. I admire Melanie more than I can say. It wasn't good enough for her.'

'Swisser-Swatter's going to be a show-stopper.'

'Only since the re-jig. Be fair. But Melly's worth better than that.'

'Since when does anyone get what he's worth, or she's worth? Except for you?'

'What you need is a bunny capsule, mate, and a beakerful of life-enhancing H_2O. The first thing we do after the show opens is put together that new cabaret act for Melly. Café de Paris? Why not? I've got a number for her that's going to be bigger than "One man, one wife!" I swear. Can I take this with me? The sooner Sall learns it, the sooner the armada can sail. Are you sure you shouldn't get some help, Larry?'

'I thought I *was* the help,' Larry said.

I turned on the sconced lights in our basement dining room with triumphant embarrassment. We had had the house remodelled with some of the money from *Family Circles*. Charlie Lehmann insisted on buying out my percentage of the profits. At first I suspected that he was trying to get a bargain, but he insisted that the film had cost too much money for even its success to make my participation worth as much as he was offering me for my share. He could afford it; I should take it. His generosity touched and disturbed me; it was easier to think of Charlie as a manipulator than a benefactor. I sensed that he was making a cash bid for my friendship. I should have been happier to give it to him than to have him think it had a price.

Annie's freckled interior decorator, Ivan Sisley (he pronounced his first name the unRussian way), had lined the basement with mirrors and, at my frivolous suggestion, had created a glassed grotto, with a bubbling fountain in it. It was hardly more than a transparent cupboard, but it was – as Benny Bligh had said one evening – somewhere to keep the fish fingers when we weren't using them. Annie and I gave quite a few dinner parties; she had become an excellent cook, and she had Maria to help her.

Rachel said, 'You were going to be a penniless playwright.'

I said, 'That was in the first draft. Before they increased the budget. *And* before I met Annie and her little boy, of course.'

'Everything that happens to Michael is someone else's fault, you notice?'

I said, 'Come on now, Annie: only the good things. The boys seem to be getting on very well upstairs. No blood yet. The worst is yet to be. Clock this!' I pressed a glass panel above the narrow sideboard and it sprang open to reveal vintage bottles from Restell's. '*Nouveau, nouveau?* Shall I say that again?'

Rachel said, 'Annie, it's really very nice of you –'

'Don't be silly.'

'I'll try not to be,' Rachel said, 'but we really won't stay with you any longer –'

'Oh finish your dinner,' I said. 'Have you seen one of these before? It works by compressed air. You have to hope the bottle is more durable than the cork. And luckily it is on this occasion.

Cheers!' The front door bell rang. I counted the three places Maria had laid and then the three of us. 'Who the fuck?'

Annie said, 'Someone with a package marked "Rush", which almost certainly could've waited. You'd better go and answer it. Maria's gone to her sister's.'

'She works for Claudia Monk,' I said, as I went up the stairs to the bell's second ring. '*Piccola* Maria, no?'

Annie said, 'I don't know why it is that all the important things have to be sandwiched between things that don't matter at all, but what happened was so horrible that I feel ashamed. I remember you both so well, forgive me, when you came back for that funeral, Mike's grandmother – *your* grandmother! – and how you didn't seem to need to say anything to each other and yet you were so together. Damn the world is all I can say.'

I opened the door and Joe Hirsch said, 'Hullo.'

I said, 'Why?'

'I'm selling life insurance: may I have a few minutes of your voluble time?'

I said, 'You might have bloody well rung.'

'I did. Twice.'

'Before you came round. We're just having dinner for Christ's sake.'

'I wanted to see you. Did you say dinner? I never eat lunch; you can imagine how hungry I am.'

I said, 'My imagination doesn't work nights. My sister's here.'

'The widow?'

'Couldn't you talk a little louder? The neighbours didn't quite catch. Can't you ever show a bit of tact?'

'She *knows* she's a widow presumably.' He was actually checking the post on the little table by the front door. 'Don't worry, I won't embarrass anybody.'

'Then how will we know you're here? There're no letters for you, blast it; this is *my* house.'

'I'd like to see her.'

'Well, we must ask you round sometime.'

He was halfway down the basement stairs. 'Godalmighty,' he

said, 'does Louis the Fourteenth know about this? Hullo. You remember me. I saved you from a flake worse than death. Joe Hirsch.'

Annie said, 'Tell you what: I'll go out.'

'I tried to stop him,' I said.

'I need your signature on something. Unless you think the Americans ought to be doing what they're doing.'

'You want them out of Western Germany, do you? When by?'

Joe said, 'Can I get myself a plate? Saigon. Read that and if you agree, bung your name at the bottom.'

I said, 'As long as we can be sure no one pays any attention, it must be the right thing to do, mustn't it?'

Joe came back with an unmatching plate. I snatched it from him and stamped into the kitchen. I came back with the Haddon Hall and the right cutlery and banged them down in front of him. He was leaning over Annie and the casserole. 'Smells good enough to eat with your bare hands. What are you using these days?'

Annie said, 'Insect repellent. I'm going to take it back to the shop.'

'She likes me,' Joe said. 'While I'm here, Rachel, you wouldn't like to do a programme for Tower T.V., I suppose, on what happened to you?'

I said, 'Joe . . .'

'I'm trying to persuade our programme controller that there's a life beyond panel games and sit. coms. The good fight! Not easy. Delicious stew. Who made it?'

I said, 'Who else is signing this damned thing?'

'The usual gangbang: all the people normally to be found pulling up privet in Grosvenor Square when weather permits.'

Annie said, 'I don't think it does much good signing things personally.'

Joe said, 'When did anyone ever ask you to sign anything?'

Annie said, 'Still hungry?'

'I won't say no if you're offering.'

I said, 'Have you met cook?'

'Let the little woman defend herself,' Joe said. 'If she can.'

'I can't,' Annie said, and poured a ladleful of hot stew directly into Joe's lap.

'You fucking cow!'

'*More?*'

'You fucking *cow*. Christ!'

'Pass the water, Michael.'

Joe unbuckled his hipsters, ripped them down and bent over to take the heat off his crotch. 'What've you bloody done to me, you prize bitch? She's completely mad.'

'You still look to be all there, most of you, on a rough count.'

'Do you think they always look like a bunch of boiled tomatoes? I could have you in court. You could have me in hospital. You could have us both in Benny Bligh's column. Have you got a spare pair of . . . well, trousers, I suppose? First things last.'

'You'd better come upstairs. That's where the fitting rooms are. How are you for socks?'

'You must be fucking mad,' Joe said. 'She must be fucking mad.'

I took him upstairs. Rachel looked at Annie and smiled. They sat in front of their floral plates and Annie began to cry.

I said, 'How's Felicity?'

'Why do you ask that?'

'I thought she was your wife.'

'We both made the same mistake. What's the matter with Annie?'

'She hasn't put a foot wrong all evening, so far as I can see.'

'You have the most unbelievable wardrobe.'

'Ivan swore it was the latest thing – slide-out rails, pull-out drawers.'

'I mean what's in it, cretin. *Turn-ups?* Felicity's gone to Greece. The *Crusader* sent her out there. Barnaby scents trouble. Have you still got your house on that island? Haven't you got any other trousers, for Christ's sake?'

448

'Not available for rental. We're hoping to go there in June.'

'She might want to borrow it. Can we?'

'I'll have to talk to Annie. You remember Annie.'

'What's she so angry about these days?'

'Unexpected guests who are bloody rude to her mostly. Silly, isn't it?'

'She resents your success. I can tell. She feels humiliated. I'm sorry, but I don't believe in being tactful.'

'Oh? When did this start?'

'If she ever went to bed with anyone else, you'd probably chuck her out. Personally I regard it as a liberation. You know about Felicity and Barnaby, presumably. I made a fool of myself, but I shall get over it.'

'Marrying her?'

'No, that was fine. Afterwards. When I fell in love with her. Fatal. Almost. I think she resents the fact that I never made a pass at her.'

'Felicity?'

'Annie, you clown. It can always be rectified, of course.'

I said, 'Why don't you get my trousers on and get the hell out of here?'

Joe said, 'Any idea what's for pudding at all?'

Annie had made a *St Emilion au chocolat*. Joe went to find a plate from the kitchen. When he returned, he drew his chair closer to Rachel.

'He won't admit it,' he said, 'but I'm the brother Michael never had.'

'And now I know how lucky I was.'

'It must be hell for you,' Joe said, dipping his licked spoon back into the serving dish for another scoop of cream, 'having everyone feel they have to lower their voices for you. I bet you long to meet some people who don't know anything about what's happened to you. Tell you what: I'm going to Israel after Easter. Come with me.'

I said, 'Joe, why don't you just behave like a pig and leave it at that?'

'Oh stop being the good hostess, why don't you, for two minutes? What do you say?'

Rachel said, 'I've got my son to settle into a new school. And a new school to settle on.'

'Not the one Michael and I went to, I hope.'

'I want it to be co-ed.'

'I should say. Michael never saw a tit close to till he was eight-een. Or did he used to come into the bathroom to get his sponge when you were in the tub? Israel needs seeing. What do you say?'

'I'll think about it,' Rachel said.

'Oh,' I said, 'Rachel, before I forget, there's a letter came for you on the hall table.'

'Interesting hand-writing,' Joe said.

Oh yes, I heard, and I saw, and I wondered what to do, and what I felt. I felt all the disreputable things you are too clever not to imagine. I thought that I ought to have the decency to keep myself to myself, and leave yourself to yourself, and then I thought again and began to write this letter, not sure whether I should send it but wanting you to know that I still exist. When my existence has to be the least of your concerns. And then I began, as I am beginning now, to have the petty hope that my writing might mean something, might even excite you when you saw it on the envelope. I read your old letters and I smiled and remembered and hoped. I have no recipes for con-solation, Rachel, no philosophy to account for the sordid plots and spiteful twists we call life. I can enumerate the ironies and taste their ferrous tang; every artist has a vulture's feather in his plumage. I write not only because it is a rest from wrestling with clay and wax, my latest toys, but also because it allows me to summon you up without pleading for attention. I am here and you are somewhere and I want to see you again. I do not, I swear, want to see the stigmata on you, nor can I offer their cure. Let me advertise only my discreet services, if required.

Can a handful of cobwebs possibly supply some balm for unhealable wounds? This old spider knows at least how to spin those. For the rest, he asks nothing better, or more futile, than to hope to be the smallest kind of comfort to one he loves.

There was a little drawing at the bottom: a spider with Guy Falcon's bearded frown.

'She can't possibly really want to go, can she? With Joe?'

'Why not? You always tell people he's your oldest friend. He certainly always tells people you're his.'

'I loved it when you did that with the stew.'

'Did you? Weren't you afraid you'd never work again for Tower T.V.?'

'When did I ever work for them? I hope she doesn't go with him just because she can't think of anything better to do.'

'Isn't that the reason ninety-nine per cent of people do ninety-nine per cent of the things they do? Including getting married and invading Russia?'

I said, 'I know it's not easy having Rachel here.'

'That's no problem,' Annie said, 'is it? Compared to having me here for instance.'

I said, 'I wish you wouldn't keep saying things and then going into the bathroom.'

'You can come in here if you want to.'

I said, 'Annie, if you weren't here . . .'

'Maria would have to come earlier in the morning, wouldn't she, or what would you do for breakfast? Oh I don't know, you could probably handle the problem, with a little help from Messrs Kellogg's.'

I said, 'You always look your most attractive when you're being like this. Why?'

'Female wiles,' she said. 'I finally filled in the coupon and got some. What's her name this time then?'

I said, 'Annie. Still Annie.'

She twisted in my arms and looked me full in the face. 'What's going to happen to us, Michael?'

'Who knows? But there are excellent chances that we shall eat, drink and be warm in our beds while it's going on. That gives us a lead on most of suffering humanity, wouldn't you say? Do you want to go away, is that it? You were astonishing tonight.'

'Never knew I had it in me did you, or when? Perhaps I am not entirely the stick you're afraid I am. Or is that what you're afraid of?'

'Please don't say things like that.'

'Or at least not so loudly? *You* say them. What's the point of having a resident tutor if you never learn anything from him?'

'We're not going to let it fall apart, Annie.'

'And have Benny Bligh find out? Rather not! The shame, the shame! That's what really terrifies you, isn't it? The great writer-director who couldn't hang on to his nonentity of a wife! You know what really hurts me? You make me feel such a *fool*.'

'Fool? You're just about the brightest, most –'

'For loving you,' she said.

The postman couldn't get an answer from Larry Page in the morning, so he went upstairs and rang the Monks's bell. Claudia had a key to the basement (Larry did not answer the telephone) and she went down in her dressing gown and slippers and unlocked the door. He was lying on the sticky floor by the piano. He seemed to be deeply asleep. Claudia and the postman were unable to wake him, so she rang for an ambulance.

Rachel said, 'Are you sure she really wanted to go to the zoo? I never wanted to, with or without William. I *hate* zoos. After Africa, I don't even like animals all that much.'

'I'm a bit ashamed not to have a dog for Daniel,' I said, 'but what would we do with it when we travelled? We did have a hamster at one point, but it got out and ate all the telephone wires. Heavenly peace! Not that I liked it. You're not seriously thinking of going to Israel with Joe, are you?'

'Serious thought is rather beyond me at the moment. I was thinking of going there anyway. He was right: I like the idea of somewhere where I don't mean anything, as far as I like any idea at all.'

'All they'll want you to do there is pick grapefruit, isn't it, and wipe the arses of under-age *kibbutzniks*? Why not get Joe to find you a job in television? Why go to Tel Aviv when you can go to Finsbury Park? He's even got an interest in a paperback house, if you want to go back into publishing.'

'Every time you run him down, you make him sound more attractive. I'm not going to sleep with him, if that's what worries you.'

'Why should it?'

'It's always easier to think of people as tragic than to accept that they're comic.'

I said, 'It always strikes me as appropriate that the masks of comedy and tragedy are often shown hanging from the same peg. Not that I would have mentioned it unless . . . Don't imagine I don't think it was tragic, what happened, whatever . . . David was extraordinarily . . .'

'Ordinary. Oh yes. I do know that.' Rachel poured more coffee from the German machine and looked defiantly at me. 'It just so happens that he was a man. Quite a rare species. He also loved me and I loved him. He was killed; I'm alive. Is that a tragedy? It's a misfortune.'

I said, 'I was always secretly rather glad you lived a long way away. You had something other people didn't, or so I always imagined. And if you did, I didn't all that much want to see it.'

'You seem very happy.'

'Do I? Is Annie?'

'Time I went to Israel,' Rachel said. 'Or shall I have another cup of coffee?'

'She isn't, is she? Did she tell you why?'

'Michael, it's your marriage.'

'And you're my sister. I'm afraid I made a fool of myself.'

'What is it daddy says? "That seldom requires any very radical reconstruction." How?'

'Screwing some woman. This was well over a year ago. Nearly two.'

'Michael –'

'Please, Raitch. I know: it's the kind of thing people do all the time. So I'm told. Often by them. It's the sort of thing people get away with every night. It's the sort of thing I don't. Some shit phoned Annie, before I'd even got home and told her any lies. I don't know who, but I'll kill them when I find out. What does it matter? It doesn't matter in the least and it's also completely changed our lives, slightly. Since that lucky day, everything's gone sickeningly right: *Family Circles* was a hit, *Maximum Security* ran ten months in the West End – only about ten years after it should have – and I got to direct *The Good of the School*. We have the house, the cottage on Iskios, the carriage at the door, the mini-Versailles in the dining room, Maria, the whole *schmeer*. Why am I telling you this? I can do anything I want except make her happy. I don't mean in bed. Bed is better than breakfast, believe me. It's crazy sometimes. Everything we don't say, we do. Anger is a better lover than love ever was. We hardly communicate with the light on, but once it goes off, we can't wait: action stations! And then the next morning . . . it's made no difference at all. War is fine; peace is hell. What do you think the answer is?'

Rachel said, 'I'm sorry but the oracle is closed.'

I said, 'I keep hoping that we're closer than we are. We've never really . . . do you think that's something we could repair?'

Rachel said, 'There's a kind of possessiveness in you, Michael, that longs to be possessed, isn't there? You want people to treat you badly, say cruel things to you, and then you feel better. More in demand.'

'Do I deserve that?'

'When was the truth deserved? And how important is it? People are a lot less individual than they suppose, don't you find? Everyone turns out to be unique in pretty well the same way as everyone else. Do you know about our mother and her American?'

'Buddy? Of course. We had Son of Buddy staying here at one point. They used to visit sites of historical interest together, didn't they? It was all perfectly innocent, wasn't it, her and him?'

'Perfectly,' Rachel said.

They went back to see the dromedary again and they watched herrings being flipped to the seals. They had ice creams and they shuddered at the spiders. They contributed to the welfare of wild animals (William and Daniel each dropped coins in the box) and then they went to catch the 74 bus. A very long-haired young man in a plaid jacket and an American cap ran over to them as they were crossing the road. 'Excuse me, excuse me, could you spare a minute? There's fame and money in it, if you could, in unbelievably small quantities!'

The unit was shooting on the edge of Primrose Hill. They needed Annie and the boys to walk through a scene in which the heroine (Sylvia Sherwood, in boots and a big felt hat) walked back to the house in which she was going to commit suicide.

'A comedy presumably,' Annie said.

The director was called Tim Galloway. He said, 'Hey, you're not a writer are you?'

Annie said, 'No, but I sometimes sleep with one.'

Galloway, who was albino and wore mauve-tinted glasses, crouched down to be mates with William and Daniel. 'I want you and your brother to run around and be a little bit naughty when your mummy calls you. Could you do that for me?'

'He's not my brother,' Daniel said.

'Just do the rest of it then, O.K., the two of you?'

The third assistant winked at Annie, as if he were a little cleverer than the director. He took Annie and the boys back to the edge of the shot while Sylvia Sherwood (Lady Corman) had some chin-up attention from a powder puff. They did a take and it was fine except that there was a technical snag. 'Hair in the gate?' Annie said.

'Who *are* you exactly?' Galloway said. 'What's keeping us, Rod?'

'Ready when you are, sir.'

The few minutes lasted for an hour.

Tim Galloway said, 'Can we possibly persuade you to stay and eat, because I'd love to have Daniel and William do something else for me afterwards?'

A voice behind Annie said, 'Look who's come up in the world. An extra at last! How are you, Annie?'

Annie said, 'Of all people.'

'Indeed! Aren't you the lucky one?' Frank Kitson had shaved his beard. He had retained the moustache which had a revolutionary droop. 'Do you know who you've pressganged into our little epic, Timothy? None other than – Mrs Michael Jordan.' He imitated the sound of an ovation and ruffled the hair of the two boys. 'No less! And this is what you've been doing since you gave us all the slip, is it?'

'This is Daniel's cousin, William.'

'Hullo, William, hullo, Daniel: do you want meat and two veg by any chance? Because see the big white van? Rod, will you escort these gentlemen?'

'William's father was killed in West Africa.'

'Didn't I read about it? I was thinking of giving Michael a friendly call, funnily enough.'

'What's funny about that?'

'You're not looking in the least maternal, Annie, I must say. Lovely coat! I've become an independent producer – hence all this – and I was thinking of shopping him as director for the next little number but three; do you think he might be interested?

'He's always interested. Ask him.'

'Are you going to the first night tonight?'

'God, I knew there was something! I've got a hairdresser's appointment at three. We'll have to go.'

'And ruin Tim's continuity? Never. Relax. I'll fix a car to take you to South Molton Street and we'll get the boys taken home for you after they've had their handouts. *Annie*, this is your uncle Frank, who loves you remember?'

'How did you know I had my hair done in South Molton Street?'

'Doesn't everyone? I might get a word with the maestro between reprises. Did anyone tell you I was divorced?'

'Who is it?'

'Telegram for you, miss, and the telegraph boy too, if you want him.'

'Aubers!' Sally said. 'I'm shaking like a jelly.'

'I'll go and get a spoon. Strawberry, I hope?'

'I should like to leave for an unknown destination.'

'Pity to miss the hit of the season,' Aubrey produced a hidden bouquet of orchids. 'Give these to the understudy on the way out, will you? She'll appreciate them, unspoiled little trouperette that she is!'

'Aubers, they're truly gorgeypoo. Perhaps I'll stay and face the music after all.'

'Nothing more than madame's due. They're booking till Christmas, in case your thumbs were pricking.'

'Careful! We'll have no hint of the Scottish play hereabouts.'

'This is for your pains.' He put a small, flat box on the dressing table. 'If you're not as good as you're going to be, I shall send the bailiff's man to repossess it.'

'It's never an original?'

'Then I'll take it back. 1588, the man promised. Let's believe him. Has Benny made up his mind yet?'

'Well, you know he prefers making up other people's. He's definitely coming and he's possibly going to review us, in his own scrutable fashion. Tease, tease, you know Big Ben.'

'I'm not asking for any favours.'

'Oh I am,' Sally said. 'He's getting them, why shouldn't I? I don't make an arse for just anybody, you know.'

'That's not what I'd heard, angel, but if you say so!'

'Aubers, you're a very naughty pussy, aren't you?'

457

'You're good enough in the show for Benny to be totally honest and above board.'

'It's not his favourite position, honey.'

'As long as it's good for you, darling. Did mother Raglan get her tickeypoos all right?'

'Bless you, the Baroness is thrilled. Aubers, it's a brilliant show and I shall do my best to do my best. I don't know how you manage to be so utterly brilliant all on your ownypoo, but I do take off my coronet to you. The numbers are wonderful. If Joe Pub doesn't like them, so much the worse for Joe Pub.'

'What do you do about income tax, Sall? Because there's someone going to be here tonight that you probably ought to meet.'

The stage-doorkeeper came in with a yellow handful of telegrams. Sally smiled at the first one and handed it to Aubrey: 'VERY BESS WISHES – LOVE MICHAEL AND ANNIE.'

'Remind me why we're going to this thing.'

'Because you've had your hair done, aren't we? Because we're in the trade. Because we were asked. Because it gives us a chance to be the happiest couple in the world.'

'Because Charlie Lehmann wants you to run the rule over the show?'

'We're going because we're going. It just might be a very good show.'

'When's he coming to London?'

'Who? Oh. Next week, I think. Why?'

'Just wondering when you're going to do your next vanishing trick.'

'Annie, what're you trying to do exactly?'

'Get this earring . . .'

'How much gall are you going to go on squeezing out of an empty rind?'

'I'm allowed to wonder when I'm next going to be a temporary widow.'

'Aren't you just a little bit ashamed of saying a thing like that?'

Annie said, 'Yes.'

I was kissing her when the front door bell rang.

'Poor Michael.'

'Rich Michael. And there's the barouche to prove it. Unless it's Joe Hirsch, of course, with something he wants me to sign.' She had the earring in. She pretended not to like dressing up, but the Ken Scott dress and the mink (we had bought it in Athens, Karegeorgi of Serbia Street) denied her modesty. 'Action?'

Our driver was an ex-squadron-leader. He played at deference with a straight-faced humour that turned using his limousine service into a kind of egalitarianism. He wore the cap and the grey livery and charged mercilessly; one had no feeling of betraying one's principles. His charges were a tax; his attitude a dispensation.

I said, 'We could just get Sandy to drive us straight on to Greece. Square one isn't really all that far away.'

Annie said, 'What would Charlie say?'

'He'd have to say *kalemera*, wouldn't he, or not say anything at all?'

Annie said, 'Frank wants to talk to you.'

I said, 'After many a summer. Have you thought of going back to work at all?'

'Am I preventing you from doing something you want to do?'

'Annie, I warn you . . .'

'You have the Riot Act with you? Read it, read it!'

'Do me one little favour. Try not to let me down tonight, all right?'

Annie said, 'It's all right: I'm not crying.'

'And I'm not lending you my handkerchief. We don't have to go to this damned show. We could go and have a quiet dinner somewhere and hope it's a flop without saying so.'

Annie said, 'Why are you wasting your life?'

Ned Corman and Sylvia Sherwood were in the foyer, talking to Lord and Lady Flam, when we walked into the theatre past the gawkers. Sandy Moxon had tipped his cap and wished us a pleasant evening, quite as if he had not heard our conversation behind his smooth neck. Bob Sander wore a narrow-lapelled midnight blue dinner jacket. His ruffled shirt had a good deal of red in it. I had never seen anything quite like it. His date was Arianne Chaunay, whose face had been on the front of *Black and White*'s most recent issue. Lovey Jellinek was in a fringed mini-skirt and a mini-top which left her Acapulco shoulders open to admiration. There was a chunky gold locket between the self-supporting breasts. 'Her hair,' Benny Bligh whispered to me, 'is the most dressed thing about her.' It was turreted and tufted and had coloured sticks thrust through it, like a savage's cheeks. 'It revives one's faith in the booboisie, does it not, to see so glittering a company at a musical comedy celebrating, of all relevant subjects, a virginity as tough as an old boot? The world writhes and bleeds without, but we are convoked to applaud a Surrey musical, with a fringe on the bottom.'

Lovey said, 'Does anyone understand a word that man says?'

I saw Melanie Tucker. She was wearing a rather long black dress, in the twenties style, and a jet choker. Her skin and throat were very white, as if they had been French-chalked. She stood at the side of the foyer, a bead bag in her long fingers. She had on black stockings and red boots, the only colour in her costume. She seemed to be alone.

'Good evening, Mrs Jordan.'

'Hullo, Barnaby.'

'You've struck us off, have you?'

Annie said, 'I'm sorry?'

'Your list of suitable people for dinner.'

'We never have suitable people for dinner.'

'But you do dish out a steaming ladleful from time to time, I hear.'

Annie said, 'Bad stews travel fast. Presumably Joe Hirsch . . .'

'. . . went home with his *bourguignonne* between his legs. To think that I always had you down as the gentle, unaggressive Mrs

Jordan. What's got into you lately? You're looking exceptionally challenging tonight, why is that?'

'Terror,' Annie said.

'What've you got to be terrified of?'

'Aggressive young editors who really wish they were talking to someone else.'

'Why not talk to the prettiest woman in the house?'

'Off you go then,' Annie said.

I said, 'How's the new one coming?'

'By very slow train at the moment,' Claudia said. 'My father died, did you hear?'

'I'm so sorry. When was this?'

'A couple of months ago. He was attacked by some people in the street. In Bologna.'

'What sort of people?'

'Young, I was told. The police said they were after his wallet. They may be right. I rather hope it was someone who knew who he was. It'd be nice to think that life had a justifiable plot, even though we know it doesn't.'

'Well, I hope they catch them, whoever they were.'

'Yeah? Personally, I like to think of people getting away with things.'

'No you don't,' I said.

'Are you still faithful to your wife?'

'Frequently,' I said.

'Don't you think that's rather selfish of you?'

I said, 'I'm longing to see the new book. What's it called?'

'*His and Hers.*'

'Sounds plangent,' I said.

Benedict Bligh said, 'Lord Flam?'

Chester turned slowly on his way into the stalls. He could contrive to be surprised as if he expected it. 'Yes?'

'You should give more money to the arts.'

'I'm sure you're right.'

'Millions more. See to it. We're entitled to reparations from people who've turned London into a place where property and

461

theft are closer together than a bishop and a boy scout. Tens of millions even. Unless you only want to be remembered as the one who got away.'

Chester Flam said, 'That had better not mean what it seems to mean.'

'What will you do? Tear me down and put an office block in my place?'

Lovey said, 'Are you usually good at getting things out of people?'

'I'm better at getting them in,' Benedict said. 'What're you doing after the Armada?'

'That isn't necessarily what I've heard,' Lovey said. 'And I hope I shall be celebrating with my husband. I happen to be married to the author.'

Benedict considered the Lovey breasts. 'Nice to have met you both,' he said.

> If you want traffic jams,
> Electric trams,
> Frozen lambs,
> The grandest slams,
> Those weren't the days!
>
> Prefer factory smoke
> To Hearts of Oak,
> Or the sort of bloke
> Who spreads his cloak?
> Those weren't the days!
>
> No income tax,
> No plastic macs,
> No knicks, no knacks,
> No Arnold Bax!
> Those weren't the days?

> Bess had a full larder,
> A fleet to guard her
> And – what was harder –
> To face the Armada!

In came the agile chorus with:

> England was England,
> A place-to-sing-land,
> An on-the-wing-land,
> Rarer-than-Ming-land!
> Ding-dong-ding-land!
> And those *weren't* the days?
>
> We were young and free;
> Never bent the knee,
> Top of the tree!
> Ruled the sea!
> Those *were* the days!
>
> The roof we'll raise,
> And sing their praise,
> Those *were* the days,
> Hip, hip, hurrays!
> Hip, hip, hurrays!

When the lights went up, Benedict Bligh was in his glasses, being professional with a pencil on the back of his programme. The other critics glanced at him with surly apprehension. They might be right, but Benedict would be quoted. The applause was loud enough to make me and Annie smile.

'Catchy tune the last one,' she said.

'And always was,' I said.

Aubrey said, 'Half-time and they love it! They love it!'

Sally said, 'We lost them for a bit about two thirds of the way through.'

'It's working a treat. You were sensational for a change! Wait till Essex gets his head chopped off. Benny stayed awake, Michael Jordan clapped, with one hand: it goeth well. Lovey's adoring it and we have the big number yet to come!'

Barnaby said, 'He must have the best rhyming dick in the biz. Watch out for moon and June in act two. It could happen.'

'I'm enjoying it,' Annie said.

'You're a thoroughly nice woman, I must say.'

'Must you?'

Claudia was saying, 'And are you bidding for the film rights?'

'I never do things like that, Claudia. It's not the sort of show I'd ever want to make a movie of myself.'

'Not even if the money was right?'

'Money doesn't mean anything to me,' I said, 'except perhaps —'

'— the freedom to do what you want. I saw the interview.'

'If I didn't love you, Claudia . . .'

'Yes, what's the apodosis?'

'It's the bit that comes after the if clause, isn't it?'

Claudia said, 'Is there a life after patter?'

'How shall we ever know? Excuse me.' Melanie Tucker had jogged my glass of *vin d'honneur*. She ignored my apology and went down the steps towards the stalls. 'She ought to be in it, really, that girl.'

'I think she's *on* it, don't you?'

We began to move back to our places. The lights were still on when I saw Melanie again. She had come in from a side door and was waiting for some people who were already seated to slant their knees. 'Excuse me.' She edged in front of them with a modest step. 'Thank you.' She was naked except for the red boots. She had left her programme in her seat, next to Benedict. She picked it up and played the fan.

'Find it warm?' Benedict said.

'Do you know who I am?'

'Puss-in-boots?'

464

'I'm the girl who loved the man who wrote the music for this show.'

Benedict said, 'You were Arthur Sullivan's mistress?'

The band had begun the overture for the second half.

Melanie said, 'His name was Larry Page.'

Aubrey had come through the pass door. His instinct for trouble, and its extinction, took him straight to Melanie. 'Darling! You look wonderful. Let's go, shall we?'

'I want to talk to Mr Bligh.'

I said, 'Less is nothing at all. What the hell . . . ?'

Annie said, 'I thought she looked strange in the foyer.'

Aubrey said, 'Melanie, come along with me.'

'And since when were you P.C. 49?'

'She's mad.'

'Me too,' Benedict said. 'Go and sit down, Aubrey.'

When Aubrey reached for her, Melanie opened her mouth, loaded with a scream which caused him to withhold his hand. The lights went down and the flamenco began.

There was a well-earned ovation as the Armada sailed on to the stage. Each ship was in full sail, built round its captain. The chorus undulated in good order as the number started.

> This is the end for Merry England:
> España's going to bury England!
> Our Duke of Medina Sidonia
> Will be London's brand new owner.
> And Good Queen Bess
> An unvirginal mess.
> We'll kick her in the fanny – hard! –
> For failing to marry a Spaniard!

The exaggerated accents and the growing biliousness of the assembled *capitanes*, as the wind section blew more and more tempestuously, were both very obvious and very funny. The audience laughed and clapped. A palpable hit was in the making. In the middle of the battle, when the little English ships were doing agile damage to the dons (magnesium flashes made vivid broadsides), Benedict rose from his seat and took Melanie by the hand and led her up the aisle. She walked like a mannequin, her little pubic apron her only, impeccable costume. The audience adjacent to the aisle blinked and wondered if she could be part of the show.

Lovey said, 'Whatever's happening?'

Aubrey said, 'Look happy. Better still, don't look at all.' When Benedict and Melanie had gone through the doors at the back of the pit, Aubrey slipped from his seat and went after them like a cigarless Groucho. When he looked through the porthole into the crush bar, he could see Melanie talking keenly to Benedict, who was using his pencil. He waved jolly fingers at Aubrey and gave another sip of lubricant to Melanie. Aubrey shouldered the door and went in.

'Hullo, *Aubrey*! Microscopic world! Do you two know each other?'

Aubrey said, 'Whatever this crazy woman tells you —'

'It's the truth,' Melanie said. 'I didn't think even you'd have the nerve to deny it.'

Aubrey said, 'I don't know what you've been telling him, and I don't much care, because I've done just about everything I can to help save your career, and how the hell did you get into the theatre anyway?'

'I had a friend,' Melanie said, 'who wasn't you. Or where would I be?'

'Think what this'll do to Larry. If you've got any sort of pride left, for God's sake . . .

Melanie said, 'Larry's dead.'

Aubrey said, 'I don't believe you.'

'Yes you do.'

'Is that Larry with a "y"?'

'You're lying.'

'I don't need to lie, not any longer, because there's no one left to protect.'

'How did it happen? When did it happen? Because I saw him yesterday.'

466

'Apparently he was quite a musician, this chap.'

'This evening. At St Mary's, Paddington. Want to check? It'll be in the paper in the morning, won't it, Mr Bligh?'

'I'm shattered,' Aubrey said. 'I'm devastated. He was an old, old friend of mine. We went back a long, long way. I did my best to help him. I gave him work when I could, copying, arranging. He could've been a brilliant composer, but he had this self-destructive thing. I don't know what she's been telling you, but you can see that she and Larry . . . same sad syndrome!'

'I've told him the truth,' Melanie said. 'And I only hope he prints it.'

'If it isn't true, he's bound to,' Aubrey said, with a wink at Benedict.

Benedict said, 'You say you've got manuscripts, proving . . .'

'Proving nothing,' Aubrey said. 'I hummed; he wrote it down. I can't be doing the crotchet work, but they're my tunes and no one can ever say they're not. And if they do, I'll sue.'

'I adore courtroom dramas,' Benedict said. 'There aren't anything like enough of them. See you in the Strand, Aubrey/ Ready to beat the band, Aubrey/ And take the stand, Aubrey!'

Over more applause, Aubrey said, 'Benedict, a lot of people have put a hell of a lot of work into this show.'

'And it shows, Aubrey. It sweateth to please.'

'Including – more than anyone – including your – including Sally –'

'All-inclusive praises are your speciality.'

Melanie said, 'And he doesn't even ask how it happened. He knows how it happened, and why, and who . . .'

'Is she going to go into the witness box like that?'

'Spare yourself, Aubrey. This isn't the Beau Bumhole we know, the man who gave us *Zenda* and wouldn't take it back again.'

'Think of Sally. Think of her.'

'You know, Aubers, I'm the sort of traitor who likes to keep the faith.'

'One word of this in print and you'll be sorry.'

'A SHIT, A SHIT, A PALPABLE SHIT. Good headline? Or too cultural in its referential field, would you say? There is a way out of all this, which might save a lot of unpleasantness. It's up to you: your money or your wife.'

As Aubrey lunged at Benedict, Melanie strolled out of the bar. Benedict lay flat on the floor and waved his legs in the air. 'She's going to need a taxi, Aubrey. Do see about it.'

There were calls of 'author, author' in the auditorium.

Rachel hired a car and drove down to her in-laws with William. There was a school near the Lucases which they thought might be suitable. Annie and I sat in the remodelled breakfast nook reading the morning papers. 'Benedict has no shame at all. Look at that. He's pissed all over it.'

'He says Sally's divine.'

'Since when was divinity enough? Look what he says about "tunes under plain wrapper" and "mail order melodies".'

The telephone rang.

'The first of the ghouls.' I picked up the receiver and before anyone spoke, I said, 'I disagree. I enjoyed it immensely and I mind who knows it. Barnaby! What can I do for you in under a thousand words? You know my every move, but I'm running – well, limping really – a little late this morning. I am talking about a new film, yes. Talk, talk, talk is the badge of all our tribe. I'd sooner not say until I'm certain, but depend upon it, you're the first person I'm not telling. Annie what? Oh yes, didn't she? I'll tell her.'

Annie said, 'Did you ever meet this mysterious Larry Page character?'

'Funny, Barnaby calling up like that. Not his usual style. I wonder what he really wanted. He said how good you looked last night.'

'I wonder,' Annie said.

'I see what you mean. Benedict does a special obituary piece, right next to the *Bess!* review, all about an unknown composer . . . Curiouser and curiouser!'

'We're expected to put two and two together, presumably.'

'That's mathematically rather ambitious for *Crusader* readers, isn't it? Aubers won't need his slide rule, though, will he, to get the point?'

'Perhaps he didn't expect you to be at home,' Annie said.

'Who?'

'Barnaby.'

'Then why would he phone?'

Rachel took William to Leinster Lodge at the beginning of the summer term. The headmaster was in Wellington boots and a corduroy windcheater (it was a chilly May day) and he clapped William on the shoulder and asked him if he knew anything about tractors.

'Not a lot really.'

'I've got one that won't start. Feel like coming to have a look at it with me?'

'I don't mind,' William said.

Rachel admired Geoff Barnett's bluff skill; she sensed that he was reassuring her more than William. There was display in his modesty: he was the honest conjuror who could make her son disappear without any fuss at all. Rachel was superfluous before there was any time for tears, at least from William. She kissed him goodbye as if she were the deserted one and he went off with Barnett.

Rachel had bought a green Mini. Hyde International had honoured all its obligations: she had been given a lump sum, a good pension and health insurance for life. The Chairman had taken her to lunch (at Les A.) and even offered her a job at Head Office. She had not liked him, but she had admired him: he flattered her only with frankness. He was afraid that David's death had been the result of nothing more tragic than muddle, though he asked her some direct questions about Trevor Flint and the timing of the mission to Porto Vic. The Chairman's grey-blue eyes had white above and below the iris. His face reminded Rachel of one of those trick drawings, to be found in children's books, which look like a face whichever way up you hold the page.

She drove across country from Leinster Lodge, which was near East Grinstead, and stopped at a village pub called The Shepherd and Dog, where workmen were re-tiling the roof. She watched the relay of tiles, lobbed from one set of hands to the next until they reached the workman at the top. It seemed that the men could continue the process and look at her at the same time.

He was sitting on a red banquette in the corner of the saloon bar. He did not stand up. He spread his arms along the top of the seat and half-raised himself. His book was face down: Montesquieu's *Persian Letters*. She turned her head to check the title before she looked at him.

She said, 'This is a funny place to choose.'

'Dull, isn't it? But then I always did hate competition. What can I get you? This is Beaujolais.'

'Immaterial,' she said.

'You're looking more beautiful than ever. Pain, the cruel cosmetic. What are you going to do, have you decided?'

'I may go to Israel. I've got the chance.'

'With a man?'

'Beside a man. What're you working at?'

'A self-portrait entitled "Man Missing The Bus". All my own fault. I always thought the bloody bus was trying to catch me.' He brought her a glass of wine and they almost touched glass against glass before sipping. 'Who is he?'

Rachel said, 'Who's who? Oh, that I'm thinking –'

'You've had someone else,' he said, 'since. Anyone I know?'

Rachel said, 'You're the only person in the world who knows.'

'Except for him, presumably. If he doesn't know, he's missing something.'

'I'm not going to ask you how you could tell.'

'I couldn't tell you even if you asked. You told me, that's all.'

Rachel said, 'He was a West Indian, a doctor. He came to the

470

house the night I got back from . . . what happened. How's Wendy?'

'Unswervingly loyal, relentlessly generous. Every time I have someone she pays me back in undiluted fidelity.'

'I can't forgive him,' Rachel said. 'For dying. That's why I did what I did with Jerome. I had some crazy notion it might fetch him. Once it started, I never wanted it to stop. I didn't want him to be human. I was only angry when he was gentle. What I wanted was for things not to be true. Not him, not anything. I wanted what was happening to be so unnatural, so unbelievable that nature would give me a reprieve, things would run backwards like a film. Nature never repents though, does it?'

'I could tell you that I still love you, Rachel, but it would only be the truth, I'm afraid, and what good did that ever do?'

'I don't know what to do with my life. I'd like to throw it away. I'm waiting for something terrible to happen to me. I stood outside, watching the tilers and thinking that perhaps they'd drop a packet of tiles on me. They thought I wanted them to pick me up. Imagine being lobbed from hand to hand, all the way to the top!'

'Get a job,' Guy said. 'Bore yourself to life. Or are you thinking of going back to your witch doctor?'

'You're the only person I can forgive for saying unforgivable things. Why?'

He took her jaw in his hand and brushed his thumb across her lips, revealing her teeth for a sharp second. She closed her eyes and her smile agreed with what he had not said.

I showed *The Good of the School* to the Venetian delegation on a Wednesday morning, at the Baronet in Wardour Street. It was like seeing it for the first time; they lent me foreign eyes. What seemed normal to an Englishman became grotesque when declared to Italians. I was shocked by the savagery of the schoolboys who, until then, had simply recalled those I had known. I was embarrassed by the figure of Solomon, who would be taken by everyone as an impersonation of myself. I had been determined from the beginning not to make him a bland victim. He might be despised and rejected, but he was not entirely innocent. The recklessness of his jokes, at the expense of those who later turned on him, deprived him of the sympathy it might have been more prudent to solicit. I saw nothing heroic in him. For all his capacity to make wounding remarks, the outcast was, it was clear, a candidate for normality: he would have liked nothing better than to belong to the clan from which he was ejected. Ambition never seemed despicable to him until he was disqualified from it. Even in the most abject moments, when he pleaded to be told why the rest of the House refused to speak to him, put shit in his bed and salt in his jam ration, he had no notion of making a world elsewhere. Cleverness by itself had no country and no arena. His agony was the proof of how he craved the approval of those he hated and who showed every sign of hating him. The scene in which he stood at bay amid indifferent persecutors was both comic and painful. They have already begun to be bored with baiting him and are not sorry to have an excuse for finding other diversions. He imagines that his courage has shamed them, but I shot the scene in such a way that it is clear they are glad of an opportunity to re-admit him to the House. The following week, he plays in the football team and receives his colours, after a battling display, from one of the ring leaders of his humiliation. In the second half of the film, when he is able to get his foot on the ladder of preferment as the result of betraying Eely and Barnes, whose closeness excludes him almost as painfully as the earlier ostracism, Solomon's conversion to the morality of a school from which he had wanted nothing more than to be removed forever was, to me, as convincing as it was abrupt. The cunning of the institution lay in its impersonal persuasiveness: the cloisters, the statues, the prize-winners' panels in Great Hall, the memorial window in the massive chapel (I had, with brazen wiliness, persuaded my old school to let me film in the chapel, and even to give it a ghostly grandeur through liberal volleys from the smoke gun), the racquets' court, the scoreboard on Big Ground, all the paraphernalia of sentimental indoctrination, were brought into a montage which parodied the scene in Eisenstein where Kerensky was tempted by the imperial insignia. Solomon's promotion to monitor and House Commander was accompanied by mocking music; in gaining his revenge, like some adolescent Napoleon, he forced the authorities to honour a code for which they assumed that no one had any serious respect. Solomon's eagerness to be good was an excess of zeal which no one who had properly learned the lessons of a public school education could ever have displayed. The last scene, in which he is made an Under Officer, after leading the House to victory in the Drill Competition, showed him in Sam Browne belt and blue shoulder flashes, a swagger stick under his arm, being applauded by the very people who had made his life hell. The folly of his complacency prevented him from seeing that he had now been more thoroughly degraded than he had ever been by rejection.

The Venetians assured me that the film was certain to be included in the Festival with a haste which seemed calculated to avoid any discussion of its content. I shook hands with them, smiling, and went to meet Charlie Lehmann at the White Elephant. As I was cutting through Soho, hoping for a taxi, I saw Sally Raglan, in a white mini-skirt, with white boots and a French sailor's hat, signing an autograph outside the Globe.

'Morning, your majesty!'

'Oh Michael, on your knees, sirrah! Why are you always there when I'm doing something I shouldn't be?'

'Nothing very irregular in honouring your contract with the public, is there? The show seems to be keeping all its promises, in spite of Benny's blast.'

'He always has to prove how incorruptible he is.'

'Are you still talking? Among other things?'

'We're just doing other things for the moment. He doesn't talk all that much when he's up the Amazon anyway. Oh Michael, have you heard about Aubers?'

'There's more? I've only heard what's been blowing in the wind ever since Benny spat into it.'

'You know they were buying this house in California, him and Lovey? And you know about this character in the Channel Islands, Archie something, who's been looking after Aubers' money? He was in town for the opening and Aubs introduced me to him, because I may be doing a film in America when *Bess!* closes, if it ever does. *Anyway*, Aubs wanted a slab of cash to take care of the living pit and stuff like that, no, you know, to top up the tank, and he asked Archie thing to disgorge the necessary. Nothing happened for a bit and then he got word from Jackie Palgrave that he could have about half what he'd put in for. He couldn't understand what Jack meant, because he'd bunged about half a million into this partnership. How could there be less than half that much in the kitty? You've heard this already.'

'I feel as if I have,' I said, 'but no. Could it be that Archie thing, D.S.C., D.S.O. and bar, had made off with fifty-one per cent of Aubers' gotten gains?'

'Can you *imagine*? Aubers finally tracked him down –'

'Wonderful what those bloodhounds can do!'

'– and he said to him, "I thought you were an officer and a gentleman." To which he said, "I thought about it and in return for a quarter of a million, I decided just to hang on to the officer part." Aubs said, "I thought we were friends, for God's sake." Thing said, "I never really liked you enough to pay that two hundred grand to stay on your Christmas card list, to be perfectly honest." Aubs is practically on a drip, I can tell you. Why are you laughing?'

'It's the way you tell them,' I said. 'Does that mean Mulholland Drive is no longer being renovated?'

'Of course not. *Bess!* is going to Broadway as soon as we can all get permits, some of us, and then there's the movie and then there's the next show after that . . . Aubs always bounces back, you know that. He's longing to work with you again, incidentally.'

I said, 'Tell me something, Sally, even if it's true.'

'*Now* . . .'

'Was it you?'

She said, 'Was it me what?'

'Someone phoned Annie from that location, before Ken had his attack, when I was down there working on the script of *Family Circles*. It was you, wasn't it?'

'Phoned Annie? What about?'

'Someone told Annie that I'd had it off with Jilly Brandt.'

'Who ever is Jilly Brandt?'

'The mother of that little boy who wouldn't cry.'

'Why would I want to tell Annie a thing like that?'

I said, 'O.K.'

She said, 'Not guilty, m'lud. Hey! It wasn't *true*, was it?'

I said, 'Give my love to big Benny.'

Charlie Lehmann had had his hair cut short. 'This is as near as I ever want to get to joining the Marines,' he said. Distress rejuvenated him: he had been in the States partly on business, partly in the hope of persuading Mireille to come back to him. As soon as things went well in Los Angeles, he suspected that they would go badly in New York. They had agreed to put up the money for me to start on the script for *Dizzy*, a film about Disraeli which, if it happened, would be my first real movie as a director. Even as it threatened to become a reality, I felt a twinge of dread. Why did I always solicit opportunities for panic? How willing I should have been to hear that Mireille had agreed to return to London, but that the studio insisted on a more experienced director! Charlie watched me eat my smoked salmon and sipped San Pellegrino. His anguish thinned and jaundiced him, but I doubt if he would have been happy to make the same exchange. The man who had supplanted him in Mireille's bed was hugely rich. Charlie might be hurt, but he was comforted by the logic of his wife's decision. There was tact in it, as well as ruthlessness: she meant him no harm and, if he was wise, he would do her none. I almost envied him the briskness with which he advised me of how things stood. He sought no sympathy nor did he expect me to say unpleasant things about his wife. There would be a divorce; it had happened before and it might well happen again. Meanwhile, luckily, there were serious things to discuss: when did I think I could have a first draft ready of *Dizzy*? Was October too soon to hope? How did I feel about Ned Corman as Gladstone? Could Sally Raglan do Victoria? He did not want to wait till she'd played *Bess!* on Broadway, and on the screen, but who else could do it as well? We sat at a corner table in the back of the panelled restaurant, ostentatiously exclusive in our dialogue, and took huddled delight in the curiosity of those who came and went and wondered what we were planning. Business could be more pleasurable than pleasure.

I walked across the park until I saw an empty taxi. I should have taken the sun and the exercise, but I could not resist raising a finger. Nothing pressed and yet, as usual, I felt in a hurry. There had to be something I had to do.

Annie was in the kitchen. I called the good news down to her. It seemed better when I told it to her than when I had heard it myself. The telephone rang while I was on my way to the basement and I went back up to the sitting room to answer it. It was a wrong number, or a burglar, to judge from the silence and the click which followed. I was dialling Ned Corman's private line, in order to begin the humble tease which would beguile him into growing sideburns for the new year, when Annie came upstairs with a large, stiff spray of gladioli in one of our Casa Pupo vases. They chafed against each other in a slightly disagreeable way as she put them on the walnut table by the window.

'Oh and we're going to Venice,' I said, 'in the autumn. Nice flowers.'

XII

Swinging London –
I'm singing London,
London's a place
Full of grace,
And flavours.
Winging to London,
Swinging to London,
Lovely birds,
Music and words,
Put the zing in London!

I went to the big window at the back of the sitting room and listened, wincing, to the sound coming from our neighbour's garden. The house belonged to Lord Horniman, a fleshy young man who went to the City in the morning, but was often home in the early afternoon. His blonde wife, Vicky, had several girl friends with whom she took coffee, accompanied on the transistor, on her paved patio. I was infuriated by the blatant noise and I was comforted by my fury. I stood there allowing Aubrey's unmistakable words to break over me like tepid turf.

London has a new face –
Less arsenic, less lace –
She's young, she's free,
And that suits me,
Swing and be swung,
Sing and be sung,
Take wing, be young!

I shut the window loudly and sighed in the silence. It was nearly three o'clock and I had had no lunch. Maria had offered to make something, but I said that I would go up to the Hungry Horse for a pie. Wanting food and yet without appetite, I sat reading about Victorian England, appalled and envious of Disraeli's nerve, virtuously postponing the moment when I should have to find a shape for the script. How many books did Flaubert read before he considered himself ready to start work on *Salammbô*? Bob had made a fat deal with the studio, but I was still waiting to hear that the first payment had come through. Never trusting anyone was an indulgence which would gild the news that all was well, as I always trusted it would be.

I heard the front door open. Annie was wearing her new Israeli fawn leather mini-skirt and jacket and the hand-dyed shoes from Elliot's. There was a brightness in her eyes which, in a movie, would have argued for a key-light perfectly aligned to bring out their hazel vitality. She was carrying a bunch of peachy long-stem roses.

I said, 'Hullo.'

'Oh hullo! Are you here?'

'I'm giving my usual unimpressive imitation.'

She said, 'I brought you some flowers.'

'Did you?' I took them from her and nosed their rich odour and then I threw them across the room. They fell like pick-a-sticks in a rude jumble.

'Was that necessary?'

I said, 'Why lie?'

'I thought you preferred it.'

'Why *him*? Do you suppose he relishes being used as a stick to beat me with?'

'I don't suppose he objects all that much, do you? In view of the history?' She winced at the thorns as she re-collected the bouquet. 'Why so petulant about someone giving me a few flowers?'

'He's given you half Kew Gardens,' I said. 'If you want to go to bed with him, you'd better go to bed with him. Before we run out of vases.'

Annie was standing under a drawing of Guy Falcon's. It showed a naked woman, sitting alone on a bed (an echo of Rembrandt's study of his wife). Its title was 'Him and Her'.

I said, 'You already have.'

She looked at me, unforgiving and unblinking.

I said, 'Annie Rose.'

She said, 'He really likes me, Michael.'

I said, '*I* really like you.'

'Not always easy to tell.'

'I know why you're doing this. And so do you. Deny it.'

'Oh, there's an element of tit for tat,' she said. 'I'm not saying there isn't.'

'Damned right,' I said. 'I'm tat and you're tit.'

'He says he loves me.'

'And that's good enough for knickers off and pillows under the tum, is it? Loves you!'

'How can you talk to me like that?'

'I just open my mouth, madam, and out it comes.'

'You don't really want me. Be honest.'

'At a time like this?'

'You'd be patient with me if you did.'

'I'll be patient with you, if you'll be nurse with me. Wasn't that always our deal?'

'I don't like deals. The truth is, you hate me to have anything of my own. Even a cold. You're the only man I know who can actually be jealous of a germ.'

'Only the kind that gets you into bed more easily than I do.'

'I've never refused you in my life.'

'Refused me? I never imagined that you could think of it like that.'

'Well, I can,' she said. 'He doesn't want to break us up, you know.'

'Then why are we in pieces?'

'All I'm asking is a little time.'

'Of course,' I said. 'How about thirty seconds?'

Annie said, 'Do you want something to eat?'

'I've just had a large portion of humble pie, thanks all the same.'

'I haven't had any lunch; have you?'

'Presumably what you did have was just as satisfying in its way.'

'We talked most of the time,' she said.

'Some do, some don't. I'm sure he gives a prompt and efficient service.'

'Actually, if you want to know, he feels very guilty about you. The first time —'

'Oh please don't feel that in the interests of the higher accuracy you have to give me a blow by blow account of how you managed to get his engine started.'

'You really want me to walk out of this house, don't you?'

'I don't know what I want,' I said. 'I wish I did. I want this not to have happened, that's what I really wish, but I don't think my fairy godmother is available just at present, is she?'

The front doorbell was ringing.

'There she is now perhaps.'

Annie did not smile. 'Are you expecting anyone?'

'It could be the florist,' I said, 'with more flowers for me. It might be Maria having lost her keys again, madam.' I left Annie looking miserable and triumphant with her flowers and went to the door. 'Next time I have to change the locks, it's coming out of her Christmas box, whatever the Mafia says.'

'Hi.' A very bearded young man, in greasy jeans, carrying a scuffed green canvas holdall, was standing on the doorstep.

I said, 'On what conceivable grounds exactly?'

'You don't remember me?'

'I might if I could see you. How are you, Jess? I never got your letter.'

'I didn't write,' Jess Nathanson said.

'No use blaming the G.P.O. then.'

'I saw your latest movie. I dug it a lot. How's Annie? Your

mother gave me your address. I called her from the airport. Sensational home.'

Annie said, 'Aren't you going to ask him in?'

'Annie, could I possibly dump on you guys for maybe a coupla days?'

I said, 'Jesus . . .'

'You look terrible,' Annie said.

'I'm more than that when you get to know me. Frankly, I'm on the lam. But chicken or beef is perfectly acceptable.'

I said, 'Still the comedian!'

'You'd sooner see my paintings? Relax! I left in a hurry: no etchings, no murals. No pocketbook even. When those F.B.I. guys come knock, knock, knocking at your door, you split before they split you.'

'F.B.I.? Are you serious?'

'I've been in a chase sequence like the Keystone Cops never dreamed of. Over the border with one coat of paint to spare. Howling *sneakers*? Phew! Canada. A thinking man can have too much of Toronto. No mean city? I'll take Tarsus.'

Annie said, 'Show Jess where he can wash. He looks like he could use some food.'

'You could start with this bit,' I said, pulling one of his ears towards the bathroom.

Jess said, 'She looks wonderful.'

I said, 'Jess, this isn't a good time . . .'

'It's a stinking time,' Jess said. 'Vietnam, Greece, Israel . . . So what can we do? Please, do you have another calendar?'

I said, 'Stay and have something to eat by all means, but . . .'

'Say, that mat of yours really doesn't have "Welcome" on it, does it? How do the Greek colonels affect your house out there?'

I said, 'They show no signs of wanting to move in for the moment. What you really ought to do is have a bath, Jess.'

'If it doesn't put you out.'

I said, 'And I'll find you some clothes. It's quite a little sideline of mine.'

Annie was putting cutlery on the table in the breakfast nook. 'He looked a little desperate.'

'And how do I look? Annie, if this is some way of shutting me up –'

'We'll need some glasses.'

'I don't want anything to eat. Only Spaniards and people who make love in the lunchbreak eat meals at half past three. How was it? Good?'

'What?'

'The meat course.'

'Do you have to be disgusting?'

'It wasn't *fish*, was it? What are you doing asking him to stay?'

'The kid is desperate, couldn't you seee that?'

Jess came down stairs with a halo of talcum around him. 'What's my best way to Paris?'

'Straight ahead that way until you come to a big ditch. Big jump and straight ahead again.'

'Buddy gave me addresses, people to rap with. People with spare beds maybe who can remind me of my heritage.'

'How about money? Did he give you any of that? What does he think about –?

'Funny you should ask that because I have a transcript of his testimony in my rucksack. Two volumes of single-spaced paternal disapproval, labelled "Doing My Best To Understand". Frankly, I'm a little radical for him: a little radical bastard who doesn't know what he's doing ruining his life just because he doesn't want to defoliate gooks or get his ass shot away doing it. Buddy, quite frankly, is turning in his gravy. His country right or extreme right is all the same to him. Meanwhile I blow my last serious chance to do something worthwhile in the world, such as being a dentist in Scarsdale and spending my time picking disused matzos out of Mrs Nussbaum's back teeth. Man's work! Now Mrs Nussbaum's *daughter*, she just might lend a whole new dimension to "Open wide", but when do I get to tilt *her* fucking chair? In summation, I fouled up, according to dad, and I don't get another Fascist penny out of him until I come to his senses.'

'There must be work on television for this kid,' I said.

Annie said, 'And what about your mother?'

'Ethel is in understandable shock. But at least having a son who's a graduate deserter from Uncle Sam doesn't yet mean they cut off your charge account at Bonwit Teller. When *that* happens . . . I'm being totally unfair, of course, but what are kids for? She's shattered, is the truth, but Revlon has preparations to take care of that. Luckily my sister Lisa is joining the Marine Corps. Please God she meets a nice Jewish commandant somewhere between the Halls of Montezuma and the shores of Tripoli.'

'Food,' Annie said, 'is what you need.'

'Beautiful *and* psychic? If you were under thirty, Annie, I'd trust you anywhere. And you probably will be quite soon if you go on doing whatever you're doing. Aren't you eating, Michael?'

'I'll enjoy watching you.'

'So what's with your Greek house right now? Is it empty?'

I said, 'We may go there in the summer. If we live so long.'

'I guess you're afraid to speak out against those Fascists in Athens in case they take it away from you, right?'

I said, 'I've signed a few things.'

'Because what was it Karl Marx said?'

'First eat, wasn't it, and then bad mouth your hosts?'

'About the economic circumstances determining the consciousness?'

'As far as Karl Marx is concerned,' I said, 'I'm waiting for the musical.'

'You're no longer a socialist?'

'I have people in Downing Street,' I said, 'who take care of that side of the business for me. I'm a socialist, but I no longer light candles on Friday nights.'

'How about Israel,' Jess said, 'do you have an alibi there as well?'

I said, 'I'm beginning to appreciate what your father sees in you, pal.'

Jess said, 'Reminds me: I guess I should maybe call them.'

'I thought you said he was a Fascist.'

'But a *concerned* Fascist. Do you think I possibly could? What time is it in Scarsdale? I'd hate to not wake them up and give them something new to resent.'

I said, 'Help yourself. And leave the money on the table.'

'Is he serious?'

'Only when he's joking, isn't he?'

I sat there watching Annie eat while Jess went upstairs to make his call. I was hungry, but I could not confess my hunger. My head began to ache. Annie managed, without any apparent effort, never to look at me as she finished her food. She had the naturalness of an actress who refrains from looking at the camera while managing to strike the closest possible tangents. She proved to me, in the most decorous way, that she was capable of sustaining an attitude, or a pretence, for just as long as she wanted. I was filled with dread and hatred and admiration and desire. She declared war in the most peaceful imaginable way.

'How long's he going to go on gabbing, for Christ's sake? We're not really going to let him stay, are we?'

'Give him some money and he'll go away,' Annie said.

'You don't want him here, do you?'

'It doesn't matter to me.'

'Well, it fucking matters to me. *I* have to work.' I glared at Jess as he came back down the stairs. His face was covered with tears. The beard shone. 'You got through.'

'I'm sorry,' he said. 'I'll be hungry again in a minute.'

Annie said, 'Oh Jess.' She put her palm on his cheek and dried it on a kitchen towel. 'Have some fruit salad.'

'I thought I couldn't cry any more. You know what he said? "Your mother hasn't been out of the house since the day you skipped. She doesn't even get dressed." Isn't that *great*? Maybe I should quickly go bomb some gooks and *then* have the fruit salad. When I hear my mother has her health and charge accounts back in synch. And for this I put a front-end load on your telephone bill.'

Annie said, 'She's still going to be glad to know you're O.K.'

'If he tells her, she is. Meanwhile, if the Arabs go ahead and

484

attack Israel, guess who's going to be responsible for that too. Can I call Nasser from here? How can I fight on two fronts and still contribute meaningfully to the counter-culture?'

'I've been pretty bloody patient in the circumstances, wouldn't you say?'

'I've got your medal in the car.'

'You and your brother,' Joe said. 'Same tongue. Why do I bother?'

Behind them, Rachel could hear the guide instructing a party of Zionists from St Louis, Missouri. 'After a heroic defence, all of the garrison agreed to commit suicide rather than surrender to the Romans. They killed each other to the last man. Today the state of Israel takes the men and women of Masada as its inspiration. It is here that the paratroopers of the I.D.F. swear their oath. Never again will we allow ourselves to be led into captivity or separated from our native land. Israel will fight to the last man. And now, over here, you will find the excavations where Professor Yigael Yadin discovered the skeletons of the original defenders . . .'

Joe said, 'And how do we know about their heroism? Because Flavius Josephus decided to be the one who lived to tell the tale. If it hadn't been for the only traitor in the bunch, it would all have been for nothing. How great an example did they set finally, frankly? And of what? So you can't be loyal to the dead without being dead yourself! Is that what we're supposed to think?'

Rachel said, 'It's astounding and it's horrible. Very lifelike.'

Joe said, 'You sometimes have to ask yourself, quietly, whether this land was really promised or whether Jehovah couldn't find anyone else to take it off His hands. Great view, but do you see any milk and honey?'

In the car, on the way back to the kibbutz, Rachel unbuttoned the top button of her shirt and made a fan of the lapel. 'I hate being told that I have to be moved.'

'Why did you come with me in the first place?'

'You know your trouble, Joe? You can't take "yes" for an answer, can you? I wanted to get out of England. I thought Israel might be what I was looking for. Now I should like to get out of this car. Your technique is a bit schoolboy, isn't it?'

He took his hand from her thigh. 'You want to get out of everything.'

'Yes, please.'

He pulled up where a bamboo frame held tatters of palm-frond and some sacking. The primitive shade had been nagged to shreds by the hot wind. 'Wait for a number thirty-six camel, if that's what you want.' He leaned across and opened the difficult door. 'It goes straight to Marble Arch.'

'Just take me back to the kibbutz, will you, please?'

'Please and thank you,' Joe said. 'Frauds we could do without. I've wanted you from the first moment I saw you, in that dreary little theatre in Colchester. It's getting to be a long time to wait. You think you're being loyal to the dead; I think you're pleasing yourself, thank you all the same. By teasing me. Deny it.'

Rachel pulled the door shut again. 'I prefer more sophisticated pleasures.'

'And what's wrong with this one? Recent theology suggests that God is less concerned than early reports indicated with who screws whom. The dead sing no psalms, you may remember, and have no feelings, least of all hard ones.'

Rachel said, 'I'd probably be more impressed if you showed me your wallet. It's fatter, isn't it?'

Joe said, 'You're not afraid you'll hate it. You're afraid you'll like it. Well, if you want me to make it a thoroughly disagreeable experience, you have only to say so. But you don't. You'd like it and you know you would. He won't mind; he won't know; he isn't around.'

Rachel said, 'What's your *un*subtle line?'

'You think I'm just adding to my score? Why not add to yours? Afraid I'll tell people? I'll tell them anyway. Think I'm going to let 'em think Joe Hirsch went away for two whole weeks with the beautiful widow and never got past the gate?'

Rachel said, 'How old were you when you left Berlin?'

'Don't bloody well change the subject.'

'Was I? Because that's how old you are now, isn't it?'

'Ever have an eight-year-old propose to you before? I want to marry you, Rachel.'

'What will your wife say?'

'As long as it doesn't affect her position as a producer with Tower T.V., hallelujah, won't she? Goodbye and good luck. Well, goodbye.'

'You know it can't be done, don't you?'

'If it can't, I'm the man to do it. I'm good at the nightwork, Rachel. Ask anyone. *Almost* anyone.'

They drove through the gates of the kibbutz and past the grey concrete of the community centre. Children were playing basket ball and volley ball in the beige yard. Someone was practising the cello in a breeze-block music room. Beyond the unpainted buildings, orchards of grapefruit and orange trees swerved past a rocky outcrop which not even determined ingenuity could render fertile. The volley ball flew over the netting and bounced in front of the Morris.

'In the Warsaw ghetto,' Joe said, 'the children didn't play; they pretended to play. Why can't we pretend to live? In view of what happened . . .'

Rachel said, 'No one can do anything in view of what happened.'

'Can anyone really do anything else? You know you need a man.'

'I'd sooner have a job,' she said.

'Why not consider our generous two-in-one offer? Do you want to work in television or would you prefer to do something worthwhile? I always look after my females.'

'It helps you to despise them, I assume.'

'That's why Felicity walked out basically. She was so sure I'd got her her job. In fact she got it in spite of me. You can imagine how eager the other directors were for my wife to have a slot. Personal empires! But try and prove that I was a hindrance more

487

than a help. When people hate you, they flatter you with all sorts of powers you don't wield. You're afraid Michael won't like it.'

'I'm afraid I won't like it,' Rachel said.

They had parked the car and were walking back to the guest house when the air raid sirens stopped the games on the playground.

'True or false?' Rachel said.

'You think I'm a shit, don't you?'

'Oh Joe, let's just say that your candidature for sainthood still needs work.'

Joe said, 'I might be different, if I lived here.'

'I'm no great believer in geography as a cure for souls,' Rachel said.

'The English only ever want us to be shits. Shits, benefactors and violinists.'

'You've forgotten comedians,' Rachel said.

'Daniel said he was sorry, but he was going to pray to his God and not to the king. The king would have to do what he liked about it. And the king said, "What I'm going to do, you won't like." And his men came and threw Daniel into the lions' den.'

Through the wall, I could hear Lord Horniman: 'You bloody little *bitch*.'

'I saw the lions' den, didn't I?' Daniel said. 'With mummy.'

'You bastard, Tristram. You total no-no.'

'And in the morning, the king went to see if the lions had enjoyed their breakfast, and there was Daniel – unsugared, unmilked and uneaten –'

'You stink, you little bitch, do you hear me?'

'We *all* hear him, don't we, daddy?'

'I'd sooner stuff a turkey.'

'And the king said, "What's going on around here?" And Daniel said, "Oh king, live for ever," which was tactful of him, considering the plans the king had for him, "but I haven't done anything wrong, and that's why the lions won't eat me for breakfast." Daniel, it seems, had small experience of the modern executive conscience, but that's another story.'

'Will you tell it?'

'Maybe tomorrow.'

I heard the brief ring of the telephone. It was answered downstairs, promptly. I waited to hear if it was for me.

'Next time I marry a woman for her money, such as it is, I hope it'll come in a tastier box.'

'Why do they shout at each other all the time, dad?'

'Because these houses are too small for jousting in full armour.'

'And what happened then? *Dad?*'

'What happened then? All the bad men were thrown into the lions' den and got eaten up like fresh cereal. The moral being: never make the king look silly unless your name is Daniel. And even then be sure you're the right Daniel, because not every lion in the zoo is familiar with this story. And now goodnight. See you in the morning.'

'Tristram, you're a bonzo, a stupid, stupid bonzo.'

Annie was sitting in the *bergère* chair under the window, with the white telephone on the carpet beside her.

'They're locking Hornimans again next door,' I said. 'What're you reading?'

'Something Jess left behind.'

'He's one of those people who bends the corners of books. He bends the corners of people too, come to that. What would you like to do?'

'I'm happy,' she said.

I picked up the telephone and put it back on the oval table we had bought from the little antique shop under the flat which she rented in Colchester. 'We were going to go to "Headquarters" sometime. I'm told the show's not bad.'

'Whatever you like.'

I took her by the shoulders and kissed her.

'What are you so angry about now?' she said.

*

489

It was a false alarm. After supper, there was a concert in the community centre. They stayed until the interval, when Joe suggested a walk in the moonlight. They were accompanied by the sound of the string quartet.

'Mozart? Haydn? Heinrich von Kitsch? Not easy to tell at a hundred paces.'

'Music doesn't mean anything to me, I'm afraid,' Joe said.

'What does?' Rachel said. 'Apart from money.'

'Aren't you at all attracted to someone you can say things like that to? And don't you like money? I do. I had breakfast in Downing Street last week and this cabinet minister asked me what use I really thought it was. I said, "For instance, it's invaluable for getting away from people like you at a moment's notice. It's worth having a helicopter on permanent stand-by just to be able to scramble when you see an idiot and his question on his way across the room."'

'You really said that?'

'Do I get any marks if I did? I did. You wouldn't be so grand about cash if they hadn't looked after you. What did you get? A quarter of a million, I hope. Less? You should have let me negotiate.'

Rachel said, 'I think I'm going back.'

Joe said, 'Is running away the best form of exercise?'

'I'm chilly.'

'I have a cure for that. Rachel, I've got eighty-five thousand "A" shares in Tower T.V. I have a three-year contract and an option on another fifty thousand shares at par in three months' time. Do you seriously imagine that I'm after the widow's mite?'

'I can think of answers to that,' Rachel said, 'but I'd sooner have the helicopter.'

She walked back under the pollarded regularity of the grapefruit trees. The windows of the community centre were tilted open, at the top, and she stood and smiled at Haydn in the heavy shadow of the building. Joe came slowly under the branches and looked at her as if she were a stranger. He had just gone into the guest house when a row of figures, in single file,

490

came out of the orchard from another direction. They were in berets and camouflaged blouses and dark shorts and they carried Sten guns. The sound of blurted instructions came from a radio carried by the patrol leader. He listened and then, with a casual gesture, indicated to the others to disperse. He took the hand of a girl and pulled her into the lee of the community centre and kissed her. Rachel moved. The couple paid no attention to her as she opened the screened door and climbed the concrete stairs towards her room.

She was reading *His and Hers*, Claudia Monk's new novel. The heroine had been more or less abandoned by her journalist husband, who spent his time in the world's hot spots, reporting other people's battles. When one of their children is seriously injured in a playground fall from a climbing frame, he is in Saigon. Nicola writes an article about her guilt-bitterness entitled 'Mummy's Boy' which creates quite a stir. The climax of the book comes when Jeremy is sent to cover a civil war in Africa (the episode must have been based on Barnaby's excursion to the West African Federation). He has not wanted to go, but his editor prevails on him to make one last trip. When he is killed, the editor himself comes to Nicola's house to break the news. She makes it difficult for him to speak at all before she has told him of Jeremy's devotion to the family and to herself and of her own conviction that a woman's place is, whatever anyone may say, in the home. Her tone suggests that she is resisting a sexual advance from the notoriously predatory editor. He is embarrassed at being obliged to sincerity. When, finally, he breaks the news, Nicola throws herself into his arms. The widow's courage is widely admired, not least by Jeremy's old friends, who hurry to recommend themselves with competitive eulogies. Everyone can imagine how she feels, but only her son, still on crutches, imagines with enough accuracy to make her dread his tongue. After the funeral, the boy accuses Nicola of wishing that he too was dead. He promises that he will know exactly why she does whatever she now does with her life. Nicola realizes that every action she undertakes will be subject to a vigilance more intense than her husband ever cared to display. She begins to fall in love with the son whom she was within a fraction of hating. (It has even occurred to her to push him down the stairs.) The death of Jeremy so shames the editor, who persuaded him to go on the fatal journey, that he offers Nicola the job of 'Women's Editor'. When she goes home and tells her son of the opportunity, he throws down his crutches and takes her in his arms and kisses her on the lips.

Rachel closed the book and put it on the grey shelf behind the bed. She linked fingers behind her head and smiled at what she had read. She altered her position just a little and was no longer smiling. She looked at her watch and then she got out of bed and put on her slippers and dressing gown. She opened the ill-fitting doors on to the terrace and walked into the moonlight. The concert was over. The lights of a lorry bent over the shallow horizon and then went straight along the desert road. She stepped over the low partition. Joe was in bed, reading a floppy script. Spying on him made her feel something she had not felt before. Doing what she should not have done put her, almost wilfully, in his debt; the small assault made her protective. She tapped on the glass.

Without looking up, he said, 'It's open.'

She pushed the door and went in.

He said, 'Want to borrow my razor?'

She walked up to the bed with a shake of her hair.

'All right if I just finish this?' he said.

'To think we used to call it making love,' she said.

'Does it matter what you call it? You enjoyed it, didn't you? You *sounded* as though you did.'

'It matters a lot.'

'Let's go back to Greece. Now. Let's get out of bloody England and go back to the house and be what we were. Just ourselves.'

'And the Colonels.'

'What do you care about the blasted Colonels? You've never

given a damn about politics up until now, have you? Where are you going?'

'What's the point of a bathroom *en suite*, if you don't make *en sweet* use of the thing?'

'I preferred the old earth closet. No charming flushing sounds.'

'You can't go to Greece. You've got Disraeli to do.'

'You accuse me of being responsible for what you want to have happen. You obviously prefer to stay here. I can do Disraeli anywhere my typewriter can be persuaded to click. You, on the other hand, can't do what you want to do unless I'm being selfish and thoughtless as usual, can you?'

Annie said, 'I never meant any of it to happen.'

'No,' I said, 'that's what's so convenient about it really, isn't it? How could you enjoy it so much if it was what you'd always wanted? Everything that happens to you has to be someone else's fault before you can get any pleasure out of it. Even orgasms.'

She said, 'How long have you thought those things?'

I said, 'You know me: new scenes dreamed up while you wait, and rewritten as required. A man's life.'

'You were resentful even when you said you were happy, weren't you? You've never really wanted to be married to me.'

I said, 'Now I'm responsible for what you've done. Always blame the writer, right? Do you seriously think he loves you?'

'I'm not sure that I'm a good judge,' she said. 'I seriously thought you did.'

I said, 'Game and first set. Oh Annie, I don't *believe* any of this; the more frightful the things we say to each other, the more it seems like a game.'

'Not to me,' she said. 'But then I don't even understand whist.'

'At least the sex is good, isn't it? Ours, I meant. Are you laughing? You're not *crying*, are you? Annie, what have you got to cry about? You're the queen of the castle. And you do know I love you, don't you?'

*

'*La fermeture du golfe d'Aqaba, prévu par le Président Nasser, risque de provoquer des vives réactions en Israel. En cas de guerre, qui de toutes apparences semble imminente, tous les états Arabes, y compris l'Égypte, la Syrie et la Jordanie, se sont promis d'unifier leurs états-majors afin d'en finir définitivement avec l'état Hébreu . . .*'

Joe turned down the car radio and looked at Rachel as though the threat of war were something which might oblige her to change her mind. They drove away from the kibbutz under a steely sky in which Israeli Mirages appeared and disappeared with unsynchronized shrieks.

'You still think we ought to leave?'

Rachel said, 'I don't know anything about what people ought to do. I just want to go home; and this is not it.'

'Headquarters' was in Dean Street. It was dark and smoky and narrow and uncomfortable and I had to negotiate at some length with the doorman before I could even have a word with Keith Harley, who ran the place, in the hope that he would rate me enough of a celebrity to deserve to be fleeced. The cabaret was already in progress when one of his slouching waitresses flashed her torch at a corner table, reserved for the house, and we were seated on kitchen chairs.

A white man in black face and a black man in white face were doing a duet. They did a little soft shoe shuffle, with comic lack of unanimity, and then they went back to words and music:

> WHITE FACE: I'll share your shitty bathwater.
> BLACK FACE: Ditto your pretty daft daughter.
> WHITE FACE: Cheeky coon!
> Try a different tune,
> Or I'll see you in hell.
> (In brackets, you smell.)
> BLACK FACE: Why so upset, Freddie?
> Since I've had her already!

As the two of them turned and began to box each other's shadows, Keith jumped on to the stage and pretended to have to separate them: 'Gentlemen, please. Gentle*man* and friend, please!'

They had to compose their differences as the pianist played a hurried God Save The Queen and obliged all three on stage to stand to attention. He then went back to the number for the two performers to say, through gritted teeth, the key word 'Harmony!'

Keith Harley affected to damp down an ovation which had, in fact, been scarcely polite. His impersonation of smug panic was so much funnier than the number it followed that it was applauded, with much keener sincerity, as if it were a separate act. Keith had the face of a corrupt March Hare; it needed more than the audience's enthusiasm to appease his wickedness. 'Keep calm, ladies and genitals, the Nuclear Deterrent will soon be here to restore peace in our tomb. Anyone shocked by the sheer banality of the last little offering is invited to apply for his money back from the muscular darkie situated directly behind this poky little clip-joint. He will treat all applicants strictly on their merits in the dark alley where he conducts his remarkably profitable operations. Do rush at once, so that we may proceed with selling overpriced victuals to the next wave of satire-hungry stupes and trend-following teeds. Thank you slightly.'

The lights grew bright enough for shadows to be thrown and the waitresses began to distribute salads and spaghetti which it would now be humourless to send back. Annie had put on a charcoal-grey Roman suit and a frothy lace blouse, with jet earrings I had bought her in Mallorca. She smiled brightly at me and made a motion with her head, a sort of controlled shake and a ripple of the lips, which I had never noticed her do until recently. I imagined, rightly or wrongly, that it implied that she was making an effort to give value for money. I hated it.

'What time is it in California, Comrade Jordan, and why are you not there?'

'I must have heard you were, Chairman Benedict. Perhaps you are. What are two places at once to a man of your ubiquity?'

'Two faces at once are all I can spring to these days.'

495

'Janus, this is still my wife, Annie.'

Benedict said, 'If she was anyone else's, I should congratulate you.' He took Annie's fingers in his languid left hand and raised them to his lips. 'I'm still Benedict Bligh, but it's proving an increasingly uphill struggle. Is this dump still proving that satire-with-its-heart-in-the-right-place is, like home cooking, home fooking and British cinema, no certain cure for most forms of cancer?'

Sally said, '*Anything*'s better than three hours of Maoist improvisation in Camden Town. The Long March in waltz time. Chu Chin Mao, Benny called it.'

'But it never called back,' Benedict said. 'Is anyone sitting there?'

'Yes,' I said, 'we are rather.'

Benedict squeezed in next to Annie. 'Now who was it who was talking about you in glowing terms the other day? Or was it after-glowing terms?'

Sally said, 'Tell me about *Dizzy*. Or aren't I supposed to know?'

Annie said, 'Excuse me.'

She was near the narrow alley that led between the tight tables to the cloakroom. I was in the corner, beyond Benedict and Sally.

Benedict said, 'Oh surely you're going to leave a forwarding address.'

I called out, 'Darling . . .'

Benedict said, 'Yes, darling?'

'Do you always do as much damage as you possibly can?'

'I never hesitate to insert whatever cracks I can in the tawdry fabric of bourgeois decorum, especially if the demolition can proceed to the popping of champagne corks.'

I said, 'The truth is you want our bloody table, blast you.'

'If you've finished bleeding on it.'

Sally said, 'Half the sweat in London seems to be here. Keith's doing brilliantly, isn't he?'

I said, 'The food's inedible, the cabaret is no sort of a joke and the tables are so close together you can't get a cheese wire between them. How can it fail?'

Benedict said, 'Do relax. She'll be back. Females piss these days, you know. It's a new dispensation.'

Annie appeared from the back of the restaurant with her white PVC coat. I stood up again. 'Have the bloody table,' I said.

'The family man, my dear Michael, is never an artist of consequence.' Benedict kept his blanched hand on my impatient sleeve. 'He's always either checking his watch or wondering why his wife is looking so particularly pretty for a change.'

'Sod you, Benedict, royally.'

'Awfully good of you to suggest it. Perhaps after the show? Or during it, if it's as well-intentioned as you imply. The moment is nigh, Comrade Jordan, when we shall all have to parade in our true colours.'

'And how does a chameleon like you work a trick like that?'

'Darling, do sit down,' Sally said. 'No one can see me.'

'Let her go,' Benedict said. 'That's my firm advice.'

'I don't go to firms for advice,' I said. 'I don't want any sentimental education from Professor Bligh, thanks all the same. And don't put your undertaker's hands all over me. I might not be up to slugging it out with ex-miners who write the Play of the Decade twice a week, but I just might fancy my chances against a stick of perfumed asparagus like you.'

Benedict said, 'Is this your witty, weighty way of announcing your retirement from the theatre? Am I being served notice that you will never again require me to oil your works?'

Sally said, 'Oh do relax, the pair of you, and sit down and vie for my favours. No one's ever had to vie very hard.'

I said, 'That's not my memory of events.'

Benedict said, 'He can't decide whether he wants to go or stay, can he? Do you notice?'

Sally said, 'Michael was so sweet, Benny, when I first met him. He thought the cause of true love had to be pleaded one button at a time.'

I said, 'If you want the table, have the table.'

Sally said, 'Darling . . .'

I started towards the door through which Annie had already passed.

'He obviously doesn't want me for Disraeli,' Sally said.

'Saves the nose-job,' Benedict said.

Annie must have found a taxi before I reached Dean Street. I had hurried and I had loitered; I could not say, even to myself, what I wanted to happen. I was sick with shame and fear, but I acquiesced in my pain and had some complicity with it. The mind too had its scabs which, like a schoolboy, I could not refrain from picking and even chewing. I wanted to catch her, or give her the chance of being caught, but I contrived to make things worse even as I sought to repair them. I told myself that I could not interfere with her liberty and, in another voice, that she would sooner or later turn back and hope that I was there. I felt sick and tearful; I was angry and determined. A static of panicky and strident words blathered in my head. I walked on towards Shaftesbury Avenue as if I had some destination in mind. The next scene of any consequence in my life had to be with Annie, but first there had to be a pause, during which she could imagine that I was never going to come home and she could weigh the consequences of what she had so far been able to enjoy with impunity. I saw that the Rialto was showing *Family Circles* as a late show. I bought a ticket and went in to hear my own words.

'Darling,' Sally was saying, 'if I didn't go away occasionally, how could I ever come back? And if I never came back, how could we keep meeting again?'

I stayed until I saw the scene in which young David Brandt had almost driven Ken Haller to despair and, even though I knew about the confusion which had led to the boy's perform-ance, I found his reaction marvellously true. The imagination, like memory, could be a matter of collage; the great cook makes scraps seem like fresh produce. I sat there in scornful admiration of what I thought I had created. When I wept, I could not distinguish between the tears which I was shedding for the character's misfortunes and those I was weeping for my own. Whatever their provenance, the tears tasted better than Keith Harley's house cup.

I kept looking at my watch, as if I were deliberately missing an appointment or was anxious to keep it. When I had left enough time to give Annie the impression that I had not in the least minded her absence, I went out into Lower Regent Street and looked for a taxi. It had begun to rain. The street glistened and hissed under the tyres of unavailable cabs. I walked steadily towards Fulham, my suede jacket darkening at the shoulders and then down the front. My knees got wet. I felt quite cheerful by the time I turned down past the grocery shop and saw Tristram Horniman's Rolls with its lights still on, parked outside number 21. He and Victoria were in the lit interior, kissing as keenly as if they had nowhere else to go. Victoria gave me a wave of petty royalty as I fumbled for my key. She had both breasts out of the top of her fairy frock.

There was a light on upstairs. I stopped in the hall and removed my jacket and my sopping trousers. In my underpants, with my shoes hooked over two fingers and my clothes clutched under my elbow, I went into the bedroom. Annie was not in bed. She was fully dressed and there was a suitcase on the sea chest at the end of the bed.

I said, 'I didn't rush after you because I thought you might want to have some time to yourself. I got caught in the downpour.'

'You'd better have a hot drink. I thought you weren't coming home.'

I said, 'The timing's a little neat, I must say. I stay out for well over an hour and when I get back, you're just about to snap the locks. If you were really going, might you not be gone by now? And if you're not really going, must we really have all this going on?'

Annie said, 'Is this really what you've come back to say?'

'This is my fucking house, lady.'

'You ought to have a hot bath,' she said.

'Please don't be thoughtful at a time like this. I rather hoped I could play this for laughs, but it doesn't seem to be getting them.'

Annie said, 'I don't think I like satire.'

'I certainly don't think I could love anybody who loved that show. Annie, this has got to stop, hasn't it, before someone gets seriously offended? Why not now? If you wanted to teach me a lesson, consider me taught. I'm a fast study when I need to be, if also a very foolish one. Why else am I saying all the things wisdom forbids? Such as please let's not go any further with this. And have I got any clean socks?'

'The other drawer,' Annie said.

'I keep hoping that incompetence will prove to be endearing. Thanks.'

She said, 'He's coming to get me.'

I said, 'Have you thought about Daniel?'

'You think about him for a few days.'

'And how many is a few?'

'Maria'll be here. She knows what to do.'

'She only knows what to do in Italian,' I said. 'What do I tell Daniel?'

'I've fixed for my mother to come up from Worthing to-morrow afternoon. She'll take him back with her. You remember my mother, don't you? She's the one who wears the 1938 hats that you put into the play about the suburban couple who imagine their daughter is a West End star when she's really a high-class tart.'

'Not particularly high-class,' I said. 'That was based on Sally's mama and her alcoholic dad and you know it was. I used that one line —'

'Oh I don't care what you did. I expect you'll use me now.'

'I'll use anything I bloody want to,' I said. 'You told your mother the full score, presumably, did you? Oh don't worry, it's probably been on the sports news by now. Once Benedict knows, the whole world knows.'

'What is there to know? I need a breathing space, Michael. It's the only sensible thing.'

'Don't we all though? They should send you to the Middle East. With your sensible skills, you'd have the Gulf of Aqaba open like *that*. Or would it be like this?'

'Every time you say you want things to get better, you make them worse.'

'Why can't we go and breathe on Iskios? Did you call him or did he call you?'

'It's funny, I called him and he was engaged and he was calling me. The minute I put it down, it rang.'

'That's hilarious. Are the rights available?'

'I hate you,' she said.

'I often have the same feeling. But you happen to be my wife. What I did, I did out of – oh vanity and – I did it without doing anything to you, whereas you are deliberately humiliating me in every possible direction . . .'

Annie said, 'Michael, I'm not going to argue with you, because you're better at it than I am. You're better at everything than I am.'

'Not arranging socks, I'm not.'

'Shut up. Shut up for two minutes. I'm not going to apologize, because I'm not doing anything wrong. I'm not going to break down and cry, which I usually do, because I don't want to. And I'm not going to not go when he gets here, because I'm bloody well going.'

The front door bell was ringing. She picked up the suitcase and walked out of the bedroom. I told myself that she did not look as if she was all that keen. The bell had rung again. I looked at myself in the mirror above the little Regency dressing table. I had the failed face of an actor who was not going to get the part. I heard Annie say, 'What the hell are you doing here?' I grinned at myself and went out on the landing.

Joe Hirsch was saying, 'Where's Michael? I have to talk to him. It's very important.' He was wearing a fawn safari suit, only

501

just freckled with raindrops. He frowned at Annie's suitcase. 'Going somewhere?'

'No,' she said, 'I always walk around the house with a suitcase.'

'Night flight?'

I said, 'What the hell do you want? It's well after midnight.'

Joe said, 'A word with you before you go.'

'I'm not going anywhere.'

'Annie just said –'

'She is,' I said. 'I'm not.'

'Good,' he said. 'Because I need to talk to you.'

'Where's Rachel?'

'She went straight down to Sussex, didn't she? She wanted to see the kid, in case he wasn't homesick.'

'His name's William,' I said. 'It might come in useful to know that.'

'I've asked her to marry me,' he said. 'Have you got anything to eat at all? A bit of chicken, some eggs – a slice of caviare perhaps?'

Annie stood there with her bag and we smiled at each other, as if we had forgotten that we were playing a hateful game and had reverted to affection. Then I heard the sound of another car in the street.

I said, 'Look, go in there, will you? And I'll have a word with chef.'

'You have a *chef* now?'

'For Christ's sake, when I ask you.'

'What the hell is going on?'

I bundled Joe into the sitting room and shut the door on him as there was a rap on the knocker.

'I can't find the light.'

'Sit in the dark.'

Frank Kitson was standing on the doorstep. He was wearing a three-quarter-length corduroy driving coat, rather enviable, and a French cap to match. 'Bloody awful traffic, I'm afraid, even at this hour. I'm terribly sorry . . .'

Annie said, 'Frank . . .'

'How are you, Michael?'

'On top of the bloody world, Frank old boy. As I'm sure your vivid imagination must have told you.'

Annie said, 'Perhaps . . . perhaps you'd better go.'

'I am going,' Frank said. 'And you're coming with me. I've driven from bloody Guildford. I'll tell you something funny, Michael.'

'You won't sing, will you, afterwards?'

'We were discussing the new season. Tony came up with the idea of doing a new production of *Maximum Security*. Out of the blue.' He picked up Annie's suitcase and sniffed the rain in the open doorway. 'Is this the lot then?'

I said, 'The classic revenge of the second-rate. Adultery on a farts council grant. The Turn of the Subsidized Screw. Ask Guildford if they'd like to put that on.'

'You disappoint me, Michael, you know.'

'I disappoint everybody, you know. I disappoint myself. I ought to be laughing and cheering, like a true man of our times, at the sight of my wife disappearing into the ground with the worm of her choice.'

'If you can't manage a little dignity on your own account, try thinking of Annie for a change.'

'That's the trouble,' I said. 'Thinking of her and looking at you makes me want to put my fingers down my throat. Or round yours.'

'Sad. Let's go, honey, shall we?'

'Honey! Do you get your dialogue from the American army surplus stores by any chance? Have you got a new car?'

'Still the Peugeot,' he said.

'It looks different in the dark. Let's hope the same is true of you.'

Frank said, 'What makes you think we do it in the dark?'

I slammed the door. I waited for Annie's knock, but the car started and backed up the street and then I saw Joe Hirsch standing in the living room doorway. 'O.K.?' he said.

'O *what*?'

'Guess who's in London.'

'Joe, you are the last person in the whole world I want to see at this particular moment.'

'No, I'm not,' he said. 'I'm your friend, Michael. Mind if we check out the kitchen? There was a delay at Lod and then there was only kosher on the plane. I got a deal from El Al, resold my B.E.A. tickets and made a profit on the trip. I flew back next to Meyer Grossman from the Embassy, which is why I'm here. They need us, Michael. They need everybody and everything they can get. Meyer wants us to set up a committee –'

'There must be something more useless we can do,' I said.

Joe found a bowl of eggs and set about making an omelette. 'Artists, writers, actors, film directors, the scum of the earth, as long as they're famous scum. The necessary lord, the required professor, the statutory judge. You wouldn't like to talk to your father, I suppose? Anyone who's willing to pull an oar or puff a little wind into the sails. Where's Ken Haller?'

'In New York. Counting houses, I expect.'

'Call him. You get the people together, I'll get them on the box for you. Step one. Should they all necessarily be Jewish, do you think?'

'What exactly are we trying to do?'

'Drum up support for this small Middle Eastern state of which you may have heard. The neighbours are ganging up on it. Fucking hell, Michael, do I have to write it on the blackboard in capital letters? They're going to have a war out there.'

'I think Nasser's bluffing.'

'What about Hitler? Did you think he was? It's not a risk we can take. Pierrette.'

'What?'

'Is in London. You've guessed. Got any other salt?'

'What's the difference between one salt and another, for God's sake?'

'You ought to put a grain of rice in it, it stops it clogging. That's a useful tip.'

'What's she doing here? Fuck the salt.'

'Your sister's not an easy woman to please, is she? Pierrette's staying at my place. Why don't you call her?'

I said, 'I'm in no hurry to call anyone.'

'She's got something she wants you to see. Do you remember Hermann Pfaff?'

'I'm not going through all that again.'

'She's got hard evidence that he's shipping precision instruments to Egypt. In violation of international law. Through shell companies. They've got a lot of ex-Nazis working in their armaments business. I think we should nail him.'

'Off you go then.'

'This is the time. It needs your help. There's nailing and nailing. I'm thinking of a T.V. documentary. In our *Small World* slot perhaps.'

'I seem to remember doing a documentary with you before. About a certain Chester Flam and his noble plans.'

'She's married an American banker and gone to live in California. Jessica. *Black and White*'s probably sold. Felicity may be going to edit. They're thinking of giving it a woman's angle. Oh for Christ's sake, Michael, this is a completely different set-up. I can deliver now. It's a red hot issue, what's more, and it could swing a lot of sympathy Israel's way. Talk to Pierrette, because she's got all the dope. It needs your kind of honesty, Michael, your uncompromising approach.'

'Trying to do uncompromising work on the box is like trying to conceive a lion in the belly of a skunk.'

'We've got to get to Pfaff in the first place, if we want to get the goods on him, face him with evidence, and that means a foot in the door, and a camera crew not far behind. His door doesn't open easily.'

'I must find out where he got it,' I said. 'Why should he open it for me?'

'Obvious. Your dad. All he has to do is write a letter. He's done Pfaff a good turn in the past, everyone knows that, not least Mr Economic Miracle. It's your dad's chance to save his bloody soul.'

'I don't trust you, Joe. I don't trust you and I don't like you.'

'Yes, you do,' he said. 'Mind if I have some cereal?'

'What the hell are you really after?'

'I'm after shits who based their fortunes on what they did in the war and said they didn't, and what they did after it and don't want people to know. Isn't that a club even someone of your fastidious tastes could consider joining?'

I said, 'I'd like to think about it.'

'And I'd like you to,' Joe said. 'Hard. And preferably fast. Meanwhile, call your friends. We need a deputation in Downing Street in time for the nine o'clock news after next, at the latest. No beards, no accents, no hand signals. Your kind of Jew.'

'He'll get over it, love. Lucky that friend of his was there.'

'Yes. Now it'll be all over town.'

'It was bound to get out.'

'It didn't necessarily have to be wearing fluorescent pyjamas, though, did it?'

'O.K., so now we have to see if we have the right keys, assuming this is the right cottage. And we do and it is! Welcome to Glamis! I shouldn't worry about Michael. He'll soon find someone else. Let's hope the rain hasn't got to the bed before we do. The roof's very ornamental, but it is a little bit porous. Mind your head. How you've stood it all these years is what beats me, with Michael the mouth going fifty to the dozen. You can see I don't get down here every weekend exactly, can't you? Some spiders really can turn out the work. Wasn't that amazing about them asking me to do Michael's play? They can't have had any idea. Sod! Forgot to put sheets on the bed last time before I departed. You'll find some in the airing cupboard, under the stairs. Mind your head. Annie . . . Welcome aboard, honey.'

My father was having breakfast when I arrived at Court Royal the next morning. He wore a silk dressing gown and stiff slippers and he was reading *The Times*. I was torn between shame and cunning over the purpose of my visit, but I could hardly pretend that it was casual. With a bad conscience and a show of tact, I said that I was interested in doing a study of some key figures in postwar Europe. I mentioned Sir Robert Godolphin and a few others before admitting, with affectations of candour, that I was still fascinated by Pfaff, who had, after all, become a symbol of adroit intelligence, a man who had admitted everything and nothing in the same sweet breath. I was keen, I said, to have his own version of the last two decades on film. 'And you're the only person I know who could just possibly get him to let me do it.'

'You're gunning for him, presumably?'

I allowed Samuel to catch a rueful smile on my face. 'And you're still hoping for a knighthood, presumably?'

'I shall ignore your impertinence,' he said.

'You always do,' I said. 'I'm not sure that it's very nice of you.'

It was his turn to acknowledge a telling shot. 'How's your wife?'

'She seems to have left me,' I said. 'Are you pleased?'

'Are you?' he said. 'I liked her. Have you been faithful to her?'

'One woman,' I said, 'who meant nothing whatsoever. Is this possibly a story you've heard, or even told, before? When it comes to swinging, I'm one of those who invariably gets hung for a lamb. Are you going to help me or aren't you?'

'Conceivably both,' he said.

My mother came in, unusually pale (I rarely saw her without make-up), and took plates and cups from the table. She looked at us as she so often had in the past, when my father and I were locked in one of our politely savage dialogues. Samuel went to the desk under the Dendy Sadler painting which had once hung in his parents' flat. 'A Lawyer and his Client'. He found pen and paper and set himself to write as if he were about to compose a judgment, his left hand steadying the paper, which was set at an angle on the blotter, the right holding his pen so tightly that the tip of his finger was whitened by the stress.

'Did you mind,' I said, 'that she wasn't Jewish?'

'Is she not? And are you?'

'Jewishness, I'm promised, is a club from which there can be no resignations.'

'Did I tell you that Kendall was dead?'

'I'm sorry to hear that,' I said.

'Are you? I'm not. It'll save me five hundred a year.'

'She knew more about the family than I ever shall.'

'More than was good for her,' Samuel said, 'or for the family. Be careful with Pfaff, if you manage to get near him. Unless you're careful, you may like him. He's upset more calculations than may well be dreamed of in your philosophy.'

'If what they say he's doing is true, I don't think I shall like him too much. His company's involved in arms shipments to Egypt, so I'm told.'

'Business is business,' Samuel said.

I said, 'Sometimes you shock me, dad. You seriously shock me. Do you know what you just said?'

'Have you any notion of the volume of trade between the Axis powers and the allies during the war? It ran into many millions. Neither peace nor war is ever quite total, is it? Don't judge her too harshly, will you, should she come back?'

I said, 'Joe Hirsch thinks it might make a difference to how the public look at Israel if they knew ex-Nazis were actively supporting the Arabs.'

'Will that come as much of a surprise?'

'The obvious is not familiar to everyone yet, is it? Would you be willing to talk about being duped by him?'

'This subject comes back more frequently than Roquefort cheese,' Samuel said.

'It could be crucially important if the war starts.'

'*If*,' Samuel said. 'There you go with your long words again!'

'Why can't you and I really talk to each other ever? How little one would have to change, don't you ever feel that, if one wanted to change everything! And yet we never do. Why?'

'Because, replied Father William, changing everything would, in all probability, change very little.'

'Jews, for instance, would still almost certainly be Jews.'

His brief smile belonged to the young man who liked to tango. 'Whatever that may be.' He came and put his arm around my waist. I realized how rarely in my life he had embraced me. 'Good luck, old boy.'

'Whatever that be,' I said.

'They're strong and they're capable and they're clever and they're probably passing ruthless. The Israelis.'

'They're also surrounded and very likely to be let down by the powers. We have to do what we can.' I kissed his unshaven cheek. 'Can't stop.'

Every time I went back to the house, I had the vain fantasy that she would be there. My mother-in-law (not wearing a hat) had collected Daniel and I was alone except for the morning minis- trations of Maria. I could not wait for her to arrive and I was eager for her to go. Once, sitting in my study overlooking the garden, I masturbated into a Kleenex For Men while she hoovered on the stairs. My imagination was so lame that I could not even accelerate myself with an erotic scenario. I made some notes about Disraeli, but I found it difficult to impersonate his capacity for triumphing over the odds. My prime ministerial illusions faded; I could not even cut bread without taking a slice from my thumb. I listened to the radio and I watched the television; the crisis in the Middle East was a painful painkiller. I wanted Annie and I wanted the Arabs to disappear. I wanted everything and did nothing. I called what famous friends I had and recruited them to the committee. I was given the numbers of other celebrities who might help, but I was reluctant to call them. It might appear as if the danger to Israel, where I had never been, was being used as an excuse for social climbing; unable to bring myself to the necessary boldness, I could not tell whether scruple or accidie inhibited me. I suffered from mental indigestion; nothing settled in my head. Yet when I spoke on the telephone, my affectations of normality sounded quite lifelike. I even deceived myself into thinking that my anguish was regres- sing, until some woman telephoned and said simply, 'Is Annie there, please?' and I was crying when I put the receiver down. My shame made me aggressive when Ken Haller returned my call to the Pierre in New York and proved wary of signing our dignified manifesto.

'For Christ's sake, Ken, you've put your name on considerably less worthwhile productions. It's not anti-British in the slightest. "We call upon Her Majesty's Government to support a fellow member of the United Nations under the threat of extinction." You can't call that much of a twist to the lion's tale. And it's certainly no re-make of the Protocols of the Elders of Zion. Where are those conniving bastards now that we need them incidentally? As tirades go, this is about six inches in the right direction . . . *Who?* You're working with that little shit? He's not banking on Arab money by any chance, is he? Thanks. I'll spell your name right. Oh, there's someone at *my* door too. But it isn't Carl. If we live.'

I opened the door fast and wide. She was changed and she was unchanged. There was the beautiful girl and there was the secretive woman.

'*Bonjour.*'

'*Bonjour.*' She carried a worn briefcase with metal handles, held against her breast, as if she had come for a music lesson. She wore a beige raincoat and a brown beret and brown plastic boots.

I said, 'You're exactly as I remember.'

'You must have a very bad memory.'

'It doesn't feel bad,' I said. 'What can I get you? Coffee? A drink?' I hung her coat over the banisters and indicated the sitting room. Her legs were longer than I remembered. Her elbows were bony. 'Tea?'

'Nothing.' She glanced round the room and took a step towards the Guy Falcon drawing and lengthened her neck for a closer look. 'You're married, yes?'

'I'm married yes and no. Just at the moment, my wife . . .'

'Well, can you get us in to see Pfaff?'

'Early days,' I said. 'My father warned me that Pfaff can be extremely plausible. We shall need to be very well prepared even if we do manage to . . .'

'We are,' she said.

'You would be. How is everything with you?'

'Everything is a great many things. Too many.' She unlatched the chapped briefcase and took out documents. My spirits fell as I tried to be businesslike. She handed me one dossier after another. 'Bogus invoices. Photographs of wartime visits to concentration camps, in S.S. uniform.'

'I think we know about these, don't we?'

'Bills of sale to South American companies, evidence of diverted shipments, letters of thanks from Nazis in Egypt and Syria, demands for special equipment ditto.'

I said, 'Your daughter must be – what? – eighteen by now. France! How is she?'

'Instructions in Arabic for shipments to Buenos Aires. Why? She's in California. She intends to be an international lawyer.'

'Like her mother,' I said.

'I thought you'd end up rich,' Pierrette said. 'Some house!'

'Joe's rich,' I said. 'I lack his single-mindedness; he always knew what he wanted. I only know what other people do. It's not very surprising, is it, if Pfaff's organization sells stuff to Nasser? If it's on sale, he's likely to be able to get it, isn't he? Business is business.'

'It's a good time to expose it,' Pierrette said, 'that's all. Now is the moment to get him. Once the Arabs attack, the opportunity won't be there any longer.'

'I'd forgotten how well you spoke English. Opportunity to do what precisely? Isn't the whole idea to help Israel?'

'If you like,' she said.

I said, 'You can't imagine how much I've wanted to see you again. I'm going to have to take the German on trust, you know; I still can't bring myself to learn it. How long have you known about this?'

'We have a lot of information, one way and another.'

'We?'

'My friends and I. He was a Nazi; isn't that enough for you? I thought you cared very deeply about these things.'

'This all seems a very cumbrous way of scoring points for Israel.'

'Cumbrous?'

'Sorry. I flatter you with . . . Elaborate; heavy-handed. Have we really got time to make a film and get it shown before the shit meets the fan? Before the war starts. We can't possibly have anything on the screen before, oh, August. Is there really going to be time?'

'You always want an excuse to do nothing.'

I said, 'You obviously still know me very well. I'd forgotten how . . . direct you liked to be. I'm going to make some tea; do you want some?'

'O.K.' Had she always chucked her head to one side like that, so that her hair shifted over her ears?

We went down to the kitchen. I filled the kettle and plugged it in as if the simple operation proved some adult competence. 'So tell me,' I said, 'about your life since our last instalment. Are you still teaching?'

'Yes.'

'I'm still learning,' I said. 'And . . . is it still Jacquot, after all these years, or . . . ?'

She said, 'That's all finished now.'

'And what else has started?'

'*Histoires personnelles!* Those things don't matter very much.'

I said, 'They do to me.'

'The important thing to me is what has to be done.'

I said, 'What are you keeping from me, Pierrette?'

'Look . . .'

'I've looked; I've listened. I like what I see. Do I like what I hear?'

'Joe said you were willing to help us.'

'You and who else? You still haven't told me.'

'Still the same jealous man? I thought you might have changed.'

'Only the socks,' I said. 'I don't like to be manipulated.'

'How else did you get this house?'

'You think I shouldn't live in a house? Quite a lot of people do. I shall probably sell it if my wife doesn't come back, if that's . . .'

'You think too much about other people,' she said. 'Why do you really want to help Israel so much? Are you hoping it will prove to people how strong you are, how much you can achieve if you want to?'

'And what are you hoping, Pierrette? Are you ever as tough on yourself as you are on other people?'

'You spend a lot of time in America, yes? For me, Israel is an excuse.'

'Do I get an explanation with that at all? An excuse for you to do what?'

She frowned at her milkless tea. 'For the Jews, for the Arabs, for the Germans. An excuse even for God perhaps. For the Zionists it proves that the good Jews survived, for the Arabs that the bad ones did, to steal their land, thanks to the Europeans who were as generous to give away what didn't belong to them as they were quick to take what didn't. It proves that God was asleep, but finally woke up and it proves that the world has a conscience after all, as long as someone else pays the bills. We want it to survive because we need it to have been braver, and stronger, than we were. We always want to avenge ourselves on a victim we can curse with all the faults of the devil but not all of his powers.'

'You sound as though you've said that before.'

Pierrette said, 'Your wife is an actress?'

'My wife is, I'm afraid, almost entirely sincere. Next time perhaps I should be less ambitious. Or more. You still blame yourself for your grandfather.'

She said, 'He was a conceited old man. He thought that being Professor Lévi was something more than being a Jew. He thought it gave him privileges. He admitted being what he was because he did not really think that he was that alone.'

'And was he?'

'His courage, I see now, was a kind of cowardice. He stood up for himself because he thought he had nothing in common with other people. He should have stood up for them too.'

I said, 'You certainly ask a lot of people. Why are you saying things to me that you don't really feel?'

'Feelings are not the only basis of what we say. Perhaps they shouldn't be any part of it at all.'

'*You*'re an actress. You loved him. And he was brave enough, by all accounts, to do for me. I shall never forget what he said to that man – that Commander, Brault. "*Mon pauvre ami.*" Never. One day . . .'

'He knew that I was there,' she said. 'He said it for me. Commandant. Another actor.'

'Who the hell have you been talking to?'

'Weakness is easy to love,' she said. 'He wanted to be admired. He wanted to admire himself. There was nothing authentic in him.'

'You wanted him to be a Jew and nothing else, is that it? Can anyone really be that, unless he agrees to be a victim and exist only in the eyes of the people who put the labels on people?'

'Oh to tell the truth,' she said, 'I'm sick of the Jews.'

'Then why all this? Why all this?'

'This has nothing to do with the Jews,' she said.

'Or Israel?'

'Israel is the end of the Jews. It was meant to be. It will be. Israel . . .'

'Is that something you want or something you don't, the end of the Jews? And what does exposing Pfaff have to do with what you want?'

'Everything,' she said.

'That's a lot of things, isn't that what you said? Everything. What are you these days, Pierrette? Don't I deserve to know?'

'Objectively we want certain things, both of us. That's all that matters for the moment.'

'Why? Why is it all that matters and why . . . ?'

'Why, why, why!'

'You're hiding something. What? Tell me.'

'You always wanted to hurt me, didn't you, a little bit? You spoke to me like that before.'

'Oh, you do remember that we had a previous meeting.'

'I don't forget,' she said.

I said, 'Nor do I.'

She said, 'I don't want to speak about me. I don't want to be what I am. I never did. He acted and I too act. I'm tired of it. I want to disappear myself.'

'Why do mistakes in grammar make me want to kiss you?'

'Kisses!' she said. 'Haven't you had enough of those yet?'

'Certainly not. Is that what's holding you back? Please don't mind me. I've wondered and wondered what would have happened if we'd stayed together then, and always.'

She said, 'Do you remember I told you how that man came back and fired that last bullet into my dead grandfather?'

I said, 'Do I? And you felt as if it went into you. I've never forgotten it. I wanted to make a film based on that moment.'

'Do it,' she said. 'Whenever a man comes in my body, I feel as if it was happening again.'

'No, you don't,' I said. 'You're talking about Jacquot, aren't you? Or was he the only man who counted with you? You miss him, is that it?'

'I used him,' she said. 'I see this now. I was a victim who wouldn't let him stop. I hid from myself how strong I could really be. I liked being 'elpless, it was my only strength, O.K.? Now I'm different. I have to be. I want to shoot that last bullet out of me, Miko. That's the only thing I have left that I truly want to do. I want to spit it out of myself, like men spit sperm into what they despise and can't stop themselves wanting.'

She looked at me as if I had been cruel. Then she crossed her hands across her mauve sweater and wrenched it over her face. She wore a rather dirty white bra and she was fumbling with the catch before she had shaken the hair from her mouth and was looking at me again.

I said, 'Please don't.'

'You've been wanting to see them ever since I came in. Why deny it?'

'I don't,' I said. 'I just don't want you to do that.'

'You want to be putting your hands under my sweater and breathing like an express train first? Do you remember in that hotel? You couldn't believe it, could you, the things a girl was willing to do? Very French! You would've spent the rest of your life with me because I licked your balls for you.'

I said, 'You don't want me to expose Pfaff really, do you, for any reason that I think worthwhile?'

'Threats!' she said.

'Tell me the truth, blast you. What are you really trying to do? Apart from having the pleasure of manipulating me?'

'The truth! You know what Bertrand Russell said about the truth?'

'*Le grand savant anglais!* Stafford Canning's a bloody knight, you know. He'll probably get a peerage once Wesley Idun gets dumped. What did he say?'

'"The truth is what the police require you to tell."'

'Does that make me a policeman in your eyes?'

'All men are policemen,' she said. 'They force women to tell them things to justify them doing what they mean to do anyway. The truth they don't want to hear is the only one that really matters: we don't want your world, at any price.'

'You know who else I remember? The fat boy with the hoop. The one playing by the lake, as if there was no sort of war on at all. The one you looked out of the window at the day your grandfather was killed.'

'*C'est un bon élève! Il n'oublie rien.*'

'You thought maybe one day you might marry that fat, ugly boy, because he was so awful. And now you want to kill him, don't you, because he never asked you to marry him? You look out of the window at the fat, bourgeois world, and you still can't decide if you want to vanish into it or to have it vanish so that it never tempts you again.'

'Disgusts me again,' she said.

'Disgust and temptation are sometimes the same. You want it to want you so that you can have the pleasure of rejecting it. Instead of which, all it does is going on bowling its stupid hoop and wearing its silly hat. And that's why you want to point yourself at it like a pistol and blow it away. And then you'll be free. You think. Do you ever dream of Hermann Pfaff bowling his hoop and wearing his awful hat?'

Pierrette said, 'We have to get him.'

'Am I of your party? I don't know.'

'Damn it all,' she said. 'They're back, where they were before. And you don't mind. If you ever cared about me . . .'

'Ah. A personal message! You'll never know how often I've imagined you, how often I've relived that moment in the hotel when you took off your black top and stood there. Not like just now. Looking at me, afraid. I've always imagined that you could have taught me all sorts of things. I don't mean in bed. We credit the French with all kinds of cleverness. When my wife . . . began to have this affair she's having – I thought, part of me, that it was my great opportunity to go back to the crossroads, to take the right road again. I didn't believe that love was enough; I thought it was a fraud, an escape. I thought you were the real thing, a proper woman. Are you?'

'Proper? I don't know.'

'You want me to be Commandant Brault. You want me to go and shoot Pfaff, softly. With a camera. But shoot him. Because he deserves it. I'm not sure that I can. Even for the Jews.'

'You survived,' she said, 'and finally that's all that matters to you.'

'And you didn't. You didn't. I used to dream of bringing you back to life. I wrote a play about you – the first act anyway – in which I almost did. The final vanity of the writer: resurrection in print. I used to think that when Orpheus looked back, after bringing Eurydice all the way up from Hades, it was because he suddenly couldn't bear the thought of living with her in the light of common day. He dreaded the moment when his love would ask him to help with the washing up or look at the spot on her bum. But now I think maybe he didn't turn round by mistake on purpose. I think she called to him. I think she tricked him into losing her forever, because she knew that her kisses came from the House of the Dead. They would always taste of ashes.'

Pierrette said, 'This is your world, is it? Stay in it.'

'Killing Pfaff would be another way of killing yourself, is the truth. You want to stay a prisoner in the House of the Dead. The last thing you can bear is the idea of freedom, for yourself or anyone else. I used to hold my wife in the dark, when I began to be afraid I was losing her, and I'd find myself imagining you, with Jacquot. I wanted to make her want the things I could give her, the safety which was the same thing as a kind of punishment, so that our relationship wouldn't depend any more on her wanting me, or not wanting me, but on wanting *it*. I'd be a little bit cruel to her, thinking that if I could make her dependent on what I knew she wanted, I would hold the key to her pleasure and she'd never want to leave, never *dare* to leave. It was a humiliation which was a kind of mastery. Perhaps the two are too close for separation, or comfort. I imagined what Jacquot did to you, and how you hated and craved it, and it was as if I had you in my hands, as if my wife had disappeared and I was in the war, with you. When you came in the door, I wanted you to be her. No, I wanted you to be the lover I thought I had in Paris, the woman who would have done any and everything with me. But you never were that woman. I made it into a romance and I embarrassed you, a little bit, I think, into being romantic with me. But you used me then, to wound yourself, just as you want to use me now to wound Pfaff. I don't blame you, Pierrette. I love your name and the shape of your ears. I loved the taste of your cunt and I've never forgotten it. But you and I were never lovers, were we? I thought you released me from my English ignorance, but you locked me into something else, an illusion of a different kind. I wanted to have it come alive all over again. I can't tell you how little effort it would have taken from you to make me a happy fool all over again! Men are nothing much, are they?'

'Halfway is a long way for some people to go, I suppose.'

'And what's the whole way, dammit? How many bodies are there at the end of the whole way? That's what always bothers me.'

'You get used to bodies,' she said. 'Alive or dead, they're something to get used to.'

'I used to think that when you'd been naked with someone, you knew them as well as you could ever know them.'

She said, 'When will you know when we can go?'

'Are you seriously interested in exposing Pfaff?'

'Very seriously.'

'Why? Tell me why. What you hope to do. What good.'

'Good!'

'You're not interested in helping Israel, so what are you interested in, blast you?'

'You want me to throw myself into your arms, don't you? You want me to say that you're the one true love of my life. Then you'll do anything I say I want you to do – go dancing, kill Hermann Pfaff, die for Israel. You don't care why I want this or that, you're only offended because I haven't been putting my finger in there for the last fifteen years and pretending it was you. I lie to you, I can have anything I want. You want a world full of people who love you and you don't care what kind of world it is as long as that's true.'

'Is it to your credit that you think that? Or that you don't want the world to be like that? Perhaps.'

'The world can't be like that. Only people like you can be like that. And every person like you in the world accepts the existence of men like Pfaff, by your indifference, by your flippancy, by your smugness.'

'Out comes the vocabulary!'

'Now you're happy, because you can hate a woman, because you can say cruel things to her. That's as far as you'll ever care to go: first love, then contempt. The real world you leave to other people to manipulate. Anyone who proves to you that it isn't as you want it you either accept, if they're strong, or laugh at, if

519

they're weak. In the end, everything comes back to you.'

'The artist –'

'Love, art, humbug, these three!'

I said, 'I feel the force of everything you say. I half believe that you're right. Pfaff should be destroyed because he deserves to be destroyed . . .'

'You understand nothing.'

'And it's sentimental to want to expose him just because Joe and the man from the embassy say it would be a help to people I don't even know or want to live with. Granted.'

'Whatsoever.'

'You'll never know, and you'll probably never care, what I felt when I heard you were in London.'

'Your wife has gone away, I was going to come back. What is there I don't know?'

'You think I'm incapable of lying too? You think I'm incapable of getting what I want except by saying that I want it and crying if I don't get it? I don't think so. If I'd only wanted to persuade you that I was the man you wanted me to be, I think I might've managed it. It's not you I don't want; it's that man.'

She said, '*Peu importe.*'

'*Justement, ma petite Pierrette, justement.*'

'Now you're free to hate me, you look at me quite kindly, don't you?'

'I'm very much afraid I don't hate anybody.'

'You won't even give me that.'

'I can't live an abstract; I can't live a programme. I can't be something because I agree with it. Because somehow a part of me always disagrees. I can't be Joan of Arc, because I don't hear one voice, I hear many. I can't be her, I can't burn her. Plus and minus.'

'Write your plays,' she said.

'It seems they've won before it's started.'

'Is that right? Trust them! What's happened? I go to look for a corkscrew and I miss the bloody war.'

'The B.B.C. man in Jerusalem says that they've destroyed the Arabs' air forces; the battle's as good as won.'

'Classic! They make us all think they're about to be pushed into the sea by the big bad Arabs and the next minute . . . They say they don't want to fight and then they up and knock the other side out before the bell's bloody well gone. Brilliant, I must say. Only next time, don't bother to come round with the begging bowl and the hard luck stories, don't you agree? They can take care of themselves and I think that's just what they may as well get used to doing. Meanwhile, honey, here's to us! You are sure you heard it right, are you? I must say, with the best will in the world, I hate to think what some of them are going to be like now. If you thought they were pushy before, imagine them in the future. Annie, what the hell's the matter with you? That's my best plonk! Not to mention my best Turnbull and Asser.'

'If you thought I was pushy before . . .'

'I didn't know you were Jewish.'

'Neither did I.'

'We don't have to guess what this'll do for the fools, do we? Make 'em think that justice and happy endings are part of the divine plan again! You and I know different. If you wonder why I bothered to get rich – and I'm going to get a lot richer in the future, a *lot* – it's so that we can laugh the last laugh, knowing that nothing's really all that funny, or lasting. Money may be a lie, but at least it's a lie you can *count*. The only kind of meaninglessness that avoids queuing! Don't love me, just be with me. Face it: having everything you don't want is the only revenge you can have.'

'No,' she said. 'Not having it is even better.'

He said, 'I should have let you marry that faggot. Then you'd've come to me all right.'

'Sorry, Joe.'

'Damn you,' he said, 'because you're not the only one who's suffered, my beautiful, unique, tragic Rachel, the love of my life.

And now would you be good enough to get the hell out of my house, always assuming that you were on your way in any case?'

My mother said, 'He's in there.'

My father was standing in the window of the flat, with his back to me. I said, 'Hullo, dad.'

He might have been whispering to someone I could not see. There was movement in his back, the slightest rumpling of the cloth of his black coat. I could not hear him: I knew he was speaking. I walked into the room and he turned round abruptly, as if to catch me. His face was wet with tears he did not welcome or acknowledge. His body had taken unwanted command. He composed his face, as I imagined he did before giving judgment. 'Shema Yisroel . . .'

I blinked with irritation at the choking threat of emotion. I said, 'We're not going to have to bother with friend Pfaff after all.'

He said, 'I did suggest . . .'

'Do you know what happened? I just spoke to Meyer Grossman. They've captured the entire shipment, still in its crates in the Sinai. They've lifted the whole lot.'

'A benefactor,' Samuel said.

'The street's where you bloody well belong, you tuppenny ha'penny tart.'

'I'll go to the police. I'll go to the police.'

'First on the right, you can't miss it. I hope they find something useful to do with you.'

'Let go of me, you total bastard.'

'Oh for God's sake, Horniman, at this hour in the morning.'

'Oh hullo, Jordan. Terrific work, I must say.'

'Let me into the house, Tristram, you utter shag.'

'Stopping Gamel Abdul in his rather slimy tracks. Ten out of ten.'

'Oh yes,' Victoria said, 'jolly good. Well done.'

'I don't honestly think much credit is due to me.'

522

'We saw you doing your stuff in Downing Street.'

'The bravest of the brave,' I said.

'Over before it's begun.'

'Like too many moonlight kisses.'

'Sorry? We were both mightily chuffed, weren't we, chicken?'

'Gosh yes,' Victoria, who was in her underclothes, ducked under her husband's arm and into the house.

'Are you off somewhere?'

'Yes,' I said.

Athens was very quiet. There were people, of course, in the streets and the cafés, but they seldom greeted each other. It was as if the Greeks had learned that dignity and resignation were the same thing. There was pride in their reticence, and a kind of abdication. They found that no one was going to do anything about what had happened, until they did it themselves. They pretended, with rare irony, that something good had happened, but only fools told you what it was. The fools did not know that they were repeating what people deprived of their liberty always say – that things were better and smoother, that officials were more polite and that there was no more corruption. The fools do not know that corruption, like everything else, takes a little while to rearrange.

You probably know that I telephoned Worthing several times. Daniel seemed fine. I thought of going down there, but I heard you were going to collect him and, because I so hoped I would see you, I thought it better to stay away. I haven't left England because I didn't want to see you; more because I did. I hoped that Iskios would be far enough away for me to think of more important things than the only thing I wanted more than anything in the world. The Friends of Israel Committee ended in numbing absurdity. I was naive enough to imagine that Israel might do something never before done by the winning side – stick to the fine promises they

523

made before they knew they had won. I actually asked Meyer Grossman, a hero of the 1948 war and a poet himself, when his government intended to give back the land they had conquered. It's hardly surprising that he looked embarrassed – not for the government, but for me. Why should the Jews behave better than anyone else ever has? He suspected that I thought that the Israelis would have to do the right thing because I'd been so obliging over having a word with the P.M. God help me, perhaps his suspicions were justified! There was a kind of relief in being disappointed, if disappointment was what I felt. How terrible to have the world respond to one's hopes! There had been talk of keeping the committee in being, a sort of permanent liaison between Israel and us, whoever we thought we were, and I dreaded having to stay in London and honour my obligations. How convenient to find oneself superfluous! Who can be a part-time referee in the world's game?

Iskios is quiet too. It was always difficult for me to imagine how people could lead such ordinary lives when terrible things were happening. When I was going back to school, I was scandalized by the smiles of those who were ignorant of my cruel fate and saw nothing brutal in the day. When I used to read scholarly articles, dated during the war and written in German universities, I could hardly go on reading them. How could educated men continue on their accurate way when the world was lurching or leaping towards unspeakable horrors? Now I can see that there can be a temptation, almost a need, to be more and more blinkered the more mortifyingly annihilating the prospect. As others cry for help, there is something very important that one must get just right! As Icarus falls, the ambitious fool, the modest ploughman curses him with his regularity. The Greeks pretend that ordinary life is an art and so dispense themselves of the shame of acquiescence or the risk of refusal. And these are the people who proved their ancient virtue, once, by saying 'no' to Mussolini; the only people who celebrate an annual negative. But then, of course, as the smart ones know, they did their nay-saying under a dictator who would probably salute today's Colonels as his own. This is certainly the bitter view of my friend Asteris, who has been exiled to Iskios for satirical articles he wrote *before* the so-called 'revolution'. Naïveté and cynicism are easy cousins here: the Colonels dignify their putsch with a noble term. At the same time, they appropriate the jargon of their opponents and tempt the weaklings with a good reason to join them. Asteris smiles at my indignation and his bespectacled dignity reminds me of Prince Mavrocordato, whose picture hangs above my desk in Seymour Walk. (We bought him in Colchester, if you remember, together with that rascal Colocotroni, who faces him across the room.) Asteris is giving me Greek lessons (Oh yes, I certainly *do* need them) and we exchange books. Am I working? Yes. I always said that I wanted to come and spend a long time here, doing what I ought to do, not what others wanted of me. Well, *eccomi*! I've abandoned Disraeli – perhaps not forever – and I'm writing a play about a fool who believes everything he is *told* about the world, its ways, its future, and not what he sees and feels for himself. He is a kind of Quixote, my 'hero', who is ashamed of loving his wife and his son, of wanting to live with those who care for him and for whom he cares, of having a single life and a simple purpose. He throws it all away to go and make gestures he is comically unsuited to and can never really manage. He is an anti-chivalrous Don, riding other people's hobby horses, the ultimate credulous cretin, who thinks that only by being a shit can one really live one's epoch and only by infidelity can one be true to oneself. Everything that goes wrong seems to him to be heaven-sent and everything that goes right is a snare and a delusion. It *should* be very funny, if only I didn't take it so seriously, but perhaps that's the source of the humour. *Tha to elpizome*. We'll hope so. I tell myself, like the fool I am, that I'm writing only for myself this time, but if I am, why do I always find myself on the quayside when the steamer comes in? (There's only one that actually comes in the *day* now.) Let me put it this way: if anyone phones and tells you that I've been seen sharing my bed with an old goat, don't necessarily believe her, will you? I wish you could see the terrace now that the rascal Dimitri has finally re-roofed it (for *more* money!). I sit in the evening, in the Wittgensteinian deckchair, looking into the courtyard where the almond is still in flower and I wonder why I was ever so interested in ghosts. Someone once told me that 'I love you' is always a question, without a question mark. If so, I'm still asking it.

'*L'objet de votre visite dans la République; vous n'avez rien écrit. Tourisme, affaires, quoi?*'

'*Comme vous voulez.*'

'*Mais non, madame*. Lady, listen . . .'

'Tourism? Tourism.'

'You be careful, lady. *Attention!* This isn't England.'

'I've been in Africa before,' she said.

'You have somebody with you? Somebody to meet you?'

She walked on with her stamped passport. The other passengers were waiting for their luggage. The customs man, in his kepi, gestured to her to return to the carousel. He did not at first believe that she had come from London with only the bag which she had over her shoulder. She walked out into the dust. The children with their sores and their stumps came towards her as if they were there expressly to greet her. She walked through them to where a 1952 Impala was waiting. It had been repainted by hand, blue and white. It had tiger-skin nylon covers on the uneven seats and gold-fringed drapes against the mounting sun. She was in the back of the taxi before the driver had finished his invitation. He looked rueful when he had to get in and start the engine. She had deprived him of the pleasure of seduction. She told him where to go and what she would pay.

When they reached the village, he turned and put a hand along the tigerskin and looked her full in the face. There was no sign of a shop or a hotel or even a car or a pavement. There were corrugated iron roofs to the huts, chickens, potholes, electric cables high above the unpaved street, carrying power some-where else. She gave him the money she had specified and walked on up the road. It soon became a track.

There was a compound with a palmette fence which made her smile, without amusement. Naked children squatted by the entrance. Women with pot-bellied babies sat on the bench by the surgery door. She sat down by them. When Jerome came out, he looked at her for a moment and then he said, '*A qui le tour?*'

She waited, chin up, the strap of her bag in both hands, feet apart.

Asteris came in the late afternoon on Tuesdays and Thursdays to give me my Greek lesson. On Monday, Wednesday and Friday, I walked up to the village and we had our conversation in Stelio's café under the eucalyptus, in the little *plateia*. It pleased me to be seen there with him by the snooping policeman. I could believe that another little war was being waged, a petty epic which I hoped would prove within the budgetary scope of my imagina-tion. Asteris and I were reading Cavafy. I made lists of clever words and tried to memorize them. I was typing my last page before setting off for the village on a Wednesday afternoon when I heard the slur of footsteps on the new stairway and then a rap on the half open door. As soon as someone came to the house, I pretended that I was at home in my solitude. I never looked up.

I said, '*Empros.*'

The light widened and whitened my page.

'*Ti nea lipon?*'

'The zoo was closed. You were the nearest lion.'

I said, 'I always hoped that if I didn't look, one day it might be you.'

'Don't look different,' she said. 'Look as you did just now.'

'If you promise you won't disappear.'

'You weren't there. You said you always met the boat.'

I said, 'You could've sent a telegram.'

'I did,' she said.

'Did I get it? *Kalos irthate*. Welcome to Greece.'

'Can I come in yet?'

I said, 'Christ Jesus, Annie.'

She said, 'Oh darling, don't.'

'*Don't? Don't?*'

'Didn't he want us to come?'

I said, 'Yes, he wanted you to come. Very much. He never wanted anything more in his life. He just happens to be a cry-baby.'

Daniel said, 'Can we go to the beach?'

I said, 'What else is it there for?'

'I saw Yorgo. He said you were here.'

'Then it must be true.'

She was wearing cream-coloured trousers and the same football shirt she used to wear in the cottage when we first came to the island. Her hair was cut rather short and it was darker than I thought it would be, almost chestnut where the scissors had been. She stood to attention when I looked at her and her lips were trembling.

I said, 'You *are* alone, I take it?'

She said, 'Please don't feel . . .' She stopped herself and put her teeth into her lower lip and then took a deep breath. 'We can't leave Daniel on his own.'

I said, 'Can we really begin again?'

'As long as it's not at the beginning,' she said.